Born in England in 1970, Santa Montefiore grew up in Hampshire. She is married to historian Simon Sebag-Montefiore. They live with their two children, Lily and Sasha, in London. Visit her at www.santamontefiore.com and sign up for her newsletter.

Santa Montefiore

The Affair

Sea of Lost Love

**SIMON &
SCHUSTER**

London · New York · Sydney · Toronto · New Delhi

A CBS COMPANY

The Affair first published in Great Britain by Hodder & Stoughton, 2010
An Hachette Livre Company
Sea of Lost Love first published in Great Britain by Hodder & Stoughton, 2007
An Hachette Livre Company

This bind-up edition first published in Australia by Simon & Schuster Ltd
A CBS COMPANY

1 3 5 7 9 10 8 6 4 2

Simon & Schuster UK Ltd
1st Floor
222 Gray's Inn Road
London WC1X 8HB

www.simonandschuster.co.uk

Simon & Schuster Australia, Sydney
Simon & Schuster India, New Delhi

A CIP catalogue record for this book
is available from the British Library

Paperback ISBN: 978-1-4711-4873-6
EBOOK ISBN: 978-1-47114-069-3

Printed and bound in Great Britain by CPI Group (UK) Ltd, Croydon, CR0 4YY

The Affair

Prologue

The human spirit is a kaleidoscope of millions of tiny mirrors, reflecting a whole spectrum of colours, depending on where the light falls. It is multi-faceted and limitless in its potential. Yet within this intricate hall of mirrors, some surfaces never get a chance to shine but lie in darkness, ignored.

We may never completely realize our capacity to love. We may never flower to our full bloom. But sometimes, something happens in our lives to give us a glimpse of what we could become were we to allow that light to find those dark and secret surfaces of our soul. Then, we realize we have wings and always have done . . .

In Search of the Perfect Happiness

PART ONE

Desire

Chapter 1

'The happiness of your life depends on the quality of your thoughts'

In Search of the Perfect Happiness

London
September 2008

Angelica Lariviere pulled on a pair of Spanx and looked at herself from all angles in the luxurious bathroom designed especially for her by Smallbone of Devizes. Mirrors encased the bath on three sides and opposite, above the two basins where Dyptique candles burned and perfumes adorned pale marble surfaces in pretty glass bottles. Angelica loved beautiful things: sunlight shining through a dew-encrusted cobweb, mist over a mirrored lake, an antique glass chandelier, birds in the magnolia tree, stars, a pregnant moon, Paris, perfume, the melancholy tones of a cello, candlelight, the stirring bleakness of a winter heath, snow. More exquisite than reality was her imagination. As elaborate as an enchanted garden, her dreams spilled onto the pages of her fantasy children's novels, where life had no limitations and beauty could be manifested at will. Most of all, Angelica loved love, for nothing was more beautiful than that.

As she mused on the swift passing of time, her thoughts lingered on that first kiss in Paris, beneath the streetlamp on the Place de la Madeleine. Olivier would never kiss her like that again, and she'd never feel the intoxicating sensation of a hundred tiny bees' wings tickling the walls of her belly. Not that he didn't kiss her – just that a husband's kiss is different from a lover's. A first encounter can never be repeated. Marriage, children, and domesticity had deepened their affection for each other but, at the same time, stolen something of their magic, leaving them as familiar as siblings. She felt a wave of nostalgia for that precious moment, and a little wistful that so intense a love would never be experienced again.

It was then that eight-year-old Joe wandered in, clean and flushed in his pyjamas, and his eyes widened in horror at the sight of her. 'Yuck!' he exclaimed, screwing up his face. 'Not *those* again!'

Angelica picked up her wineglass and scrunched her tousled blonde hair between her fingers.

'Sorry, sweetie, tonight I need my big pants,' she told him, taking a sip of chilled Sauvignon. 'It's Big Pants or Big Tummy, and I know which I prefer.'

'Daddy doesn't like them, either.'

'That's because Frenchmen appreciate beautiful underwear.' She thought of the drawer of exquisite Calvin Klein lingerie she never opened, preferring to wear simple cotton underwear from Marks & Spencer, and felt sad that after two children and a decade of marriage she had given up trying to be sexy. She slipped on her black Prada dress. 'Better?' she asked, striking a pose and smiling at him coquettishly.

'Phew!' he sighed melodramatically. She crouched down to kiss him. 'You smell nice,' he added.

'That's better. Remember, if you want to be popular with the girls, only ever tell them they look beautiful. Good training to get a wife someday.'

'I'm never going to marry anyone.' He put his arms around her and rested his head on her shoulder.

'Oh, you'll change your mind when you're bigger.'

'No, I won't. I want to be with *you* forever.'

Angelica's eyes welled with emotion. 'Oh, darling, that's the nicest thing you've ever said.' *Who needs magic when I have you!* 'Give me the Full Joe.' He pressed himself against her with a giggle. 'That's so nice!'

'Can I watch *Ant Bully* now?'

'Go on then.' She watched him grab the television control and climb into her bed. He shouted for his sister to join him, and Angelica heard six-year-old Isabel hurry across the landing.

She turned back to the mirror and wiped away a smudge of mascara. *That boy is going to break hearts one day,* she thought. She stood back and appraised herself. *Not bad, thanks to the Spanx.* She actually looked quite slim. On a wave of enthusiasm, she hurried into the custom-made dressing room and reached for a vintage black belt with a pretty gold buckle in the shape of a butterfly she had found in the Portobello market. Back in front of the mirror she put it on, slipped into open-toed black stilettos, and admired the transformation.

Joe and Isabel chattered on the bed, their voices erupting into the uninhibited laughter exclusive to small children. The door opened and Olivier strode in with the insouciance of a man used to being the dominant power in the house.

'It smells like a bordello!' He turned up the lights. 'The children should be in bed.'

'They *are* in bed – *our* bed.' She laughed. 'Hello, darling.'

He scowled and blew out the candles, knowing that she would forget. 'I see you've got a glass of wine. I could do with a drink myself.'

'Bad day?'

Olivier took off his tie. 'It's a difficult time. The mood in the City is very depressed.' He went into the dressing room and slipped his jacket onto a hanger. 'Did you pick up my dry cleaning? I want to wear my Gucci jacket tonight.'

Angelica flushed. 'I forgot. Sorry.'

'*Merde!* Sometimes I wonder what goes on in that cotton wool head of yours.'

'There's a whole world in here, beyond the cotton wool, of course.' She tapped her temple, trying to be upbeat. 'I get paid to imagine.'

'You remember the plots of those fantasy novels of yours, but you don't remember to pick up my dry cleaning. You still haven't collected my trousers from the tailor, and I asked you weeks ago. If you had my job, we'd be broke!'

'Which is why I don't have your job. Look, I'm sorry.'

'Don't apologize. I'm obviously not a priority.'

'Darling, don't be angry, please. We're going out to dinner, it'll be fun. You'll forget about the City and your Gucci jacket.' She walked up behind him and put her arms around his waist. 'You *know* you're my priority.'

'Then be an angel and get me a drink – and put the children to bed. The summer holiday is too long. When do they go back?'

'Thursday.'

He sniffed irritably. 'Not a moment too soon.' He stepped out of his trousers and hung them up carefully. Olivier was meticulously tidy. 'I'm going to take a shower.'

'So, how do I look?'

Olivier glanced at her as he removed the gold-crested cuff links from his shirt. 'Why the belt?'

'Fashion, darling!'

'Why would you want to emphasize the widest part of you?'

Angelica stared in astonishment. 'The widest part of me?'

He chuckled and kissed her neck. 'You always look beautiful, Angelica.'

She watched him remove his shirt and toss the cuff links into the leather box on the trouser press. Though slightly built and not very tall, Olivier was an attractive man. He was athletic, playing regular games of tennis at Queen's, or running off his excess energy around Hyde Park when one of his four couldn't make it. He was typically Gallic, with thick brown hair swept off his face in waves and smooth olive skin that never paled, even in winter. His features were fine, his nose long and aristocratic, his eyes a startling cornflower blue against lustrous black lashes. It was his mouth that had first attracted her to him, the way it curled at one corner. Now it took a lot to make it curl at all. He wore his clothes with the panache of a true Parisian, paying special attention to his shoes, which were always polished, and his suits, which were always beautifully tailored. Appearances were important to Olivier, and he spared no expense at Turnbull & Asser and Gucci. He liked to look good and he liked *her* to look good, too.

With the help of Sunny, the housekeeper, Angelica put the children to bed and served her husband whisky on the rocks as he came out of the shower smelling of sandalwood. He didn't notice that she had removed the belt, replacing it in the drawer along with her joy. She no longer felt like going out to dinner, even though Scarlet was one of her closest friends. She felt like a sack of flour.

As she reached for her handbag, her mobile telephone bleeped with a message. **Please come quickly. I need you. X Kate**. Angelica's heart lurched. Kate was in trouble, again! She looked at her watch. Kate lived in Thurloe Square, on the way to Scarlet's house in Chelsea. If she was quick, she could jump in a cab and meet Olivier there.

Olivier's reaction was predictable. He sighed grumpily and swore, clipping his words to emphasize his annoyance. 'She is such a drama queen! And you run to her like a lady-in-waiting who cannot see that without her drama the queen is not a queen at all.'

'She's fragile. She's obviously in a state.'

'She spends her whole life in a state.'

'It's not her fault that Pete is having an affair.'

'I sympathize. If I were married to her, I'd have an affair, too.'

'I hope that's not a threat.'

'Not to you, my angel. The very fact that we are opposites is good for my soul. I am material, you are ethereal.' He laughed, pleased with his analysis. 'Go on then, I'll meet you there. But don't be later than eight-thirty. I'll let them know that you are dealing with a crisis. No doubt your fellow lady-in-waiting will understand!' he added, referring to Scarlet. 'Though, I'm sure she won't want you to be late for dinner.' As she left the room, he noticed her handbag, thrown carelessly on the bed with her lip gloss and compact. 'Angel, you cannot pay the cab without your purse!' he called impatiently. She rushed back, gathered it all up, and hurried out again.

Angelica wrapped her pashmina around her shoulders and hailed a cab on Kensington Church Street. It was a chilly night for September. Grey clouds filled the sky like porridge, and the evenings were now setting in early. Some trees were even beginning to turn orange. The streets were bustling with people having returned from their summer holidays for the start of the school term. The traffic was heavier, too, slowing down to near gridlock opposite Kensington Palace. She was grateful to be going in the opposite direction.

The cabbie interrupted her thoughts with glum comments on the lack of sunshine, the misery of yet another wet summer. 'Global warming,' he said gloomily. 'Still, Boris is mayor and Cameron will sweep Brown down the proverbial drain. It's not all bad.'

He dropped her off outside Kate's white terraced house where two bay trees stood on either side of the shiny pink door like sentinels. She rang the bell. From inside came the sound track of *Mamma Mia* and voices. She tried to peep in, but the curtains were drawn. Maybe the text message was old and she was interrupting a dinner party.

Finally, the door opened, and Kate appeared in a cashmere

dressing gown, a bottle of Chardonnay in one hand, cigarette in the other. Her face was tear-stained, mascara smeared over blotchy skin, her spiky brown hair pulled off her face with an Hermès scarf. She looked like a little girl in her wretchedness.

'Oh, Angelica, thank you for coming. You're a real friend.'

She wasn't the only real friend. There in the sitting room sat Letizia and Candace, apparently as bewildered as she was.

'What's going on?' Angelica hissed as Letizia enveloped her in a cloud of Fracas.

'Not sure, darling,' she replied, her Italian accent curling seductively around her words like a soft cat's tail. 'Your guess is as good as mine!'

'Where are the children?'

'With her mother.'

'And Pete?'

'In Moscow.'

'Lucky.'

'*Esatto,* darling. No man likes to see a woman in tears, especially if they are shed for him.'

'Let me get you a drink,' said Kate, wandering unsteadily out of the room.

Angelica sank into a chair. 'If I'd known you two were here, I wouldn't have bothered. Olivier will be furious if I'm late for dinner.'

'You think that's bad?' said Candace, raising a perfectly shaped eyebrow. 'I'm meant to be at the theatre.'

'You're so good to her,' said Letizia.

'No, I'm a schmuck!' A born-and-bred New Yorker, Candace never minced her words. 'I've texted Harry that I'll meet him in the interval. He's so mad, he hasn't replied. If I continue like this, he'll divorce me.'

'She looks so thin,' said Letizia, sliding her green eyes towards the hall. 'Like she hasn't eaten a carbohydrate in weeks. I'm a little jealous, actually.'

'Misery,' quipped Candace. 'They should sell it by the bottle.'

'Has Pete left her, do you think?' Angelica asked.

'Of *course* not. They're *addicted* to each other. They make each other *equally* miserable.' Candace glanced impatiently at her pretty pink nails. 'What's she doing in there, treading the grapes?'

'This is going to be a long night; I just know it,' sighed Letizia.

At last Kate returned with the bottle of wine. 'Couldn't find the bottle opener,' she said with a drunken giggle, dragging on her cigarette. 'You're probably wondering why you're all here.'

'It's your birthday and we've all forgotten!'

Letizia shot Candace a look. 'What's happened?' she asked kindly, patting the sofa. Kate sat down with a sigh.

Candace took the bottle from her and twisted off the cap. 'I think I need a little fortification.'

'I'm late,' Kate stated darkly.

'Honey, we're *all* late,' said Candace.

'Not for the theater. *Late* late.' She gave a meaningful look.

'Oh, *that* kind of late. Well, that's a surprise!' Candace continued. 'I thought you two were at each other's throats, not in each other's pants!'

'Have you done a test?' Angelica asked.

'No, that's why I invited you all around. I need the moral support to do it.'

'You haven't done a test?' Angelica was annoyed. If it turned out to be negative, what was the point of dragging them all out tonight?

'So, you have another child, what's so bad about that?' asked Candace, pouring herself some wine.

'Yes, another child will bond you back together again. There's nothing more romantic, darling,' Letizia purred encouragingly.

Kate shook her head, her eyes welling with tears. 'Not in this case.' She bit her bottom lip. 'If I'm pregnant, I don't know whose it is.'

'Have I missed something?' asked Candace, stunned.

'You're not the only one,' said Angelica. All three women looked at Kate.

'I had a one-night stand. It was a mistake. Pete was with The Haggis, and I was in despair. I'm an idiot. Now look at me. I'm a wreck. To think I'm a model. No one will employ me now except those ugly agencies.'

'In this state? I think you'd be lucky to be employed at all,' said Candace, teasing her gently.

'It was only once, and now I'm going to be punished for the rest of my life.'

'So, who is he?'

'I can't tell you. I'm too ashamed.'

Angelica narrowed her eyes, considering possible candidates. Letizia put her arm around Kate's skinny shoulder and gave her a reassuring squeeze, enveloping her in pale cashmere and perfume.

Candace looked at her watch. 'I don't mean to be rude here, but Jeremy Irons isn't going to wait for me to turn up to Act Two. Can we move this along, please?'

'Sorry, Candace, you're really good to me.' Kate sat up, bracing herself for the moment of truth.

'Have you got the kit?' Letizia asked. 'There is no better time than the present.'

Kate pointed to four boxes on a side table. 'Just in case . . . you know . . .'

'Sure, they lie all the time!' said Candace, striding over to get them for her. 'Come on, Kate. Let's get you upstairs.'

Letizia fetched her a glass from the kitchen, Candace handed her the tests, Angelica helped her up the stairs and pushed her into her en suite bathroom.

'Right, give it your best shot!' said Candace, throwing herself onto Kate's super-king-size sleigh bed. She ran her hand over the brown furry bedspread. 'This is nice.'

'Who do you think it is?' Angelica hissed.

'Must be Ralph Lauren,' said Candace.

'No, not the bedspread. Her *lover*?'

'Oh, well . . .'

'Robbie?' Letizia suggested.

'Robbie who?'

'Her trainer!'

'Oh no! That's such a cliché! She'd have told us if it was him.' Candace waved her hand dismissively. 'It'll be someone we all know. *One of us*.'

'I can't pee! I'm too nervous!' Kate wailed from the bathroom.

'Run the tap,' Letizia suggested.

'I'll kill her if this is all a false alarm,' said Candace.

Angelica glanced at her watch. 'Not if Olivier gets here first. It's eight-thirty!'

'Is it coming?'

There was a long pause, then finally a shriek. 'Now I can't stop! Help, the glass is too small!'

They all waited without uttering another word. Kate poked her head around the door. 'Are you still here?'

'Of course we're still here. It's not like we've got anything better to do!' said Candace.

'Well? What does it say?' Letizia asked anxiously.

'I haven't done it yet. I'm too scared.' She emerged with the glass.

'Oh really! Too much information!' Candace cried, hiding her eyes.

'You must all have a test,' insisted Kate, handing them each a box.

'This is insane!' But Candace took one anyway and opened it.

Letizia threw her empty box on the bed. 'I'm confident it will be negative. What are we looking for?'

'Were you born yesterday? A blue stripe,' said Candace. 'And you're going to have to look at mine for me.'

'This takes me back a few years!' said Angelica, studying the device with nostalgia. 'I should have had another one.'

'You can have mine,' groaned Kate.

'Don't say that, darling. You might not even be pregnant.' Letizia was a natural optimist.

'Let's see,' said Angelica. 'All together now.'

'Oh Lord, can I do this with my eyes closed?' said Candace.

'You're making more of a fuss than me,' said Kate.

'That's simply not possible!' said Candace.

The four women dipped the sticks into Kate's urine. 'I think I'm going to be sick,' moaned Kate.

'*You're* going to be sick. At least it's *your* wee!' Candace grimaced.

Angelica pulled hers out and watched as the little window turned blue. She felt a wave of pity for her friend. 'But it's *your* baby, Kate,' she said quietly.

They all stared at their tests. Then they all stared at Kate.

'Any negatives?' Letizia asked hopefully. They all shook their heads.

Kate sank onto the bed. 'Hell! What am I going to do?'

'What do you *want* to do?' asked Letizia, sitting beside her and putting her arm around her again.

'You don't know how hard I've worked for this stomach,' she exclaimed, then burst into tears. 'Now I know, I can't even have a fucking cigarette or a glass of wine. I might as well enrol in a convent!'

'It's a little late for that!' said Candace.

Kate put her hand on her belly. 'If I could be sure it was Pete's, it wouldn't be so bad, would it? But what if it's not

Pete's. I mean, he'll *know*. Men always know. Babies always look like their fathers, don't they?'

'Not always,' said Letizia.

'Oh, they always do. That way the fathers don't eat them,' Candace retorted.

'You don't have to make your mind up now, Kate,' said Angelica, aware that she was now running very late indeed. 'Think about it for a few days.'

Kate ran her rheumy eyes over Angelica's dress. 'You need a belt,' she said with a sniff.

'I put one on and Olivier said I was emphasizing the widest part of me.'

For a moment Kate was drawn out of herself. 'He said what?'

'I hope you cut off his balls!' said Candace.

'No, I took off the belt.'

'You sop! What are you? A doormat?' Candace laughed fondly. 'What are we going to do with you?'

'I think I need a new body.'

Letizia sighed. 'No, darling, you just need a new husband.'

Kate managed to stagger over to her chest of drawers and pulled out a belt. 'Don't argue with me. I'm dangerous when drunk.' She slipped it around Angelica's waist. 'This is *not* the widest part of you, whatever Olivier says. You look fabulous!'

'You really do,' agreed Letizia. 'Olivier should be ashamed of himself. You should have married an Italian. They love curvaceous women.'

'The widest part of you, my ass! His ego's so wide he can barely make it out the door! Tell him that and see how he likes it.' Candace smiled at her affectionately. 'Go knock 'em dead!'

'Now we've sorted you out, let's talk about me,' said Kate.

Candace gave her a big hug. 'Angelica's right. Sit on it for a few days. Call me in the morning. Letizia will put you to bed.'

'You're leaving?' said Kate in a small voice.

'*I'm* not,' said Letizia, stepping in dutifully.

Candace beckoned Angelica with a brisk wave. 'Come on, honey, we're out of here.'

Angelica put her arms around Kate, whose face crumpled like a child being left at boarding school. 'I'll call you in the morning – if I'm still alive!'

'Thank you for coming, you two. I really appreciate your support.'

'I know,' cried Candace as she hurried down the stairs. 'We expect huge rewards in heaven! Birkin bags and Louboutin shoes by the truckload – in every colour!'

'What a mess!' Angelica sighed as they stepped onto the pavement.

'This time it really *is* a mess,' agreed Candace. 'Where do you have to go?'

'Cadogan Square.'

'I'll take you.' She summoned her driver with a wave. The glossy black Mercedes pulled out into the street.

'But you're late for the theatre.'

'I'll say I crept in at the back – what's the difference? He's mad already. Anyway, you know what? I've seen enough theatre for one night.'

'You think she's acting?'

'Her whole life is theater, God love her. And we do love her, don't we!'

As they climbed into the car, Kate's front door flew open and Letizia hurried down the steps waving Angelica's bag.

'Oh Lord!' Angelica sighed. 'Not again!'

'If your brain wasn't in your head, you'd be leaving it all over the city,' said Candace.

'You sound like Olivier.'

'No, honey. Olivier doesn't think you *have* a brain!'

Chapter 2

'Buddha says that pain or suffering arises through desire or craving and that to be free of pain we need to cut the bonds of desire'

In Search of the Perfect Happiness

Angelica arrived to find the dinner had already begun. She was led by a young man in a black Nehru jacket through the candlelit hall to the dining room, where the sound of chatter and clinking glasses rose into the lily-scented air. When she entered, those she knew called out and waved, teasing her for being late. She dared not catch Olivier's eye; it was enough that she could sense his staring at her furiously from the far end of the table. The hostess in tight leather trousers and shiny black boots was more forgiving. She leapt up and strode around the table to embrace Angelica affectionately, wrists jingling with bracelets and bangles.

'Hi, doll. I got a text from Kate but couldn't leave the house.' Scarlet lowered her voice. 'Is she okay?'

'I'll fill you in later. Long story. But she's alive!'

'Well, that's something. You look like you could do with a drink?'

'I've already had one.'

'Then have another. You're as pale as a pancake. I'll get Olivier suitably wasted. He'll be love's young dream by dessert!'

'Thanks, Scarlet. Right now he's a grumpy old nightmare!' Olivier was now in conversation with the ravishing Caterina Tintello. There was nothing that lifted his mood as surely as a beautiful woman.

'Now, you've got the delicious Jack Meyer from South Africa on your right – give that husband of yours something important to worry about – and my slightly less delicious husband on your left.'

'Oh, Scarlet, William is very delicious!'

'Well, he is to me, I suppose, but Jack's delicious to everyone. Now, let me introduce you.'

Scarlet tapped Jack on the shoulder. He said something to Stash Helm, the vivacious woman on his right, then stood up politely, towering over them like a bear. Angelica felt her spirits jolt back to life, recharged by his big shaggy head and wide, infectious smile as he grinned down at her appreciatively. She smiled back, the tension melting away in the warmth of his handshake.

'Jack, meet Angelica Lariviere. Jack's a notorious flirt,' Scarlet teased. 'Don't say I didn't warn you.'

'While the cat's away . . .' he replied, without taking his eyes off her. Angelica was enchanted by the humorous twinkle behind his glasses.

'There's no keeping this dog on the porch,' Scarlet added with a chuckle.

'Some dogs aren't made for porches,' said Angelica.

'You seem to know a lot about dogs.'

'She knows a lot about everything. Angelica's an author, a very successful one, too! Jack loves books. That's why I put you next to each other.'

Scarlet returned to her place, and Jack pulled out Angelica's chair.

'You smell of oranges,' he said.

'Is it overpowering?'

'No. It's delightful.'

She basked in his accent. It wasn't strong, but she could feel the sun and smell the rich red soil in those gently clipped vowels.

He sat down and scrutinized her. 'You seem familiar,' he murmured.

She shook her head and looked away, disarmed by the intimacy of his gaze. 'I don't think so.'

'We haven't met before?'

'Definitely not.'

He laughed it off and spread his napkin on his knee. 'Funny, I feel I know you. A past life, perhaps.'

Before Angelica could respond, William turned to greet her on her left. Reluctantly, she swung around to kiss him, hearing Jack resume his conversation with Stash. 'You look well,' William commented, running his eyes over the glow Jack had just ignited. 'Where have you spent the summer?' William was reserved in that cool, phlegmatic way for which upper-class Englishmen are notorious. Angelica had known him and Scarlet for years: they were part of the London social scene, and Scarlet had become one of her inner circle of friends. However, as fond of him as she was, right now Angelica wished she could turn away and talk to Jack.

She was aware of every movement he made and most of William's conversation went unheard. The first course was eaten, the plates taken away, and, although Jack passed her only a few comments about the food or the wine, she felt they were isolated from the rest of the guests on a little island of their own, acutely conscious of each other. She could feel his arm against hers, and it was warm and strangely familiar. Neither moved away, and she wondered whether he, too, was aware of it. She could hear his voice, the foreign way he articulated his words, but having to respond convincingly to William made it impossible to tune in to what he said. His laugh was infectious, and she laughed herself, deliberately feigning amusement at something William had said. Her host felt witty, growing uncharacteristically animated as a result of her encouragement.

Finally, with reluctance, William turned to Hester Berridge, a buxom, rosy-cheeked Englishwoman who bred horses in Suffolk while her husband worked at the Tate. Angelica was cast adrift for a moment while Jack continued to talk to Stash. She sat back and sipped her wine, the sense of anticipation causing her stomach to fizz. She glanced at her husband, who was still deep in conversation with Caterina. Their heads were almost touching, and he was grinning roguishly. He had once looked at her like that, before they had married and their conversations had been dragged into a more domestic domain. He threw his head back and they laughed together. Angelica didn't mind – Olivier was always better company after a good flirt.

'So, now I get to talk to the authoress,' said Jack, turning his heavy gaze on her as if she was the only woman in the room he wanted to talk to. She noticed the deep lines around his mouth and across his temples, slicing through his rough and weathered skin as he smiled, and felt something she hadn't felt in a very long time: the stirring of tiny bees' wings in her stomach. 'What sort of books do you write?'

'Fantasy novels for children. Probably not your thing, unless you're into sorcery and time travel.'

'I'm definitely into those. I love Tolkien, and I've read all the Harry Potters. I suppose I'm just a big kid.'

'Most men are. The only thing that changes as they grow up is the cost of their toys.' He laughed and the crow's feet deepened across his temples. 'They're a bit of fun, that's all,' she added modestly.

'Children's books are far harder to write than adult fiction.'

'I think I'm just too fanciful to stick to reality.'

'Which writer is your role model?'

'I'd hate to sound like I'm comparing myself to the greats. But I suppose I aspire to be Philip Pullman in the same way a painter aspires to be Michelangelo!'

'It's good to aim high. If you focus hard enough on your goal, I'm sure you'll get there. Philip Pullman's a genius. Your imagination must be exceedingly fertile.'

'You have no idea.' She laughed. 'I get lost in there sometimes.'

'I'd like to get lost in there, too. Real life is way too real most of the time.'

'Oh, I don't think it's a place for a man like you.'

'Why not?'

'Far too fluffy. You have to swim through an awful lot of cotton wool to get to it.'

'I'm a good swimmer.' He smiled, running his eyes over her features appreciatively. 'What name do you write under?'

'Angelica Garner. My maiden name.'

'I'll look out for your books. I need a good book for the journey home.'

She blushed with pleasure. 'So, what do you read?'

'While I'm on the porch?'

'While you're on the porch.'

'Lots, simultaneously. I have books in every room of the house. I like mystery, adventure, love.'

She raised her eyebrows. 'Love?'

'I have a strong feminine side.' He pulled a soppy face.

'Now that surprises me.'

'Why? A book without love is like a desert without flowers.' His gaze grew intense. 'What is more important in life than love? It's what it's all about. Why we're all here, and, when we go, it's all we take with us.'

'Well, I agree with you, of course.' She was stunned by the emotion in his words.

'I'm a frustrated writer,' he confessed sheepishly, playing with his spoon. 'Never had anything published, though. Not for want of trying.'

'What have you written?'

'Rubbish, clearly.'

'I don't believe that.'

'I'm Jack of all trades, master of none.'

'What are the other trades, besides writing?'

'There was a time in my youth when I wanted to be a pop star.' He pulled a face, anticipating her amusement. 'I had long shaggy hair and leather trousers and smoked joints while I strummed my guitar. Now I make wine.'

'Not a poet then.' He gave her a quizzical look. '"A book without love is like a desert without flowers."'

He laughed and shook his head. 'Just a hopeless old romantic.'

She watched him help himself to food, admiring the leonine strength in his profile, the big, pawlike quality to his hands, the very male ruggedness of his skin – so unlike Olivier's polished European glamour – and wished the night could go on forever.

'Do you have a vineyard in South Africa?'

'How well do you know South Africa?'

'I've never been.'

He looked surprised. 'Then you must come. I own a beautiful vineyard called Rosenbosch in Franschhoek. You would love it. You can set your next novel there.'

'I need something to inspire me. I'm growing tired of what I do. Right now I'm considering doing something a little different.'

'Which is?'

She hesitated. Olivier teased her about her fascination with the esoteric; she didn't want to look foolish in front of Jack. 'I'm not sure I'm ready to discuss it,' she replied, embarrassed.

'A love story?'

'No.'

'Murder mystery?'

'No.'

'Erotica?'

She laughed throatily. 'Not yet.'

'I'm determined to find out. I'm a Scorpio: once I set my heart on something, there's no stopping me.' His gaze was too intense: she had to look away.

'I'm not even sure how I'm going to do it, if at all. Olivier thinks it's too ambitious.'

'That's not very supportive.'

'But it's honest. Olivier is very honest.' She looked down at her belt and sucked in her stomach.

'He must be proud of your writing, though.'

'Of course he is,' she replied, but even she could detect the lie in her voice. Olivier didn't think there was much of a challenge in writing for children; she rather hoped she'd prove him wrong with her new idea.

'Is he the good-looking Frenchman over there?' He nodded in Olivier's direction.

'That's the one.'

'Does that dog stay on the porch?'

'I think so. He does a lot of barking, though.'

'Dogs need to bark, makes us feel butch.'

'Give them long leads and they generally don't stray farther than the edge of the porch. If it's a big porch, which Olivier's is.'

'Lucky Olivier.'

'I know. It's the biggest porch in London.'

He frowned. 'No, he's lucky to be married to the most beautiful girl in London.'

Angelica laughed and looked down at her plate. 'Scarlet's right – you're an incorrigible flirt.'

'Not at all, my bark is bigger than my bite. But you *are* very beautiful.' She dismissed his comment with a toss of her hair, but he continued without taking his eyes off her. 'I like sensual women. Women with big hearts. Passionate women.'

'Like your wife,' she teased.

'Exactly, like my wife.' But his eyes twinkled again with mischief, and Angelica smiled into her glass.

'So, what's the new subject?'

'I can't discuss it with you.'

'That's where you're wrong. I'm the perfect person to discuss it with, because you don't know me. I won't judge you, because I don't know you, either. In fact, I am the only person here you *can* discuss it with.' He replenished her wine-glass and sat back in his chair expectantly.

'You're very persistent.'

'When I know what I want.'

'All right.' The wine had made her reckless. 'I'm not sure I want to continue writing children's books that are simply good adventure stories. I want to explore the deeper meaning of life. Perhaps add another layer, like a parable, for me as much as for my reader. I want to find the elusive happiness we're all searching for.' She stopped his interrupting by raising her hand and continuing at great speed, wishing she'd never begun. 'Before you laugh at me, I want to add that I've read all those self-help and esoteric books. I know all the clichés. We *all* know those. The secret is putting them into practice in a practical way. We can't all become hermits and meditate in distant caves. There must be a way of finding heavenly peace while living in the material world. I just feel there's more to life than living it mechanically. There, I've said it. Now it's your cue to laugh.'

He let her finish, then nodded gravely. 'I'm not laughing. It's probably the best idea you've ever had.'

Her face lit up at his unexpected approval. 'You really think so?'

'Absolutely. Everyone is driven by a desire to be happy.'

'Yet so many people are miserable.'

'The secret you're looking for is love.'

'Well, I know that much.'

'Then you don't need to write the book.'

'It's not that simple. Pure, unconditional love is near impossible.'

'No, it isn't. You feel it for your children, don't you?'

'Well, do I? Of course I'd kill for them and die for them. But I'm not sure it's completely unselfish. I need them. That's ego driven, isn't it? I mean, it might be better for them to go to boarding school, but I can't bear to be parted from them, so they'll go to London schools. That's *conditional* love, isn't it? True happiness comes from loving *unconditionally* – and I don't just mean our own children, I mean everyone.'

'Well, I do see there's a problem there. I find most people intolerable.'

'You see? Jesus loved everyone unconditionally. All the great teachers and avatars preached unselfish, absolute, un-reserved love. The kind of love that loves no matter what. Impossible for we less spiritual creatures.' She grinned at him playfully. 'I certainly don't love Olivier unconditionally.'

He laughed and glanced across the table at Olivier, now in animated conversation with Scarlet. 'So what are the conditions?'

'They're too many to list. We don't have all night.'

'Which is a great pity.' He turned his eyes on her again and lowered his voice. 'Loving your husband is dependent on how he makes *you* feel. So you love him on condition that he makes you feel alive, beautiful, and valued.' She was surprised by the wisdom in this analysis – Olivier wouldn't even discuss such a subject. 'If he ceases to make you feel good about yourself, you will cease to love him. You might not leave him, but the essence of your love will change.'

'You're so right. Olivier has the power to make me feel good about myself or bad about myself. His love can wound me or uplift me. Unconditional love would love him no matter what, even if he didn't love me at all.'

'Pure love loves even the hand that strikes it.'

'I couldn't love like that.'

He leaned towards her conspiratorially, and she felt the flame of his charisma as if his body were made of fire. 'I think it's a great idea.'

'You're very sweet to say so.'

'You should have been called Sage, not Angelica.'

She laughed in astonishment. 'Most people don't know that Angelica is a herb.'

'I'm a countryman. I know my herbs, flowers, shrubs, and trees. I know my birds, too. I love nature with a passion. I can't be in a city for too long, the concrete depresses me.'

'I love nature, too. I just don't spend enough time in it.'

'I suppose the park doesn't quite satisfy.'

'No, it doesn't. But I grew up in Norfolk. My parents still live there. It's beautiful, by an estuary. There are all sorts of birds on the beach.'

'Ah, Norfolk, the bird-watching capital of Britain.'

'How do you know that?'

'Because I love birds and I've been to Norfolk. I remember thousands of geese in winter, marsh harriers, bearded tits, avocets, terns, and the odd bittern.'

'You're joking!'

He grinned, pleased that he was able to impress her. 'Don't they have the most wonderful names!'

'You recognize all of those?'

'Of course. As I said, I know my birds.'

'You really do.'

'Come to South Africa. We have all sorts of exotic breeds there: the little malachite kingfisher with her electric-blue plumage and the cheeky hoopoe who calls "poop poop poop" across the garden.'

'Wow, you're a fount of information. How come you're so wise about life and nature?'

'If you love nature, you automatically ask yourself the big questions. You're constantly faced with the death and rebirth of trees and flowers. And when you gaze over vast distances, that prompts you to think of your own mortality and makes you feel very insignificant.'

'I'm going to wipe the dust off my binoculars!'

'I'm glad I've inspired you.'

She sipped her wine thoughtfully. 'You've *really* inspired me, Jack, and not just in the feathered department. I'm going to try to add a deeper layer to my books. I'm going to search for the perfect happiness.'

'You should. I'm not just saying so because I find you attractive. Most people go through life as if they were blind, mechanically, as you say, without ever questioning what it all means. Trust me, I ask myself that question every day.' His face darkened as if a sad thought had passed through his mind. 'We're all going to die. I'd like to find out what I'm doing here before I go. I'd certainly like my last years to be happy ones.' He drained his glass, which was promptly filled by a hovering waiter.

'Let's talk about something happy. Tell me about your children?'

So Jack told her about Lucy, Elizabeth, and Sophie: the three jewels in his crown.

'I bet they've got you well wrapped round their little fingers.'

He laughed as he thought about their wheedling and manipulating. 'They're young women now. Even Lucy,

who's just fifteen, is going on twenty-one. It's hard for a
father like me. I want to wrap them in pink candyfloss and
hold on to their innocence. I'm a terrible old rogue, so I
suspect all the young men in their lives of the worst
intentions.'

'Judging them by your own standards.'

'Exactly. I keep a shotgun under my pillow, and woe
betide anyone who lays a dirty hand on one of my girls.'

'It's going to happen, you know.'

'Oh, it already has. Elizabeth is eighteen and has a boyfriend
at Stellenbosch University. Sophie is sixteen, and who knows
what mischief she's already got up to. Lucy's a knockout, and
I can see a knowing shadow in her eyes. She's tasted the fruit
of good and evil, I'd bet my life on it. There's nothing I can
do.'

'Children come through us, but they don't belong to us.'

'That is a hard lesson for me to learn.'

'For all of us. Mine are still little, but Olivier will find it
hard, especially with our daughter.'

'You never forget what they were like as little girls. In spite
of their makeup and grown-up clothes, they're still the same
underneath. And they don't know how naïve they are. They
think they know everything. I want to stand at the helm of
their lives and steer them through the mines.' Angelica felt a
wave of tenderness. She, too, wanted to steer Isabel and Joe
through the mines. 'When you find the secret of happiness,
let me know.'

'You, Jack, shall be the very first person I tell.'

After dinner Olivier remained at the table with Caterina and
a few others while the rest of the guests adjourned to the
sitting room, where a fire burned in the grate.

'Isn't it a little early for fires?' asked Hester, flopping onto
the sofa.

'It's been the most miserable summer on record,' Scarlet replied, lighting a cigarette. 'I've spent the last month in Italy, and I'm really feeling the cold. You horsey people never feel the cold.'

'It's all that rolling around in the hay,' said Hester, laughing huskily.

'Do you really get up to all that?'

'As much as one can without frightening the horses,' Hester replied, glancing at her husband, who was standing by the window talking to Stash.

'I'd expect you to be burning up in those leather trousers,' said Angelica, joining Hester on the sofa.

Scarlet gave her a hand. 'See, I'm as cold as a fish! I have terrible circulation.'

'You could eat more. You're so skinny, you have no insulation,' said Angelica.

'Thank you for the compliment!' Scarlet puffed out a ring of smoke.

'I'd happily give you some of mine!'

'At our age, women have to choose between their faces and their figures,' said Hester, who had clearly chosen her face.

'So they say, but if my arse expands, my misery pulls my face down, so I choose my figure, every time. A little nip here or tuck there will take care of the face. As it is, I'm so riddled with Botox I can only just pull a smile.'

'I've sacrificed my figure by default, and it's done nothing for my face,' said Angelica, noticing Jack talking to William in the library.

'Oh, I'd love your face, Angelica,' said Scarlet, warming her bottom at the fire. 'We'd all love to look as wholesome as you. Trouble is, no amount of makeup can disguise my unscrupulous past.'

'Oh, I don't think I look wholesome!'

'You do, like a field of golden wheat. You look like a fresh bun just out of the oven. In fact, I'm surprised you haven't been discovered to star in a Hovis advert.'

They all laughed, and Angelica caught Jack's eye as he turned to see what was amusing them. His attention was like sunshine, and she basked in the delicious warmth of it.

Coffee and tea were brought in on a tray, and William and Jack joined the group in front of the fire. Angelica tried to behave naturally, but her whole body tingled with a pleasure as unfamiliar as the taste of a long-forgotten fruit. Jack's smile was contagious. His hair, the colour of wet hay, fell over his forehead until he pushed it back into shaggy waves like a lion's mane. She admired the generous width of his face, his dark eyebrows that knitted together when he frowned, and his almond-shaped eyes that seemed to see the humour in everything. He dominated the party, his comments wittier than everyone else's, his charisma brighter, and everyone laughed at everything he said.

'Jack, why don't you play something?' Scarlet asked, lighting another cigarette. Scarlet was classically trained and never missed an opportunity to show off her talent. 'Because if you don't, I will.'

Jack needed no encouragement. 'Bring me a glass of red wine, and I'll play anything you want.' He went into the library and sat on the piano stool. The baby grand, a wedding present to Scarlet from William, was covered in silver photo frames and a large vase of tuberose. If Jack had impressed Angelica during dinner, it was as nothing compared to the sight of him at the piano. He began with jazz, his fingers dancing deftly over the keys, his powerful body moving in time with such grace and confidence it was as if the piano were an extension of him. Then he played their requests, and they all sang the songs of the Beatles, Abba, and Billy Joel. Angelica joined in, blushing each time he caught her eye, hoping he couldn't hear her pitiful effort. Whether he did or not, he seemed to smile for her alone.

When Olivier sauntered in with Caterina and declared that it was time to go home, she was disappointed. There was no point trying to persuade him to stay. Once Olivier had made up his mind to go there was no changing it. He looked pointedly at his watch, indicating his impatience with a brisk toss of his head.

Angelica said her goodbyes. When she got to Jack, he took her hand and kissed her on both cheeks. 'Come to South Africa. You might discover the secret you're looking for riding across the veld.'

'You don't give up, do you?'

'Life is short.' He pleaded with his eyes.

She laughed and removed her hand. 'It's been fun meeting you and I loved your piano playing. You're not Jack of all trades, you're Jack, master of music. You have a wonderful gift.'

She could tell he was disappointed at her departure, and she was flattered. She hadn't received such attention in years. She couldn't wait to tell Candace.

Olivier was in a good mood. He didn't mention her tardiness nor ask about Kate, and she didn't volunteer any information.

'What a great evening,' he said, opening the car door and climbing in. 'Scarlet always gives good parties.'

'She's a pro at throwing people together and leaving them to get on with it. There are always new people, which is fun.'

'What was that South African like?' he asked. 'He looked a bit pleased with himself, if you ask me.'

'Charming, actually.'

'I bet. He's the sort of man who's strong on charm and weak on brains. I suppose girls like that rugged Clint Eastwood appeal.'

'He was amazing on the piano. You should have joined us.'

'I didn't think you liked singing.'

'I do. I just have a terrible voice. How was Caterina?'

He grinned. 'Caterina is a naughty monkey.'

Angelica was relieved to change the subject. She didn't want to discuss Jack with her husband. 'You've met your match with her.'

'She's an atrocious flirt. Her husband should keep an eye on her.'

'Nothing wrong with a flirt.'

'It's different for a man.'

'In what way?' Angelica bristled.

'I'm afraid there are double standards. A woman flirting in front of her husband is humiliating.'

'Oh, and it's not humiliating for a man to flirt in front of his wife?'

'It's different.'

'Says who?'

He turned into Gloucester Road. 'Boys will be boys. It means nothing. I flirted with Caterina, but she knows I am devoted to you. Whereas if you flirt with a man, he assumes you're not happy with your husband and that you are looking for an affair.'

'You're so wrong!'

'Did you mind my flirting with Caterina?'

'Not at all, but that's because I'm not possessive. I trust you.'

'And you are right to.'

'Are you saying that you wouldn't trust *me*?'

'Yes.' He put his hand on her knee. 'If you flirted with another man like I flirted with Caterina, I'd be crushed like a grape under your foot.'

'You're ridiculous.'

'No, just a hypocrite. Unlike you, I am very possessive, and my heart is very tender.' She laughed. 'The South African flirted with you, naturally. I would be surprised if he didn't. You are a good-looking woman, Angelica. But did you assume he is unhappy with his wife?'

'Of course not.'

'But if you had flirted with him, he would have assumed you were unhappy with me.'

'I didn't flirt with him,' she said quickly.

He stopped at the traffic lights at the bottom of Kensington Church Street. 'I would never accuse you of that, *mon ange*. But don't think I wasn't watching you.'

She wanted to say that he was too busy watching Caterina, but she bit her tongue. Caterina had done her a service.

As luck would have it, Olivier found a parking place a few yards from their house in Brunswick Gardens, beneath a leafy cherry tree that had not yet begun to turn. Angelica hurried up to the front door and waited for Olivier to join her with the key. She smiled as she thought of Jack and how close she had come to getting into trouble with her husband. There was nothing wrong with a flirt, she thought blithely. She felt more alive than she had in years. Perhaps the secret of happiness was in living dangerously. But how to make that feeling last?

Chapter 3

'Thinking positively will attract positive things into your life'
In Search of the Perfect Happiness

The following morning Angelica was awoken by the children climbing into her bed. Olivier had risen early to go to work, turning on the light and waking her up, but once he had gone she had drifted back to sleep and into Jack's big embrace. She had felt a warm sense of belonging there, like a ship docking after a long time at sea. The children's voices seemed distant, like gulls in a faraway sky, and she yearned to remain in those strong, protective arms. But the cries had grown into loud squawks, forcing her back into the present, where Joe and Isabel were fighting over the television control.

Sleepily, she took over and chose *Tom and Jerry* for them, then lay back on the pillow to savour the remaining traces of her dream. It was a new feeling to fancy someone. Since meeting Olivier in Paris in her mid-twenties she had had eyes only for him. Sure, he could be difficult and demanding, like a petulant child who expects his every whim to be indulged and sulks when he feels unappreciated, but she had always been dazzled by him. He had the power to send her spirits soaring and, as so often happens with mercurial men, the same power to pull her down. Her attraction to him had never waned, and she had always relished his touch, even though it was rare these days.

Jack had made her feel attractive in a way Olivier no longer could. There was nothing like the first spark of desire. She had forgotten the magnetic pull of another human being, the invisible force that held her attention wherever he was in the room, the sense of loss when he was out of sight. Those bees in the pit of her belly that made it impossible to eat or sleep. It had been a decade since Olivier had made her tremble with nerves. Her meeting with Jack was like an invigorating wind sweeping through her sails, shaking them out, reminding her that she was still attractive.

She breakfasted with the children, a dance in her step, an Abba tune on her lips. Then they skipped off to play in the garden, leaving her alone with her thoughts. She sat in front of the newspaper, a cup of tea in her hands, lost in the sunlight flooding the kitchen. It didn't matter if she never saw him again: he had caused something to shift inside her and now everything looked more radiant.

She jumped when the telephone rang at nine. It was Candace. 'Hey, Angelica, you're still alive!'

'Oh God, I'm more alive than ever.'

'So you had a fight, then made up in the most degenerate way possible.'

'No.' She sighed dreamily. 'I fell in love last night.'

'I get a feeling this isn't about Olivier.'

'You're right. It was nothing more than an innocent flirt, but God, I feel fantastic this morning.'

'Who was he?'

'Some friend of Scarlet and William's from South Africa.'

'Sounds interesting.'

'It's just that I haven't fancied anyone in years, and I'd forgotten how good it feels.'

'Did Olivier suspect?'

'No, he was too busy flirting with Caterina Tintello.'

'Oh, that old reptile. She's anyone's!'

'Well, he was welcome to her. She diverted his attention, so I had Jack all to myself. God, he's attractive. Scarlet warned me, and she's absolutely right, he's bad news, but . . .'

'But?'

'There's nothing wrong with a harmless flirt.'

'After that belt comment I'd say it's what Olivier deserves!'

'He doesn't think before he speaks. He's so French.'

'Well, honey, I'm glad you've realized you've still got it. It won't do Olivier any harm. He takes you for granted. I'm not saying you need to do anything drastic, but a little flirt every now and then will remind him that if he doesn't play his cards right, you might find someone else who does.'

'What about you? Has Harry forgiven you?'

'I told him I'd been at the back for the whole second half. Fortunately, I heard a couple of old biddies discussing it in the ladies' room afterwards and just repeated their opinions.'

'Have you heard from Kate?'

'Yes, she rang at dawn, God love her. I was fast asleep!' She growled a laugh. 'Pete gets back tonight, so she's got to pull herself together. I suggested we all meet up for lunch at Cipriani tomorrow to console ourselves after the kids have gone back to school. I know most mothers long for the end of the summer vacation, but I'm going to be bereft. I'm dreading it.'

'She might listen to some advice.'

'Not old Groundhog! Oh, she'll listen as if her life depends on it, but the minute you walk out that door she's forgotten all the wise words you've given her and is off to make the same mistakes all over again. I have more success reasoning with my dog.'

'What's she going to do?'

'I know what she *should* do.'

'Which is?'

'Get rid of it.'

'She'll never do that.'

'God will understand.'

'Hers won't.'

'It's better than the alternative. If Pete finds out it's not his, he'll leave her. Period. I'd hate to have to support her through a divorce. Besides, I don't think she'd survive it. She's very fragile.'

'But what if the baby comes out looking like someone else?'

'Depends who that someone else is.'

'Any ideas?'

'No, but I'm working on it. Whose shoulder does she cry on?'

'Not *my* husband's, at least. Olivier finds her intolerable.'

'But it could be anyone else's!'

'I'd better call her.'

'Then bring the kids over for lunch.'

Angelica went upstairs to dress. She put on a CD, and the throaty voice of Amy Winehouse filled the house. Sunshine flooded her bathroom, bouncing playfully off the marble and mirrors, a rare sunny day in what had been the very greyest of summers. She knew she should start on a new book, but continuing in the same mould didn't inspire her at all, and today, she felt wildly free from care. Perhaps she didn't have it in her to write any more novels. Five was a decent number, after all, and they had done pretty well. She hadn't hit the big time, but they sold all over the world, and she had broken into America with the last one, which was based in Arizona. Her latest, *The Silk Serpent,* was due out in March, and her publicist was trying to get her to go and promote it in

Australia. She was big in Oz, apparently. Perhaps she should quit while ahead and float about having lunches with her girl-friends and pondering the meaning of life. Olivier didn't like her working anyway. He made no secret of the fact that she was a wife and mother first and that her writing was merely a hobby. But what would she do if she didn't write? Candace was busy with her charities; Letizia was a contributing editor for *Vogue;* Scarlet ran her own PR company, Bright Scarlet Communications; and Kate modelled, for catalogues mostly. Writing was the only thing Angelica was good at. She brushed her doubts away. Today, she was free of care. Jack's memory hadn't faded, and when she looked in the mirror she saw an attractive, sensual woman, Spanx or no Spanx!

She slipped out of her nightie and opened her underwear drawer, where the neat rows of matching Calvin Klein lace panties and bras lay unused. With a shiver of guilty pleasure she chose a set in ivory. So, she didn't have the lean, slender figure of her youth, but she was undeniably All Woman. Riding on the crest of this most enthusiastic of waves, she decided to join Candace's Pilates class in Notting Hill. It was about time she took a grip, and David Higgins's classes prom-ised quick results. Candace was blessed with height and the long legs of a racehorse, but she insisted her flat stomach and sculpted waist were down to David's rigorous regime. Angelica would never be tall like Candace and no miracle could lengthen her legs, but she could tone up and lose weight. Not for Olivier, not even for Jack, but for herself. The handsome South African had inspired her to get in shape.

She pulled on a pair of jeans, pink trainers, and a floral blouse from Paul & Joe, leaving her unruly hair to fall over her shoulders in shiny curls. She felt the underwear clinging to her skin and smiled at her own daring, as if she were wear-ing it especially for Jack to take off.

Before leaving the house she telephoned Kate, who sounded a lot better in spite of her hangover. 'Candace asked me for lunch today as well,' Kate said, 'but Mum is bringing the children back and having lunch with me here. I have an idea, which I'll share with you tomorrow at Cipriani.' Angelica wished she'd share the identity of the Other Man. 'Thank you for coming over yesterday. You didn't get into too much trouble with Olivier, I hope?'

'No, he was fine,' she lied.

'He knows how much I need you. I don't know what I'd do without all my friends.'

Without an audience there'd be no play, thought Angelica cynically. 'That's what friends are for,' she said. 'To pick you up when you fall.'

'I've fallen very hard this time.'

'Nothing you can't cope with.'

'I'm not sure, this time. I think I've really gone and blown it!'

'No, you haven't. These things are sent to make us stronger.'

'Would it make me stronger to lose Pete . . . and the children?'

'You're not going to lose anyone. Look, you said you had a plan.'

'Yes, I do.' The strength returned to Kate's voice.

'Hold that thought until tomorrow, then we can all discuss it over a glass of wine and a delicious meal.' She forgot that Kate didn't eat.

'Okay, thank you again, Angelica. I owe you one.'

Angelica put down the telephone and wondered what it was that compelled them all to buzz around Kate like worker bees around the queen. Was it her vulnerability that inspired them all to look after her? Or her charm, of which she had an inordinate amount? How could someone like Kate be taught the art of happiness – or even the art of serenity?

*

Angelica spent the morning in Harrods buying shoes for the children and picking up the uniforms she had ordered in July but forgotten all about. Efficient mothers, like Candace and Letizia, had complete winter sets in the right sizes by June, all name-taped and folded in the children's cupboards for the beginning of the autumn term. They returned to London from the South of France or the Hamptons with nothing more than the odd haircut to organize. Angelica, on the other hand, squeezed all the back-to-school tasks into the week before term started, dragging the children around town in a fever to buy the long list of things they required. They'd return from each shopping trip armed with toys that Angelica had been too weak to deny them. Every year she cursed her lack of organization, but every year it was the same last-minute rush.

She arrived late for lunch at Candace's, the boot of the car filled with shiny green Harrods bags. Candace lived in leafy Notting Hill, where the pavements were wide and tree lined, and shiny Mercedes and BMW four-by-fours were parked among Porsches and the odd Aston Martin. Her silver Great Dane greeted them at the door, alongside the Filipina maid in a pink-and-white uniform. Candace's children scampered upstairs excitedly to hide, followed by Joe and Isabel, who hurried past their mother to chase after them. Candace was on the telephone in the immaculately weeded garden, lying on a sun lounger, a glass of fruit juice on the table with the October issue of American *Vogue*. When she saw her friend, she waved. 'Isn't this glorious!' She pushed her Dior sunglasses to the top of her head, sweeping her thick hair off her face.

'I see you're making the most of it,' said Angelica, descending the steps to join her.

'It'll rain tomorrow.' Candace had the sleek brown skin of her Latina mother and the pale green eyes of her father, a stunning combination that enhanced her fine features. 'Come and join me. How hungry are the kids?'

'They've all disappeared upstairs.'

'Great, let's lie out a little longer. They'll come down when they want to eat.'

'Mine had doughnuts in Harrods.'

'Did you get everything done?'

'Just about.' Angelica dropped her handbag to the grass, ignoring the lip gloss that rolled out, and flopped onto the lounger beside Candace. 'I spoke to Kate. She says she has a plan.'

'I wonder what that could be?' Candace laughed dismissively. 'I'm not holding my breath. You do realize we've got nine months of this soap opera?' Candace sipped her juice. 'Ringside seats.'

'Why do we all flock around her? What is it that makes her so compelling?'

'Because our lives would be dreadfully dull without her little dramas to entertain us.' Candace grinned mischievously. 'Why don't *you* have a little drama for a change?'

'My life is very drama free, thank God.'

'It was until last night.'

'Where it began and ended.'

'It just shows that you're ripe for an affair.'

'Oh really, Candace, the sun has gone to your head.'

'No, I'm just putting it out there.'

'Well, pull it back in again, fast! You think I have time for an affair?'

'What? Too busy, like JFK, Lloyd George, and Clinton?'

Angelica laughed. 'You think I'd risk all that I have for a fling?'

'That's the fun of it, apparently. The risk, the excitement.'

'I prefer sitting in the audience watching Kate's life spiraling out of control. I couldn't live like that – it's exhausting.'

'You'd be surprised how many women have affairs at our age. Ten years of marriage, bored of the monotonous plod, plod of their daily lives. Then some handsome, dashing stranger walks in and ignites a flame they thought had died.'

'The flame Olivier ignited all those years ago is still burning strong, I assure you.'

'I hope so. But you felt the frisson of attraction last night, didn't you?'

'Yes, I did. But I can leave it at that. I really don't care if I never see him again.'

'But there might be another Jack around the corner. You're on receive. I'll bet there have been countless Jacks in the last ten years, but you haven't noticed them because you haven't been on receive. It doesn't mean you don't love Olivier, just that you are ready for a little excitement. Just warning you to be careful.'

'You sound like you're speaking from experience.'

'I have the knowledge but not the experience. I just observe what goes on around me. I don't know what it is about me, but people confide in me. Look at you. I'll bet you haven't told Kate, Scarlet, or Letizia about last night.'

'You're right. I haven't told anyone.'

'There you go. I'm the keeper of secrets, the sacred vault.'

'You should be the one writing the book.'

'How's that going by the way?'

'It's not.'

Candace put her glasses back on and curled her glossy lips into a smile. 'All you need is a little inspiration.'

That evening Angelica and Olivier had dinner alone together in the kitchen. Angelica had cooked a root vegetable soup and Thai noodles with ginger, but not even his favourite dish could raise her husband's spirits. He told her about his day, his fear that the City was on the brink of collapse, speculating that thousands of jobs were under threat. The financial world was about to implode, and Olivier was right in the middle of it. He looked grey and tired.

'I've got a sore throat,' he added gravely, as if that was the worst thing to befall him. 'I had it this morning when I woke up.'

'Have you taken anything for it?'

He shrugged helplessly. 'Only aspirin.'

'You should gargle with TCP.'

'I can't abide the taste of that stuff. I'll have an inhalation and sleep in the spare room.'

'You don't have to do that.'

'If I can't sleep I want to watch television.'

'Take Night Nurse, that'll knock you out.'

'And make me feel drugged in the morning.' He took a spoonful of soup. 'This is very soothing.'

'Good.'

'I'm sure I'll feel better in the morning. I can't afford to take time off work at the moment.'

'Oh, you'll be fine after a good night's sleep.'

'I don't know . . . these things tend to linger.'

Angelica recalled the times she had been nearly incapacitated with flu and still managed to look after the children. She grinned into her bowl. Throughout history, men had fought bloody battles with incredible acts of bravery, and yet nothing could slay a man more surely than a sore throat.

Olivier retreated to the spare room after fumigating the kitchen with his Karvol inhalation. Angelica had a bath, lighting candles and scenting the water with aromatherapy oils. She lay back and closed her eyes, letting her mind wander wherever it chose, reining it in when Jack's face surfaced and his arms spread wide to hold her. It was still early when she climbed into bed. She didn't have the will to read – other people's books just reminded her of her current lack of imagination – so she put on a DVD instead. An old movie, one of her favourites: *Falling in Love,* with Meryl Streep and Robert De Niro. She had seen it countless times but still managed to cry when they found each other on the train at the end.

She switched off the light and lay in the semi-darkness listening to the distant drone of cars and the sudden roar of a motorbike as it sped up Bayswater Road. The bed was large, and she felt small lying there, alone. When the children were younger, they'd pad across the landing to climb in beside her. She had relished those nights snuggled up against their warm little bodies, listening to the reassuring rise and fall of their breathing. Now the children slept soundly down the corridor, and Olivier was wallowing in self-pity in the spare room upstairs. Tonight, there was no one to hold but in her dreams.

Chapter 4

'If you love yourself, you open yourself up to being loved in return'

In Search of the Perfect Happiness

The following morning Angelica woke the children early for their first day back at school. They had spent the whole summer going to bed late and waking up at eight, so she had to open their curtains and stroke their faces, coaxing them out of their deep sleep with gentle words of encouragement. They lay inert, their warm bodies curled up beneath their duvets, their pale faces buried into their pillows. She felt sorry for them. There was nothing pleasant about being woken for school, even if it was the most luxurious in London.

Isabel rolled over and stretched like a cat, blinking in the weak light of a grey day. Joe staggered into the bathroom, where he hovered dangerously by the loo, eyes half closed, barely aware of his aim. Angelica rushed to steady him so that he didn't wee all over the floor.

Once awake, they recovered quickly, rushing about with excitement, throwing their pillows at each other while Angelica struggled to get them washed and dressed. She knew how important it was for them to look polished for their new class teachers. She hadn't expected them to be concerned about *her*.

'Mummy, I hope you're not going to wear *that* into school,' said Joe.

Angelica looked down at her wide-leg jeans and trainers. 'What's wrong with what I'm wearing?'

'All the other mothers will look cool. You look like you haven't tried.'

Angelica was mortified. Her jeans weren't *any* old pair, but Hudson's most fashionable, and her trainers were shiny new silver ones. 'What do you think, Isabel?'

'I want you to wear your big shoes.' She meant the new Tory Burch platforms Letizia had brought back from America.

'Well, if you really mind, I'll change.'

'Zeus's mummy's very cool,' said Joe.

Angelica couldn't disagree. Jenna Elrich was famously glamourous, if somewhat overdone in Angelica's opinion. She was one of those girls who wore cream in midwinter, real fur, a lot of big gold jewellery, and oversized sunglasses even when there was no sun.

'She *is* cool, Joe darling, but I'll never be as cool as her. I haven't the time to spend my mornings being blow-dried at Richard Ward.'

Joe wasn't listening: he was too busy sneaking his favorite Power Ranger toys into his backpack. Angelica changed into a pair of J Brand jeans, the brown platforms Isabel had requested, and a Burberry khaki jacket.

When Joe saw her, he nodded his approval. 'That's better,' he said.

She threw on a gold Yves Saint Laurent necklace for good measure and wondered whether other mothers were dictated to by their children.

The scene at the school gates was pandemonium. The road was partially blocked by shiny chauffeur-driven cars. One or two bodyguards with important-looking devices plugged into their ears trailed their small charges, while handsome fathers in suits and long-legged Prada-clad mothers, with straightened blonde hair and suntans, tried to control their excited children as they greeted their friends and gossiped on the pavement. The air was thick with perfume and voices and the odd irritated mutter from a local trying to get to Kensington Gardens to walk his dog. Angelica lived close enough to school to walk and stopped to chat to those she knew on the way.

They shook hands with the headmistress, who remarked how much they had grown and how much the sun had bleached their hair. 'We spent the summer with Olivier's family in Provence,' Angelica told her, aware that it sounded far more glamourous than it really was. The women in his family were a coven of grumpy, dissatisfied witches bent on making everyone around them as miserable as they were. The only consolation was his father, who was dashing and charming, with old-fashioned manners and a dry, cynical wit that made her laugh, mostly at his wife's and daughters' expense.

She was happy to find Candace and Letizia in the hall, talking to Scarlet. When she saw her, Scarlet grabbed her arm exuberantly. 'You have a fan, Angelica!'

'She has many fans,' Candace interjected.

'Sure, but this one's very smitten.'

'Who is he?' Letizia asked.

'A devilishly handsome South African I put her next to at dinner. I didn't notice that you two had hit it off.'

Angelica blushed and tossed her hair casually. 'He was fun.'

'Well, he thinks you're gorgeous! He called to tell me what a rare and special woman you are. Duh! Tell me something I don't know!'

'I hope he knows she's married,' said Letizia.

'He's married, too, but it doesn't stop his flirting as if he were single.' Scarlet laughed huskily. 'You know, I was in Clapham yesterday seeing my acupuncturist, and I spotted him knocking on a little door at the end of the street. He looked really nervous. I was about to shout out and wave, but knowing him as I do, and what a terrible old rogue he is, I left him to his business.'

'A lover perhaps?' asked Candace.

'Without doubt,' Scarlet agreed. Angelica was surprised to feel the twist of jealousy in her gut. Scarlet continued, 'He might be badly behaved, but he's very attractive.'

'He wasn't badly behaved with me,' Angelica retorted nonchalantly. 'He just flirted a little.'

'I hope Olivier noticed,' said Scarlet. 'It would do him good to swallow some of his own medicine.'

The four of them took the children to their new classes. None of them looked as immaculate as Candace's children, with their perfectly ironed uniforms and polished shoes, their hair shining like silk. When it came to saying goodbye, Candace bent down and hugged them as if they were embarking on a long voyage rather than a short day at school. 'I hate leaving them,' she said, her eyes glittering with tears as they walked back down the corridor.

'They love it here,' said Angelica.

'Oh, I know *they* do, but what about me? I'm a wreck.'

Angelica laughed at the absurdity of such a suggestion. Candace, with her manicured nails, sleek hair, and beautiful face was nowhere near a wreck. She looked typically pristine in skinny jeans and flat shoes, an olive cashmere vest worn over a crisp white shirt. Her beloved Birkin handbag hung on her arm, almost eclipsing the enormous diamond ring Harry had bought her on his last business trip to Hong Kong. Angelica doubted Candace's children had ever criticized *her* choice of clothes. 'They'll be out in less than seven hours.'

'I know, but the first day is always hard. I hate the emptiness in the house. All I can hear is the scuffle of feet as Florencia goes up and down the stairs to clean and Ralph lies in his basket sulking because the children aren't there to play with him. Thank God we're having lunch somewhere nice today. I don't think I could bear being at home on my own watching the clock.'

'I'm going to get to my desk, finally,' said Angelica, wondering what she was going to do there.

'I'm going shopping. Screw the credit crunch!'

'I would say the credit crunch demands it. There's no point adding to the misery by denying the shopgirls their commission.'

'I'm so glad you see it that way. I thought I'd pop into Harvey Nichols – fancy a little wander around the first floor?'

'Much as I'd love to, I'd better try to do something. Besides, I haven't checked my emails in weeks.'

They made their way through the throng of parents to the street, where Candace was met by her chauffeur. She climbed into the front seat and waved a bejeweled hand at Angelica. 'See you later,' she shouted, already pressing her telephone to her ear.

Angelica turned towards home, imagining Joe and Isabel settling into their new classes, when a voice shouted at her from the other side of the street. It was Jenna Elrich. Her heart sank. Jenna held her son's hand and crossed the road without a glance at the Range Rover that had to brake suddenly to let her pass. 'How are you?' she asked.

'I'm great,' said Angelica, taking in the big hair and giant sunglasses that made her look like an insect. She was tanned the colour of her Gucci handbag, but her face had the remains of a frosty beauty.

'How's Joe?'

'Thrilled to be back.'

'Zeus didn't want to come to school today. I had to drag him out of bed complaining. *"Mais Maman, je ne veux pas aller a l'école!"* Isn't that right, Zeus?' Angelica was startled by such pretentiousness. Her own children had a French father, but she wouldn't dream of showing off so shamelessly.

'Oh, he'll be fine when he gets inside. Miss Emma's incredibly sweet.'

'We've had such a busy summer. I'm exhausted. We've just finished the house in Mustique, but there are terrible delays on the chalet in Gstaad. I've told John that if they don't finish it by Christmas, I don't want it. Then Jennifer got sick and had to be flown back to London, so I had to have the children on my own for two weeks in Biarritz without a nanny! Imagine the horror of it! So now I'm interviewing for a new nanny, if you hear of anyone who's looking.'

'I'll keep my ear to the ground.'

'Well, I'd better get on, or Zeus will be the last boy to arrive, and that won't be a good way to start the new year.' Then as an afterthought, she added, 'You look great, by the way. I wish I could do that tousled, just-got-out-of bed look, but I always end up looking polished.' Angelica watched her stride off in her leather boots and big coat and hoped she'd boil to death in the heat of the school building. *Tousled, just got out of bed!* she thought indignantly, marching up the road. *If there's one woman I can't abide, it's Jenna Elrich.*

At last she sat down at her desk in her office at the top of the house overlooking the garden. With its pale walls and New England furniture, leafy plants and bookshelves, it was her little sanctuary, where Olivier couldn't complain about the scented candles and her choice of music, a room of her very own where she could meditate without disturbance and dream without distraction. With a sigh of pleasure she sat in her chair and switched on the computer. It had been a long

summer away, and it felt good to be back. While the computer was starting up she lit a candle and switched on her iPod.

The sight of the seventy emails was alarming at first, but
after scanning the list she realized that most were spam and
could be swiftly deleted. There was one from her agent,
Claudia Hemmingway, and a couple from her editor in New
York. She replied briefly, skipping the ones from friends
asking them for dinner and printing out long epistles to read
later. Then her eyes caught sight of a familiar name: Jack
Meyer. With a rush of curiosity she clicked on his name.
How on earth had he found her?

> Dear Sage, I hope you don't mind my writing to you. I've
> been thinking about the idea for your book (which I think is
> great, by the way). I'm back in Rosenbosch now. It's spring.
> The air is infused with the smell of flowers and camphor. I
> love this time of year: everything is new and exciting. I think
> you should come out – it would really inspire you. I enjoyed
> meeting you in London very much. I love your website by
> the way, though there aren't enough pictures of you and the
> ones that are there are not as beautiful as the real woman.
>
> From Dog Safely on Porch

She stared at the words in amusement. What a devil to
have taken the trouble to find her website. He knew she was
married. Judging by his adventures in Clapham, he obviously
got a kick out of living dangerously. She read it again, dwelling on the best bits. She could hear his voice in her head, the
lilt of his accent, his gravelly tone, and she smiled. She could
imagine the Dutch vineyard of Rosenbosch settled beneath a
bright blue sky, surrounded by camphor trees and budding
flowers, and visualized his lying on the grass with a pair of
binoculars, watching the birds.

So, what to do? It would be rude not to reply. After all, there was nothing wrong in lighthearted emailing. Wasn't it possible for two married people to be friends? Wasn't it presumptuous to assume he wanted to sleep with her? He hadn't overstepped the mark at dinner, and she hadn't encouraged him. She looked at the date: he had sent it yesterday. With a mounting sense of guilty pleasure, she placed her fingers over the keys and pressed Reply.

Dear Dog on Porch, Thank you so much for your email. It's nice to hear from you. I'm sitting at my desk pondering my new idea, but feel blocked and uninspired – if you come up with any gems, do send them. I need all the help I can get! How heavenly to be enjoying spring. We're in autumn as you know, and it's only going to get bleaker! Oh for sun and the smell of camphor! Rosenbosch sounds delightful. Olivier and I would love to visit you there one day.

She crinkled her nose at the mention of her husband. *That's very childish,* she thought, and swiftly deleted it.

Rosenbosch sounds delightful. Would love to see the porch! It must be as big as Olivier's. Sage

She read it over a few times. It wasn't flirtatious; she didn't want him to think that she fancied him. Her finger hovered a moment over the Send icon. *What harm can it do to have a cyber friend?* She pressed the key and watched the message disappear off her screen, suffering a sudden, though fleeting, stab of regret.

She imagined his receiving it. Would he write back immediately? She waited a moment, staring at the screen, expecting to hear the ping of a new message, but none came.

Finally, she clicked out and went into Word, opening a new blank document on the screen.

There was nothing more disconcerting than a blank document with nothing to write on it. So she typed the working title: *In Search of the Perfect Happiness* by Angelica Garner, then played around with the typeface, settling on large flowery letters in pink. This took up a few minutes, during which time she listened for the ping of an incoming message.

After writing down as many ideas as she could think of on the big subject of Life, she picked up the telephone and called Candace. Her friend was in the McQueen department at Harvey Nichols.

'He's emailed me,' she stated simply. 'He found me through my website.'

'Oh my God! What did he say?'

'I'll read it to you.'

'Wait, I have to sit down. Wait, wait, wait! Oh, for a chair . . . Don't they have anywhere to sit in here? What about the old or disabled, or simply demented like me! Okay, I'm sitting down, fire away.'

Angelica read her the email.

'He's mad about you.'

'Do you think so?'

'Of course. The fact that he went to the trouble to find you speaks for itself.'

'He's just being friendly.'

'You're just being naïve.'

'I've written back.'

'You're crazy!'

'There's nothing wrong with a little cyber chatting. After all, it's very presumptuous of me to assume that he wants to get into my knickers.'

'No, it's not, it's intelligent. I told you, you're ripe for an affair.'

'I'm not going to have an affair.'

'Look, they always start like this. A little chatting, a little flirting, then it's lunch . . .'

'He lives in South Africa.'

'He was in London. Trust me, Angelica, he'll ask you to lunch. Would you tell Olivier?'

'Sure.'

'No, you wouldn't. Are you going to tell him about this email? Of course not. It'll be your little secret, and you'll love every minute of having one. Every time Olivier loses his temper or gets grumpy or whatever, you'll have your little secret to smile about.'

'Are you suggesting I shouldn't email him?'

'No, I'm just warning you. Keep him at a distance. Don't write anything you wouldn't want your husband to read and don't ever, ever write an email under the influence of alcohol!'

'You know your stuff.'

'Like I said, I'm the sacred vault.'

'Well, Sacred Vault, I'll call you if he emails back.'

'Honey, it's not a question of if but when.'

Angelica checked her emails once more before leaving to meet the girls for lunch, but there was only spam offering her discounted Viagra. The sun had come out, shining through a break in the clouds, and Angelica turned her face to it, wondering whether it was shining on Jack, too, safely on his porch.

She wasn't the last to arrive at Cipriani. Candace, Letizia, and Scarlet sat discussing Kate over Bellinis.

'Darling, we've ordered you one,' said Letizia, reaching out to greet her.

'Guess who I bumped into this morning?' Angelica said, kissing Candace and Scarlet in turn.

'Who?'

'The ghastly Jenna Elrich.' She sat down next to Letizia and recounted how Jenna had imitated her son speaking to her in French. 'It was so pretentious,' she complained.

'You know what? You should have replied like this,' said Candace, clearing her throat. '"Why, that's so funny, Jenna, because Isabel woke up this morning and said *'Mama, tengo ganas de ir al colegio,'* then Joe piped up: *'Anch'io voglio andare a scuola!'* "' She pulled a face, clearly pleased with herself.

'Brava!' Letizia declared in delight.

'Now *you're* showing off.' Angelica laughed.

'I'm a natural linguist,' said Candace. 'What can I say?'

Angelica leaned into the table. 'You know what else she said? That she wishes she could have my tousled hair that looks like I've just got out of bed and haven't bothered to brush it, but every time she tries she just ends up looking perfect and polished.'

'And plastic,' Scarlet added.

'How rude!' said Letizia.

'I think she's hilarious.' Candace laughed. 'She's barely able to say a sentence without bigging herself up. If she mentions a man, he fancies her; if she mentions a woman, she's jealous of her; if she pays you a compliment, it's a back-handed one designed to pull you down. She came for dinner once and complimented me on my "quaint country cooking."'

'I find her infuriating,' grumbled Angelica.

'Don't worry, darling. She'd kill for your tousled locks,' said Letizia.

'No, she'd like your marriage,' said Candace. 'Hers is a deeply unhappy one, and that's the core of her bitterness.'

'Last year she admitted to me that she was well past forty, but she's clearly forgotten, because she keeps referring to the approaching "Big Four O" and asking what she should do to celebrate,' said Scarlet.

'Correct her,' Candace suggested. 'Honey, it's the Big *Five* O!'

'Her husband works at Lehman's. I don't think she'll be doing anything to celebrate,' said Angelica.

'Maybe selling her vast collection of shoes and handbags,' said Letizia.

'The Birkins are fakes,' said Candace. 'Believe me, I *know*.'

At that moment, Kate strode into the restaurant in a knitted minidress and boots, her eyes hidden behind big Chanel sunglasses. Every eye turned as she looked around for her friends, then waved vigorously when she saw them. Women envied her lithe body and striking face, and men sensed something wanton that women did not. She weaved through the whispering tables like an enchanting snake, savouring the attention.

'Sorry I'm late.' She blew them all kisses. 'It's just been one of those mornings.' She flopped into a chair, dropping her Anya handbag to the floor. 'I need a drink.'

'I didn't think you were drinking,' said Letizia.

'I'm not meant to be, but one little teeny weeny Bellini won't hurt the baby.' She smiled at the waiter, who blushed.

'So Pete got back last night. Did you tell him?' Candace asked.

'No. I'm too scared.'

'So what's your big idea?' Angelica asked.

'I'm going to wing it.'

'You're not going to get rid of it?' Candace was astonished.

'I can't.'

'It's only a teeny weeny bundle of cells.'

'I know, Candace, but still it's a life. I've always been anti-abortion. There's a child in here.' She touched her belly.

'Not that you'd know,' said Letizia.

'It's smaller than mine,' Angelica observed.

'Not for long,' said Candace. 'Angelica's joining my Pilates class.'

Scarlet grinned at her. 'Make sure you have a pedicure first – that David is delicious.'

'Trust me, that's the last thing on your mind when you're trussed up, in agony, and sweating like a pig.'

'You don't sweat, Candace, for sure!' Letizia laughed.

'Of course she doesn't,' replied Scarlet. 'She glows like a princess, of the Park Avenue variety.'

The waiter came with Kate's Bellini. She took a sip and smiled. 'That's better. You see, I was thinking, my lover has similar coloring to Pete, so hopefully, unless there are any hideous kickbacks from previous generations, the baby will look enough like Pete to fool him.'

'That's optimistic,' said Candace.

'It happens all the time,' said Scarlet. 'Apparently a vast percentage of children in this country do not belong to their fathers.'

'I think you should come clean,' Letizia advised.

'And risk losing Pete?' asked Angelica.

'Is he worth keeping?' Candace asked. 'What's your lover like?'

'Not the marrying type,' said Kate.

'Already married?'

Kate shook her head. 'I can't say. I haven't told him about the baby, and I'm not going to. To be honest, he's rather embarrassed about the whole thing. As far as we're both concerned, it never happened.'

Candace growled, 'There's someone in there who says it did.' She pointed a manicured nail at Kate's stomach.

Kate grinned. 'But he's not telling.'

'Not *yet*,' said Angelica.

★

At half-past three they picked up the children from school, standing in a huddle discussing Jenna Elrich, who was barking into her telephone in French to one of her staff. When she got the children home, Angelica went upstairs to check her emails. Never before had she been so eager to read them. With an expectant grin she clicked on her mail. There was one from her agent suggesting lunch – and one from Jack Meyer.

Dear Sage, Your email is the most exciting thing to happen to a poor old dog lying on the porch, bored and neglected! I can hear your voice in your sentences and your laugh, as I imagine you must have laughed when you suggested that my porch is as big as Olivier's. If Olivier is clever, he won't require a big porch, but lie next to you in complete bliss on a porch the length of his nose to his wagging tail. (Wagging, I stress, because he's married to you!) As for my ideas, I'm putting them together for you, looking back over my life and experiences. It's not ready yet. Perhaps I'll give it to you when you come out to South Africa, which I hope you will, very soon!

From Dog on Porch

Chapter 5

'Search for the beauty in everything because it's there if you look hard enough'

In Search of the Perfect Happiness

Angelica stared at Jack's email, a mischievous smile playing guiltily about her lips. She knew she shouldn't be encouraging him. But the chance of their meeting again was very slim. He lived a safe distance away in South Africa. Even if he came to London, she'd never be able to explain away lunch, and she certainly wouldn't dare go behind Olivier's back. She'd be sure to bump into someone they knew and be found out. She toyed with these ideas for amusement, for the sheer pleasure of the impossible dream.

With a recklessness that was quite out of character, she wrote a reply.

Dear Dog on Porch, I think the first secret to happiness is acceptance. Isn't the desire to have what one can't have the root of our unrest? Sage

Pleased, she pressed Send without hesitation. She waited a while for a reply. She'd have to go down to the playroom in a moment to beg, bribe, and coerce her children into doing their homework, but she was reluctant to tear herself away

from the computer. Just as she was about to get up, the telephone rang. It was her agent, Claudia Hemmingway.

'Hi there, Angelica. How's the writing going?'

'It's great,' she lied. 'Just began today.'

'Fabulous. Can't wait to read the first draft.'

'Don't hold your breath. I won't have anything for you
until after Christmas.'

'That's okay, so long as you're pushing on. Listen, I think
we should have lunch. There are a few proposals I want to
discuss with you.'

'Nice proposals?'

'*I* think so.' She paused. 'I haven't seen you all summer.
Let's say it's time to regroup.'

'Oh God, you're going to try to persuade me to go to
Australia again.'

'I promised I wouldn't.'

'I can't leave the children for that long – you know that.'

'And I totally understand; it's just that . . .'

'It would be so good for my career. Olivier doesn't consider
it a career.'

'The money you make certainly classes it as a career.'

'You talk to my husband.'

'Look, I'm not going to try to persuade you to go to
Australia. I promise. Let's have a nice lunch and put together
a battle plan for the next book. When can you do it?'

'Can we put something in at the end of November? I
know it's a long way off, but I'm reluctant to leave my desk
while I'm on a roll.' *Gives me more time to get something
written.*

'That's fantastic. I don't want to interrupt your creative
flow.'

As Claudia was looking through her diary, Angelica heard
the ping of a new message. There, highlighted in bold, was the
name: Jack Meyer. 'What about Thursday the twentieth?'

Claudia suggested. 'We can go to Sotheby's Café. I know you like it . . .' There was silence. 'Angelica? Are you still there?'

She tore her eyes away from the screen. 'Yes, yes, I'm here. Sorry, just got distracted by an email.' She flicked through her diary, eager to finish the call so she could read what he had written. 'The twentieth of November. It's in.'

'Great. I'll leave you to your writing and that email!'

Angelica put down the telephone and turned back to her computer screen.

Dear beautiful Sage, In my case the desire to have what I can't have poses a tremendous challenge, which generates a great deal of happiness in the form of anticipation. Perhaps acceptance in its purest form is the key to *lasting* happiness. The trouble is that there is nothing pure in my form of acceptance, only frustration and rebellion as I fight against it. Surely if I accept my lot, I will never raise myself up to my true potential? What do you say to that? From Dog on Porch

With an increasing sense of guilt, she read it again. 'Dear beautiful Sage . . .' He obviously wasn't worried that his wife was going to read his emails. She knew the rest of what he wrote referred to her and the challenge she posed. She was the object of his desire and quite unobtainable. Yet she didn't feel she was in danger. Email gave their letters a comfortable detachment. It wasn't like speaking on the telephone, or talking across the table at lunch. It enabled her to flirt in a way she would never have dared flirt in person.

She was aware that she was encouraging Jack for her own amusement, which wasn't really fair. She should stop it before it went too far. But she managed to convince herself that it was as much a game for him as it was for her. He probably had email 'friends' across the globe – what was one more?

So how should she respond to his thoughts on acceptance? She sat back and considered, chewing on a pen. The happiness of which he spoke was temporary, more of a high than a state of inner peace and harmony. She posed a challenge, and the desire to win her gave him the anticipation of happiness, but, having won her, the challenge would be gone and happiness would elude him once again.

Her fingers hovered over the keys. She knew she should wait a few days before replying. She didn't want to look keen. But the temptation was too great to resist, and besides, didn't she deserve a little innocent fun?

Dear Dog on Porch, The happiness you speak of is a temporary happiness. Imagine a dog on his porch. If he's straining at the lead and yearning for what is in the garden, he will only feel frustrated and unhappy. If he strays into the garden in chase of a rabbit, he might experience the pleasure of the chase, but then his happiness evaporates until the next rabbit. If he accepts that he must stay on the porch and lies there feeling the wind through his fur and the sun on his skin and doesn't yearn for that rabbit, surely then he will feel the deep inner contentment of just being. From a rather confused Sage

She was wrenched from her ponderings by Joe shouting up the stairs that he wanted to watch *Ben10* but that Isabel had stolen the control to watch *High School Musical*. 'No television until you've done your homework,' Angelica replied, skipping down the stairs. 'Joe, you're first. Look, the sooner you do it, the sooner it's over, then you can watch *Ben10*.'

While Sunny made spaghetti bolognese for tea, Angelica sat with Joe at the dining-room table. *Happiness is loving my children,* she thought as Joe read out loud. She watched her son's earnest face as he concentrated on the words and tried to imagine what he was going to be like as a man: handsome like his father, certainly, with her light eyes and fair skin. Outspoken like his grandfather. Unique in the way that every human being is a one-off.

Her mind drifted to Olivier, and she felt a twinge of guilt, though there was no fear of his reading her emails; he never set foot in her office. He wouldn't imagine her having a cyber friend like Jack. No one would. Olivier had a reputation for loving women. After all, he was French. In fact, if Olivier didn't chat up girls at every turn, people assumed he was ill or in a bad mood, and they were probably right. It didn't mean that Olivier didn't love her above all others, just that he needed the adrenaline rush of a flirtation and the confirmation that at forty-eight he was still attractive. But she, being English and less flamboyant, was reputedly a paragon of virtue.

Angelica drew Joe into her arms and gave him a bear hug. 'You're brilliant,' she exclaimed, savouring the smell of his hair and his soft skin against her cheek. Her children were still little, but it wouldn't be long before they were pushing her away, not wanting to be cuddled, and then she'd have no one to wrap her arms around, because Olivier was never here and when he was, his mind was still in the office.

'So, can I watch *Ben10* now?'

'Go on, then. Tell Isabel it's her turn.' She watched him disappear into the hall. *My happiness depends on the health of my children,* she thought. *Not a lasting happiness because it is always clouded with fear. I fear things that might never happen. Wasted energy and yet, I can't stop myself. For every moment of bliss I fear the pain of loss. How would I cope without them? Happiness is like small islands in a sea of fear. Why can't fear be small islands in a sea of happiness? Why fear at all? Can't I just* accept *things as they come and deal with them as they arrive?* She smiled wistfully as Isabel padded into the room.

★

When Olivier arrived home, the children were in bed and Angelica had cooked dinner. The table was laid in the kitchen with place mats and napkins, wineglasses and a single candle.

'This is romantic,' he said, dropping his briefcase on the hall table.

'It's just the two of us.' She noticed the silk and cashmere scarf around his neck.

'Good. I'm too tired to talk to anyone but you, and my head is still full of rampaging elephants.'

'Have you taken anything for it other than aspirin?'

'Besides Nurofen, no. I think I'll have another inhalation before bed.'

'Take Night Nurse.'

'All right. I'll do that. Tomorrow, I'll stagger into work with a hangover.'

'How's it been?'

'Terrible. Everything is down. This is serious, Angelica.'

'I know, I've read the papers.'

He sighed and sank into a chair. She poured him a glass of Bordeaux. He took a sip, and his shoulders relaxed.

'Take off your scarf and jacket, and I'll give your shoulders a rub.'

'What's going on?' he asked, loosening his scarf. 'Are you having an affair?'

'Silly! You just look so tense.' She felt her cheeks redden.

'I *am* tense.' She put his scarf and jacket on the back of his chair and proceeded to massage his neck. 'That feels so good.' Her fingers worked deep into the muscles, feeling them soften beneath her touch. She felt guilty about her secret emails, and her guilt made her a geisha to make up for it.

'I haven't given you a massage in years.'

He laughed. 'You never gave me massages even when we were courting. I was the one with the oil.'

'And the magical hands.' She was surprised to feel herself grow hot with desire.

'They still are magical, you know.' He closed his eyes, and slowly his tension drained away, replaced by a physical yearning for a more primitive form of release.

He took her hands and pulled her round in front of him, pushing out his chair so she could sit astride him. 'I want to make love to you,' he murmured. 'I have a beautiful wife. I should take more notice of her.'

'With your sore throat!'

'It's feeling better.'

Hypochondriac, she thought affectionately. 'What about the children?'

'If we worry about the children walking in on us, we will never make love.'

He pulled her head down and kissed her, letting her hair fall about his face. His lips were warm and tasted of wine. He was a good kisser; he always had been. He pulled her shirt out of her jeans and slipped his fingers inside. She felt his hands undo the clasp on her bra and then the sensual feeling of his thumbs on her nipples. It had been so long, they responded eagerly to his touch. She threw back her head and allowed his bristly chin to scratch the delicate skin on her neck as he kissed her. Aware of the danger of being caught by a sleepy child, Angelica wriggled out of her jeans and panties and sat astride him again, slipping him inside her with a well-practised hand. They lost each other for a while, alone in their pleasure, until they reached the peak together. They remained entwined a moment longer, hearts racing, heads spinning with the sudden rush of adrenaline.

'That was spontaneous,' she said, kissing his temple. It was damp and salty.

'It is like we are young and in love again.' He stroked her hair. 'We should make love more often.'

'Life is busy,' she said, climbing off and reaching for her clothes.

'We should make time for the important things. Now what's for dinner?'

Angelica watched him tuck into the lamb cutlets with relish. Sometimes it was as if food was his meaning for living. An unsatisfactory meal could ruin his whole week. She sipped her wine and ate slowly while he talked about himself. He didn't ask her about *her* day. There was nothing unusual about that: there wasn't a great deal to report, but suddenly it mattered that he wasn't curious. 'Lehman's has crashed. Other banks are sure to follow. This is really going to affect everyone, even us.'

'I know. I'm being careful.'

'No unnecessary indulgences.'

She stiffened. 'I said, I'm being careful.'

'I know you are.'

'I've got money coming in.'

'Sure, but the publishing world is going to be hit, too. People are going to cut out things they don't need, and books will suffer.'

'Children still need to read.'

'But you won't be paid such big advances in future. You watch: everyone is going to be pulling in their belts.' She raised a reproachful eyebrow at the mention of the word 'belt' and wanted to remind him that he didn't like her to wear one.

'The City will recover. It always does,' she said instead.

'But it could take years.'

'Well, until it does we'll just be careful.'

'You'll see, even those big-time spenders like Kate and Candace will have to close their purses.' She couldn't imagine their doing anything so rash.

'So how are the children? How was their first day back at school?'

'They had a fabulous day. Loved every minute.'

'Who did you see?'

'Usual crowd. Scarlet, Letizia, Candace . . . Oh, I bumped into the dreadful Jenna Elrich.'

'Now, she's a sexy woman.'

Angelica's mouth fell open. 'God, Olivier, have some taste!'

'She's very stylish. I like her look.'

'You and Joe both,' she muttered. 'I suppose she looks glamourous to the uninitiated.'

'She's well dressed.'

'Overdone like a Christmas tree.'

'Talking of which, I suppose we're going to spend Christmas with your family.'

'I'm as unenthusiastic about them as you are.'

'And then visit mine in France.'

'I don't know whose is worse.'

'Oh, yours win, hands down. No contest! But they redeem themselves by giving me lots of amusement!'

'I'm glad they amuse you. They depress *me*.'

'So, cheap presents this Christmas.' He wiped his mouth with his napkin. 'This isn't the year for spending money, so don't go mad.'

'I know, it's the thought that counts.'

'If it were the thought that counted, they'd get nothing at all! If I remember rightly, you forgot to bring presents for my sisters last year, which just goes to show how little you think of them.'

'They're charming, adorable women,' she said, sucking in her cheeks. Olivier narrowed his eyes, but his lips curled up at one corner.

★

After dinner Olivier retreated to their bedroom with a mug of hot tea and honey. He switched on the news and ran a bath, taking his clothes off and hanging them neatly in the closet, scowling at his wife's clothes carelessly discarded on the floor along with Joe's Ben10 toys and damp bath towels.

Angelica went to check on the children. They were fast asleep in their bedrooms, their faces innocent in the darkness. She pulled the duvet up over Isabel's exposed shoulders and stroked Joe's flushed cheek. Then she heard Olivier turn off the tap and climb into the water. Conquered by curiosity, she climbed the stairs to check her emails one last time before bed. If Olivier knew she was in her office, he would think it very strange. She never worked in the evening, let alone read her emails. But there, as she had hoped, was one from Jack.

Dear beautiful Sage, I think the dog would rather slit his throat than face a life of no rabbits. I know I would! Besides, doesn't it depend on the rabbit? Who's to say the rabbit can't keep the dog interested? I think you should consider the rabbit and not just dismiss her as a plaything for the dog! As for yearning, it is part of the pleasure of life. Without yearning there are no dreams – as a writer you should know the importance of dreams – and without dreams how can we reach our full potential?

Sleep well, lovely Sage. I am on my porch, but my dreams are making me a happy dog. DOP

The City might be collapsing around her husband's ears; she might have to stop shopping; they were probably going to spend a miserable Christmas with her eccentric parents – but Jack made her feel desirable. He shone a light onto a part of her that no one else saw, and in the glow of that light she felt that hidden part awake and stir into life.

Chapter 6

'Being generous and loving spreads happiness that is then returned to you tenfold'

In Search of the Perfect Happiness

Olivier had gone to the spare room again, so Angelica lay in bed alone, composing her next email to Jack. She wished Joe or Isabel would come to keep her company. She missed the gentle sound of their breathing and the warmth of their bodies beside her. She didn't miss Olivier; he smelled of Vicks and snored.

By Saturday morning she had caught Olivier's sore throat. She heaved a sigh and staggered into the bathroom, her eyes heavy with sleep, and rummaged in the medicine cupboard for some Day Nurse. Unlike Olivier, she wouldn't moan and groan, but treat the symptoms with the right drug and push through her day with typical British stoicism. She knocked back a little cup of orange liquid and retched at the taste.

She returned to bed and squeezed in between the children, who had come to join her, a pillow over her head to drown out the sound of *Bug's Life* on the television. She thought of Olivier asleep upstairs and felt her heart harden. He accused her of running around Kate like a lady-in-waiting, but she was expected to run around *him* like a devoted mother.

They had met at a summer wedding in Paris and spent all night dancing in the cobbled courtyard beneath a canopy of stars. Knowing how much she loved books, he always went out of his way to find her things he thought she might like to read. He had been spontaneous then, always one step ahead of her desires, surprising her with his thoughtfulness. He had taken her to the opera and the ballet, out for dinner at the Ivy, for romantic weekends in the Georges V, holidays on the Riviera. He had bought her little presents whenever he had travelled abroad on business, and left notes on her pillow telling her how beautiful she was and how much he loved her. Occasionally, his notes had been more imaginative: *Claridge's, 3:30 p.m., room 305* and they had met like strangers and made love all afternoon, ordering dinner from room service. Then they had married and had children, and she had morphed into his mother. He no longer took her out for dinner or arranged treats, but complained about his throat or his stomach or whatever was troubling him, and asked her advice on which medicine to take. Yes, she had morphed into his mother. No wonder Jack made her feel attractive; it wasn't very hard to make her feel like a woman.

It was a bright, clear day, so she took the children into Kensington Gardens. The sun was warm and the park filled with children on scooters, people walking their dogs, joggers running along the paths, cyclists weaving down the Broad Walk. *If only the summer had been like this,* she thought, basking in the heat. Isabel and Joe made a beeline for the Diana Memorial Playground, scaling the mast of the pirate ship like monkeys. She sat on a bench and watched them, marvelling at how much they had grown over the summer months. Then her mind sprang back to Jack and the email she was going to send him. The anticipation of a reply was enough to cure her sore throat.

When she got home, Olivier had left a message on the kitchen table. 'Gone for coffee. Be back at midday. What shall we do for lunch?' She imagined him sitting in Starbucks on the High Street reading the papers and munching on a croissant, wrapped in his scarf and jacket, and wished she had the nerve to take the children off to Birdworld, leaving him to organize his own lunch. Instead, she left them climbing the magnolia tree in the garden and went up to her office.

Poised over the computer, she felt her irritation dissolve in the excitement of this small, secret act of defiance.

Dear Dog on Porch, You see how difficult it is to put these things into practice!

As a little aside and something else to get your teeth into, isn't suffering part of this great school of life? Doesn't it make us wiser, stronger, and more compassionate? If life was a blast without pain or sorrow, would we die any better for having lived?

It's a beautiful day here in London – I hope the sun is shining on your porch and that all the rabbits are safely in their burrows. From your ever more confused Sage

She turned off her computer and joined the children in the sunshine, sitting at the table to watch them play. It wasn't long before Olivier returned with the newspaper. As predicted, he wore a scarf to emphasize his ailing throat.

'I had a bad night. It was agony this morning, I couldn't lie in. I'm feeling much better now I'm up and have had my coffee.'

'I was thinking of taking the children to Birdworld.'

'Good idea. I'll stay here and take it easy.' She didn't bother to mention that she, too, now had a sore throat. Olivier never liked to share the limelight when he was unwell.

'I might take them off now. We can have lunch there.'

'Is there anything for me to eat?'

'There's some soup in the fridge. That'll be good for your throat.'

'What time will you be back?'

'I don't know. Fourish.'

'Okay.' He looked disappointed.

'You can always come with us. It's not very strenuous walking around Birdworld.'

He put his hand to his throat. 'No, I'd better rest. You know what my sore throats are like.' He hunched his shoulders, looking sorry for himself.

'Why don't you watch a DVD or something? You need to give your body a chance to recover. I'll make you a hot drink before I go.' He seemed to swell beneath her apparent concern.

'Perhaps I will have a spoonful of that Manuka honey.' He didn't make a move to get it.

'Good idea,' she said getting up dutifully. 'That's meant to be excellent for sore throats.'

Angelica didn't really want to go out on her own. She would have liked Candace to go with her, but Candace spent every weekend at their house in Gloucestershire. Kate and Letizia were bound to be doing something more glamourous. Then she had a bright idea. She'd ask Scarlet. *She* was the sort of girl who relished a plan cooked up at the last minute, and William was notoriously easy-going.

As fortune would have it, Scarlet thought it a fabulous idea. She suggested all going together in her BMW, as it had ample room for two adults and four children. When she rang the bell, Olivier answered to find her in a denim miniskirt and pale brown suede boots. His mood lifted at the sight of her tanned thighs, and for a moment Angelica thought he might change his mind and come with them.

'I'm a little under the weather,' he explained, torn between his desire to see more of her legs and his inclination to sulk in front of the television feeling sorry for himself.

In the end it was Scarlet who made the decision for him. 'I don't want you infecting my children with whatever undesirable bug you happen to have,' she said firmly. 'I think you'd better go back to bed and sleep it off.'

Olivier watched them drive away, wondering what he was going to do all afternoon without Angelica to look after him. He resented her for deserting him when he was ill. The least she could have done was rustle up something more interesting for lunch. As it was, he faced boring old soup. He brightened a little at the thought of dinner, certain that she would cook something more inspiring to make up for having abandoned him.

'I bet you're pleased to be out of the house,' said Scarlet as they drove down Holland Park Road.

'He's like a bear with a sore head.'

'More like a sheep!'

'I know, he's pathetic when he's sick. He brings out the worst in me. I'm irritated that he can't look after himself and guilty that I'm not nursing him as I should.'

'All men are the same. It's Man-Flu. When William's sick, he starts talking like his old nanny. "I think I need a *little* Vicks on my chest and a *little* lemon and honey." Everything in the diminutive and delivered in his most wretched voice.'

'Do we blame their mothers? Are our sons going to end up the same because of our over-indulgence?'

'I hope not, but I fear so.' Scarlet glanced at the four children in the back. The boys were playing Nintendo, the girls flicking through Isabel's owl book.

'I don't know whether Olivier's more annoyed that I'm

abandoning him for the day, or that I haven't cooked him anything for lunch.'

'Oh dear, what's he having?'

'Soup.'

'Shame on you, Angelica!'

'I know. I haven't got round to filling the fridge. I'll find something more substantial for dinner, even if it means ordering out. You know what's annoying, though?'

'That he wouldn't cook for you if you were ill.'

'Exactly. It's all one way. I'm the one who has to buy the food, put meals on the table, take his jacket to the dry cleaner – which reminds me, I still haven't picked up his Gucci jacket and trousers. Damn!' She sighed in frustration. 'There's so much to do and so little time in the day! I have to think of all the domestic stuff, and yet I have a career, too.'

'William's the same. I'm at the office all day, juggling my clients and my children, and yet he expects dinner on the table when he gets home – and not just soup and salad. That's men for you. Especially an old-fashioned man like Olivier.'

'A *French*man like Olivier.'

'At least you have that sexy French accent to listen to on the pillow.'

When he's there, Angelica thought bitterly.

Once at Birdworld in Farnham, the children rushed into the shop, picking up furry toys of exotic birds and squeezing them to make them tweet. Scarlet's son Charlie made straight for the sweet stand. Scarlet strode in after them in her high-heeled suede boots and large sunglasses, turning every head.

Outside, Charlie munched from a bag of jelly beans while the others ran from cage to cage feeding the birds from the packets of seeds and dried worms their mothers had bought for them at the admissions desk. Scarlet and Angelica wandered after them, chatting, enjoying the sunshine and the sight of their happy children entertaining themselves.

'This was a fine idea, Angelica,' said Scarlet, impervious to the stares she was getting, even from the birds.

'It's easy entertainment. I'd like to have a country place like Candace.'

'We once rented a cottage near Tetbury, but now we've bought a place in Mustique there's no point. I can't cope with too many homes.'

'I'd like to take the children somewhere hot for Christmas, but Olivier has decided to stay here and spend a long week-end in cold Provence with his ghastly family.'

'He's wise: the depression's only going to get worse, and he's right in the thick of it. Glad we bought our house in Mustique before things went apeshit.'

'I need sun at Christmas. I can't bear the short days. It's night-time by three in the afternoon.'

'You should come and stay with us in Mustique.'

'If only. I had already looked into renting a house near Cape Town.'

Scarlet's face lit up. 'Oh, you could go and visit your friend Jack Meyer.'

Angelica laughed casually. 'He's not my friend.'

'He'd like to be.'

'I think he probably has enough "friends."'

'I'm sure he does.'

'What's his wife like?'

'Lovely. She's South African, too. Very bright and clever, but really nice. They met at Harvard.'

'Sounds rather terrifying.'

'God no! She's so laid back she's practically horizontal – does a lot of yoga and meditating.'

'Well, that's just up my street.'

'She's a little too New Age for my taste. You know, crystals, incense, and angels! But she's a saint. Jack was very sick a few years back. He had cancer.'

Angelica was shocked. 'How awful. Is he okay now?'

'Oh yes, totally. He shrugged it off in that effortless way of his. You'd never have known there was anything wrong with him, except that he lost all his hair.'

'My God, that must have been terrible. He has fabulous hair.'

'A fine head as any I've seen. Now he's like a shaggy old lion again. He might be an incorrigible flirt, but he's devoted to Anna. He owes her a lot.' Angelica didn't want to hear how much he loved his wife. 'I think men just need to flex their muscles every now and then. They're not monogamous by nature. In fact, I think it's quite a struggle for most of them. So long as they feel attractive to other women, they're content to stay on the porch.'

Angelica smiled at her friend's reference to the porch. 'I'm sure Jack stays firmly on his.'

Scarlet grinned at her mischievously. 'I'm not so sure. Some dogs can't help themselves, however devoted they are to their wives. It's in their blood, like wolves or foxes. There's simply no taming them.'

They had lunch at the café, then sat on little benches to watch a demonstration with owls. Scarlet hid behind a tree to make a phone call while the children watched the owls, enraptured. Angelica thought of Jack suffering from cancer and wondered whether his ordeal had inspired his reflections on life and its purpose. An illness like that could change a person profoundly. He hadn't mentioned it, so she decided she wouldn't, either. She wondered whether he had replied to her message.

★

They got home from Birdworld at six. Charlie and Joe fell asleep in the car. The girls listened to *High School Musical* and stared out of the window in silence. The day had exhausted them. Olivier appeared at the door, took in the delicious sight of Scarlet's smooth thighs, then asked Angelica what was for dinner.

'Steak,' she replied, waving Scarlet off, a sleepy Joe leaning against her hip.

'Good, I'm ravenous!'

'How are you feeling?' she asked.

'So so.' He shrugged in that French way of his. She noticed his scarf was still tied around his neck. 'I think I'll have another hot drink.' She knew she was expected to make it.

'The children loved Birdworld,' she volunteered, irritated that he hadn't asked.

When she finally managed to get to her desk after putting the children to bed and making Olivier a Lemsip, there was no email from Jack. She pressed Send and Receive again just to make sure, but no messages were displayed. She bit her bottom lip and frowned. Perhaps he had gone away for the weekend. No one checked their emails on a Saturday. She'd look again tomorrow, but realistically there was no point looking until Monday.

She went downstairs to run a bath to find the room filled with a cloud of eucalyptus. There, slouched in the armchair, a towel thrown over his head, sat Olivier inhaling a bowl of boiling water and Karvol. *My knight in shining armour,* she thought, rolling her eyes. *Sometimes I want to kick this dog right off the porch!*

Chapter 7

'People treat you according to how you allow yourself to be treated'

In Search of the Perfect Happiness

On Monday Angelica met Candace in the reception room at Ten Pilates in Notting Hill. Candace, immaculate in a beige tracksuit, smiled broadly and dropped her mobile telephone into her chocolate-brown Birkin.

'You look glamourous for the gym,' said Angelica.

'This isn't just a gym, honey. This is the hottest ticket in town!'

Angelica looked around at the tall, willowy girls coming out of their classes, dabbing their necks and faces with towels. Among them she saw a face she recognized.

'Hey, doll,' said Scarlet breathlessly. 'It was hell today. David's on a roll.' She turned to Candace. 'Have you warned her about the Higgins Ten?'

'What's that?' Angelica asked nervously.

Candace enlightened her. 'It's David's trademark. He counts ten and you think you're going to die, you've already done a minute or so and your ass is killing you. But just when you think it's over, he demands ten more. Does it every time. Don't be fooled by the countdown. There's *always* another ten.'

'Hence Ten Pilates,' said Angelica brightly.

'I'm not sure that's exactly what he had in mind,' said Scarlet. 'More likely the ten torture beds you see before you.' She registered Angelica's anxious face. 'Don't panic, he'll be kind to you as you're a beginner. Have you had a pedicure?'

'No!'

'Keep your socks on then. Don't embarrass yourself!'

'She's joking,' said Candace. 'Trust me, he's not looking at your toes – that man's only interested in muscle!'

Angelica filled out the required health form, then followed Candace into the studio, where ten Reformer beds were lined in two rows in front of an enormous mirrored wall. Candace dropped her bag on the sofa and put her long hair into a ponytail. 'Hey, David, I want you to meet my friend Angelica Lariviere.' A lithe Australian with a thick mop of dark brown hair extended his hand.

'Good to meet you,' he said with a smile. Angelica was not encouraged. *I'm going to have to sweat and heave and groan in front of that Adonis?* 'Have you done this before?' he asked, and Angelica tried to look past his boyish good looks to the professional instructor who was going to turn her into a supermodel.

'No, it's my first time.'

'Well, let me show you how these Reformers work.' *Thank GOD he didn't say bed.* She followed him over to what looked like a rack of torture with ropes and springs, trying to take it all in so as not to make a fool of herself. 'How fit are you?' he asked.

'Not fit at all. Two children, too much cake, sitting at a desk all day – you get the picture.'

'No worries, we'll get you in shape.' Angelica wished she'd had that pedicure.

'If you get confused, just watch me,' said Candace, taking the Reformer beside her friend and lying on her back. 'It'll soon become second nature.' She put her legs in the air, threw a ring over her feet, and proceeded to stretch. 'So, what's the news on the email front?'

'Hot and heavy,' Angelica replied, lying down and trying to stretch like Candace but barely managing to straighten her legs.

'You're crazy, Angelica. Where's it going?'

'It's not going anywhere. It's just fun.'

'Perhaps, but be careful.'

'Olivier's driving me insane at the moment. This is a distraction.'

'It might get out of hand. Has he asked you out for lunch yet?'

'Of course not. He's in South Africa.'

'Don't say I didn't warn you.'

'Right, girls!' It was David, striding into the room, which was now full of stretching women. He turned the music up loud: Madonna singing 'Hung Up' to the Abba sound track. 'Let's get going. One foot on the foot bar and push it away.'

'My leg's aching already,' Angelica moaned.

Candace made it look easy. 'Remember the Higgins Ten.' Angelica began to sweat. 'And by the way, this is just a warm-up.'

'I'm in hell. Did you say it's an hour?'

'Just under. But think of the body you're going to have.'

'It had better be worth it.' *Think of Jack. I'm doing this for you, Jack. One, two, three, four . . .* By the end of the hour Angelica could barely stand, her legs were trembling, and the muscles in her stomach ached, even in repose. Her inner thighs had never worked so hard. 'So how do you feel?' David asked. There was a mischievous curl in his smile.

'I think I'd rather give birth than go through that again.'

'If you can just get through a couple of weeks, your body will adapt and you won't find it so hard.'

'Or painful?'

'Or painful.'

'He's born in the wrong century,' said Candace. 'He'd have found his niche in the Tower of London manning the rack – and probably enjoyed it!' She took a swig from her water bottle. 'Look at him! He'd be so disappointed if we skipped out having not even broken into a sweat.'

'No chance of that!'

'We keep coming back because you're the best, David,' said Candace, raising her bottle in a toast.

'If I looked like you, Candace, I'd keep coming back, too,' said Angelica.

'You will,' David encouraged.

'No amount of lunges can give me those legs.' She looked at her friend, beautiful in spite of the sweat that stained her T-shirt.

'Everyone's different,' said David. 'The point is to be the best you can be. So do you want to sign up for more classes?'

'I'll buy fifty,' said Angelica. 'God help me!'

'A woman on a mission.' Candace gave Angelica a knowing look. 'D'you think I can get you to Richard Ward as well?'

'Not if I come out looking like Jenna Elrich.'

'Only Jenna can look like Jenna, and she's stuck with that for life, poor darling!'

When Angelica got home, she ran a hot bath and poured a whole sachet of Elemis Musclease under the tap. The water went brown and smelled as medicinal as Olivier's Karvol inhalations. She restrained herself from going upstairs to check her emails, not due to any lack of enthusiasm but because she didn't think she'd make it, her thighs hurt so much. She put on Dolly Parton and lit a couple of candles, dimming the lights because she loathed looking at her flesh in such an unforgiving glare. With a sigh, she slid into the water and rested her head, letting the warmth ease away the pain. In spite of her discomfort she was inspired by the Pilates class. David had a gift for motivating his clients, and she had left invigorated and determined to get back into shape. Candace had told her that it would take three weeks to see a real difference, but she could already feel it working. She closed her eyes, ashamed to find Jack's face bobbing to the top of her thoughts like a cork. The anticipation of another witty message from him sent a pleasurable ripple through her cramping stomach.

She climbed out of the bath and dried herself, taking her time. The wait would make his email all the more satisfying. She rubbed cream into her body, adding a few drops of juniper essential oil for water retention, and sprayed herself with Jo Malone Red Roses. Feeling sensual, she delved into her Calvin Klein underwear drawer, choosing a bra and panties in dusty pink. It gave her a thrill to know that beneath her jeans and shirt she was wearing exquisite lingerie.

Angelica wore little makeup. She had naturally youthful skin and the pink cheeks of a girl raised in the fresh country air. With a touch of mascara and lip balm, she was ready to read her mail. Her excitement mounted as she climbed the stairs, her pace quickening in spite of her painful muscles. It took a while for her computer to start, but finally, the screen went blue and her icons appeared in neat rows. She clicked on Mail and the list appeared. She scanned the names in bold, but there was nothing from Jack. She pressed Send and Receive just to make doubly sure, but the words 'No New Mail' appeared at the bottom of the page.

With a sinking heart she had no option but to face the blank page of her next novel. For a moment she considered writing to *him*. Did it matter that he hadn't responded to her last email? Did their emails have to go back and forth like a tennis game? Even in tennis the opponent didn't always return the ball; often he missed, or hit the ball in the net. This was like a friendly tennis match – winning wasn't the aim. And she wasn't playing hard to get – she wasn't expecting to be got at all. This was an innocent friendship, and friends could write when they felt like it.

But then doubt set in. Perhaps he had got bored. Maybe his wife had found out and banned him. Or he might have gone away for a few days and forgotten to take his BlackBerry. What time of year was it in South Africa? He had said it was spring. He must be busy with the vines, surely. God, the list of possibilities was endless. The fact was, he hadn't replied and that was that. She was surprised by the depth of her disappointment.

She clicked onto *In Search of the Perfect Happiness* by Angelica Garner and sat staring at the pink letters and white page that followed. She sat there for half an hour without writing a single word. It began to rain. Light drizzle was blown about on the breeze like dust. Celine Dion sang 'All by myself . . . don't wanna be all by myself . . .' and Angelica felt empty, like a well of dried-up ideas. As often as she lowered the bucket it came back as light as when it went down. Her agent was expecting another fantasy novel for children, laced with magic and monsters. She was never going to be Tolkien – she didn't have the patience or the genius to write such powerful allegories – but she usually enjoyed sinking into her imagination and spinning any reality she desired. But her imagination was as cloudy as cauliflower soup.

Her fingers hovered over the keys. The blank page stared back at her, goading her to spoil its perfection. Then an idea popped into her head from nowhere. An evil, unhappy sorceress falls in love with a good man and attempts to attract him with spells and potions. Nothing works because nothing ever does on good people. So she has to learn how to be good like him, because only a pure heart will win him. For every good deed she does she loses a little of her evil nature. Gradually her good deeds begin to make her happy and the less evil she becomes. She sets out on a quest and learns the secret of happiness.

Angelica was *quite* pleased with her idea. It was a mere husk – she'd have to fill it in and build it up – but at least it was a start. Forgetting her empty mailbox she began to develop her magical world, inventing names and language, customs and laws.

By three o'clock she had a better idea of her fantasy land, and, feeling happier for having started, she saved what she had written and closed down her computer. She clicked on her mailbox to find Jack still hadn't replied. She shrugged it off bravely; perhaps it was for the best.

It was raining, so she walked under an umbrella to pick up the children. It felt autumnal. The leaves in the park were beginning to turn yellow and brown. The skies were grey, the pavements shiny and wet. Only the pigeons seemed not to notice and hopped about cheerily as if every day was a picnic.

Outside the school, mothers gathered among nannies, huddling under umbrellas or sitting in their cars parked on yellow lines. As she approached she heard her name above the rumble of engines. It was Candace, waving exuberantly out of the window of her car. 'Get in, Angelica.' As she crossed the road Candace hissed at her. 'She's told Pete she's pregnant!' Angelica peered through the window. Letizia and Kate sat in the backseat deep in conversation. The driver stared ahead, pretending not to listen. 'Get in!'

'He doesn't suspect it's not his?' Angelica asked, squeezing in beside Kate.

'Why on earth would he? He's the philanderer in our marriage, not me – well, at least that's the way he sees it. He's over the moon. He says we've got to have marriage counselling, though, so we're strong for the new baby. A friend of his has recommended this woman called Betsy Pog.'

'Great name,' said Letizia with a giggle.

Candace laughed cynically. 'You don't need marriage counselling, he just needs to keep his pooch in its pouch.' They all laughed.

'No, really, Betsy Pog is my kind of woman. She's meant to be fantastic.'

'She *better* be fantastic,' Candace added.

'We're going tonight for our first session.' Kate shivered with excitement. 'What shall I wear?'

'A hair shirt?' asked Candace.

'Oh, I was thinking much more along the lines of a little Prada dress with my red Louboutins.'

'Well, at least it'll look like you're trying,' said Angelica.

'I *never* try,' Kate retorted. 'My style is effortless and effervescent.'

'You might as well wear it while you can,' said Letizia.

'God, don't remind me. The thought of maternity trousers and big shirts again! Hideous!'

'Darling, pregnancy is no excuse to dress badly,' Letizia reproached her. 'A woman is at her most beautiful when bearing a child.'

'Sometimes you are so Italian!' Kate retorted, envisaging flat shoes with dismay.

'So is it public knowledge yet?' asked Candace.

'Have you told your mother?' Angelica added.

'Same question,' said Candace.

'No, I haven't had my twelve-week scan. Don't breathe a word to anyone.'

'Does your lover know?' Candace asked more keenly.

'He's not my lover.'

'Whatever. Does he know?'

'No.'

'You don't think he'll work it out when he hears you're pregnant?'

'I *know* he won't work it out.'

Candace raised an eyebrow. 'That's interesting, what is he? A priest?'

'Look, he's forgotten it even happened.'

'But *we* haven't,' said Candace with a grin.

'I'm not going to tell you,' Kate retorted. 'Not because I don't want to. You know I share everything with you three. But I promised him I wouldn't, and I must keep my word.'

'What, because you always do?' said Candace. Kate was notoriously feckless.

'No, because I owe it to him and because the consequences of it getting out are too horrible to imagine.'

Angelica narrowed her eyes. 'So we know him.'

'The plot thickens,' said Letizia. 'He's not one of our husbands, is he?'

Kate laughed. 'You'd have to *pay* me to sleep with one of your husbands!'

'Me, too, honey,' Candace joked, lifting her finger into the light. 'I think I'm due another diamond.'

The week passed without an email from Jack. Angelica continued her Pilates classes and bore the consequent stiffness with fortitude. She buried herself in her writing and tried not to be too disappointed about Jack's sudden disappearance. It was inevitable that their correspondence would end at some stage. She had been naïve to imagine they could continue flirting indefinitely. He had probably moved on to someone else he had met at another dinner party – someone who was prepared to take the flirtation further, like his 'friend' in

Clapham. It had been fun. He had made her feel alive. She picked up the children from school, listened to Candace and Scarlet worrying about the credit crunch's effects on fundraising and spending, and tried to shrug off the heavy feeling of anticlimax.

Then on the following Wednesday morning the world shifted back into place. She received a large royalty check from Holland and an email from Jack:

> Dear beautiful Sage, I'm sorry I didn't reply earlier, I've been away. I think we need to discuss things in person. This dog is getting restless here on the porch and was wondering whether he might persuade you to allow him to take you out for lunch when he comes to London in October. You're no ordinary rabbit. DOP

Oh my God, oh my God, oh my God! What to do? Angelica wanted to have lunch with him more than anything in the world. But what would Olivier say? No, she knew exactly what he would say: *'Mais non, mon ange.'* NO. *That* had to be avoided at all costs. But she couldn't lie, in case she was spotted. They couldn't go somewhere low-key in the back of beyond because if they were discovered they'd look even more suspicious. They'd have to go out in Chelsea and risk it. *What am I doing? I don't want an affair! I really, really don't. I just want a little fun. I just want to feel attractive. He doesn't want an affair either, for sure. Of course he doesn't.*

She reread the email twenty times. Her mind was as clear as glass and whirring away like a new clock. *If I say no, I'll look churlish and presumptuous. And besides, I want to see him. I'm nearly forty years old. I think I'm entitled to do what I want. So Olivier can't be told. I'll say I'm having lunch with the director of my publishing house, then I'm covered if I'm spotted with a strange man. Olivier has never met my publisher, let alone my agent – actually,*

*he's never met anyone from my working life. Schmuck! as Candace
would say. Serves him right!*

Dear Dog on Porch, I think it's about time you used up that
slack on that lead of yours. *Too flirty! What am I thinking?
I've gone mad!*

Dear Dog on Porch, I'd love to have lunch. It will be fun to
see you again. Where do you want to go? Let me know
when you're over and I'll book . . . *No, that's far too keen!
Typical woman wanting everything tied up neatly with a
bow!*

Dear Dog on Porch, I'd love to have lunch. October is a
good month for dogs. So many leaves to truffle through in
the park! I think you'll find I'm actually a rather ordinary
rabbit. On the subject of lunch – shall I put it down to
research? From Curious Sage

As soon as she sent it she telephoned Candace. 'Candace,
it's me.'
'Hi, honey, what's up?'
'Book me into Richard Ward at once.'

Chapter 8

'Think, speak, and act for the Higher Good, and you will be a lucky person'

In Search of the Perfect Happiness

So the emails began again. Jack was coming to London for five days beginning the week of October 13, and Tuesday, October 14, would be a fine day for lunch. He'd book somewhere and let her know nearer the time.

Angelica went into a spin, torn between her desire to see him and her sense of loyalty as a wife and mother. Her moods swung from ecstasy to panic. Her head throbbed with the weight of her dilemma. As she lay awake at night unable to sleep, her nails bitten down to the quick, her heart raced with that elusive, mislaid magic.

She stopped eating cake and worked out four times a week at Ten Pilates. David began adjusting the springs to make the exercises more challenging, and soon she found that her body no longer suffered such agonizing stiffness afterwards. Her toenails shone fuchsia pink, and her figure began to change. The waist that wasn't now was, and she belted her dresses with pride. The Calvin Klein underwear drawer was opened on a daily basis, but Olivier, so preoccupied with the FTSE 100, didn't notice. It didn't matter. The girls did, and even Jenna Elrich found something nice to say.

'You look great!' she commented at the school gates one afternoon as they waited in the autumn sunshine to pick up their children. Jenna was taking advantage of the cooler weather to show off her new Burberry cape and boot-cut purple trousers. Her shiny Gucci loafers were so high she towered over Angelica. Around her neck she wore a silk Hermès scarf with just the right shade of purple flowers on it to tie in with the trousers, and hiding most of her face was a large pair of brown Chanel sunglasses. 'What have you been doing? You've lost *so* much weight.' *That* was classic Jenna, insinuating that Angelica had previously been the size of a hippo.

'Pilates.'

Jenna looked her up and down. 'You're unrecognizable.'

'Hardly.'

'No, really. I barely recognized you. You look fabulous. I'm surprised. Is it just Pilates, or is there something you're not telling me?'

'Sex,' Angelica stated simply. 'I'm just having an awful lot of sex.'

Jenna's face crinkled with sympathy. 'You *poor* darling. You need to go to the pharmacy and ask for some husband repellent.'

Angelica laughed at the absurdity of the woman. 'Does it work for you?'

'If only such a thing existed! I give my husband a minute. I'm like, "Okay, darling, you've got sixty seconds. Go!" and I close my eyes and think of those Manolo shoes I want or that perfect little cashmere from Ballantyne. 'Right, minute over! Enough!"'

'Sounds like you're ready for an affair.'

'Oh, there's no shortage of men who admire me.' She laughed as if *that* idea was preposterous. 'But John would divorce me, and right now, the way things are, I don't think I'll find anyone richer.'

'Better hang on to him, then.'

'Until he tells me to stop shopping. Really, if I was one of those wives, I would take a lover, for sure.'

Angelica managed to extract herself and found Kate huddled in a group with Scarlet, Candace, and Letizia, telling them about her latest advice from Betsy Pog. 'It's going really well. We have to tell each other three things we like about each other over breakfast and before we go to sleep at night.'

'Can you find three things first thing in the morning?' Angelica asked.

'Can you find three things, period?' added Candace.

'It's a struggle, but I make them up if I can't.'

'That's naughty, darling,' said Letizia. 'You have to give it a chance and do it properly.'

'What does he say about *you*?' Scarlet asked.

'Oh, that's easy. The list is as long as the Mississippi.' She giggled. 'I think he's falling in love with me all over again. Then, we have to whisper a word, just a single word, into the other's ear when we're in public.'

'Like what?' Candace asked.

'Sexy, horny, delicious, manly . . . that sort of thing.'

'That's hilarious!' Scarlet laughed. 'What does he whisper to *you*?'

'I can't say – I'm too embarrassed!' She bit her bottom lip, then relented. 'It really turns me on. He'll sidle up and whisper "Juicy" then wander off again, leaving me quivering with excitement.'

'Oh *p-lease*!' wailed Candace.

'There are many roads to Rome. Besides, it must be working,' said Letizia. 'You're glowing like an oven.'

'He can't get enough of me. I think being pregnant turns him on. It makes him feel virile.'

'Little does he know,' said Candace.

Kate shot her a look. 'It's his. I'm sure it's his. I was just being overdramatic.'

'Not you,' Candace added with a grin. 'You're *never* that.'

The day before Angelica's lunch with Jack, she sat beside Candace at Richard Ward's Metro Spa in Duke of York's Square, sipping Earl Grey tea and waiting for Thomas to come and highlight her hair. The ruggedly handsome James was already adding lights to Candace's rich brown locks. Being a natural blonde, Angelica had never felt she needed dye, but Candace had convinced her that Thomas would lift her look while keeping it natural.

'Thomas will hide all your little flaws. He's a genius,' she told her, extending one hand to the manicurist, who sat on a stool at her feet. 'And he's a vault like me. He knows where all the elephants lie buried and will take that knowledge to his grave. Trust me, no code breaker can crack him.'

The salon was vast – room upon shiny room of mirrors and sleek black chairs; legions of black-uniformed juniors washing hair and standing to attention behind the technicians, who were all frighteningly cool, suntanned, and good-looking; the air infused with the smell of Kérastase. 'Ah, you must be Angelica,' said Thomas, breezing in followed by a pretty junior with waist-length blonde hair.

'This is she,' said Candace. 'You're to make her even more beautiful than she already is.'

'Oh really!' Angelica protested, embarrassed.

Thomas scrutinized her hair. 'I know just what you need. You have lovely hair, by the way – very thick and in good condition. You're lucky, it has a natural wave, but not frizzy – a cross between Farrah Fawcett circa 1974 and Meg Ryan of *When Harry Met Sally* fame. Leave it to me.'

Angelica glanced at Candace, terrified. 'Relax. Thomas knows what's good for you. Lie back and enjoy it.' She grinned at James in the mirror. 'She's a virgin, but she'll learn to be a hair whore like me.'

James laughed. 'The word "whore" sounds strange coming from your pretty lips.'

'You'd be surprised what I can come out with when pushed,' she replied, giving the manicurist her other hand. 'My angelic face fools people into thinking I'm a pushover, but my acerbic tongue gets me what I want.'

'So, Angelica, you're determined to have lunch with Jack?'

'You think I'm mad.'

'You know what? I do think you're crazy, but I also think you're entitled to have some fun. Just be careful.'

'I will.'

'You have a nice life. Don't go screw it up over a flirt. It's not worth it. Once you lose Olivier's trust, you'll never get it back.'

'I won't lose it, Candace. I'm not intending to have an affair.'

'Few women go out with the intention of having an affair. One thing leads to another, but it usually starts with lunch.'

'He's a nice guy. I'm enjoying the attention. But that's all it is, I promise.'

'I don't want to have to pick up the pieces.'

'You won't have to. It'll just be lunch.'

Candace caught James's eye in the mirror. He didn't look at all surprised. In his seven years at Richard Ward he had heard just about everything.

Thomas returned with bowls of dye and sheets of tin foil, and began pinning up her hair. Duffy's husky voice rang out from the sound system: 'I'm begging you for mercy, why won't you release me.' Candace flicked through *In Style* magazine with her free hand. 'So where's he taking you?'

'Daphne's.'

'That's a little dangerous, isn't it?'

'It's better to go somewhere normal than be seen in some obscure restaurant in Richmond.'

'You have a point. What are you going to tell Olivier?'

'That I'm having lunch with my publisher.'

'Whom he's never met.'

'Correct.'

'And if you see someone you know? How will you introduce him?'

'As Jack.'

Candace raised an eyebrow. 'You're really playing with fire.'

'I know.'

After Thomas had finished colouring her hair, a junior led Angelica into a room full of sinks and reclining chairs that looked more like beds. Vast flat-screen televisions playing CNN were set up on each wall. She lay back and let the girl wash her hair and give her a deep conditioning treatment and massage. She shut her eyes and emptied her mind of thoughts.

'Are you dead?' Candace leaned over her. 'Oh, you can't be, you're snoring.'

Angelica awoke with a start. 'God, did I doze off?'

'You certainly did.'

'Was I really snoring?'

'No, that was a joke. When you're finished, I want you to meet Robert. He usually does my hair. Today, he's going to do yours.'

'I don't know how you find the time to do this every six weeks.'

'Every six weeks? Honey, you've got to be kidding! I'm in here every week for a wash and blow-dry! Don't forget your bag,' she added, dropping it into Angelica's lap. 'You left it in the other room – with your brain!'

Angelica followed Candace through a couple of rooms full of clients reading magazines; having lunch in their chairs; getting pedicures, manicures, blow-dries, and haircuts. It was a glamourous world she was excited to be part of. Robert awaited her, a cherubic-looking man with grey hair and a bashful smile. 'Over to you, Robert,' said Candace, waving her manicured hand. Robert combed her hair into a middle parting. 'You should have had a manicure,' said Candace.

'That's one beauty treatment beyond me.' Angelica looked at her short nails. 'I can't do the Park Avenue princess look.'

'You wouldn't want to, honey. That look is so over. The trick is to look polished without looking like you've had the sex appeal ironed out of you.'

'You want to keep your curls?' Robert asked, scissors poised.

'I'd like to look like I've just got out of bed – looking perfect,' Angelica replied.

Angelica buried herself in the October issue of *Vanity Fair*, trying to read an article on Marilyn Monroe and not sneak a look at her hair before it was finished. Her stomach was in a knot, and she wasn't sure whether it was at the thought of having lunch with Jack – or of having lunch with Jack with horrid hair. Their emails had heated up over the last few weeks. She hadn't gone too far, but she had certainly said things she might not have dared say to his face – with her husband sitting at the other end of the table. She was now worried that she would disappoint him. That she had looked better in candlelight. That in the bright glare of day she wouldn't look like the girl he had been flirting with by email, and suddenly wish he hadn't.

'What if he doesn't fancy me?' she said to Candace, without taking her eyes off the page.

Candace shouted over the roar of the hair dryer. 'It doesn't matter. You're not going to have an affair with him anyway.'

'That's not the point. I want him to think I'm beautiful.'

'If he doesn't fancy you, he'll stop emailing you and that'll be that – and a good thing, too.' She looked across at her friend, and her face fell. 'Oh dear.'

'What?' Angelica nearly dropped her teacup. She was too afraid to look at her reflection. 'Is it bad?'

'Bad, bad, bad.'

'How bad?'

'Take a look.'

Angelica's stomach swam on a wave of nausea. She raised her eyes. Then her fears evaporated at the sight of her ravishing bed head. 'Oh my God. It's stunning.'

'Go figure!'

'Robert. You really *are* a genius!'

'Thank you.' He fluffed it up with his fingers. 'The colour's good, too.'

'It really is.' Angelica was thrilled. 'Clever Thomas. I must thank him as well.'

'There's no chance he won't fancy you. Unfortunately!' said Candace, staring at her with approval.

'I hope you're right. I just want to be adored.'

'From afar.'

'From afar.'

Candace put down her magazine. 'I think I should go with you.'

'Well, think again,' said Angelica, getting up with a new confidence. 'I'm nearly forty years old. It's my time to have fun. The first step to happiness is good highlights and haircut.' She delved into her wallet and pulled out a crumpled note. 'This is for you, Robert, for putting down the foundation stone of my inner temple of happiness.'

★

Angelica picked up the children at three-thirty. The only person not to compliment her hair was Jenna Elrich, who was too busy shouting into her mobile telephone like a sergeant major. But Angelica noticed her glance in her direction a couple of times, her face as green as granite. Letizia, Kate, and Scarlet were very impressed. 'Anyone would think you were having an affair,' said Scarlet.

'If they didn't know her better,' Letizia added.

'She's married to a Frenchman. Looking good is what he expects,' Kate said. 'Betsy Pog told me to dress for Pete, so I went to Selfridges and bought a whole heap of lingerie. Pete is a real silk-and-lace man. Betsy says it's worth putting on just so that he can take it off.'

'So what have you got on now?' asked Angelica.

Kate pulled down her jeans to reveal red lace knickers. 'The bra is adorable.'

'Divine,' breathed Letizia.

'Nice,' agreed Scarlet. 'But I'm more fascinated by your stomach.'

'*What* stomach?' Candace exclaimed.

Kate pulled up her sweater to show off her belly, still brown from her summer in the Caribbean, but as flat as a board. 'Oh, it's growing,' she said, patting it.

'Only you'd know,' said Angelica.

'Has Betsy Pog told you to eat more?' asked Candace. Kate frowned at her. 'She should. There's a starving baby in there!'

'It's early days,' said Kate.

'Well, the poor creature can't survive without food.'

'Speaking of which, don't forget my surprise dinner for Art next Thursday.' Art was Kate's best friend, married the year before in a gay ceremony to Tod. 'He hasn't the slightest idea, which is astonishing. I'm not known for my ability to keep secrets!'

'You're on your way,' said Candace. 'Which is a great shame.'

When Angelica returned home, she set about doing the usual duties: homework, tea, bath, and bedtime stories. Every time she passed a mirror she glanced at herself with pleasure and a growing sense of unease. What on earth was she doing having lunch with Jack Meyer? And without telling her husband? She didn't dare consider the consequences were she to get caught. Candace was right, she was crazy. But she was confident that she would be able to keep it to a friendly flirt. That she'd be in control. That the last thing in the world she would do would be to risk the good life she had.

Olivier came home early to find her sitting on Joe's bed with Isabel on her knee, reading *Stone Soup,* her favourite children's book. Olivier stood in the doorway watching the trio in the soft light of the bedroom, noticing at once his wife's new hair and appreciating her changing figure. She caught his eye and smiled, registering the admiration in his gaze.

She finished the story and took Isabel to her room. As she walked past her husband, he took her arm and looked at her intensely. 'You look really good, Angelica.' She walked on, guilt clawing the inside of her stomach. She kissed her daughter and tucked her in, placing Splat the duck against her chest for her to cuddle. Then she put her son to bed, wrapping her arms around him for the Full Joe. He liked the routine and held her tightly. Olivier kissed their foreheads and chatted a little about their day and what they'd been doing. It was rare that he returned home in time to see them before bedtime.

They met in their bedroom. Angelica recognized the look on her husband's face from those long-ago trysts at Claridge's and the irony was not lost on her. He had taken off his jacket and tie and stood appraising her lasciviously.

'You look different tonight,' he remarked, narrowing his eyes.

'I've had my hair coloured.'

'It's not just that. You're looking slimmer, too.'

'I noticed you didn't like me wearing belts.'

He looked surprised. 'So you decided to make an effort for *me*?'

'Why not?'

'I'm flattered. Women don't often go to the gym for their husbands.'

'What are you suggesting? That I have a lover?'

He dismissed such a ridiculous idea with a laugh. 'Of course not. Women go to the gym to compete with their friends.'

'I couldn't begin to. They're all taller and thinner than me.'

'But you have sex appeal, Angelica. That's what I like about you. So you worked out for me, eh?'

'Yes.' Her lie prevented her from looking him in the eye. She made to walk past him, but he pulled her into his arms.

'Just because I told you not to wear a belt?'

'You said my waist was the widest part of me.'

'I did not!' He was genuinely apologetic. 'Did I?'

'You did.'

'I'm sorry. What a careless thing to say. If I hurt you, I apologize. So what do you do?'

'Pilates, Olivier. I realized I'd let myself go. I didn't want to be voluptuous anymore.' She squeezed his firm shoulders. 'Especially as *you* work out. I didn't want to end up looking ten years older than my buffed husband.'

He laughed, and she remembered why she had fallen in love with him; he looked so handsome when his eyes were full of mirth.

'Take off your clothes,' he demanded, turning to lock the door. 'Let the children sleep.' She began to unbutton her shirt. When he turned around, he noticed her pretty lingerie and frowned in bewilderment, his eyes tracing her body. 'I've been sleepwalking for the last few months. That's what the City has done to me. I'm a man who loves beautiful women, and yet I sleep beside one every night without realizing how fortunate I am!' He slipped his hands around her waist and she stood tall so he could feel how firm it was. 'You look like the girl I met all those years ago, but with the maturity of a woman.' She felt her spirits rise with satisfaction. He traced his fingertips across her stomach. 'You've worked hard.'

'I'm glad you can see the difference.'

'*Ma chérie,* it's not the outside that's important but the inside. However, seeing as you've managed to get your figure back, permit me to appreciate it!'

He kissed her, raking his fingers through her hair – her *perfect* new hair. For a moment she feared he might ruin it and tossed it out of his reach. But what was she doing having lunch with Jack Meyer when she had finally managed to win her husband's approval? Her stomach churned with regret. It was too late to cancel. She'd enjoy a nice lunch, then scale down the emails. Jack had inspired her to get back in shape. Now she had her husband's attention, she no longer needed him.

Chapter 9

'Reach for the stars with your dreams and desires'
In Search of the Perfect Happiness

The following morning Angelica walked the children to school, bumping into Candace on the street on the way back. Effortlessly glamourous in a Ralph Lauren tweed jacket under a cashmere cape and tight blue jeans tucked into leather boots, Candace struggled to restrain her silver Great Dane as he tried to sniff the bottom of a passing Jack Russell. 'He's obsessed with small dogs!' she wailed as Angelica approached her. 'Enough, Ralph!' She took off her sunglasses and ruthlessly scrutinized her friend. 'You're not going to wear *that* to lunch, are you?'

Angelica was scruffy in baggy jeans and trainers. 'No.'

'I'm pleased to hear it.'

'I'm having second thoughts. What am I doing, Candace?'

'You tell me.'

'Olivier came home last night and was so sweet. It suddenly dawned on me that it's *his* attention I'm craving – not some sexy stranger's.'

'We all know that.'

'So what do I do? Cancel?'

'No, it's too late.'

'I feel awful. I've encouraged him. I'm a prick tease!'

'Yes, you are. But you still can't cancel.'

'I'm such an idiot.'

'Look, go have fun. Now that you know where your priorities lie, there's no danger of your getting into trouble.'

'What if I get caught?'

'You won't. Olivier's hardly likely to walk into Daphne's in the middle of the day, is he?'

'I hope not – unless he's fired! I haven't told him I'm going.'

'D'you fancy coffee?'

'Why don't you come home with me and help me select something to wear?'

'Okay, let's go choose something cool and understated. But not trainers, please.' Candace gave the lead a tug. 'And you, Ralph, can sit in Angelica's garden and not chase squirrels.'

At home, Sunny made them coffee and brought it up to Angelica's bedroom on a tray, while Ralph bounded about the small garden defying the instruction about squirrels. Candace took off her cape and began to go through Angelica's closet.

Angelica put on her favorite Dolly Parton CD and slipped out of her jeans and sweater.

'Wow, you really have slimmed down, Angelica. And I like your underwear, too. Where's it from?'

'Calvin Klein.'

'Nice. What does Olivier think?'

She flashed her friend a bashful smile. 'Let's just say he's rediscovered it.'

'Well, that makes two of you.' She pulled out a Vanessa Bruno floral blouse with an extended collar for tying in a bow. 'This is cool. Just don't tie the bow, let it hang.' Angelica put it on. 'I think you should wear jeans. You don't want to look like you're trying too hard. This is just a friendly lunch:

you're not interviewing for an affair. Wear these Rupert Sanderson shoes – they're fabulous and they'll give you height.'

'That's the one thing Pilates can't do for me.'

'But these can.' She grabbed them off the shelf and threw them at her. 'Where are those Stella McCartney jeans with cute little pockets at the front?'

Angelica studied herself in the mirror. 'God, I don't recognize myself when I dress up. I still feel like I'm pretending to be someone else.'

'Honey, you look fabulous.'

'Only because of you, Candace.'

'I'll happily take all the credit. I couldn't let you slip into that old cliché of the scruffy writer. Writers don't have to be badly dressed.'

'I'm loving myself!' Angelica threw her arms up and laughed.

'And of course, you don't give a rat's ass about Jack anymore.'

'I'm a little sad I'm already over him. What am I going to do now for entertainment?'

'Come shopping. It's safer.'

'Now I know why you do it.'

'There's method in my madness.'

She looked at Candace steadily. 'Have you ever been tempted?'

'I wouldn't be human if I wasn't tempted every now and then. But I love Harry, period. And you know what? If there's something positive I inherited from my mother, it's her backbone of steel. I've never found it hard to say no and walk away from trouble. You must learn to do the same.' She tossed her her jacket. 'Today is your first lesson.'

Angelica parked her car in Draycott Place. It took a while to find a parking space, and when she did, she was so anxious she rolled into the Range Rover in front, knocking its bumper with hers. 'Oh Lord!' she exclaimed, hastily reversing. She hurried out to assess the damage. To her relief, the Range Rover was unscratched. Her own car was already grazed from past blunders; if she had just acquired one more scratch, she couldn't tell. She walked unsteadily up the road towards Daphne's, breathing deeply to calm her nerves.

She looked at her watch, not wanting to arrive before Jack. She was fashionably five minutes late. Inhaling a large gulp of air, she pushed open the door and strode in, holding her head high to convey a confidence she didn't feel. She lowered her voice at the desk and articulated his name with care as if it were a loaded gun. As she was led through the tables she glanced about her, relieved that she recognized no one.

Then she saw him sitting in the corner, reading the *Evening Standard,* and all her reservations evaporated at the sight of him, so broad he dwarfed the table. He sensed her approach, and his face opened into a wide smile. 'The wise sage,' he said, standing up to greet her. He dwarfed her, too, even in heels. She kissed him, breathing in the lime scent of his cologne and relishing for a fleeting moment the rough sensation of his cheek against hers. It was almost too intimate to bear, and she drew away, her face flushing crimson.

She sat down and laughed nervously. 'So, the dog's been let off the porch.'

'You can't expect a dog like me to stay at heel when there's the most delicious-looking rabbit in the garden!' The warmth of his expression brought him back to her in a sudden rush of desire. *What am I doing?* she thought anxiously. *When I'd lifted almost every paw out of the mud!*

'Oh really! You are funny!' she exclaimed, trying to brush off his comment with nonchalance.

He swept his eyes over her face. 'You look different.'

'Do I?'

'Yes. Your hair's lighter. I like it. You look great, Angelica.'

'Now you're embarrassing me.'

'Good.' He grinned and leaned towards her, peering at her over his glasses. 'You look even prettier when you blush.'

In an attempt to keep the conversation under control, she said: 'How long are you in the UK? I mean, are you here on business?'

'Kind of.'

'Does your wife ever come with you?'

'Sometimes, but right now she's at home with the children. She doesn't like to leave them.' He grinned at her mischievously. 'Does Olivier know you're having lunch with me?'

'No, I never got around to telling him.' He shot her a quizzical look, and she couldn't help grinning back at him. 'Okay, so I lie. I knew he'd say no, and I wanted to have lunch with you. I mean, why not? There's nothing wrong with having lunch with a friend, is there?'

'Nothing wrong at all.'

'It was just easier not to mention it. He's very jealous. But I won't have my wings clipped.'

He gazed at her a moment longer than was comfortable, then laughed heartily. 'Now *you're* funny!'

'Why?'

'Because you know as well as I do that there's *everything* wrong with having lunch with a man you've only just met. It's not wrong in itself, only wrong because your husband wouldn't like it. If it wasn't so, you would have told him and he would have told you to have a good time.'

'Then the secret to happiness is not honesty,' she rallied.

'I'd agree with you there, but that's a selfish kind of happiness, not the pure happiness you're searching for.'

'Okay, so I'm selfishly taking my pleasure.'

'Let's drink to that. What will you have?'

'A glass of white wine, please.' She needed fortification.

'Then let me choose a bottle of good South African wine.'

The waiter brought the wine, and Angelica took a swig, immediately feeling more confident. She began to relax as the conversation moved on to more mundane subjects and she no longer felt like a small prey in the shadow of a formidable predator. They discussed the menu, then he hailed the waiter and ordered for her. Olivier had done that, too, when they had first courted. Now he simply ordered for himself.

'So how's the book coming along?' he asked.

'Not well.' She laughed. 'It's amazing how much time can be wasted writing one's own name.'

'I read your last book, by the way.' He was clearly pleased by the surprise on her face.

'Which one?'

'*The Caves of Cold Konard*.'

'And . . .?'

'I really enjoyed it. In fact, I couldn't put it down. At first I thought I'd take a look just so I could say I'd read it. But I was hooked – on the second page, to be precise, when the cave isn't a cave at all. It's very clever. Then Mart carried me away. I identified with him even though he's just a boy. I suppose we're all children at heart, aren't we? Those Yarnies are dreadful, disguising themselves as Enrods to fool Mart into trusting them. They're the worst sort of enemy, and I know a few Yarnies back at home. It's all very magical, but at the same time very true to life. Really, I was impressed.'

'Thank you.'

'Olivier should read it. I think he'd be astonished by your talent.'

'Oh, he's so busy.'

'That's no excuse. You can always make time. He's probably jealous of your creativity.'

'Oh, I don't think so.'

'Trust me. He's working all hours in a bank churning
figures. You're sitting at home, listening to music, surfing the
waves of your imagination. How fantastic is that? I bet he's
jealous you make money doing something that looks so easy
and is so pleasurable.'

'Except it's not easy at all, because I'm not sure that what
I've written so far is any good. I can't seem to think of a single
brilliant idea, just rather ordinary ones.'

'Yet.'

'I'm almost tempted to ask for time out to recharge.'

'So you can work out the deep layers beneath the story?'

'Yes.'

'Think of Tolkien. You almost do it with *The Caves of
Cold Konard*. It wouldn't be difficult to add another layer. To
make it more spiritual for those who want to read beneath the
surface.'

'I'm anxious about it. I've never done it before. It would
be easy to continue on the same road.'

'But good for you to challenge yourself. If you're bored of
your books, your readers are going to be bored, too.'

'I know. I've got to find something I'm passionate about.'

'You're a woman of great passion, Sage. That comes across
in *The Caves,* and it's contagious, which is why it's hard to
put down. Even for an old book veteran like me!'

'You really think so? You're not just saying that?'

'Because I fancy you? No. I'll buy *The Silk Serpent* even if
this is the last time we ever lay eyes on each other.'

She stared at him a moment, a heavy sense of disappointment sinking to the bottom of her belly like a stone. The
thought of never seeing him again caused her physical pain.
She hadn't anticipated still being so attracted to him. She had

hoped to have lunch and leave, drawing a line under a fun but innocuous flirt. But he drew her to him, like the hypnotic allure of a long-forgotten melody whose notes resonated deep within her soul.

He took a sip of wine. Neither spoke for what seemed like a long while. The waiters brought their first courses and, as Angelica looked up to thank them, she noticed a familiar face at the other end of the restaurant. 'Oh Lord,' she exclaimed, shrinking back.

Jack followed her gaze. 'Who have you seen?'

'Jenna Elrich. A Yarnie.'

'The one with big hair and sunglasses?'

'That's the one. Don't be fooled: she's pure malice.'

'She's either very insecure or her husband's given her one in the eye.'

'Could be either, actually.'

'She can't see you.'

'Oh, she will. She's the sort of woman who can spot some-one she knows a mile off. She'll be desperate to know who you are.'

'I'm your publisher.'

'Yes.' She flushed at the flaws in the lie. 'You don't look anything like a publisher!'

'I don't think you can generalize. My name is Leighton Jones and I'm your publisher from South Africa. If she comes over, leave me to do the talking.'

She laughed into her glass. 'That makes me tremble with fear. She's a wicked gossip.'

'I'd like to give her something to gossip about.'

'And ruin my marriage?'

He turned serious. 'Do you want to go somewhere else? We can leave if you're worried?'

'No, we can't leave now, it'll look suspicious. Let's pretend we haven't seen her. If she comes over, you're my publisher in Johannesburg, simple as that. The more we make of it, the guiltier we'll look.'

'You've got it all worked out.'

'You don't know my husband. He's more jealous than you can imagine.'

'You should be flattered.'

'It doesn't work that way. Possessiveness is a ball and chain around our ankles. It curtails our freedom and makes us unhappy. The secret to happiness is to love without conditions.'

'Which we know is impossible.'

'We can at least try.'

Jenna Elrich sat beside the window with a couple of women Angelica didn't know. The three of them were bad examples of too much Botox and not enough mirth. They picked at their food and sipped their water and lemon through tight, joyless mouths. Angelica turned her back, but she knew Jenna would recognize her. It was only a matter of time before she tottered over in her six-inch heels to find out who Jack was. If he wasn't so devilishly handsome, she wouldn't bother.

The wine Jack had chosen was very good. Angelica didn't like to drink at lunch, especially as she was driving, but Jack refilled her glass, and she felt pleasantly relaxed and soon forgot all about Jenna. They discussed love and the secret for happiness, and the more they talked the more Angelica entered his magnetic aura until she no longer saw or heard the other people in the restaurant. They were both stimulated by the arguments: she could see the enthusiasm in his eyes like a bright light behind them shining through. By coffee they had identified some of the most endemic obstructions to happiness.

'We should write a book together,' Jack suggested. 'It would be a big best seller.'

'I think you're right. I'm feeling very inspired.'

'Perhaps I can be your mentor. Whenever you need to discuss something, you can call me.'

'I don't have your number,' she replied with a shrug, knowing she was now cruising across another frontier.

'Then give me your phone.' She rummaged through the chaos in her handbag and pulled it out. Her heart raced at the obvious step she was now taking. Candace had been right. Lunch was not just lunch. He took her mobile and began to punch in his number. Then he held it up to her with a grin: *DOP*.

'Dog on Porch,' she said, smiling back.

'Wrong! Dog *off* Porch,' he corrected.

'You're very naughty.'

He flicked open his phone. 'Give me yours.' She read out her number. He held it up. 'Sage. Nothing naughty about that,' he said, replacing it in his jacket pocket. 'Now, when am I going to see you again?'

Angelica was flustered. 'I don't know,' she said. 'Aren't you going back to Rosenbosch?'

'Not until Friday.' He lowered his voice. 'We haven't even touched on desire.'

Angelica's cheeks flamed, and she dropped her gaze into her empty coffee cup. She thought of his secret lover in Clapham and reminded herself that flirting was just a game to him. 'Desire is a basic animal instinct that should be avoided at all costs.'

'Why?'

'Because it doesn't last.'

'But it's a good place to start.'

'If it's the appropriate journey to make.'

'I'm already off the porch.'

'But you're still on a lead.'

'Sometimes desire is out of our control and the lead is broken.'

'We shouldn't let it get out of control. We should raise ourselves up to higher thoughts, not succumb to our primal instincts.'

He laughed affectionately. 'Who are you kidding? You sound like a bad textbook.'

'I know what's wrong, that's all.'

'Don't try to analyze it. I know you feel attracted to me, too.'

'I would never admit to it. I'm a married woman.' But she felt the blood rush to her cheeks to give her away.

'It doesn't matter whether you admit it or not. I can sense it, like a dog. I know it's wrong, but I can't stop desiring you. It's not just your beauty – there are many beautiful women in the world – it's something else. Something unique to you that I won't even try to limit to a word. I felt it the first moment I met you. It hit me hard and left me reeling. I know I should walk away, but I don't want to.'

'Well, hello, Angelica.' It was Jenna, towering over the table in a blousy blue shirt with billowing sleeves, obviously the height of fashion. For Jack she took off her sunglasses, pushing them up into her hair.

'Leighton Jones,' he said, coolly extending his hand.

'Nice to meet you,' Jenna replied, smiling coyly. 'You're from South Africa.'

'Johannesburg.'

'Beautiful city and such friendly people.'

'Thank you.'

'So, Angelica, how come you're having lunch with such a handsome stranger?'

'He's my publisher – aren't I lucky!'

'You certainly are. You know, I've always wanted to write a book.'

'You should,' said Jack. 'Everyone has a book in them.'

'Oh, I know I'd write a best seller. My life is full of incredible stories, and I've met the most amazing people.'

'An autobiography, then?'

'Un roman à clef,' she replied in a flawless French accent.

'Well, when you do, let me know?'

'Do you have a card?'

Angelica was astonished by her forwardness. Jenna held out an expectant hand.

'You write the book first,' said Jack with a smirk. 'Then, once you've finished, get in touch. Everyone has good ideas; few manage to write them into anything resembling a book.'

Jenna wasn't used to being rebuffed. She faltered a moment, then regained her composure. 'Okay, I'll do that. Well, it's been nice meeting you. See you at the school gates, Angelica.' Jack watched her walk away, which was what she intended, because she walked deliberately, swinging her hips.

'She's a good-looking Yarnie,' he said as she disappeared round the corner.

Angelica rolled her eyes. 'If that's what rocks your boat.'

He chuckled. 'It doesn't, as it happens. But I can appreciate good legs.'

'How far off the porch would she tempt you?'

'Little more than a sleepy glance.' He leaned back in his chair and sighed. 'Anyway, I'm already off the porch. Remember, I know my Yarnies from my Enrods, and you, my darling Sage, are an Enrod through and through.'

They remained at the table until after three o'clock. The restaurant was almost empty. Waiters bustled about clearing tables and laying up for dinner. Angelica reminded him that the children came out of school at half past. 'Then I suppose I have to let you go,' he said, waving for the bill.

'Thank you for lunch.'

'The pleasure is all mine.'

'I hope you have a good few days here.'

'They will be good if you let me see you again.'

'Jack . . . I don't know . . .' The effects of the wine had worn off, and she remembered who she was. 'I have a family.'

'I'm only asking for your friendship. I like you.'

'And I like you, too. But it's not appropriate.'

'Look, I've put my cards on the table, but I'm man enough to have you on your terms. As you observed, I'm still tied to the porch. Let me have a bark; I'm not asking for more than that.'

She thought about it a moment. 'All right, I'll see you again. You can call me.'

He took her hand, and Angelica's spirits soared as his smile shone a light into the neglected recesses of her soul.

He paid the bill and accompanied her out into the street. It was still sunny, but long, damp shadows fell across the tarmac to remind them that it was autumn.

'So,' she said, suddenly feeling awkward. 'It's farewell.'

'So long, Sage,' he replied, putting his hand in the small of her back and bending down to kiss her. For a moment she felt unsteady as he pressed his lips to her cheek, taking his time. The lime of his cologne was subdued by the natural spice in his skin, and she breathed it in dreamily.

'Back to the porch,' she said softly, pulling away.

She walked down the road towards her car, arms folded, head bowed, her thoughts still with him. She dared not turn around. When she reached her car, she unlocked the door and climbed in. Risking a look now that she was behind glass, she saw that he had gone. She remained a moment at the wheel, reflecting. If infidelity extended to thoughts, then she was guilty already.

Chapter 10

'It is only with darkness that one can appreciate light'
In Search of the Perfect Happiness

'So how did it go?' Candace was waiting for Angelica at the school gates. 'Don't do that!' she snapped at Ralph, whose nose was buried once again in the bottom of a far smaller dog. 'Really, I can't take him anywhere!'

Angelica was about to divulge the details when something snuffed out her intention, like a sudden pail of water thrown onto a bonfire. Her exuberance fizzled away beneath her friend's formidable gaze. Candace was her confidante – she could normally tell her anything – but this foolhardy leap over the marital border line was beyond her comprehension and approval. As much as Angelica longed to share, she knew what Candace would think – and she couldn't bear to incite her condemnation – or be persuaded to delete Jack's number from her telephone.

'It was really nice,' she replied cagily.

'Nice?' Candace crinkled her nose. 'Lunch with the vicar is nice!'

'Okay, it was fabulous. He's everything I remembered him to be. He's gorgeous, handsome, funny, clever, sensitive, witty, and thinks I'm delicious – which is almost the best thing about him . . .'

'But? I can hear a but . . .'

'He's married, and so am I. It's not going any further.'

'I'm pleased to hear it.'

'I don't know what I was thinking. I was a little embarrassed actually, sitting there as if I was about to embark on an affair.'

'Look, you had a great lunch. You had a flirt. You feel good about yourself. Now go home and wrap yourself around Olivier. I'm not Catholic, but a few Hail Marys won't hurt.'

Angelica laughed. 'At least he propelled me into getting into shape.'

'I thought it was Olivier's comment about the belt.'

'I lied. It was Jack.'

'Well, you can thank him for that, and Olivier will never know.'

Angelica's mobile telephone bleeped in her handbag with a message. She thought of Jack's number hidden in there and felt a quiver of guilty excitement. Candace restrained Ralph, apologizing to another mother who picked up her terrier in disgust. Angelica delved into her handbag for the telephone while Candace summoned Kate, Letizia, and Scarlet with a wave. 'Over here, girls!' she shouted into the throng of perfume and Prada. Angelica flushed as she read the text: Loved our lunch, Sage. Fancy taking this dog for a walk in the park tomorrow morning? X DOP

Candace looked at her quizzically. 'Who's that from?'

'Sunny. She wants me to pick something up on the way home,' Angelica lied, clicking the telephone shut and replacing it in her bag. It shocked her that she was able to fib with such ease.

The three girls came over to join them. 'Hi, dolls. I'm just telling Kate and Letizia about this lad from Yorkshire I've hired for half term to teach the children football and tennis. If any of yours want to join them, they're most welcome,' said

Scarlet, who thought nothing of wearing tight black hot pants with boots to pick up her children from school.

'A manny?' said Candace. 'I'm loving the sound of that!'

'Sort of – he'll keep them busy so I don't have to.'

'Sounds perfect,' Kate interjected. 'We were going to go to St Lucia, but Pete now has to go to Moscow, and I don't relish the idea of taking the children on my own, in my condition.'

'It's an inspired idea, darling. How did you find him?' Letizia asked. 'Might he be available for the Christmas holidays? Does he ski?'

'He's the son of a friend of mine. A fine young man who's nuts about Manchester United and sufficiently handsome that I won't tire of looking at him. I don't think he skis, Letizia, but I'll find out.'

'Oh, will you, darling? I need someone to help over Christmas. Maria isn't legal, so she can't travel. Such a bore. A skiing manny would solve all my problems.'

'Pete and I are thinking about renewing our marriage vows,' said Kate, who knew just how to grab everyone's attention.

'Don't you think you should wait nine months?' Candace replied. 'In case the baby looks like someone else.'

'It won't,' Kate retorted swiftly. 'It's Pete's, I just know it. Mothers *know* these things,' she added, as if she were the only one among them to have experienced motherhood.

'That's *so* romantic,' Letizia sighed. 'I love weddings.'

'I thought it would be a good excuse for a beautiful new frock. Vera Wang sprang to mind, and I'd love all your children to be bridesmaids.'

'So the credit crunch hasn't reached Thurloe Square,' said Candace.

'If we're going to proclaim our love to each other, I want it to be monumental to reflect the size of our hearts.'

'So are we talking St. Paul's?' said Candace.

'No, that place is jinxed. I thought something less royal and more glamourous. After all, our first wedding was in Cornwall – hardly the height of glamour.'

'So where's this one going to be?'

'Mauritius!' She clapped her hands with excitement. 'And I want all the children in floaty white dresses and breeches. Can you imagine how cute they're all going to look? And me in my Vera Wang dress.'

'Sounds like an Estée Lauder advert,' hissed Candace to Angelica, who rejoined the conversation after having drifted off into the park with Jack.

'It's just what we all need,' she said. 'A holiday in the sun.'

'I thought June, just after the baby is born, then we return to London with suntans, ready for the summer.'

'Has Pete agreed?' Scarlet asked.

'He'll do anything for me at the moment. He's feeling very macho and protective.'

'It's a great idea. Not often that a girl gets married for the second time to the same man,' said Angelica brightly.

'You know what I really, really want?' said Kate, biting her thumbnail. 'You won't laugh?'

'We wouldn't dare!'

'To come up the aisle on a beautiful white horse.'

They stared at her in disbelief. Even Candace was silenced. Kate looked from one to the other, waiting for someone to say something. Letizia made to speak but faltered.

'You're not serious,' said Candace at last.

'I'm very serious.'

Letizia recovered her enthusiasm. 'I think it's a fabulous idea. Only *you* could get away with it, darling.'

'And what? The kids come up behind in a cart?'

'No, they skip up in bare feet, scattering shells and flowers on the sand.'

'You're joking,' said Scarlet.

'No, I'm not.' Kate looked hurt. 'I thought it would be so romantic.'

Candace dropped her shoulders and smiled. 'You know what, honey? I'm with you all the way. If that's what you want, you go for it. It's your dream. Just don't put us in floaty white dresses with shells in our hair, please.'

'Well, I had hoped . . .' Kate began, then giggled. 'What do you take me for? You think I'd give you all the opportunity to outshine me at my own wedding?'

Isabel and Joe rushed out of the big doors, throwing themselves at their mother. Angelica wrapped her arms around both of them at once. 'Good day at school?' she asked, as they competed to tell her about their day.

'You forgot my gym bag!' Isabel accused.

'Did I?'

'Silly Mummy. I had to sit out and read a book!'

'I'm so sorry, darling. But if I had the choice, I'd much prefer a book than the gym!'

She waved to the girls, then made her way up the street laden with the children's book bags and backpacks. They ran on ahead, hanging on lampposts and skipping over the lines in the pavement. Angelica strolled behind in a daze, reliving lunch with Jack and deliberating how to respond to his text.

She would love to go for a walk in the park, but the chances of bumping into someone she knew were high. She had got away with lunch, in spite of having been accosted by Jenna; she didn't dare risk it again. Her mind ached as she tried to devise ways of unpicking the Gordian knot: how to engineer a meeting without risking her marriage and reputation? How to see him without leading him on? How to enjoy the flirt while maintaining her distance? How to restrain herself? She couldn't deny that she was very attracted to him and was reminded of her teenage years and the crushes she had suffered at school. This was different; it was reciprocated. The feeling of being desired was intoxicating. She wanted to feel like that again. She couldn't fool herself; she was sliding down the slippery slope into adultery, and she knew it.

By the time she reached the house she was no nearer a solution. Sunny opened the door, and the children tumbled in, running into the kitchen to help themselves to the biscuit tin. The smell of fish fingers wafted out into the autumn air, and Angelica was reminded of where she belonged. She closed the door behind her and felt a sense of security within the four walls of her home. Her mobile burned in her handbag, but she ignored it, setting the dining-room table for homework by way of a distraction.

Finally, bath time was over, and the children were in her bed watching an old DVD of *Robin Hood*. She stood alone in her bathroom in her pretty lingerie. The lights were dimmed, music playing softly, Dyptique candles burning. In the sensual atmosphere of her sanctuary, she decided that she would simply respond that she would love to see him again before he left for South Africa. What was the harm? He'd be gone in a week – this might be her last opportunity to see him, ever.

So she leaned against the sink and wrote a text: **Dear DOP, Park sounds good, weather permitting. X S**

She climbed into the bath, reluctant to get changed and go out. Olivier was going to meet her for drinks at Sotheby's, then they were joining friends at Harry's Bar for dinner. Another late night she didn't need. She'd have much preferred to stay at home, watching an old episode of *Frasier*.

Now that she was slimmer she could get into a favourite silver Ralph Lauren skirt and pale grey top. She admired her reflection, scrunching her hair between her fingers. She wished Jack could see her now, all dressed up, looking her best. What would she wear to the park? She couldn't ask Candace. A stab of guilt weakened her resolve for a moment. She hated to keep anything from her friend, but she didn't want anything to spoil her fun, not least her conscience.

She kissed the children, stroking their hair and soft faces. Engrossed in *Robin Hood,* they barely noticed her. 'Be good for Sunny,' she said, slipping on silver stilettos. 'Hey, how do I look?'

Joe tore his eyes from the telly. He appraised her a moment while Angelica struck a pose. 'Cool,' he replied.

'As cool as Zeus's mum?'

He grinned. 'Cooler.'

'What good taste you have, sweetheart.'

She waved at them. Joe turned his attention back to the television. Sunny was coming up the stairs to put them to bed. Angelica yearned for her own bed but picked up her clutch bag and left the room with a determined stride.

She sat in the taxi staring at her mobile telephone, willing Jack to send her another message. When it bleeped, her heart leapt with excitement, only to be disappointed when she read that it was from Olivier: he wasn't going to make Sotheby's but would meet her at Harry's Bar instead. She wasn't surprised and found that she didn't care, either. As the taxi turned into Bond Street she retrieved Jack's message and read it again.

Sotheby's turned out to be more fun than she had expected. William and Scarlet were there – Scarlet in the tightest pair of black leather trousers and transparent Chanel blouse – and a whole host of other friends. Everyone she talked to complimented her on her appearance, asking whether she had been away, or what she had had done, and she felt light-headed with all the attention.

At half past eight she took a taxi to Harry's Bar. The club was already full of diners, sitting in the dim light at small round tables surrounded by paintings and mirrors and plants. Her friends were already there, but not Olivier. She weaved her way to the other end of the restaurant and greeted them all warmly.

'You look marvellous,' said Joel de Claire, Olivier's oldest friend. 'Why don't you sit there between Antoine and Roberto,' he said, pointing at the empty chair at the far end of the table. 'That way you can see into the club, and when Olivier arrives, you can scowl at him for being late.'

'Angelica doesn't scowl!' protested Joel's wife, Chantal, flicking her wavy chestnut hair off her shoulder.

'Oh, you have no idea,' Angelica quipped, edging around the back of the chairs. Antoine and Roberto stood up politely, and she kissed them both. They all sat down. Then Angelica felt her telephone vibrate with a message. While Antoine and Joel conversed across the table, Angelica sneaked a look at her text. To her astonishment it was from Jack: **Raise your beautiful eyes and look to ten o'clock.** A ripple of excitement washed over her. Suppressing a smile, she glanced through the gap beside Chantal, where Olivier was to sit. There, with his back against the wall, sat Jack, in an open-necked white shirt and jacket, his rugged face dark and handsome, his unruly hair swept off his face so that the blond streaks in it caught the light and glistened as if he had just returned from a day at sea. She was thankful for the dim light as her cheeks burned with pleasure. She turned her attention to the elderly couple at his table, a distinguished-looking pair, diligently reading the menu, and wondered who they were. When she looked back at Jack, he was grinning.

Her line of vision was suddenly blocked by Olivier, who stood before them in a navy Gucci suit and sensible tie, his face ashen in the candlelight.

'Bad day at the office?' Joel joked in French, patting him firmly on the back.

Angelica watched him unbutton his jacket and sit down. He blew her a weary kiss. The table all began to talk at once. Angelica's French wasn't very good, but she wasn't listening anyway. Her telephone vibrated with another message. **I'm bored stiff. Wish I could sit with you!** Without hesitation she typed back: **They're all speaking French! Mine is terrible. X** She was exhilarated when he replied instantly: **Meet me at ten by the restrooms.** She lifted her eyes and bit her bottom lip. **Yes.**

The remainder of the meal passed in a blur. Every time she looked at her husband she could see Jack sitting behind him. They caught eyes once or twice, but Angelica was quick to look away, afraid that Olivier would notice and turn to see whom she was flirting with. Antoine and Roberto were old friends of Olivier's, and, in spite of being charming and good-looking, they had the unattractive habit of speaking across her. She was weary of the financial crisis, but Antoine and Roberto both worked in the City and found the subject hard to resist. She rolled her eyes at Carla, Antoine's wife, who was being ignored by Joel for the same reason. She glanced at her watch to see that it was nine-thirty. *Half an hour to go,* she thought impatiently, picking up her wineglass and taking a sip. Her stomach churned with nerves. A dish of grilled sole was put in front of her, but she didn't feel hungry.

'Don't you think you should leave your work in the office?' said Chantal to her husband.

'I apologize,' said Joel good-naturedly. 'We're boring the girls.'

'They might be bored to listen, but they are not too bored to spend,' said Roberto without humor.

Veronica, his wife, rose to their defence. 'There is nothing more boring than *not* spending.'

'Darling,' Roberto cut in, his Italian accent comic, 'it is worse than boring – it is a disaster. I predict that wives will take lovers when their husbands no longer make the money for them to whittle away.'

'You must think us all very shallow,' said Angelica stiffly.

'Most women are,' Roberto continued. 'I am afraid to say that a vast majority of women marry men for their money.'

'I married Antoine for his genes,' said Carla. 'I needed to erase from the gene pool my father's family's famous nose. Antoine has the nose of a Greek god.' They all looked at Antoine, and he dutifully lifted his chin.

'I married Olivier because he is a good lover,' said Angelica, aware that she was about to deceive him.

Olivier preened. 'What can I say, boys?' He laughed, the colour now returning to his cheeks. 'I might lose my money, but I'll always be a good lover.'

Angelica glanced at her watch and placed her napkin on the table. 'Excuse me,' she said, getting up. 'Won't be a minute.' As she passed Olivier, he took her hand.

'Where are you off to?'

'The ladies'.'

He pulled her down and whispered in her ear. 'You're the best-looking girl in the room.'

She glanced at Carla, Chantal, and Veronica, none of them famed for their beauty. 'Not a great deal of competition,' she replied, then walked off in the direction of the powder room, too frightened to glance at Jack, who watched her go and placed his own napkin on the table.

She walked downstairs, unsteady with nerves, and stood there waiting, heart pounding with anticipation and fear. It wasn't long before Jack appeared. Neither could contain their exhilaration at finding themselves in the same restaurant. 'The Fates are on my side,' he said, drawing her into his arms and kissing her cheek. Her head spun, but she didn't hurry to pull away.

'This is an incredible coincidence. Out of all the restaurants in London.'

'I love Harry's. It reminds me of my mis-spent youth.'

'How much of it did you mis-spend?'

'Not enough.' He devoured her features from behind his glasses. 'So are you going to meet me in the park tomorrow?'

'Don't you have any work to do?'

'Sure, but when there's a will there's a way. Actually, I don't have a meeting until the afternoon. Why don't we walk around the Serpentine? A morning stroll. I like to be near water; it is good for the soul.'

Aware of the little time they had and reckless in his presence, she replied hastily. 'Why not?'

'I'll bring some bread for the birds.'

'I thought dogs ate birds.'

'This one is a benign dog; you should know that by now.' He looked at her in that intense way of his.

'And no chasing rabbits?'

'Why would I want to do that, when the most desirable rabbit is right here?' He raised his eyes to see Veronica, Chantal, and Carla coming down the stairs towards them. 'You've got company. I'd better go. See you in the café on the Serpentine at ten.' Before she could reply he had disappeared into the gents.

'We've decided to leave them to it,' said Chantal.

'Men can be so boring,' Veronica complained.

'Let's go outside. I need a cigarette,' Carla suggested. 'Besides, it's far too hot in here. Look at you, Angelica, you're burning up.'

Angelica was indeed burning up, but not because of the heat in the club. She waited for them to come out of the ladies' room, then followed them back upstairs and outside, where the cool night air chilled her cheeks and the darkness hid her desire.

Chapter 11

'Have faith and you will succeed'

In Search of the Perfect Happiness

Angelica walked to the park, hands in pockets, her Moschino navy peacoat wrapped tightly around her. The sun shone golden in the autumn sky, setting the tops of the trees alight in a blaze of oranges and reds. The air was crisp and fresh, the roar of the morning traffic rising with the flight of pigeons. She put her head down, letting her hair fall about her face to hide her shame. It was useless denying her intention. She was on her way to meet the man with whom she was now falling in love.

Biting her bottom lip, she considered Olivier, her children, and her comfortable life. She hadn't done anything wrong – yet. Jack was merely a friend. Her life was still safely in her grasp, in one piece. She knew the consequences of having an affair; she had seen them in the shattered lives of friends who had been through the mangle of the divorce courts. She didn't want that. She didn't want to lose Olivier.

There was still time to walk away, but Jack's allure was too great. Surely it was possible to enjoy his company without sex? To look from afar and dream of another life without having to taste it? He lived in South Africa. As painful as it was to think of his leaving, it was also a relief; the distance would save her from herself.

She reached the café by the Serpentine a little early, so she sat on a bench and watched the ducks. She smiled as she thought of his promise to bring bread. She still derived pleasure from feeding them with her children, and he clearly did, too. It was an attractive quality to enjoy the natural world. Olivier only ever noticed birds when he had a gun in his hands. A jogger ran by, his breath misty in the morning air, his face red with exertion. A group of young mothers with toddlers in strollers sat drinking coffee at a round table in the sun, their eyes red-rimmed with exhaustion. Angelica remembered interrupted nights and was grateful that her children were now old enough not to disturb her sleep.

Then Jack came striding purposefully through the trees, and she stood up to meet him. He waved when he saw her, his face creasing into a joyous smile. She felt at once uplifted, her heart filled with light. She waved back, glancing around furtively to see if she was being watched.

'I feel like a schoolgirl playing truant,' she said when he reached her. But he pulled her into his arms without a care for secrecy and kissed her cheek. The electricity of his touch was so powerful that she caught her breath. In that brief moment she forgot all about Olivier.

'You *look* like a schoolgirl playing truant.' He laughed. 'Relax.'

'Did you bring bread for the ducks?'

'Of course.' He delved into his coat pocket and passed her a plastic bag of bread crumbs. He watched her dip her fingers in and come out with a handful. 'So how was last night?'

'Dull. All anyone wanted to talk about was the financial crisis.'

'I nearly fell off my chair when I saw you walk into the club. You looked like a silver angel floating through the darkness.'

'I didn't see you when I came in.'

'I saw *you*. God bless mobile telephones, and God bless you for breaking the rules and leaving it on.'

'I always leave it on vibrate in case the children need me. It was an extraordinary coincidence.' She threw crumbs onto the water and watched the ducks swim swiftly over to eat them.

'I couldn't take my eyes off you. I can't take my eyes off you now, either.'

'Really, you are funny.'

'You always say that when you're embarrassed. It's an endearing defence mechanism.'

'It's just that I'm not used to being complimented.'

'I don't believe that for a second.'

'Really, I'm not.'

'Look, I'm holding back here. If I could, I'd shower you in compliments.'

Her heart accelerated like a trapped bird's. 'I thought we were just going to be friends.'

'We are. I never said I wouldn't say what's on my mind.' He took her hand, sending a shiver all the way up her arm. 'You know how I feel.'

'I'm still surprised that you can talk so openly about your feelings. Men usually don't. They're usually muzzled.' She slipped her hand out of his grasp.

'Englishmen perhaps, not South Africans. But I've learned to say what's on my mind because I might never get another chance.' He poured the last crumbs to the pavement, where a gaggle of fat pigeons waited eagerly to peck them up. 'Let's walk.'

They set off around the pond. The water shone like a gilded mirror as the sun rose higher in the sky, and Angelica felt the warmth on her face. 'It's beautiful, isn't it?' she said, reluctantly putting her hands in her pockets so that he couldn't hold one, wishing that they were in some distant city so he could.

He took a deep breath. 'Very beautiful.' They walked on in silence, taking in the glory of such a magnificent morning.

'I'm mad, you know,' she said after a while.

'I know. You're married. I'm married. What we're doing is crazy. But I can't help myself. If I can't be your lover, I'm content to be your friend.' He laughed and shook his head at his own dishonesty. 'No, I'm not content to be your friend. I'm smitten with you, and all I can think about is making love to you. Don't say I'm funny and brush me off with a laugh. I'm not at all funny. I'm a very sad man.'

'Jack . . . don't . . .' She remembered his lover in Clapham. Perhaps Scarlet had got it wrong.

'Listen, I'm a terrible flirt. I'm the first to admit it. But this is beyond a flirt and a first for me, if you can believe that. I'm walking into unknown territory with a great big FORBIDDEN sign hanging across the pathway. But I know that if I don't seize the moment, it might never present itself again. Life is short.'

'You have a wife, Jack, and children. Let's just be friends. Isn't that what a really wise sage would advise?'

'If that's all you're prepared to give me, then I have no choice but to accept. I'd rather see you as friends than not at all.' He bent down and picked up a small stone, throwing it into the water so that it bounced three times before sinking. 'It's wrong of me to try to persuade you to give me anything more. I'm going back to South Africa on Friday. I wish you could come with me.'

'You know that's impossible.'

'I'd say come out with Olivier and your children, but I don't think I could stand to see you both together.'

'I'd never get away with coming out on my own.'

'So it's walks around the Serpentine.' He looked away. 'Why do I have to meet you at this time in my life?'

'If we had met fifteen years ago, we might not have liked each other.'

He looked back at her, his eyes dark and sad. 'Oh, I'd always have liked you.'

They changed the subject and discussed the previous evening. Angelica made him laugh as she imitated her friends. He told her of the people he would introduce her to in South Africa – fun, bohemian people who didn't talk about finance, but discussed books and films and art. 'As ironic as it is, you'd get on very well with my wife.'

'I don't think I'd want to meet her. Not now.'

'We haven't done anything wrong except declare a mutual attraction.'

'That would be reason enough for Olivier to explode into a jealous rage!'

'Anna would shrug it off with a smile.'

'Broken on the wheel, I suppose.'

'Indulgent, actually.' She didn't like the sound of Anna, or the look on his face when he spoke about her. 'Take me out of the equation, and you two would find you had a lot in common.'

'I'll never know,' she replied tightly.

He grinned as if he could see her jealousy as colours swirling around her head. 'I'm flattered you mind.'

'I don't mind, actually. You can tell me all about Anna if you wish.' Her voice sounded tense even to her.

'She's not a beauty like you, but she's beautiful on the inside. There are many different ways of loving, and I'd be lying if I told you I didn't love her. I don't know you well enough to love you, but I'm *in* love with you, and right now I think about you more than I think about anyone.'

'Am I meant to take that as a compliment?'

'Yes, the fact that I'm being honest with you sets you apart from any other woman I've ever fancied. It's easy to tell someone you love them to get what you want, but that's not love. That's desire, lust, attraction, or fascination. You only start to truly love someone when you fall *out* of love with them, when you love them in spite of their faults, most often *because* of them.'

'Well, that is honest, I suppose.' She felt her spirits sink.

'It's the greatest compliment I can give you.'

'Then it's true to say that I love Olivier. I'm not sure that I'm *in* love with him anymore. Wouldn't it be nice to experience both at the same time? The constant comfort of love and the exciting thrill of in love. Are you in love with Anna?'

'No.'

'But you love her. So surely you don't want to hurt her?'

'No. I don't want to hurt her.'

'Wouldn't she be hurt if she knew you were, as you put it, falling in love with me?'

'I think she would.' He stopped walking and rubbed the back of his neck, looking up at the sky as if he'd find an answer there. Finally, he shook his head and stared at her thoughtfully. He suddenly looked old. 'It's complicated, Angelica. I wish I could explain, but if I did, I'd ruin the magic of our meeting. Right now, all I really care about is being with you. I'm aware that I'm leaving soon, and I want to feast my eyes on you for as long as I can before I go. I wish we had met twenty years ago.'

'I was a very unattractive twenty-year-old,' she replied with a laugh, relieved that they weren't going to talk about their spouses any more.

'I don't believe that for a second.'

'You'd have tossed me a glance and moved on to someone prettier. I know your type.'

'Then if you believe in karma, what goes around comes around. You are my penance for all the irresponsible flirting I've done over the years.'

'I'd hate to think of myself as a penance.'

'I've met someone I really want but can't have. That's the most bittersweet penance there is.'

'I imagine a man like you has women tucked away in every corner of the globe.'

'I don't tuck people away, and I don't intend to. If you think this is a game to me, you're wrong. It might have started out as an entertainment, but it's got a hell of a lot more serious.' He thrust his hands into his pockets. 'I didn't plan to fall in love, Sage. Not at this stage in my life.'

They sat on a bench beneath a chestnut tree, watching the world move around them. People met and parted, and Angelica wondered how many were illicit meetings like theirs. By lunchtime neither could believe that three hours had gone by. In an effort to prolong the morning, they found a small café in Knightsbridge and ate a simple lunch of smoked salmon and salad. Angelica no longer worried about being caught. Having lunch with Jack felt like the most natural thing in the world. She didn't glance around like a fugitive but focused on his gentle brown eyes and listened intently to everything he said. If anyone had bothered to look at them, they would have thought them lovers by the way they gazed at each other, oblivious to the rest of the city, and by the natural way he occasionally took her hand or played with her fingers, and by the way they laughed with such abandon.

In a short time they'd both return to their separate lives. It seemed incomprehensible sitting there together that they had lives beyond each other. But that time eventually came. Jack had an appointment, and Angelica had to pick up the children from school. Their conversation dwindled as they felt the heavy anticipation of their parting. He took her hand across the small table and leaned towards her. 'I want to see you again before I go.'

'Is that wise?'

'That's irrelevant. If we were always wise we'd never enjoy making mistakes.'

'I don't know, Jack.'

'I'm only asking for one more morning. Don't pretend you're doing any writing at the moment.' His grin was persuasive – and she did want to be persuaded. 'Aren't you feeling inspired?'

'Yes, you're very inspiring – for a different genre altogether.'

'Then write something different. Follow your instincts.'

'I don't dare.'

'Why?'

'Because Olivier will know.'

'No, he won't. He'll think it's your imagination – if he reads it.'

'Sod's law, this will be the first book of mine he reads.'

'It'll be the best book you've ever written.'

'So I suppose you want a dedication?'

He chuckled, but she thought she saw sorrow in his eyes. 'No, I just want to see you again before I leave.'

'You'll be coming back, won't you?'

He shrugged. 'Who knows where life will take us? I don't want to take any chances. Please, Angelica. I won't pounce, I swear it.'

'Maybe.'

He grinned in that roguish way of his, and Angelica wondered whether she had imagined the sorrow.

They parted in the street. He hailed a cab, and she watched him wave through the back window until he was swallowed by traffic. She turned and set off towards Kensington, the scent of his cologne still fresh on her skin.

Grey clouds now moved across the sky, driven by a chilly wind that whipped through the trees, causing the orange leaves to fall to the pavement like rain. Their morning together seemed nothing now but a sunny dream. It must have drizzled while they were in the café, for the tarmac glistened and the air was damp. Autumn had snatched the magic that had been theirs so briefly. Now that they had parted, she longed for him with every fibre in her body. She regretted her reluctance to see him one last time before he left for South Africa and wanted to text him to reassure him that she wanted him as much as he wanted her. But as she approached the school, she remembered once again who she was and where she belonged.

She met her friends with a heavy heart, knowing that she was unable to share her predicament. Candace noticed it at once. 'Are you all right, Angelica?'

'I'm fine,' she replied, shrugging it off. 'I went out last night, so I'm a bit tired.'

'You don't look tired.'

'Makeup.'

She wasn't convinced. 'I didn't see you at Pilates this morning.'

'God, I totally forgot!'

'You were missed.'

'I'm going mad.'

Candace looked at her friend suspiciously. 'So what were you doing?'

'Trying to write my book.'

'How's it going?'

'I've begun at least. A meagre plot that seemed good at the time, but now, on reflection, is rather old hat.'

'Well, at least you've started. It's more important to write than work out.'

'I know.'

Candace raised her eyes to see Jenna striding towards them. 'Oh Lord, it's a gaucho. Doesn't that girl ever take off her sunglasses?'

'Hi!' Jenna gave a little wave. 'Isn't it cold all of a sudden?' She didn't look in the slightest bit cold in her cowboy hat, cashmere poncho, and riding boots.

'It was lovely this morning,' said Angelica.

'I've already begun,' said Jenna with a triumphant smile.

'Begun what?' asked Candace.

'My novel. Didn't Angelica tell you? I'm writing a novel based on my life.'

'Wow! Best seller,' said Candace flatly.

'I didn't realize how easy it is to write a book. I always thought of you toiling away, Angelica, fighting to get it done before your deadline. It's a piece of cake.' She gave a little sniff. 'At least for me.'

'Well, you're not quite Tolstoy,' said Candace, her jaw tensing with irritation.

'No, it's more like a modern Edith Wharton.'

'I can't wait to read it,' said Angelica, trying to keep a straight face.

'You will read it, then you can put me in touch with that delicious publisher of yours . . . what was he called? Leighton something.'

'Leighton,' said Angelica with a blush. She couldn't remember what he had said his last name was. 'Jenna met him when we were having lunch at Daphne's,' she said to Candace, whose bewildered expression was replaced by a knowing smile.

'Oh, *him,*' she said. 'He *is* delicious. Such a shame he's gay.'

'Gay?' Jenna was appalled.

'Yes. He breaks hearts all over the world. Only a man can win him.'

'God, I would never have guessed!' Jenna had gone pale.

'Good luck with the book,' said Candace, tapping her arm. 'We could all do with a little Edith Wharton.'

The big doors opened and one by one the children were handed over to their mothers or nannies. Jenna pushed her way to the front of the queue.

'I don't think we'll ever see that book of hers,' said Candace. 'Shame!'

'I forgot to tell you I'd bumped into her!'

'What else did you forget to tell me, Angelica?' Candace looked at her sternly. 'Are you seeing him?'

'No!'

'It was just lunch?'

'Yes. I told you, it was just lunch. I'm sad, that's all. Life is a little less bright without his emails to keep me going – and I really liked him.'

'It's for the best, though, Angelica. You have a nice life.' Candace was now satisfied. 'You'll get over him.'

'Of course. But I can't tell you how much I'd like to see him again.' That, at least, was true.

Chapter 12

'You can't control what happens to you in your life but you can control how you react'

In Search of the Perfect Happiness

Angelica took the children for a playdate at Letizia's house. She sat in the airy green sitting room drinking tea with her friend while the children played upstairs. Letizia looked glamourous in a pair of grey flannel trousers and a dove-grey cashmere top, a few inches taller thanks to Tod's pumps.

'I love the idea of the manny,' she told Angelica, playing with the array of Van Cleef gold necklaces that hung down to her navel. 'I mean, Maria is a nightmare! She's got to go. I cannot cope with that sour face at the breakfast table every morning, and I know she thinks I'm a tyrant.'

'You *are* a tyrant, Letizia,' said Angelica with a grin. 'But it's not her place to judge you. You pay her to do a job; she should at least do it with a smile.'

'I've spoiled her, darling; that's the trouble. At the beginning I gave her every goodie bag from every party I went to, and I bought her a really generous birthday present from Links. Now she thinks I owe her a living.'

'They all have a sell-by date.'

'Well, she's well past hers; she's beginning to smell!' She

waved a hand under her nose. '*Schifosa!* I feel unwelcome in my own home.'

'See what this manny of Scarlet's is like. If you like him and Scarlet's not employing him over Christmas, take him skiing with you.'

'It's such a great idea, especially for Alessandro. He's too old to have a nanny now, but a boy who can teach him football sounds ideal.'

Angelica's mobile rang with a message. She knew instinctively that it was from Jack. While Letizia continued talking, she pulled it out and read: **I'm pining for you, Sage. When can I call you? DWOP** She bit her bottom lip, wondering what DWOP stood for. Letizia didn't notice the colour in her cheeks. 'And what about Kate's wedding?' Letizia continued. 'I'm so excited. It's wonderful that they're patching it up. Although I wouldn't trust Pete as far as I could throw him. I mean, it's shocking. He's married to one of the loveliest girls in London, and he has to skulk around having affairs. It's disgusting and disrespectful.'

Angelica wanted to repeat what Olivier had said: that in spite of Kate's beauty, she was neurotic and flaky and probably very hard to live with. But she held her tongue. Letizia was fiercely loyal about her friends. The only one with whom Angelica could really speak her mind was Candace.

'Let's hope that's all over,' she said instead.

'Do leopards change their spots?'

'Some do.'

'I'm not sure Pete's one of those. Still, it will be a great wedding. We're all going to stay in the Saint Géran . . .'

'. . . and waft about in white linen.'

'Yes.' She laughed. 'With shells in our hair! *Madonna!*'

When she got home, Angelica perched on the loo seat while the children played in the bath. She read his text again, ignoring Joe, who threw one of his big dinosaurs to the bath mat with a loud clunk. She tapped in her reply: **Don't pine. I hate to think of you sad. Call me at 8, if you like. X Sage.** Another dinosaur landed on the mat, covered in foam. 'Do you want to watch TV before bed?' she snapped.

'Yes, but . . .'

'No buts, Joe. Stop throwing things out of the bath, or you'll go straight to bed.' She knelt down to wash their hair, now on a mission to get them both into bed by eight.

Joe got to watch *Scooby-Doo*. Isabel sat at her pink dressing table while Angelica dried her long brown hair. She opened her drawer and played with the tray of makeup she had collected from her mother's old lipsticks and eye shadows. Angelica watched her daughter's reflection fondly, determined that she would never do anything to jeopardize her secure little world.

At last they were in bed. She had read them a couple of chapters of *Despereaux,* which she had enjoyed almost more than they did, then lovingly kissed their foreheads. A Full Joe from her son had completed the bedtime ritual before she had turned off their lights. With a sigh of relief she walked back into her bedroom and lay on the bed, her mobile in hand, awaiting his call.

At five minutes past eight it rang. She could see from the DOP in the display screen that it was Jack. Her belly lurched with guilty pleasure. 'Hello,' she said in a soft voice.

'I miss you,' he replied with a sigh.

'I miss you, too.'

'That makes me feel a lot better.'

'What does DWOP stand for?'

He chuckled. 'Dog Well off Porch.'

'Dog Soon to Be Back on Porch,' she replied wryly.

'I don't like to think of going home without you.'

'I'm a little big for your suitcase.'

'I'd buy one big enough if you said you'd come.'

'It's not going to happen, Jack.'

'I'd love to show you Rosenbosch. It's so beautiful at this time of year. It's spring. Everything's so fresh and new. I'd take you riding across the veld, into the mist on the hills, and we'd sit at the top, and, once the mist had lifted, I'd show you the whole valley. It would take your breath away.'

'It already has.'

'Do you ride?'

'I grew up in the country and was obsessed with ponies.'

'Good. Then I have just the horse for you. A chestnut so sweet natured you could gallop at full speed and never fear falling off or being run away with.'

'I'd love that. I haven't felt the wind in my hair for years.'

'Then let me. Make up an excuse. I'll organize your ticket.'

'How would you explain that to your wife?'

'You're my friend.'

'She'd be a fool if she believed that, and I don't think she is a fool.'

'She's not, but she's tolerant.'

'She really wouldn't mind if I pitched up to stay?'

He hesitated a moment. 'I really don't think she would. Look, I would behave myself. I respect her a great deal. I just want you *near*.'

'There would have to be a very good reason for Olivier to let me go. There are practicalities you haven't even considered. I don't have a nanny. Who'd pick up the children every day? It's not as easy for me to leave as it is for you. My children have homework every evening, and, unless Olivier gets sacked, which I hope he doesn't, I'd have to hire someone to cover for me, and Olivier hates having strangers in the house.'

'Then it's really impossible.' His voice sounded so low she felt a stab of pity.

'I'm sorry.'

'Me, too.' There was a pause. She could hear his breathing down the line. Then his tone lifted. 'What are you doing tomorrow night?'

'Kate's giving her friend Art a birthday party.'

'You have to go?'

'Yes, I do.'

'You can't cancel?'

'Absolutely not.'

'Tell them you're sick and come and have dinner with me.'

'I couldn't.'

'Which part couldn't you do?'

'Both, Jack. I couldn't lie to my friends, and I couldn't have dinner with you. It would be folly.'

There was a pause while he devised a plan. 'Then let's meet after the party.'

'I don't know . . .'

'Look, I leave on Friday.'

'It's too dangerous.'

'What about Friday morning? We can walk around the park again.'

'We got away with it once. I can't do it again.'

'I have to see you, Sage. What's the harm in two friends meeting for the last time?'

At that moment she heard the front door slam. She sat up with a start. 'Oh Lord, I think Olivier's home.'

'Text me. I'll meet you tomorrow night. You can leave the party early. We can go someplace, a bar . . .'

'It's risky.'

'I know.'

'If I get caught . . .'

'London's a big city.'

'You'd be surprised.' She heard Olivier's footsteps on the stairs. 'Got to go,' she hissed urgently. She heard him hang up without saying goodbye, and said loudly for Olivier's benefit, 'Better go, Mum, Olivier's home.'

He came in looking moody, tossed his jacket onto a chair, and loosened his tie. She got off the bed.

'What's for supper?' he asked.

'I thought we could order in something. What would you like?'

'A Chinese. Ring Mr Wing now, I'm ravenous.'

'Fancy a glass of wine? I do.'

'Yes, be an angel and bring it up here, will you? I've had one hell of a day. It's very tough.' He sighed heavily. 'I hope you're writing your book, Angelica. We might need your earnings if I'm laid off.'

'You think you might be?'

'Nothing is certain.'

'God, Olivier. That's terrible.'

'I know. Things are really bad.'

'But you're going to be okay, surely?'

'Didn't you hear what I just said?' he snapped impatiently.

'Yes, I'm just being optimistic.'

'Well, now isn't the time to be optimistic. If I'm laid off, we'll be in trouble. Your earnings will be important.'

'My new book comes out in the spring.'

'Good. Let's hope it sells well.'

Angelica went downstairs to order the food and pour the wine, seething with resentment. She didn't imagine Jack would come home in such a foul mood and demand that she order the food and pour the wine. He admired her books, he had even read one, which was more than Olivier had ever done. Now he had the cheek to tell her that what *he* considered a small home industry might actually be important. Well, she knew it was important. Her fans all over the world knew it was important. Jack knew it was important. If Olivier bothered to read her royalty statements, he'd realize just how important it was. But compared with his vast banker's salary, her earnings were as raindrops in a lake – inconsequential.

Furiously, she ordered the dinner then sat in silence as they ate it at the kitchen table.

'Thank God we're not going out tonight. I'm shattered.'

He didn't notice that she hadn't laid the table or lit a candle. She no longer felt guilty about fancying Jack. In fact, she felt she deserved a flirtation. If her husband wasn't going to cherish her, Jack would – and if he really pushed her, she'd find a way to get to South Africa. In the gloom of Olivier's bad mood the thought of riding across the veld was extremely enticing.

'Are you going to talk to me, or are you just going to sit there sulking?' Olivier asked.

'You don't need to get at me just because you've had a bad day.'

'Haven't you read the papers? It's not just a bad day. Things are really going sour. We're careering headlong into a recession. Probably the worst we've had in one hundred years. I need your support, not your condemnation.'

'I'm not condemning you, Olivier. I just don't like your implying that my books are some kind of last resort if we hit bad times.'

'I'm grateful for them. We might need them.' He spread plum sauce onto his pancake, then piled it up with duck and onion slices.

'But your implication is that they can be brushed aside. I might as well be knitting bootees for the local children's shop by the tone of your voice.'

He put his hand on hers and sighed resignedly. 'I would never imply that what you do has no value. It has tremendous value not only to you spiritually but to us financially. All I'm saying is that they might become our only source of income.'

She withdrew her hand. 'You've never read one.'

'No, it's true. I haven't.' He took a large bite and began to chew. As he did so, his hostility lifted and he smiled. 'I will.'

'Don't bother. You're busy.' She no longer cared whether or not he read one. In fact, she rather wished he wouldn't so that she could continue to hold the grudge, justifying her seeking consolation from Jack.

'I'm sorry I'm hard to live with at the moment. Ask any of your friends who is married to a banker. It's not fun any more. I can't even tell you to go and spend a few grand in Gucci.' He shrugged helplessly.

'I'm far too busy writing anyway.'

'This is very good.' He rolled another pancake. 'We should have this more often. I had forgotten how much I like Mr Wing.'

Before she went to bed she sent Jack a text: **I'll meet you at eleven tomorrow night. X Sage.** No sooner had she sent it than a message came winging back: **I'll wait at the end of the street in a taxi. What's the address? DOP.**

Olivier slept beside Angelica, but the gap between them was as big as Siberia. Angelica lay on her side facing away from him, dreaming of Jack and riding across the South African veld on a beautiful chestnut mare. Everything about him was romantic. The way he was so happy to discuss life. The way he spoke about his feelings. The way he loved nature. The way he noticed *her*. With him she felt attractive, feminine, mysterious, and cherished. With Jack she was someone totally different, someone Olivier had forgotten. And she liked that someone very much.

The following morning felt unlike any other. Olivier had gone to work. The children were getting ready for school,

Sunny was preparing breakfast downstairs, she was dressing . . . but the air around her had changed; it was now charged with possibility. She walked the children to school and kissed them at the door. She had coffee with Candace, Letizia, Scarlet, and Kate. She listened to Kate's arrangements for Art's party: she had filled the house with silver helium balloons so that you couldn't see the ceiling; she had ordered a cake from Jane Asher that was 'to die for'; she had Mustard doing the catering; and she had hired a karaoke machine for all those aspiring singers to show off their talents – and yet Angelica moved through her day knowing that, whatever happened, at eleven o'clock her world would change. She sensed it like a bird sensing an earthquake.

She had lunch with Scarlet at Le Caprice, then picked up the children at three-thirty. They walked through the park, feeding the geese on the Round Pond. She sat on a bench while the children played with the birds, considering her life and the fork in the road that lay ahead of her. She didn't want to leave Olivier; in spite of his moodiness she loved him. But Jack had injected her life with excitement and given her a high from which she was reluctant to come down.

The children grew tired and hungry. They walked back past Kensington Palace, Joe bending down to pat every dog, Isabel hanging off the railings like a parrot. Sunny gave them tea. Angelica supervised their homework at the dining-room table. Everything was the same as always, except in her head, where everything was different.

She dressed for dinner, choosing a vintage midnight-blue dress Olivier had bought her in Paris the first year of their marriage. She had always loved that dress, but it was only since losing weight that she was able to wear it. Olivier threw a shadow across the room. He stood in the doorway, watching her. Without asking he turned up the lights and wandered in, taking off his jacket. 'So you're going out.'

'Yes, to Kate's party for Art.'

'Oh yes, I forgot.' He ran his eyes up and down her body. 'You look *très jolie*.' He pulled a face. 'Shame you're going out. I'd like to take that dress off.'

'No time, I'm afraid,' she said, slipping past him.

'You smell nice, too.'

'Oranges.'

'Nice.' He looked at her longingly and a little lost.

'Thank you.'

'Don't be too long.'

'Why, are you going to miss me?' She hadn't meant to sound so sharp.

'Of course. I like your company.' He narrowed his eyes. 'You're not still angry with me for last night?'

'Of course not.'

'I haven't seen you for ages.'

'You saw me last night.'

'That doesn't count. We should spend more time together.'

'Sure.' She grabbed her evening bag and tossed her hair.

'I'm sad that you look so ravishing, but not for me.'

'It's not my fault you're not coming. You still can.'

He dithered, and for a terrible moment she thought he might change his mind and go with her. 'No, I'm tired. Just don't be too long.'

'It'll go on all night, Olivier. You know what Kate's karaoke evenings are like.'

'Karaoke! I'm definitely not coming to hear a bunch of Hoorays singing out of tune to YMCA!' He laughed unhappily. 'Let's go out for dinner tomorrow night, just the two of us.'

'No, let's stay in. I'll be tired.'

'I thought you might like a night out, just us.'

'I would, but not tomorrow.'

He threw himself onto the bed, crossing his feet. 'What's for supper?'

Angelica arrived at Kate's just as Scarlet and William were ringing the doorbell.

'Where's Olivier?' William asked.

'Not coming. Hates karaoke.'

'Well, that makes two of us. That's the point where I think I'll leave you all to it,' he added.

'And when the party will really get going.' Scarlet giggled as William nudged her playfully.

Inside, the guests waited in the sitting room for Art and Tod to arrive. The effect of all those silver balloons was magical. Candles covered every surface and were reflected in the big ornate mirrors that hung above the mantelpieces. Waiters weaved through the throng with trays of champagne and cocktails. Angelica took a glass of champagne and found Candace talking to Letizia and Kate. All the husbands were there except Olivier, but Angelica wasn't in the least bit upset. All she could think about was eleven o'clock.

At last the couple arrived. Tod flung open the door and Art's face was a picture of astonishment and pleasure. He swept his eyes over the faces of his friends and settled finally onto Kate's. 'You naughty girl!' he said, throwing his arms around her small frame and lifting her off the ground. 'I love you, I love you, I love you!' he breathed into her ear.

'Happy birthday!' she exclaimed, raising her glass, and everyone in the room raised theirs.

'Let the party begin!' Tod shouted, and, as if by magic, the lights were turned up and music resounded through the rooms.

Chapter 13

'Live in the present because it's all there is'

In Search of the Perfect Happiness

'Angelica, darling, you look peachy,' said Art, towering over her. At six feet four he was handsome in an aristocratic, chiselled way, with intelligent grey eyes and glossy brown hair that flopped over his face.

'Happy birthday, Art,' she said, smelling his spicy perfume as he bent down to kiss her.

'What is that scent? It's delicious,' said Candace. 'Though kind of overpowering!'

'State secret,' he replied. 'I don't want you all smelling like me.'

'You don't look anything like fifty,' said Angelica.

'Don't mention the five, please, it hurts. You're as old as you feel.'

'Or as old as the woman you feel,' said Angelica with a giggle. 'That's what my father always says.'

'Not in my case. Tod is nearer the six, but don't tell him I said so.'

'Kate has really pushed the boat out on this one,' said Candace, gazing around the room.

'She loves me,' he said casually.

'Don't we all?' It was impossible not to think the world of Art.

'You two are enough to turn a gay man straight. I'd better circulate, or I'll get into trouble. There's no such thing as a free dinner.'

'Isn't he adorable?' Candace asked as he made his way through the throng.

'Adorable!'

'You don't think . . .?' She scrunched up her face as if trying to conjure an impossible mental picture.

'What?'

'That he's the mystery man?'

'You mean, Art and Kate?'

'Yes.'

'Absolutely not. He's devoted to Tod, and he's gay. Anyway, she's convinced herself that Pete's the father.'

'Well, she might be right. But we'll know when he's born and doesn't look anything like Pete!'

'I wager he looks nothing like Art.'

'Come on, let's take a look around. He's sure to be in here somewhere.'

They worked their way through the room. Candace sized up every man with eyes as sharp as an eagle's. Angelica watched the clock. Minutes passed slowly, and sometimes, when she looked, they seemed not to pass at all. She felt dizzy with nerves, unable to concentrate on what anyone said. She forgot people's names and blundered into more than the odd faux pas. Raising her glass cheerfully, she blamed the champagne. Due to her somewhat daffy charm, she got away with it.

Dinner was buffet style, and Angelica helped herself to a small portion of salad, which she picked at on the sofa with Candace and Letizia, too anxious to eat. Kate flitted about in a short cashmere dress that barely covered her bottom. Her belly was still as flat as a biscuit, which prompted the girls to question whether she really was pregnant.

'It wouldn't surprise me if she's making up the whole thing,' said Candace. 'Then we'll all be swept into the drama of the miscarriage.'

'She's just skinny. I showed even before I was pregnant,' said Angelica.

'She should be showing by now, especially as it's her third child. But that stomach is as tight as a trampoline.' Candace watched her take Art's cigarette and sneak a quick drag. 'Would she be smoking if she was pregnant?'

'I don't think she's making it up. She was in a real state, remember? And we all saw the lines go blue on the tests,' said Letizia.

'True, you can't manufacture that,' Angelica agreed.

'She's not holding back on the alcohol, either. Actually, I'd go further and say I think she's tipsy.'

'If the child is like his mother, he'll have the constitution of an Irish navvy.' Angelica laughed.

'She's a mystery. Where's Pete, by the way?'

'Probably with Olivier – they both hate this sort of party.'

'He's in Russia,' Letizia interjected. 'But you're right: he hates karaoke, and he's not fond of Art, though I can't think why. Everyone loves Art.'

'Look, Art's a ladies' man,' said Candace. 'Heterosexual men don't get him. He makes them feel nervous because he's such a beautiful creature. It's a crying shame for women that the best-looking men are gay.' *Not all,* Angelica thought, and glanced at her watch.

It wasn't long before the karaoke started. William left with a few other husbands who found the sound of tuneless shriek-ing too much to bear. Kate kicked off with 'It's a Heartache,' followed by Scarlet and Tod singing a harmonious rendition of 'I Got You Babe.' Nothing could persuade Angelica to take to the floor, even fortified with champagne and the anticipation of disappearing into the night to meet Jack. She

sat back on the sofa and laughed at the sight of her friends
blithely making fools of themselves.

The next time Angelica looked at her watch it was eleven
o'clock. The world stood still as her stomach plummeted. She
had waited so long for this moment, but now that it was here
she shied away, like a pony at too high a jump. She paled and
drained her champagne glass, driven by the sense of inevitability that had propelled her through her day. Without a word
to anyone she got up and slipped out into the hall. A waitress
retrieved her coat, and she wrapped it tightly around her as
she stepped out into the cold. It was crisp and clear outside,
the sky studded with stars; at the end of the street a taxi waited
beneath a bright lamp.

Angelica walked towards it, her steps accelerating, tap-
tapping over the pavement. She could see him through the
back window, silhouetted against the light of the lamp, and
her heart inflated like one of Kate's silver balloons. She
reached the cab, and the door flung open. Glancing back to
make sure she wasn't being watched, she climbed in. Jack
didn't wait to ask permission. He pulled her into his arms and
pressed his lips to hers hungrily. Angelica wasn't surprised or
horrified that he had broken his word; his kiss felt like home.

The old cabbie looked in his rear-view mirror and grinned.
If he wrote about everything he'd seen going on in the back
of his taxi, he'd have a best seller to boast of. The trouble was,
he could barely manage to write a shopping list, let alone an
entire book. He shook his head regretfully and pulled out
into the street.

Jack's mouth was warm and soft, his chin rough against
hers, his embrace the firm hold of a man reluctant to let her
go. He slipped his hand beneath her coat, and she felt the heat
in it up and down her dress. She yearned for him to touch her
skin, to feel his fingers caress her dark and secret places, and
her desire made her forget herself. He kissed her neck and

throat, sending an exquisite tremour through her body, and she let out a deep moan, pressing herself against him.

As the taxi swung around corners and stopped at traffic lights, Jack and Angelica clung to each other, savouring the magic, aware that tomorrow a plane would take him away to the other side of the world.

The taxi drew up outside Number 11 Cadogan Gardens, and Jack climbed out. The sight of the hotel and the rush of cold air as he opened the door brought her to her senses. She shrank back into the seat in terror. 'I can't . . .' she faltered. He leaned in and reached for her hand. But she shook her head and looked away, embarrassed. 'You know I can't.'

He said something to the cabbie, but Angelica couldn't hear for the ringing in her ears. For a dreadful moment she thought he was telling the man to take her home, that he was going to walk away in displeasure, but he climbed in beside her, closed the door, and drew her back into his arms, kissing her temple and nuzzling her cheek.

'It's okay,' he said gently. 'I shouldn't have presumed. I couldn't help myself. Forgive me.' She lay against him, relieved that he didn't think less of her. 'I have all these good intentions when I'm not with you, then the minute I see you I just want to carry you upstairs and make love to you.'

She lifted her face. 'I can't go home to Olivier smelling of you. What will he think if I turn up in the early hours of the morning? I'm the kind of girl who's in bed by eleven.'

'You don't have to explain. I'll take you home. But not before I've kissed you again. Just drive, cabbie. Anywhere you like.'

The taxi drove around Bayswater and Notting Hill, while Jack and Angelica sat entwined in the backseat, nuzzling and kissing each other like young lovers. It was past midnight when it rattled up Kensington Church Street and into Brunswick Gardens.

'So, it's goodbye, Sage.' He took her face in his hand, and she pressed her cheek against it. It had all happened so quickly. A few meetings, a dozen emails, and now a brief taxi ride, and yet they felt there had never been a time when they hadn't known each other. His eyes were sad as they swept over her features, as if this was the last opportunity he'd ever have to feast on them. His sentimentality moved her, and she turned her head to kiss his palm. 'I'm already missing you,' he murmured. 'Let me memorize every feature so I know you by heart.'

'Come back soon,' she whispered, fighting back tears.

'You come to South Africa. I'll take you up to Lowry's Pass, and we'll drink wine and watch the sunset. There's no place more romantic. I'll hold you until the last flicker of light disappears behind the hills.'

'Oh, Jack. If only . . .' She felt her throat constrict.

'Promise me you'll come.'

'I can't.'

'Then just pretend. I want to hear you say it.'

She stared into his pleading eyes. 'All right. I'll come. I promise.'

The tension in his face melted. 'Then I'll wait for you there.'

He cupped her face and kissed her for the final time, then watched her open the door and step into the street. She took a moment to compose herself, standing beneath the street-lamp, smoothing down her coat. He would have walked her to her door, but it was too risky. Instead, he watched her walk quickly up the pavement, arms folded, shoulders hunched against the cold, her figure growing smaller as she was swallowed into the darkness. At last, she arrived at her house. She turned and stood there a moment, staring back at him. Then she gave a small, cautious wave. Reluctantly, he told the driver to take him back to the hotel.

Angelica watched until the taxi was out of sight. She remained on her doorstep for a few minutes, wiping her face and scrunching her hair between her fingers. Then she took a deep breath and unlocked the door. Stepping into the light of her home, she should have felt guilty, but she just felt sad. The dream dissolved in the glare of reality, and once more she was reminded of where she belonged.

She took off her coat and kicked off her stilettos, then padded up the stairs in her stockinged feet. Olivier was lying in bed watching television. It was midnight: he had waited up. He glanced at her and registered at once her stricken face. 'Are you all right, Angelica?' He sat up in alarm.

'I'm fine. Just desperately tired.'

'You look like you've been crying.'

She forced a laugh. 'Crying with laughter probably, at all those terrible karaoke singers!'

She walked into the bathroom and closed the door behind her. She undressed, watching her reflection with grim satisfaction, as if it didn't belong to her but to a deceitful, conniving stranger. She didn't care that Olivier would think it odd that she showered in the middle of the night: she felt compelled to soap away her guilt. It hurt to think of Jack flying off the following day, but she knew it was for the best. She had played with fire and nearly burned her whole family. Standing under the water, her hair squashed into a shower cap, she closed her eyes and emptied her mind. The burden of so much emotion was too much to carry. She listened to the water fall about her like rain and felt the comforting warmth wash over her skin.

Olivier slept pressed up against her, his arm resting protectively over her stomach. She could feel his breath on her shoulder and was reminded of those early days when she had treasured each second of their closeness. Now she wished he were Jack. She sank into her imagination, visualizing riding across the South African veld with him beside her, grinning in that raffish way of his that made her heart swell with happiness. Eventually, she slipped into sleep – a seamless transition into Jack's world, where it was just the two of them.

In the morning Olivier was gone. He hadn't woken her up by turning on the light as was his usual habit, but had crept into the bathroom and dressed quietly. The children alerted her to the time by climbing into her bed and turning on the television. She opened one eye to see the clock on her bedside table. It was a quarter to eight. She sat up in panic, switched off the television, and sent the children downstairs to Sunny. Then she dragged herself into her closet, pulled on a pair of jeans and sweater, and sat over a cup of coffee while the children wolfed down their breakfast as fast as their small teeth would allow.

She was late getting them to school. The front door was closed, and she was forced to ring the bell and apologize for her tardiness. It was clear from her pale face and bloodshot eyes that she had overslept. She kissed them hastily and watched them run down the corridor, hoping that she had remembered Joe's games kit and Isabel's ballet bag. No sooner had she set off back up the road than her mobile rang. Her heart stalled when she saw that it wasn't Jack but Candace.

'Good morning,' her friend said chirpily.

'Hi, Candace.'

'You sound flat.'

'Hangover,' she lied. 'I could barely get up this morning.'

'I didn't see you leave. What time did you go?'

'About eleven-thirty. I didn't want to break up the party.'

'It got rather debauched, actually. We got an ass shot from Art.'

'What, he mooned?'

'I kid you not. Totally hilarious. He pulled down his trousers and flashed his backside.'

'Why?'

'He sang the finale, totally pissed. There were only a few of us left. But you know what?'

'What?'

'He has a birthmark on his butt cheek that looks like a strawberry.'

'Really?'

'Huge, you can't miss it. He said his father has one, too, in exactly the same place. How weird is that?'

'Weird.' She tried to lift her voice, but she felt leaden.

'You sound like you should go back to bed.'

'I think I might.'

'Don't even bother trying to write today. You know what you need?'

'Tell me.'

'Lunch with the girls. Kate's already called, suffering from anti-climax. Alessandro was up being sick in the night, so poor Letizia barely got a wink. Scarlet has declared that she is spending all day in bed, but the rest of us could do with a Bellini and a gossip.'

'And an early night.'

'You're sounding like me.'

Angelica walked slowly up the road, eyes on the pavement, hands in pockets. There was a cold wind, and heavy clouds threatened rain. She wondered what Jack was doing, whether he was at the airport. Perhaps he was already in the air. Their snatched moments the night before had only made things worse. Instead of fizzing with excitement, she felt flat and abandoned. Life without Jack lay ahead, bleak and long, like the dead of winter. Before she had known him she had been content with her lot. Now she found it lacking; she had tasted the forbidden fruit and found her regular diet bland by comparison.

She reached the house and put her key in the lock. Sunny stood in the hallway all wound up like a clockwork doll. 'Is everything all right?' Angelica asked, bewildered. The air smelled of summer.

'A man came round,' Sunny explained.

'What man?'

'A man with a van.' She pointed into the dining room. 'He brought these.' Angelica peered into the room and her jaw dropped in amazement. The entire room was filled with red roses. She could barely discern where the table was for the vases of flowers. 'Was there a note?'

Sunny shook her head. 'Nothing. He just brought them in and left.'

She felt her telephone vibrate in her handbag. 'It's okay, Sunny. I think I know who they're from.'

I will never forget last night. Your loving Dog. I'm afraid
the porch is no longer in my vision.

Angelica blushed. 'Oh, Sunny. What am I to do with all these flowers?'

'We'll place them through the house.'

What will Olivier think? 'I'll take three with me to lunch. Put the rest wherever there's a space. My godfather is full of surprises.' *Why would my godfather give me flowers? And so many? Think!* Sunny began to take vases of blooms upstairs while Angelica called Jack.

The sound of his voice renewed the intimacy between them, and she was transported back to the night before. She could hear the metallic noise of the airport in the background; he was already on his way.

'You're very naughty, filling my house with roses,' she said tenderly.

'I'm glad you got them.'

'The dining room is filled with them!'

'I won't get you into trouble, I hope.'

'He won't even notice. He's rather distracted by work at the moment. How did you get them to me so fast?'

'I bribed a friend to go to the flower market and buy as many as he could carry in his van.'

'That's very resourceful.'

'He owed me one.'

'Must have been something big to get up that early in the morning.'

'It was.' He paused. 'I wanted to show you how much you mean to me.'

'I'm convinced.' Love was like a game of snakes and ladders: one moment you're sliding down a snake, only to find a ladder to carry you back up to great heights.

'I'll never forget our night in the taxi.'

'It wasn't what I had in mind.'

'Nor me. I was going to be good.'

'I'm glad you weren't.'

'So am I. I'll take that memory back home with me, so on lonely nights I can replay it over and over and remember the beautiful English girl I've left in London.'

'I wish you didn't have to go.'

'I wish you could come with me.'

'Impossible.'

'I know. Fools' dreams. You get writing your book now.'

'I don't know what to write about.'

'Of course you do. Write about us.'

'I don't write adult fiction.'

'Now is the perfect time to start. You said you wanted to do something different.'

'I don't like unhappy endings.'

'Then give us a happy ending.'

'I don't know how to do that.'

'You work it out. You're the novelist.'

'Things don't always work out in fiction. Look at all the great love stories, *Gone with the Wind, Anna Karenina, Romeo and Juliet* – they don't end happily.' There was a long pause. For a moment she thought she had lost the signal. 'Are you still there?'

'Still here,' he said at last, but his voice had changed. He sounded as miserable as she had felt that morning. 'Give us a happy ending, Angelica. I don't know how you can do it, but do it for me. I'm afraid, in reality, there *is* no happy ending for us.'

She felt a lump at the back of her throat. 'As long as we're friends, I think I can live with that.'

'I'll email you. You let me know when I can call you.'

'Mornings,' she replied hastily. 'After I've dropped the children at school. I'll be at my desk, trying to think of a happy ending.'

When she hung up, she retreated to her bedroom and closed the door behind her. With a groan she flopped onto the bed and cried into the pillow. She knew it was ridiculous to cry over a man she barely knew, but it was as if his departure had sucked the air out of the city. There was nothing left to breathe.

Chapter 14

'It is only with darkness that one can appreciate light'
In Search of the Perfect Happiness

Angelica drove to the West End with three vases of roses in the back of her car. She parked in Albemarle Street and made her way down to the Wolseley, situated in the magnificent old motorcar showroom on Piccadilly. With its high ceilings, chiselled arches, and elegant stairway, the restaurant echoed the grandeur of Renaissance Italy.

It was already buzzing with London's most fashionable. Their chatter echoed off the pretty yellow walls and black-and-white chequerboard floor. Angelica looked around for the girls, recognizing a few friends in the sea of faces. Jason at the front desk put down the telephone and greeted her by name, but Angelica had already spotted Candace waving her bejewelled fingers from a round table in the centre of the room.

'There you are!' she said as Angelica joined them.

'You look like I feel,' said Kate, taking in her drawn features and shadowy eyes.

'You'd better feel fabulous, or I'm walking straight out of here,' Angelica joked.

'Let's face it, we all feel pretty rough,' Candace conceded.

'But don't *ever* say I look it!' Kate drained her Bellini. 'Hair of the dog.' She raised her empty glass to the waiter. 'Another one for me and one for my friend.'

'That baby's going to be break-dancing by dessert!' said Candace.

'It's mostly peach juice,' Kate defended herself. 'Besides, I read somewhere that champagne is actually really good for a baby.'

'Like, what, a Jordan interview in *Hello!* magazine?'

'No, something far more highbrow, like *Vogue.*'

Letizia applauded her. 'It's amazing what little gems one picks up in that magazine. Most of them mine, of course. Not *that* one, I hasten to add!'

'Oh, give me a break,' said Candace, rolling her eyes. 'If champagne is good for your baby I'll eat my Birkin.'

'The lizard one that's particularly chewy?' asked Kate.

'I'd even go as far as to suggest the croc – not only outrageously expensive, but totally indigestible.'

'Imagine that coming out during a colonic?' Kate suggested.

'I'm sure they've seen a lot worse,' said Angelica.

'Like the salami you ate at your twenty-first birthday party,' Letizia cut in.

'Oh, please. I'm looking at the menu!' exclaimed Candace, fanning her face.

'Darling, last night was amazing,' said Letizia. 'I never thought I'd get into karaoke, but actually, I got quite competitive.'

'You were the dark horse, Letizia. Your rendition of "Stand by Your Man" with that husky Italian accent made me want to cry,' said Kate.

'Tears of pain?' interjected Candace.

'No, I thought, *That's me.* I could have kicked Pete out, but I chose to win him back. I stood by him. I *am* that song.'

'And you deserve a medal after that emotional battle!' Candace smirked cynically.

'I think we all deserve medals,' said Angelica. 'As much as I love my husband, he can be very demanding.'

'There's no one more demanding than Olivier,' Candace agreed.

'But he's so handsome,' Kate gushed. 'I wouldn't mind waking up to him every morning.'

'Be my guest.' Angelica laughed. Candace raised a thoughtful eyebrow.

'There's more to a man than his looks,' said Letizia. 'At our age, we get the faces we deserve.'

'Which is why I still retain my beauty,' said Kate with a giggle. 'I'm a thoroughly splendid human being.'

'And you have a splendid face, darling,' Letizia agreed.

'When it moves,' Candace hissed under her breath for only Angelica to hear.

'What are you going to do for Olivier's birthday?' Kate asked. 'It's next week, isn't it?'

Of course, she was absolutely right. 'How on earth do you know when his birthday is?'

'I have a funny memory when it comes to the names of people's children and birthdays. I never forget.'

'So when's mine?' Candace asked, quick as a flash.

'I'm not at my best after a glass of champagne, but if I remember rightly, you're a Virgo.'

Candace was surprised. 'You're spot-on, but that's not difficult: I'm a typical Virgo.'

'Letizia's June twenty-eighth – home-loving Cancer; Angelica's March sixth – typical, idealistic Pisces; Scarlet's August twenty-first – very Leo; and you, Candace, are somewhere in late September.'

'The twentieth, actually. I'm more than impressed, I'm astonished you remember anything about anyone else!' said Candace.

'I have a few gifts.'

'Well, I'd completely forgotten Olivier's birthday,' said Angelica. 'I don't even have a gift.'

'Book a table at the Ivy and say it's been booked for ages,' Letizia suggested. 'A surprise. We can all emerge from under the table, if it would help.'

'Oh, I think he'll be too stressed out to even remember. If it wasn't for his adoring mother, who will ring at dawn, it would be just another day.'

'For Pete's, which is at the beginning of December, I'm going to whisk him off to Rome for the weekend. He loves opera.'

'Which bores you to tears,' said Candace.

'That's not the point. It's *his* birthday.'

'That's surprisingly selfless of you, Kate.'

'I can be generous.' She grinned wickedly. 'After all, he's being very generous to me.'

'So? Out with it? What did he get you?'

The waiter brought the Bellinis. Kate took a sip, enjoying making them wait. 'He's giving me a lot of his *time,*' she said with emphasis.

'Not his wallet?' Letizia asked.

'Oh, anyone can buy a girl presents, but not all men are good lovers.'

'Now you've got me,' said Candace, leaning forward. 'Go on.'

'Twice he's woken me up in the middle of night. *Down there!*' The girls looked from one to the other in astonishment.

'You're kidding!'

'Wouldn't you rather sleep?' asked Letizia, who needed at least eight hours a night.

'I don't really wake up. I just ride a beautiful wave without ever opening my eyes.' She looked dreamy – and more than a little tipsy.

'So what's in it for him?' Candace demanded.

'The pleasure of giving,' said Kate sanctimoniously.

'I think *he* deserves the medal!'

In the wake of that revelation, they all buried their faces in the menus and ordered. Angelica felt flat in spite of being with her best friends in the glamour of the Wolseley, having left the dining room back at home filled with flowers. While Jack's visit to London had been in the future, she'd had something to look forward to; while he'd been in the city there had been the possibility of meeting him. Now that he had left the country, all chance and anticipation were gone. Nothing in the future except an enticing mirage made up of their impossible desires.

'Angelica, you're very quiet,' said Letizia, smiling at her sympathetically.

'Hard to get a word in when Kate's on form,' said Candace.

'I'm feeling a little down, actually,' Kate retorted. 'Though one would never know, of course. Have another Bellini, Angelica. I'm suffering a terrible anti-climax after my party, too.'

'Art's party,' Candace corrected.

'Whatever,' said Kate. 'All that preparation, one blissful night, and blink – it's gone.'

'I'm just tired, but I can't complain. It was a tremendously good party.' Angelica smiled weakly. She felt as if the slightest comment would make her cry. 'I have three big vases of roses for you all,' Angelica continued in order to change the subject. 'My godfather filled the dining room with them.'

'Nice godfather,' said Letizia.

Candace was unconvinced. 'What's your godfather doing sending you flowers?'

'He's a bit eccentric. He hasn't remembered my birthday in ten years. The flowers, he said, were to make up for it.'

'Well, I'll happily take them home. Might tell Pete they're from a secret admirer,' said Kate.

'Isn't that a bit close to the bone?' said Candace, but she was looking at Angelica.

'Oh, that's all in the past, and besides, he's not an admirer. Never was and never will be.'

'Well, that narrows the field.'

'It was a silly mistake, and I'd really appreciate it, Candace, if you'd drop the subject now that I'm preparing to renew my vows with Pete. I have my first meeting with Vera Wang next week, and Christian Louboutin is going to make me a pair of shoes especially.'

'Do you need shoes on a beach?' Candace asked.

'All girls need shoes, wherever they are,' Kate replied tartly.

'Sandals, then,' said Angelica, trying to get into the spirit of things.

'Flats? God, no!' Kate exclaimed. 'I won't have Candace towering over me on my wedding day.'

'Imagine having everyone towering over you all year round,' said Angelica, taking a gulp of her Bellini and feeling a little better.

'Good things come in small packages,' Letizia reassured her kindly. 'I don't even think Gaitano knows my real height. Mind you, I'm not that familiar with it, either. My heels are almost stuck onto my feet.'

'Well, I like to tower over everyone, especially you, Candace. That way I always feel at a slight advantage,' said Kate with a grin.

'It's not Candace's height you need to worry about, darling,' said Letizia. 'It's her tongue.'

'Someone has to keep all your pretty little feet on the ground,' Candace replied. 'Roses, eh, Angelica? Nice godfather.' She gave Angelica a knowing look, and Angelica knew she had been discovered.

After lunch Angelica led the girls back to her car and handed them each a large bunch of roses.

'*Madonna!* These are amazing!' Letizia exclaimed, burying her face in the petals.

'The whole house smells of them,' said Angelica. 'I'll keep one for Scarlet.'

'What's Olivier going to say?' Candace asked gently.

'He won't even notice now I've given some of them to you.' But Angelica couldn't look at Candace. Her friend was far too clever not to work out what had really gone on. Candace took her roses, kissed Angelica goodbye, and hailed a taxi with Letizia and Kate, whose long bare legs shivered in the cold. Angelica watched them go, consumed with guilt.

She didn't see Candace at the school gates. The four-by-fours double-parked and jostled for the few free parking places, packed high with luggage for the weekend in the country. Isabel and Joe ran out excitedly, throwing her their book bags and backpacks, waving goodbye to their friends. Jenna Elrich swept up the pavement in a fur-lined cape and cap, her hair falling down her expensive back in a glossy ponytail. 'I'm so stressed out,' she complained to Angelica. 'I've got to go to Paris this evening for a concert in honour of the Sarkozys tomorrow night, and the dress I wanted to wear is lost somewhere over the Channel.'

'How do you mean, lost?'

'I sent the luggage ahead, but it hasn't arrived.'

'Where did you send it?'

'To the Georges Cinq, of course. Lord knows what I'm going to wear.'

Angelica didn't have the patience for this ludicrous woman. 'Oh, I'm sure you can find some old frock in those cupboards of yours.'

'That's just it. They're all so last season!'

'Oh, God forbid!'

'Exactly. Carla will be in Chanel couture, for sure. I'm going to have to leave the kids with my mother and go shopping.'

'What hell!'

'I hate shopping.'

'You disguise it well.'

'Just because I always look elegant doesn't mean I enjoy the process. In fact, I positively loathe running around department stores. I've called Selfridges Personal Shopping. They should be able to find me something, don't you think?'

'Have a glass of champagne and let them do all the running?'

'Quite.'

Angelica edged away. 'I hope you find something to wear and enjoy the concert. Sounds very glamourous.'

'No, it's a bore. I so hate travelling.'

'The train is rather convenient, I think.'

'Train! Dear God, no. NetJet, but even so . . .'

'A plane's a plane,' said Angelica, fully aware that a NetJet plane *wasn't* simply a plane but a luxurious penthouse with wings.

'Better hurry. Have a good weekend.' She rushed off in her five-inch-heeled boots, leaving a whiff of Dior in her wake.

Angelica called her children. 'We're going to have a great weekend,' she said, taking Joe's hand.

'What are we going to do?'

'Nothing,' she said with a smile. 'Absolutely nothing.'

As Angelica had predicted, Olivier didn't question the flowers. He was used to her filling the house with white roses and assumed that she had gone a little over the top with red ones for a change. The City was a sterile place to work; it was heartening to come home to warmth, colour, and music. He usually hated her scented candles and blew them out the minute he walked into the room, but now he viewed them with a fondness that surprised them both. The financial crisis was changing the world so fast he found himself clinging to the one place that didn't change at all: his home – complete with flowers, scented candles, and Dolly Parton.

That night, while Olivier sat in the study watching the news and chatting to friends on the telephone, Angelica reflected on her marriage. Olivier loved her. Naturally, after so many years of marriage, they took each other for granted, but she didn't doubt that he loved her. Jack didn't love her in the same way. His love was fuelled by lust and the allure of the forbidden. She loved Olivier in that deep, familiar way that is no longer aware of itself. Her feelings for Jack fed off the way he made her feel as a woman. She was two people. The woman Olivier knew and the woman Jack knew. Were they to meet, neither would recognize the other.

PART TWO

Experience

Chapter 15

'Darkness serves the light; it is our greatest teacher'
In Search of the Perfect Happiness

It snowed over half term. A thick layer of sparkling white sugar covered the countryside like icing on a Christmas cake. Angelica took Joe and Isabel to stay with Candace in Gloucestershire for a couple of days while Olivier remained in London trying to keep his head above water as the City sank with the share prices. The children built snowmen and swam in the indoor pool while Angelica and Candace curled up by the log fire, drank tea, and gossiped. Candace didn't mention the roses, nor did she refer to Jack, although the handsome South African stood between them like a neon elephant in the room. Angelica knew she had been discovered – Candace had the instincts of a panther – but she didn't want to hear advice; she knew what it would be and would ignore it. She read her texts in the privacy of her bedroom and spoke to him late at night after everyone had gone to bed, sharing the minutiae of their day, their thoughts, and their dreams, but mostly they whispered the sweet nothings of lovers. The deeper Angelica became embroiled in her secret, the further she drifted from her friend, for honest intimacy was the glue that bonded them.

She spent Halloween with Scarlet and Ben Cannings, her manny, the exuberant lad from Yorkshire whom Scarlet had employed to teach her children football. Tall and handsome, with a thick mop of dark hair and soft brown eyes, he was mature for his age and chivalrous in the tradition of well-educated northern men. He whisked the children into Battersea Park and entertained them while Scarlet and Angelica went to Hamleys to buy them costumes for the trick-or-treating street party they were to join after dark. Isabel wanted to go as an owl, which was the only costume Hamleys didn't have, while Joe was content to dress up as one of the skeletons displayed in every shop window in town. Scarlet's children wanted to go as Harry Potter and Hermione Granger and kill all the witches.

As they left the toy shop laden with shiny red bags they bumped into Jenna Elrich climbing out of her chauffeur-driven car in a flurry of leather and fur. 'Great minds think alike,' she said, mobile telephone clamped to her ear. 'Zeus now wants to go as a bat, and Cassandra has demanded another princess dress. Pink is the only colour she'll wear. Thank God the twins are too small to demand anything except chocolate! I hope you haven't bought the last bat!'

'They're all yours,' said Scarlet, looking her up and down disdainfully.

'I'm taking them to the Louis Vuitton party. Are you going?'

'Trick or treating for us,' said Angelica.

'Oh, I hate all that ringing bells and running around. One bumps into so many dubious people coming into Chelsea to check out the big houses. I'd be very careful if I were you . . . Hello!' she barked into the telephone. 'Yes, it's Mrs Elrich. Am I speaking to the manager? Must go,' she mouthed at the girls and flounced off into the shop, leaving her chauffeur in the cold, standing to attention beside the shiny blue Range Rover.

'Well, *she* won't have to dress up. She already looks like a witch with those poor animal tails hanging off her cape,' said Angelica, linking her arm through Scarlet's.

'The perfect target for Charlie and Jessica! Perhaps we'd better pop into Louis Vuitton for some target practice before we hit the streets. Let's go and find your owl.'

'But where?'

'The Disney Store.' She waved at an approaching cab. 'If we don't get lucky there, you can always buy her a pretty brown cape from Marie Chantal.'

At the beginning of November Barack Obama became the first black president of the United States, and Kate hired a healer to cleanse her house of all the negative energy emitted during the acrimonious years of her marriage. Candace rolled her eyes at Kate's latest fad and ordered another Birkin for Christmas. Having worked for seven years before her marriage in the Ralph Lauren press office in New York, she was well plugged into all the stores and was immediately placed at the very top of the waiting list. Scarlet bribed Ben to move in over Christmas as her children's official coach and tutor, in spite of Letizia's pleas to loan him to her for her skiing holiday over New Year's. And just when Angelica was resigned to never seeing Jack again, her agent made an unexpected proposal over lunch at Sotheby's Café on Bond Street.

Claudia ordered champagne and raised her glass to Angelica. 'This is to you,' she said, her eyes twinkling with excitement. 'And to the successful optioning of *The Caves of Cold Konard*.'

Angelica was stunned. 'You're not serious?'

'Totally serious.'

'Who?'

'The Cohen-Rosh brothers — Stephen and Marcus.

They're the hot new producers in Hollywood. Very now, very happening, *very* cool.' She liked to emphasize the important words in a breathy whisper. 'Toby will be calling you to discuss the details. I think he wants to tell you himself, so act ignorant. We have *not* had this conversation.'

'Fine by me.' Angelica's head swam, already visualizing the red carpet at the Oscars and panicking about what to wear.

'On another note, I know you won't go to Australia, but what about South Africa? They really want you, and the book is doing so well out there. It'll give *The Silk Serpent* such a boost.' Angelica blanched, which Claudia mistook for refusal. 'Before you say no, it would be a week, not a minute more – a few days in Jo'burg and a few in Cape Town. Back-to-back interviews, radio, and a few talks to literary groups. They love you out there. They're a big market for you. Think about it.'

'I'll go,' Angelica replied steadily.

Claudia nearly choked on her champagne. She dabbed her mouth, leaving red lipstick on the napkin. 'You what?'

'I'll go.'

'Right, okay, great.'

'I didn't want to go to Australia because it's too far. I can't be two days away from my children. But South Africa is nearer and the same time zone, almost.'

'You'll love it. The South Africans are so friendly and warm. They'll put you up in the nicest hotels and treat you like a queen.'

'I'd like a couple of days at the end to visit a friend.' She could barely control the tremour in her voice.

'Sure.' Claudia was surprised. 'I mean, if that's not too long for you to be away. We can arrange anything you want.'

'Research.'

'For the next book?'

'Yes. I'm feeling inspired.'

'Good.'

'I'm going to do something different, Claudia.'

'Not too different, I hope. Your readers will expect more of the same, and you don't want to disappoint them.'

'I'm writing this one for me.'

'Okay.' Claudia looked a little anxious, but she couldn't complain: she'd got Angelica to agree to South Africa. 'Can't wait to read it.'

After lunch, Angelica kissed her agent goodbye and walked down Bond Street towards Piccadilly. Her legs felt unsteady, as if she were walking on jelly, and her head spun. She had agreed to go on a book tour to South Africa. What would Olivier say? How would she manage to tell him without giving herself away? She wasn't a very good actress. This was going to be the lie of her life. Anticipation rising with each step, she found a bench in Green Park and sat down.

The gardens were littered with crispy brown leaves, the sky was a dull pigeon-gray, but she felt as happy as if her heart were flooded with sunshine. She pulled out her telephone and pressed Jack's number. It rang a few times before he answered.

'Hello there, you.' His voice was full of affection.

'I'm coming to South Africa.'

'My God, when?' His excitement rippled down the line, and she smiled into the telephone.

'Next year.'

'I have to wait that long?'

'Only a few months.'

'How have you managed to pull that off?'

'Book tour. My agent just told me. I'm going to promote the new book.'

'So what are we looking at? February?'

'Maybe.'

'February is beautiful. You must come and stay.'

'I'd love to.' She thought of his wife and her exuberance deflated.

'Come for a long weekend.'

'I've requested a couple of days at the end of the trip.'

'A couple of days? That's too short. Come for a long weekend. Four days.'

'I don't know . . . What will your wife think?'

'It doesn't matter. I want to spend time with you. Where will you be before?'

'Jo'burg and Cape Town.'

'I'll come and see you.'

'I'd love that.'

'I couldn't bear to think of you in the same country as me without being able to see you. I'll pick you up at the airport.'

'I'm going to have to work.' She laughed at his enthusiasm.

'All work and no play . . .'

'I'll make time to play.'

'I can think of a few games.'

'Will you be allowed off the porch?'

'I'm already off the porch, darling. I was off the porch the moment I laid eyes on you at Scarlet's.'

'Then we'll meet in Johannesburg.'

'I can't believe it.'

'Neither can I. I haven't told Olivier yet.'

'He won't ban you from a book tour, surely?'

'I hope not. But I'll have to convince him that it's really necessary.'

'Darling, it is more necessary than you know.'

'Not sure he'll agree with you.'

'When are you going to tell him?'

'Tonight.'

'Let me know what he says.'

'I'll text you.'

'I love your texts.' He paused, then lowered his voice to barely a whisper. 'I think I'm falling out of love with you, Sage.'

She remembered their conversation by the Serpentine: that you truly start to love someone only when you fall *out* of love with them. 'You don't know me well enough to fall out of love with me,' she replied softly.

'I feel I've known you forever.'

'But you haven't, Jack.'

'True, and we don't have forever. But I'm living for now. And at this very moment, you're here with me, and that's more than I could wish for.'

She put the mobile in her handbag and smiled to herself, the warmth of their conversation wrapping her in a pair of invisible arms. An old tramp in a ragged black coat was sitting on the next bench. He stared at her, his arms folded against the cold, a bottle of something toxic in a brown paper bag beside him. At his feet a skinny greyhound shivered in a dirty little coat of its own. Her heart buckled with compassion. Aware of her own good fortune and fuelled by happiness, she delved into her handbag for a five-pound note. When she gave it to him, he blinked at her in surprise. 'You're a pretty lady,' he said, shoving the money into his pocket.

'Thank you,' she replied.

'I'd like to fuck you.' He grinned at her toothlessly, and Angelica's stomach churned in disgust. She hurried away, wishing she hadn't parted with that five-pound note. *No good deed goes unpunished,* she thought as she hailed a taxi outside the Ritz Hotel.

That night she went to see the new James Bond film in Leicester Square with Olivier, Joel, and Chantal. At dinner afterwards at the Ivy, Angelica decided to tell Olivier about her book tour in front of his friends. That way he'd be less likely to refuse her.

'Darling,' she said after he had eaten a healthy portion of lobster and drunk almost a whole glass of Sancerre, 'my publisher wants me to go to South Africa on a book tour in February.'

'That sounds fabulous,' Chantal enthused.

'It's not all that fabulous. Book tours are really hard work,' Angelica replied, watching Olivier nervously. She took a sip of wine and hoped he couldn't see her heart jumping through her sweater.

'I didn't think you wanted to go on book tours.' Olivier's face clouded.

'Well, I have to go sometime, and I've said no to Australia.'

'I agree: that's too far for a mother to travel,' said Chantal. 'But South Africa is so pretty.'

'Pretty and dangerous,' interjected Joel.

'Oh, I'll be perfectly safe.'

'I had a friend who was nearly murdered in Johannesburg.'

Chantal rolled her eyes. '*Mon cher,* everyone has a friend who was nearly murdered in Johannesburg. Being held up with a gun is as common as being accosted by those *Big Issue* people over here. They are on every street corner. But don't worry, Angelica, I'm sure you will be well looked after.'

'I don't like the sound of it,' said Olivier, having considered it. 'Who's going to look after the children?'

'I'll get someone. Chrissie, for example, or Denise – the children trust them.' She hoped those nannies who had worked for her in the past would be available.

'Do you want to go?' Olivier asked.

'I'd like to. It'll be good for my career, although I'll miss the children dreadfully.'

'And your husband,' Chantal reminded her. 'Husbands need their wives more than children. Especially French husbands.' She gave Joel a playful nudge.

Joel laughed. 'I don't like to let Chantal out of my sight.

But what can I do?' He shrugged. 'I'd do anything to avoid her sulking.'

'I don't sulk!'

He let his jaw drop. 'Chantal, you were *born* sulking! If you didn't get your seasonal shopping trip to New York, your face would be in a permanent scowl that no Botox or collagen could cure.'

'You're so silly!' She laughed. 'Well, Olivier. This is a dilemma. What are you going to do? A girl needs a bit of freedom from time to time. It's good for the marriage.'

He thought about it a moment. 'I agree. It is good to be apart every now and then. How long will you be gone?'

'I don't know. Just over a week.'

He pulled a face. 'More than a week?'

'It's a one-off,' said Angelica hopefully. Joel refilled Olivier's glass.

'I don't think you've ever been away for so long.'

'Which is why she deserves to go. You men are always travelling,' said Chantal. 'We, on the other hand, stay at home, look after the children – '

'And spend our money,' interrupted Joel.

'There has to be some compensation, surely!' Chantal protested. 'I gave up a good job to be a mother. Angelica has a good job as well as being a good wife and mother. For that she deserves a break.'

'It's not fun, I promise you. But apparently these tours really boost sales, and my next book is out in February.'

'It's not the money I care about,' said Olivier, whose pride prohibited him from admitting that he might be struggling financially. 'As long as the children are taken care of. You can't expect me to come home early to help with their homework. And as long as you are safe. I want you back in one piece, Angelica.' He took her hand. She noticed how tired he looked around the eyes.

'It'll be fine. I'm hardly going to be roaming the streets at night, or lurking in dangerous places.'

'Perhaps you should go with her!' said Joel.

Angelica was horrified. 'And leave the children without either parent?' she exclaimed. 'In which case I'd rather not go. Forget it, Olivier. It doesn't matter. Besides, I haven't said I'll go.'

It was a gamble, and she held her breath. He took a gulp of wine. The waiter came with their main courses and placed them on the table. Olivier's mood lifted at the sight of his steak.

'Go,' he said, picking up his knife and fork. 'I'll survive without you for a week or so. At least I won't have to contend with all your makeup littered around the bathroom.'

'No dimmed lights and scented candles, Leona Lewis and Neil Diamond.'

He raised his eyebrows. 'I might even surprise myself and miss them.'

Angelica knew she would have to tell Candace that she was going to South Africa. There was no point lying about it. Candace would find out one way or another. But instead of telling her immediately, as she normally would, she decided to wait until nearer the time. She confirmed the dates with her agent: February 7–15, just before half term, and agreed to stay at Jack's vineyard for the last three days.

At the beginning of December, the girls gathered at Scarlet's house for a Christmas lunch. Scarlet had decorated her home with a large fir tree in the hall, its branches heavy with gold tinsel and big glass balls that shone like glittering bubbles amid the fairy lights. On the top sat the silver star Charlie had made at school out of tin foil. The bannisters were interwoven with garlands of holly and berries, and mistletoe laced the door frames. Choirs singing carols resounded from invisible speakers, and a fire raged in the grate beneath a row of cards draped decoratively on ribbon. On the hall table a tray of tall purple flutes fizzed with the finest champagne.

Candace arrived bearing a big scented candle from Jo Malone, which Scarlet placed in the middle of the coffee table and lit. Letizia bought faux-diamond collars for the cats, while Kate had gone to SpaceNK and filled a bag with her favourite beauty products. Angelica bought *The Shopaholic's Guide to Buying Online* and some cookies from Ladurée.

'Well, dolls, isn't this a fine way to spend a rainy afternoon?' asked Scarlet, sinking into the sofa, a glass of champagne in hand. 'I love all the presents. Must make a point of throwing lunches more often!' Outside, the wind swept through the plane trees, whipping away the last remains of autumn.

'It's been an exhausting few months,' said Kate, who now looked like she'd swallowed a football. She patted her belly that strained against her little Ralph Lauren cashmere dress. 'Amelia wants me to call it Jordan. Phoebs says that if it's a boy, he can go back. She absolutely doesn't want a brother.'

'Just call the stork,' said Candace.

'If only one could put in an order and have it delivered like a pizza.' Kate laughed. 'I'm bored of being the oven!'

'What does Pete think?' Letizia asked, pulling Taz onto her knee to attach her new collar.

'Naturally he wants a Russian name.'

'Very romantic,' said Angelica, envisaging Lara from *Dr Zhivago*.

'Vladimir,' Candace suggested in her best Russian accent.

'Please, no,' said Kate. 'For this one I want a name that no one else has.'

'You'll have to make it up, then,' said Candace.

'Angelica, you're good at names. Your novels are full of weird words.'

'How do you know? You've never read one!' said Candace.

'I read the back-of-the-hovel one in Waterstone's,' Kate retorted.

'Caves, not hovels,' Letizia corrected.

'Whatever, I saw a whole lot of extraordinary names.'

'On your way to the magazine section,' added Candace.

'I have ADHD – I can't possibly get through a whole book. Anyway, the point is that Angelica is good at names. She has a wild and wonderful imagination.' She turned to Angelica. 'Will you think of a name for my baby?'

Angelica laughed. 'That's too much responsibility.'

'You don't want to get it wrong,' Candace warned, drawing a line across her neck with her fingernail.

'Don't be ridiculous,' said Kate. 'I only want suggestions.'

'Which you'll disregard,' said Candace.

'Just flick through *Grazia* for inspiration,' Scarlet interjected. 'I don't think there's a celebrity who hasn't chosen a mad name for her child.'

'Like Apple, Suri, and Bluebell.' Kate knew them all.

'If you want a name that no one else will give their child, try Jane or Mary,' said Candace. 'Trust me, she'll be the only one of her generation.'

Lunch was in the dining room. They gossiped about the people they had in common, dragging up the same old names to peck at like vultures. Scarlet thought Jenna Elrich's husband was having an affair with Caterina Tintello, having seen them together at Annabel's. Letizia was sure Hester Berridge had had a face-lift, although Scarlet disagreed, claiming that she'd never put that sort of money into anything other than her horses. However, they weren't the only group of women to gossip: London was visibly vibrating with rumour. 'I hear that you're going to South Africa,' Kate said to Angelica. Angelica was caught off guard.

'South Africa? When?' Letizia asked.

'Book tour,' Angelica replied casually, unable to look at Candace. 'The dates haven't been finalized yet.'

'I was in Michaeljohn yesterday, having my hair cut by the fabulous Enzo, and found myself sitting next to Chantal de Claire.'

'Karma,' said Candace. 'What goes around, comes around.'

'Sounds very glamourous,' said Scarlet. 'There's a fabulous spa near Cape Town – now, what's it called?'

'It's not at all glamourous. It's really hard work, giving talks and interviews. It's relentless. No fun at all. I'm literally spending a few days in Jo'burg and a few in Cape Town.'

'Wedgeview,' said Letizia. 'It's in Franschhoek. My mother went there last year and said it was fabulous. Maybe we should all go with you!'

'A fine idea,' said Scarlet. Then to Angelica: 'You can pop in and visit your old flame Jack Meyer.' Angelica felt her cheeks flush and took a big gulp of wine. 'They have the most beautiful vineyard called Rosenbosch.'

'I don't think I'll have time for that, sadly. Olivier will only let me go for a week, and it'll be packed with work.' She caught Candace's eye.

Candace put down her knife and fork and placed her hands in her lap. 'You know what, Angelica, if you want to go to that vineyard, you'll make time. No one ever turned down an opportunity like that because they didn't have the time.'

By that, Angelica knew she meant an affair. And as always, she was right.

Chapter 16

'Count your blessings and watch them multiply'
In Search of the Perfect Happiness

Angelica dreaded Candace's confronting her about Jack. But it was inevitable. Candace was not the sort of girl who swept things under the carpet and dissembled when she was furious or upset. Angelica knew she'd always tell her the truth, even though the truth hurt. The only consolation was that her friend had a big heart, and her advice was never for her own selfish ends. Candace was immune to jealousy, secure in her own skin and solid in her beliefs.

The moment came over coffee in Starbucks on Kensington High Street an hour before picking up the children for the Christmas holidays.

'Look, Angelica,' Candace began, stirring her cappuccino. 'I know you're still communicating with Jack. I've known it for months. I don't mind that you haven't told me. I shouldn't expect you to tell me everything.' Angelica made to speak, but Candace stopped her. 'No, let me finish. I also know that you're going to see him in South Africa. I have strong instincts, so don't deny it. And I know you saw him the night of Kate's party for Art, and I know you've been texting – and probably calling, for all I care. The point is, I'm your friend, and I'm concerned about you. I can't let you walk into something that has the potential to tear your family apart. I have to warn you because you don't seem capable of seeing the pitfalls yourself.'

'I know the pitfalls.'

'No, you don't. You *think* you know the pitfalls. If you really knew them, you'd make damn sure you avoided them at all costs. Right now, you're in love. You can't see beyond your desire, which is totally understandable. Desire clouds a person's judgment. But I beg you, cancel your trip and stop communicating with him. This is way more dangerous than you can imagine, in your state of mind.'

'Firstly, I'm not having an affair.'

'An affair is not simply sex, Angelica. You're having an affair of the mind, and that's almost worse. If it was just sex, I'd say, do it, finish it, and leave it alone. An affair of the mind is an addiction and therefore far harder to quit.'

'We're friends.'

'No, you're not. Friends want the best for each other. If he's pursuing you, then he's not your friend: he's only thinking of himself and his desires. If he really cared about you, he'd leave you to your husband and your children.'

Angelica began to bite her nail. 'I probably won't see him in South Africa.'

'Bullshit. You've already arranged to see him. Don't tell me that you haven't already told him you're going and that he hasn't already invited you to his farm. What on earth does his wife think? Will she be there? Have you asked? Will his children be there? What will Olivier say when he finds out? Which he will, because they *always* find out, one way or another. Are you the only one he's chasing? From what Scarlet says he has a girl in every town.'

'No, he doesn't,' Angelica replied quickly.

Candace raised an eyebrow. 'Oh dear, you have got it bad. Look, you have to ask yourself the questions: What does he want from you? Where's it going to go? Do you want to leave Olivier and the children and run off with him? Are you going to break up two families to be together? Is that what you want?'

'Of course not!'

'Then drop it, Angelica.'

They drank their coffee in silence while both digested what had been said. Finally, Candace drained her cup. 'Are you and Olivier having problems?'

'No.'

'Things are really bad in the City at the moment. Olivier is probably terrified of losing his job. He must be beyond stressed out.'

'He is very stressed and completely self-absorbed,' Angelica replied bitterly.

'So he's not listening to you. You're not listening to him. He's not giving you attention. Look, it happens. Romance gives way to domestic life. That's what marriage is. But you have to work at keeping the romance burning. Maybe you should both go away without the children. Be a man and woman together rather than a mother and father. Remember what attracted you to him in the first place. If your lives are running parallel but not touching, then you have to rebuild the tracks. Olivier's a really great guy, and he loves you. Isabel and Joe depend on you. Their entire world rests on you and Olivier. You break up, the foundations crack beneath them. The simple truth is that you can't have everything you want in life. Duty has to come first when you've brought two little people into the world. It's your responsibility to give them a solid base camp for life. Don't think it isn't.'

Angelica sighed heavily. 'I hear you.'

'You know, we live in a disposable culture. We run a hole in a sweater, we don't mend it like our mothers used to do, we trash it and buy a new one. We want something we can't afford, we buy it anyway, on credit, and pay later, because you know what? We think we deserve everything we want. We think our happiness is a right, like our right to live on this planet. We're the "me" generation, and it's all about how to make "me" happy. So we desire another woman's husband, we feel we have a right to him, because our happiness is paramount, and God forbid anyone stand in the way of that. There's no sense of duty or responsibility any more, and I know I'm sounding like my grandmother, but she lived a more moral life, where she made her vows before God and kept them, whether she was happy or not. It wasn't all about "me" – but about taking responsibility for one's choices and putting duty before personal gratification. I don't want to preach, but you're happy with Olivier. Sure, he's not an easy man, but he makes you laugh when he's on form, and you love him. Do you really feel you deserve another woman's husband? Do you really feel Olivier deserves to be a cuckold? Do you really feel your happiness is more valuable than Joe's and Isabel's, that you have a right to have an affair whatever the cost?' She sighed and took a sip of coffee while Angelica stared forlornly into her cup. 'Selfishness is all part of the sickness of our world. The crazy idea that we have a God-given right to be happy all the time and if we're not, something's not right – but hell, it's not our fault!'

'Wow, you should run for president!'

'I'm good at rhetoric.'

'You sure say it like it is.'

'I just don't want to be the person who says I told you so. By then it's too late and all the eggs in the basket are broken – and they're such fine eggs!'

'You won't be that person, I promise.' *You're the sage, not me,* Angelica thought bleakly. 'You should write a book.'

'Of course I should write a goddamn book, but I can't write like you. I don't have that gift, unfortunately. Besides, why share my wisdom with the rest of the world?' She shrugged on her cape and hooked her caramel Birkin over her arm. 'It's not ready for me yet!'

Candace gave Angelica a lift to school. The pavement heaved with leggy mothers with sheepskin jackets and Anya Hindmarch handbags, and pale-faced children in immaculate green coats and hats, waving goodbye to their friends and teachers. The street was blocked with shiny Mercedeses and BMW Jeeps, solemn-looking chauffeurs in navy suits idling beside their vehicles. Joe and Isabel bounded out like excited puppies and flung their arms around their mother.

Candace kissed Angelica affectionately. 'You have a good Christmas,' she said, giving her a sympathetic look.

'I'll be fine. Christmas with my ghastly parents. New Year's in Provence with Olivier's ghastly mother and sisters. No texts to get me through it all. No warm Caribbean sea to lose myself in. But I'll be fine. I'm made of strong British stock!'

'There you go,' said Candace, smiling. 'You hold on to that great sense of humour.'

'If I can't cry, I might as well laugh.'

'Call me if you need me.'

'I will.' She looked at her steadily. 'Thank you.'

'Don't mention it. What are friends for?'

Angelica had no intention of giving up Jack. As far as she was concerned, she hadn't done anything wrong. He made her laugh, and he made her feel attractive, and she didn't see anything wrong with that. So they were falling in love with each other, but they were wise enough to know when to stop, weren't they? And a little flirt with danger was not a crime; it made her happy.

She was relieved the holidays had arrived at last. She never wrote when her children were home, so she had the perfect excuse to abandon her desk. Claudia was in for a shock. She had barely started her new book and what she had written wasn't satisfactory. Meanwhile, sales of her paperback were good and she had received proof copies of *The Silk Serpent,* which had a fabulous shiny snake on the front with bright red eyes and a green forked tongue. She immediately sent one to Jack.

The children were very excited to be home. They played in the garden, climbing the magnolia tree and feeding the birds. She took them to Kew Gardens, where they walked along the celebrated treetop walk, holding hands to reassure Angelica, who was afraid of heights. They made daily trips to Kensington Gardens to give bread to the swans and scale the pirate ship in the Diana playground. Angelica took them for a walk around the Serpentine, remembering the morning she had spent there with Jack and allowing her heart to flood with nostalgia. It was now bitterly cold, and frost hardened the ground and froze the trees into bent and twisted shapes like crippled old men. The skies were grey, darkness came early, and crows cawed into the icy air as they pecked the grass for worms.

Angelica turned her thoughts to South Africa. She googled images of vineyards and dreamed about riding across the veld with Jack, the sun on their faces, the wind in their hair, their cares boxed up and left behind. They spoke often.

On Christmas Eve Angelica and Olivier drove up to Norfolk to spend a couple of days with Angelica's parents and sister. Angelica always dreaded going home but returned yearly out of duty and a misplaced sense of pity. She began to feel anxious the moment they left the city. Her stomach contracted into a tight ball, and she had to wind the seat down and lie flat to stop it from hurting. Isabel and Joe sat in the back quietly playing Nintendo while Olivier listened to Radio Four.

★

Angie and Denny Garner lived in a bleak grey house on the edge of an equally bleak estuary. They had bought the house in the 1960s when Denny, who would have preferred a big house in Gloucestershire, could only afford a big house in an unfashionable corner of Norfolk. Angie longed to be part of the glamourous set who danced the night away at the Café de Paris. But she settled for her husband's swinging parties at Fenton Hall, where she wore little dresses from Biba and faux-fur coats from Carnaby Street, hopping from lap to lap like a bunny, glass of cheap champagne in one hand, joint in the other. Her hair had been piled into a blonde beehive then, her lips pale, eyes heavy with kohl and fake lashes. She had once been chocolate-box pretty. Now her face was swollen with the excesses of alcohol and cannabis, her beehive badly dyed an unsavoury orange to match her skin. While his wife had expanded like a soufflé, Denny was as slim as he had been in his youth, though his long hair was now grey and tied into a thin ponytail. For Denny and Angie the world had stopped turning in about 1975. Angie staggered through their tasteless home in silk kaftans and bell bottoms, Denny in high-waisted tight trousers and big-collared flowery shirts from Deborah&Clare, always unbuttoned to expose his narrow chest and gold chains. They still held parties where cannabis cake put everyone in the mood for sex. There was nothing less redolent of the glory days than Angie and Denny's impoverished and meagre swinging scene, where the main subject of conversation was ill health and death.

Angelica was embarrassed by her parents. She'd rather die than introduce them to her friends in London, keeping them secret like a stain on the carpet hidden beneath a rug. As a teenager she had longed for them to be like other people's parents – sensibly dressed in Barbour jackets and green wellies, with sleek dogs misting the glass of their Volvo estates. Olivier, on the other hand, found them entertaining and couldn't understand why his wife was so appalled.

'You didn't grow up with them,' she explained. 'I'd hide in my room and play music really loudly so I didn't have to listen to them all downstairs. What was acceptable when they were teenagers became grotesque as they grew older. I didn't want to think of my mother having sex with other men. I just wanted them to be normal like everyone else.'

'No one's normal,' Olivier reassured her. 'People present as normal, but really everyone hides some sort of weirdness behind closed doors.'

'There's weird and weird – my parents' weirdness is a unique brand.'

'Which is why they're such fun. They're originals.'

'Thank God He broke the mould after He made them; otherwise, I'd be just the same. Mercifully, I was spared that life sentence.'

'At least they were loving parents.'

'I suppose. But all children need boundaries. We never had any. I longed for proper family meals at the table and regular bedtime. We just did what we wanted and saw too much. They thought it was natural for children to see their parents having sex.'

'It explains why you were so prim when I met you.'

'They almost put me off for life.'

Olivier grinned mischievously. 'I gave you a taste for it.'

'I needed an older, continental man with experience.' She took his hand and smiled back. 'Otherwise, I might have remained a virgin all my life.'

'You're too sexy for that. Someone would have snapped you up.' He glanced at her. 'You're looking very good these days, you know.'

'Thank you.'

'I'm glad I married you.'

'And I'm glad I married you.' She pushed thoughts of Jack and Candace to the back of her mind. 'We're lucky, you know. What we have is very special.'

'I might be a bad-tempered devil sometimes, but I do love you, Angelica. Things haven't been easy these past months, and I know I've been neglecting you. But I've never regretted marrying you.'

'I know. And together we have made the two sweetest children on the planet.'

She turned to find them fast asleep. She squeezed his hand, and he squeezed it back. In that fleeting moment she saw her life with clarity, as if she were above her body, looking down. Jack didn't belong there. But the moment didn't last. Soon they were motoring up the drive of Fenton Hall and the children were waking from their nap. Olivier slipped his hand away and replaced it on the wheel. Angelica wound up her seat and prepared for the worst.

The car pulled up on the gravel, setting off security lights that lit them up like actors on a stage. Denny appeared in the porch with a cigar between his lips, hands in the pockets of his jerkin. A flurry of fluffy dogs scurried out like big rats, sending the children into squeals of panic. Angelica coaxed them out of the car, bending down to stroke the dogs to prove that they weren't going to bite. Olivier waved at his father-in-law and went round to the boot to see to the bags. Angelica took Joe and Isabel by the hand and led them inside.

'Hi, Dad,' she said.

He put his arm around her and planted a smoky kiss on her cheek. 'You look smashing, darling. Go and see your mother – she's in the kitchen with Daisy.' Angelica took the children through the hall, where a grand piano stood in front of a sweeping staircase and pale green sofas clashed with the blue patterned carpet. She recalled the times she had sat at the top of those stairs watching the parties below. Her father at the piano, a girl on his knee, her mother in a miniskirt and platform boots singing Marianne Faithfull songs, the hall smoky enough to hide where people put their hands.

On the walls were large black-and-white photos of Angelica and her sister Daisy as children in white hippie dresses with buttercups in their hair, big Andy Warhol prints in psychedelic colours.

She heard her mother's voice before she reached the kitchen. 'Well, he's not going to be worth a great deal now, love. You should have squeezed him for as much as you could get out of him a year ago at least.' Angelica sighed and stepped into the room.

'Ah, Angelica.' Angie left the Aga and sailed across the room like a galleon to press the children to her spongy bosom. Both Isabel and Joe recoiled as they were smothered in red lipstick and Yves Saint Laurent's Opium. 'You've grown so big. Look at you! You're adorable. Both of you.'

Daisy was sitting at the kitchen table looking pale. 'My lot are upstairs in the attic, if yours want to join them. They're playing with Dad's trains.' Joe's eyes lit up, remembering the gigantic model railway from the year before.

'Come on, Isabel,' he hissed, taking her by the hand. Angelica watched them go, hoping they wouldn't bump into the dogs on their way through the hall. As there was no screaming, she deduced that her father and Olivier were still outside chatting.

'Hi, Daisy,' she said, kissing her sister. Daisy looked her over in surprise.

'You've lost weight,' she said.

'Have I?'

'Yes, you have, love.' Her mother appraised her admiringly, taking a drag of her cigarette. 'It suits you. After all, you have to be careful: you have my genes. Daisy's lucky she's skinny like her father.'

'So how are you, Daisy?' Angelica asked, pouring herself a glass of Chablis.

'Well, since I last saw you, which was, what? Oh, a year ago!' She laughed, trying to make light of it.

'I know, it's crazy, but life has been so busy.'

'Streatham isn't the other side of the world.'

'I know. We should make more of an effort to see each other.'

'Ted and I are now officially divorced, but he won't settle.'

'I told her, she's missed the boat now. I can't imagine he has much money to give you,' interjected Angie.

'He's been made redundant,' Daisy informed her.

'I'm sorry to hear that,' Angelica replied truthfully. She knew Daisy didn't get paid much as a piano teacher.

'Life's a bummer.'

Angelica took a gulp of wine and braced herself for her sister's defensiveness. Ever since she had married Olivier and made a better life for herself, Daisy had resented her. 'I know how hard it is, Daisy,' she said sympathetically.

Daisy sniffed. 'I don't think you have the slightest idea, Angelica.'

'I've made a delicious fish pie,' said their mother cheerfully, opening the Aga door to look at it. 'Denny loves fish pie. I've asked a few friends over for drinks tonight. Just locals. Jennifer and Alan Hancock, Marge and Tony Pilcher. I've always had a bit of a thing about Tony. He's a dreadful old roué!' She laughed throatily.

Angelica caught Daisy's eye and knew they were both thinking the same thing – remembering their parents' parties with horror.

'You look good,' said Daisy, defeated by the onslaught of memories that only Angelica shared. 'I love your blouse. Where's it from?'

'Oh, Harvey Nichols, I suspect,' she replied vaguely.

'I bet it was expensive. I mean, too expensive for me.' Daisy fiddled with the buttons on her Gap shirt.

'You can borrow it anytime, Daisy.'

'I don't know how that's possible, seeing as we never see each other.'

'I gather your books are doing very well, love.'

'They are. Actually, I'm going on a book tour in February.' Angelica brightened at the thought.

'Really, how wonderfully glamourous. Where are they sending you?'

'South Africa.'

'Goodness me! Denny and I went to Cape Town one year when you were little. We stayed in a charming little boutique hotel – it was a delight. I lay beside the pool all day while Denny showed off on the diving board. He had a very sexy pair of red swimming shorts in those days. I wonder whatever became of them.'

'Who's going to look after the children?' Daisy asked.

'I have Sunny, of course, but I'll need someone to come and supervise the children's homework. I'll find someone.'

'It's easy if you have money. I could never go away like that, being a single mother and having to do it all on my own.'

'I don't know how you do it, Daisy. You're brilliant: cooking, cleaning, looking after the children, and working as well. You're a domestic goddess as well as a talented musician. You're amazing, really.'

'It's what I do. I don't know any other way. You know, I couldn't have your life. I couldn't get up every morning and . . . do my hair.' She shrugged and gave another little sniff.

Angelica stared at her. Once she might have been quietly offended by such an aggressive comment. But now she just laughed. 'Well, of course. I mean, my books write themselves. I have all the time in the world to do my hair.'

Chapter 17

'Laughter is the greatest healer'

In Search of the Perfect Happiness

The following morning, Joe and Isabel ran into their parents' bedroom at dawn carrying stockings full of presents. Angelica had taken enormous pleasure filling a pair of Olivier's shooting stockings for each child, and the wool was stretched to capacity. Angelica wondered what Daisy had bought her three children and felt a wave of pity at the thought of them opening their meagre stockings on Angie and Denny's bed, without their father to enjoy it with them.

She remembered opening her own stocking with Daisy: her mother fighting a hangover with a bottle of pills, chain-smoking in bed in a silk nightie that barely contained her bosom, her naked father on the floor doing press-ups. There were always lots of dogs, and the room smelled of damp fur and Opium. Their presents had been generous. Her mother was extravagant. Denny wasn't rich, but he couldn't deny her anything, and he liked her to look good. And she did, in those days. Her nails were always manicured, her hair in an updo. Her clothes had been cheap, but somehow she had pulled it off. Not a lot had changed. Her father still did press-ups, her mother still wore Opium, the dogs still slept on their bed. Only now Angie's nails were false, her hair badly dyed, the fake tan too orange for her skin, and of course her once voluptuous figure had ballooned so that her clothes had to hang around her like drapes over an ugly table. Angelica didn't want to imagine the sight on the bed and thanked God it wasn't her own children having to witness the pill-popping and chain-smoking and her mother's breasts, sagging like old udders.

The night before had been a trial for Daisy and Angelica. Angie had appeared in a blue silk kaftan that fell over her bosom like a waterfall. Her turquoise eye shadow shimmered from her false black lashes to her overplucked eyebrows, and her lips were pale beige, clashing against the copper tones of her skin. Denny's trousers were tight, emphasizing the unseemly bulge that clearly excited his wife, for she grabbed it with a pudgy hand and gave a dirty laugh. 'Hey, handsome!' she breathed, pressing against him.

'I think I've pulled!' he said to Olivier, raising his eyebrows suggestively.

Olivier caught Angelica's eye and grinned. Angelica smiled back, grateful for his support. For the first time she realized what a unique man he was for not thinking less of her because of her appalling parents.

Jennifer and Alan Hancock arrived first, a mousy couple clearly in awe of their hosts and very nervous. Jennifer sat on the club fender, unable to take her eyes off Denny's crotch, and Alan agreed with everything Angie said, however ridiculous. When Marge and Tony Pilcher arrived, Angie was transformed into a coy little girl. Her voice went soft and babyish, she pouted and giggled, she even blushed through her tan. Denny stood with one foot on the club fender right in front of Jennifer so that she had a clear view of what he obviously believed were his most significant assets. He smoked a cigar, showing off the gaudy signet ring that sat on his little finger like a Quality Street toffee. His nails were too long to be masculine. Olivier filled glasses with pink champagne and passed around the nuts, observing the party with amused detachment.

Angelica talked to Marge, a sturdy woman who liked gardening. She tried not to look at her father, whose crotch was now so close to Jennifer it was indecent.

'Did you know Trudy Trowbridge died last week?' asked Tony, dragging on a joint and handing it to Angie.

'Oh goodness,' she breathed. 'How old was she?'

'Seventy-three,' said Tony.

'Too young,' said Marge. 'I'll be seventy-eight in March.'

'You're as young as you feel,' said Alan, looking at Angie for approval.

'As young as the *woman* you feel,' added Denny.

Angelica rolled her eyes, then gasped as Tony gave her a squeeze.

'Then I'm very young indeed,' he chortled.

'I'm not even seventy,' Angie lied. 'You can feel me anytime, darling.'

Tony released Angelica and tossed a glance down the ravine of Angie's cleavage. In spite of her cheap hair and copper tan, her plumpness made her skin relatively wrinkle free. She could easily have passed for a sixty-year-old.

Daisy found them all intolerable and went to play the piano. Angelica remained on the sofa a while, listening. She admired her sister. Angelica hadn't picked up her flute since leaving school. She wasn't even sure where she'd put it and, were she to find it, if she'd remember how to play. She exchanged a glance with Daisy and smiled encouragingly. Her sister smiled back; the same complicit smile they had shared as children. But after a few pieces Angelica excused herself to check on the children, not that anybody cared, and Olivier followed her upstairs.

'Bloody hell, I can't believe they still behave like this! They're in their seventies!' Angelica exclaimed as they walked down the corridor towards the children's bedroom.

'They don't think they're dinosaurs,' said Olivier with a grin. 'They've all grown old together. To each other, they are the same as they've always been, and I know you won't agree, but your mother was obviously very pretty in her youth.'

'I thought I was going to be swept into an orgy when Tony grabbed me.'

'I'd never let that happen.'

'The old lech.'

'I'm a young lech.' Olivier swung her around and kissed her.

'How can you feel horny when *that's* going on downstairs?'

'I only have to look at you to feel horny.'

'I feel nauseous.'

'Thank you!'

'Not because of you, silly.'

'Let them get on with it. They are not you. They just brought you into the world. And I toast them for that.'

Angelica laughed. 'That's all you can toast them for. They're an embarrassment. Thank God I'll never have to introduce them to my friends. Can you imagine what Candace would think?'

'Her commentary would be priceless. But she's your friend, so she would sympathize. No one who loves you would condemn you for having wacky parents.'

'I'm very grateful *you* don't,' she said seriously.

He kissed her forehead. 'Are you crazy? There's nothing of your parents in you that I can see.'

'Wait until I'm seventy!'

★

Now she lay in bed as the children opened their stockings, taking pleasure from being just the family, away from London and all the stress Olivier seemed to bring home with him every evening. She cast a thought to Jack and wondered whether he was trying to contact her. Her mobile telephone had no reception in Fenton, unless she went down to the estuary, where, for some reason, it worked on a small and desolate bit of beach. She had warned him she might not be able to communicate, and right now she didn't mind. Olivier had made love to her after dinner, and she had relished his attention. He had always been a sensitive lover. Afterwards, they had lain entwined, laughing about her parents and their atrocious friends. Then they had imagined how things might have gone had they not been there. Laughter had enabled her to talk about it without the usual stab of embarrassment. Once she detached, there *was* something very funny about Denny and Angie's swinging scene; it was tragic only if she identified with it.

Joe and Isabel were delighted with their presents. Joe's had been wrapped in red; Isabel's in pale blue. Neither could understand how Father Christmas had known exactly what they wanted, but accepted that it was due to the letters they had written over half term and sent up the chimney at Candace's house in Gloucestershire. Olivier lay half asleep in spite of the racket around him. He grunted every once in a while to prove he was awake and slipped his hand over his wife's leg to give it a squeeze. Angelica couldn't remember the last time they had lain in bed like that, all together. On weekends he usually slept in the spare room to get a lie-in. She smiled to herself and remembered Candace's advice. She was absolutely right, of course. What she had was indeed precious – a fragile flame she should do everything in her power to nurture.

Joe and Isabel ran off to get dressed. Angelica lay in her husband's arms, savouring the warmth of his body and the comfort of that familiar place on his shoulder. There was no place for Jack there in the marital bed. At that moment she seriously considered cancelling her trip to South Africa and deleting his number from her telephone. It had been fun, but not fun enough to risk destroying her marriage.

After a while she got up and opened the curtains. The countryside was covered in a crisp coating of frost. The sky was a pale, watery blue, the rising sun shining weakly down on the frozen earth. Seagulls wheeled over the estuary beyond the gardens, their cries haunting the wide stretch of dirty sand where smaller birds pecked on debris left by the retreating tide. It was a lonely scene, but beautiful in its desolation, and Angelica stood a while watching it, longing to be able to describe it in her writing. She imagined small creatures emerging from the rocks, long slimy legs striding over the little rivers that ran down to the sea, round bellies as green as the weeds that lay carelessly over the sand, bulbous eyes scanning the expanse for trespassers. Troilers, she thought: greedy, nasty Troilers, and suddenly she had the beginnings of a story. The story she had been trying to write.

With a rush of excitement she rummaged in her handbag to find a pen. While Olivier showered, she sat on the bed, scribbling furiously as the ideas came in quick succession. It was as if a dam had broken, allowing inspiration to flow freely once again.

At breakfast, in a pair of J Brand jeans and a Phillip Lim blouse, she sipped coffee while the children played with their new toys, too excited to eat. Daisy watched her enviously. The lost weight gave her cheekbones definition and her eyes seemed bigger and brighter. Her clothes looked expensive, especially the Yves Saint Laurent coin necklace Olivier had bought her for her last birthday. Daisy scowled into her bowl of cereal. Denny and Angie were still in bed, having practically slept through five grandchildren opening stockings on top of them. 'I bought most of their presents in the sales,' said Daisy. 'There were great bargains because of the credit crunch.'

'Clever you. Olivier would love me to be a little more economical,' Angelica replied.

'I was rather extravagant before the divorce, but now that Ted is refusing to give me any money, I have to be really careful.'

'He'll have to settle in the end.'

'If he has any money left.'

'He can't squirrel it all away.'

'You'd be surprised. I always thought I'd make millions as a concert pianist. I thought you'd be the penniless writer. Funny how wrong one can be.'

Angelica didn't attempt to contain her impatience, even though it was Christmas. 'You know, Daisy, if you stopped looking at your glass as half empty all the time, you'd find that you are incredibly blessed. You have three beautiful children and a roof over your head. A smile might attract a nice man, and who knows, if you're fun to be with, he might even marry you.' She got up. 'I'm going for a walk. I'm not going to apologize for being who I am. If you have a problem with me, it's *your* problem. Don't try to make it mine. I've only ever been kind to you. Olivier can look after the children for a change.'

'I'll look after them,' Daisy volunteered, not knowing how to react to her sister's melodramatic outburst. Joe and Isabel were too busy playing with their cousins and their new toys to notice.

Angelica marched down to the estuary in a state of outrage, to that little bit of beach where her telephone would work. She wanted to call Candace and let off steam. She buttoned up her navy peacoat, buried her face in her cashmere scarf, and thrust her hands into a pair of gloves. A woolly hat kept her head warm, leaving her curly hair to bounce over her shoulders and down her back as she walked. The wind whipped against her cheeks, but it felt good. She inhaled the icy air and felt it burn the bottom of her lungs. The sun was a little stronger now, and she could feel it when the wind relented.

Her booted feet crunched the frost as she strode down to the beach. Besides a few birds, the landscape was dead. It was hard to believe that bulbs slept beneath the frost and buds would later emerge from those lifeless branches. She loved winter. It was bleak and forlorn and somehow extremely beautiful.

Daisy infuriated her. The way she made sneering little comments designed to cut her down to *her* size. The way she only ever saw the negative – what she *didn't* have, *couldn't* do, *wouldn't* enjoy, instead of celebrating her good fortune.

It was cold and damp in the enclave. She sat on a rock and pulled out her phone. At least she was out of the wind. An intrepid seagull approached in the hope of stealing something to eat, but Angelica had nothing to offer. She watched the gull with its long yellow beak and black eyes and thought of Jack. He'd know the name of every bird on the estuary. She found herself smiling as she scanned the sand and sky for others, envisaging Jack with his pair of binoculars and pockets full of crumbs.

She could see her breath on the air as she scrolled to find Candace's number, but before she could finish, the phone bleeped with a message. She knew it was from Jack. **Happy Christmas, Beautiful. I miss you. Try to call me if you can. If I don't answer, it's because I can't. My thoughts are with you all the time these days – can you feel them? I'm sending them straight into your heart. Yours always, DOP**

Moved by the lonely beauty of the beach and the longing that loneliness induced, she cancelled Candace's number and pressed the speed dial for Jack's.

With a thumping heart, knowing she was more than

foolish, she listened to the ringing tone. A small part of her just wanted to hear his voice and leave a short message. That small part knew it would be wiser to call Candace instead. But the larger part wanted to speak to Jack and feel cherished on that dull, colourless day. *I'm only going to wish him a Happy Christmas,* she thought.

At last he answered, and his voice, now as familiar as her favourite cashmere sweater, resonated with sunshine. 'I was hoping you'd call.'

'Happy Christmas, Dog on Porch,' she said, feeling warm all over.

'Where are you? It sounds windy.'

'Down on the bleakest beach in Norfolk. The only place my mobile works.'

'I'm in the garden. It's really hot. I'm glad you called. I miss you.'

'I miss you, too.' And she meant it, the fire in her heart now rekindled. 'You sound so close, like you're right here with me.'

'I *am,* in thought.'

'If I close my eyes, I can feel you.'

'I wish you were here. February is so far away.'

'It'll come quickly.'

'It had better. I can't wait too long.'

'Why is it that time goes fast when you're having fun and slow when you're miserable?'

'Because there is no such thing as time. It's simply a way of measuring one moment to the next. It's all in our minds.'

'You're turning into a philosopher.'

'I'm morose these days, my darling. I need you here to make me laugh.' His voice sounded so flat, she felt her heart flood with compassion.

'Don't be morose. You're in a beautiful place, with your lovely daughters. It's Christmas.'

'That's why I'm morose. Beauty often makes one melancholy. It's all transient. Nothing lasts.'

'There's always the promise of something better around the corner.' He didn't reply, so she continued, determined to make him happy. 'Your daughters are growing up, but think of the pleasure in watching them blossom.'

'Right now I'm dwelling on the past, not the future. The past is solid. It's happened. No one can take it away from me.'

'Focus on the present, Jack. The present is the only reality. Yesterday is gone, tomorrow doesn't exist but in your imagination. Now is really here.'

'No, I'm focusing on February and what I'm going to do to you when I see you.'

'You are funny.'

'I've embarrassed you,' he said brightly, and she smiled, knowing she had cheered him up.

'Yes, you have.'

'I've never made a secret of wanting to make love to you.'

'Perhaps you should have.'

'And miss out on your embarrassment? I'd love to see you right now. I bet you're blushing.'

'I'm not telling.'

'You're lovely to kiss.'

'Thank you.'

'I bet you're lovely to kiss all over.'

'Really, Jack, stop!'

'This is working. I'm feeling better already.'

'So it's true, the secret of happiness comes from one's state of mind.'

'I suppose it does. Before you called I felt so depressed. But now, with the simple thought of taking your clothes off, my misery has lifted and I'm in a better mood than I have been in in days.'

'Don't get too excited. You might get into trouble.'

'Anna and the children have gone to church.'

'Why aren't you with them?'

'I'm not feeling like snuggling up to God today.'

'Okay. I've never heard that excuse before.'

'Let's just say He's not in my good books at the moment.'

'Now, why's that?'

'For a number of reasons. But I don't want to ruin my mood by discussing His shortcomings. Let's talk about making love again. Where was I? Oh yes, I was unwrapping you like a Christmas present . . .'

After she had hung up, Angelica sat gazing out over the estuary. Her spirits had soared up there with the gulls, and she felt as if her heart would burst with happiness. Right now she loved who she was. She felt deliciously wicked, a femme fatale, capable of doing anything she wanted, as if the world turned for her and her alone. She took off her woolly hat and ran along the sand, arms outstretched like a bird. She relished the sensation of letting herself go. The wind swept in from the sea, cold against her skin, raking rough fingers through her hair. Laughter bubbled up from her belly, and she released it into the air with the furious squawking of seagulls, their breakfast interrupted. She didn't feel guilty and she didn't sense danger. She rode the wind without a care for those on the ground.

Chapter 18

'Move with the current, it is resisting the flow that causes
problems'

In Search of the Perfect Happiness

Angelica and Olivier accompanied the family to church. Joe
and Isabel mucked about with their cousins, giggling at the
vicar's booming voice, whispering loudly about the dandruff
on the collar of the old man in front, until they had to be split
up. Daisy smiled apologetically, aware that she was in God's
house, where resentment had no place, and Angelica smiled
back, relieved that her outburst had caused her sister to be
contrite.

She dreaded lunch and present giving. Daisy would apologize for not being generous, then make Angelica feel guilty
for spending so much. Her nephews and nieces would wait
impatiently for her gifts, which were always more exciting
than their mother's: another gripe Daisy would add to her
long list of resentments. Joe and Isabel were always given
things they didn't want and had to thank their aunt through
gritted teeth, whining later to their mother, who always left
hers and Olivier's gifts until last, for that very reason.

Later Olivier and Angelica would take the children for
a walk with Daisy and her three. Once out of the house
things would improve. The sea air would sweep away their

irritation, the sight of the horizon draw them out of themselves, and at last they'd manage to discuss their parents, the
shared horror being the only thing they really had in common.
Sometimes Daisy and Angelica could laugh together at Angie
and Denny's expense, but more often they couldn't. Daisy
hadn't escaped like Angelica had; like it or not, Daisy needed
them.

By the time Olivier packed up the car, the suitcases having
been in the hall since breakfast, Angelica was desperate to
leave. She was even looking forward to staying in Provence
with Olivier's ghastly mother and sisters. At least with them
she could detach – they weren't *her* family. Unlike Daisy,
Marie-Louise and Marie-Celeste were extravagant and spoiled
and grumpy in the way only the French can be. Olivier's
mother, Marie-Amalie, worshipped her son, treating him like
a prodigal prince, elbowing Angelica out of the way as if she
were an unwelcome appendage and not his wife. Olivier
adored his mother, which blinded him to her faults, leaving
Angelica alone with her gruff but delightful father-in-law,
Leonard, which was where she was entirely happy to be.

During that week Angelica called Jack more frequently
than ever. The texts flew back and forth, giving her a vital
lifeline to hold on to while Olivier sat chatting to his mother,
and his sisters bitched about their friends beside the fire in the
coldly elegant drawing room. Sharing her stories with Jack
enabled her to see the funny side of her situation. She enjoyed
hearing him laugh down the line as she imitated Marie-Louise
snorting disapproval and Marie-Amalie chastising her for writing books when she should be seeing to her husband's needs.
'It is not right for a woman to work when she has a husband
to look after,' she said. 'And anyway, who reads them?'

Jack's laugh was satisfyingly loud. 'I do,' he said. 'I've just
finished *The Silk Serpent* and loved it. Even better than *The
Caves of Cold Konard*. Tell her that!'

'I think you're my biggest fan.'

'You *know* I'm your biggest fan! I think you need rescuing, darling.'

'It'll be over soon, and life will go back to normal.'

'I think you should take a stand. No more in-laws. You didn't marry them when you married Olivier.'

'You want to bet?'

'Don't be afraid to speak your mind. At worst you'll just offend them; at best you'll offend them so much you won't ever have to see them again.'

'I love my father-in-law – he makes it bearable.'

'Don't let them walk all over you, Angelica. You're far too nice.'

'I'm learning to be nasty.'

'Just keep your boundaries strong. Don't let them break through. And smile as if you know something they don't. It always works. A little secretive smile always does the trick!'

'How do you know that?'

'Because my mother has that look on her face all the time, and it drives me mad!'

It was a relief when the children went back to school for the Easter term and Angelica found herself once again reunited with her four friends, at the centre table in Le Caprice. Jesus, the charming Bolivian manager, sent them a round of Bellinis on the house, and Angelica savoured the sensation of being back in civilization after what had been an extremely un-civilized Christmas.

'Thank God that's over for another year,' she said, raising her glass to Candace, Scarlet, Kate, and Letizia.

'You think yours was bad? Do you want to know what Pete gave me?'

'No, let me guess,' said Candace, narrowing her pale eyes. 'An ironing board.'

'No, he gave me a boob job.'

'What?'

'He said I might need one after having the baby. Either that or a tummy tuck.'

'Did you give him a penis extension?' said Candace scornfully.

'Or a good clip around the ear,' Scarlet added for good measure.

'I hope you told him where he can stick his vows?' said Angelica.

Kate grinned mischievously. 'No, the ceremony is still on. You think I'm going to let him worm his way out of my big day by starting a fight?'

'I'm curious, darling. What *did* you say?' Letizia asked.

'That my body is a temple carrying his precious child.'

'Or someone else's precious child . . .' Candace added wryly.

'No, it's definitely Pete's. No question. Don't know why I ever doubted it.'

'A teeny weeny insignificant thing like a date?'

'I'm not a total idiot. So, it could possibly be Mr X's baby. Possibly. But right now I'm not prepared to go there. I want to have a serene pregnancy. Look what happened when I had Phoebe? Pete and I fought all the time, and she came out in a right state, poor thing. She's still very temperamental. So I meditate daily and take deep breaths through the nose, like this.' She placed a hand on her belly, closed her eyes, and inhaled through flared nostrils.

'Oh God, it's the Virgin Mary.' Scarlet laughed.

'Nothing immaculate about *this* conception,' Candace interjected.

'You're not going to tell us, are you?' asked Angelica.

'No,' Kate replied firmly. 'Look, I'd happily tell you, but I have to think of *his* feelings. My New Year's resolution is to put others before myself.'

Candace arched an eyebrow. 'It's going to be a tough year.'

'You'd be surprised how altruistic I've become.'

'Go on, surprise us,' said Candace.

'I've already turned a blind eye to a text Pete received from The Haggis.'

'You cannot be serious!' gasped Letizia.

'She's still hanging around?' Candace was astonished. 'I thought she was well past her sell-by date.'

'So did I!'

'How did you manage to see it?' Angelica asked.

'Did you sneak a peek?' Candace added.

'*I* wouldn't dare!' Letizia interrupted. 'My marriage exists on trust. If I mistrusted Gaitano for a second, the whole thing would unravel.'

'Honey, Kate's marriage exists on *mis*trust. As soon as they start *trusting* each other, the whole thing unravels!'

'I think you have a point, Candace,' Kate conceded, draining her Bellini.

'I'd love William to get a few sexy texts,' said Scarlet. 'Then I wouldn't feel so guilty when I get mine.'

'*You* get sexy texts?' Kate rounded on her jealously. 'Why don't I get any?'

'Really? Who from?' Angelica asked.

Scarlet shrugged nonchalantly. 'Oh, loads of people. You'd be surprised. In my line of work I meet men all the time.'

'Gay men,' said Candace. 'I didn't think the fashion world was in the business of straight men.'

'I'm talking about the men behind the scenes. They're very naughty! They have my number. It's very easy to flirt that way. I'd never take it any further, but it makes me feel good.' Candace caught Angelica's eye. Angelica dropped her gaze into the menu as the waiter came to take their orders. 'It's got nothing to do with what I feel about *them,* but how they make me feel about *myself*. Complete, unadulterated vanity,' she continued breezily.

'You dark horse, Scarlet!' Letizia was impressed.

'Not called Scarlet for nothing,' Candace added. 'I'll have crispy duck salad to start, then the chicken,' she told the waiter. 'No mashed potato.'

'So do you want to know what The Haggis said, or not? Soup to start, duck salad as a main course and make it big. I'm hungry.'

'Ah, I see eating is a New Year's resolution as well as altruism,' said Candace. '*Now* I'm surprised.'

'Well, go on. We're listening,' said Letizia. 'Did you sneak a peek?'

'Not exactly. I mistook Pete's telephone for mine. They're identical.'

'Sure they are,' Candace commented under her breath.

'Well, mine has a sticker on it, actually. But the ring tone's the same, and he was in the shower, so I opened it and read it.'

'And?' said Scarlet.

'What did it say?' Letizia and Angelica asked in unison.

'Hey sexy, you haven't been in touch . . .'

'In touch. That's a good one,' said Candace. Kate didn't understand. 'Well, surely she meant that he hadn't touched her for a while.'

'Goodness no! She's far too stupid to think up something witty like that.'

'It doesn't necessarily mean that Pete's been cheating on you since he agreed to stay on the porch,' said Scarlet.

Angelica thought of Jack on his porch and brightened at the prospect of seeing him again in only a few weeks. She glanced at Scarlet and knew that *she* could enlighten them a bit on the advantages of texting. In comparison to her, Scarlet was an amateur.

'She's stalking him,' said Kate.

'I hope she's not a bunny boiler,' Letizia added.

'No bunnies to boil.' Kate laughed coolly.

Candace looked at her through narrowed eyes. 'You don't seem upset?'

'Valium,' said Kate simply, taking a calm breath and smiling serenely. 'It's a wonder what a teeny weeny little pill can do for one's stress levels. Really, I've never felt better. Highly recommended.' They all stared at her. 'Got you!' She laughed, but no one joined her. 'Just a joke. You think I'd be so irresponsible?'

'Honestly? Yes,' said Candace a little nervously. 'At this rate your baby will come out laughing.'

'Well, he'll have a good sense of humour if he's anything like his father,' Kate replied.

'Which one?' asked Candace, then she added with a chuckle: 'Or are they both comedians?'

Angelica picked up the children from school in a good mood. She felt light-headed after three Bellinis, and happy to be back in her comfort zone. She was even pleased to see Jenna Elrich, whose suntan and sea-bleached hair were usually enough to deflate her joy. But her spirit was flooded with generosity, and she listened sympathetically as Jenna moaned about the beach house in Mustique and the chalet in Switzerland, the inefficiency of builders and decorators, and she didn't mind a bit when Jenna told her how pale she looked. She had put Norfolk and Provence behind her and was looking forwards, to South Africa.

When she got home, there was a man sitting on her doorstep in a pair of khaki trousers and a blue shirt. Around his waist was a tool belt. As she approached, he lifted his eyes and smiled sheepishly. 'Hi, love, I hope you don't mind me hanging out on your doorstep for a moment?' His accent was East

End, as was his affability. He didn't look dangerous. In fact, his face was boyishly good-looking, with big blue eyes brimming with honesty.

'Of course not,' she replied, smiling back politely.

She unlocked the door and let the children run inside. She closed it behind her and threw the children's backpacks onto the dining-room table. The children ran off to the playroom. Just as she put the kettle on to make a cup of tea, the doorbell rang. She knew it was the man on her doorstep before she opened the door.

'I'm really sorry to bother you, but I'm in a bit of a pickle. I'm a carpenter. I'm working on that building opposite.' He moved so she could see the house covered in scaffolding. 'Big job, that is.'

'I bet it is,' she replied.

'Anyway, Steve has run off with my jacket by mistake. It's got my wallet and phone inside. I've been waiting for him to come back, but it's been an hour. He must have gone home without realizing.'

'Oh, that's awful. Do you want to borrow our telephone? My husband's upstairs, I'm sure he won't mind,' she lied, thinking that was the sort of thing Candace would do, if she was ever foolish enough to let a strange man into her house – which she most certainly wasn't. But this man didn't look dangerous.

'That's really good of you. Look, my name is John Stoke.' He put his hand in his breast pocket. 'Here's my card.' She looked at it. John Stoke, carpenter. *Might be useful,* she thought, *if ever I need one. Which I most certainly will at some stage.* She noticed his hands were big and rough and splattered with paint. 'If you don't mind, I'll just call my mobile and see if he picks up.'

Angelica showed him into the kitchen, where he pushed in the number. She made two mugs of tea. 'Damn! He's not picking up.' He sounded desperate. 'I live in Northampton. I don't even have money for the train. Would you mind if I call my wife?'

'Go ahead. Milk or sugar?'

He looked embarrassed. 'You don't have to make me a cup of tea.'

'You're freezing.'

'Well, it *is* cold out there without a coat! Milk, two sugars. Thank you.' He rang his wife. 'Hello, love, it's me . . . I've been bloody stupid, Steve's run off with my coat . . . Good question, he left his on-site, but it's all locked up now. I thought he'd come back once he'd discovered his mistake . . . Yes, I'll get home . . . I'm not sure, I'll think of something . . . Yes, I know it's Robbie's birthday, I'll make it, don't worry . . . I'll call you when I've worked out what to do . . . This nice lady has let me use her phone . . . She lives opposite the site . . . Yeah, I know, I'll tell her . . . Okay, 'bye . . . She says thanks for looking after her old bloke!'

'Not at all. Why don't you call your boss?' She handed him his mug of tea.

'I don't have his number. It's in my phone.' He shrugged. 'I'm self-employed. I have a different boss every week.'

'Look, how much do you need? I can lend you some money to get you home, and you can pay me back tomorrow. You're working opposite, after all.'

'I can't ask you to do that! You don't know me. For all you know I might run off and never come back.'

'The small amount I have in my wallet won't get you very far, I'm afraid.'

'Well, it's very kind of you. I feel bad, but I won't refuse your offer, because I don't know how I'm going to get home otherwise. It's our Robbie's birthday. He's going to be six.'

'Same as our daughter.'

'You know how much it means to be there.'

'I certainly do.' She opened her handbag and delved inside for her wallet. 'I have fifty quid. Will that get you home?'

'That's more than enough. I'll pay you back tomorrow, I promise.'

'I trust you.'

'Thanks for the tea. Just what I needed. I feel much better now. It's cold out there.'

'You can't go out in just a shirt.'

'Oh, I'm strong. I'll survive.'

'But it's freezing. I was wearing gloves and a hat, and I was still cold.'

'But you're a lady. I'll bet you're not used to labouring outside like I am.'

'Why don't you borrow a coat?' She marched into the hall and opened the cupboard where Olivier's coats hung in a neat row. She pulled out a navy one. 'I won't tell him if you don't,' she said with a grin. 'Give it back tomorrow, and he'll never know.'

'I couldn't.'

'Go on. It's sub-zero, and it's only going to get colder.' She looked outside. It was already dark.

'Well, all right. You're really kind. Not many people like you around these days. People are so guarded. The world is a less friendly place than it used to be.' He shrugged it on. 'Nice.'

'Cashmere.'

'Very nice.'

She handed him the money. 'You go carefully now, and I'll see you tomorrow.'

'I look like a real gent in this.' He laughed, and she opened the door. 'I start at seven in the morning.'

'I'll be up. You know what children are like, and I have to get them ready for school. Just ring the bell. If I'm not here, give it to Sunny, my housekeeper.'

'God bless you.' He smiled at her gratefully and thrust his hands into the pockets. ''Bye now.'

Angelica felt virtuous helping out a stranger in need, and still a little tipsy. She called the children into the dining room to do their homework and forgot all about him in the pile of Kipper and Biff books and maths. When Olivier returned, she didn't bother to tell him. She certainly didn't want to admit that she'd lent a total stranger one of his favourite coats. In the morning she was so busy getting the children dressed and down to breakfast that she didn't give the carpenter a thought. They were late for school, distracted by the snow that had fallen in the night. It was only when she returned home that she remembered him.

She expected Sunny to mention that he had dropped in with the coat and money. But Sunny said, 'No one has rung the bell.'

'How strange.'

Sunny shrugged. 'Perhaps he is over there,' she said, pointing to the building, teeming like a hive with builders.

'I'll go and ask them,' she replied, already feeling a little sick, expecting the worst, envisaging Olivier's rage. She wrapped her coat around her and hurried across the street. The snow had melted on the road, but the pavement and gutters were still white – as white as her anxious face. She approached a builder standing in the doorway in grubby overalls. 'Excuse me,' she said. The man looked her up and down appreciatively. 'Is there anyone who works here called John Stoke?'

The man frowned. 'No John Stoke. John Desmond, but no John Stoke.'

'Carpenter. Young, blue eyes. Charming?' She faltered a moment, before continuing optimistically. 'Is there, by any small chance, anyone called Steve?' The blank look on his face made her stomach swim. 'No Steve,' she murmured helplessly.

'No Steve.' He smiled at her sympathetically. 'Madam, have you been had?'

Chapter 19

'The outer world is a reflection of your inner, so focus on the beauty within you'

In Search of the Perfect Happiness

When Angelica called Candace and told her what had happened, her friend erupted into peals of laughter. 'Oh my God, Angelica!' she exclaimed, catching her breath. 'What on earth possessed you to let a strange man into your home? With your children in the house? Are you crazy?'

'The builder opposite says he's notorious. The clever thing is he never asks for money. He didn't ask me once.'

'But you offered anyway.'

'I was being kind.'

'I do love you, Angelica!'

'I'm not loving myself a great deal this morning. And Olivier's going to love me a lot less.'

'You're not to tell him!'

'I have to . . . It's his favourite navy Ralph Lauren coat. I am in such deep shit.'

'You know what? I wouldn't tell him. I know I don't often advocate lying, but in this case, when his reaction is so predictable, I'd make something up. You lost it at the dry cleaner's.'

'That *is* believable.'

'I'm not sure telling him the truth will do your marriage any good. Especially when you're about to go off to South Africa.'

Angelica ignored her insinuation. 'How could I be so gullible?'

'It's not in your nature to be cynical.'

'I even pretended Olivier was upstairs.'

'So you didn't totally trust him.'

'I tried to think what you would do in the same situation.'

'You know exactly what I would do. I'd send him down to the nearest pub to ask the publican to borrow his phone. A woman alone in the house with children? You've *got* to be kidding me!'

'If he'd just run off with my money, I wouldn't have minded. Whatever possessed me to give him Olivier's coat? Why didn't I give him one of mine?'

'At least you were sane enough not to do that.'

'I'm such an idiot.'

'Don't torment yourself! It could have been so much worse. He could have taken the children.'

'Now you're really frightening me.'

'Good. Now you won't be so naïve again. You can't go around trusting people, just because they have nice faces and seemingly honest blue eyes.'

'Do you think he'd been watching me?'

'Of course he'd been watching you. He chose you because he knew you were a sucker.'

'I hope he won't come back.'

'He's too smart to make *that* mistake. But you have to go to the police and tell them exactly what happened. He's probably working his way through Kensington and Chelsea. They have to catch him before he gets to Kate's!'

Angelica spent an hour at the police station on the Earls Court Road, telling a nice young officer exactly what had happened. It was of little consolation that the man was a notorious thief, preying on the kindness of women like her, who felt sorry for him. The fact that she had lost Olivier's coat remained. However, she resolved not to tell him. She'd make something up when he discovered that it was missing. His wrath over her vagueness was a lot better than the alternative.

She did, however, tell Jack. His reaction was unexpected. He didn't laugh like Candace. His first thoughts were for her safety. 'It could have been really nasty, Angelica. You mustn't ever let anyone you don't know into your home.' He sounded really anxious. 'Promise me you won't do that again!'

'You can be sure of that. I can't afford to lose another coat!'

'Who cares about the coat! I care about you.'

'You're very sweet.'

'You've got to take better care of yourself. Have you got good locks on your door?'

'I think so.'

'Don't be vague and British about this. The world is a dangerous place.'

'We live in a very safe area.'

'Don't kid yourself. Nowhere is safe. You have to put good locks on the doors, a camera outside so you can see who's there, and don't ever open the door without asking for ID if it's a deliveryman. Don't trust a van and a uniform. They can be copied as easily as a child's fancy-dress outfit. Keep your wits about you.'

'This isn't Johannesburg.' She laughed, feeling a surge of tenderness towards him.

'I thank God for that.'

★

Inevitably, Olivier discovered the coat was missing a couple of days later. She said she'd ring the dry cleaner's and find out whether they could locate it. 'They can pay for a new one if they've lost it,' he said, then forgot all about it. Angelica was relieved.

A couple of weeks went by. Now she was able to laugh about it, sharing the story with the girls, who teased her affectionately until Kate told a story about giving two hundred pounds to an Indian fortune-teller on Sloane Street who told her not to wear black on Tuesdays, and knew her mother's maiden name and the name of her favourite flower. Who would have guessed red peonies, after all? He showed her photographs of his orphanage in Delhi, and when she said she had only twenty pounds in her wallet, he informed her politely that there was an ATM machine around the corner. Angelica's story was forgotten, and Kate was back where she was happiest, at the centre of everyone's attention.

Angelica began to pack for South Africa. She was so excited, laying everything out on the bed before folding her clothes carefully into her suitcase. It would be sunny and hot, so she packed pretty Melissa Odabash kaftans and white palazzo pants and sandals, and booked into Richard Ward for highlights and a pedicure.

The children weren't happy that she was leaving them, but she had managed to bribe Denise, their old nanny, to work the week with strict instructions to spoil them rotten. She felt a painful wrench at the thought of separation.

The evening before she was due to leave, a policeman arrived at the door. Olivier was home. She was in the kitchen with Joe, listening to him read *Harry Potter*. Olivier happened to be in the hall looking through the post, so it was he who answered the bell. She strained to hear their conversation. Although she couldn't make out every word, she picked up enough to know that Olivier was being told about the carpenter and the coat. She felt the earth give way beneath her and cursed herself for going to the police station. Why hadn't she kept her mouth shut? Joe pressed her to listen. She swallowed her anxiety and managed a smile of encouragement. 'I'm listening,' she said. Joe read on, but Angelica wasn't listening. She was frantically planning her excuse. She knew Olivier would be furious.

She heard the door close, and a gust of cold wind blew into the kitchen. She shivered. Olivier stood in the doorway. His face was grey. 'Joe, go and play with your sister, I want to talk to your mother.' Joe knew something was wrong. He glanced at his mother anxiously.

'We'll read later,' she said, wanting to save her son from any disquiet. She closed the book and watched Joe reluctantly leave the room. With a heavy sigh she raised her eyes to her husband. Unlike Jack, his first thought was not for her safety but for his coat.

'It was my favourite. I'd had it for twenty years. Why didn't you tell me?'

'I was too ashamed,' she replied truthfully. No point in pretending otherwise.

'You lied. You said it was at the dry cleaner's.'

'Yes, I'm sorry for that. I wanted to avoid your fury.'

'Well, you only delayed it.'

'So I see.'

'Why didn't you show him the safe and offer him your jewellery? Why did you stop at the coat?'

'Don't be sarcastic.'

He frowned and leaned against the sideboard. 'Sometimes you baffle me, Angelica. Your dippiness is sometimes charming. But now it's just worrying. I'm not sure that I can trust you.'

The insult struck her. 'This isn't about trust. Or rather, it's not about your trusting me, but my trusting a stranger. It happens to people all the time. I'm sure Kate would have done exactly the same.'

'Kate would have given the keys to her house. That is not a good comparison.'

'Look, I made a mistake. It's only a coat.'

'You let a total stranger into our house. He could have hurt the children!' He sighed melodramatically. 'Well, I suppose I should be thankful that you didn't hand them over so guilelessly.'

'Now you're being ridiculous.'

'I don't know that I can trust you where they are concerned. You put them in danger.'

Angelica stood up, fists clenched at her hips as if she were about to strike him. 'How dare you question my ability to look after the children! You don't know the half of it. You're in the office all day, returning late in the evening in a bad mood. Who looks after them on a daily basis? Who's there to make sure they are picked up from school and fed? Who does their homework with them lovingly, every day, so that they understand their lessons? Who picks them up when they fall? Who kisses them better? Who tucks them in at night?' Then she fired her most lethal weapon. 'Who do they run to when they need reassurance or when they hurt themselves? Don't *ever* call me a bad mother. I'm a bad wife, sure, I'll accept that. And you know what? Right now I don't care. I gave your coat away . . . I wish I'd given *you* away!'

Olivier watched her stride out of the room and into the hall. She grabbed her coat and handbag and marched into the cold street. Olivier heard the door slam and remained rooted to the floor in astonishment. When he had calmed down, he realized that he had gone too far.

Angelica ran down Kensington Church Street, turning right at the church to sit on one of the wooden benches in the garden behind. It was dark, and she was alone. The old York flagstones glistened with damp. Not even pigeons ventured out on such a cold night. She wrapped her coat tightly around her shoulders and sobbed uncontrollably. The injustice of his accusation had wounded her deeply, as if he had taken a blade and sliced through the roots of her identity and pride. Joe and Isabel meant everything to her.

When she had stopped crying, she pulled out her mobile telephone and dialled Jack's number. The rings seemed to go on forever, but when he finally answered, the sound of his voice assuaged her anger, replacing the hate in her heart with love. A mental picture formed of Jack on a mountain flooded with light, while Olivier dwelt in a valley of shadow. Her spirit longed to join Jack up there where it was warm and radiant.

'Olivier is the sort of man who says things he doesn't mean in the heat of the moment. Don't begrudge him for feeling frightened, Angelica,' he advised after she had told him what had happened.

'He's hurt me,' she said, her eyes again welling with tears.

'My darling, don't cry. You'll be out here the day after tomorrow and in my arms as soon as you get to the hotel.'

'If it wasn't for my children, I'd never want to come back.'

'When you told me the story, you frightened me, too.'

'But you were kind.'

'That's my nature. I'm not hot-headed. I'm philosophical, and besides, I don't imagine you'll ever let a stranger into your home again, or give away one of Olivier's precious coats.'

'He's very proud of his clothes.'

'There's no point getting angry with someone when they know very well how foolish they have been. There is no better teacher than experience.'

'I wish Olivier felt like that.'

'Experience is *his* best teacher, too. I bet he regrets saying that to you. He'll learn to think before he speaks.'

'I don't want to go home.'

'You have to face him and make up before you fly out tomorrow.'

'I don't have the heart to.'

'Then take a walk, let the wind blow your anger away. Think about positive things.'

'Like you.'

'If that helps.' He chuckled, and she felt the gloom lift a little.

'Life is too short to waste even a moment being angry. Every second is precious. Go home, wrap your arms around your children – that'll make you feel better. Then wrap your arms around Olivier and make up.'

'I'll do no such thing. He should apologize first.'

'Perhaps you have to be the bigger person this time.'

'I'm not feeling big at all. I'm feeling hurt and furious and very small.'

'Not the Sage I know, debating the secret of happiness, talking so fluently about the need to love unconditionally and detach from our egos. If you detach now, your pain will disappear because it is attached to your ego. No ego, no pain.'

'How simple that sounds. But I have a very long way to go.'

'Perhaps, but you could take a great big leap forward right now and make that distance shorter.'

'Why have you suddenly become so wise?'

'I'm only telling you what you would tell me in the same situation. I am the voice of your Higher Self.'

'If my Higher Self sounded like you, I'd listen to it all the time.' She laughed and took a deep breath, no longer angry.

★

In comparison to Olivier, Jack shone like a knight in shining armour. While Olivier had exploded with fury and accusation, Jack had cared only for her safety. For the first time she allowed herself to wonder what it would be like to be married to Jack. She didn't attempt to work out how such a thing could be achieved, but she fantasized about it. She remained on the bench a while, arms folded, gaze lost in the dark, imagining what life would be like with Jack. Her visualization infused her spirit with joy. Did she love Olivier? Or was she so used to being married to him that she mistook familiarity for love? Right now, she felt no love at all, just resentment and the desire to wound him back.

She looked at her watch. She had been gone an hour. There was no avoiding going home. Slowly she walked back up the road, head bent against the wind and drizzle. She saw the lights on and thought of the children wondering where she was. Their need pulled her home, as if she were attached to them by an invisible cord, rooted in her heart.

Olivier heard the door close and appeared in the hall looking anxious. His face was white, and his eyes had lost their shine. 'Where have you been?' He sounded defeated.

'For a walk. I had to get out.' He watched her take off her coat and hang it in the cupboard.

'I'm sorry I overreacted.' She shrugged, unable to dislodge her resentment. 'I should not have accused you of being a bad mother.'

'No, you shouldn't have.'

'I didn't mean it. I was just angry. I can buy another coat.'

'Whatever.'

'I can't buy another wife and children.' He grinned sheepishly, hoping for a sign that she had forgiven him, but she remained stiff and unyielding. 'Do you want to know what the policeman said?'

'Not really.'

'They've arrested the man. You have to go down tomorrow morning to identify him.'

'I'll ask him for your coat.'

'I don't care about the coat!' he growled impatiently. 'Besides, he won't see you.'

'That's a blessing.'

'I care about you. I'm sorry, *ma chérie*.'

She let him draw her into his arms but remained detached, as if she were above, watching him hold someone else. 'Aren't you going to forgive me?' he asked gently, pulling away to look into her eyes.

'I'm hurt, Olivier. I can't simply snap out of it like you can.'

'What more can I do?'

'You said the most awful thing. I can't pretend I didn't hear it.'

His face reddened with frustration. 'I wish I hadn't said it. Let's throw that moment away. It never happened.'

'You should think more carefully before you accuse.'

'I know. I'm an idiot! But you can't fly off to South Africa feeling angry. What if something happens? The last words we will have said to each other are in anger. I would never forgive myself.'

She stared at him a moment, as if seeing him anew. 'It's always about *you*,' she said boldly, empowered by the apprehension on his face. 'Everything is always about you.'

'What do you mean?'

'I'm going upstairs to bathe the children. I don't want to talk about this anymore. I think a week in South Africa is just what I need – what *we* need. I'm tired of running around you, Olivier.'

Angelica climbed the stairs without glancing back. When she had disappeared, he walked into the kitchen and poured himself a large whisky, leaned back against the sideboard, and hung his head.

Angelica bit her lip, suppressing her guilt. She had allowed herself to drift past another frontier, down the river towards the inevitable waterfall – and she hadn't even tried to grab the hand outstretched to stop her.

Chapter 20

'One often finds one's destiny on the road one takes to avoid it'

In Search of the Perfect Happiness

The following evening Angelica was in the plane, on her way to South Africa. She sat in her business-class seat, drinking a second glass of Sauvignon Blanc, trying to dull the ache in her heart as she replayed the parting scene with masochistic fervour. Joe had cried, burying his face in her neck, asking her over and over why she had to leave him. His stricken face and unyielding grip had weakened her resolve, and it had taken all her strength to pull away. If the book tour hadn't been so meticulously planned, she would have cancelled, but so many people depended on her now, it simply wasn't possible. And it was only a week. She had pressed her lips to his wet cheek and whispered, 'I'll be back for the Full Joe.' Isabel had cried, too, but only because Joe cried and she didn't want to be left out. Although only six, Isabel was made of stronger stuff. She was content with her bribes and the fact that she'd have her father to herself. He had promised to come home early every evening in time to read them a bedtime story. Isabel was happy to be left with her father; for Joe, only his mother would do.

Angelica felt light-headed. It was a welcome feeling, masking the bruising caused by her row with Olivier and her parting from the children. She had kissed her husband coolly. He had held on to her for longer than was necessary, hoping for a softening in her demeanour. But her resentment was such that even though she willed herself to be loving, her heart refused to give in, remaining as tight as a clenched fist. Now that she was suitably tipsy, she could convince herself that she didn't regret her behaviour, that she had every reason still to begrudge him. The balance of power had never tipped so far in her favour before, but it was a hollow victory. Candace would have said that she had prolonged their row to give her the perfect excuse for adultery. She took another swig of wine and tried not to think of Candace, or to question her motives for prolonging her sulk. She drained her glass, almost convinced that given the way Olivier had treated her, she deserved someone to cherish her.

She ate dinner, watched *Vicky Cristina Barcelona,* then lay flat beneath her blanket and fell asleep. She didn't dream of Jack or Olivier, but of Joe and Isabel, their anxious faces pulling her heartstrings so hard they tore the flesh and bled.

When they landed in Johannesburg, it was early morning, but already the light was dazzling. Used to the grey, cloudy skies of England, she squinted in the glare of the royal blue sky and let the sunshine lift her battered spirits.

Sweeping her family to the back of her mind, she turned her thoughts to Jack. She had told him not to meet her at the airport as the publisher's rep was going to pick her up and take her to her hotel. She'd have time only to shower before having to go downstairs for a lunch event. Although she had an afternoon talk with a ladies' reading group in Pretoria, she had made sure that dinner was left free, explaining to her agent that she'd be tired after her flight and would go straight to bed. Jack was meeting her for dinner, somewhere quiet, but they had arranged to speak beforehand as she wasn't sure what time she'd make it back from Pretoria.

The thought of being on the same continent as Jack filled her with nervous excitement. She was moving inexorably towards an affair, and, even if she had second thoughts, it was too late to stop now; she hadn't the will to turn the tide. It was that sense of inevitability that turned her stomach to jelly. But Candace was safely tucked away on the other side of the world, her voice of reason lost in the great distance that separated them, and she didn't think of her family. She was in South Africa, far from anyone she knew, far from the *Angelica* she knew. Here, she could be anyone she wanted to be and somehow it wouldn't count – she'd step back into her own skin on her return.

As she walked into Arrivals, a pretty, brown-faced girl stood holding a handwritten sign with her name on it. Angelica waved, and the girl smiled in recognition, weaving nimbly through the crowd to greet her. 'Hi, I'm Anita,' she said, laughing bashfully at her crude sign. 'Sorry about this. I wasn't sure I'd recognize you. Welcome to Jozi.' They shook hands.

Angelica delighted in her accent. It reminded her of Jack. 'It's good to be here,' she said truthfully, inhaling the foreign air and tasting in the atmosphere the anticipated sweetness of forbidden fruit.

'You look radiant, considering the long flight. Was it okay?'

'I slept most of the way.'

'Good, so you're not too tired for your lunch event?'

'Not at all.'

'We're fully booked, which is great. We even had to turn a few people away. It's going to be fun.'

They walked through the airport and out into the car park, where the midsummer heat was luxurious. Frothy trees shimmered in the breeze as birds flew in and out of the branches. Anita was cool in a black sundress with red pumps, and

Angelica couldn't wait to change out of her jeans into some-thing lighter. They climbed into the hot car, and Anita turned on the air-conditioning. Piles of papers and files lay across the backseat, and at her feet was a bag containing bottles of water and shiny red apples. 'In case you get thirsty,' she said, hand-ing her a bottle. 'Now, we're going straight to the Grace. It's really pretty. I think you'll like it. It has a lovely garden behind with a swimming pool, so if you want to lie out this after-noon for an hour, be my guest. We'll be leaving for Pretoria at four.'

'Busy schedule!'

'Claudia made it very clear that you wanted to squeeze as much as possible into these five days. I gather you have chil-dren to get back to.'

'And an irate husband.'

'Oh, he doesn't like you to go away?'

'No. He likes the domestic routine to stay the same. He's very pernickety. He likes things neat and tidy, from the way he folds his shirts to the way I slot into the home, looking after the children.'

'Then it's good for you to get away.'

'Absolutely.' She breathed heavily, savouring the novelty of being unencumbered. 'I'm going to enjoy having "me" time.'

'Spaces are good for relationships. You realize how much you miss each other.'

Angelica laughed and put on her sunglasses. 'I'm not miss-ing him yet!'

She turned her gaze onto the leafy streets of Johannesburg, devouring the exotic sights with fascination. Anita gave her a tour of the city as they drove into the centre. What struck her immediately was the lack of people on the pavements. There were no mothers pushing prams, no joggers on the way to the park, no dog walkers. Houses hid behind tall, forbidding walls fitted with spikes and alarms; security guards stood at the gates, suspicious and watchful. No one seemed very keen to get out and enjoy the frothy plane trees and rampant bougainvillea.

'There's a terrible problem with crime. Everyone has a story to tell. It's very sad, and it's not getting any better. The only thing you can do is fortify your house so it's as safe as a castle. If you're a woman on your own, you don't drive at night, and if you do, you don't stop. Not even at robots.'

'Robots?'

'Traffic lights.' She laughed. 'I know, foreigners always find that funny.'

'So life goes on in people's houses?'

'Behind those walls you will find some of the most beautiful homes you have ever seen. Luscious gardens with palm trees and swimming pools, bright flowers and exotic birds. They live well. But for all that, they sacrifice their freedom.'

'Is it worth it? Why don't the rich move somewhere safer?'

'Because their friends are here. Their lives are here. The climate is perfect. But don't forget, we can't take much money out, and Europe is very expensive. If you're wealthy, what can you do? Leave it all behind and start again?'

'Is Cape Town as bad?'

'No, Cape Town has less crime. It has a more European feel, being on the sea. I'd prefer to live there, but my work is here, so I have no choice.'

'But there's still a problem with crime?'

'Wherever you get a vast divide between rich and poor, you're going to get crime.'

'And in the countryside?'

'It's everywhere. You have to be constantly vigilant. For us, it's second nature. Talking of which, don't wear those rings.'

Angelica glanced at her diamond engagement ring and diamond eternity ring. 'Really?'

'Unless you want your finger sliced off.' Anita watched her blanch. 'Don't panic, you can wait until you get to the hotel. But then I'd put them away somewhere safe.'

'I've never taken them off.'

'No time for sentimentality. Better to be safe than sorry.' Angelica toyed with them. *I'll put them back on with my skin.* But somehow, removing her wedding ring felt worse than removing her skin.

They arrived at the Grace Hotel through a shopping mall. 'Safer than walking outside,' Anita said, and after their conversation about crime, Angelica was grateful. The mall was busy with shoppers, like an ant colony where all the action takes place underground. Sweeping her eyes over the shop fronts, she thought she'd rather spend the afternoon there than lying by the pool, burning. 'There's a really good African market around the corner. If you like, I'll take you there this afternoon. Full of jewellery and fabrics. It's quite touristy, but you can haggle and get the prices down. There are some really nice things, once you get your eye in.'

The Grace was an elegant, old-fashioned hotel with comfy red sofas, gilt mirrors, mahogany furniture, and brass fittings. Angelica was reminded of London. They checked in swiftly, and Anita left her with the porter. 'You have an hour or so to relax. I'll call you from here when it's time to come down.' Angelica was happy to be left on her own in her room. She tipped the young man, who smiled appreciatively, left her suitcase on the luggage rack, and departed. The room was tasteful and airy, with tall windows, pale green walls, a king-size bed, and a mahogany desk. They obviously valued her highly to put her in such a grand hotel. She went to the telephone to call Olivier. She longed for news of the children. But as she picked up the receiver she felt her resentment resurface. In spite of wanting to hear news of Joe and Isabel, she didn't feel ready to speak to her husband. She put the receiver down and went into the marble bathroom for a shower. She'd leave Olivier to stew and call Jack instead.

Any doubts about her intentions were carried away with the soap. She closed her eyes and let Jack's broad face surface in her mind. She found herself smiling with guilty antici-pation at the prospect of kissing him again. She could almost feel his bristles on her skin, his breath on her neck, and his big arms around her body. After showering, she sat in her towel and took off her rings. They were not easily removed, and she had to twist and turn and pull. With a sigh of resignation she slipped them into the pocket of her wash bag. Her hand looked naked without them, but she felt free.

She switched on her mobile and reluctantly sent a text to Olivier with the hotel telephone number, adding that he wasn't to call her as she was busy at an event. Jack had called three times. She pressed redial. It rang only once before he answered. 'There you are!' His voice was so cheerful she forgot all about Olivier.

'At last.'

'At the Grace?'

'Right here.'

'I can't believe you're in the same city as me.'

'Neither can I.'

'So you've got this lunch event.'

'Here at the hotel.'

'Then what?'

'Nothing until four, when I have to go to Pretoria for a teatime event.'

'Then dinner with me.' She sensed his grinning into the telephone.

'Dinner with you.'

'I don't think I can wait that long.'

'Well, you have to.'

'My God, you're here in Johannesburg. It feels so surreal.'

'It's beautiful.'

'It is now, because you're in it.'

She laughed, embarrassed. 'You are funny!'

'What's your room number?'

'Two-o-seven.'

'I'll call you this afternoon.'

'I can't wait.'

'Neither can I.' He seemed in a hurry to go. Reluctantly, she hung up.

Her spirits high with excitement, she rummaged in her case for something to wear, pulling the contents onto the carpet, where they remained in an untidy heap. She chose a duck-egg-blue sundress from Heidi Klein and wedge espadrilles. Her skin glistened with body oil and an abundance of Stella McCartney rose and amber eau de toilette, and she scrunched her hair dry so that it fell over her shoulders in thick curls. In spite of the creases on her dress she was pleased with her appearance. She waited for Anita to ring from downstairs. Looking at her watch, she had twenty minutes to kill. She went and stood at the window, looking out onto the sunny gardens below, smiling at the small birds that played merrily among the trees and gardenia bushes.

The sound of the doorbell made her jump. Expecting Anita, she strode over to open it. To her astonishment, Jack stood in the corridor like a shaggy brown bear, his mouth curled into a triumphant smile.

'I couldn't wait,' he said, taking her in with one greedy sweep of his eyes. Before she could reply, he pulled her into his arms, shuffled into the room, and closed the door behind him. 'My God, you smell delicious.' He buried his face in the crook of her neck and inhaled hungrily. Angelica laughed with delight, then gave in to the sensual feeling washing over her like a tide of warm honey. Her legs weakened and she felt her stomach lurch, as if plummeting from a great height.

He placed his lips on hers, and she felt his bristles scratch her chin, then the warm, wet sensation as he parted her lips with his tongue. She forgot about Anita and the lunch event as he unzipped her dress and ran his hands up her back and around to her breasts, caressing her nipples with his thumbs. She let out a low moan and threw her head back. Her dress floated down to her feet, where it remained like a blue pool around her ankles. Before her legs gave way, he lifted her in his arms and carried her to the bed. For once her mind was lost for words, neither condemning nor justifying her infidelity. It remained empty and detached, allowing a sensual wave to wash her into a transient paradise where it was just her and Jack, at liberty to love each other.

He took off his glasses and placed them on the bedside table. She laughed. 'Can you see me?'

His eyes looked bigger without them, the colour richer, with a shade of sage green making them almost gray. 'My sense of touch is more than enough to satisfy my need to savour you.' Gently, he brushed her hair off her face, tenderly kissing her forehead, her temples, her cheeks, and her chin, tracing her jawline with his tongue. While he played with her ear his hand stroked her belly and hips, moving down to her thighs and over her silky Calvin Klein panties. She closed her eyes, parted her legs, and invited him in with a wantonness that surprised her. With an ecstatic sigh she was swept over the final frontier.

A little later, the telephone brought them back to reality with a jolt. They lay entwined, their naked limbs thrown over each other casually, hearts slowly decelerating with their breathing. 'That's my call for lunch,' she whispered with a laugh. 'How do I look?'

'Glowing.' He pressed his lips to hers with a smile. 'Shame you have to go. I could do that all over again.'

'We have an hour this afternoon.' She sat up and picked up the telephone. 'I'll be down in a minute,' she told Anita.

'I can think of a lot of mischief we can get up to in one hour.'

'That was pretty good for twenty minutes.'

'Tonight, I'll take my time.'

She got up and hurried into the bathroom, picking up her dress on the way. When she saw her reflection, she laughed throatily. Her hair was wild, her cheeks raw, her mascara smudged beneath her eyes. She washed herself with a flannel, repaired her makeup, and sprayed another cloud of scent across her chest. When she emerged, Jack was already dressed in a biscuit-coloured suit with an open-necked blue shirt. 'You look smart,' she said, walking over to kiss him again. 'I was so shocked to see you, I didn't notice.'

'I've got a grand lunch to go to.'

'Oh?'

'There's a really hot speaker who's come all the way over from London just to talk to us.'

She narrowed her eyes. 'You're not coming to *my* talk, are you?'

'Believe me, there's only one hot speaker in the whole of Johannesburg.'

'You can't!'

'Why not?'

'There isn't room for you. It's fully booked.'

'I know. I must have been the last person to get a ticket.'

'How?'

He shrugged. 'I'm your cousin.'

'My cousin?' She looked incredulous.

'They have to make space for family.'

'You're going to distract me.'

'I hope so. I'd be very put out if I'd gone to all that trouble not to have any effect at all.'

'Now I'm really nervous.'

'Don't be. I'm your biggest fan, and besides, I've read *The Silk Serpent,* which is more than can be said for the rest of the guests downstairs.'

'They can buy their copies today.'

'And they will, when I tell them what a work of genius it is.' He pulled her into his arms and kissed her again.

Anita was waiting in the lobby downstairs. They walked out of the lift together as if it was the most natural thing in the world. 'This is Jack Meyer, my cousin,' said Angelica. Anita shook his hand, but she was more concerned with getting her author to the event on time.

'Everyone's here waiting. Let's go.' Angelica caught Jack's eye and grinned.

'Good luck,' he said. 'I'll put up my hand and ask the first question.'

'That would be really helpful,' said Anita. 'People are often a little shy.'

'Not in Johannesburg,' said Jack.

'Well, that's true. We're a pretty outspoken lot. But still, it'll be good to get the ball rolling.'

The dining room was full of eager-looking children with their parents and grandparents. Jack and Angelica were immediately separated. Anita led Angelica into the crowd to meet her fans, while Jack wandered over to the other side of the room, where he stood by the window, watching her. She felt his eyes upon her like the sun, and once or twice raised hers to lock comfortably into his gaze like a sunflower that automatically finds the light. *This is what it would be like if I had another life,* she thought, staring at the handsome man who, only moments ago, had been making love to her. She pulled away and turned her smile on the children, thanking them for coming out to meet her on a Sunday, shaking hands with their parents, who told her how they had read *The Caves of Cold Konard,* too, and couldn't put it down. All the while she was fizzing inside because Jack was there, in the same room, breathing the same air.

Chapter 21

'Joy is not in things; it is in us'

In Search of the Perfect Happiness

Later that afternoon, Angelica lay in Jack's arms on the hotel bed, her naked body pressed against him, her leg wedged comfortably between his. They moulded together perfectly, like intertwining branches of a gum tree. She didn't feel guilty. It felt so natural, and they were so far from her London life and the risk of getting caught. It wasn't hard to pretend she was single again.

Her talk had been a success. Jack had been true to his word and asked the first question. She had struggled to maintain her composure as the room had grown quiet and everyone had turned their attention to her. She was barely aware of what he asked, so distracted by his charisma that lit him up like some supernatural being – or perhaps it had been the sunlight streaming through the French doors behind him that had made it almost impossible to see him but in silhouette: his shaggy, unkempt hair framing his darkened face, his imposing stature that dwarfed the two women sitting on either side of him, the granular tone of his voice that resonated with the intimacy of their lovemaking. She was filled with gratitude that, for the moment at least, this leonine man belonged to her.

Marjory Millhaven, who had organized the event, clapped her hands exuberantly, announcing to everyone that Jack was the speaker's cousin. A shadow of anxiety had passed across his face as the entire room had strained to get a better look at him. A few young mothers had tittered appreciatively, and Angelica had hastily answered his question, moving swiftly on to the next. So pleased was she with her lunch that Marjory was reluctant to let Angelica go, insisting at every attempted departure that she stay another ten minutes. Aware that the clock was gnawing through her afternoon with Jack, she hastily signed more books, talked to each child who approached her, and finally extricated herself by promising to come back another year.

'You were a real pro today,' Jack said, running his fingers through her hair. 'As your cousin, I was very proud.'

'You were brave to come.'

'I know. South Africa is a small place. There was a chance I might have known someone, but I didn't.'

'What would you have done?'

'Pretended you were my cousin,' he replied nonchalantly, as if it really wasn't such a big deal.

'Does your wife know you're here?'

'Yes, and she knows I'm taking you out for dinner.'

Angelica was astonished. 'She doesn't mind?'

'You're my friend.'

'Do you sleep with all your friends?'

'Only you.' He kissed her forehead. 'I can't lie to her.'

'So you've told her how you feel about me?'

'No, she hasn't asked.'

'But if she did ask, what would you tell her?'

'She won't. She respects my boundaries.'

'Isn't she at all possessive?'

'We've been married twenty years. She knows me well enough to give me my freedom.'

'She sounds extraordinary. Do you offer her the same freedom?'

'She doesn't require it.' He sounded like Olivier. Were all men such hypocrites?

She sat up to challenge him. 'So it's all right for you to have an affair, but not for her?'

'She doesn't want one.'

'How do you know?'

'I know.'

'You have a very peculiar relationship.'

'You'll understand when you meet her. She's unique.'

Angelica had no desire to meet her. 'Are you sure it's a good idea?' she asked, seeking reassurance.

He pulled her back into his embrace and squeezed her. 'Are you crazy? You're coming to Rosenbosch whether you want to or not. Don't think about Anna.' Sensing her unease, he added: 'Live in the moment, Angelica. Leave my marriage to me.'

Angelica tried not to think about Anna as she sat in the car with Anita on the way to Pretoria. The traffic was heavy on the highway, shantytowns quivering in the heat and close enough for her to get a stirring sense of their poverty. Anita told her about the history of her country, what it was like living under apartheid, and the positive future she so passionately believed in. Angelica made all the right noises, half listening, half replaying the stolen hour she had enjoyed with Jack. She knew she should telephone Olivier, if only to put him out of his misery. Perhaps she had been unfair to treat him so coolly. But Joe would want to talk to her, and she dreaded hearing his voice, knowing it would drag her back to the reality she had so deliberately left behind. While she was removed from her family, she felt disconnected, as if she were living another woman's life.

Anita parked the car in the parking lot, bribing the attendant to watch it, as was the custom.

'What would happen if you didn't pay him?' Angelica asked, following her towards the restaurant.

'He'd probably steal it himself!' She laughed.

The restaurant was a log cabin. Angelica took a deep breath, bracing herself for another talk. But as she stepped into the foyer she was transported into the world of Cold Konard. The lights were dimmed and the walls decorated to look like the inside of a cave, hung with extravagant garlands of fake green weeds and purple and red crystals the size of footballs. She peered into the dining room, which had been cleared for what was obviously a children's tea party. About fifty children were running around in fancy dress – as Mart and Wort, Yarnies, Elrods, Mearkins, and Greasy Grouchoes.

She laughed with delight. 'This is how it must feel to be J. K. Rowling,' she said to Anita as an oversize Wort strode over to welcome her.

'I'm Heather Somerfield, or Wort,' she said, snorting in amusement at her effort to dress in character.

'You look terrific!' said Angelica, though the Wort she had invented was a five-foot elf, not a monumental egg. 'I'm so flattered by all the trouble you've gone to.'

'The children love you. They're so excited you're coming. And so are we. I wanted to dress up as a Mearkin, but they don't make green leotards in my size.'

'You look great as Wort.'

'Come and meet the children. There are some more convincing Worts in there.' She marched into the dining room and clapped her hands like a headmistress. 'Girls and boys, it gives me great pleasure to introduce Angelica Garner, the author of *The Caves of Cold Konard*.' The squeals petered out as the children stopped their games and stared at her shyly. Angelica wished she had come in costume. It was clear that

the talk she had planned for a ladies' reading group would not
be appropriate here. She'd lose their attention in the first
sentence, and it would be horribly embarrassing. 'So, Angelica,
what would you like to do?' Heather looked at her
expectantly.

Good question ... what indeed? Angelica thought
anxiously. She gazed back at the fifty pairs of painted eyes
and hesitated momentarily. They all looked so keen and
expectant, waiting for her to speak. But she couldn't talk
about inspiration to a group of small children who had all
made the effort to dress up. They required enchantment.
She peered through the fog in her mind, trying to find
something to grasp. Then, as if by magic, the fog lifted,
and her mind was clear.

'I want them all to sit around me,' she said excitedly. 'I
have a story to tell.'

'A chair, Megan, now, now,' instructed Heather to a
celery-thin Mearkin. Megan hurried over with a chair and
placed it in the middle of the room. Both women gently
pushed the children forwards. They shuffled towards her and
sat down in a semi-circle, nudging one another and whispering behind hands.

Angelica leaned forwards and lowered her voice dramatically. 'Have any of you heard of Troilers?' The children shook
their heads. The whispering ceased. 'Fat, slimy, ugly, greasy
Troilers, who inhabit the estuary where an oily black river
meets the sea. These Troilers, who live in holes in the banks
of the river, eat creatures of light called Dazzlings. Beautiful,
ethereal, weightless creatures, without whom the world
would descend into the hands of these evil Troilers. The
more Dazzlings they eat, the stronger and more powerful
they become and the darker the sky grows as, little by little,
all the light in the world is consumed. So the Dazzlings need
help, and who better than Conner and Tory Threadfellow of

London. Why them? you might ask. Especially as they are humans and the only way to get to this plane of existence, which is here, around us all the time, is in dreams. Well, let me enlighten you on how it is done and why two children – oh yes, they have to be children – are the only people in the whole world who have it in their power to restore the Dazzlings and their light . . .'

The children stared unblinking as Angelica wove the tale she had conceived in Norfolk. She was astonished at how fluidly her ideas came to her and how clearly she saw them, like gazing through a limpid pond into a magical world below. It was as if it had always been there, only before the water had been cloudy.

Heather and Megan sat drinking tea at a round table, as enraptured as the children. Anita caught her eye and shook her head, incredulous that she was capable of weaving such a tale off the cuff. Angelica felt her imagination released at last and propelled into vibrant colour. Her spirits soared. The more the children responded, the more ideas came. She had her story. It was simple and so obvious, and yet her own apathy had prevented her from seeing it.

At the end the children remained seated, hoping for more. The celery Mearking and egg-shaped Wort thanked Angelica, and the whole room erupted into applause. She glanced around to find the doorway filled with restaurant staff and parents.

'What a wonderful story you have shared with us today,' said Heather, her cheeks rosy beneath the face paint. 'I hope that's a little taster for the next book?' She raised an eyebrow, and Angelica nodded. 'Oh good!' She clapped her hands again. 'We're very fortunate to have lots of copies of Angelica's new book, *The Silk Serpent,* which she has agreed to sign. And I'm glad to see some parents over there who have money to pay for them!' She snorted again and showed

Angelica to a table and chair in the corner that had been set up for her to sign books. 'Would you like a cup of tea?'

'I'd love one,' said Angelica, sitting down. She rummaged unsuccessfully in her bag for a pen.

'Megan? A cup of tea for Angelica, now now.'

Megan returned with a cup of tea and a pen, and Angelica signed books and chatted with the children. They had all lost their shyness and found a great deal to say. The party continued, and trays of sandwiches and pretty pastel cupcakes were brought in. Angelica sipped her tea, light-headed with all the compliments. She felt the warm glow of success and basked in it. The prospect of spending the night with Jack just added to the surreal charm of the day.

'So what are you going to do tonight?' Anita asked as they drove back towards the city. The evening light had mellowed into a soft, amber glow, settling over the buildings like a diaphanous veil.

'My cousin is taking me out for dinner.'

'Jack? He's very handsome. Is he married?'

'Yes. He has three children. They live on a vineyard in Franschhoek. I'm going to stay the weekend at the end of my tour.'

'Oh, that's where you're going. I knew you were off somewhere. You'll love Franschhoek; it's really beautiful.'

'I'm looking forward to it.' Once again she nudged Anna to the back of her mind.

'Do you ride?'

'It's been a while. But hopefully it's like riding a bicycle – you never forget.'

'I'm glad you're having time to see a bit of our countryside while you're here.'

'Oh, I couldn't just dip in and out, and family's family. I couldn't leave without spending time with Jack.'

Anita dropped her off outside the hotel, and she hurried up the steps, two at a time. A pair of uniformed doormen opened the doors, and she burst into the foyer, where Jack stood up to meet her. He dropped his newspaper on the coffee table and grinned broadly, striding towards her. She ran into his embrace without a care for who might be in the room. He kissed her ardently, enchanted by her enthusiasm.

'How did it go?'

'It was amazing. All the children had dressed up as my characters, and they had decorated the restaurant like a big, slimy cave. They had gone to so much trouble.'

'Wow! You've hit the big time.'

'I'm a big fish in a teacup.'

'Better than no fish.'

'I'm a *hungry* fish.' She noticed he had changed out of his suit into a pair of jeans and a green polo shirt. 'Where are you staying?'

'Here.'

'No, I mean, where have you put your things?'

'Here.' He shrugged casually. 'I've taken a room here, too.'

'You've got it all planned, haven't you!'

'A dog needs to know where he's going to lay his head at night.'

'But you know you're laying it next to mine.'

'I wasn't sure you'd want me to.'

'After London?'

'Well, I wasn't going to take you for granted.'

'That's very gallant of you.'

'Of course. I've managed to entice you here – the last thing I want to do is scare you away.'

He led her into the street, where a taxi awaited them. The sun had dipped behind the buildings, leaving a gentle heat. The African driver got out to open the door, and they climbed in. Jack took her hand. The way he looked at her was almost bashful.

'I'm very happy you're here, Angelica Garner.'

'I'm happy to be here, Jack.'

'I never believed you'd come.'

'It was a fluke.'

'Or destiny.'

'Perhaps.'

'I can't really believe you've pulled it off. I dreamed of this, but never expected it to come true.'

'Dreams so often don't.'

'Have you made up with Olivier?'

'No, I'm still angry with him.' She shuffled closer. 'Let's not talk about Olivier, or Anna, or our children. Let's enjoy this short time we have together. I want to enjoy being this fabulous woman I am when I'm with you.'

'Do I make you feel fabulous?'

'Yes, I feel sensual, liberated, witty, sexy, *alive*. I feel bigger and better than I do when I'm me.'

'You're still *you,* my darling,' he said, laughing at her exuberance. 'You are all of those things. They have always been part of you. If you focus on your right arm hard enough, you forget that your left arm exists. That's all it is. You're focusing so hard on being Angelica that you've failed to notice the Sage beneath.'

'You've brought her out. Imagine how many people go through life without discovering all that they can be.'

'We all have the potential to be many things. But life might not necessarily give us the opportunity to play those parts.'

'I'm glad it's given me the opportunity to play *this* part, even if it's just for a week.'

'The secret to happiness is living in the moment.'

'I know,' she teased, rolling her eyes. 'It's all there is.'

★

Jack took her to a cosy little restaurant in the centre of town. It didn't matter if he bumped into someone he knew for he had already told his wife he was going to take her out for dinner. Angelica didn't understand their marriage. Surely, no self-respecting wife would allow her husband to fly to another city to take a woman out for dinner. She wondered what story he had concocted and how easily she had swallowed it.

They sat at a table in the corner. The restaurant was full of colour. In London women wore so much black; in Johannesburg they were like fine birds of paradise, in turquoises, oranges, and reds. She sipped her wine and gazed at him across the candlelight.

He smiled at her from behind his glasses, his eyes full of affection. 'Are you happy?'

She sighed with pleasure. 'Very.'

'Because you're living in the moment, at last.'

'I don't want it to end.'

'That's very female.'

'What? Wanting a moment to last forever? Don't you?'

'Yes. I love life. I want to live forever. I have a very strong feminine side.'

'Yes. I remember now. *A life without love is like a desert without flowers.*'

'You have a good memory.'

'For things I consider important.'

'I'm flattered.'

'My happiness is always marred with sorrow. I anticipate the end of it, or the loss of it. I wish I could really enjoy the moment without that fear.'

'How about if you just let go of that fear? After all, what will happen will happen, and your negative thoughts won't change that. You have a choice to enjoy dinner with me, or sit here worrying about leaving. The fact remains: you *will* have dinner with me. It *will* end. We *will* go home. The choice is yours as to whether you enjoy it or not.'

'But it's very human to crave continuity and reassurance. If someone could tell me that my children will reach old age in good health, I could enjoy them without this terrible fear of losing them or of their getting sick.'

'Look, life deals you a set of cards. You don't know what they are, but they determine what happens in your life: whether you get sick, knocked over by a car, face bereavement of some kind. Those things are here to teach us about ourselves, about love and compassion, and to test us so we grow into better human beings. So how do you maintain any control? By the way you *choose* to react. Think about it: a postman comes with a letter containing news. The fact is that the letter contains news. Whether it's good or bad depends on how you look at it.'

'But if it says my mother is dead?'

'Then your reaction would be one of sorrow . . .'

'Depends on how I view my mother.'

'You've answered your own question. It depends on how you feel about your mother. The news isn't inherently good or bad, it just *is*. It's your attachment to your mother that makes you happy or sad. The point is that the happiness of our lives depends on the happiness of our thoughts. Think positively, and life will be positive.'

'You should write a book on this. You're much more of a philosopher than me. I am totally in the dark.' She drained her glass. 'I thought I had life taped. But then I realized that life's trappings, life's luxuries, although they make living easier – and no one likes luxury more than me – they don't create happiness in themselves. It's the sunshine, the trees and flowers, beautiful scenes, music, the embrace of loved ones, that create happiness. They fill us up inside with something magical and intangible.'

'It's loving *yourself,* Sage, and giving love.' He reached across the table and took her hand. 'You ask a man who's survived a brush with death, and he will tell you that happiness is just in loving life and appreciating living. But most people take life for granted and crave more and more material things in the hope that a smarter house or a better car will fulfil them. You ask a woman who has lost a child and she will tell you that the only thing in the world that will make her happy is to hug her child again. Of course, we can't all live like that, but there are lessons to be learned from those people. Love is the only thing that can make us happy. Love is like a bright light that burns away resentment, fear, hate, and loneliness. Life is so precious. The tragedy is that people only realize that when they are on the point of losing it.'

He stared at her for a long moment, his face suddenly sad. She stared back, her stomach cramping with dread. He looked as if he was on the point of telling her something important but hesitated.

'Your fish, madam,' said the waiter, and the moment passed. Jack sat back to allow the waiter to place the dish in front of him, and to compose himself.

'That looks good,' he said, smiling. The sorrow had passed, like a rain cloud, leaving him sunny again. Angelica felt a sense of foreboding but couldn't detect from where it came.

Chapter 22

'The bend in the road is not the end of the road, unless you
fail to make the turn'

In Search of the Perfect Happiness

That night they made love again. A warm breeze slid in
through the open window like a silk ribbon caressing her skin,
bringing with it the scent of gardenia from the garden below.
In the pale moonlight she was able to lose herself and her fear
as she and Jack feasted upon each other. She could focus on
the sensual pleasure of his touch and forget the look that had
passed across his face. She could dwell in the present because
that was all they had. But daylight soon flooded the room with
the eagerness of a new day crammed with possibilities, and
there was nothing they could do to hold it back. Her fears
returned with the sunshine, and her sense of loss engulfed her.

'I don't want you to go,' she whispered, pressing her sleepy
body against his. 'I've just found you.'

'I don't want to go, either. But you have to work. I can't
hang around all day.' He swept her hair away from her face
and kissed her temple. 'And I have work to do, too.'

'I can't live in the present, Jack. I can't do it. I think about
the future, and my fears overwhelm me.'

'You have to try. None of us knows the future. We might
think we do, but Fate holds the cards and we can't see them.'

'I know what's on the cards. I will return to London on Sunday and leave you here. I can't bear it.'

'But we will have a wonderful few days at Rosenbosch.'

'I want a lifetime of wonderful days.'

'We all want that.'

'Why do you have to live so far away?'

'Don't analyze everything, Sage. Let it go.'

He got up and opened the curtains, filling the untidy room with daylight. Her clothes lay strewn across the floor and over the chair, spilling out of her case like entrails. Since arriving in South Africa, she hadn't had time to catch her breath, let alone unpack. She watched him gaze at the gardens below and take a deep breath, as if he were inhaling the trees and bushes and flowers and birdsong. He stood with his back to her, his magnificent physique broad and tanned, except for the paler marks left by his swimming shorts. She wanted him to take her again and stretched out on the bed expectantly. He turned around and grinned.

'You're coming to Rosenbosch, and that's all I'm thinking about. One step at a time. If you look too far ahead, you lose the Now. I've been looking forward to Now for a very long time. Let's just live it.'

'Show me how.' She reached out and laughed as he climbed onto the end of the bed like a shaggy lion, burying his head in her stomach.

Then he was gone and she was alone in the shower, wondering how she was going to get through the next few days of events without Jack there to come back to. The room looked bigger without him filling it. The emptiness was as loud as the silence. She was happy to leave it and get on with her day. The sooner she began, the sooner she would finish and the sooner they'd be together again. Rosenbosch stood at the end of the week in a magical aura of light, like the Disney fairy-tale castle at the end of a dark tunnel. Without losing her focus, she'd slowly make her way towards it.

Anita waited for her in the foyer. They had a brunch at eleven, a literary lunch at one, and a book club tea at four. Angelica's heart sank at the prospect of having to be enthusiastic and gracious when all she wanted to do was curl up beneath the duvet and wait for the few Jackless days to be over. If she could just get through Monday and Tuesday in Johannesburg, Cape Town on Wednesday would be one giant step towards Thursday evening, when Jack would pick her up from the Mount Nelson Hotel and drive her to Franschhoek. She had done what she had promised herself she would never do: fallen in love.

She climbed into Anita's car and opened a bottle of water, staring blankly into the car park. At that moment her telephone buzzed with a message. While Anita organized her files in the backseat, Angelica stole a quick read. **I love everything about you, Sage. I'll call you tonight at eleven. X Dog Happily on *Your* Porch.** She smiled with gratitude that Jack had found his way into her life and injected it with such enchantment. His texts and telephone calls would carry her through to Thursday. Beyond that was just unthinkable.

However, there was one telephone call that she was unable to avoid. At midday, when they were en route to the literary lunch in Pretoria, Olivier called. 'Hi,' she said coolly.

He sounded nervous. 'Are you okay? You didn't call. I've been worried.'

'I'm fine. Just on my way to an event. All gone well so far.'

'*Bon*. Are you still angry with me?'

'I've just been run off my feet.'

'No, you're still angry. I understand. Will you accept my apology now you're on the other side of the world?'

'I'm not angry with you, and of course I accept your

apology. We all say things we don't mean. Let's forget it ever happened. How are the children?'

He answered in detail, which was uncharacteristic for Olivier. 'They're on great form. Joe got mentioned in dispatches for hard work. He was very pleased and showed me the newsletter himself. He's missing you. We all are. But he's not unhappy, so you don't need to worry. He's just counting the days for you to come home. Isabel has fallen out with Delfine, but there's nothing unusual about that. They seem to break up and make up ten times a day as far as I can see. She's made a paper caterpillar with Joe for the days you are away, and each day they tear off a segment. Every day I give them a treat. Yesterday I took them for tea at Patisserie Valerie. They loved it and ate those raspberry tarts. They made a terrible mess, but what the hell. They had a good time.'

'You must have left work early.'

'I'm happy to leave work early at the moment. There's not much to do except damage control, and there's no pleasure in that. I'm enjoying spending time with the children, actually. They are highly entertaining. Candace has asked us for the weekend, which is very kind of her and a great help to me, as I'm not very competent on my own, as you know.' Angelica felt a wave of compassion. He was making an effort to be a committed father.

'Give Candace my love. I'm very grateful to her for rescuing you. The children will have a great time in the country.'

'I'm going to take the morning off on Monday so I can pick you up from the airport.'

'You don't have to do that.'

'I know. I want to. I've had time to think and reflect. I'm not too proud to see the error of my ways and make a change. Sometimes it takes a little distance for us to realize how much we care.'

'Let's just forget the whole incident.'

'Yes, please.' He sounded relieved. 'So tell me, how have your events gone so far?'

While Angelica talked, Anita drove, trying to look like she wasn't listening. But once she hung up, Angelica felt she had to explain.

'We had a row before I left. My husband's very temperamental. I'm glad that he's apologized.'

'Ag, shame,' said Anita, her face crumpling with sympathy.

'No, it's not a shame at all. It's really quite an achievement. He's French and very proud.'

'Here we say "shame" when something is very sweet.'

Angelica laughed. 'Shame and robots. I should start putting together a little dictionary.'

'And your children?'

'They've made a paper caterpillar with segments for every day I'm away. Each day they tear a segment off.'

Anita grinned at her. 'Shame!'

'If you saw my husband in a temper, you wouldn't be so quick to say shame.'

'Sounds like he's missing you.'

'He is.'

'They're always the same. As soon as you're away and they have to run the household and look after the children, they stop taking you for granted.'

'He's full of appreciation.'

'At least you had your cousin here to look after you.'

Angelica contained her amusement by opening her telephone to text Candace. 'I know, if it wasn't for Jack, I wouldn't have been allowed to come at all.' She hesitated over the letters. Perhaps it would be a good idea to mention Jack and Anna and their invitation to Rosenbosch to Olivier the next time he called, just to cover herself. The way the grapevine worked in London there was no chance she'd manage a weekend there without its getting back somehow.

Dear Candace, thanx for having my lot for the weekend. You're a star. Olivier is so grateful! Missing you. All well out here. Beautiful weather – glorious! Catch up on my return. XX Angelica. A few minutes later, Candace replied. **Glad it's going so well. Can't wait to hear all about it. We're missing you here. Kate's latest crisis will have you in hysterics! Love, Candace X** She clearly couldn't resist adding a word of warning: **Be careful!**

Although Angelica was curious to know about Kate's latest drama, she didn't want to think about next Monday. She didn't want it all to be over. She wasn't ready for her old skin, and she certainly wasn't ready to see Candace and the mirror she held up to reflect her guilty conscience.

Sustained by Jack's texts and his late-night telephone calls, the week went faster than she had anticipated. She said good bye to Anita in Johannesburg and flew to Cape Town, where she was met by a rep called Joanna. As they drove towards the city, Angelica was horrified by the endless sea of shanty townships that seemed to lay siege to it. The heat shimmered off the corrugated iron roofs that gave pathetic shelter to the multicoloured boxes that people called home, and telephone poles rose into the air like masts of beleaguered ships after a terrible battle. She wasn't sure she could live in a country where such poverty was so visible and so overwhelming. Surely it would be impossible to find happiness in the shadow of such misery.

Angelica was relieved to leave the shantytowns behind for the immaculate, gleaming prettiness of the city. It was almost possible to forget that such ugliness existed as they drove up the palm tree-lined avenue to the Mount Nelson Hotel, settled in the shadow of the magnificent Table Mountain.

Angelica loved Cape Town on sight. The city smelled of freedom after the claustrophobic sense of fear in Johannesburg. Azure skies stretched out above the ocean, where gleaming white yachts and brightly coloured fishing boats bobbed about on the water, disturbed occasionally by sleek cruise liners and vast containerships bringing produce from all around the world. The rocky coastline reminded her of the French Riviera, and yet the differences were unmistakable. The sun blazed down upon the mixture of gabled Dutch architecture, noisy African markets, and cobbled streets resounding with the sound of the muezzins calling the faithful to worship. The delightful concoction of European, African, and Islamic influences gave the city a unique exuberance. It was hard to imagine an angry underbelly of poor Africans seething on its outskirts, as menacing as any outside Johannesburg.

She sat on the terrace of the Mount Nelson in the sunshine, inhaling the sweet scents of freshly cut grass and neat borders of bright flowers where fat bees buzzed contentedly among the lavender and roses. She drank Coca-Cola and sat comfortably back in her chair, her spirits buoyant now that she was on the final leg of her tour, with only a day and a half of back-to-back interviews before she would be released at last to spend time with Jack.

They lunched with a journalist from the *Mail & Guardian* newspaper, an eccentric woman with the steady, forbidding gaze of an exotic bird of prey. Angelica chatted happily about her impressions of South Africa and her desire to come back. The bird of prey tucked into her lunch, enchanted by Angelica's ebullience and charm. While Angelica felt her heart swell with love for Jack, she radiated love to all around her, and it was hard to finish the interviews, so happy were the journalists to bask in her luminosity. She felt love for everything and everyone, and, with her heart so charged, there was no room for fear.

They had a window of free time in the afternoon, and Joanna drove her to the graceful white beaches of Camps Bay. They motored up the long, palm-lined avenue that ran parallel to the sea and bought grenadilla ice cream from an exuberant African seller, shouting, 'Grenadilla lolly, make your life jolly.' The sea was freezing, and Angelica pulled her foot out with a surprised yelp.

In the evening, after an interview in town, Joanna took her up Table Mountain, where she stood in humble silence at the splendour of the view before her. All humanity lay below in miniature, from the myriad of ships in the bay to the elegant mansions in the wealthy suburbs. Wide sandy beaches, rocky slopes, towering skyscrapers, and the grim shantytowns shimmered beneath a cloud of dust. She stood in awe, feeling the wind on her face and the diminishing heat as the sun descended slowly below the horizon. Up there she felt small and insignificant, and yet she felt part of everything – as if she were made of air. She wished she were a bird so she could open her wings and fly on the breeze, high above her cares.

The following day she sat at the hotel giving interviews. After lunch they had a couple of hours to go shopping. Joanna drove her to a vast African market, where she wandered contentedly among the richly coloured fabrics, wooden carvings, and beaded jewellery. She chatted to the sellers, bought embroidered white pyjamas for her children and a beautiful game of Solitaire, whose base was carved out of dark wood and whose balls were made of many different types of crystal. She envisaged it sitting proudly in her sitting room and laughed at the thought of Joe and Isabel playing with the pieces and losing them under the sofas. The image of her children caused her heart to twist with longing.

Her last interview finished at four. She packed her suitcase, struggling to fit everything in and having to sit on top in order to zip it up. Finally, she waited in the lobby for Jack. Having put off telling Olivier about her weekend plans she realized that if she didn't do it now, it would be too late. So she called him on his mobile. It rang a few times. She mentally rehearsed what she was going to say, concentrating on making light of it. When he didn't answer, she was relieved to leave a message. 'Hi, darling. It's me. Just to say that I bumped into Jack Meyer and his wife Anna here in Cape Town. You remember him from Scarlet's dinner? Probably not. Anyhow, they've asked me for the weekend, which is really nice of them considering my Saturday afternoon event has been cancelled and I would have had to hang around here on my own. So I'll be on my mobile if you need me. Give my love to the children. Have a great time at Candace's and give her my love. My plane gets in at seven-thirty on Monday morning if you're still keen to come and pick me up. Totally understand if you're not. It's a schlep. Big kiss. 'Bye.' She hung up and winced. Had she gone on too much? Would he believe her? She ran over what she had just said, trying to remember it word for word, searching for any slip-ups. *Tant pis,* she thought. *What's said is said*. She hoped he wouldn't detect that she was lying.

While she waited, her thoughts turned to Anna. She had no desire to meet Jack's wife. She wished they could spend the weekend together alone, without the jealous glances of another woman who had more claim on him than she did. It would be easier, she thought, if Jack moaned about her, but he hadn't made even the smallest derogatory remark. He had made it clear that he loved his wife. He had also suggested that the two of them would get on very well. But Angelica had no intention of liking her. She was anxious about having to hide her feelings, having to skulk about, stealing moments while Anna was in another part of the house or perhaps in the garden. She hoped that Jack had made plans so that she didn't have to spend time with his wife.

When Jack finally strode into the lobby, her fears melted in the glow of his cheerful smile. Aware that she was in his town, she was careful not to throw herself at him like she had in Johannesburg, although her heart was ready to burst with joy. He bent down and embraced her affectionately, raising his eyes over his glasses to case the room for anyone who might know him.

'You all right, Sage?' he asked, his gaze softening. 'You look radiant.'

'I love Cape Town.'

'I knew you would.'

'Everyone is so friendly.'

'The sunshine makes everyone smile.'

'Do you think Londoners would smile more if we had sunshine all the time?'

'You don't need sunshine, Sage. It's already inside you.' She laughed and watched him pick up her case and walk outside. 'What have you got in here? The entire contents of the African market?'

'I bought some lovely things.'

'So I see.' He glanced at the necklace dangling over her breasts.

'Pretty, isn't it?' She grinned. 'How long to Rosenbosch?'

'Just over an hour.'

'So I have you all to myself for an hour?'

He smiled at her mischievously. 'We might have to stop en route. I don't think I can sit all the way to Franschhoek and not touch you.'

Jack put the suitcase in the back of the car and climbed in. Before driving off, he pulled her into his arms and kissed her.

'You're more beautiful than you were in Jo'burg,' he said, caressing her face with his eyes. 'Just the sight of you is enough to restore my spirits.'

'Did they need restoring?'

'They did,' he replied, nuzzling her. 'I can't wait to show you my home. And we'll be just in time for a sundowner at Sir Lowry's Pass.'

'That sounds enticing.'

'Oh, it is. I've brought a picnic. Tonight, the sunset will be more spectacular than ever.'

Chapter 23

'Keep your face to the sunshine and you cannot see the shadows'

In Search of the Perfect Happiness

They drove out of Cape Town, past the monumental panorama of rocks known as the Twelve Apostles, jutting sharply towards heaven. The dual carriageway cut through the vast, flat plain beneath a cornflower-blue sky. In the distance, velvety green hills rose to meet the horizon, where feathery clouds caressed their voluptuous curves as they moved swiftly on down the valley. They passed rich farmland, where the soil was red and the crops tall and golden, and vineyards with vines planted in neat rows giving the impression of thick fields of corduroy. Jack held Angelica's hand, glancing at her occasionally and smiling. The scenery was so dramatic and so vast that Angelica yearned to be part of it. How romantic to live surrounded by such beauty, all the time.

Finally, they arrived in Franschhoek. The name was written up on the hill ahead in big grey stones. Angelica felt her belly cramp with anxiety at the thought of meeting Anna. By now the sun was setting, turning the hills flamingo pink. Sensing her nervousness, Jack squeezed her hand.

'I want to take you up to watch the sunset before I show you Rosenbosch.'

She smiled at him gratefully. 'I'd love that.'

With the window down, she could smell the fertile soil and camphor trees. The air was warm on her face, the light soft and wistful on her skin. She gazed at the gleaming white houses and picket fences adorned with pink and white roses, the neatly mown lawns and pretty verandas, and loved Jack all the more because he was part of it.

He took a left turn and drove up a dusty track, leaving the town behind. The valley darkened around them, but the horizon blazed with liquid gold, setting the sky aflame. After a while he pulled over and they climbed out. He opened the boot and extracted a small green hamper. 'We can't watch the sunset without a drink. Follow me, I have the perfect spot for our sundowner.' Angelica hurried after him. 'We don't want to miss it.'

Up there on the hillside they were alone with the sound of roosting birds and crickets chirruping in the grass. They sat down, and Jack took out the bottle.

'One of ours,' he said proudly, showing her the label. 'A particularly good 1984 Chardonnay.'

Angelica laid out the glasses and Jack uncorked the bottle and poured. They sat in silence a moment, savouring the taste. Angelica felt the chill all the way down into her belly, followed by the pleasant lightness in her head. She felt the cramp slacken in her stomach and took a deep, satisfied breath.

'So what do you think, Sage?'

'Just as I expected: delicious,' she replied truthfully.

He was pleased, holding up his glass triumphantly. 'It's not bad. Not bad at all.'

She took another sip. In the distance the gold had darkened to a deep red, as if a giant furnace blazed just beyond the hills. Grey clouds hung heavy in the white sky; the valley was swathed in a shadow of dusky pink.

'I love it here, Sage. It fills me up inside in a way that nothing else can. I suppose I feel close to nature. Close to heaven.'

She took his hand, feeling a sense of melancholy wash over her. 'Why is it that beauty makes us think of heaven?'

'Perhaps it reminds us that the beauty of nature far exceeds anything that human beings are capable of creating. It makes us feel small and insignificant and in awe of a Higher Power.'

'Or perhaps it connects with the divine inside us, so on some deeper, unconscious level we feel part of it all. Maybe it simply triggers a long forgotten memory of where we all come from and for a moment we are gripped by a yearning to return home.'

'Whatever the reason, it makes us sad.'

'Because it's so fleeting.'

'Like life.'

She frowned, reminded suddenly of the cancer that had brought him so close to death. 'Which is why we have to live in the moment,' she said, smiling at him gently. 'I'm living in the moment right now, Jack. I'm not thinking of yesterday or dreaming of tomorrow. Right now I'm here on the hillside with you, among the birds and crickets, and I couldn't be happier.'

Jack took her wineglass and placed it on the grass with his, then drew her into his arms to kiss her. She lay against him and closed her eyes, relishing the sensation of his rough chin and warm lips. The spicy scent of his skin blended with the lime of his cologne – a smell that was becoming familiar to her. She fantasized that they were married, living in this stunning country, drinking their own wine, watching the sunset every evening and never growing tired of each other.

Finally, the furnace died away, leaving the grey clouds to hang snugly over the hills like blankets. It was twilight when they walked back down the hill. The magic was over, and

Angelica was left with the unsettling prospect of meeting Anna. They climbed back into the car and drove down the hill into Franschhoek.

'So what am I to expect?' she asked, staring ahead at the little flies caught in the headlights.

'She'll love you. You're just her type.'

'I'm sure you're wrong.' She glanced at him, but he didn't reply. 'So are your children going to be there, too?'

'No, only Lucy, our youngest. Sophie and Elizabeth are staying with friends in Cape Town.'

Angelica began to bite the skin around her thumbnail. 'I feel guilty, coming into your family like a cuckoo.'

He took her hand and squeezed it. 'Don't feel guilty, Sage.'

'I do. I mean, I'm going to meet your fifteen-year-old daughter. She'll shake hands and smile, not knowing that I've been sleeping with her father. It's so deceitful. It's not what I wanted.'

'It's not what I would choose, either. There's a lot about my life that I wouldn't choose. But there it is.'

She glanced at him and noticed his jaw tense. His anxiety made her feel a lot better. That was the first time he had implied that things weren't all well with Anna. *But how could they be?* she reflected. For if he were blissfully married, would he have room in his heart to fall in love with her? If she were blissfully married, would she have fallen in love with him? She gazed out the open window and tried tossing her fears into the darkness.

'Here we are.'

He turned the car into the driveway, a long, straight dust track overhung with an avenue of towering camphor trees. Ahead, the lights of the house blazed into the semi-darkness.

'Home sweet home,' she said, bracing herself.

The house was a pretty whitewashed building constructed in the mid-eighteenth century in the Dutch style, with dark green shutters and gables sealing the pitched roof at both ends. In the middle, above the front door, an elaborate gable framing the upper-storey window was the house's main feature. Big terracotta pots stood against the wall planted with what looked like fruit trees. Dogs began to bark as the car drew up in front.

'You have a lot of dogs,' said Angelica, her stomach as tight as a ball of elastic bands.

'We love dogs. Some are rescue animals, others we've bought, one or two have just joined us for a while because they like the food.' He turned off the engine. 'So what do you think?'

'It's really lovely, Jack. I can't wait to see it in daylight.'

'Tomorrow I'll give you a guided tour of the whole estate. We'll take the horses out and have a picnic lunch on the hill. You're going to love it so much, you won't want to go home.'

Angelica inhaled the exotic scent of camphor. 'I think I already do.'

Her attention was diverted by the front door opening to reveal a slight woman in floppy white trousers and a man's shirt, her brown hair tied casually in a loose ponytail. What struck her, though, was not her elegance but the warmth of her smile. It was the smile of a woman who knew nothing of her husband's infidelities and had swallowed his explanations without a single, questioning chew.

'Welcome!' she cried, almost bouncing down the steps to greet her. She was the same height as Angelica but half the size. A delicate woman with fine, chiselled features; a long aquiline nose; strong chin and jaw; and bright, twinkling eyes the colour of the grey clouds that Angelica had just seen from Sir Lowry's Pass. 'Jack has told me so much about you. I feel I know you already.'

Angelica was caught off guard. She allowed Anna to embrace her and couldn't help but smile back, albeit apologetically. 'It's so nice to be here, finally,' she replied. 'I've been looking forward to it all week.'

'Well, come on inside.'

Jack remained outside with the dogs, hauling her suitcase out of the car. Anna disappeared into the house. Angelica followed her over the polished wooden floorboards, past a round table adorned with a heavy brass pan of gardenia that filled the air with its sweet, sultry scent. The walls were off-white and quite bare but for a couple of large paintings of fruit set in heavy wooden frames. 'How was the sunset?' Anna asked.

Angelica tried to answer casually, but her mind was whirring with all sorts of questions. 'The most beautiful I have ever seen.'

'Sir Lowry's Pass is one of my favourite places in the world. I told Jack to take you, if you arrived in time. It's never the same. Sometimes the sky is pink, other times orange, gold, even purple. What was it tonight?'

'Molten gold.'

Her smile was almost triumphant. 'Good. So you saw it in all its glory. I'm so pleased.' Angelica searched for some hint of bitterness, however small or well disguised, but found none.

Anna led her upstairs, across the landing decorated with bookcases and into a large bedroom with tall old-fashioned windows such as one might see in English Tudor houses, divided into many smaller square panes. In the centre of the room stood a high four-poster bed, made of the same rich reddish-brown timber as the floorboards.

'This is a stunning room,' Angelica enthused, inhaling the smells typical of a house cooling down at the end of a hot day.

'I'm glad you like it. That bed's very comfortable. I've had guests who have failed to get up for breakfast because they don't want to get out of it. If you'd like breakfast in bed, just let me know.'

There were attractive lines around her mouth and eyes. She wasn't beautiful, but her face was arresting as her vibrant personality shone through. Angelica couldn't help but like her. She doubted there was a single person on the planet who didn't like her.

The sound of Jack's heaving her suitcase up the stairs made them both turn around. 'Here come the whole contents of the African market.' He laughed and lifted it onto the antique wooden chest at the end of the bed.

'I hope you came with an empty suitcase,' said Anna.

'I should have. I didn't expect to shop. I was meant to be worked like a donkey. I didn't think I'd have time.'

'Well, at least you brought a big case.'

'And there's a man in the house strong enough to carry it.'

'Only just,' said Jack. 'How about a drink on the terrace?'

He strode past them and descended the stairs. Anna followed lightly behind, and Angelica felt a wrench in her heart. They both belonged here; she didn't. She cursed herself for having the audacity to feel envious when it was she, not Anna, who was the impostor.

Outside, they sat on green gingham cushions at a table overlooking the gardens. The moon lit up a pagoda in the middle of a small, ornamental lake. White roses wound their way up the poles, and lilies floated on the water like pretty little boats. Beyond, the range of rocky mountains was silhouetted against the sky. The croaking of frogs and clamour of crickets were carried on a warm breeze, and jasmine scented the air beneath the awning. Anna had already laid the table for dinner and placed a vase of freshly cut roses in the centre. Angelica couldn't fail to notice her sense of style. Everything – from the black-and-white-tiled terrace to the chunky crockery decorated with painted green elephants – was touched by her self-assured good taste. She was one of those rare women blessed with flair: whatever she touched was rendered attractive, whether it was the way she decorated her house, the way she dressed, or a simple gift she might wrap for a friend, slipping a pretty butterfly under the ribbon. Angelica knew her type and admired her.

'I love your pagoda,' she said.

'That's my little space. It's where I meditate. My family know not to disturb me when I'm there.'

'You meditate?'

'Every morning and every evening. At sunrise and sunset, for an hour.'

'You have amazing self-discipline. I only manage once a week. I never find the time.'

'You have a busy London life. You write books, you have small children, you have a husband and a house to run. I didn't meditate for two hours a day when our children were little, more like twenty minutes, snatched at the end of the day and then with half an ear on the children in case they woke up and needed me. Try to find ten minutes at the beginning of your day, before you start working. Just a little time to go within yourself and find that quiet place. It's very restorative, and keeps you looking young.'

'Well, that's an incentive.'

'You wouldn't think I was nearly fifty, would you?'

'You're joking!' Anna didn't look older than forty.

'No, it's true. I can only put it down to meditation and trying to find serenity in my day-to-day life.'

Angelica looked across the table at Jack, who was pouring the wine. 'Anna should write the book on the quest for happiness.'

She laughed, and there was a sweet charm in the way her nose crinkled. 'So many books have been dedicated to that elusive subject. If I knew the secret to happiness, I'd have levitated into nirvana by now. But I'm here, very human and full of flaws.'

At that moment Lucy appeared from the sitting room with a scruffy dog in her arms. She was tall and pretty, with curly light brown hair and big brown eyes, like her father. 'Ah, Lucy,' said Jack. 'I want you to meet Angelica Garner, a friend of mine from London.'

The girl's eyes lit up. 'I love your books,' she said, extending her free hand.

'Who's that?' Angelica asked, nodding at the dog.

'This is Domino. He found his way into our garden – '

'And into Lucy's heart,' continued Anna.

'Come and join us,' said Jack.

'Do you mind if I don't? I've already eaten, and I want to do some more on my project.'

'What project is that?' Angelica asked.

'I'm doing a project on the Russian tsars for school.'

'That sounds interesting.'

'A lot of work.'

'Do you have to cover all of them?'

'Just the important ones.'

'Cherry-picking.'

'Yes.' Lucy laughed. 'I'd rather be reading your new book. I gather Daddy's already read it.' She raised her eyes to her father and grinned. 'When will you give it to me?'

'If I give it to you now, you'll never finish your project.' Jack's eyes were full of affection as he watched his daughter. '*The Silk Serpent* is your reward.'

She shrugged. 'Better get back to my laptop. Are you staying all weekend?'

'Leaving on Sunday.'

'Good, I'll see you tomorrow, then.' She kissed her parents and retreated inside.

'You have a beautiful daughter,' Angelica said to Anna.

'There's not a lot of me in her,' Anna replied. 'She's her father's daughter.'

'Lucky girl to be so tall.'

'She is lucky. They're all tall like Jack. It cannot be said that my husband hasn't improved my family gene pool.' Angelica noticed the way she gazed at her husband. There was something sad in it, wistful perhaps. His eyes slid away as if not wanting to see.

They drank wine, ate from a spread of salads, chicken, and bread, and talked about life. Angelica forgot to be jealous of Anna. It was as if she were a mythical enchantress blinding Angelica to her own fears and resentments. There she sat in her white linen shirt, her skin radiant and brown, her compassionate eyes glittering in the light of the hurricane lamps, smiling with a gentle peacefulness as if nothing bad or unpleasant in the world could touch her. When she looked at Angelica, she did so with affection, as if she were looking at her own daughter. Angelica wanted to feel antipathy. Anna stood between her and the man she loved, but she could find nothing but gratitude for the warm welcome, and the desire to hear her talk more.

When Anna disappeared into the house with the dishes, Angelica was left at the table with Jack. She lowered her voice and leaned towards him. 'Anna's a very special woman,' she said. She wasn't sure whether she was asking a provocative question or making a genuine statement.

But Jack smiled triumphantly. 'I told you you'd like her.'

'She's very wise.'

'Like you.'

'I'm not wise, Jack. If I was wise, I'd walk away from here right now and return to my husband and children.' She dared touch his hand across the table. 'Why do you want me, when you're married to such an amazing woman?'

'Don't compare yourself to Anna. I don't.'

'What does she think I'm doing here? Doesn't she suspect anything?'

'She doesn't have a possessive bone in her body.'

'So she knows.'

He shrugged. 'I don't know what she knows. But she likes you.'

'I can't imagine her disliking anyone.'

'Oh, she does, believe me. She can turn very frosty.'

'I think she sees the good in everyone.'

'I've seen her turn frosty if she feels her children are threatened, for example. She's not all sweetness and light.'

'You know, the most ridiculous thing is that I want her to like me. Yet here I am sleeping with her husband. It's awful. I'm a really bad person.' *Candace is right: I'm thinking only of myself and my right to happiness.*

'Don't let me hear you talk like that. I told you, leave my marriage to me. It's not your problem. If you want to feel guilty, then feel guilty about Olivier. Anna is *my* wife and *my* responsibility. Does she look unhappy to you?'

'No.'

'Then don't worry about her.'

'I didn't go into this considering your wife. I was only thinking about us. If I'd met Anna before, I'd never have entertained an affair. Never.'

He let go of her hand, sensing Anna returning from the kitchen with dessert. 'Then it's my good fortune that you are only meeting her now.' He grinned mischievously. 'When it's too late to back out.'

After dinner Jack played the piano in the sitting room. A cool breeze slipped in through the French doors, bringing with it the sweet scent of jasmine and damp grass. Anna and Angelica sat on the sofa drinking coffee, listening to the music, the dogs sleeping on the carpet at their feet. Jack played sad tunes that made Angelica's hair stand on end. His face was anguished, as if the music was coming directly from a tormented soul. He didn't play from a score but from memory, and he closed his eyes to allow the melody to transport him. Angelica was so enthralled she didn't notice Anna, wiping away tears, until he had finished. 'Now I'll play something happy,' he said, as if making a conscious effort not to look at his wife.

'Anything,' Angelica replied, feigning cheerfulness. 'Just don't ask me to sing.'

Later, when Angelica was in bed trying to sleep, she heard the doleful sound of the piano again. She didn't dare get up in case Anna was with him. She lay listening, carried on the notes to a dark and melancholy place where dreams were unfulfilled and wishes hung suspended in the air, never to be granted. She felt a heavy sense of loss and the wetness of tears on her pillow. She could fantasize as much as she liked, but she and Jack would never ride off into the sunset and live happily ever after. Her thoughts sprang back to her children and made her feel suddenly quite desolate. What was moving Jack to such sorrow? When she finally drifted off to sleep, she dreamed of him, a distant, misty face in the sky. The faster she ran, the farther away he drifted, until she cried out in her sleep and woke herself up in panic.

Chapter 24

'Expand your view beyond the ego's range'
In Search of the Perfect Happiness

The following morning Angelica was awoken by the excited clamour of birds in the plane trees outside her window. A dog barked in the distance, and guinea fowl exploded into a round of indignant complaint. She lay a while, relishing the foreign sounds, barely daring to believe that she was there at Rosenbosch. She climbed out of bed and crept across the squeaking floorboards to open the curtains. The sunshine tumbled into the room, and she squinted and threw an arm across her eyes. Blinded for a moment, she held on to the wall for balance. Then she tentatively opened her eyes.

The beauty of the view was breathtaking. The gardens glistened in the dawn light, beneath the bluest of skies. Towering pine trees and extravagant red flowering gum trees threw shadows onto the immaculately mown lawn, where white and blue hydrangeas grew in the borders, intermingled with forget-me-nots. Beyond, the vineyard stretched out to the hills beneath an eerie layer of mist that lingered like smoke. She noticed a lone bird of prey circling high in the sky, silently watchful for signs of breakfast below. The pagoda stood in the tranquillity of the morning, in the middle of the ornamental lake. The surface of the water shimmered like a mirror, reflecting the perfection of the heavens above, and small, energetic birds fussed about the roses. She wondered whether Anna was in there meditating. She didn't think there was any place on earth as peaceful as that little pagoda.

Not wanting to miss a moment, or give herself time to dwell on her children, she dressed in a pair of white trousers and light plimsolls, throwing on a diaphanous floral shirt. She left her hair to fall about her shoulders and sprayed herself with scent. She had noticed that Anna wore no makeup. Her style was effortlessly glamourous, though she doubted Anna would ever use that word to describe herself. So she didn't bother with her usual morning ritual and skipped downstairs, bare-faced.

She went into the kitchen to find a jovial-looking African woman in a bright yellow headdress, piling up a tray with coffee and bread. 'Good morning.' Her smile was dazzling against the rich brown of her skin.

'Good morning. I'm Angelica.'

'Very nice to meet you, Miss Angelica. My name is Anxious. Master is out on the terrace if you want to join him.'

'Thank you. I will.'

'Would you like some coffee?'

'I'd love tea . . .'

'I have a pot of tea ready. Madam likes jasmine tea in the morning, but I have Earl Grey if you would prefer.' The tray looked heavy, but Anxious lifted it off the table with ease and bustled efficiently towards the terrace. Angelica followed her.

Jack was at the table reading a newspaper, surrounded by his dogs. When he saw her, he jumped to his feet.

'Good morning, Sage,' he said, taking her around the waist and kissing her cheek.

He smelled of shaving foam and lime cologne. His hair was damp and pushed off his forehead into a thick froth of unruly curls. Behind his glasses his eyes shone with enthusiasm, the crow's-feet searing through his temples like deep scars. He looked more handsome than ever.

She withdrew, afraid that his wife or daughter would notice their intimacy, and took a seat beside him. 'Where's Anna?'

'Gone off with Lucy to help with the harvest.'

'I thought she might be meditating in her pagoda.'

'She's done with that by six.'

'Don't you have to help, too?'

'Technically, yes. But as you're here I'm going to entertain you.'

'I'd be more than happy to pick grapes.'

'I know, but I want you to myself. Besides, they started hours ago and will be finished by half ten. If the grapes come in too warm, they're useless for good wine. You shall survey the harvest from the comfort of a pretty chestnut mare. Faezel and Nazaar are bringing them around at nine-thirty.'

'That sounds like heaven. I've dreamed of riding over the hills with you.'

'Anxious is making us a picnic, aren't you, Anxious?'

Anxious lifted her eyes over the teapot and grinned at him affectionately: 'Yes, Master.' She poured into Angelica's cup.

'I'm going to show Angelica the estate.'

'Tell her to wear cream: the sun is very hot, and she is very pale.'

'You'd better do as Anxious says,' he teased, watching her big body vibrate with a chuckle. 'I've done as Anxious says for the past thirty-five years, haven't I, Anxious?'

She shrugged. 'Some of the time. Most of the time, no.'

'When will the picnic be ready?'

'Just now, Master.' She put the teapot down and went to fetch it.

'She's a real character. I love her like my own mother.'

Angelica sipped her tea and helped herself to toast. Across

the garden she could see a couple of dark-skinned men working in the borders, their heads protected by white hats. The sound of their chatter floated across the lawn with the twittering of birds.

'It's so beautiful here, Jack. I don't ever want to leave. I hate to think of returning to our winter: the short, bleak days; the cold, damp air; the bare trees and borders of dead flowers. Here it's so lush and fragrant. The light is so bright, the sky so blue, the green greener than I have ever seen it. Everything is an extravagance of colour and scent. Even you look browner and glossier out here.'

He took her hand. 'I'm so happy it's touched you like it touches me. I love this place more than any other. When I die, my ashes will be scattered beneath those hills.'

'A fine resting place.'

'I'll never leave.'

She looked alarmed. 'You'll come back to London soon, I hope.'

'If you're there, then I'll devise a good excuse.' He looked at her fondly, but his smile faltered.

'I'm looking forward to riding out. I haven't ridden a horse in years.'

'Don't worry, Fennella is very placid. She'll look after you. And so will I!'

At nine-thirty two men appeared with the horses. Jack's was a fit-looking grey mare, with the legs of a racehorse, while Angelica's was smaller and sturdier, with a gentle face and soft brown eyes. She approached Fennella and stroked the white blaze down the centre of her nose; the mare nodded with pleasure, snorting through dilated nostrils.

'She likes me,' said Angelica, patting her thick neck.

'She's a good girl,' said Faezel.

'Just the sort of horse I need.'

Jack took her foot and lifted her into the saddle. 'How does it feel up there?'

'Oh yes, it's all coming back to me now.'

'All right?'

'Yes. Lovely view.'

She took the reins and tried to remember what to do with them. Jack swung into the saddle with the artlessness of a man who has spent most of his life on a horse. He thanked the boys, then trotted up to the terrace, where Anxious stood with the picnic basket. He heaved it behind the saddle, then tied it securely in a specially tailored harness. 'Thanks, Anxious. We're all set. See you later.'

'I'm glad your friend is wearing a hat. That skin is like an orchid.'

'Anxious wants to be reassured that you put on sun cream.'

'Of course,' Angelica shouted back.

'Does she know how to ride?'

'If she doesn't, she will by sunset.' He chuckled as Anxious shook her head disapprovingly, and cantered back to Angelica, who hadn't yet dared move. 'Let's go.'

Tentatively, she gave the horse a squeeze. She needn't have bothered. Fennella knew to walk alongside Jack's horse, Artemis.

'You know Franschhoek was once known as Olifantshoek, Elephant's Corner, because, being bordered on three sides by mountains, the valley was ideal for elephants to raise their young. They liked the isolation.'

'Are there any elephants here now?'

'No, but we have loads of other wildlife. We might see some steenbok, and of course there are plenty of birds where we're going.'

They made their way up a dusty track, alongside a thicket of pine trees. The vineyard stretched out lush and luxuriant, and in the distance they could see the grape pickers among the vines like giant bees, the buzz of their chatter rising into the still air.

'All this is yours?'

'All mine,' he replied proudly. 'Before me it belonged to my father and before him to my grandfather, who bought it as a young man.'

'Is your father still alive?'

'No, he died when I was a teenager.'

'It can't be easy growing up without your father.'

'I still miss him. He was a wonderful man.'

'And your mother?'

'She lives in Denmark. She tried to make us all leave with her, but I don't hold the same fear of the place as she does.'

'She fears it? Why?'

'South Africa is very troubled. You know that. Crime is rife. It's not a safe country to live in any more. But we've been lucky.'

'Your mother went far.'

'She's Danish, so she went home. She lives in the countryside, in a crumbling old farmhouse, with my brother and his wife and their children. They come out every year, and I've made the detour to see them on the way back from London. Wild horses wouldn't drag her here. Email has reduced the gap between us, and we speak a lot on the telephone.'

'So you have no family here any more, besides Anna and your daughters.'

'That's right. It's just us now.'

'How sad that so beautiful a place is marred by crime.'

'When you see the differences between the haves and the have-nots, it's really not at all surprising. But it's the price you have to pay to live in such glory.'

'It's a hive of activity over there,' she said as they approached.

'We're two weeks late in starting this year due to the unusually long winter rains.'

At the end of each row was a red or white rosebush, planted to reveal the first signs of disease before it hit the vines. A flurry of butterflies fluttered in the air, dropping onto the flowers to sip the nectar.

'Look, there's Lucy.'

Lucy looked up over the vine and waved vigorously. Beyond her, Anna was busy picking and chatting to the African women who came from nearby towns to help. The sound of singing drifted down the narrow avenues between the vines with the chuckling of black guinea fowl.

'What happens once the grapes are picked?'

'You're really interested?'

'Of course. I've never thought beyond my glass of Sauvignon.'

'Then I'll give you a tour before we head off into the hills.'

Angelica was enchanted by everything at Rosenbosch, from the beauty of the countryside to the functional charm of the winery. They tied the horses in the courtyard outside the farm buildings, designed in the same Dutch style as the main house, and Jack took her inside to show her the winemaker, stopping to chat with workers on the way. Finally, down in the dank darkness of the barrel cellar, they were alone.

Jack pulled her into his arms and kissed her hungrily, as if he had been waiting all morning for an opportunity, holding her close and inhaling her scent.

'You smell so good,' he breathed into her neck, and the warmth on her skin made her shiver. 'I really love you, Sage.'

He swept her hair off her face and gazed at her features as if committing them to memory. She allowed herself to be enveloped by his giant frame and nestled happily there, his words echoing in her ears and in her heart.

★

They rode up into the hills, where low shrubs and bushes, known as fynbos, grew in abundance, pollinated by birds. Jack pointed out the orange-breasted sunbird and the yellow-fronted bee-eater with its yellow wings and bright red throat. The mist had lifted, leaving the way open for the sun to blaze down ferociously. Angelica could feel it on her forearms and through her shirt. The horses walked at a steady pace, and she began to feel confident in the saddle. As they climbed higher a light breeze swept across her face, and she was grateful for its cooling fingers. After a while, they arrived at a small plateau, where a copse of tall pines gave shelter from the sun. They dismounted and led the horses into the shade.

'We'll set up our picnic here,' he said, lifting down the basket. 'Let's see what old Anxious has prepared for us.'

He laid out a green tartan rug and put the basket in the middle. Angelica sat down and fanned her face with her hat, pushing her sticky hair off her forehead. Jack opened the basket and took out a bottle of wine in a cooler. Anxious had packed a small bucket of ice, smoked salmon, lemon, bread, pâté, and salad. Everything was neatly wrapped and insulated with ice packs.

Hungrily, they tucked into their picnic. The wine was refreshing, mixed with ice, and there was grenadilla juice to quench their thirst.

'So how's your book going?'

'I've come up with a brilliant idea.'

'About the secret of happiness?'

'No. About greasy green Troilers.' She pulled a face. 'I don't think I'm qualified to write about happiness.'

'Sure you are.'

'I love exploring ideas, but I can't put them into any coherent order. They're scattered thoughts and arguments, like we've been having over the Internet. I'm still searching.'

'Keep a diary. Perhaps you could turn that into a book one day.'

She laughed. 'And risk someone's reading it?'

'Would Olivier really read your diary?'

'No, I don't think so. But things haven't been good between us recently, so he might be tempted were he to see it lying around.' She bit into her pâté sandwich. 'This is really good.'

'Homemade duck liver pâté.'

'You should sell it.'

'We do, only locally.'

'Quite industrious, aren't you?'

'We have to be resourceful. It's not easy at the moment.'

'Maybe *you* should write the book. You're much wiser than me.'

'I think we should write it together.'

'Now you're talking. You can do the serious stuff, and I'll do the fluffy stuff.'

'You're not fluffy, Sage.'

'You know what I mean. You're more intellectual than me.'

'I wouldn't say that. But we would make a good team, bouncing ideas off each other all the time.'

'Okay, what if we did write a book together, what would we call ourselves?'

He thought about it a moment, chewing on smoked salmon. 'D. O. Porch.'

She laughed. 'That's hilarious! What about Fido Porch?'

'Doesn't quite have the right ring to it.'

'No, you're right, it doesn't.'

'Let's think laterally.'

'I'm rather light-headed, I'm not sure I can think at all.'

'Go on. Wine loosens up the imagination.'

'You think?' She looked doubtful. 'Just makes me silly.'

'The sillier the better. We want something that's eye-catching.'

'Like Marmaduke Picnic?'

'Now you're on the right lines.'

'Marmalade Pickthistle. Migglethwaite Harp. Humpfink Danwit.'

'Now I see how you get all those crazy names for your characters. A few glasses of wine and you're at your most creative.' He helped himself to another slice of bread and spread it with pâté. 'Tomorrow we've asked some friends over from a neighbouring vineyard for a braai.'

'What's a braai?'

'A barbecue.'

Her face lit up. 'That's it! Something Braai.'

He nodded thoughtfully. 'I like Braai. It has an eccentric ring to it, doesn't it?'

'Braais are symbolic of happiness, because we all love our food.'

'What about the Something?'

'*I've* thought of Braai. *You* have to think of the Something.'

'All right. Leave it with me. I'll come up with something for Something.'

They finished lunch and drained the bottle. Lying on their backs, holding hands, they gazed up into the kaleidoscope of pine needles to the glimpses of bright blue sky above. The wind picked up. Known as the southeaster or Cape Doctor, it took the edge off the searing heat. Down in the valley Anna, Lucy, and the grape pickers would be enjoying lunch. Angelica was pleased to be alone in the quiet with Jack, where time seemed to stand still. Nothing else seemed to matter but Jack and her and this precious afternoon without commitments or cares. They could lie in the shade, talk about life and love, and pretend they had forever.

At five, they sat up and watched the sunset. Angelica

thought of Anna and how much she loved the changes of light and colour at the end of the day. It perplexed her to think that she had suggested Jack take her up to Sir Lowry's Pass the night before. It was as if she was pushing them together. She didn't seem to be watching out for stolen glances, hoping to catch them in a romantic tryst, willing them to trip up so that she could throw accusations as she had every right to do. She left them to their own devices, as if she didn't care what he did.

As the sun turned the sky pink and gold, Angelica hugged her knees, the bubbly feeling in her belly souring with melancholy.

'Have you had many lovers?'

He frowned at her. 'What kind of question is that?'

'Does Anna tolerate them?'

'My darling, what's inspired this line of thought?'

'I don't know. The sunset makes me think of her.'

'She'll be enjoying it down there with the workers.'

'You should be with her.'

'We have enjoyed thousands of sundowners together. I only have one more with you.'

She inhaled the fragrant air, filling her lungs before letting it out in a rush. 'Anna knows we're lovers, doesn't she?'

'If she does, she hasn't said anything.'

'But she suggested we watch the sunset last night. Isn't that behavior a little odd for a wife?'

'Anna's not like other wives. We make our own rules.'

'Are there others like me?'

He put his arm around her and pulled her towards him. 'Don't be silly. There's no one else like you.'

'Really? Scarlet suggested you had a lover in Clapham.'

He stared at her. 'She said what?'

'She saw you with a woman in Clapham.'

The horror evaporated. 'Ah, the lovely Mrs. Homer.'

'Who's Mrs Homer?'

'An old lady of eighty. Scarlet needs her eyes tested. You don't need to be jealous of Mrs Homer.' He placed his lips on her temple and left them there for a long while. 'You don't need to be jealous of anybody.'

'Not even of Anna.'

He sighed. She sensed he was deliberating how to respond. Finally, he pulled away and gazed at the hills on the other side of the valley.

'Look, she's her own person. She's a free spirit. She doesn't own me, and I don't own her. We love each other, which is a choice we make, not conditions imposed on us by an institution, and how we choose to love each other is our own business and no one else's. We conduct ourselves in a manner that respects the other. She doesn't judge me, and I don't judge her. We're friends and soul mates. But the way I feel about you is different from the way I feel about anybody in the world. You have to trust me.'

She leaned her head against his shoulder and let the amber light warm her face. 'I do trust you, Jack,' she said. But still something wasn't quite right. There was something he wasn't telling her.

Chapter 25

'When you love unconditionally, there is nothing to forgive'
In Search of the Perfect Happiness

That evening, they had dinner on the terrace with Lucy, Anna, and a friend of Lucy's called Fiona. Anna was lively, despite having toiled all morning in the fields with the grape pickers. Her eyes were bright, her smile uninhibited. Angelica watched her closely, trying to decipher her. But she seemed to have no side, and she certainly didn't seem to be hiding anything.

In the middle of dinner the telephone rang, and Anxious came onto the terrace to tell Angelica that her husband was on the line from London. Angelica was brought back to reality with a jolt. Her first thoughts were for her children, and her chest compressed with fear. Why on earth would Olivier be calling her at Rosenbosch? How had he got the number? It must surely be an emergency. She hurried after Anxious into the sitting room.

'Hello, Olivier?' She could barely restrain her impatience.

'Hi, darling? How are you?' His casual voice dispelled her anxiety.

'Is everything all right?'

'Everything's fine. I tried to call you on your mobile, but it's always switched off. As you didn't call me back, I got the Meyers' number from Scarlet.'

'You had me so worried. I thought something terrible had happened to the children.'

He laughed. 'They're here. They want to say hello.' Angelica's eyes brimmed with tears. She felt the familiar pull in her chest and swallowed hard. 'I'll pass you over. They're really missing you.'

Angelica waited tensely as Olivier passed the telephone to Isabel. 'Hello, Mummy.'

'Hello, my darling. Are you having a nice time with Daddy?'

'I miss you.' Her voice was small, and Angelica felt the tears spill onto her cheeks.

'I miss you, too, darling. But I'm coming home on Monday. We can have tea together. Shall we buy a cake at Patisserie Valerie on the way home from school?'

'The raspberry ones with cream?' The thought of cake cheered her up as Angelica knew it would.

'Any cake you like.'

'I've painted you a picture.'

'I can't wait to see it.'

'Have you seen any animals?'

'Lots.'

'Elephants and lions?'

'Lots of birds.'

'Will you bring me back a bird?'

'There's a really pretty one called the orange-breasted sunbird. Sometimes they fly in a flock of thousands.'

'Can I have one for my birthday?'

'I'm not allowed to take them out of South Africa. But I've bought you some pretty things.'

'Do you want to speak to Joe?'

'Pass him on. I love you, darling.'

'Love you, too, Mummy.'

She wiped her cheeks with the back of her hand and waited

while Isabel dropped the telephone, picked it up, and handed it to Joe.

'Come home, Mummy.' Joe's voice was even more pathetic than Isabel's had been.

'I'm coming home on Monday.'

'Why can't you come home now?'

'Because I have to take a plane, darling.'

'Will you sleep on the plane?'

'Yes, for a whole night. Has Daddy been looking after you well?'

'He takes us to Patisserie Valerie.'

'That's nice.'

'But I want you to come home, because you're my best friend in the whole world.'

'I miss the Full Joe.'

'I'm empty.'

'I'll be home on Monday to give you a great big cuddle and fill you up. You only have three more segments on your caterpillar, don't you?'

'We tear one off tonight before we go to bed.'

'Then you'll only have two left.'

'Yes. One more, then you come home.'

'And give you the Full Mummy.'

'Yes.'

'I love you, darling. Will you pass me back to Daddy now?'

Joe kissed the telephone. His breathing was so close to the receiver that Angelica could almost touch him. 'I love you in my heart,' he said, before passing her back to Olivier.

Angelica could barely speak for the ball of emotion lodged in her throat. The longing to hold her children was visceral. For a moment she came to her senses. What was she doing out there with Jack, when her children were in London, needing her?

'So how's it going out there?' Olivier's voice reminded her of the old life she wasn't sure she wanted any more.

'It's been a whirlwind,' she croaked.

'I bet the Meyers' vineyard is really beautiful.'

'It is. It's the most beautiful place I think I've ever been to. The sunsets are just magical.'

'We miss you, Angelica. *I* miss you.'

Something inside her cramped with fear. The echo of the children in the background made her want to hurry home with her guilty tail tucked between her legs in remorse, like a disgraced dog.

'I miss you, too,' she replied automatically. But she didn't miss him at all; she was envisaging her children in South Africa where they could run wild like the steenboks of the veld.

She hung up and sat a while on the sofa, the image of Joe and Isabel playing among the vines burning a hole in her imagination. It was there that Jack found her.

'Is everything all right?' he asked, sitting beside her. She looked up, and a shadow of concern darkened his face as he registered her drying tears. 'What's happened, Angelica?'

'Nothing. He just had me worried, that's all.'

'The children are fine?'

'Yes. Everything's fine. I didn't expect him to call me here. He got your number from Scarlet. I truly thought something dreadful had happened. He frightened the life out of me.' She placed a hand across her pounding heart.

'Do you want a drink?'

'Or two?'

He put his arm around her and pulled her close. 'You'll see them on Monday.'

'I know.' She lowered her voice. 'That's what terrifies me, Jack. I want to see my children, but I don't want Monday to come. I want to stay here with you.'

'Don't think about Monday, my darling. It's still a long way off, and we still have many hours together.' He stood up and offered her his hand.

She took it, rising to her feet. 'I want you *and* my children, Jack.'

'I know.' He squeezed her hand reassuringly. 'Come on, let's finish dinner, then we can sit in the pagoda and look at the stars.'

Angelica felt she had to explain her tearstained face, so she repeated what she had told Jack about Joe and Isabel and how much she missed them.

'I hope I'll worry about them less when they're older.'

Anna smiled serenely. 'You worry about them more as they get older because the dangers get worse the more independent they become.'

'Oh, Mum!' Lucy complained. 'Come on, Fiona. I think it's a good time to leave.' The girls excused themselves and disappeared into the house.

Anna laughed. 'The trick is to worry about things where you have a certain degree of control, not about things over which you have no control at all.'

'I worry about *everything*,' said Angelica hopelessly.

'Worry is a negative emotion. It does nothing but eat away at you. If worry changes nothing except your state of mind, then it is better cast aside. Do you pray?'

'Yes. Mostly when things are bad.'

'That's okay. But you pray for your children?'

'Of course.'

'Then worry is like *negative* prayer. You're simply wrapping them in your dark thoughts. If you send them love, your thoughts reach them as light. Don't send them your fears, send them your love. Be constructive.'

'Do you really believe in the power of prayer?'

Angelica looked at Anna and Jack, who were holding each

other's gaze for a long moment; she felt the chill of an outcast. They shared an understanding with which she could never hope to compete.

'I believe in miracles,' Anna continued. 'But I also believe there are things in our lives that are set in stone, things we cannot change, even with the power of prayer.'

'Such as?'

'Death. When we have served our purpose, it is simply time to go home, whether we are young or old.'

'I fear losing my children, all the time,' Angelica confessed.

'So do I. But everything life throws at us is to teach us important lessons. We can't control what happens to us, but we can control how we react. The greatest freedom man has is choice.' Angelica looked at Jack. Now she knew where he got his ideas. 'Nietzsche said, "He who has a *why* to live can bear with almost any *how*."'

'Do you have a why?' Angelica asked.

'Yes. My life has purpose. There is purpose in everything life throws at me, good or bad. But no one can tell anyone else what their purpose is. Everyone must find it out for himself.'

Angelica wondered what Scarlet would make of this conversation and smiled inwardly at the thought of her cynical face and rolling eyes.

'Let's go and look at the stars,' said Jack, draining his glass.

'You go. I'm tired from picking all those grapes this morning. Tomorrow will be the same, so I think I'll go to bed early. I hope you don't mind.'

Angelica felt guilty that her spirits lifted at the thought of being left alone with Jack. 'Can I pick with you tomorrow?' she asked, getting up.

Anna looked pleased. 'Of course. More hands the better.'

'Then that is settled,' said Jack, pushing out his chair. 'We'll be up at dawn to pick. We'll have a braai here for lunch. Then I want to take Angelica into Stellenbosch.'

'Good idea,' Anna agreed.

'We can stop at Warwick on the way back for a sun-downer.'

'What's Warwick?'

'A beautiful vineyard about half an hour's drive from here.'

'Don't forget I'm taking Lucy into Cape Town tomorrow afternoon. We won't be back until late.' Anna embraced Angelica affectionately. 'No more worrying, okay?'

'I'll try.'

'Think positively. You won't help them by worrying about them. But you can help them by sending them positive thoughts of light and love.'

'Then that is what I'll try to do.'

'Good night. It's an early rise tomorrow, with the sun. You don't mind if I knock on your door to wake you?'

'Not at all. I want to join in. I've never picked grapes before.'

'Sleep well, then – and enjoy the stars from my little pagoda.' She smiled at her husband, a smile so loving that Angelica was left more confused than ever.

She walked down the garden with Jack and his dogs, cradling the cup of peppermint tea that Anxious had brought her. A bright moon threw long shadows across the lawn from behind the pine trees. Frogs croaked loudly from the lily pads, and crickets chirruped in the grass. The air was infused with the aromatic scent of damp soil and the heady perfume of gardenia and rose. They walked across the stepping-stones to the pretty white pagoda. In the centre was Anna's meditation mat. Around the edge was a sofa and four big, comfortable armchairs in navy and white ticking. They sat together on the sofa, and Angelica slipped off her shoes and curled her legs beneath her. Jack lay back, stretched out his long legs, and threw an arm behind Angelica, pulling her close.

'You get all your ideas from Anna, don't you?'

He feigned ignorance. 'What ideas?'

'Existential ones. Don't pretend not to know what I'm talking about. Either that or she's got her ideas from you.'

'Okay, so she's taught me a lot about life.'

'I thought it was something special that we shared.'

'It is.'

'Well, not exclusively.'

'Does it matter?'

'I suppose not.'

'I'm just as wise.'

She sighed. 'None of us is as wise as Anna.'

'You're ten years younger than her. When you're her age, you'll be just as wise.'

'I don't know. She was born wise, I suspect. Some people are. I'm just on a search.'

'We're searching together. Don't forget Somebody Braai – *In Search of the Perfect Happiness*. Our groundbreaking work in progress.'

'So what shall our first chapter be about?'

'The happiness of your life depends on the quality of your thoughts.' He kissed her hairline. 'When I think about you, I'm happy.'

She took his hand and wrapped it around hers. 'When I think about you, I'm happy, too.'

They watched the stars twinkling above the shadowy silhouette of the mountains, discussing their book with zeal. The dogs lay on Anna's mat, lulled to sleep by the low mono-tone of their voices and the warm night air. When they retreated inside to go to bed, they crept up the stairs like schoolchildren returning from a midnight adventure. Jack followed her into her bedroom and pressed her against the back of the door to kiss her. He didn't attempt to do anything more than that.

'You need to sleep. We have a big day tomorrow.'

'I wish we could curl up in bed together,' she whispered.

'So do I. But you wouldn't get much sleep.'

'I want you to make love to me again.'

'I will.' He kissed her nose. 'But not tonight.'

'It should be enough just to be near you. But it isn't.'

His smile was so tender, her stomach seemed to flip over. 'Just one more kiss, then I have to release you.'

Once Jack had gone, she undressed and brushed her teeth, humming contentedly. She resolved not to think about Monday. After all, it wasn't the end of the affair, just the end of the weekend. There would be many more. Their love would grow, and they'd cross the world to be together.

She slipped on her nightdress, feeling the sensual pleasure of the silk against her skin, and wished Jack was waiting for her in her bed, his arms outstretched. She went over to the window, where a sugary breeze swept gently through the gap between the curtains. She pulled them aside and leaned on the sill. The valley had a romantic allure, set in shadow beneath a luminous navy sky, glittering with stars. She listened to the crickets, the distant croaking of frogs, the secret scurrying of nocturnal creatures hiding in the undergrowth. Then she saw a figure lit up in the moonlight, walking across the lawn. It was Jack. She caught her breath. Where on earth was he going at this time of night, and why hadn't he asked her to go with him? He was alone, but for one of his dogs, who trotted along beside him. It was a strange time to walk the dog. She went to bed feeling uneasy.

It seemed like the middle of the night when Anna knocked on her door to wake her. She mumbled something incoherent and opened her heavy eyes. It was still dark. Reluctantly, she got up and staggered over to open the curtains. The lawn was haunted by the memory of Jack walking across it during the night, and she felt her insides twist with anxiety. Now a light mist hung in the valley, replacing the luminous night. The air was cool, dogs barked in the distance, the chatter of guinea fowl added to the dawn chorus. She sensed the vine-yard stirring to life with the smoke wafting up from the labourers' cottages. She dressed hastily and made her way downstairs, where Anxious had prepared a light breakfast on the terrace. She found Jack at the table. He didn't mention his nocturnal adventure, so she didn't, either, but she was relieved to find him in a happy mood. She dismissed her fears; there was nothing wrong with a man walking across his own lawn in the middle of the night if he felt so inspired. Perhaps he couldn't sleep. They ate quickly and headed out to the farm buildings as the first rays of dawn bled into the sky.

The air was charged with anticipation. The burly Afrikaans farm manager was barking instructions to the farmworkers as they prepared to head into the Sauvignon Blanc vineyards to pick the fruit. A bakkie drew up with a truckload of women and children from town to help with the picking, their sing-ing rising merrily out of the mist. Jack strode about, talking to the workers, taking the manager aside for a quick word, deriving pleasure from being busy. Angelica stood with Anna, Lucy, and Fiona, thrilled to be part of the scene.

The tractors started up, and they were all carted off into the fields as the sun began to rise. Angelica was given gloves, a pair of cutters, and a crate. Anna explained how to use them. Then they set to work side by side, chatting as the guinea fowl waddled up and down the aisles, pecking at the soil. It was strenuous work, but invigorating, and Angelica's spirit swelled with pleasure as the light expanded and flooded the valley.

When the crates were full, they carried them to the tractor, which rattled back down the track to the winery. By ten o'clock the mist had lifted and the sun blazed down unobstructed. Half an hour later they were called to a halt, the sun now too hot to carry on. Finished for the day, they returned to the farm for refreshments. A table was spread out in the shade with traditional Cape food: bobotie, breyani, ghema curry, and koeksisters, washed down with wine. Angelica mingled with the workers, chatting and laughing, asking questions about their lives and listening with interest to their answers.

Angelica and the girls swam in the swimming pool to cool off before lunch. The pool was concealed behind a hedge with a pretty white hut to change in. Sun loungers were set in a row on the paving stones, and Anxious appeared with grenadilla juice on ice. Angelica wallowed in the cool water, taking in the fruit trees and climbing roses, listening to the girls' light chatter and the twittering of birds. She felt stiff from riding the day before, and her arms ached in a pleasurable way from her morning's work.

Just before lunch, Kat and Dan Scott arrived from the neighbouring vineyard. Kat was athletic and blonde, with pale blue eyes and full pink lips that curled into an infectious smile. Her long legs stretched out slim and brown beneath a miniskirt, and her toenails were painted bubblegum pink. Her handsome husband was unable to take his eyes off her and grinned indulgently at everything she said. Jack cooked the braai beneath a shady plane tree, the dogs circling like greedy wolves in the hope of scraps. Anna held court in the pagoda as Kat and Dan told them about their honeymoon in Brazil, and Dan, never one to miss an opportunity to amuse, told stories against himself that had everyone holding their stomachs from laughing. Angelica remembered when she and Olivier had been so happy. She glanced at Jack and knew that *they* could be happy like that, were they ever given the chance. Was it beyond probability that one day they might end up together, holding hands and flaunting their love like Kat and Dan?

Kat turned to Angelica. 'Jack tells us you're going to Warwick this afternoon.'

'Yes, I hear it's beautiful.'

'Oh, it really is. It has a stunning view of Table Mountain. You must go for a sundowner.'

'It produces the most delicious wine,' said Dan knowledgeably. 'The Sauvignon Blanc is unique because of a special hybrid of peach tree planted by a horticulturist called Professor Black. They were the first variety to withstand the south-easter. After the professor's peaches were removed they planted the first Sauvignon Blanc. You can definitely taste peach in it. It has a unique bouquet.'

'Oh, and they have that gold cup that two people can drink out of at the same time.'

'Tell her the story,' Dan encouraged his wife.

Kat took Dan's hand and smiled at him fondly, stirred by a happy memory they shared. 'It's a lovely story. Once there was a beautiful maiden called Kunigunde, who fell in love with a young, ambitious goldsmith. She refused the hand of many rich suitors and finally confessed her secret love to her father, a powerful nobleman. He was so angry that he threw the young goldsmith into the dungeon. Kunigunde's heart was broken. She pined for him and began to fade away with grief. Finally, her father relented and told the goldsmith that if he could make a chalice from which two people could drink at the same time without spilling a single drop, he would be free to marry his daughter. Of course, he never believed such an invention was possible. But the goldsmith was inspired by love, and with love anything is possible. So he set about making this special cup. His fingers formed an exquisite skirt-shaped chalice, the like of which no one had ever seen before. At the top stood a model of his virtuous and beautiful Kunigunde, who, with upraised arms, held a small, movable cup. It was simple, yet ingenious. Two people could easily drink from it at the same time without spilling a single drop. The king was astonished but stood by his promise. No one was happier than the young couple, who earned his blessing to marry and lived happily ever after.' She gazed languidly at Dan. 'We've drunk from it, haven't we, Danny?'

'And not a drop was spilled,' he replied.

'Thank God! I imagine it's very bad luck if it does!'

'I can't wait to see it.' Angelica felt inspired by the story that showed how with love anything was possible.

'Shame your husband isn't here with you.'

Anna laughed lightly. 'Don't worry. I'll lend her mine.'

They all laughed with her, except for Angelica, who didn't know how to respond. She sipped her grenadilla and tried to hide her blushes behind her hair.

'And don't forget to toast good old Professor Black!' Dan added merrily.

Chapter 26

'The best way to predict the future is to invent it'
In Search of the Perfect Happiness

That afternoon Jack and Angelica drove to Stellenbosch. Jack parked the car, and they wandered up the harmonious streets of Cape Dutch houses, beneath avenues of leafy plane trees. The white buildings gleamed in the dazzling sunshine, beneath an uninterrupted cerulean sky. They stopped at a café, sitting at a small round table on the pavement in the shade of a green-and-white umbrella.

Their mood was buoyant after their morning in the fields. They chatted about their book, and Angelica bought a few more presents for Joe and Isabel. It hadn't occurred to her to buy anything for Olivier. At four they drove to Warwick Wine Estate for tea. Nestled beneath the shadow of Simonsberg Mountain, Warwick was a charming old vineyard in the Cape Dutch tradition.

They were met by James Dare, a laid-back Englishman with a hearty laugh and irrepressible sense of humour. They drank the famous Professor Black Sauvignon Blanc on the veranda as Jack and James discussed the quality of the grape. The sun threw a vibrant palette of reds and golds across Table Mountain, and fish eagles circled the dam in search of supper.

Before they departed, Angelica requested a drink out of the famous marriage cup.

'So you know the story?' said James.

'Kat Scott told me at lunch. It's a lovely tale.'

'I'll ask Belle to go and get it.' He called to his wife.

'Is it bad luck to drink with a man who is not my husband?'

'Not at all. It's not just a symbol of love and faithfulness, but of good luck, too.'

'Wonderful! We all need good luck,' she said.

'How long are you staying?'

'I leave tomorrow evening.' She pulled a face. 'Don't! I can't bear it. I've had such a magical time. South Africa is the most beautiful country I've ever been to. The countryside is spectacular. I've never seen such magnificent sunsets. If it wasn't for my children, I think I'd stay forever.' She avoided Jack's eye, although she felt his gaze as surely as if it were sunshine.

Belle brought out the marriage cup, a shiny chalice just as Kat had described.

'How very clever!' Angelica exclaimed, taking it so she could get a closer look.

The metal was intricately engraved and highly polished. She gave it to James, who turned the skirt upwards. 'Professor Black Sauvignon Blanc 2008 vintage,' he said, pouring. 'Right, Jack, you hold it towards you at an angle. Angelica, this is for you.' He poured a little into the movable cup. Angelica, dizzy from the wine she had already consumed, began to giggle nervously. She looked into Jack's brown eyes and put her lips to the cup. Without taking their eyes off each other, they both drank. She didn't know whether it was nerves or the alcohol, or the silent words she read behind his glasses, but she began to laugh, snorting through her nostrils so that her cup tipped and wine dribbled down her chin. This made her laugh all the more. Infected by her amusement, Jack and James joined in as Belle put her hands on her hips and shook her head.

'I hope you're not superstitious,' she said with a grin.

'What will be, will be,' said Jack when he managed to control his mirth. 'Spilled wine won't make the slightest bit of difference.'

'Oh dear! I'm so sorry,' Angelica apologized, wiping her chin. 'Has that ever happened before?'

'No,' James replied, chuckling. 'Most people take it very seriously.'

'Luckily, you're not married,' said Belle. That made Angelica laugh all the more. *If only they knew,* she thought. *If I wasn't laughing so much, I'd cry.*

Jack and Angelica were still laughing in the car on the road back to Rosenbosch. It was now dark. The sky was almost purple, the valley lit by a round, pregnant moon. Stars shone bright as cut glass. They held hands, aware that this was their last night together.

'Anna won't be back until late.'

'What are you suggesting?'

'That we make love in the pagoda.'

'Anna's pagoda?'

'It's not hers. It's *ours.*'

'I'm not sure it's the place to commit adultery.'

He glanced at her, frowning. 'You leave tomorrow. I don't know when I'll see you again. I want to have you tonight.'

She smiled and squeezed his hand. 'We'll think of something.'

They drove down the avenue of camphor trees. The lights were on in the house. Jack looked at his watch. It was seven-thirty.

'I had hoped Anxious would have gone home by now,' he said.

'You can send her home, can't you?'

'Of course. I just want to be alone with you.'

They drew up and climbed out. He stood a moment, staring at the door, a frown lining his forehead.

'What's wrong?'

'I don't know. Nothing.' He shrugged off his doubts and opened the front door. 'Anxious!' The house was silent. He glanced at Angelica, his face suddenly pale.

'Are you all right?'

'I don't know. Get back into the car.'

'I'm not leaving you alone.'

'Do as I say.'

But she followed him through the house to the terrace. As he opened the kitchen door Angelica saw blood on the tiles and caught her breath in horror.

Before she could scream at the sight of the dead dogs, a gang of Africans swept onto them like birds of prey. They seemed to materialize from nowhere, wrapping grubby hands over their mouths and pointing guns to their temples. Jack didn't struggle, knowing they would have no compunction about shooting them, too. The men whispered urgently to one another in a language she didn't understand and marched them through the hall into the dining room. Angelica was so paralyzed with fear they had to drag her. There, in the corner, sat Anxious, her bright smile reduced to an unhappy line of fear. She raised her bloodshot eyes to Jack.

'I'm sorry, Master.' She began to cry.

'It's not your fault, Anxious. Angelica, don't struggle, and do everything they tell you to do. For God's sake, don't look at their faces.'

He proceeded to speak to them in their own language. Pleading for their lives, she assumed. Telling them to take everything but their futures. Even in that moment of deepest terror, Angelica couldn't help but be impressed.

They bound their hands behind their backs and their feet

together with ties they must have found in Jack's bedroom, then ordered them to sit on the floor beside the dining-room table, back to back.

'Those are my favorite ties,' he hissed at Angelica.

'God, Jack. How can you joke at a time like this?'

'Fear.'

'The dogs . . .'

'Don't.'

'Are they going to kill us?'

'Not if we do as they say and remain calm.'

'I'm so frightened.'

'We're in this together, Angelica, and we'll come out of this together. I won't let them hurt you.' His voice was so full of conviction, she believed him.

A gang member with bulging black eyes knelt beside Jack. 'Where are your mobile phones?' he demanded in English. His breath smelled of spirits.

'In my shirt pocket,' Jack replied calmly. He delved into Jack's shirt and removed his phone.

'Where's the safe?'

'We don't have a safe.'

'You're lying.'

'There's cash in the study, top right drawer. We have nothing to hide.'

'Everyone has a safe.'

'We were robbed ten years ago. After that, we decided not to have a safe. Take what you want and go.'

Bulging Eyes hissed at another gang member standing by the door and ordered him to go to the study to find the money. Angelica was petrified. She thought of her children and how much they still needed her. *Remain calm, don't cry, hold it together for Joe and Isabel. They won't kill us. They'll take everything valuable and leave.*

Bulging Eyes leaned over Jack. 'We're going to tear your

house apart, and if we find a safe, I will personally cut your throat like an animal.'

Angelica was too shocked to cry. She felt as weak and vulnerable as a little bird. Was it naïve to pray for help? Was it possible that someone might have seen them enter and called the police? She closed her eyes and prayed.

'There's no safe,' Jack repeated.

Angelica opened her eyes and looked over at Anxious, the personification of her extraordinary name. She was somehow smaller than before, as if the air had been punched out of her. Her right cheek was beginning to bruise. Angelica sent a hasty prayer to God, requesting only that their lives be preserved. *I'm not ready to leave my children,* she pleaded. *Or Olivier. Oh, Olivier, what have I done? Please God, forgive me. I promise from now on I'll be good. Don't let them separate me from my children, I beg of you. Let us live. Please God, let us live.*

A moment later the man appeared with a cash box and spoke to Bulging Eyes, who grew red with fury. 'Is that all you have?' he spat. 'A few thousand dollars?'

'The rest is in a bank. We don't keep much cash in the house. There's silver in the pantry.'

Another man rushed in with Anna's jewellery box.

'There must be more than this!'

'My wife doesn't wear jewellery.'

Bulging Eyes turned his attention to Angelica and her bound hands hidden from view. He grabbed her arm, yanking it out from behind her back with such force she thought it would dislocate. 'All women like jewellery.' He clearly thought she was Jack's wife. He grabbed her fingers and noticed they were bare. She silently thanked Anita for making her hide her diamond rings in her wash bag, although, in the circumstances, she would happily give them up in exchange for their lives.

'I'm going to ask your wife where the safe is. If she doesn't tell me, I'm going to enjoy her.' He ran the barrel of his gun up her naked leg, hovering on her thigh. His grin was so lascivious she knew he meant it.

Her heart stalled, but she felt Jack's hot back against hers and was encouraged. 'There is no safe,' she repeated bravely.

Overcome with impatience, Bulging Eyes called out, 'Somebody!' Somebody appeared at once – a tall, lanky African with cheekbones as sharp as polished granite. Bulging Eyes ordered him to watch the prisoners while he disappeared into the hall. Somebody jiggled from one foot to another, pointing the gun at Jack.

'He's not going to find a safe that isn't there,' said Jack impatiently. 'Help will arrive at any minute. Why don't you take what you have and go before it's too late?'

'Sorry about the dogs,' Somebody replied. 'I like dogs.'

'Listen, Somebody. I don't care about money or possessions. They are replaceable. I only care about my family. If I had a safe, I'd open it for you and give you everything inside. You have to believe me.'

'The boss heard that you have a safe.'

'Then it's misinformation.'

Somebody shrugged. 'He'll kill you. He's killed before, many times. He enjoys it.'

Angelica closed her eyes, drowning in a sense of helplessness.

Bulging Eyes returned looking more livid than ever. In his hand he held a kettle. Kneeling down, he hissed into Jack's ear. 'If you don't tell me where you hide your money, I'm going to boil your penis.' He plugged the kettle into the wall and turned his bloodshot eyes to Angelica. 'Then I'm going to kill your wife like a pig.'

Angelica's head swam as she gazed into the abyss. 'Oh God!'

'Be calm!' Jack hissed. 'You are a sensible man. Why would I risk my life and that of my wife and servant for something as unimportant as money and jewellery? I've told you, there is no safe.'

He then began to talk in their language once again. A heated discussion followed as the kettle began to steam. Suddenly another man appeared in the door. A shout resounded from the front of the house like a bullet. Bulging Eyes stood up in alarm. He hurried into the hall a moment, then returned, his face taut with panic.

'Where are the keys to your car?'

'On the table in the hall. By the front door.' There was hope in Jack's voice. Angelica clung to it like a rock climber to a rope.

'I know you're a liar!' he accused. His face looked like a swollen bladder about to burst. Pointing the gun at Jack, he fired.

Angelica wasn't aware of the gang leaving the house, piling into Jack's car, and speeding down the drive. She heard Jack cry out, then saw the stream of blood making a pool around them. She froze in terror, her mind flooding with fear.

'Jack!' she cried, desperately trying to wriggle her hands out of the tie. 'Jack! Speak to me.' Jack began to laugh. 'Oh, Jack! Please don't die!' She shuffled around so that she could see him, all the while working on her hands.

'They shot me in the shoulder.'

'Are you in pain?'

'Not really.' He looked at the puddle. 'I'm ruining the rug.'

'You're going to be okay.'

Anxious whimpered in the corner.

'They cut the phone lines. No one will find us now,' she wailed.

Finally, Angelica's hands slipped through the tie. She didn't feel the pain as they were forced through the material. She released her legs and set about doing the same for Jack.

'Hold on, Jack. You're going to be fine. I'm right here.' From somewhere she found a strength she didn't know she had. 'We're going to get out of this, my darling. You're going to be fine.' She pulled off her shirt and wrapped it around the wound, pulling it tightly to stave the blood flow. 'I'm not going to let those bastards take you from me. I've just found you, and I intend to keep you.'

She got up, staggered over to Anxious, and untied her hands and feet.

'Go and get help, as quickly as you can!'

Angelica's voice was commanding, and Anxious gathered herself, grateful to be of use once more. She hurried out of the room, determined to raise the alarm.

Angelica ran into the kitchen, past the pile of slaughtered dogs, to the telephone. As Anxious had informed her, the line was dead. For a moment she slumped over the sideboard, defeated. The dead dogs lay like sodden coats, reminding her of the gravity of their predicament, and she gave in to a wave of helplessness. *This is not happening,* she thought, closing her eyes. But it *was* happening, and she had to be strong for Jack. Pulling herself together, she grabbed some tea towels and returned to the dining room. As she pressed the towels into Jack's shoulder, she noticed he had gone very pale.

'Hang on, Jack. You're going to be all right. Help is on its way.'

'I have something to tell you, Sage.'

'Nothing matters, darling. Don't waste your energy.'

'I'm dying.'

'You're not. You're going to be okay.'

'Listen to me, Angelica.' His tone was firm. She stopped

talking. He held her naked arm with a blood–soaked hand and stared into her eyes. 'I've been dying for years.'

Her stomach lurched with his constant reference to his own mortality. 'What are you talking about?'

'I have lung cancer, Angelica.'

Her hands began to tremble as she mopped his shoulder with a tea towel. 'I know. Scarlet told me. But you're better now.'

'No, I'm not.' He winced with pain as she put pressure on his torn flesh. 'It came back. There was nothing more the doctors could do for me. I'm dying, Angelica, whether I die of a bullet to my shoulder or from the cancer in my lungs. The truth of the matter is, I have very little time to live. That is why I wanted to live it fully.'

'It's not true!' She began to shake with frustration. 'I'm not going to listen to this! We need to get help! I'm not going to let you die.'

'It doesn't really matter one way or another. We've had fun, haven't we?'

'And we'll have more fun. More sundowners. More rides across the veld. Our lives are just beginning.'

But Jack shook his head forlornly. 'No, my darling Sage. My life is ending.'

'I won't believe you! I've dreamed of growing old with you. I've fantasized about leaving Olivier for you, bringing the children out here, starting afresh with the man I love. I've dreamed of sacrificing everything for you. Don't tell me you're dying. I won't believe you!'

'You must. I didn't want to tell you and spoil everything. But there's a very good chance, by the size of this pool of blood, that I might die at any minute. So I want you to know the truth: that you have kept me going these last few months. That without your love and laughter I would have sunk into depression as my life slowly ebbed away.'

She stopped attending his wound and slumped beside him. 'Are you telling me that all the while we've been together, you've known that you're dying?'

'Yes. I should have told you, but for my own selfish reasons, I couldn't. At first you were just another beautiful woman who captured my attention. But you are different from every other woman in the world.' He rested his head against hers. 'I love the way you make fun of yourself and the way you laugh. I love your vagueness and your vulnerability, and yet your intelligence shines out in spite of your lack of confidence. I love the way you challenge yourself and the way you write, allowing your heart to spill onto the page. I love the way you blush when I compliment you and the way you make love with such abandon. There's no one else like you, Sage. Before I knew what I was doing, you crawled beneath my skin and I realized I couldn't live without you. I thought I knew what love was, but I hadn't a clue until I loved you. You gave me the will to live. You made me feel strong enough to beat anything life threw at me, including my cancer. But not even your indomitable spirit could beat that.' He winced again as the pain seared through his body. 'I wasn't in London on business, but seeing a healer I hoped might save me.'

'Mrs Homer.'

'Scarlet's scarlet woman!' He chuckled weakly.

'Oh, Jack.'

'I was clutching at straws. I so want to live. I haven't done half the things I want to do.'

'You'll do all those things and more.'

'No, I won't. I won't live to take my daughters down the aisle. I won't watch them become mothers. I won't be there to support them when they fail, to knock the lights out of boyfriends who treat them badly. I won't ride with you across the veld and picnic at Sir Lowry's Pass and make love to you.

I just won't be here any more, and that is impossible to comprehend or accept.'

'And Anna?'

'My darling Anna . . . Every time I look into her eyes I see my own death reflected in them. I see her pity and her sorrow. When I look into yours, I see the man I always was. I see myself as you see me. If I had told you the truth, you would have looked at me in the same way that Anna looks at me. I couldn't bear that.'

'So, it *is* true.'

'I wish it wasn't.'

She fought back tears, determined not to let Jack see her cry. 'I don't want you to leave me, Jack. I've only just found you.'

'It is better to have loved and lost than never to have loved at all.' He smiled, knowing they would usually laugh at such a cliché.

'Better for whom?'

'I'm sorry, Sage.'

'Did you ever think about *me*?'

'I thought about you all the time. I wanted to tell you.'

'But what? You couldn't find the words?'

'The only words that matter are that I love you.'

'I'm not sure, Jack. The truth matters if we are to trust each other.' She waited for him to reply. When he didn't, she turned to look at him. His eyes were closed. 'Jack?'

Suddenly, the house was swarming with people: farm-workers, police, ambulance men, and Anna, ashen with terror, bending over her husband as he was carried out on a stretcher. Lucy was crying over her dead dog, being comforted by Anxious, now restored and keen to be of use. The farm-workers' wives handed around mugs of tea and biscuits. Angelica sat on the sofa in the sitting room with the chief of police, recounting what had happened, while he made his

way through a large plateful of shortbread. Now that it was all
over, she began to tremble with the aftershock, as cold as if it
were the middle of winter in spite of the blanket that had
been placed around her to protect her modesty. She suddenly
wanted more than anything to call Olivier. She longed for
home with a yearning so powerful it overwhelmed her.

Anna left Jack in the capable hands of the ambulance staff
and came back to the house. She looked small and frail, but
her face remained composed.

'Is he going to be okay?' Angelica asked apprehensively.
The chief of police went in search of another biscuit.

'He's lost a lot of blood, but he's going to live.'

Angelica bit her lip and began to cry. Anna sat beside her
and put her arms around her. 'But he's still going to die?' she
whispered into Anna's ear, clinging to her like a shipwrecked
sailor to a piece of driftwood.

'Yes. He's going to die.'

A vise tightened its grip on her sinking heart. 'I didn't
know.'

'I'm sorry.'

'How long has he got?'

'Not long. A few months. No one knows.'

'I feel such a fool.'

Anna pulled away and looked at Angelica with compassion. 'If you're a fool to love Jack, then so am I.'

'No, you're a good person, Anna. *I'm* bad.'

'My dear Angelica, you've made him so happy. There's
nothing bad in that, at least, not from my perspective.'

'It doesn't make you unhappy that I love him?'

'Why would it? There are many different ways to love, and
the human heart has an unlimited capacity. If that wasn't so,
you wouldn't have the space to love both your children, *and*
your husband, *and* Jack. But you do. You love them all. I
don't begrudge Jack for loving you, either. Even if he wasn't

sick I wouldn't hold him back. We don't own each other, Angelica. We just choose to be together while we live this life here on earth. I don't possess his heart. I have no right to. But since he is dying, he knows he has my blessing to live his last months, weeks, days, hours, as he chooses.'

'You are a truly exceptional woman, Anna.'

'I don't feel at all exceptional, but I do know that my love for Jack has made me a better human being. It's a good feeling to know that I love him enough to take pleasure from his happiness.'

'Olivier isn't anything like as generous spirited as you. If he knew about . . . well, he'd be furious.'

'The greatest measure for good and bad is not a book of laws. They differ from culture to culture. What is bad in one country is considered good in another. No, the best gauge is whether or not you are hurting someone else. Adultery is not a sin in my marriage, but it is in yours because Olivier would be deeply hurt by it. Therefore, it is not right.'

'I should call him.' Angelica felt contrite.

'Yes, you should.'

'I'll go upstairs and see if those bastards have taken my passport. I hid it in my wash bag with my rings.'

Angelica got up. Her legs felt unsteady. Anna accompanied her into the hall. Now that they were being honest with each other, she felt she could ask her anything. 'I saw Jack walking across the lawn in the middle of the night. Where was he going?'

'Jack doesn't like to sleep, Angelica. He fears that there is always a chance he might not wake up. So he walks. It makes him feel better.'

'I sensed something wasn't right. I just couldn't put my finger on what it was.'

'I see it in his eyes every time I look into them.' Angelica frowned at her. 'Fear, Angelica. I see his fear of dying, and it breaks my heart.'

'I didn't set out to fall in love with him, Anna.'

'I know. But you have a family who need you. You must go back to them.' Angelica nodded and made to leave, but Anna stopped her.

'One other thing,' she said, taking Angelica's hand.

'Yes?'

'Jack has had many lovers during our marriage, as I'm sure you know. But he's never lost his heart before. They've always come and gone with the seasons. But you?' She smiled kindly. 'You're beyond the seasons, Angelica, like the sun.'

PART THREE

Wisdom

Chapter 27

'Life is a celebration'

In Search of the Perfect Happiness

Angelica sat at the kitchen table in her house in Brunswick Gardens, hugging a mug of tea. It was raining, the clouds thick and grey like gruel. The trees were bare, twisted and gnarled in the cold. One or two people hurried past beneath umbrellas, their footsteps disappearing as they strode down the pavement towards the High Street. Olivier poured himself a cup of coffee.

Sunny went upstairs tactfully to tidy the children's bedrooms. Olivier had told her the terrible news about the robbery the night before, and she had taken the children to school that morning while Olivier had driven to the airport to meet his wife. He had never seen Angelica look so pale and thin. It was as if she hadn't eaten for the entire week – and Olivier, usually so imperturbable, had stayed up all night watching television, unable to sleep for worry.

Angelica had dreaded going home to the bleak winter weather, but now she embraced it. Those low hanging clouds and the light, persistent drizzle were as familiar to her as family. Heathrow had felt like home, the friendly English passport controllers like relatives. She had run into Olivier's arms and clung to him, hoping that if she pressed herself close enough there'd be no space for her adultery. He need never find out. Nothing would come between them to prize them apart.

He had asked about Jack on the way back in the car. 'He's going to live,' she had replied, then collapsed into violent sobs. How could she explain that while one wound healed, the other in his lungs would surely kill him? How could she explain the depth of her love and the degree of his betrayal? Would she have chosen to love him had she known he had only months to live? Would she have allowed herself to get so close only to lose him in the end? Had he really loved her at all?

She sipped her tea and felt better now that she was home. She had climbed back into her skin with haste and remorse, only to find that it no longer fit so snugly. It didn't matter. It felt familiar, and she was pleased to put it on again with her rings. She longed to hold her children, but knowing they were in the same city was good enough. Her old life was where she had left it, and nothing had changed but her heart, which no one could see.

She watched Olivier pour hot milk into his coffee. While she had focused on Jack, she had ignored the fact that Olivier wasn't only her husband, but her best friend, too. She had chosen not to see his good qualities and concentrated solely on the qualities that irritated her in order to justify her affair. He had apologized for their row about the coat, but she hadn't forgiven him: while she was still angry she felt entitled to Jack. The truth was that Olivier, in spite of his impatience, was funny and charming and affectionate. He was suffering at work, in the very centre of the crisis that was shaking the financial world, trying to hold it all together for her and the children, and she hadn't been there for him. She had shirked her responsibility to her family for a fleeting, dead-end affair. She stared into her tea, plagued with guilt.

'I think you need to talk to Candace,' said Olivier, sitting down at the table. She looked into his clear blue eyes and realized that she had forgotten how beautiful they were.

'Not yet, Olivier. I want to talk to *you*.'

He looked surprised, but she knew he was pleased. 'Do you know what I was thinking when I was tied up there in the dining room not knowing if I was going to live?'

'Joe and Isabel.'

'And you, Olivier.' Her eyes glittered. 'I felt remorse. I wished I had never said a hurtful word to you in our entire marriage. I wished I'd appreciated you, not grumbled about your imperfections. After all, I married you for those.'

'Did you?' He grinned, and she was reminded of the first time that smile had captivated her all those years ago in Paris. It hadn't changed; she had just grown used to it.

'Yes, because it's your imperfections that make you different from everyone else. Without them you wouldn't be you.'

'That's very sweet of you, but I'm not sure that's true.'

He took her hand across the table. It was smaller and smoother than Jack's. For a moment she longed for the rough, calloused hand of the rugged South African, but she had to put him behind her now. She belonged with Olivier. If she concentrated on him hard enough, would she forget Jack had ever existed?

'I have had time to think while you have been away, and certainly, last night, I did more thinking than ever. When you went to South Africa and we had had that fight, I worried I was losing you. But last night, I felt close to losing you in a different way. I just wanted you home, where you are safe. I love you, Angelica, but I also need you. I am nothing without you. I'm half a man. I know I am difficult, selfish, and demanding, but I am going to make a conscious effort to be a better husband and a better friend.'

'We'll both make an effort.'

Angelica lowered her eyes in shame. She hadn't even bothered to remember his birthday back in October. It would have passed like any other day had his mother not called at seven in the morning. Angelica had rushed to Gucci and bought him a jacket and a pair of brown lace-ups, and Kate had managed to book her a table for two at the Ivy.

He lifted her hand to his lips and kissed it. 'Before you call Candace, you'd better call your mother.'

Angelica looked at her husband in horror. 'You told her?'

'Of course. She's your mother. You could have been killed, Angelica. She has a right to know. Besides, I didn't know what state you'd be in once I got you home. Don't be angry. At least I fended her off. She threatened to drive down this morning. She's worried sick.'

'Sure she is.' Angelica chuckled cynically.

'Just call her.'

Angelica dialled Fenton Hall with a sinking heart. The last thing she needed was her mother fussing over her. It rang only twice before Angie picked it up and breathed down the line in a little-girl-lost tone of voice. 'Is that you, love?'

'Yes, it's me.'

'Thank the Lord you're safely home. My God, we've been worried about you. I'm coming down right away.'

'You don't need to.'

'I'm your mother, and I want to!'

'I'm fine. It was horrid, but it's over.'

'I'm coming. There's nothing you can do to stop me. Your father and I have been beside ourselves with worry. This is a wake-up call, as loud as any I've ever heard.'

'I promise you, I'm fine,' Angelica protested.

'But I'm not. I need to see you, love. Surely *you* understand a mother's need?'

Angelica did, indeed, understand a mother's need. Grudgingly, she relented. 'All right, I'll see you later, then.'

News travelled fast along the buzzing network of grapevines that crossed oceans. Anna had called Scarlet, who had called

Kate, who had called Letizia, who had called Candace, who had waited tactfully for Angelica to call her.

'Oh my God, Angelica, are you all right!' she exclaimed down the telephone. 'You don't know how happy I am to hear your voice!'

'Oh, Candace, you're going to say I told you so.'

'I promise I won't. I'm coming over right now. Oh, and the girls are coming over for lunch, but don't panic, we're bringing our own food.'

'Now, why doesn't that surprise me!'

She put down the telephone and hurried upstairs to take a quick shower. There was no point moping about. The sooner life got back to normal, the better. The thought of her friends brought on a strange craving, like homesickness – a longing for what was routine and familiar.

Olivier went to the office. Angelica cried in the shower. She thought of Jack in his hospital bed, and she cried for the cancer in his lungs and for the inevitability of his demise. She recalled the last thing he had said to her, that the only important words were that he loved her. So why did she doubt him? Then she cried with fury at his concealing the truth and taking his pleasure without any regard for her tender heart. Did he not once consider what impact his death might have on *her*? Was he just going to satisfy his own need for validation and then leave her adrift? Or didn't it matter, seeing that he'd be gone and no longer responsible for the lives destroyed?

Angelica was still in her bathrobe when Candace rang the bell. Sunny let her in, and Angelica called to her from the landing. The moment she saw Candace's concerned face she began to cry all over again.

'Honey, it's going to be all right,' said Candace, opening her arms. 'Hearts get broken, but they mend.' Candace was so tall, she hugged Angelica as if she were a child, then walked with her into the bedroom.

Angelica curled up against the pillows. Candace took off her Ralph Lauren tweed jacket and laid it carefully on the upholstered armchair in the corner. The room smelled of figs from the Dyptique candle Angelica had lit in the bathroom. The television was switched on to the Top 40 music videos. Candace took the control and turned it down, then kicked off her shoes and joined Angelica on the bed.

'Okay, so what happened out there?'

'I lied to you, Candace. I went out to South Africa with the intention of having an affair. I encouraged the row with Olivier to justify it. We met the moment I set foot in my hotel.' Angelica picked up the cord of her dressing gown and began to play with it like a cat's tail.

'Well, I know all that.' She laughed gently. 'I know *you*, silly. But you know what? You can teach a person knowledge, but you can't teach her wisdom. That can only come from experience.'

'Now I have the wisdom of an old woman.'

'You look like an old woman with all that crying.'

'I daren't look!'

'It doesn't matter. We'll sort you out before the girls get here.'

'I'm glad they're coming.'

'I thought you would be.'

She sighed. 'I just want things to go back to the way they were.'

'They can never do that, but you can learn to live with the experience.'

'I was so frightened.'

'Wait, you're getting ahead of yourself. So you met him in Johannesburg?'

'He was staying in the same hotel. We made love. It was perfect and heavenly, and I forgot about Olivier and the children . . .' She raised her eyes, ashamed. 'You'd be surprised how easy it is to forget yourself.'

'Go on.'

'He went back to his farm; I continued my events. We met again in Cape Town when he drove me to Rosenbosch.'

'His farm?'

'Yes, the most beautiful vineyard you have ever seen. Oh my God, Candace, it's like paradise.'

'I can imagine.'

'But first he took me up to this pass to watch the sunset. He'd brought wine, and we drank and laughed and watched the sky turn red and gold. It was amazing. Then we went to his house, and I met Anna, his wife, and she asked me about the sunset. She had told Jack to take me up there.'

'A little odd, didn't you think?'

'It gets even stranger. I got the feeling that she was purposely leaving Jack and me on our own, as if she knew we were having an affair and condoned it.'

'What's she like?'

'She's incredible. I liked her the moment I saw her. I didn't want to, but I couldn't help myself. She has an extraordinary charisma, as if she's a glowing lightbulb and I'm a fly.'

'Honey, you'd *never* be a fly!'

'A moth.'

'A butterfly.'

Angelica smiled and sniffed. 'A very small creature. There's no side to her. She is wholly good and kind and generous, and there's nothing she doesn't know about.'

'Where's the catch?'

'There *is* a catch.' Angelica tried to control her tears by blinking. 'But wait. We spent two magical days together, and Anna left us alone all the time. Then, on Saturday evening, we drove back from a neighbouring vineyard. Jack sensed something was wrong. But we were so determined to spend our last evening alone together that we marched in. Anxious wasn't there . . .'

'Anxious?'

'The maid.'

'She's really called that?'

'She really is.'

'I *love* it!'

'Poor Anxious. She was tied up and dumped in the dining room. They had slaughtered all the dogs. They were piled up there in the kitchen like skins. It was horrible. This gang of blacks descended on us. I thought we were dead. I was so scared. But Jack was very calm. They wanted to know where the safe was, and Jack kept telling them there wasn't one, but they didn't believe him. You know, one of them was called Somebody.'

'Wow! That's a cool name, too! Shame I've finished breeding.'

'He didn't really want to be there, you could tell. Anyway, the leader shot Jack on his way out, for no reason. Jack was bound and helpless, and he just shot him.'

'Is he going to be okay?'

'Yes. He bled a lot. Oh my God, the amount of blood. You wouldn't believe a person could bleed so much and live. But he is stable. Now for the catch.'

'Here, let me get you a tissue.'

'I don't have any.'

'Then loo roll will have to do.' Candace padded into the bathroom and came back with a whole roll. Angelica dabbed her eyes gratefully. 'So what's the catch?'

'Jack is dying of lung cancer.'

Candace's jaw swung open in astonishment. Even she couldn't have foreseen that. 'He's dying of cancer?'

'Yes. He told me as he bled onto the rug. He said it didn't matter one way or the other because he was going to die anyway.'

'Holy shit!' Candace shook her head. 'This is *really* heavy duty.'

'I know. I didn't believe him at first, but he insisted. He said he was sorry that he hadn't told me earlier, but he hadn't wanted to spoil things.'

'Hold on. He encouraged an affair *knowing* that he only had a limited time to live?' Now Candace was cross.

'Yes. He said I made him feel like the man he used to be, whereas his wife looked at him with pity.'

'Oh great! So he uses you to forget his illness?'

'I suppose so.'

'How *selfish* is that? I *told* you he was selfish. You know, if he had *once* considered you and your family, he would *never* have pursued you. I *knew* he was selfish right from the start.' When Candace got angry, her nostrils flared and she emphasized her words with verve, as if punching them out with her anger.

'I believe he loves me.'

'Of *course* he loves you! What isn't there to love? But he shouldn't have made you fall in love with *him*.'

'If I had listened to you that day in Starbucks, none of this would have happened.'

'And the girls would have nothing to talk about!' Candace laughed.

'That's not true. I imagine Kate has kept you all busy this past week.'

'And some!'

'Oh dear.'

'I'll let her fill you in. The last thing I want to do is steal her thunder, and besides, I'm not done yet.'

'Okay, so the last thing he said to me before he passed out was that the only important thing was that he loved me.'

'And you haven't spoken to him since?'

'No. But get this? Anna told me that she loves him enough to take pleasure from his happiness.'

'From his screwing around?'

'I wouldn't put it quite like that. She isn't possessive. She really isn't.'

'She's clearly not from this world.'

'I think you're right. She told me that he has had many affairs but that he's never lost his heart to anyone like he lost it to me.'

'Generous of her to share that with you.' Candace raised an eyebrow cynically.

'I'm not sure that he does though. I feel wretched and betrayed. I left yesterday evening on my scheduled flight without a word to him. I'd hidden my passport and rings in my wash bag.' She fingered her diamonds fondly.

'Clever you.'

'Only because the rep in Jo'burg told me to. Thank God for her.'

'I'd hate to think of those brutes running off with your beautiful diamonds.'

'So would I. I don't know what they ran off with. Not much, I suspect. South Africans don't keep large quantities of money and jewelry in the house for that very reason.'

'I don't know whether to admire Anna or mistrust her.'

'If you met her, you certainly wouldn't mistrust her. She's the real thing, I tell you.'

'So what are you going to do?'

'I'm hoping you're going to tell me.'

'You really want my advice?' She chuckled. 'I'm rather wary of giving it to you, after all you've been through.'

'No, I want you to tell me what is right. I'm ready to listen now.'

'Okay, if you're sure.'

'I am. I should have listened to you months ago.'

'You love him, that's obvious.'

'Yes, I do. But I feel hurt, and I don't want to risk losing Olivier or the children. I know I've been foolish and selfish, too. I'm definitely part of the "me" generation. I want to call him now . . . more than anything in the world. I want to make him better. But I know it's got to end.'

'Well, here's the deal. You write him a letter, and you tell him it's over. I don't think it would be wise to speak to him, considering he's in the hospital recovering from a bullet wound, and it'll be harder on you if you hear his voice. Then you go upstairs to your office and block his emails and delete his address from your system and his number from your telephone, and you make a conscious effort to send back any letters he writes to you and any emails that he manages to send you. Trust me, he'll try to find you.'

'This isn't going to be easy.'

'Of course it isn't. But it could be a whole lot worse. Think about the mess if Olivier found out.'

'Right, I'll do it.'

'You've got away with it, which I never thought you would.'

'My fingers have been burned.'

'Honey, your whole life could have gone up in flames! Now, we'd better tidy you up. If the girls see you looking like this, they'll think you've given up on life!'

Angelica put on a pair of skinny flare jeans from Gap and a cashmere sweater from Paul & Joe. She dried her hair and applied some makeup. Candace sat on the loo seat watching her.

'Phew, it *is* you after all. I wasn't quite sure.' They both laughed.

'You're a great friend, Candace.'

'Well, I hope so.'

'Joking apart. You've made me feel so much better about the whole thing.'

'You just needed to make sense of it . . . then deal with it.'

'I was so confused. I love him, and yet I feel so hurt.'

'And angry.'

'A little.'

'If it were me . . .' She sighed heavily and flared her nostrils. 'Well, it just *wouldn't* be.'

At one o'clock the girls arrived on her doorstep en masse. Even Kate was on time for once. Loaded with presents and bags of lunch, they marched into the house, embracing Angelica with such fervour one might have been forgiven for thinking she'd just risen from the dead.

'You're so pale!' Kate cried, studying her face to check her features were still in place. 'I want to hear every detail. Then I want to fill you in on *my* life, which couldn't get any stranger.'

'We've brought sushi,' said Scarlet, dumping her bag on the dining-room table.

'I'm ravenous,' said Letizia. 'Let's spread it out and tuck in.'

'Not before a glass of wine. I don't know about anyone else, but the sight of Angelica's white face has scared the life out of me.' Kate opened the fridge and pulled out a bottle of Chardonnay.

'I think Angelica needs a shot more than any of us,' said Scarlet, going to the cupboard and grabbing the glasses by their stems. Her jeans were so tight they could have been painted on. She stood on tiptoe in spite of her high-heeled black PVC boots, which gave her at least another three inches.

'Thank you all for coming,' said Angelica, laying the table.

'Are you crazy? They've been dying to come all morning,' Candace exclaimed.

'We've been so worried, darling,' said Letizia kindly. 'When Kate called me, having heard from Scarlet, I had to sit down. I mean, to have all those horrible men on top of you!'

'On top of me?'

Kate pulled a face. 'So I exaggerated a little,' she admitted sheepishly.

'They weren't on top of me. They tied me up and dumped me in the dining room. Besides that, they didn't touch me.'

'Oh! I'd have been offended,' Kate quipped. 'Just joking! Had any of them come anywhere near me, I would have died!'

'No, you wouldn't. The prospect of telling all your friends afterwards would have sustained you,' said Candace.

'It must have been a real nightmare,' said Scarlet, placing the maki rolls in neat lines on the serving dish.

Letizia had found a vase for the purple tulips she had brought and placed it in the centre of the table, taking a step back to admire her creation. 'Now, isn't this divine. Spring is just around the corner.' She tossed her glorious mane off her shoulder. 'But an early spring is in your dining room, darling.' Angelica thanked her.

'I bet it was stunning in Franschhoek,' said Scarlet.

'It was.'

'It's a crying shame there's all that poverty and homelessness,' mused Letizia. 'I mean, if it wasn't for the crime, which is beyond anything we have here, it would be the perfect place to live.'

'It's so easy to forget when you're there, in someone's home. I drove past shantytowns of such squalour, but the minute I was at the vineyard it was as if that squalour belonged to another country. Then it invaded their home, and I realized why people leave and start again on other continents.'

'I'd like to live in Italy,' said Kate brightly. 'In a magnificent palazzo.'

'Well, of course you would.' Letizia laughed.

Candace rolled her eyes. 'You'll have your moment, Kate. But right now the spotlight's on Angelica, and you know what? I think she deserves it.'

Chapter 28

'Vulnerability is your strength'

In Search of the Perfect Happiness

They all sat around the dining-room table, listening to Angelica recounting her adventure. She didn't get emotional this time, having processed the experience with Candace. Besides, none of the others knew about her affair. They finished the bottle of wine. It was only the prospect of having to pick up their children from school that prevented them from opening another. Kate insisted her baby enjoyed alcohol in spite of Candace trying to convince her otherwise. Finally, after they had devoured all the sushi and the gory details of dead dogs and bullet wounds, Kate's moment arrived.

'Go on, tell her,' said Candace.

'You mean, you haven't already?'

'Of course not. It's not my story to tell.'

'That never stopped anyone,' said Scarlet.

'What's happened?' Angelica asked, glancing at Kate's belly. At least the baby was still in the right place.

Kate said melodramatically, 'I've walked out on Pete once and for all.'

'You haven't!'

'I have. It took a lot of courage – '

'And a few drinks,' interrupted Candace.

'But I couldn't take his philandering anymore.'

'The Haggis is still in the picture?'

'Honey, she *is* the picture.'

'What about the baby?'

'It might not be his,' Kate conceded.

Candace shrugged and raised her eyebrows at Angelica. 'Still no name.'

'It's irrelevant. Pete is the father of all my children.'

'Unless you have any more,' Scarlet added.

'You never know,' said Kate with a smirk.

'So where are you living?'

'When I said I walked out on Pete, I didn't mean I *literally* walked out of the house. God forbid! I walked out of our *marriage*. *He* walked out of the house. He's camping at a friend's.'

'What about Betsy Pog?'

'That old harridan!' quipped Candace.

'At least we can say we both tried.'

'To be fair,' said Scarlet, 'you tried more than him.'

'Darling, he didn't try at all,' agreed Letizia.

'He's trying to win me back, but I've already moved on.' The secretive smile indicated that she literally had.

'Go on, Angelica, ask!' Candace demanded.

'Who is he?' she complied.

Kate's grin swallowed her entire face. 'He's, now wait for it . . . Count Edmondo Augustino Silviano di Napoli. And he comes with a beautiful palazzo overlooking the sea.'

'Are you sure he's not making it up?' Angelica asked.

'Sounds like he owns the whole of Naples.' Scarlet laughed.

'Counts are two a penny in Italy,' said Candace.

'He's the real thing,' Letizia insisted. 'I promise you.'

'It really doesn't matter,' Kate replied. 'He's gorgeous.'

'So what are you going to do about the Vera Wang wedding dress?'

'Maybe she'll make use of it in her palazzo,' said Candace.

Kate was appalled. 'If you think I'm going to hurry down the aisle with another man after all I've been through, you don't know me at all.'

'Such a waste of a beautiful dress!' Letizia sighed.

'I'll give a wedding dress party. Everyone has to come in their wedding dresses.'

'Honey, half the guests won't be able to get into their wedding dresses!' said Candace.

'They can have them let out,' said Kate.

'Why don't you put it in a box? You're young. I can't believe you're going to go through the rest of your life as a single woman.'

'Single no, unmarried yes. I'll never trust men again.'

'They all say that,' said Candace.

'I'm having fun. Pete is trying to woo me back. Edmondo is whisking me off to Rome and whispering sweet nothings to me in Italian, not to mention the flowers and jewellery. I'm enjoying the attention.'

'That, I can imagine,' said Candace.

'I'm dying for you to meet him.'

'So what have you done with your tickets to Mauritius?' Angelica asked.

'Given them to Art and Tod. They're so excited. Two weeks at the Saint Géran hotel, business-class flights on Virgin, all paid for by Pete.'

'They struck it lucky!'

'I think Art deserves it. He's seen me through the rough times.'

'And Tod deserves it for having put up with him sitting on the telephone with you night after night,' Candace added.

'Well, exactly,' Kate agreed. 'After all, it's my New Year's resolution to be generous. This is the new generous me.' She smiled angelically.

'It's so easy to be generous on other people's money!'

Kate turned to Candace and pulled a face. 'I've got to begin somewhere. Small steps for me, giant steps for mankind!'

When Angelica picked the children up from school at half past three, she forgot about the robbery at Rosenbosch in the comforting familiarity of her old life. Joe and Isabel flung themselves at her, clinging to her coat like monkeys, competing to be heard. The three of them held hands and walked up the street and into Kensington Gardens, where the pale, winter sunshine had managed to find a break in the clouds and stream through. They walked up the path towards the palace, and Angelica listened to their news. They had so much to tell her, and she gave them all her attention, soaking up their love and letting it revive her.

Once they got home the children rushed upstairs to see what presents their mother had brought them. They bounced on the bed as she unpacked her suitcase, delving through her memories to pull them out. Joe and Isabel tore at the paper excitedly. But nothing delighted Isabel as much as the little bottles of shampoo and body lotion that Angelica had taken from the hotels. She ran to her bedroom, her arms full of loot, to try on her pyjamas and to put the bottles in her dressing table drawer in tidy rows. Joe was happy with his gifts, but it wasn't until he had given his mother the Full Joe that he was able to put the week behind him. He lay against her, nuzzling into her neck, and Angelica held him tightly, thanking God that she was alive to enjoy her children.

While they played in their bedrooms, Angelica went upstairs to her office. She switched on her computer and began to sort through her post. It was surreal how quickly life returned to normal. Rosenbosch began to feel like a dream. With a suspended heart she clicked on her emails. She barely dared breathe as the list came through. She scanned it, wishing for an email from Jack, knowing that he hadn't sent one.

There was only one thing to do: write her letter and send it off. Delete his details from her email and telephone. She should have done it months ago, before she had fallen so far, before her vanity had overpowered her. She pulled out a sheet of monogrammed writing paper and turned on her iPod, choosing Ennio Morricone's sound track to *Once upon a Time in the West*. She wrote in turquoise ink to match the printed address at the top of the page, and she wrote with care, choosing her words judiciously.

My darling DOP, this is the hardest letter I will ever have to write, but for my own sanity and the good of my husband and children, I feel there is no other ending for us – with all the will in the world I am unable to find a happy one. As you said when you lay bleeding beside me, 'We've had fun, haven't we?' We've had more than fun, Jack, we've shared something rare and magical. You've shown me my wings and taught me how to use them.

I am trying to understand why you chose not to be honest with me and to forgive you, but I'm not like Anna; I'm full of human frailties while she has surely been touched by the angels. My heart bleeds for you and for us as I leave you in the loving arms of your wife and daughters. But it's just not meant to be. We were given a glimpse of paradise, but now the clouds have closed and that glimpse has gone forever. I know I will never see you again but in my dreams.

Rest well, my love. There's no one more qualified to accompany you along your final path than Anna, although I will be with you in my thoughts. Please don't try to contact me; it will only make it harder for both of us. I will always love you. Sage

She wept as she wrote it, wiping her eyes on her sleeve so that she didn't smudge the ink. So it really was goodbye. She wrote the envelope and sealed it, staring at the address and remembering those camphor trees, the pavilion on the lake, the mountain range, the sunsets, and Jack with his wavy hair swept off his broad face, his gentle brown eyes, and his roguish grin. Then she cried all over again because it hurt so much to think of his dying.

She deleted his details from her computer and mobile telephone and gave the letter to Sunny to post. She felt as if an invisible rope connecting them across the globe was now severed. Hugging her children was the greatest medicine for her injured heart. When she went into Isabel's room, she found her at her dressing table, applying makeup.

'Darling, look at you!' She laughed, putting her arms around her daughter from behind. 'That's the reddest lipstick I've ever seen!'

'Kate left it behind,' said Isabel nonchalantly. 'I stole it.' She grinned mischievously.

'Really? Today?'

'No, while you were away. She came to see Daddy.'

Angelica's stomach cramped. 'Did she?'

'Yes.'

'Did you say hello?'

'No, we were meant to be in bed. But Joe and I watched from the top of the stairs.'

'You spy!' she tried to sound lighthearted, but her instincts were screaming at her. 'What were they talking about?'

'I don't know. They were having a glass of wine.'

Angelica felt sick. Why hadn't Olivier told her? Or Kate, for that matter? She thought Olivier loathed Kate. She hurried from her daughter's bedroom to seek refuge in the bathroom. Leaning against the marble, she stared at her stricken face in the mirror. Little by little, comments that Kate had made, that had meant nothing at the time, now added up to something far more sinister. The fact that she knew his birthday, the time she had said how much she'd love to wake up to him every morning – and countless more. Was Olivier having an affair with Kate? Was Olivier the father of Kate's child? Was that why Kate was unable to name her lover? She sank onto the loo seat and put her face in her hands. It suddenly made an awful lot of sense. And she had been so smug in assuming that *her* husband was the last person in the world to whom Kate would turn for comfort.

Tormented by these thoughts, she muddled through the children's homework until the doorbell rang to relieve her. She opened it cautiously. On seeing Angie standing there wringing her hands, she fell into her mother's arms with a sob. Angie immediately grew in stature, responding to her daughter's need with efficiency and self-importance. She helped her into the kitchen, sent the children upstairs to watch television, and put the kettle on, taking down two cups and a teapot from the cupboard. It had been years since she had set foot in Angelica's house. She had forgotten how pretty it was.

'My life is unravelling,' Angelica sniffed, slumping in her chair.

'I'm here now, love. Everything is going to be all right.' Angie opened the fridge and took out a bottle of milk. 'I want you to tell me exactly what happened. Get it all out. Cry as much as you need to. You'll feel so much better. A problem shared is a problem halved.'

Angelica didn't have the heart to tell her that she'd already shared it with Candace, which must mean that it would now be quartered. She watched her mother bustle about and felt a surge of gratitude.

'Thank you for coming.'

Angie placed the cups on the table. 'I needed to make sure that you were all right.' She narrowed her eyes and scrutinized her daughter's face as only a mother can. 'Which, you clearly aren't. But you're going to be fine. We're going to discuss this until you feel strong again.' She filled the teapot and placed it on the table, then sat down. 'Nothing like a cup of tea to revive the spirits.'

'You're so English, Mother.'

'What do you expect?' She chuckled throatily. 'So tell me, what happened?'

Angelica took a sip of tea, revived indeed by the hot liquid. Then she told her mother about the robbery. To her surprise, her mother listened without saying a word. Her face showed her horror, but she didn't interrupt, not once. Angelica felt the full force of her mother's attention and blossomed beneath it. Riding a wave of confidence, she confessed her adultery. Before she knew it, she was confiding everything, knowing that no one would understand like Angie. After all, Angie had just about done it all.

'I'm so sorry your heart has been broken, love,' she said, her orange skin crinkling with compassion. She placed her pudgy hand on top of Angelica's and gave it a squeeze. 'You think when you marry that broken hearts are a thing of the past, gone with your misguided youth. But the truth is, you're never too old to have your heart broken. I assume Olivier doesn't know?' Angelica nodded, blinking through tears. 'Good. Don't tell him. Honesty is not always the best policy.'

'Should I forgive Jack for betraying me?'

'He didn't betray you, love. He lost his heart to you and did all he could to protect it. There's nothing wrong with that. Don't feel aggrieved. Forgive him for being fallible, but don't blame him for being dishonest. You've lived a wonderful love affair, such as most people never experience in an entire lifetime. What a privilege to have loved like that. Denny and I had to sleep with other people to feel a sense of adventure.'

Angelica wiped her face with her sleeve. 'Don't you love each other enough?'

'We love each other enough to trust each other, if that's what you mean.'

'I hated your swinging parties as a child. I felt they were more important than us.'

'I know you did, love. That's why I wanted to come and see you today. I nearly lost you in South Africa, and that would have meant that I never had the opportunity to tell you how sorry I am that you felt like that. It's been bothering me for years, but I was too proud to talk to you about it. The robbery concentrated my thoughts. Life is too short to spend it with one's head under the carpet, avoiding the important things. The truth is that Denny and I were very selfish in those days. We let you down when you needed us most. I wanted to come now, because you're never too old to need your mother, and it's never too late for your mother to come to your aid.'

Angelica took Angie's hand. 'It's never too late, Mum.'

When the doorbell rang again, Angelica looked confused.

'That'll be your sister, Angelica. She's come to pick me up. She also wanted to see you.'

'You can stay here if you like,' Angelica suggested.

'You need to be with your husband. I can't have two sons-in-law falling by the wayside. Go and open the door, love. Daisy's been worrying, too.'

Angelica unbolted the door. Daisy stood on the doorstep looking pale and ashamed. Her big eyes shone with regret that so many years had been wasted in bitterness. Without a word they embraced. They understood each other without the need to articulate in syllables what they both felt in their hearts. Angie went to the cupboard and took down another cup.

After they had gone Angelica bathed the children and put them to bed. She lingered over their bedtime stories and smothered their smooth faces with kisses, taking pleasure from every moment, however small. She enjoyed the Full Joe and the Full Isabel, savouring the smell of their skin and the warm feel of their bodies as they wrapped themselves around her, begging her to stay just a little longer. She shoved Kate to the back of her mind as she made every effort to live in the present.

Downstairs, she poured herself a large glass of wine. She sat at the kitchen table and deliberated whether to confront Olivier. If he was innocent, wouldn't her suspicion lead him to suspect *her*? She was afraid even to mention adultery in case he questioned why she was considering it. Olivier was very astute and rarely missed a trick. It wasn't beyond the realm of possibility that he might start doing sums of his own.

As she prepared dinner, she thought of Anna, trying to channel some of her wisdom and tolerance. Say Olivier and Kate *had* slept together: Kate had said it was a one-night stand that had meant nothing, something they both regretted, it wasn't going to happen again, in which case it wasn't an *affair,* but a *mistake.* How could she pass judgment when she herself had fallen in love with Jack and had an affair lasting months? At least Kate and Olivier weren't in love with each other. She could forgive that. But what of Kate's baby? *Please God, let that baby belong to Pete.*

At last Olivier arrived. He swung open the door and called her name, a vast bouquet of lilies in his arms. 'I thought these would make you feel better,' he said. Angelica tried to behave normally and took them from him with a smile. *The actions of a guilty man?* she wondered.

'They're lovely, thank you.'

He kissed her. 'How are you feeling?'

'So much better. Mum came and we talked. Then Daisy joined us. It was good. We should have done it years ago.'

'Sometimes it takes a scare to frighten everyone into real-izing what's important.' He looked at her intensely.

She returned his look, searching for any indication of *his* adultery. 'You're so right.'

'I bet the children were pleased to see you.'

'So pleased.'

'They missed you.'

'And I missed them.'

'Did you miss *me*?' he asked, pulling a sheepish face.

'Of course I did.' She watched him take off his coat and hang it in the cupboard. In all his years of flirting she had never feared he'd leave her. Now she was no longer sure of him. 'Would you like a glass of wine?'

'I'd love one.' He followed her into the kitchen. 'So what's up?'

'Kate has left Pete,' she said, watching his reaction carefully.

'I'm surprised he didn't leap first.' He shrugged. 'It was always going to happen.'

'I don't know. I thought they were trying to make it work.'

'No one could possibly stay married to her.'

She stood at the stove and stirred the tomato sauce for the pasta. 'I thought the baby might help them patch it up.'

'I did, too.'

'It might not be Pete's.'

He looked interested. 'Really? Whose does she think it might be?'

'Someone she had a one-night stand with at the end of the summer.'

He didn't look at all ruffled. 'Does Pete know?'

'No, Pete thinks it's his, which, of course, it might be.'

He shook his head and tutted disapprovingly. 'She's a very careless girl.'

'I'm not even sure that the man she slept with has a clue that he might have got her pregnant.'

'Let's hope it *is* Pete's, then.' He took a sip of wine. 'Or someone is going to get a shock when the baby is born.'

Angelica was confused. If Olivier was the man Kate had slept with, wouldn't he have been a little more flustered at the prospect that he might be the father of Kate's unborn child? Unless he already knew, in which case he would have had plenty of time to hatch a plan. Perhaps that was why Kate had come around. Maybe she had seized the moment, as Angelica was away, to confront him and tell him about his possible child. Still, he was remarkably cool for a man keeping such a terrible secret.

The following week, Angelica avoided Kate as much as she could. Every time she saw her belly she imagined Olivier's baby inside, looking just like Joe or Isabel. Her fear distracted her from thinking about Jack, but it inhibited her creativity. Much as she tried, she was unable to get back into her book, in spite of the flood of inspiration she had received in South Africa. To keep herself busy and away from her desk, she continued her Pilates classes three times a week and spent as much time as possible with Candace, for her friend confirmed over and again that she had done the right thing in cutting all contact with Jack, even though the absence of his texts and emails hurt her daily.

At the beginning of March, Kate invited Olivier and Angelica for dinner to meet Edmondo, the now infamous count. Diluted in the company of Art and Tod, Letizia and Gaitano, Candace and Harry, and Scarlet and William, Olivier gave no indication of intimacy with Kate, and Kate, all over Edmondo like a wiry octopus, barely tossed him a glance. If they shared a secret, they deserved Oscars for their ability to dissemble.

Edmondo was a central casting count: dark and handsome, with thick glossy hair, smooth brown skin, and a large, sensual mouth, almost bruised from so much kissing. He spoke with a strong Italian accent that Angelica found as attractive as Olivier's French one, and he gesticulated with his hands. He was confident and funny and wild about Kate. Having expected an awkward evening pretending they all liked him, they were surprised to discover that no pretence was necessary.

Kate dragged the girls into her bedroom after dinner to discuss him. 'I'm so grateful that he likes me, belly and all,' she said. 'I mean, he's never even had a child of his own, so having to put up with my two, and this one in here, is Herculean.' She looked so pathetically grateful that even Candace was unable to find anything cynical to say.

It was only when Kate texted her friends in panic a week later that Angelica pushed aside her suspicions and ran to her aid, leaving the children to have tea with Sunny. Kate opened the door and grabbed her by the wrist. 'You have to hear this. You won't believe it.' She didn't look tearful and bedraggled like she had the day of the pregnancy test. Instead, she almost looked amused. The doorbell went again, and Candace walked in with Letizia. Angelica found Scarlet in a pair of black velvet hot pants drinking a cup of tea on the club fender. She beckoned her over with a wave of her hand, the rows of bracelets jingling on her arm like armour.

'Hi, doll. This is hilarious!' she said, flicking her blonde bob.

'At least she hasn't split up with Edmondo.'

'God, no, to the contrary, that seems to be rocking.'

'So what's happened now?'

'I'm not going to spoil it. She has to tell you herself.'

'Did we all need to schlep out to hear it?'

'Yes. Trust me, it'll be worth it.'

Letizia and Candace came into the sitting room. 'Tea, anyone?' asked Kate breezily.

'Yes, please,' said Candace. 'You can lace it with something stronger if you think we need fortification.'

'I'm the one needing fortification, but I've given up booze.'

'Really?' asked Letizia, sitting down on the sofa.

'Really. I've clearly got a problem, so I've joined AA. Edmondo is supporting me all the way.'

'I'm impressed,' said Candace. 'Generous *and* sensible.'

Kate knelt on the floor beside the coffee table and poured the tea into mugs. 'Biscuit, anyone?'

'No, just tell us what this is all about,' said Angelica, trying not to look too hard at her protruding belly.

'Okay, here, take your tea.' She handed Angelica a mug.

'Are you going to tell us who the mystery man is?' Angelica hadn't meant her voice to sound so edgy.

'I wish I could say it was Edmondo's. I'd love a little Italian child.'

'I highly recommend them,' said Letizia cheerfully.

'So what is it, then?' Candace asked.

'So I'm called in to see Mrs Moncrieff.'

'She called you?' Letizia asked.

'The secretary did. I thought *I* was in trouble. I'm in my forties, and I felt like a schoolgirl again, called in to see the headmistress. So in I go. She asks me to sit. She's looking really embarrassed. Actually, I'm feeling sorry for her. She puts her elbows on the table and knits her fingers. "I'm very sorry to have to mention this, Mrs Fox, but I feel I should explain before you see Amelia's form teacher. You see, Amelia brought something quite inappropriate for Show and Tell this morning." As you can imagine my mind was racing with all sorts of possibilities, but I could never have guessed it would be my vibrator!' She watched with pleasure as they all stared at her.

Finally, Candace shook her head and grinned. 'How do you do it!' she exclaimed. 'Just when I think you've exhausted every possible drama, you find another one even more entertaining than the last.'

Kate giggled. 'She pulled out the drawer and handed it to me in a bag, wrapped in paper. Can you imagine? It was horribly embarrassing. Someone had actually wrapped it up!'

'Did Amelia take it out and show everyone in assembly?' asked Scarlet.

'Thank God her teacher got to her before she got into assembly. As it is, I'm never going to live it down!'

'What did she say it was for?' Letizia added.

'Oh, I should think she thought it was a clever little massage device,' said Candace with a cackle.

'Do you think Mrs Moncrieff knew what it was?' asked Angelica.

'Oh yes,' Kate replied. 'She knew exactly what it was. She suggested I find a more suitable place to keep it. I wanted to die. I couldn't look at Amelia's class teacher. I couldn't look at anyone. You can bet the whole school knows about it by now.'

'It's hilarious,' said Scarlet.

'For you!' Kate reminded her. 'For me, it's a nightmare.'

'What are you going to say to Amelia?' Angelica asked.

'I'm going to tell her that she mustn't take Mummy's things into school.'

'Tell me, what does the vibrator look like?' Candace asked.

'A rabbit,' Kate replied.

Candace shrugged. 'Easy mistake.' She sipped her tea.

Scarlet grinned over her mug. 'Tell me, does it rock?'

Chapter 29

'Surrender to the flow of life'

In Search of the Perfect Happiness

Angelica couldn't shake off her suspicion that Olivier was having an affair with Kate. She recognized the irony, but still, the idea that her husband had betrayed her with one of her closest friends was like a knife to her heart. She clung to him at night, wrapping her tentacles around him, waking in the early hours to check that he was still there. He assumed her neediness sprang from the robbery, not from her fear of losing him. The more she thought about it, the more she regretted her own affair and the more she realized how much she loved him.

Olivier started coming home earlier in the evenings, and they bathed the children together and took turns reading to them. She listened to his worries and tried to give advice, or at least support. He, in turn, went into her office and took down a paperback copy of *The Caves of Cold Konard*. At first he read a little every night, and she knew he was struggling, but she was grateful for his effort. But then he kept the light on later and later as it became harder to put it down. 'I just have to find out what happens to Mart!' he exclaimed, without taking his eyes off the page. Angelica grinned into her own book with pride.

Then, on March 5, Olivier mentioned her birthday over supper. 'I thought you'd forgotten,' she said, pleased that he hadn't.

'I thought we could go out for dinner at Mr Wing.'

'Sure.' She had rather hoped for something a little more exciting.

'I've been so busy I haven't had time to arrange anything better. Why don't we go and spend a weekend in Paris in spring? A kind of belated birthday weekend.'

'I'd love that.'

'We can go shopping, and you can choose something . . .'

'I don't need a present,' she said humbly, knowing that now was no time for extravagance but disappointed all the same.

'We'll choose it together. Have the girls planned anything?'

'I haven't mentioned it. To be honest, I've been busy, too . . .' She thought of the book she had to write and the wasted hours staring at her email, willing Jack to find a way of contacting her. Hoping he'd make the effort in spite of all the obstacles she had erected to stop him. 'I wouldn't expect them to remember.'

'Well, I've remembered, and the children have got something for you.'

She smiled at the thought of Joe and Isabel's gifts. They'd be more precious than anything bought in a shop.

The following morning, the children woke her up to cries of 'Happy birthday, Mummy.' They had made cards and plates at the Pottery Café in Fulham. Isabel's was prettily painted in pinks and blues with butterflies and flowers around the edge and one glorious bumble bee in the middle. Joe's was a mess, but Angelica could make out a red train, puffing smoke. She cuddled both children, holding them for as long as possible before they wriggled away. Nothing could beat those delightful plates; she would hang them on the wall in her study.

Olivier was already dressed for work. He kissed her tenderly. 'Be ready at seven-thirty. I'll come home early to change. I've reserved Mr Wing for eight.'

She walked the children to school, bumping into Candace as she left them at the door. 'Happy birthday!' she said, Ralph straining at his lead as he attempted to follow a scruffy little bitch down the pavement.

'Thank you!' Angelica was surprised.

'So what's Olivier got you?'

'Oh, nothing yet. We're going to go to Paris in the spring. He's busy at the moment.'

Candace pulled a face. 'Too busy to buy you a present? Honey, there's a Tiffany in the City.'

'Don't tell me!'

'Is he taking you somewhere nice tonight?'

'Mr Wing.'

'A Chinese?' Candace crinkled her nose in disgust. 'I think he could do better than that.'

'I love Mr Wing.'

'We *all* love Mr Wing, but not on our birthday.'

'Oh, it's fine,' Angelica said, laughing it off. 'Things are really good between us now – I shouldn't complain. At least he didn't forget.'

'I'd take you out for lunch if I didn't have a meeting.'

'I've got to get down to some writing anyway.'

'Go have a massage or something.'

'Not today. I'm not in the mood.'

'I'll see you at pick-up.' Candace gave the lead a yank and Ralph loped back reluctantly.

Angelica returned home and took a cup of tea up to her office. Claudia called at nine to find out how the book was doing, impatient to see what she had written so far. Angelica lied and told her she was halfway through it. Her mother telephoned to wish her a happy birthday, and Daisy called, suggesting they have lunch together. Angelica didn't hesitate but invited her to Le Caprice, thrilled to be doing something exciting on her birthday.

She scanned down her emails, disappointed to find that Jack hadn't written. She couldn't remember whether or not he knew it was her birthday. She had asked him not to contact her, and he had obviously respected her wishes. She had to summon all her strength to restrain from emailing *him*. She longed to find out how he was. But he was dying, with Anna at his side, guiding him towards the last leg of his journey home. There was no room for her there. It was well and truly over.

She opened her novel about the greasy Troilers who live on the estuary, and turned on her iPod. Engulfed in grief, she channelled her feelings into her novel. Her resentment formed the ugly, slimy Troilers; her love, the weightless, phosphorescent Dazzlings. The story would be an allegory of her love for Jack, and no one would ever know that but her. The music carried her into her fantasy world, where she gave vent to her emotions and thus created a captivating story where love battles to save the world from evil. She knew her theme was not original, but equally no one else could write it like she could.

After an agreeable lunch with Daisy, during which they had laughed about their ludicrous botanical names and their parents' disastrous attempts to hold on to their youth, she picked up Joe and Isabel and brought them home for tea. She hadn't seen any of her other friends, and none of them had called, which surprised her. Kate had prided herself on remembering birthdays; after all, she had remembered

Olivier's, Angelica thought bitterly. The least she could have done is remember *hers*. Sunny bathed the children as she showered and slipped into a black Prada dress. As she applied makeup and sprayed herself with scent, she reminded herself that happiness was a state of mind. That the quality of her life depended on the quality of her thoughts. If she dwelled on the negative aspects of her day, they would only pull her down. Instead, she concentrated on the positive things: The fact that her children had gone to such trouble to make her cards and presents. The fact that Candace had remembered her birthday. The fact that she had made peace with Daisy. The fact that she was now close to her mother. The fact that Olivier hadn't found out about her affair. The fact that she had such good friends. The fact that her husband and children were healthy. The fact that she had so much to be grateful for. After a while it began to work. She lit her scented candles and played *Back to Black* by Amy Winehouse. Her spirits rose with the perfume and filled the room.

When Olivier appeared, he found her in the bathroom singing loudly. He came up behind her, pulled her hair aside, and kissed her nape. She laughed at him in the mirror. He was handsome in the golden glow of the candlelight. She was surprised when he placed a pendant there, fastening it at the back. The diamonds fell against her chest, glittering against the black of her dress. She gazed admiringly at the heart that rested behind the letters O, J, and I, dangling on the end of a thick white-gold chain. 'You've been to Chopard,' she said, astonished.

'Of course. I know that there is nothing that excites a woman more than diamonds.'

'How very right you are,' she replied, turning round to kiss him tenderly. 'Thank you.'

'You look more beautiful than I have ever seen you, my darling.'

'I'm ready for Mr Wing.'

He scoffed. 'As if I'd take you to Mr Wing!'

She stared at him. 'Where are you taking me?'

'A surprise.'

'Oh my God. I'm already surprised!'

'You're going to love this one.' He took off his jacket and tie. 'Give me a few minutes to shower and change, and then we'll go. There's a car waiting for us outside. Tonight, I intend to party hard!'

So he had never intended to take her to Mr Wing. It had all been a ruse. She couldn't wait to tell Candace.

Olivier appeared on the landing in a pair of jeans, a white shirt beneath his favourite gunmetal blue Gucci jacket. His skin was brown against the collar and his dark hair still wet and tousled, pushed off his forehead. He took her hand and they walked downstairs together. She decided that she would forget about his supposed affair with Kate and enjoy the evening. Tomorrow she would confront him and hopefully dispel her fear once and for all. If he admitted it, she would cope somehow. She would not let it destroy her marriage or her friendship with Kate. Anna had proved that was possible.

They climbed into the back of the car. It pulled out into the street. The trees were still bare but the park was full of crocuses and daffodils, the air warmer, the days longer and brighter. Angelica was exhilarated with the suspense. She smiled all the way down Kensington Church Street, trying to work out what restaurant he was taking her to from the direction of the car. When they turned into Thurloe Square, she realized they were headed to Kate's.

'What's going on?' she asked, narrowing her eyes suspiciously.

'I promised to pop into Kate's on the way. She's got a present for you.'

'This is all very fishy.'

'She's bought you something special. She called me tonight on my mobile. She said she hadn't seen you at school today.'

'No, but she could have called me herself.'

'You know Kate,' he said. Angelica wondered whether he knew her better than any of them.

The car drew up outside the house, and they stepped onto the road. Kate had changed her window box, filling it with an elaborate display of red geraniums. Before Olivier had time to ring the bell, the door swung open. A uniformed butler stood at attention. 'Good evening, sir,' he said. 'May I take your coat?' Angelica was more suspicious than ever. She slipped out of her sheepskin and handed it to the butler, who folded it over his arm. 'Mrs. Fox is in the drawing room.'

The house was strangely quiet. Angelica noticed that the double doors were closed. She could feel the silence of a room full of people seeping out from beneath them. The butler strode ahead and flung them wide to reveal a sea of faces before her, all smiling in the semi-darkness. None was more radiant or triumphant than Kate's. 'Darling! Happy birthday!' She waddled over in the sexiest little Miu Miu dress, her big stomach protruding like a globe, and embraced her affectionately. Angelica swept her eyes over her friends, all of them, even her parents, Daisy, and the terrible Jenna Elrich, who had somehow inveigled her way into the party. Kate had even found friends she had lost along the way. 'Are you surprised?' Angelica nodded, dumbfounded. 'I'm so pleased no one gave it away. Olivier and I have been planning this for weeks, tracking down your old friends. I had a horrible feeling Joe and Isabel might let the cat out of the bag. I could have sworn they were sitting on the landing listening to our secret meeting.'

Angelica hugged Kate again, for the guilt of having doubted

her and for the relief that now overpowered her. 'I thought you had all forgotten.'

'Good!'

'And it's not a big birthday, either.'

'Every birthday is big in importance, and besides, this is my year of being generous. Make the most of it while it lasts. I'll be back to Selfish Me next year.'

Angelica wrapped her arms around Olivier. 'Thank you,' she said. He would never know the depth of her gratitude.

Candace approached her with Letizia, Scarlet, and Tod. 'Fooled ya!' she said, handing Angelica a glass of champagne.

'You guys!'

'As if we'd forget your birthday,' said Letizia.

'I should have known,' Angelica replied, taking a gulp of champagne.

'Honey, what's with the diamonds?'

'Olivier's present.'

'Now we're talking,' said Scarlet.

'They're way over the top!' Tod added. 'I thought we were in the middle of a financial crisis.'

'I know. I can't imagine what got into him,' Angelica laughed, toying with the sparkly letters.

'Absence makes the heart grow fonder!' said Letizia.

'And I thought he was having an affair with Kate.'

'What?'

'Isabel mentioned that Kate had come over while I was away. I just couldn't understand why they were meeting at all and why neither had bothered to tell me.'

Candace put her arm around Angelica. 'That's a stretch of the imagination too far!'

'Kate would never betray a friend,' said Letizia.

'Only her husband!' Scarlet added.

'I thought that baby might be Olivier's.' Angelica's relief made her almost delirious with happiness.

'Why wouldn't it be Pete's?' Tod asked, confused.

Angelica put her hand to her mouth. 'You don't know?'

The three women looked at each other guiltily. 'I would have thought she would have told *you*!' Angelica gasped.

'Told me what?' Tod's bewildered expression spoke volumes.

'Okay, here's the deal, but don't say a word.' Candace looked at him steadily. 'Kate had a one-night stand. The baby she's carrying might or might not be Pete's. There, I've let the great big jungle cat out of the bag. If it bites us, we'll blame you!'

'Christ! That's heavy,' said Tod, scratching his head.

'Don't think you'll get a name out of her. She hasn't told a soul. But at least we can rule out Olivier,' said Scarlet with a laugh.

'I won't breathe a word,' he assured them. 'For God's sake, don't let on that I know.'

'Are you kidding me!'

'Happy birthday, darling,' he added hastily, looking past her. 'Now I've got to go and tell Art.'

'We are in serious trouble,' said Letizia anxiously.

'Can Art keep a secret?' Angelica asked.

'It's not Art I'm worried about,' said Candace. 'Tod clearly can't.'

After the buffet, Kate stood on a chair and clapped her hands, demanding silence for her speech. The noise died down, and everyone waited. She stood there in the tightest jersey dress that barely reached midthigh and patted her pregnant belly fondly. 'Good friends, old friends, new friends, special friends like you, Angelica, Scarlet, Letizia, and Candace, and family friends, Daisy and Angie. Welcome to my humble abode, and thank you for keeping the party a secret and making it fabulous with your glittering presence. Angelica, you're very dear to me. You're a *true* friend, so I wanted to return your kindness with a party to celebrate *you*. Your birthday is a good excuse, but frankly, I would have done it on any other day for the simple pleasure of honouring *you*. You're loyal, you're wise, and in spite of you being a little absentminded, you never forget your friends. Please, raise your glasses to Angelica!'

'To Angelica,' they all repeated. Angelica blushed with pleasure.

Kate leaned over and took Edmondo's hand. 'And just in case you think this isn't about me, you're wrong. I couldn't let an opportunity like this pass me by. Can you please raise your glasses to Edmondo and me, the future Contessa Edmondo Augustino Silviano di Napoli.'

'Yes! Edmondo and I are getting married.' She looked sheepish a moment and giggled. 'Well, as soon as I'm divorced!'

'To my wife to be!' said Edmondo, raising his glass, and no one had any choice but to follow suit.

As soon as the speeches were over, the dancing began. Kate remained in the centre of the dance floor, which had been set up downstairs in the children's playroom, swinging across the wooden floorboards with her count. Angelica drank too many cocktails in a bid to forget the last party she had attended here, when Jack had waited for her in a taxi down the road. In a blissful alcoholic haze she allowed Olivier to sweep her onto the dance floor. After one in the morning, when most of the guests had gone home, Art took to the karaoke machine, singing 'Crazy.' At least this time he didn't pull down his trousers to expose his strawberry.

At three o'clock Olivier took Angelica home. 'That's the best party I've ever been to,' she said, climbing unsteadily into the waiting car. 'And it was all for me!'

'I'm happy you enjoyed it.'

'I didn't think you liked Kate.'

'It's not that I don't like her. Just that I find her dramas exhausting.'

'She's a girls' girl.'

'Clearly.'

'But you got together to organize *this*.'

'For you.'

'You're so sweet, Olivier.'

He kissed her as the car drove up Kensington Gore. 'I love you, Angelica.'

'And I love you, Olivier.' She sighed dreamily as she realized how much she really did.

As the car drew onto the street a hunched figure lumbered drunkenly down the road, hugging his coat tight to keep out the cold. 'Oh God!' Angelica gasped. 'It's Pete.' They both stared as they passed him, making his way to Kate's. 'I'm so pleased we're not there to witness the scene.'

'He really wants her back.'

'If he hadn't been such an idiot, she would never have kicked him out.'

'I think he'll find he's missed the boat.'

'People make their lives so complicated.'

Olivier took her hand. 'I'm lucky to be married to you. I see shipwrecks all over the beach and thank God that we're still afloat, sails billowing.'

Angelica snuggled up to him guiltily. 'Still afloat,' she replied. Closing her eyes, she envisaged the leak in the timber and mentally patched it over. If it remained below the water-line, he might never notice it.

Chapter 30

'All things happen at the perfect time'
In Search of the Perfect Happiness

The following morning Kate was on the telephone at dawn to report the arrival of Pete banging on her door, demanding to see the children, begging her to take him back. By the excited tone of her voice she was thrilled that he cared and triumphant that he had been brought to his knees. 'Why would I want him back?' she asked. 'When I have Edmondo, who worships me? Who would have thought that I'd walk down the aisle again, me of all people? The Vera Wang dress is just too beautiful to leave languishing in a cupboard.' Angelica listened sadly, thinking of the children and the little one not yet born into the chaos of Kate's dramatic life. It didn't really matter who the father was, for Pete would gather him into his brood and give him his name and probably never suspect that he didn't belong to him. As for Edmondo, if he ever made it down the aisle, he'd find Pete standing between him and the altar. Angelica suspected that Kate still loved him and that she probably always would. Pete wasn't going to give her up without a fight.

At the end of March, the children broke up from school, and the friends dispersed across Europe for their Easter holiday.

Olivier rented a chalet in Klosters, where Letizia and Gaitano had an apartment with a splendid view down the valley. Letizia had managed to bribe Scarlet's manny, Ben, to look after her boys for the fortnight, so while the children skied together with Ben and an instructor, Angelica and Letizia were able to enjoy long lunches on the Chesa terrace in the sunshine and gentle descents down the Klosters Path. Olivier was a powerful, experienced skier, but instead of disappearing with skins in his backpack to spend the morning climbing and the afternoon descending in untracked powder, he took time to ski with his wife and children and found, to his surprise, that the pleasure he derived from watching Joe and Isabel stem down the piste far exceeded the pleasure of yet another perfect turn of his own.

They dined at the Wynegg on snails and cheese fondue and discussed Kate and the count. Letizia and Gaitano had many friends in the village, and they swept Angelica and Olivier into their social whirl, dining at friends' chalets and dancing at the little Casa nightclub into the early hours of the morning. Angelica felt revitalized, her marriage rejuvenated, her memory of the robbery faded and shunted to the back of her subconscious. But her first waking thoughts were of Jack.

She dreamed of him often, always with the same sense of loss. Awake in bed, recapturing the sense of him, she'd remember the sunset at Sir Lowry's Pass and the gentle way he had looked at her. Above all, she remembered the way he had made her feel. But that woman was gone forever now, along with the future they had embroidered with the fine threads of delusion. A future had never been in the stars for them. Although her life had returned to normal, she carried within her a small part of Jack, like a warm nugget against her heart, comforting and grazing her simultaneously.

★

The children returned to school at the end of April and the girls' lunches resumed. Angelica settled into her writing groove and inspiration flowed. Her Troilers and Dazzlings took on lives of their own beyond the pages and began to dominate her thoughts. Dreams of her book on happiness were forgotten in the flurry of her new fantasy. She didn't know what the secret was; if anything, her affair with Jack had left her more confused than ever. What she *did* know was that loving her work, her children, her husband, and her friends gave her a cosy sense of contentment. If it wasn't for the little nugget rubbing on the tender tissue of her flesh she would have believed herself as happy as any person could hope to be.

But then Anna gave her the news she had dreaded.

Angelica was alone at her desk. The children were at school, Olivier at work. She had felt uneasy all morning, unable to write for a heavy sense of foreboding that strained every nerve, unable to decipher why she felt so low and so flustered. When the telephone rang, she knew. Her throat had constricted with grief even before she heard Anna's voice.

'Angelica? It's Anna.' Angelica sensed her sorrow bleeding down the line from Rosenbosch, and tears rose from behind her carefully constructed dam and spilled freely onto her cheeks. 'Jack passed away this morning.'

'Oh God.' Angelica's hand shot to her heart.

'He was very calm and very submissive. I held one hand, the girls the other. We told him how much we loved him and that, although we wouldn't be able to see him any more, we'd feel his spirit here among the vines and in the sunsets he so loved. He smiled. He had no strength left, but he smiled, and I saw our old familiar Jack there for the briefest moment. Then he took his last breath, peacefully, without any pain.'

'I'm so sorry.'

'It's worse for the girls. They loved their daddy so much. I knew you'd want to know.'

'I should have called him . . .'

'Don't say that. Put your energy into positive things. Send him loving thoughts for he hasn't gone far, just out of sight.'

'I deserted him at his most needy.'

'He understood.'

'I think of him every day, Anna.'

'And he thought of you. He talked about you often, but never with regret. So you must do the same. Treasure the memories. Your short time together was precious. Love and longing will be the forces that reunite you one day. Don't worry about that. You *will* meet again.' She laughed in that light, untroubled way of hers. 'I hope *we* do, too, Angelica. You're more than welcome here at Rosenbosch whenever you feel ready. Jack would want you to come back.'

She swallowed hard. 'When's the funeral?'

'Tomorrow. We're going to bury him on the hillside above Rosenbosch.'

She knew it was impossible for her to be there. 'Will you do something for me, Anna?'

'Of course.'

'Put a sprig of sage on his coffin.' She closed her eyes. 'With that I'll bid him goodbye.'

Angelica spent the rest of the day crying into her pillow. She had accused him of selfishness, but her own selfishness was shameful. Would it really have hurt to have telephoned him once in a while and emailed her love? Surely, the wishes of a dying man were more important than her own. She had the rest of her life to give to Olivier and their children; Jack had had only months.

At three she went to pick up the children. Candace was standing talking to Scarlet and Letizia, waiting for the big doors to open and release their offspring into the bright spring sunshine.

Candace hurried over when she registered Angelica's stricken face. 'What's happened?' she demanded. 'Who's died?'

'Jack . . .' Angelica could not speak.

'Oh my God. Jack's dead? Truly?'

Angelica nodded and fell against her, sobbing.

Letizia and Scarlet gathered round, concerned. 'What's happened?'

'Jack Meyer has died,' Candace replied, wrapping her arms around Angelica.

'Christ!' Scarlet swore, blanching. 'I don't believe it.'

'Who's Jack Meyer?' Letizia hissed.

'A South African friend of ours,' said Scarlet. 'The people Angelica stayed with on her book tour. I knew he'd had cancer, but I thought he was in remission.'

'It came back,' said Angelica, pulling away and wiping her eyes. 'He died this morning.'

'You remember, he had the hots for Angelica,' Scarlet reminded Letizia.

'But of course,' said Letizia emphatically, putting her hand on Angelica's shoulder. 'Why don't you let me take Isabel and Joe?'

'Let's all go to tea at your house, the children can play downstairs and we can give Angelica a stiff drink in your sitting room,' Candace suggested. Angelica nodded gratefully, feeling the warmth of friendship envelop her like a beloved old rug.

Candace gave Angelica, Joe, and Isabel a lift in her car, calling her housekeeper on her mobile to change the arrangements she had made for her own children's tea. When they arrived at Letizia's terraced house, Joe and Isabel were delighted to find themselves in the company of all their friends and rushed off in a rowdy gang to the playroom downstairs. Angelica flopped onto the sofa in the first-floor sitting room, curling her feet under her and hugging the mug of tea Letizia had laced with whisky. Scarlet joined her on the sofa. Letizia was on the point of sitting down, having brought up tea and biscuits on a tray, when the doorbell rang. 'That'll be Kate,' she said, hurrying downstairs to open it. The girls glanced at one another in silence, listening to the slamming of the door and Kate and Letizia talking in low voices in the hall.

'Not me!' said Candace, raising her hands.

'Letizia, of course,' said Scarlet with a chuckle. 'She was texting in the car.'

'If I'm going to pour out my soul, it might as well be to *all* of you,' said Angelica, smiling feebly. 'Save you from gossiping about it later.'

'Don't bet on it, honey! What you're about to divulge will give us all months of gossip!'

'I'm so sorry about Jack!' Kate exclaimed as she rushed in on a wind of perfume, her pregnant belly stretching the fabric of her vintage Mary Quant minidress. Since her love affair with the count, her dress had got more lavish, her jewellery more brash, and her scent overpowering. She sat down and crossed her long legs so that the gold buckles on her Roger Vivier shoes glinted in the sunlight streaming through the tall sash windows. 'So who is he?'

Angelica smiled through her tears. 'He was my lover,' she said simply, and for once there was nothing Kate could say to bring the conversation around to herself.

The girls listened, spellbound, as Angelica confessed to loving Jack. She told them the story from the very beginning. From the moment she had felt the frisson of attraction at Scarlet's dinner party to the telephone call that morning, ending it all. They asked questions, probed into her feelings and her thoughts, and the strange thing was that the more Angelica talked about him, the less she hurt. Sharing her pain reduced the inflammation. Sharing the memories filled her heart with joy, for the love they had forged and the fun they had had. She trusted them to keep her secret: after all, they only gossiped to one another.

'The irony is that my affair with Jack has made me appreciate Olivier more. Our marriage has been strengthened because of it, and I salute Jack for that. He taught me to live in the present, and that is what I'm trying to do. None of us knows what's around the corner.' She looked at her closest friends sitting around her, listening without judgment, understanding with compassion, supporting with humour, and realized that there was nothing in the world more healing than friendship.

'Oh my God!' Kate cried, holding out her teacup and staring down at her lap. 'My waters have broken.'

'Really? Are you sure?' Letizia asked, horrified.

'I don't know why else a torrent of water would gush out of me!'

'I hope they haven't discontinued that fabric,' said Candace, glancing at the William Yeoward armchair that was now drenched with Kate's fluids.

Angelica laughed at Kate's immaculate sense of timing. 'I didn't think anything could upstage *my* story.'

'Foolish woman, you should know better,' said Candace. 'The time of reckoning is now upon us.'

'Darling, do you want me to call Pete?' Letizia asked.

'Do you have to?'

'I think I should. It's his baby, isn't it?'

Kate pulled an anxious face. 'I'm still not sure.'

Letizia shrugged helplessly. 'Do you want me to call the *other* father?'

'No,' Kate snapped. 'I'll call Edmondo.'

'You can't have Pete *and* Edmondo at the birth!' Candace exclaimed. 'There'll be a god-awful fight.'

'What shall I do?' Kate wailed, suddenly ashen with panic. She grabbed Letizia's arm. 'You have to come with me. I'm not giving birth on my own. You must *all* come with me!' Kate demanded. Letizia pulled her up to stand shakily, holding on to Letizia's arm as if it were her lifeline.

'I'll take you to the hospital,' Letizia volunteered. 'Someone has to stay with the children.'

'I'll stay!' Candace put up her hand. 'I'm not very good at childbirth. I don't *do* pain.'

'Pain? For God's sake get me to the hospital quick. If I'm too late for an epidural, I might die.' Kate began to stagger down the stairs.

'Where's your overnight bag?' Scarlet asked, following after.

'It's in my bedroom. Take the key from my bag and let yourself in. Thank God my waters didn't break in the Chanel department at Selfridges.'

Letizia rushed Kate to the Portland Hospital, where she gave birth to a baby boy. Letizia was pale, having held Kate's hand for the duration. 'Now I know why husbands prefer to pace the corridor outside,' she said when Candace, Scarlet, and Angelica arrived armed with flowers and White Company bags of presents. 'It's a bloody battle scene!'

The girls crowded into the small room. Kate lay serenely in bed holding Hercules in her arms, the two looking like the Virgin and Child. They gathered around curiously and gazed into the small face, searching for Pete in the squashed pink features of the baby. 'He looks like you,' said Candace, disappointed.

'He looks *just* like Pete,' Kate replied happily.

'No, I can't see Pete in there. He's totally you.'

'I've called him. He's on his way.'

'What about Edmondo?'

'As Hercules is Pete's, it's only right that he gets to hold him first. A son. Imagine that! I've given Pete a son.'

'You sound like Anne Boleyn,' said Angelica. The door swung open.

'Ah, here's King Henry,' said Candace, stepping aside.

Pete walked through them to gaze at his child as if they weren't there. His face flushed with emotion. 'A son!' he exclaimed proudly.

Kate handed him over. 'Hercules,' she said.

'Hercules?' Pete wasn't convinced.

'A suitably heroic name,' said Kate.

'The poor little thing hasn't done anything yet,' Pete argued.

'Oh yes, he has,' said Candace under her breath, nudging Angelica. 'I think now would be a good time to leave.'

'Do you think it *is* Pete's?' Angelica asked Candace and Scarlet as they descended in the lift.

'Absolutely not,' Candace replied.

'Oh, I think it probably is,' said Scarlet.

'Doesn't look anything like him.'

'But it doesn't look like anyone else,' Scarlet reminded her.

'That's because we don't know what we're looking for. Give it time. The truth always comes out in the end.'

The birth of Hercules changed nothing with respect to Kate and Pete's divorce. The lawyers fought it out, and Edmondo distracted Kate with promises of palaces and parties and a lavish wedding on the beaches of Mauritius, which had always been her dream. A year went by. Angelica finished her book and handed it in. Claudia called as soon as she had read it to say that it was even better than *The Silk Serpent*. Olivier read the manuscript and took her out for dinner to celebrate, raising his glass to his gifted, beautiful wife, and Angelica realized that, with time and love, it was possible for emotional scars to heal. Life went on like a train that waits for no one; she couldn't alter its course, but she could alter the way she chose to travel.

★

Then, one spring evening, as Angelica sat in the garden watching the blue tits fly in and out of the feeding cage that swung from the magnolia tree, Olivier came out with two glasses of wine, having just returned from work. The children were playing on the painted wooden playhouse, jumping off the roof, frightening the squirrels away from the bird food with their noisy chatter.

'You're home early,' she said, pleased.

'I want to spend more time with my family.' He handed her the wine and a little blue book, the size of his hand.

'What's this?'

'I was in Waterstones, buying a book on Roman emperors for Joe, when I saw a pile of these on the counter. The funny name and pretty cover caught my attention. When I read the title, I thought it was something you'd like.'

She stared at the words, her eyes misting with the sudden cascade of memories. 'Thank you, darling,' she replied. 'How thoughtful of you.'

'Daddy, watch me!' shouted Joe, swinging from the branch. Olivier went over to help him down.

Angelica gazed at the words emblazoned in gold on the front of the little blue book:

In Search of the Perfect Happiness
by J. A. Braai

She ran her fingers over them, sure that she could smell the scent of camphor trees. Her heart pounding, she opened the first page to find a simple dedication:

To Sage
The only words that matter are
that I love you

She didn't cry. She was too full of happiness for tears. So he had written the book in the months before he died, for *her*. He had loved her after all. She flicked open to the first chapter and laughed to herself:

> The quality of our life depends
> on the quality of our thoughts.

She was sure she could hear him laughing, too; his irreplaceable voice carried on the wind.

Epilogue

Two years later

The small gathering of friends and family sat on white chairs on the fine, sandy beach, just below the Saint Géran Hotel in Mauritius. Palm trees rustled gently in the breeze that swept in off the calm, turquoise sea, and red and yellow flowers gave up their scent to mingle with the heady smell of ylang-ylang that characterized the island. The sun had set behind the hills inland, no longer visible to burn their skin, but it was still hot enough for the guests to sweat beneath their summer dresses and shirts and for the children to fidget in their bridesmaids' dresses and pages' shorts. The reef roared in the distance and purple clouds gathered dramatically above the horizon as Kate cantered down the beach on a gleaming white horse.

Candace, Scarlet, Letizia, and Angelica stood in simple ivory strapless dresses, holding bouquets of white flowers, watching Kate approach in her Vera Wang gown and veil.

'I still don't know how I got to be here, in this dress, watching this charade,' hissed Candace.

'I can't believe they've made it down the aisle,' said Angelica.

'The fat lady hasn't sung yet,' Candace reminded her cynically.

'There's no stopping her now.'

'She looks stunning,' Letizia gushed, blinking away tears.

'You're not crying, are you, Letizia?' Scarlet was appalled. She was even more appalled to be posing at the entrance to the aisle in a conventional white dress that reached her ankles. 'I feel like crying,' she muttered, shuffling uncomfortably. 'But for an entirely different reason.'

'Me, too,' Candace agreed. 'At which point did we actually agree to be maids of honour? But smile, for here she is, looking like an Estée Lauder advert.'

Kate beamed down at her friends, her eyes glittering with happiness. She smiled at her audience, then slipped off the horse, allowing an attendant from the hotel to lead it away. The girls dutifully smoothed out the creases in her dress and shook her train. The children shuffled into position behind her, holding little baskets of shells and petals to throw on her as she walked back up the aisle with her husband. The girls followed. Only Letizia, eyes filled with tears, was unable to see the intricate detail on the back of the bride's dress. Linking her arm through Art's, Kate proceeded to walk down the aisle between the chairs, decorated with garlands of white flowers and lush green leaves, towards her count, who stood with his chest puffed out like a fine peacock. Tod sat in the front row with Kate's mother and siblings, little Hercules squirming on his knee in the heat in a white linen shirt and shorts from Marie Chantal. Art handed Kate over to Edmondo, and, after exchanging affectionate glances, they turned to the priest to make their vows.

Suddenly, there was a strong gust of wind and a wail from the beach. Kate glanced at Edmondo. Edmondo glanced behind him. His face fell. The wail had come from Pete – and he was coming their way. 'Told you the fat lady hadn't sung,' Candace hissed to Angelica as the wail turned into 'Kate, I love you' and got louder as he staggered towards the wedding party.

'What's she going to do?'

Kate collapsed in tears. Then she lifted her beautiful dress, kicked off her elegant Louboutin shoes, and ran back up the aisle towards him with a melodramatic sob.

'Well, I've seen everything now!' Scarlet exclaimed, throwing her flowers to the sand.

'This is so moving,' Letizia sniffed. 'She's always loved Pete.'

'Now's a really great time for a reconciliation,' said Candace sarcastically.

'Should we just wait? Perhaps she'll exchange the count for Pete,' Angelica suggested.

'This isn't *Mamma Mia*!' Candace retorted.

Art stood up and put his hands on his hips. 'Why didn't we see this coming?' He turned to the girls. 'I think Tod and I are in for another honeymoon!'

At that moment, Hercules wriggled off Tod's knee. While no one was paying him any attention, he pulled his shirt over his head and kicked off his shorts, then headed naked down to the sea.

'Oh God!' Candace exclaimed, noticing the little toddler.

'What?' Angelica followed the line of her vision. 'Oh my God,' she repeated in amazement. 'Isn't that . . .?'

One by one the girls turned away from the sight of Kate and Pete falling on each other like animals, and stared at the little boy's bottom as he trotted down the sand.

Art's jaw fell open. 'Good Lord!' he exclaimed. 'Well, I'll be damned.'

On Hercules's right cheek was a big red birthmark, the shape of a strawberry.

Don't weep for the dead. Keep all your love for the living. As one grows older one should escape from the captivity of physical belongings, for all is lent to us: possessions, friends, loves, even time.

In Search of the Perfect Happiness by J. A. Braai

Acknowledgements

This novel was inspired by my book tour to South Africa a few years ago. I fell in love with the countryside that strangely reminded me of Argentina, perhaps because of the monumental skies and magnificent horizons. I met some wonderful people and visited a stunning Cape Dutch vineyard in Constantia. Having based my previous books in Latin America and Europe, I relished the change. So, a big thank you to all my dear South African friends, who patiently answered my endless questions and showed me their beautiful country with such enthusiasm and generosity: Cyril and Beryl Burniston, Julia Twigg, Gary Searle, and Leighton McDonald. I also want to thank Pippa Clarke for being an inspiration in herself! I took advantage of my cousin Katherine Palmer-Tomkinson, who went to Cape Town last Christmas. I wrote her a long list of questions about vineyards, and she very kindly came back with photographs plus almost an entire manuscript written by the sales and marketing manager of Warwick Estate, James Dare, about the harvest there. I can't thank him enough for going to such trouble. If I have brought that delightful season to life, it is only thanks to him. I thank my father for setting such a fine example – wherever there's a wise character in my books, there's a little of him – and my mother for her perceptive editing and ideas.

Thanks to my agent, Sheila Crowley, at Curtis Brown, and

to Suzanne Baboneau and her brilliant team at Simon & Schuster for republishing this book with a beautiful new cover. Most importantly, I'd like to thank my husband, Sebag, who not only helps me construct my plots but makes me laugh like no one else in the world!

Sea of
Lost Love

PART ONE

Chapter 1

Cornwall, August 1958

As Father Miles Dalgliesh cycled up the drive towards the Montague family home, Pendrift Hall, he took pleasure from the golden sun that filtered through the lime trees, casting luminous spots of shimmering light onto the gravel and surrounding ferns, and swept his bespectacled eyes over lush fields of soft brown cows. A fresh breeze swept in off the sea and gulls wheeled beneath a cerulean sky. Father Dalgliesh was new in town. Old Father William Hancock had recently passed away to continue his work on the Other Side, leaving his young prodigy in the hot seat rather sooner than anticipated. Still, God had given him a challenge and he would rise to it with gladness in his heart.

Today he would meet the Montagues, the first family of Pendrift.

Pendrift Hall was a pale stone mansion adorned with wisteria, tall sash windows, and frothy gardens that tumbled down to the sea. Pigeons cooed from the chimney pots, and every year a family of swallows made its nest in the porch. The house was large and somewhat shabby, like a child's favourite toy worn out by love. It had an air of contentment, and Father Dalgliesh's spirits rose even higher when he saw it. He knew he'd like the family, and he anticipated an enjoyable afternoon ahead.

He stopped cycling and dismounted. A sturdy, white-faced Labrador bounded out of the front door, wagging his tail and barking excitedly. Father Dalgliesh bent to pat him and the dog stopped barking, sensing the young priest's gentle nature, and proceeded to sniff his shiny black shoes instead. The priest raised his eyes to the butler, who now stood in the doorway, dressed in a black tailcoat and pressed white shirt. The man nodded respectfully.

'Good morning, Father. Mrs Montague is expecting you.'

Father Dalgliesh leaned his bicycle against the wall and followed the butler through a large stone hall dominated by a sleeping fireplace and a large set of antlers. The air in the house was sweet with the memory of winter fires, cinnamon, and centuries of wear and tear. He noticed an open chest beneath the staircase, full of tennis rackets and balls, and an old grandfather clock that gently ticked against a wall like a somnolent footman. Classical music wafted from the drawing room with the low hum of distant voices. He took a deep breath.

'Father Dalgliesh, Mrs Montague,' the butler announced solemnly, indicating with a gesture of his hand that Father Dalgliesh should enter the room.

'Thank you, Soames,' said Julia Montague, rising to greet him. 'Father, welcome to Pendrift.'

Father Dalgliesh shook her hand and was immediately put at ease by the warmth of her smile. She was voluptuous, with soft white skin, ash-blonde hair, and an open, gentle face. Julia Montague radiated so brightly that when she was present it was always a party. Wearing large beaded necklaces in pale greens and blues to match her eyes, with a laugh so infectious no one was immune – not even that sourpuss Soames – and a sense of humor that always made the best out of the worst, Julia was like a colourful bird of paradise that had made her nest in the very heart of tweedy Cornwall.

'The family are waiting to meet you on the terrace,' she

continued with a grin. 'Can I get you a drink before I throw you to the wolves?'

Father Dalgliesh laughed, and Julia thought how handsome he was for a priest. There was something charming in the lines around his mouth when he smiled, and behind his glasses his eyes were deep set and intelligent. He was surprisingly young, too. He couldn't have been more than thirty.

'A glass of water would be fine, thank you,' he replied.

'We have some homemade elderflower cordial; why don't you try some?'

'Why not? That would be very nice.'

'Soames, two glasses of elderflower on the terrace, please.'

Soames nodded and withdrew. Julia slipped her arm through the priest's and led him through the French doors into the sunshine.

The terrace was a wide York stone patio with irregular steps descending to the garden. Between the stones wild strawberries grew and tiny blue forget-me-nots struggled to be seen. Fat bees buzzed about large terracotta pots of arum lilies and freesias, and drank themselves dizzy in a thick border of lavender that grew against the balustrade lining the terrace. In the garden a gnarled weeping willow trailed her branches into a decorative pond where a pair of wild ducks had made their nest.

The family fell silent as Father Dalgliesh emerged with Julia. Archie Montague, Julia's husband, was the first to step forward. 'It's a pleasure to meet you,' he exclaimed heartily, shaking the priest's hand. 'We were very sorry when Father Hancock died. He was an inspirational man.'

'He was indeed. He has left me with the unenviable task of following in his footsteps.'

'Which I'm sure you will do valiantly,' added Archie

kindly, running his fingers down the brown moustache that rested on his upper lip like a neatly thatched roof.

'Let me introduce you to Archie's sister, Penelope, and her daughters, Lotty and Melissa,' said Julia, still holding on to Father Dalgliesh's arm because she knew her husband's family could be a little overwhelming. Penelope stepped forward and shook his hand. He winced as she squeezed the life out of it. Large-boned and stout, with an arresting bosom and double chin, she reminded him of one of her brother's Jersey cows.

'Very nice to meet you, Father.' Penelope's voice was deep and fruity, and she articulated the consonants of her words with relish, as if each one were a pleasure to pronounce. 'You're a great deal younger than we expected.'

'I hope my age does not disappoint,' he replied.

'To the contrary. Sometimes the old ones have had too many years listening to the sound of their own voices to be sensitive to the voices of others. I doubt you will fall into that trap.' She turned and ushered her daughters over to meet him. 'This is Lotty, my eldest, and Melissa, who has just turned twenty-five.'

She smiled at them proudly as they greeted the priest. Dressed beautifully in floral summer frocks, with their long hair pulled off their faces and clipped to the tops of their heads, they were pleasant to look at and very presentable. However, they were vapid girls, their heads full of frivolities, encouraged by their mother, whose main concern was marrying them off to well-bred young men of means. According to Penelope, they were two of the most eligible girls in London, and nothing less than the very best would do. She scoffed at the idea of marrying for love. That was a highly impractical notion, not to mention foolish: one's heart could not be trusted to fall in love with the right man. She, herself, was a prime example of her theory. She had grown to love Milton Flint over time, though she secretly hoped her daughters would make better matches than she had made. She might have married a Flint, but she remained in her heart a Montague.

'This is Milton, Penelope's husband, and David, their son,' continued Julia, leading the priest farther onto the terrace. Milton was tall and athletic, with thick blond hair brushed back off a wide forehead and lively blue eyes.

'Good to meet you, Father. Do you play tennis?'

Father Dalgliesh looked embarrassed. 'I'm afraid not,' he replied.

'Dad's obsessed,' interjected David apologetically, 'though he does put the racket down for Mass!' David laughed, and Father Dalgliesh was reassured by the presence of a young man of his own generation. Julia let go of his arm and sat down.

Father Dalgliesh took the seat beside her and crossed one leg over the other in an effort to look casual. He felt a little nervous. His conviction was as solid as rock, his knowledge of the scriptures and philosophy unsurpassed, his command of Latin exceptional. His Achilles' heel, however, was people. Father William Hancock had once told him: *'It's no good being so heavenly minded as to be no earthly good. You have to learn how to relate to people, Miles, on their level, otherwise you might as well become a monk.'* He knew the old priest was right. The bishop had sent him out to be among the people to spread the word of God. He pushed his glasses up his nose, determined not to let him down.

'Our young sons are out in the woods with their cousin, Harry, setting traps for vermin,' said Julia. 'The gamekeeper gives them sixpence a rat, if they bring it to him dead. They're getting rather rich, I believe. My three-year-old son, nick-named Bouncy because his feet are made of springs, is down on the beach with Nanny. They should be up soon, and Celestria, my niece . . .' Julia looked around. 'I don't know where she is. Perhaps she's with her mother, Pamela, who's married to Archie and Penelope's brother Monty. She's in bed with a migraine. She suffers from them, I'm afraid. She might come down later. She's American.'

Julia hesitated a moment, for Pamela Bancroft Montague, as she liked to be called, was extremely pampered, often spending whole days in bed, complaining if the light was too bright, moaning when it was too dark, insisting on being left alone with Poochi, her powdered Pekingese, while at the same time demanding as much attention as possible from Celestria and Harry, and constantly ringing the bell to summon the staff. She doubted whether Father Dalgliesh would meet Pamela at all, as she wasn't Catholic and abhorred the Church, which she thought a waste of time. 'Monty arrives this evening on the train from London. He's a wonderful character, and I hope you'll meet him. You'll certainly meet Harry and Celestria, their children. Harry sings rather beautifully and is in the choir at school.' Julia lit a cigarette and inhaled deeply. Soames stepped through the doors with a tray of drinks. When he handed Father Dalgliesh a glass of elderflower, Julia noticed that the young priest's hands were trembling.

It wasn't long before Wilfrid and Sam, Julia and Archie's elder sons, returned from the woods with Harry. Exuberant after a morning building camps and setting traps, they were ruddy cheeked and sparkly eyed. 'We found three dead rats!' exclaimed Wilfrid to his mother.

'How wonderful!' she replied. 'Darling, I'd like you to say hello to Father Dalgliesh.' The three boys fell silent at the sight of Father Dalgliesh's white Roman collar and held out their hands cautiously.

'What did you do with the rats?' Father Dalgliesh asked, endeavouring to put the boys at their ease.

'We hung them on the door by their tails!' said Sam, screwing up his freckled nose with delight. 'They're enormous – the size of Poochi!' he added.

'You better not hang him up by *his* tail!' laughed David.

'You'd have to hang Aunt Pamela up with him,' added Archie with a smirk. 'She never lets him out of her sight.'

'Oh, you are wicked, darling!' said Julia, eyeing Harry. It was all too easy to make jokes about Pamela without considering her children.

'Where's Mama?' Harry asked.

'She's in bed with a migraine,' Julia replied.

'Not again!'

'I'm afraid she does suffer from them.'

'Not when Papa's home,' said Harry innocently. It was true. When Monty was there, Pamela's migraines miraculously disappeared.

Amid the idyll that was Pendrift, Monty came and went, arriving on the 7.30 p.m. train from London, in time for a whiskey and a smoke and a set of tennis with Archie, Milton, and David. He'd arrive smiling raffishly beneath the brim of his panama hat, his pale linen suit crumpled from the train, a newspaper clamped under one arm, carrying only his briefcase and all the cheerfulness in the world. Pamela's moods would lift like the grey mist that sometimes hung over Pendrift before the sun burned through, but she behaved as badly as ever, making demands, swinging the conversation around to herself at every opportunity. She was spoiled and self-centred, being the only daughter of wealthy American businessman Richard W. Bancroft II.

The boys took Purdy the Labrador down to the beach to play cricket just as Nanny returned up the path with Bouncy and Celestria. Father Dalgliesh's lips parted in wonder as he watched the celestial figure of the beautiful young woman walking towards him. To his shame his heartbeat accelerated and the colour rose in his cheeks. He hoped it was the midday heat that had caused his sudden agitation. Celestria wore a short red-and-white polka-dot skirt and a halter-neck top that exposed her midriff. Her blonde hair was loose, falling in waves over smooth brown shoulders, and she walked as if she had not a care in the world. He could not see her eyes, which were hidden behind large, white-framed sunglasses.

'Ah, Celestria, come and meet Father Dalgliesh,' Julia called out as she approached. When Bouncy heard his mother's voice he let go of Nanny's hand and ran up the path, squealing with excitement.

'Mummy!' he cried.

'Hello, darling!' Julia replied. When the little boy realized he had an audience he put his hands on his hips and began a funny, jaunty walk, wiggling his bottom and grinning, peering up from under thick lashes. Everyone clapped and roared with laughter. Bouncy was the child who united them all. His mischievous smile, inherited from Julia, could melt an entire winter. He had thick sandy hair and soft brown eyes the colour of homemade fudge. He loved to show off and was encouraged to do so, though it exasperated Nanny that he tore his clothes off at any opportunity and ran around naked. He spoke with a lisp that was irresistibly sweet. Julia and Pamela, who had little in common besides the fact that they had married brothers, had discovered a bridge in Bouncy. 'Darling, you're so adorable!' enthused his mother, pulling him onto her knee and nuzzling him lovingly. Celestria followed, still laughing and clapping her hands. Father Dalgliesh stared at her as if bewitched.

'This is my niece, Celestria, Harry's elder sister,' said Julia, without taking her eyes off her son. Celestria removed her

sunglasses and hooked them into her cleavage, then extended
her hand to the priest.

'You're much younger than I imagined. Father Hancock
was as old as Nanny!' she said.

'Really, Celestria!' Penelope exclaimed disapprovingly.
'Nanny is as fit as a fiddle.' As the priest's colour deepened,
Celestria's haughty face broke into a warm smile.

'You look like you could do with a swim, Father. The
sea's delicious this morning. Cold but refreshing.'

'Do take off your jacket, Father,' said Julia, suddenly noticing the poor man's discomfort.

'I'm fine, really,' he replied. 'I'm used to the heat, having
lived in Italy.'

'There's nothing like an English summer,' said Archie.
'Just when you think it's going to be cold and grey the sun
comes out and burns you. Unpredictable, that's what it is.'

'I'm going upstairs to see Mama and change out of my
bathing suit,' said Celestria, weaving nimbly through the
chairs. Father Dalgliesh watched her go and found he was
able to breathe again.

Celestria's beauty was indeed remarkable. It wasn't just her
thick blonde hair that glistened like the cornfields around
Pendrift, or her clear grey eyes that had never been marred
by a single moment of unhappiness, or her generous mouth
and fine bones that gave her face definition, but the way she
held herself. Her poise was cool and confident and superior,
nothing so brash as arrogant, simply that she was aware of
her place in the world and confident of other people's high
regard for her.

She was twenty-one and, according to her mother,
'balancing precariously on the edge of womanhood.' But
Celestria didn't feel at all precarious and, if Pamela only
knew the half of it, how she had let Aidan Cooney slip his

hand into her knickers and how she had felt the hard excitement through his trousers, she wouldn't have entertained such silly ideas. She was already a famous beauty, well established on the London party scene, having come out when she was eighteen. There was many a hopeful man who entertained ideas of marriage. Most looked at her intensely and treated her like porcelain, which she found rather silly, except for Aidan Cooney, of course, whose eyes were filled with something darker than admiration.

But Celestria was more than an English beauty. She had something of the exotic about her, which men found irresistible. Concerned for her safety, her mother had taken her to New York when war broke out. They had lived with Pamela's parents in a Park Avenue penthouse with ceilings so tall Celestria could barely see them and splendid views over Central Park. For six years she had been her grandfather's delight. He had long since lost his daughter to Monty and England, so he relished having a little girl around the house and showered her with attention and presents that came in boxes, wrapped with tissue paper, smelling of new. He was the father she had lost to the war, the father she could embrace while hers was overseas and in wafer-thin envelopes that arrived sporadically to make her mother cry. Celestria learned to weave her charm and throw it over whole roomfuls of people like a fisherman setting his net, drawing it in little by little until she had ensnared each and every one. She learned to enchant and enthral, understanding very early on what her grandfather expected of her. His applause was addictive, and she drank his love and grew dizzy. She was shown off to guests before dinner, presented aged seven by her governess with her hair in ringlets, her dress pressed, and her shoes shiny, and her grandfather's pride was as sweet as candy. She sang songs and blushed when they all clapped. It was easy to manipulate people.

They thought she was too young to be aware of her charisma, but she knew how pretty she was, and it didn't take long to realize that by mimicking adults she could win their admiration. 'What a funny child!' they'd coo. 'A clever little darling!' And the more precocious she became, the more everyone loved her.

Amid all the pretence her grandfather was never fooled. He knew her better than her own mother did, and understood her more compassionately. He took an interest in every aspect of her life, inspiring in her a love of books by reading to her every night before bed, and later lending her the classics he had adored as a child. He was not a musical man, lamenting that he had never had the luxury of learning an instrument, but he had a deep appreciation that he nurtured with regular evenings at the opera. He took Celestria to the ballet when she was only five and personally supervised her piano lessons. No detail escaped him, however small. He encouraged her at school, praised her triumphs, and showed his disappointment when she let herself down. But he never once let her forget how fiercely he loved her.

Pamela Bancroft Montague seemed incapable of loving anyone more than she loved herself. It wasn't her fault. The trouble was her parents had spoiled her. She had learned to be selfish, to believe she was the centre of the universe, so there wasn't much room for anyone else. She loved Celestria as an extension of herself; that was a love she instinctively understood. Her husband spoiled her, too. She shone like a jewel, and he treasured her as one. She had a captivating beauty, the sort of beauty that struck fear into the hearts of both men and women. Men found such loveliness indomitable, and women knew their own beauty lost its lustre in the light of hers.

★

Celestria didn't miss her father in those early years. She had arrived in America as a two-year-old and returned to London when she was eight. She couldn't even remember what he looked like. She had missed her grandfather when she left New York, treasuring the week they spent every autumn at the fairy-tale castle he had bought in Scotland to shoot and stalk, and the annual holiday at the Bancroft family home on the island of Nantucket. Like her mother, she learned to love herself more. When Monty tried to make up with presents for the years of estrangement, she accepted them gladly, manipulating him with little kisses and charming smiles of gratitude. Then he gave her mother a little boy: Harry. From the moment Harry was born, Pamela Bancroft Montague discovered that she could love someone more than she loved herself. Celestria didn't feel eclipsed by her new brother; she was still basking in the bright glare of her grandfather's love.

When Celestria returned, wearing a simple white dress embroidered with daisies, the family were taking their seats for lunch at a long table beneath a big square sunshade. Father Dalgliesh was placed at the head, Archie at the foot. Julia put herself next to the priest, with Penelope on his other side.

Pamela's place was discreetly taken away by Soames. He found Mrs Bancroft Montague exceedingly tiresome. Cook's son, Warren, had already been up to her six times that morning, with trays of hot drinks and little bowls of food and water for her wretched dog. He had a good mind to muffle her bell so he couldn't hear it.

Father Dalgliesh made the sign of the cross, then, with his head bowed and his hands folded, he said grace. '*Benedict, domine, nos et haec tua dona quae de tua largitate sumus sumpturi.*' As his hands made the sign of the cross for the second time, Celestria raised her eyes and caught those of the priest. He reminded her of a startled fox. She was about to smile at him with encouragement when Archie invited everyone to sit down with the words: 'Let battle commence!'

Celestria was placed between Lotty and David, but she was aware of the priest's attention even though he made an effort not to look at her again. It came as no surprise. Most men found her alluring. It was quite fun catching the eye of a priest and almost tempting to lead him astray for sport. She had had few rivals, but never one as powerful as God. The concept of celibacy fascinated her, especially in a man so good-looking. He had intelligent brown eyes, an angular face with chiselled cheekbones, and a strong jawline. In fact, if he took off those glasses, he'd be quite dishy.

'Father Dalgliesh,' she said, concealing a smirk. 'What called you to serve the Church?' He looked shocked for a moment and pushed his glasses up his nose, appalled at the effect this young woman had on him. Hadn't his faith and dedication built a resistance to this sort of thing?

'I had a dream as a little boy,' he replied.

'Really? Do tell,' she encouraged.

He raised his eyes and looked at her steadily. 'An angelic being came to me and in the clearest voice told me that my future was in the Catholic Church. It was a vision, a light so powerful it left me in no doubt that God was calling me to serve Him. Since then I have only ever wanted to be a priest. I have never forgotten that vision, and during moments of doubt, I remember it.'

'Like the light on the road to Damascus,' said Archie, chewing on a sausage.

'How miraculous,' exclaimed Penelope, her voice fruitier than ever.

'And how wonderful that miracles happen in the modern world,' added Julia.

'Yes, it is, isn't it?' replied Father Dalgliesh.

'Do you suffer doubts, Father?' Celestria asked to a sharp intake of breath from her aunt Penelope.

Father Dalgliesh struggled with the impertinence of her question. 'We are, all of us, human beings,' he said carefully. 'And it would be wrong to assume myself superhuman because of a vision and a calling. God has given me a challenge, and, at times, it seems great. Just because I'm a priest doesn't mean I am immune or even excluded from life's obstacles and pitfalls. I have weaknesses like everyone else. But my faith gives me strength. I have never doubted it or my conviction, only my own aptitude.'

As he spoke, he grew in stature. He seemed older than his years, as if he had a maturity gained over decades of experience, and yet, somewhere in the darkest corner of his heart, a menacing little seed was sown.

Later, back at the presbytery that stood next door to the Church of the Blessed Virgin Mary, Miss Hoddel brought Father Dalgliesh his tea on a tray. He sat in silence in the sitting room, his eyes far away from the book that rested on his knee. She looked about her, at the piles of papers and books squeezed into the bookshelves and heaped onto every available surface, and wondered where to put the tray. With an impatient snort she shuffled over to the coffee table and placed it on top of a tower of letters. Father Dalgliesh was shaken out of his trance and rushed to help her.

'I can't clean this place if it's always in a mess, Father,' she said, rubbing her hands up and down her wide hips as if to clean off the dust.

Father Dalgliesh shrugged apologetically. 'I'm afraid even this house isn't big enough for all my books,' he replied.

'Can't you sell some of them?'

He looked appalled. 'Absolutely not, Miss Hoddel.'

She sighed heavily and shook her head. 'Well, I've left you

and Father Brock some cold ham in the larder and a little salad for your dinner.'

'Thank you,' he replied, bending to pour the tea.

'I'm taking your vestments home to mend. I've got my trusty Singer, you see, so I can do the job properly. We can't have you looking shabby in church, can we, Father?' Again, he thanked her. 'I'll be going, then. See you tomorrow, bright and early, to tackle all that dust. I'll just have to clean around your clutter. It's not ideal, but what can I do?'

He watched her go, closing the panelled wooden door behind her. He breathed a sigh of relief. Miss Hoddel was a godly woman, of that he had no doubt. The trouble was her ill humour: there was nothing godly about that. Still, no one was perfect, not even him. A spinster in her late sixties, Miss Hodder was dedicated to serving the Church, happy to look after him and Father Howel Brock for very little. People like her were a blessing. He asked God for patience. He also asked God for strength and forgiveness. He hadn't been able to stop thinking about Celestria Montague since the moment he had seen her walking up the garden in her polka-dot swimming dress. Once again he pulled his rosary out of his pocket and began to move the beads slowly through his fingers, mumbling, in a low voice, ten Hail Marys.

Chapter 2

As far as the Montague family knew, there was nothing out of the ordinary that summer of 1958. No scent of discontent. No trail of unhappiness. Nothing. That year, like every year before, they decamped to Cornwall for the whole of August. The season was over. London looked tired and more than a little ragged, like a fairground in the early hours of the morning once everyone has had their fun and returned home. Monty still considered Pendrift home even though Pamela hated it. 'Too darn cold,' she complained, even when the sun smouldered in mid-August and her children complained of sunburn. Perhaps it was only natural that she missed her childhood summers in Nantucket, and there *was* something about Cornwall that rendered it damp, whatever the weather.

She opened the curtains and let the sunshine tumble in, irritated that she still felt cold in spite of it. She pulled on a sweater and threw a soft wrap over her shoulders. She hoped the priest had gone by now. She didn't like the Church and she liked men of God even less; they were always trying to convert people. Pamela believed only in things she could touch, and those things she could touch were often found wanting. She looked at her watch. Monty was coming down earlier than expected, having been away for ten days on business in France. He travelled a great deal, but business was business, and Pamela had to live with his achingly long absences.

She considered her husband. No one had a bad word to say about Monty – they had enough to challenge a thesaurus when it came to her, but Monty was loved by everyone. In his youth he had been the jaunty youngest child, known affectionately by the surname that suited him so well. That name had duly stuck, so now no one ever referred to him by his real name, Robert, except for his widowed mother, Elizabeth, who lived in the dower house on the estate, heaving herself up to the big house for a grumble at every opportunity. No one was more cantankerous than Elizabeth Montague. They expected every summer to be her last, but the old girl hung on as if afraid heaven would be a place where complaining wasn't allowed. A woman seemingly devoid of compassion, she loved Monty the best of her family. When he entered the room, her eyes would light up and the usual pallor of her cheeks would take on a blush. It was as if she saw the shadow of her beloved husband in the countenance of her son and was falling in love all over again.

Being the younger son, Monty was free of the responsibilities that came with owning Pendrift Hall. Those responsibilities had weighed heavily on Archie's shoulders since he'd inherited the estate fourteen years before, so that he now stooped a little when he walked and often disappeared into his office for hours, where no one ever dared disturb him. Archie Montague might have appeared benign, but beneath the gentle coating a ferocious temper lay in wait for the slightest provocation. He suffered a gnawing anxiety from the pressure of maintaining such a large property and looking after all the employees who worked on it, not to mention the education of his three sons and his wife's well-known extravagance. While Monty had always done as he pleased, Archie had had to learn about the farm and the maintenance of the family estate that had been purchased by his great-grandfather in the eighteenth century. Archie had

toiled on the farm with his father while his brother had whistled his way across the world, seeking pleasure in sunny
countries. Then, one day Monty had returned to ask his
father to lend him money to invest in a sugar venture in
northern Brazil. Archie thought the idea preposterous, but
Monty had a way about him. A charm that not only dazzled
his mother, but enchanted his father, too. Unlike poor
Archie, Monty could do no wrong. Everyone else feared the
boy had lost his mind and was about to lose the Montague
family fortune as well. But his parents believed in him blindly
and would not hear a word of doubt from anyone. Their
erratic son disappeared for a year, during which time the
Montagues held their breath. He returned a rich man, and
everyone was able to breathe again. Elizabeth crowed and
Ivan was repaid with interest. Later, on hearing the story,
Pamela was impressed by his courage. She wouldn't have
considered marrying a man who was lily-livered, nor would
she have considered marrying a man who was poor.

She withdrew from the window and went downstairs,
carrying Poochi like a baby. Soames was in the hall gathering
the silver from the mantelpiece to polish. 'Good afternoon,'
he said politely, hiding his irritation. He had hoped to avoid
her when she finally emerged from her room.

'Ah, Soames. I'm ravenous. Would you be very kind and
bring something out for me on a tray?'

'Of course, Mrs Bancroft Montague,' he replied.

'Has the priest gone?'

'He left over an hour ago.'

'Good. Where's Mrs Julia?'

'On the terrace with Mrs Penelope.'

'And Celestria?'

'Miss Celestria is down on the beach with Miss Lotty and
Miss Melissa. Master Harry is in the woods with his cousins,
setting more traps.'

'Good. Poochi would like something, too. Bring him
some leftover sausage. You love sausage, don't you, sweetie.
Yes, you do.' She rubbed her nose into the dog's fur. Soames
pitied the poor dog, being nuzzled like that. Her perfume
alone was enough to knock anyone out.

Pamela walked through the French doors onto the terrace.
Julia sat in the shade, a cigarette between her fingers, while
Penelope held forth about marriage. 'You're lucky, Julia,' she
was saying. 'This won't ever concern you, having only boys.
But, my dear, it concerns me day and night. There are a good
many scoundrels around who would be perfectly unsuitable.
The trouble is, young girls love scoundrels.'

'Nothing wrong with a scoundrel, as long as he's a *rich*
scoundrel,' said Pamela, squinting in the sunlight. She put
Poochi down, then arranged herself before sitting on the
cushioned bench. 'Sometimes a scoundrel is rather fun.'

'Oh, Pamela,' exclaimed Julia. 'You're only saying that to
be controversial.'

'You wouldn't want Celestria marrying a scoundrel,' interjected Penelope.

Pamela smiled the smug smile of a woman certain her
daughter would marry nothing of the sort. 'Oh, Celestria, I
think she's got what it takes to tame a scoundrel.' Penelope
looked at Julia and rolled her eyes 'Oh, I think it's a very
good thing for a man to keep a woman on her toes. There's
something kind of elusive about Monty. I might not like it,
but it sure prevents me running off with somebody else!'

Before Pamela could continue, the scrunching of wheels was
heard on the gravel at the front of the house. From up in the
woods Purdy heard, too, and galloped off down the field, barking. A car door opened and slammed shut. A moment later,
Monty appeared, his panama hat set at an angle on his head, his
briefcase in his hand and the *Daily Telegraph* under one arm. He
was smiling, his smooth brown face crinkled with merriment.

'Good day, ladies,' he said, taking off his hat. Then he strode over to where his wife lounged on the bench and bent down to kiss her. 'And you, my darling. A very good day to you!'

Down on the beach, Celestria lay on the sand with her cousins. The tide was high, the sea benign, like a great lion having an afternoon snooze. Gulls circled above, resting on the cliffs that sheltered the east end of the beach, pecking at the odd crab foolish enough to have climbed out of its rock pool. The sun blazed down, making them feel sleepy. Celestria turned onto her back and put her hands behind her head.

'Do you think he's never had sex?' she said, referring to Father Dalgliesh.

'Of course not,' replied Melissa. 'If he had his vision as a boy, there wouldn't have been time.'

'Do you think he'll be tempted?' Lotty asked. 'He's not an old codger like Father Hancock was.'

'Definitely,' Celestria stated, remembering the way he had looked at her. 'The trouble is, the unknown enemy is the most dangerous. It's easier to fight something if you've tried it.'

'But he's made vows of chastity. He can't break them,' said Lotty. 'That must be very hard on a man. After all, even he said he has weaknesses like the rest of us.'

'Shame. He's attractive, isn't he?' said Celestria, sighing heavily.

'You don't really fancy him,' said Melissa.

'She just likes the challenge,' Lotty added with a giggle. 'There's no greater challenge than to win the heart of a priest.'

'That would be very cruel,' said Melissa seriously. 'I hope you wouldn't be so irresponsible, Celestria.' Both sisters knew that if anyone had the power to do it, Celestria did.

'Well, if I don't get swept off my feet really soon, I just

might have to give it a try, out of boredom. Nothing much else happens around here.'

A voice called out from the top of the path that snaked its way down the rocks from the house. They raised their eyes to see Monty, followed by Wilfrid, Sam, and Harry. Purdy bounded down in front of them, wagging his tail excitedly. Purdy loved the beach; it meant games. This afternoon it meant boating, which he adored. The girls stood up and, shielding their eyes from the sun, watched the small group approach.

Monty greeted his daughter with a big smile. 'What are you three witches plotting?' He laughed, kissing her hot cheek.

'Terrible things,' replied Celestria, grinning at her cousins.

'Do you want to join us?' he asked. Although there wasn't enough room in the boat for all of them, Monty liked to please everyone.

'Can't think of anything worse,' said Celestria, looking at the boat lying forlornly on the dunes. It was a small red motorboat, her father's passion. He called it *Princess,* and both wife and daughter believed it to be named after her.

'You'd love it if you gave it a try. Little better than sitting in the middle of the ocean with nothing to see but sky and water.'

'We're going fishing,' said Harry, proudly showing off his rod. Monty held a bucket of live bait and the rest of the nets and rods.

Celestria peered inside the bucket and recoiled. 'Don't bring those ghastly creatures near me. I'm staying here on dry land, which is where I'm happiest!'

'Come on, boys!' Monty announced heartily. 'Let's get going. We don't want to keep the pirates waiting.'

Monty put the rods, bucket, and nets in the boat, then, with the help of the entire group, dragged it down the beach to the sea. As the girls waved, the motor spluttered and gurgled until it finally choked into a rhythmic chug, cutting through the waves to carry Monty, the boys, and a very keen Purdy off into the dark blue sea.

It wasn't long before they were dots on the horizon.

'I don't like the sea,' said Celestria suddenly. 'It makes me feel nervous.'

'Don't be silly,' said Lotty. 'Nothing much can go wrong. Uncle Monty's an expert.'

'That makes no difference,' she replied gravely. 'The sea's bigger than the biggest expert. One gulp and they're gone.'

Monty watched his daughter from the boat. Her slim, elegant shape reminded him of Pamela when she was young. They stood in the same way: thrusting their weight onto one leg, one hand confidently placed on the waist, emphasizing the feminine curve of the hip to its best advantage. They were very alike, although Celestria wasn't so hard. She was soft, like clay ready to be moulded, and the hand that styled her would decide her final texture. It wouldn't be his hand. It never had been. He had spent too much time abroad, trying to keep all the balls in the air, trying to be everything to everyone, spreading himself so thin that sometimes, in the silence of his dreams, he was no longer sure who he really was. But now wasn't the time to indulge in sentiment. He had three excited boys in his boat and a sea full of fish and crabs to catch. He watched until Celestria had blended into the sand, and for a moment his heart, once so carefully contained, swelled with regret. But things were now out of his control. He was no longer a free man. It was time to reap what he had sown. His gaze fell onto the water, and he was momentarily hypnotized by the murky green depths below him.

★

The highlight of the holiday for Celestria was her uncle Archie's birthday party at the end of August. Julia always threw a ball in the garden and invited their friends from far and wide to dance the night away in a glorious tent she'd decorate with flowers from her own borders and greenhouses. This year was even more special because it was his fiftieth.

Celestria longed for the party. She was bored by the countryside and yearned to return to the city. She didn't like to play tennis. The enjoyment of showing off her long legs in shorts passed quickly, and she was left with the tedium of the game. She had grown weary of sitting on the terrace with her aunts and cousins, listening to their repetitive gossip. She had spent many a morning down on the beach with Bouncy. Nanny had been grateful for the company. Celestria watched the little boy build sandcastles and play with his digger in the sand, and she understood why her mother loved Harry so much; little boys broke hearts. Later she'd learn that when they grow to be men, they break them all over again.

It was the end of the summer. Archie's ball was only a week away. Celestria had taken to spending the evenings reading in the little secret garden that was known as Penelope's, for when her aunt was a baby, Nanny had always put her pram there for her afternoon rest. Lying directly beneath the library window, she was suddenly drawn out of *Frenchman's Creek* by the sound of her father's voice. He was talking to Julia, who sounded as if she was crying.

'He's in terrible trouble. Oh, I do hate to burden you with it all, dear Monty, but I didn't know whom to turn to.'

'I'm glad you felt you could come to me.'

'You're such a good man.' She emphasized the word *good* so that it weighed heavily with all sorts of connotations. Celestria knew she was thinking of her mother.

'How much trouble is he in?'

Julia sighed heavily. Celestria leaned back against the wall like a spy and dared to peek in through the window. Her father had lit a cigar and was standing against the far window-sill on the other side of the room. His voice, firm and confident, seemed to soothe Julia's anxiety.

'Well, the farm was doing very well,' she continued with a sniff. 'But you know Archie, he's always had one eye on the City. He felt it wasn't wise to have all his eggs in one basket, so he decided to put some of them into equities.'

Monty nodded gravely.

'He made some bad investments. Then he bought some of Tom Pritchett's land, adjacent to ours, in order to expand the farm. He borrowed money, and now, well, he's having trouble paying it all back. I think the interest is high and what with taxation.' She sank onto the sofa and began to cry again.

Celestria was aghast. It was horrid to see Julia, usually so cheerful, now crumpling with despair. She'd had no idea her aunt and uncle were strapped for cash. Well, she thought, Papa will put it all right. He's got pots of money.

Monty crossed the room and sat down beside Julia. 'Don't worry, Julia, old girl,' he said, smiling. 'I'll sort it all out for you. First, let me pay for Archie's party. I know how much these things cost. It would be a pleasure, but must also be our secret. I'd hate Archie to know. He's a proud man.'

'I'll pay it all back . . .'

'Consider it a gift. After all, you entertain me and my family here at Pendrift every summer; it's the very least we can do.' Julia sat up and took a deep breath, dabbing her eyes with a handkerchief.

'Thank you, Monty. I knew I could rely on you. You're always there, a wonderful knight in shining armour. What would we do without you? You're a real brick.'

'You're a splendid woman, Julia. A terrific wife and mother. I'm glad you felt you could ask.'

'I know Archie would hate me to sneak about behind his back. But I'm desperate. I can't stand to see him so burdened. It depresses him, weighs him down as if he's carrying this heavy backpack all the time, full of unpleasant worries.' She smiled affectionately as she reminisced. 'He was very different when I married him. Of course, when one is young, one believes one is invincible, and he never anticipated inheriting Pendrift until he was an old man. He certainly never realized it would be such a load. We all imagined Ivan would last forever. He might have a ghastly temper at times. I've never minded that. It's the troubled silence that sends alarm bells ringing. I'd far rather he tore the place apart in fury than fumed alone in his study. I can't reach him there, you see.' She sighed and placed her hand on her brother-in-law's arm. 'I do love him so very much. I just want my old friend back. I know you understand.'

'I do. More than you know. And I want to do all I can to help.'

'I won't ask again, I promise.'

'You can ask as often as you like. You're family, and family must stick together.'

There was a noise from the hall. Julia jumped to her feet and smoothed down her blouse. 'Goodness, that's Nanny with Bouncy. They must be back from the beach.' Before she hurried out she turned. 'Our secret,' she repeated, smiling at him gratefully.

Celestria remained by the window, watching her father. He slouched back into the sofa and crossed one leg over the other. He continued to puff on his cigar, toying with it between his fingers and staring through the thin curl of smoke that wafted into the air. His eyes grew lazy, his thoughts far away, his face unusually solemn. She longed to know what he was thinking. Why he looked so grim. He didn't look himself at all. Suddenly she felt uncomfortable spying on him like that, eavesdropping and hearing things she was not supposed to. She retreated to her book and soon forgot all about it.

Instead of reading, she considered Archie's birthday party. She had two options of dress; one was pale blue silk, which brought out the colour of her eyes, and the other dusty pink with a dashing red sash, which emphasized her small waist. The decision was agonizing. After all, Julia had invited the Wilmotte boys, who were all holidaying in Rock, and, if she remembered rightly, Dan Wilmotte was rather debonair.

Chapter 3

Celestria should have noticed that things weren't as they should be. The repercussions of Archie's predicament would touch them all in ways she could never have imagined. But she was young and selfish. All she could think about was the party. Her frocks hung in the cupboard like magic cloaks ready to spirit her off to a ballroom glittering with chandeliers and crystal, where men in white tie watched her with admiration, and women with envy. Where music echoed off mirrored walls and champagne bubbled in long-stemmed glasses. She was twenty-one, and she wanted to be in love.

Julia busied herself with her husband's birthday party as she did every year, and no one would have guessed that beneath her smile she was strangled with anxiety. A van load of men arrived to put up the tent, and caterers began to appear with boxes of glasses and crockery. Celestria watched them construct her fantasy with great excitement. It wouldn't be sophisticated like London parties, but she was so starved of distraction that she didn't mind. There would be plenty of people to admire her, and she would dance the night away with Dan Wilmotte in whichever dress she chose to wear. Finally something would rouse this sleepy crevice of Cornwall into action, and who knows, she might even fall in love. Her mother always said that love came when you least expected it.

Lotty and Melissa were just as excited as Celestria and faced with the very real concern of finding husbands. With her long auburn hair Lotty was the prettier of the two, but, as Pamela cruelly used to say, 'in the kingdom of the blind the one-eyed man is king.' Neither dazzled, poor creatures. Like so many English girls they had oval faces with small chins and watery blue eyes, all inherited from their mother, Penelope. Pamela referred to that type of girl as 'egg-faced.' Often the egg face was a sign of aristocratic blood – though not in Lotty and Melissa's case, of course. Milton had a strong, handsome face with big eyes and a firm, angular jaw, inherited by the fortunate David, who was also tall and athletic. What a pity his daughters hadn't been so lucky. Pamela was melodramatic and selfish, but at least she had given Celestria a beautiful face.

Down on the beach, the morning of the dance, Celestria escaped having to help Julia with the flowers. Melissa was too good-hearted to hide out with her, but she had managed to coerce Lotty into joining her. The girls lay on towels in the sunshine, while Bouncy dug a hole with Nanny and the boys played cricket with Purdy. Celestria wore a pair of white shorts and a turquoise shirt, knotted at the breast, that turned her grey eyes blue. Lotty wore white slacks – she didn't like to show her legs, they were as sturdy as a pony's – and a sunhat hid her fair and freckled skin.

'Are you sure we shouldn't be helping out?' she asked with a frown.

Celestria stretched lazily. 'We'd only get in the way. Too many cooks spoil the broth. Besides, someone has to look out for the boys, as Nanny only has eyes for Bouncy.'

'Don't we all? I long for a baby,' added Lotty with a sigh.

'You have to find a man first, or didn't Aunt Penelope tell you the facts of life?'

A small smile crept across Lotty's face. 'You can keep a secret, can't you?'

'You know I can,' Celestria replied, propping herself up on her elbow.

'I haven't even told Melissa.'

'Oh, I doubt she'd be able to keep a secret from your mother, and Aunt Penelope's got a voice like a foghorn.'

'So I can trust you?'

'Of course.'

She paused, then plunged in. 'I'm in love, Celestria. Really and truly in love.' Her eyes shone with happiness.

'Who with? Do I know him?'

'That's the problem. He's not one of us.'

'Not top drawer?' Celestria was appalled but at the same time intrigued. If he was rich, what did it matter? 'New money?'

'I don't think he has very much. He's a pianist.'

'Francis Browne,' said Celestria jubilantly.

Lotty looked startled. 'How do you know?'

'He's your new piano teacher. Mama's considering getting rid of old Mrs Gilstone and replacing her with him, which would be a blessing from my point of view. Mrs Gilstone had bad breath. Your mother says he's rather good. He's obviously *too* good!'

'He's talented, sensitive, and kind.' Lotty's face, lit up by love, looked almost beautiful.

'Oh dear. I suppose he loves you back?'

'Yes. He wants to marry me.'

'You could always elope. That's very romantic and the kind of thing his sort do all the time, I should imagine.'

'Mummy and Daddy would die. I couldn't do it to them.'

'Well, you can't have both. Is he handsome?'

'Very. He's fair with a long nose and the loveliest brown eyes you ever saw. He calls me "Aphrodite."'

'I bet he does. Has he kissed you yet?'

Lotty's face turned the color of a beetroot. 'Yes. Only once. I'm longing to return to London to see him. He can't even write to me down here. Mummy would find out immediately. She wants me to marry Eddie Richmond.'

'Because he's rich and will inherit his father's estate in Northumberland.'

'He's perfectly nice; I just don't find him attractive.'

'There's more to a man than his chin, Lotty,' said Celestria facetiously. Lotty didn't smile. 'He's got nice eyes. His front teeth stick out a little, but he's got pots of money. You have a nasty choice to make: love or money?'

'In that respect there's no contest. I'd choose love every time. It's Mummy who's the problem.'

'And a very big one, too!'

'It's the 1950s. A girl should be able to marry whomever she likes. We've come a long way since Emmeline Pankhurst chained herself to the railings.'

'If you marry Francis Browne, we'll all have free piano lessons!' Celestria added brightly.

'Don't be ridiculous, Celestria, we'll have to charge you double in order to live! Mummy and Daddy will disown me.'

'Oh, I don't think so. It could be worse. You could be in love with Father Dalgliesh!'

Lotty laughed. 'Against all my principles, and I hope against all of yours, too!'

An icy wind blew in off the sea. Celestria shivered. Purple clouds gathered on the horizon, and Nanny pulled out a jersey for Bouncy. He saw her waving it at him and ran off down the beach, headed for the water. His laughter was carried on the wind like the cry of a gull. In front of him the waves had grown large and angry, pounding the sea like great lion paws. He dropped his spade, which Purdy seized with delight, casting aside the cricket ball. Nanny struggled stiffly to her feet and hurried off in pursuit of the increasingly distant figure. Celestria and Lotty watched in horror as Bouncy continued, seemingly deaf to the great lion's roar. Harry, Wilfrid, and Sam continued their game of cricket, oblivious. Only Purdy dropped the spade and began to bark in alarm.

The little boy reached the sea and stopped suddenly. Turning to his nanny, he began to cry. Beneath the darkening sky, the waves looked even more menacing. She grabbed his hand and led him away, scolding him fiercely for running off, which made him cry all the more. 'You can't swim,' she was saying when she reached the girls. 'The sea is dangerous for little boys like you.'

'Thank God he's okay,' hissed Lotty to her cousin. 'That frightened the life out of me.'

'And Nanny. She's gone green! Look.' Celestria turned to Lotty, suddenly feeling rather chilly. 'Don't make any rash decisions. I can't imagine it's much fun being poor. It certainly isn't romantic. You've grown up with money. You're used to it. You'd have a good life with someone like Eddie Richmond. He'd look after you and make life comfortable. You might even grow to love him over time.'

Lotty shook her head. 'For a selfish creature, you can sound very sensible occasionally.'

'In the olden days women married men for money and land and took lovers on the side. I think that makes perfect sense, don't you?'

'But most of the time you're full of nonsense! Marriage is a sacred thing, Celestria. One makes one's vows before God. When I marry, I will vow to love my husband with all my heart. Adultery is out of the question, and it should be for you, too.'

'Where do I get these terrible ideas from?' Celestria said with a wicked smile.

'Must be your mother. She *is* American, after all.'

Nanny had brushed the sand off Bouncy, dried his tears, and
put him in his navy blue jersey. 'It's getting cold,' complained
Harry. 'We're going back to check the traps.'

'I bet we've caught a few,' said Wilfrid enthusiastically.
'We stole Mummy's best cheddar.'

'And dipped it in Papa's whiskey,' Harry added with a chuckle.
The three of them looked as smug as a band of triumphant thieves.

'Come on!' Sam shouted, already setting off up the path to
the house.

'We'd better get you home,' said Nanny to Bouncy. 'You'll
need a nice cup of hot milk after your fright. I won't tell Mrs
Julia; it'll only worry her. Gives me the willies living so close to
the sea.' Her face looked lined and pale as the wind caught the
stray wisps of silver hair that had come away from her bun. 'I
knew a man once that drowned. They found his body on the
rocks a week later, what was left of it. Nasty business. Didn't
matter that he could swim. Made no difference at all. Poor sod.
Come Bouncy, put that seaweed down, it's dirty.'

The girls walked ahead as the path was narrow and Bouncy
walked slowly after them, his little hand in Nanny's old one.

'Do you think Nanny would have caught up with him if
he hadn't stopped on his own?' Lotty asked quietly.

'No,' Celestria replied. 'And I don't think she'd survive in
that cold water, either. They'd both drown.'

'Should I tell Aunt Julia?' Lotty was shaken by what she
had seen.

'No. Bouncy won't rush off like that again. He got a terrible fright. The sound of the waves was enough to put him off.
Besides, Papa and your mother grew up all right, didn't they?'

'Nanny was younger then.'

They arrived at a house buzzing with activity. Julia had

been transformed into a bossy sergeant major, shouting instructions to her small army of helpers. The tent was up, the floors laid, tables with white cloths adorned with glasses and plates piled high for the buffet. The smell of cooking wafted through the hall, causing Purdy to salivate greedily and make haste to the kitchen. Milton was carrying in chairs with Monty, while David made signs to put on the lavatory doors and Melissa and her mother helped Julia arrange the flowers. Lotty immediately volunteered to join her, gushing apologies for not having done so earlier. Celestria had one ally left: her mother. She knew for certain that she'd be as far as possible from all this hearty helping. When Celestria inquired after her, her father replied that she was feeling a little poorly and had retired to the small sitting room to read. Determined not to be roped into helping, Celestria said she would go and check on her. In the hall, she passed Harry, who was looking glum. 'No rats?' she asked brightly.

'Got to help Aunt Julia,' he replied.

'Well, you're a man, and they need strong pairs of hands.'

'Where are you going?'

'Oh, I'm helping, too,' she lied. 'Aunt Julia needs some cotton; there's a hole in the tent.' She pulled a face to fool him into believing that she was as exasperated as he was, then hurried off to find their mother.

Sure enough, Pamela was lying with her feet up on the sofa, a cup steaming on the table beside her, classical music giving the room a sense of serenity, her Pekingese curled up on her lap while she stroked him with long white fingers. 'Poochi is terrified of the bustle out there. It's like a railway station at rush hour, and he hates railway stations,' she said when she saw Celestria in the doorway. 'Your cheeks are pink. Where have you been?'

'On the beach.'

'In this weather?'

'Oh Mama, it's not cold.'

'That's your father in you. To me grey clouds, drizzle, and wind mean nothing but misery. I can't imagine anything worse than sitting out in it for fun.'

'It's not drizzling.'

'It will be in a minute. Look at those clouds, they're furious. Gives me a chill just looking at them. Why don't you join me in here; it's terribly dull on my own.'

Celestria slumped into the armchair.

'Ring for Soames. He can light us a fire.' She seemed to sink deeper into her white cashmere sweater. Celestria looked around for the bell. 'Isn't there one in here? Why don't you run and tell him, darling, before your poor mother dies of hypothermia.'

Celestria was reluctant to go back into the hall for fear of being put to task, but her mother was determined to have her fire. So she did something quite out of character and bent down to light it herself. Pamela was appalled.

'You can't do that, Celestria. You'll get all dirty, and your nails! Do go and get Soames, he'll do it in a flash. That's what staff are for. Really, darling, I insist.'

But Celestria was already on her knees, striking a match and lighting the little balls of newspaper that Soames had stuffed under the grate. It was easy. The wood was dry and caught fire immediately. No dirty hands and no broken nails. She stood up and looked at it in triumph.

'I don't know why you're so pleased with yourself, Celestria; it's not ladylike to do men's jobs.'

'I don't want to get caught by Aunt Julia,' she explained, flopping into the chair again. 'I'll be exhausted by the time everyone arrives.'

'Quite, darling, let everyone else do it. Too many cooks spoil the broth. Have you decided which dress you're going to wear? I did tell you to bring a bigger selection. You'll freeze in those flimsy things.'

'I think I'll wear the pink. I'm feeling pink today,' she replied.

'We'll have to tone down your cheeks a little. This Cornish weather does nothing for a woman's complexion.'

'I was lying in the sun with Lotty.'

'I hope she was wearing a hat. That girl is dreadfully pale.'

'She was. But guess what? She's lost her heart.'

Pamela's eyes widened. 'Is he suitable?'

'Not at all.'

'Well? Who is he?'

'I can't tell you, Mama. I'll be breaking my word.' Pamela's face fell. 'I can tell you that he's ordinary.'

'Common?'

'Not one of us, no.'

Pamela Bancroft Montague allowed a small smile to flourish on her lips. 'Oh dear,' she said, looking delighted. 'What will Penelope say when she finds out?'

'Aunt Penelope wants her to marry—'

'Edward Richmond, I know. Edward would be a good catch for Lotty. After all, she's no oil painting, but then, neither is Edward. They are definitely on the same level of the food chain.'

'What do you mean?'

Her fingers stopped stroking Poochi's powdered fur as she deliberated a moment. 'Well, Lotty is not a panther, or a tiger, is she? She's more like a deer. Sweet and guileless. There are plenty of her sort. Edward is neither a lion nor a leopard; he's also a herd animal, being not very original and of a type. I'd say he's a wildebeest.'

'Oh, that's so clever, Mama! What am I?'

'You, Celestria? You're a lioness, of course, and only a lion will do for you. You're at the top of the food chain, darling. It simply wouldn't be right for you to marry a buffalo or a weasel or even a stallion.'

'So it's a combination of beauty, class, and intelligence?'

'Exactly. You are not a herd animal. You have a beauty and grace that set you apart from the rest, and, although you are not the daughter of a duchess, you have all the qualities of one in abundance.'

'Except the egg face!' she laughed.

'You get your strong chin from me.'

When Monty entered, they were busy going through the family, placing them neatly into the food chain one by one, beside themselves with amusement. 'What's Papa?' Celestria asked as he looked at them indulgently.

Pamela narrowed her eyes. 'He's a cheetah,' she said in a throaty voice. 'Because he's the fastest animal in the world.'

'And you, my darling, are a white tiger: beautiful, solitary, and very, very rare.' He smiled at her tenderly. 'So this is where you've been hiding out!' he said to Celestria. 'It's safe to come out now. It's all done. Julia's gone up to have a bath. I should think you ought to be doing the same.'

'Perhaps I'll meet my lion tonight,' she said, getting up.

'Don't accept anything less, Celestria. I didn't.'

'It's a good fire, isn't it?' she added.

'She lit it herself, silly child,' Pamela said to her husband. Monty didn't bother to point out that it was still summer. 'I packed my mink stole this year,' she continued. 'Tonight I shall wear it.'

'If you're lucky, it will ward off any lesser beasts,' Monty said good-naturedly.

'Oh, I don't think she needs the stole for that,' Celestria quipped as she left the room. 'Lesser beasts can recognize a tiger when they see one.'

Chapter 4

Celestria stood in front of the window to watch the sunset. The days were slowly shortening, summertime forced into retreat by an overzealous autumn. The light was amber. Soft and warm and sad somehow. The sea glittered and sparkled like copper beneath a sky darkening prematurely with clouds. Of all the nights, the drizzle had chosen tonight. There may even be a storm, she thought with rising excitement, envisaging pressing herself against Dan Willmotte for comfort as claps of thunder ripped apart the heavens. The water was calm. Ominously so. As if holding its breath for the inevitable tempest.

She studied her reflection in the mirror and smiled with satisfaction. The pink dress looked stunning, complemented by the sparkle of her mother's diamonds. She pulled her shoulders back, admiring the gentle sheen of oil on her skin. She would shine the brightest tonight. Only a lion would do, she thought smugly. She'd leave the buffalo to Melissa. Poor Lotty, so foolish to allow herself to fall in love with an unsuitable man, she thought gleefully, certain that she was too cunning ever to make the same mistake.

She waited in her room until she was sure that the rest of the family was downstairs. It was always fun to make an entrance. She heard them in the drawing room, their voices a low murmur, punctuated by sudden bursts of laughter. She closed the curtains. The sky was now a deep mauve, like a bruise, the sea already rousing itself for the oncoming storm. As she left her room she heard the first drop of rain break against the window pane.

The noise of voices grew louder as she walked up the corridor. She reached the stairs to be met by Poochi and a strong whiff of tuberose. They could only mean one thing: that her mother had waited to make an entrance, too. She might have known. When Pamela saw her daughter, her face shone with pleasure. 'Darling, you look beautiful!' she exclaimed, casting an admiring glance over the dress. In her daughter she saw the beauty she had once been and could be all over again, vicariously. 'You're going to slay them all, Celestria.'

'You look lovely, too,' Celestria replied truthfully, although *lovely* was without doubt too soft a word for her. At forty-eight, Pamela Bancroft Montague was still strikingly beautiful. Her blonde hair was pulled back into a shiny chignon, accentuating her now fuller face and cool aqua eyes, carefully framed by jet-black lashes. Diamonds swung from her earlobes and around her neck where the skin was still firm, and a large diamond brooch was pinned to her bosom. She was wise enough to know that, at her age, being thin only made a woman appear older. Her lips were the colour of blackberry juice, against which her teeth sparkled a dazzling white. Her shoulders were wrapped in the mink stole, which complemented the deep green silk of her dress; rich colours were kinder to her skin, making it seem to glow by contrast. She wore black gloves that reached her elbows and held a small black pouch with a diamanté clasp in the shape of a flower. Inside she kept her Elizabeth Arden lipstick, a gold powder compact, and a small flask of perfume. Pamela knew how to make the best of herself, a talent she had passed on to her daughter. Taking Celestria's hand, her smile was full of pride. After all, her daughter was an extension of herself, a living reminder to everyone of the magnificence of her youth.

They entered the drawing room at the same time. Their presence, resplendent in diamonds and silk, caused a sudden hush to come over the room. The family all turned at once, their conversations trailing off as their lips parted in silent admiration. Only Bouncy continued to chatter as he tried to persuade Purdy to play with him by pulling his tail. Finally, Monty strode over. 'What glamorous girls!' he exclaimed jovially. 'Do they really belong to me?' He took Celestria's hands and kissed them with a bow before slipping his arm around his wife's waist and planting a kiss on her cheek. He looked handsome in white tie, his sandy hair brushed back off his forehead, his skin brown from being at sea all afternoon. His face glowed with pride as he led them into the room. The two women floated into the crowd like a pair of swans.

Julia wore a gown of pale turquoise. She looked poised and graceful, her bubbling laughter rising above the chatter of her excited family. Had it not been for the frenetic dragging on her cigarette, Celestria would not have known how nervous she was. She recalled the conversation she had overheard in the library and wondered whether Archie wasn't perhaps a little uneasy at the extravagance of his party. There he stood with Harry and his two elder sons, laughing about their recent rat-catching expeditions, stroking his moustache. He clearly adored his boys. He took time to listen to them, prompting them patiently with questions and chuckling in amusement at their stories. He patted Wilfrid's head and ruffled Sam's hair, and the boys gazed up at him admiringly. Celestria wondered whether he knew about her father's gift, or whether Julia had kept it to herself, as she'd said she would. She turned her attention to her smallest cousin. Little Bouncy was sitting on Monty's knee, pretending to ride a horse as his uncle bounced him up and down over imaginary fences. 'Again!' the child demanded after each 'race,' and Monty obliged without the slightest indication that he might be tired or bored.

Celestria assumed she was the last member of the family to arrive until the room fell silent once again. Put out, she craned her neck to see who stood in the doorway. There, sucking the air out of the room with inflated nostrils, stood Elizabeth Montague. 'It's the bad fairy,' Celestria hissed to her mother when she saw the solid black figure of her grandmother planted firmly between the double doors.

Pamela whispered back, 'On the food chain, I'd say your grandmother is a hyena, wouldn't you?'

'But she produced a lion?' Celestria retorted.

'Only *one* lion, and that was on account of your grand-father, who was a lion, too,' Pamela replied with emphasis. 'Now there is only one lion in this family, and I married him. Archie's a badger, and, as for Penelope, she's a wild boar.'

'Mama, you're so cruel!'

'The animal kingdom is a cruel world, darling. Dog eat dog, but the hyena eats the remains of everyone else's meal.'

Elizabeth Montague was escorted into the room by her first cousin, Humphrey Hornby-Hume, a large barrel of a man with ruddy cheeks and bulbous eyes that glistened like under-cooked eggs. Elizabeth's face was set in its usual scowl. Years of indignation had corroded any memory of joy. Her face had simply forgotten how to smile, and she was now too old to be re-educated. She always wore black in the evening, claiming that it was the most flattering colour for a woman with one foot in the grave, and she walked with a stick, one hip stiff and painful due to arthritis. She smoked incessantly, reminding everyone that cigarettes and food were her only remaining pleasures – except for Monty, whom she worshipped with a fierce and possessive love, and her grandson Bouncy, who she claimed to be the image of her dear brother who was killed in the Great War. Elizabeth adored men, perhaps because the envy she felt for women younger and prettier than herself was too much to withstand. It was impossible to imagine that this full-figured woman with wide, lopsided hips and stout legs had once been handsome, and a terrible flirt.

As they entered the room, Monty, the dutiful son, strode up and kissed her gnarled hands, followed hastily by Archie, the birthday boy. The old woman's face thawed at the sight of her favourite son, and her mouth twitched with the beginnings of a smile. Archie backed away, used to being eclipsed by his more charismatic brother. Julia noticed, as she always did, and her heart buckled with compassion.

Nevertheless, she greeted her mother-in-law with the same warmth with which she greeted everyone. There seemed to be no side to Julia; she was a ray of sunshine beaming down on everyone indiscriminately. If she disliked her mother-in-law, she certainly never let it show. Instead, she flattered her, echoed boisterously by Humphrey, who seemed never to notice his cousin's sour humour.

'Now the most important member of the family is here, I think we should proceed into the tent. The guests will be arriving shortly,' Julia suggested.

'Ah, you are too generous! I don't deserve such praise!' Humphrey quipped in his thin, reedy voice.

'Your jokes have never been funny, Humphrey,' Elizabeth replied with a dismissive snort. 'I'm certainly the oldest person here. I only come to Archie's party to remind the world that I am still alive.'

'Well, let's go and show them,' Julia persisted, trying to usher them through the room.

'I don't want them all celebrating when there's nothing to rejoice about,' the old woman continued.

'My dear cousin, if ever there was a woman so full of life . . .' Humphrey began.

'And laughter,' Elizabeth cut in sourly. 'I know, Humphrey, I'm the life and soul of the party. Get me a drink and a chair, or I shall quite literally be the soul of the party, and we don't want that, do we?'

'Archie, darling, perhaps you could make an announcement,' Julia proposed, suddenly looking rather weary.

Archie cleared his throat. 'Attention everyone!' he exclaimed, puffing out his chest importantly. No one seemed to notice.

'Speak up, boy, we can't hear you!' shouted Elizabeth, bashing her stick repeatedly on the wooden floor until the china began to wobble in the glass cabinet against the wall. At once everyone stopped talking and turned to Archie.

'Julia would like everyone to proceed to the tent now.' He sounded rather sheepish. By contrast, Monty's voice was firm and commanding.

'Before we all disperse into the tent, I'd like to wish my brother most happy returns of the day. This is, after all, a very special birthday. It gives me great pleasure to be among my family, and I know it gives Archie a great deal of pleasure, too. Blood is thicker than water, and there is nothing like the sharing of blood to unite us all in an unbreakable bond. Archie, my dear brother and friend, father, husband, and son, we wish you a very happy birthday and many more in the years to come, and whatever the future brings, know that I, your brother, have always admired you.' Julia's face softened at Monty's kind words, and Archie lowered his eyes with embarrassment. He didn't feel at all worthy of Monty's admiration.

While everyone clapped Elizabeth managed to bring the conversation once more around to her. 'I think this will be my last, Humphrey. Next year, they'll have double the reason to celebrate.'

'Hello, Grandma,' Celestria exclaimed, taking her elbow so that she walked into the tent between her granddaughter and Humphrey. Before she could reply, her cousin, whose rheumy eyes had lit up at the sight of young flesh, broke in, his reedy voice a few notes higher with excitement.

'Ah, the most charming and radiant Celestria. I thought I sensed the room exude a light more heavenly than earthly. You look more glorious than ever.' He dropped his eyes to her chest, where they delved a moment into her cleavage.

'Are you admiring my diamonds, Humphrey?' Celestria teased. He withdrew his gaze with difficulty.

'They are exquisite, but you shine far brighter than they do.'

'Don't listen to the old bore!' Elizabeth interrupted. 'If he was fifty years younger, I'd be concerned.'

'I'm struck in the heart, Cousin. How cruel you are!'

'Celestria, that dress is almost indecent!' she stated. 'In my day only tarts wore dresses that revealed so much. A dress like that will only get you into trouble.'

'But I love trouble, Grandma!'

'With a man of experience, my dear, trouble can be a great deal of fun.' Humphrey had begun to perspire.

'A dress like that sends out the wrong messages,' her grandmother continued. 'You're a Montague, and you should behave with more discretion. Look at your cousins. Now, *those* dresses are most suitable. I brought Penelope up with a strong sense of morality, which I am glad to see she has passed on to her daughters. I brought your father up in the same way. The only trouble with your father is your mother. Americans have no sense of decorum.'

Celestria laughed as Humphrey winked at her over Elizabeth's heavily coiffed grey head. 'I love Americans,' he said. 'And your mother is splendid. In fact, I'm going to reserve a dance with her right away before she gets booked up. I'd like one with you, too, Celestria. Will you promise to make an ugly old man happy?'

'Of course,' she lied with an easy smile. The thought of

being pressed up against that swollen belly, already steaming with sweat, made her blood curdle.

Humphrey disappeared into the tent to find Pamela, a futile expedition, for Celestria knew her mother would decline his offer before he had even finished his sentence. Pamela hadn't the patience for men like Humphrey; after all, she was a white tiger, and white tigers were very disparaging of warthogs.

'Let's get you to a chair, Grandma,' Celestria said, eager to deposit her charge quickly so that she could mingle among the guests, who were now arriving in droves.

'Get me an ashtray. I'd like a cigarette.' She sat down stiffly, leaning her stick against the table, and scratched about in her bag for a cigarette. Elizabeth always smoked through an ivory cigarette holder her father had brought her from India for her twenty-first birthday. While Celestria went to find an ashtray, a waiter struck a match and lit it for her, placing a bubbling champagne flute on the table in front of her.

As Celestria made to return to the table her eyes caught sight of a most attractive man. She remained frozen to the carpet for a moment, careful not to let her jaw drop like Melissa's had a tendency to do. He didn't see her. He was too busy talking to Dan Wilmotte, whose debonair looks now faded by comparison. They were both laughing, throwing their heads back in the insouciant manner of men who have no cares. There was something about the squareness of his jawline that she found very attractive. His lips were twisted into a lopsided grin, his nose was irregular, and his dark brown hair, rather long and flopping over his forehead, suggested a delicious arrogance. His charisma reached her from the other end of the room like a lighthouse signal to a ship, indicating land yet warning of danger. She was immediately transfixed by it, promising as it did a whole heap of trouble. A warm feeling of excitement curled up her spine like a hot snake.

'Celestria!' She turned to see her furious grandmother, now accompanied by a couple of elderly men, holding out her dropping cigarette with indignation. 'My granddaughter is unbearably dizzy,' she said, her lips pursed. Celestria held the glass dish beneath the older woman's cigarette so she could flick ash into it, then placed it on the table. By the slack-jawed appreciation of the two elderly men, she could tell they weren't at all bothered by a little dizziness. Much to their disappointment, she didn't wait to be introduced, but turned on her heel in search of the handsome stranger.

She might have guessed that *he* would find *her.* They all did, one way or another.

'Celestria!' Dan exclaimed, embracing her like an old friend. Had Celestria not set eyes on his handsome companion, she would have welcomed his eagerness. However, she patted his shoulder as he kissed her cheek, not wanting to humiliate him. 'Let me introduce you to Rafferty,' he said. Rafferty took her hand and raised it to his lips, not withdrawing his eyes even for a moment. Celestria was enchanted.

'It's a pleasure to meet you, Rafferty,' she replied, looking up at him from under her lashes in a manner that was most certain to ensnare him and exaggerating the slight twang in her accent.

'You're American,' he said in surprise, releasing her hand.

'Mama's American; I'm English.' She relished the exoticism of her two cultures.

'I'm Irish, from Cork. It's my first visit to Cornwall.'

'He's staying with us,' said Dan, beaming with pleasure.

'Dan, darling, will you get me a glass of champagne?' Celestria suggested, touching his arm with a gloved hand. Dan responded with zeal, turning on his polished black shoes and weaving his way through the crowd to the table Julia had set up as a bar.

Rafferty grinned at the transparency of her ploy. Celestria was too shameless to blush. 'Do you live here?' he asked. 'Stunning place.'

'It's the family home. We all descend on Uncle Archie for most of August. The rest of the year I live in London, in Belgravia. I imagine you've been to London?'

He laughed incredulously. 'You must think me very parochial!'

'Are you? One can't always tell.'

'I'm at Oxford studying law. I spend a great deal of time in London.'

'Staying with the Wilmottes?'

'They're old family friends.'

His eyes strayed a moment and lingered lazily on her breasts. 'You're very beautiful,' he murmured, suddenly serious. She noticed his eyes were an unusual shade of green, like lichen.

'Thank you, Rafferty.'

'I suppose you get told that all the time.'

'A girl never tires of compliments.'

'You don't blush, which suggests you've received far too many.'

'Would you like me to blush?'

'Yes.'

'Why?'

'Because then I'd feel in with a chance.'

She laughed, uncertain whether or not he was teasing. He gazed at her steadily. She held her ground and gazed right back, trying to ascertain what lurked behind the lichen while that hot snake curled up her spine again. Then Dan returned with a glass of champagne and the moment was lost.

She hoped she'd be placed next to Rafferty at dinner. They continued to talk, the three of them, light and frivolous chat on top of a hidden undercurrent of desire that ran between

Rafferty and Celestria. His eyes lingered on hers longer than was normal, and once or twice his fingers touched the skin on her forearm, causing her belly to turn over with excitement. She remembered the delicious sensation of Aidan Cooney's fingers, and her belly tumbled again, all on its own.

Father Dalgliesh watched her from the other side of the tent. Surrounded by elderly ladies who were delighted to have the opportunity to talk to the handsome new priest, he was unable to restrain his eyes from drifting over the heads of the guests to where Celestria was speaking to two young men. Her beauty was breathtaking. The voices around him blended into a distant buzz, like a swarm of mosquitoes, as he reassured himself that his attraction to her was only human, a temptation sent by God to test him, thus rendering his resistance all the more commendable. *I am a priest*, he told himself. *But I am also a man. The devil may tempt me, but I will not yield.* 'I told my grandson that it was no good going to Mass once in a while, one has to fulfil one's Sunday obligation. It cleanses the soul. I just don't understand the young of today.'

'Indeed,' Father Dalgliesh replied vaguely. The others were quick to agree, competing with one another to add their own stories. But Father Dalgliesh did nothing to untangle them. His mind was elsewhere, and the seed in his heart had begun to grow.

Suddenly the tent was struck by a violent gust of wind. The sides flapped, straining the cords that tied them down, and a sound like falling pebbles rattled on the roof. All eyes turned upward as the downpour threatened to break through the canvas and drench them all. Julia dragged furiously on her cigarette, masking her nervousness behind a wide and carefree smile. Pamela was clearly relishing the drama, holding forth in the centre of a group of admirers, pulling her mink stole tighter around her shoulders to keep warm. 'I hope the tent doesn't slip down the garden into the sea,' Celestria said.

'If it continues, we shan't be able to drive home,' said Dan happily. 'We'll all have to stay the night.'

'Oh, what fun!' Celestria exclaimed, longing for the party to continue into the following morning.

'Let's drink to the storm, then,' Rafferty suggested. 'That it continues all night with thunder and lightning, too. It'll be like the Blitz all over again.' Not that any of them had much memory of the war. He fixed her with those moss-green eyes, and the corners of his mouth twisted into a mischievous grin. She raised her glass.

'To the storm,' she replied, smiling flirtatiously. 'And to new friends. It's always nice to meet new people.'

Her eyes lifted and caught those of Father Dalgliesh, staring at her intently from behind his spectacles. She raised her glass at him and smiled. He flushed with embarrassment at having been caught watching her and raised his glass of lime cordial with an awkward nod. Quickly he turned back to his ladies, endeavouring to join together the fragmented pieces of conversation in order to respond convincingly.

To Celestria's irritation, Julia had seated her next to Dan, not Rafferty, but she forgave her because Dan had introduced her to the mysterious Irishman. On her other side sat Humphrey, now puce in the face with alcohol and excitement. Her heart sank. Judging by the breadth of his smile he was clearly triumphant with his placement.

'Ah, Celestria,' he gushed, planting his hand on her bottom. 'The lovely Celestria!' He wriggled his hand and let out a theatrical groan. 'What do you do to me, you naughty girl.'

She placed the object of his desire on the chair and covered her knees with a napkin. She was about to respond with rudeness when her attention was drawn to the next-door table, where Rafferty was sitting next to Melissa, trying to catch her eye. While Melissa radiated joy, Rafferty gave Celestria a look of desperation, to which she responded by raising her eyes to heaven. There was no doubt about it, Rafferty and she had an understanding and were united already by their unfortunate placements. *It is clear that he would have preferred to sit next to me*, she thought happily and threw him a coy smile. He grinned back, using only one side of his mouth. Her stomach flipped again. Oh, how delicious it was to be in love.

Chapter 5

Father Dalgliesh was ill at ease with people. In front of his congregation he sparkled. He commandeered the nave, recited Latin as if it were his first language, and filled everyone with enthusiasm to go out more virtuous than they came in. That was why the bishop had appointed him to this parish and the two neighbouring ones, despite his relative youth and inexperience. In his professional capacity he had charisma: he inspired people, stimulated them, poured oil on the rusty chinks in their faith. But when it came to everyday conversation, relating to the mundane toils of his congregants, he felt he was sitting behind a pane of glass, unable to reach them. This made him nervous. Yet he recognized the challenge before him, and, as he sat between Penelope Flint and a lively woman in her late sixties, he knew the only way to improve his social skills was to practise. He watched Celestria take her seat at a table on the other side of the tent and felt his heart deflate with disappointment. How he wished he were sitting next to her. Suddenly, he caught sight of his feet. His stomach lurched in horror as he noticed one red sock and one green. He quickly pushed them under the table, thus concealing them from Penelope's incisive gaze. It was shameful to be so distracted as to forget to dress properly.

★

'Your grandmother is right, Celestria. You're asking for trouble in a dress like that. But, as you said yourself, you like trouble. You like it a lot, don't you, my dear?'

'I don't know what you're talking about, Humphrey. Really, the champagne has gone to your head,' she replied. She felt the old man's hand squeezing her knee.

'You don't fool me,' he whispered.

'Why would I want to fool you, Humphrey?'

'Because you look like butter wouldn't melt in your mouth. But you've been a naughty girl, haven't you?'

'Now you're boring me,' she said wearily. His hand remained firmly on her knee.

'I can smell naughtiness on a girl, you see. I have the smelling power of a dog. You like a little hanky-panky, don't you? But then, it runs in the family. Your grandmother liked a little hanky-panky, too, when she was young. She wasn't as beautiful as you, but she was sexy. I was her cousin, so no hanky-panky for me. But you, you . . .' She could feel his hot breath on her cheek. 'You like the pleasures of the flesh, don't you, Celestria? You're a sensual woman, I can tell.' His hand wandered up her thigh. 'You like the feel of a man's hand on you, don't you? You tease.'

'Where are your manners, Humphrey? Have you forgotten yourself?' she asked in a loud voice. She noticed she had attracted the attention of a few other guests, among them her cousin David. 'What will my grandmother say when I tell her you've had your hand on my thigh?' The hand was hastily removed and placed on the table.

'Is everything all right, Celestria?' David asked from across the table. He was grinning, but she could tell from his eyes that he was genuinely concerned.

'Only a little fun, right, my dear?' Humphrey chortled.

'For you, perhaps,' Celestria replied sharply. Once again she caught Rafferty staring at her. She hoped he had seen the errant hand. It was always a good thing to stir a man's sense of gallantry. There lurked in most men a little of the knight in shining armour. She pulled a despairing face. Once again she raised her eyes to heaven, then turned to talk to Dan, satisfied that as soon as the dinner was over, she would be in Rafferty's arms, being swung around the dance floor.

Celestria usually dreaded the speeches, preferring to talk to the men on either side of her. But that night she couldn't have welcomed them more. While Dan was a delight, Humphrey certainly was not. Drunk and lecherous, his hand straying from the table to squeeze her thigh an inch or so higher at every venture, he was determined to take advantage of the rare opportunity of having her captive for the entire length of dinner. She knew if she told her grandmother she'd only blame the dress. She could hear her voice very clearly: 'My dear, if you had worn something a little more discreet, Humphrey wouldn't have been tempted.' As her uncle took the microphone, Humphrey's hand crawled once again to her thigh. That was enough. She couldn't tolerate it a second longer. While Archie tested the microphone by tapping it with his finger, she fled into the drawing room that led off the hall. She could feel Rafferty's velvet eyes upon her and hoped he would follow.

It was quiet in the drawing room, except for the rattling sound of rain behind the curtains. A few waiters bustled through with trays of coffee and china cups, muttering 'Good evening, miss,' as they passed. She heaved as deep a breath as the corset of her dress allowed and wandered into the hall. It was clear that Rafferty wasn't going to come. She was disappointed, but understood that his departure from the table would be considered disrespectful to her uncle, not to mention ungallant to the ladies on either side of him. One of whom was her cousin Melissa.

Celestria folded her arms and stuck out her bottom lip, swinging her hips from side to side to see the skirt of her dress dance. 'Psssst!' came from the landing above. Harry, Wilfrid, Sam, and little Bouncy crouched at the top of the stairs, peeping through the banisters.

'Look at you!' she exclaimed in delight. She had never seen a more adorable group of pink faces. They were dressed in their pyjamas, their hair brushed with neat partings by Nanny.

'W-w-w-w-we're thpying,' exclaimed Bouncy in a loud voice, his stammer more pronounced due to tiredness. She doubted he had ever stayed up so late.

'Shouldn't you be in bed, Bouncy?' she replied, climbing the stairs to join them.

'It's too noisy to sleep,' complained Wilfrid earnestly. 'The tent is right below our window.'

'We want to watch the party!' said Harry.

'W-w-w-w-we're thpying,' repeated Bouncy, his large brown eyes wide with excitement.

'Does Nanny know you're here?'

'She's not *my* nanny,' Harry corrected.

'Nor ours! She's Bouncy's,' agreed Sam.

'Can you hear the rain?' said Wilfrid. 'It's very loud.'

'Will it thunder?' Sam asked.

'I'm sure it will, and lightning, too. You're not afraid of thunder and lightning, are you, Bouncy?' The little boy looked anxious. 'Do you know what thunder is?' He put his finger in his mouth and nodded slowly. 'It's angry clouds having a jolly good fight. That's all. Nothing to be frightened of.'

'I bet the rain will drown our traps,' said Harry despondently.

'It'll drown all the rats if you're lucky,' Celestria replied. 'Then you can take them to Cyril and he'll reward you handsomely.'

'Is the party fun?' asked Harry, a little enviously.

'Great fun. But this is the boring bit when Uncle Archie and Papa give speeches. Much more fun up here, I can promise you.' She ran her fingers through Bouncy's thick hair. 'As for you, young man, I think you should go to bed. It's very late. What will Nanny say if she finds you?'

'Thee w-w-w-won't find me, because I-I-I-I-I'll hide,' he said with a naughty grin. Celestria smiled back. It was impossible not to smile at everything Bouncy said. She leaned forward and planted a kiss on his rosy cheek.

'You run off now, darling. Good night.' She skipped down the stairs, holding up the skirt of her dress so it billowed about her legs like a parachute.

She waited on the sofa in the drawing room like a patient lioness for her lion, half listening to the drone of speeches as first Archie and then her father settled into their strides and clearly grew to relish the sound of their own voices amplified above the roar of the rain. She threw herself back against the cushions and dreamed of dancing with Rafferty.

Soames peered over. 'Are you all right, Miss Celestria?'

'Just a severe case of boredom, Soames. Nothing a little music and dancing won't cure.'

When at last the speeches were over, she hastened to the bathroom to check her appearance before embarking on a night of romance with her handsome new admirer.

Her hopes were dashed, however, by her cousin Melissa, whom she found in front of the mirror in a state of extreme excitement. 'I'm in love!' she breathed, staring at her flushed face in the glass. Celestria noticed the slack jaw and reminded herself never to allow hers to fall so.

'With Rafferty?' she asked. It was too tiresome to have to feign ignorance.

'Do you know him?' she replied, surprised.

'I met him before dinner. He's a friend of Dan's.'

Her face brightened. 'You like Dan, don't you? Lotty said you did.'

'Not really,' Celestria replied breezily. 'He's very sweet, but not my type, after all.'

'Well, Rafferty has promised me the first dance,' she said hurriedly.

'Perhaps he'll promise me the second,' Celestria replied, and her cousin's face showed her mortification. She knew as well as anyone there simply wasn't any point competing with Celestria.

'Oh, I can hear the music,' Melissa exclaimed, her voice almost a wail, and left the room in a flurry.

'What's she crying about?' asked Pamela, rustling in to powder her nose and apply lipstick. 'It must be a man. It's always a man!'

'She's in love with Rafferty.'

'Who?' her mother asked.

'He's Irish and more handsome than you can imagine. Dan Wilmotte brought him.'

'He's clearly not on her level of the food chain.' Pamela placed her little bag on the marble and pulled out her gold powder compact.

'He's a lion,' Celestria replied proudly.

Pamela dusted her nose. 'Now I understand the tears. Poor Missy, she shouldn't aim so high; she'll only get bruised when she falls. I suppose you like him.'

'He's been making eyes at me all evening.'

'How presumptuous of him.'

'I've been encouraging him, Mama.'

'Is that wise? You know nothing about him.'

'He's gorgeous and charming.'

Her mother sighed and replaced the little powder puff in its case, closing it with a snap. 'That doesn't mean he's got the qualities that make him worthy of you.'

'If you mean money, I don't know.'

'I'm not entirely shallow, darling. I mean, is he kind? Loyal? Has he got integrity? Does he respect you? Or is he just after a little tumble in the flower beds?'

'Really, Mama. He's not like that at all. At least, I don't think he is.' She recalled Humphrey's hot hand on her thigh and decided to tell her mother.

'Humphrey! How ghastly!' Pamela replied, suitably appalled. 'He's a dirty old man. You see, Celestria, men are all the same. They all want a little flesh. You just have to decide whether or not you want to give it to them.'

'Not Papa!'

'Yes, Papa. That's why I have to keep myself looking beautiful – so I don't lose him to some lovely young thing.'

Celestria was horrified. She had never heard her mother talk about her father like that. 'I'd hate to think of Papa being as fresh as Humphrey.'

'Of course he's nothing like Humphrey. Good Lord, no! Your father's far too well-mannered and decent. He'd never flirt so coarsely with a girl his daughter's age, though your father does like to flirt.' Celestria noticed an edge of bitterness in her mother's voice. She swayed a little in front of the mirror, tidying her hair with her hand. She was tipsy. Celestria was startled; it was so unlike her mother. 'Your father gave me this when he made his first fortune,' she said, tracing her hand across the diamond brooch that was pinned to her dress. 'He said he had to find stars big enough to outshine the stars in my eyes. So typical of Monty.' She laughed, the brittleness now softened by the warmth of her memories. 'I told him even my father couldn't have chosen better, and he was so proud. I know he felt the pressure of marrying an heiress. He wanted to make his own money, to stand on his own two feet. He accepted nothing from my father, only me! Well, he made money all on his own. My father's very proud of him, though he's never told him so. Men! They're not very good at being sentimental.' Celestria watched the two interwoven stars glitter in the yellow light. That was how she saw her parents, interwoven with glitter. 'Wouldn't life be wonderful if one could freeze it before one falls off the peak and sinks onto a less satisfactory plateau?'

'What do you mean?'

'Well, it's not a bed of roses, even with your father. Marriage has to be worked at, and work of any sort doesn't suit me.' She took a tissue and dabbed the corner of her eye with a trembling hand. In a small voice she added, 'I'll give it a try. Your father's worth the effort, don't you agree? I just wish he was around more. He's growing into a stranger.'

'He just works too hard. Perhaps if you talked to him—'

'All work and no play makes Jack a dull boy.'

'Papa's not dull.'

'His absence is making my life dull, darling. After the war we had to get to know each other again. Now I feel we're going backwards, but there's no war to give it a veneer of acceptability. It's all very well being off all the time if you're fighting to save your country. Making money doesn't cut it. Not any more.'

Celestria placed her hand on top of her mother's. It wasn't easy discussing her father like that. She had placed him so high on a pedestal she was barely able to see him, let alone know him. She wasn't ready to accept that he had flaws.

They returned to the tent as the first rumble of thunder vibrated through the air. The band had begun to play Frank Sinatra and couples were already dancing, led by the birthday boy himself and Julia. She saw Rafferty and Melissa pressed up against each other and was sure the Irishman was just being polite. After all, Melissa was no looker.

'May I?' came a voice behind her.

'Dan!' Pamela exclaimed. 'How lovely to see you. Who's this very dashing friend you've brought with you?'

'Rafferty O'Grady, Mrs Montague.'

'Is he as charming as they all say?'

'*Wild* would be a more appropriate word, I think,' he replied with a chuckle, looking at Celestria. 'The Irish are all wild.'

'In that case I'm happy to leave my only daughter in your capable hands.' She raised her eyebrows as if to say I told you so, then moved off, weaving unsteadily around the tables to find her husband. Celestria was intrigued. Dan was sweet and handsome, but Rafferty was dark and mysterious. The very idea of his being 'wild' gave him greater allure.

They stepped onto the dance floor and took up positions, although Celestria didn't feel inclined to press up against Dan as Melissa had so presumptuously done to poor Rafferty. The rain pelted down outside, and the thunder roared above them. She imagined the sea was roaring, too, those great big lion's paws rising up in waves and pounding the shoreline. She wondered whether little Bouncy had gone off to bed like she'd told him to, or whether he was still sitting at the top of the stairs, afraid of the storm. Then Rafferty caught her eye and she ceased to wonder about anything else.

She pretended to be enjoying her dance with Dan. It wasn't good for Rafferty to believe he had already won her, and, besides, a little chase would render the catch all the more enthralling. She danced on, and then, when she had grown bored of the game, she retreated to her table on Dan's arm, grateful that the tedious old lecher had vacated his chair and disappeared into the throng. Dan refilled her glass with champagne. In order to cope with the agony of waiting for Rafferty, she took a large swig. 'Darling, you don't know how good that tastes. Why not fill it up again? After all, it's Uncle Archie's birthday, and he'd be most offended if I didn't drink to his good health.' Dan did as he was told. For some reason, tonight she resented his attentiveness. She suddenly longed for him to tell her she was drinking too much, to take command, to put her in her place. They were all putty in her hands. So she took another swig. And another. Then another, until her glass was empty. 'Just a little more. One mustn't offend the birthday boy!' she insisted, aware that her head was beginning to spin. To her intense irritation, he kept pouring without a moment's hesitation. She was on the point of telling him off for indulging her when Rafferty appeared with Melissa.

'May I ask the lady for a dance?' he said, his mouth twisted in amusement.

'If I can dance with *your* lady?' Dan replied, standing up. Celestria watched him take Melissa by the hand and lead her off towards the dance floor.

'Celestria?' said Rafferty, and her name had never sounded so lovely. She held out her hand, aware that she must have taken off her gloves and that she would feel his skin against hers. Their fingers touched, and that hot snake stirred at the foot of her spine. She suppressed a giggle, conscious of the champagne bubbles that tickled her belly. With an arrogant smile that she found devilishly seductive, he proceeded to lead her across the tent.

Once on the dance floor he swung her around and pulled her against him, pressing his cheek to hers. 'Now I have you all to myself,' he murmured. 'I'm where I've wanted to be all evening.' Celestria was flattered. They swayed to the music, and the more they swayed the more dizzy her head became. She couldn't recall how many glasses of champagne she'd had, and she was too happy to care.

She saw her parents dancing, and, even through the hazy, alcohol-induced blur, she could tell that they were not happy. Her father was looking stern, while Pamela's face was pinched and miserable. Celestria closed her eyes and inhaled the spicy scent of Rafferty's skin. Aroused by the proximity of their bodies, she began to rub herself against him in a sleepy rhythm, barely aware of what she was doing. It wasn't long before she felt the hard evidence of his excitement. Unaware of the dangers of arousing a man, she was curious and a little careless with the power her beauty gave her. 'Let's get out of here,' he whispered into her ear, and led her out of the tent.

As they hurried through the hall Celestria glanced up to the top of the stairs where the children had been hiding. They must have all gone to bed. 'Where are you taking me?' she giggled, feigning resistance.

'Somewhere we can be alone,' he replied without glancing back. He opened the door to the little sitting room and crept inside. He didn't bother turning on the lights. 'It smells of wood smoke in here,' he said, closing the door behind her.

'I lit a fire this afternoon for Mama. She hates the cold.'

'I can't see a thing. Damn, where's the sofa?'

'Now it's your turn to follow me.' She led him carefully around the coffee table, upon which Julia had stacked art books in neat piles, alongside a large bowl full of postcards collected over the years.

Rafferty wasted no time. He threw off his dinner jacket and fell back onto the cushions, pulling her with him so that she was squeezed between his body and the back of the sofa. Without another word he began to kiss her. The hot snake was wide awake by now and curling madly up her spine, causing her skin to tingle all over and a warm aching feeling to grow between her legs. The sound of rain tapping against the window enhanced the romance of it all, and her heart swelled with happiness.

His hands were warm as he caressed her face, tracing his fingers down her cheek and neck and onto the swell of her breasts, now barely contained beneath the bodice of her dress.

She arched her back by way of encouragement. He pulled away a moment, and she could sense him smiling through the blackness. 'You're a dark horse, aren't you, Celestria?' He ran his tongue across her lips. For a hideous moment she was reminded of Humphrey and his wandering hand.

She tried to push Humphrey's sweaty face out of her mind and concentrate on Rafferty, now caressing her breasts and nuzzling into her neck. His bristle scratched her skin, his wet tongue slid over it, and the snake, having been cooled considerably by the thought of Humphrey, now grew hot again. Rafferty took her hand and pulled it down to where his own ardour was straining for attention. He placed it on the stiff rod between his legs and groaned as she touched it. So this was it. This insistent thing that fathered generations, ruined reputations, started wars, inspired heroism and adventure, discovery and conquest, but, more often than not, caused the downfall of many a brilliant man. This, which she now held in her hand, was it. She felt like Delilah with a pair of scissors. One snip and that would be the end of his power. 'You're beautiful,' he murmured urgently. She wanted to laugh at the way men lost themselves in the flesh of beautiful women. Aidan Cooney had been the same: the heavy breathing, sweating brow, writhing hips, urgent whisperings, as if driven mad by the rod that wouldn't be quiet until satisfied.

Now his fingers found their way up beneath the skirt of her dress. With a gentle touch he traced along the silk top of her stocking until they lingered enticingly at the fastening of her suspender belt. 'You like this, don't you?' he breathed, lifting his head to look at her through the darkness. All she could see were two shiny pearls where the light from under the door reflected in his eyes. His fingers circled the flesh at the top of her thigh until they reached the lace of her knickers. She remembered the delicious sensation of Aidan's fingers and opened her legs a fraction to allow him access. 'I could tell you like it from the moment I met you,' he continued, and his voice resonated with the same smugness as Humphrey's. Furious at his comment, she clamped her thighs together, trapping his hand between them. He laughed, enjoying the game. 'Don't pretend you're not excited. We're the same, you and I.' He tried to wriggle his hand free, but her thighs remained firmly shut. 'Come on, Celestria, let me in.' He hadn't noticed that she wasn't laughing.

She sat up. He withdrew his hand. 'What's the matter?'

'You've obviously misunderstood. I'm not that sort of girl. I'm a virgin, of course!' She smoothed down her dress.

'I didn't mean to offend you.' He seemed genuinely mortified.

'You think I'm fast, don't you?'

'It's just a bit of fun.'

'That's what Humphrey said!'

'Who's Humphrey?'

'The disgusting old bore who had his hand on my knee the whole way through dinner. I think this has gone quite far enough!' she exclaimed angrily, climbing over him. Feeling frighteningly sober and as much out of love as a girl could possibly be, she stumbled towards the door.

'Was it something I said?' he stammered in bewilderment.

'It's a misunderstanding,' she replied, fumbling for the handle. Then he was behind her, wrapping his arms around her waist, nuzzling into her hair.

'I didn't mean to go so fast. I'm sorry, I just got carried away. You're a beautiful woman and I'm just a hot-blooded Irishman. You make a man crazy!'

'I got carried away, too,' she said coldly, finding the handle and turning it. 'But we've had our fun. Let's go back to the party.'

A woman's heart is a deep and complex thing, she thought with a sigh. Even she didn't understand it. She left the sitting room more than a little disappointed at not, after all, being in love. But she couldn't love a man who didn't respect her. Rafferty wasn't a lion after all; he was a dog in lion's clothing.

As she walked through the hall, she noticed the light was on in Archie's study and the door had been left ajar. When Rafferty had disappeared back into the tent, she turned and wandered into the study.

To her surprise she saw her father standing by the window, staring out into the storm, his fingers toying with the cigar that smoked into the warm, musty air. He did not notice her at first, and once again she found herself in the awkward position of spying on him. His profile was solemn, his mouth set into a hard, grim line. It was as if he played the role of being the jovial, good-natured husband, father, and uncle when he was in company and then became someone very different when he stepped off the stage and was alone. For a moment Celestria wondered which was the real Robert Montague. After the unsettling conversation with her mother in the ladies' room, the idea made her head spin.

Suddenly he turned and caught her watching him. She gasped, but her father's face softened and broke into a wide smile. 'My darling,' he said, leaving the storm and his heavy thoughts to join her at the door. 'It's unlike you to be so quiet!'

'And it's unlike you to be so serious, Papa. Are you all right?'

He chuckled and shook his head. 'There's one hell of a storm out there tonight. Very unusual for this time of year.'

'You looked so sad,' she persisted. Monty looked at his daughter quizzically. 'You are all right, aren't you?'

'I've never been better,' he replied, and his grin convinced her that this was true.

'I prefer to see you smile,' she said.

'Then I shall make sure I always do.'

'Where's Mama?'

'Will you dance with me, Celestria?' he asked suddenly, and Celestria didn't know whether he had ignored her question or whether he hadn't heard it.

'I'd love to. I'm one "young thing" Mama won't mind your taking in your arms.' He was astonished. Celestria grinned up at him, aware that the wine had made her reckless. She felt a frisson of excitement at having caused such a reaction. He shook his head and patted her hand.

'Come, let's get you onto the dance floor before you say something you'll regret.'

Later that night Monty stood again by the window in his brother's study. The rest of the household had retired to bed. The smell of cigarettes and wine lingered in the air, turning it sour as the hours passed. He held an empty champagne bottle in his hand. He had opened his waistcoat and undone his bow tie so that it hung loose about his neck. The rain still rattled against the glass, and the wind moaned eerily as it raced around the house to catch its tail. He was no longer the jovial Monty whom everyone knew and loved, but a man dogged by his past and the empty reality of his future. He had sown the fields of his life without a thought for the harvest. The fun had been in the growing, but he had lost control of the crop. There was only one way out.

Chapter 6

The morning after the party, Julia burst into Celestria's bedroom, her face as grey as cold porridge, declaring in a voice husky with anxiety that Bouncy was not in his room and hadn't been seen since his young cousins had left him on the stairs the night before. 'You saw him, too, didn't you, Celestria?' Her voice broke, and she began to cry. She looked suddenly very small standing in the doorway in her dressing gown, her hair unbrushed and sticking out like a feather duster. Celestria staggered out of bed.

'I told him to go to bed,' she replied, wincing at the pain in her head. She pulled her dressing gown off the back of the door and yawned loudly.

'Did you see him get up? Did he go to bed?'

'No.'

'He's not with Nanny. I could murder the silly woman for allowing this to happen.' She rubbed her forehead with the palm of her hand and took a deep breath. 'It's fine. It's a big house. We'll find him.'

'Didn't Harry and the others see him to his room?'

'Of course not. They're just boys.'

'Let's search the house from top to bottom. He must be somewhere!'

Julia shook her head helplessly. 'We've scoured the place. Everyone's looking, but he's nowhere.'

'He was frightened of the storm. He wouldn't go outside, surely!' Celestria remembered his running towards the sea the day before, and a sickness rose up from her stomach.

She joined in the search, starting with the attic. She opened every cupboard, looked under every bed, chest of drawers, sofa, and chair. She called his name, but she knew instinctively that he wasn't there. The house felt empty. Her heart hung suspended as horrific possibilities surfaced in her mind. She pressed her nose to the window. The rain had stopped, and the sky was pale and blue in the innocent light of dawn. Below, the sea was calm. Had Bouncy ventured down to the beach on his own?

They all searched together, silently, their greatest fear unspoken. Celestria had a terrible vision that the sea had taken him. Swallowed him up. Dragged him down to the bottom, where he now lay, still and unbreathing. She saw Nanny, like a spectre, calling his name in a frail and hopeless voice. She dared not catch her eye. They shared a secret that was now heavy with implication: how close she had come to losing him the day before.

Archie stalked the gardens, his expression troubled. Every now and then he would stop, hands on hips, and shake his head in despair. How could a small boy disappear in the middle of the night?

Celestria ran down the wet path to the beach. Her bare feet hurt on the stones, but she was in too much of a hurry to go back for her shoes. She had to find out whether little Bouncy had drowned. She couldn't tell anyone why she suspected he was there; she didn't really know herself. Just that something was pulling her there, trying to tell her that the answer lay in the sea. The sun was warm on her face, although it was early. The air smelled clean and grassy after the storm. She reached the rocks and scanned them for her little cousin. Her heart thumped, her chest grew tight, but the beach stretched out before her, empty but for the odd seagull pecking at shells left behind by the tide.

Then she noticed it, or rather the absence of it. Her father's boat. She looked up the beach to where it usually lay on the dunes, tied to a stake sticking out of the sand. It wasn't there. The stake stood, forlorn. At first, she imagined the storm had taken it. But the dunes had been untouched by the waves, and the marks left by the boat being dragged down the beach were still fresh in the sand. They disappeared after a couple of hundred yards, indicating that it had been taken out only a few hours before.

She had to tell her father immediately that someone had stolen his boat. Perhaps they had taken Bouncy, too. She ran as fast as she could, stumbling up the path, blinking away tears as the realization hit her that something was really very wrong. Because her feet were wet she decided to enter the house through the scullery door that led into the rooms that housed Purdy and the game larder and Julia's butlers' sinks. The lights had not been switched on, so she knew Purdy would be after his morning biscuit. In the panic of searching for Bouncy, everyone had forgotten Purdy. She opened the door and crept inside. It smelled strongly of dog. Through the gloom she saw him lying in his basket. Then, to her astonishment, she saw a small figure curled up beside him, his muslin pressed against his mouth, his little hands holding it tightly. It was Bouncy. The relief was intoxicating. Overwhelmed, Celestria began to sob. Purdy opened his eyes and sighed. He had obviously been awake for some time, waiting for his young friend to wake up so he could move. The child did not stir. Celestria crouched down and stroked his brow. His skin was warm and silky. He nuzzled his muslin and gave out a long sigh.

'Bouncy,' she said softly. He opened his eyes and sat up, looking dazed and disorientated, a frown heavy on his forehead. Purdy seized his chance and moved away, wagging his tail happily. 'Bouncy, darling. What are you doing in here? We've all been looking for you.'

'I was frightened of the th-th-th-thtorm,' he replied in a small voice, rolling his muslin into a ball and pressing it under his chin. 'Where's Mummy?' She scooped him into her arms and kissed his temple. He smelled of Purdy.

'Let's go and find her. You can't imagine how happy she's going to be to see you.'

Julia had prepared herself for the worst. Her youngest, most precious child had wandered off into the night and drowned in the sea. It was only a matter of time before they discovered his small body washed up on the sand. She envisaged the policeman at the door, the funeral, the tiny coffin, and her grief, which would plunge her into eternal darkness and despair.

'Aunt Julia!' Celestria exclaimed, finding her in a heap on the sofa in the hall, surrounded by Archie, Penelope, Milton, Lotty, and a terrified-looking Nanny.

'Mummy!' cried Bouncy when he saw her, holding his arms out for her. Julia's face opened like a sunflower before she collapsed in tears.

'Darling Bouncy!' she sobbed. 'Where have you been?' She held him against her chest, wrapping her arms around him and burying her face in his hair.

'He was asleep in the dog basket with Purdy,' said Celestria.

'With Purdy? What on earth were you doing there?' Julia began to laugh.

'I was f-f-frightened of the th-th-thtorm,' replied Bouncy, snuggling into his mother's embrace. 'Purdy looked after me.'

'Clever Purdy!' exclaimed Archie, patting his son's back a little too hard. 'He's a good chap. A fine gun dog and a nanny, too! Lotty, be a good girl and call David off the search. He went to look in the pond.'

'I'll go and get the boys up,' said Nanny in a quiet voice. 'Shall I leave Bouncy with you, Mrs Julia?'

'Thank you, Nanny.' Julia watched the old woman walk away. 'Nanny,' she added. Nanny turned, her hands clamped together as if in prayer.

'Yes, Mrs Julia.'

'It wasn't your fault.'

'Thank you, Mrs Julia.'

Celestria watched Nanny walk up the front stairs, her steps heavy and slow. She had a good mind to tell her aunt about the day before. Lotty was right; Nanny was too old. There were homes for people like her. Then she remembered her father's boat.

'Where's Mama?' she asked. 'Someone has stolen Papa's boat.'

'What do you mean?' said Archie.

'It's gone.'

'Been washed away by the storm, I suspect,' said Milton. Monty's boat was of minor concern compared with the near tragedy of Bouncy's disappearance.

'No, it's been dragged down the beach. The marks are still there.'

'I'll tell your father when he comes down for breakfast,' said Archie.

Bouncy was now thoroughly enjoying the attention. Sitting on his mother's lap, he was recounting his adventure.

'Ahem.' It was Soames. He stood stiffly in the doorway, pressed and polished in a crisp white shirt and tailcoat, out of place in the midst of dressing gowns and unbrushed hair. 'Breakfast is served in the dining room, Mr Archie,' he said, nodding slightly, embarrassed to find Mrs Julia in her night-gown. His attention was diverted to the top of the stairs, where Pamela suddenly appeared draped in a pink silk dressing gown that reached the ground, her blonde hair brushed back off her face, Poochi nestled under one arm. Without more ado, he discreetly withdrew.

'I hear we've lost Bouncy,' she said, then smiled in relief at the sight of her small nephew playing on his mother's knee. 'Thank heavens he's safe. Poochi's been up for hours scratching the door. Dogs know when something's wrong. There, you silly pooch, you can relax now, he's been found. Where was he?'

'With Purdy,' said Milton. 'I'm going to have breakfast,' he declared, setting off in the direction of the dining room, where Cook had laid out fried eggs and bacon, toast, porridge, and sardines. 'After last night, I'm ravenous. How about you, squire?' Archie nodded at his brother-in-law.

'It's been one hell of a morning,' he said. 'Breakfast, everyone. Don't want it all to get cold.'

'Where's Papa?' Celestria asked her mother as she glided down the stairs.

'I don't know. Haven't you seen him this morning?' She seemed unconcerned.

'His boat has been taken out,' Celestria continued.

Pamela looked confused. 'I don't think your father would sail out so early.'

'I think it's been stolen. It's been dragged down the beach. Probably a couple of hours ago.'

'Well, you'd better tell him when you see him. Don't worry, darling, he can buy another one. It was a rather scruffy old thing.'

Celestria followed her mother into the dining room. Archie and Milton were already sitting at the large round table tucking into their cooked breakfasts. The room smelled of coffee and bacon, and Poochi began to salivate. 'Oh, you're hungry, little man,' said Pamela, placing him on the floor with a gentle pat. 'How about a piece of bacon?' She proceeded to lift a slice with her fingers and dangle it above his nose. Archie raised his eyebrows as the little dog took a large bite and the whole piece disappeared in a single gulp.

'Shame to waste such a delicacy on that animal,' he said, eyeing the depleted dish of eggs and bacon on the sideboard.

'He's been very unhappy this morning,' said Pamela, pouring herself a cup of coffee. 'Small dogs are very sensitive.'

'If you're not careful, Purdy will think he's a piece of bacon and gobble him up for breakfast.'

Pamela didn't laugh. She was totally humourless when it came to her beloved pet. She flashed her icy blue eyes at her brother-in-law and proceeded to sip her coffee. 'That dopey dog is no match for my Poochi. He may be small, but he can be vicious. He has teeth like nails.' Archie couldn't be bothered to argue.

'Did everyone enjoy the party?' he asked as the grown-ups took their places at the breakfast table. Celestria noticed that Melissa blushed a deep scarlet. Even her ears began to throb.

'It was delightful,' enthused Penelope. 'Melissa, you're blushing!'

'Melissa?' said Lotty in surprise. Then she recalled seeing her sister dancing with that irresistibly handsome Irishman who came with the Wilmottes. Celestria was now only too delighted to hand Rafferty over to Melissa, if he was what she wanted. Their tumble on the sofa had proved, in spite of being rather enjoyable at the time, that he wasn't good enough for her.

'I think Melissa's in love,' Celestria stated coolly, forgetting all about her father's boat. Milton turned to his daughter.

'Melissa?' he said.

The poor girl could no longer contain her embarrassment. 'He's very charming,' she said in a quiet voice.

'Who is?' asked Pamela stridently.

'Rafferty O'Grady,' said Celestria. 'He's very handsome.'

'*Your* Rafferty?' said Pamela, turning to Celestria.

'He's not my Rafferty. We danced, that's all. He's charming. He had eyes only for Melissa.' Melissa seemed relieved to hear this, and the blood drained from her face, leaving her as pale as a pancake.

'I'm glad the girls aren't fighting over a man,' said Archie good-naturedly.

Pamela laughed, dropping another piece of bacon into Poochi's mouth.

'Oh, I don't think they're after the same type of man,' she said smugly, recalling Lotty's unsuitable love affair and her daughter's certainty of marrying better than all of them put together.

After a while Julia came down dressed in white slacks and a long, pale blue cardigan. Around her neck large aquamarines matched her eyes, which were bright with happiness. She drank her coffee and indulged in a cigarette, which calmed her nerves and stopped her hands from shaking. Smiling in her usual radiant way, she entertained everyone with stories of the night before. Harry, Wilfrid, and Sam sauntered in, red faced, having been into the woods to check on their traps. They announced that the rain hadn't drowned any rats, but kept them in their burrows, so the traps were empty. David sat in front of a large helping of eggs and toast while Lotty and Melissa whispered to each other, giggling behind their hands. Lotty's wide eyes and Melissa's pink cheeks told Celestria that Rafferty had done more than dance with her cousin. She couldn't have cared less. At least *she* had rebuffed him, so her pride was undented. She looked around the table. The atmosphere was joyous. The party had been a success. Julia was relieved it was over. But the family was incomplete.

'Mama,' said Celestria.

'Darling, I think you and I should go into town today.

There's going to be an awful lot of clearing up to do, and we don't want to get in the way.'

'Where's Papa?'

Pamela looked around. 'Why, that is a little odd. I can't imagine where he's gone. He doesn't like to miss breakfast. Perhaps he's having it in town. You know how he likes to chat to the locals.'

Celestria leaned across the table. 'Uncle Archie? Did Papa take your car this morning?'

'No. It was still in the garage when I checked inside for Bouncy. Thought the little devil might have sneaked in during the night. Who'd have thought he'd have snuggled up with Purdy, eh?'

Celestria tapped her fingers on the table with impatience. 'Isn't anyone going to do anything?' she exclaimed hotly.

'I shouldn't worry,' said Archie. 'He'll come in when he smells the bacon.'

'But his boat's been taken out. What's he doing in the middle of the ocean at this time of the morning?'

'Fishing?' said David with a smirk. 'Perhaps he wants a herring for breakfast.'

'Don't be ridiculous. Something's wrong; I can feel it.'

The table fell silent. They all looked at one another, then all eyes settled on Pamela.

'Did Monty go to bed last night?' Archie asked, mopping up the last of his egg yolk with a piece of toast. He didn't appear at all concerned; rather, he was making a show of it for his niece.

'Of course he did.'

'Was he tipsy?'

'Weren't we all?'

'Was he there when you got up?'

'No.' She looked uncharacteristically ashamed. 'But then he rarely is, seeing as I often don't get up at all!'

'I think we should look for him,' said Celestria, rising.

'I'll help you!' volunteered Harry excitedly, echoed boisterously by his two cousins. 'Maybe he's got caught in one of our traps.'

'This isn't funny, Harry!' Celestria snapped.

'I don't think there's anything to worry about,' said Milton. 'If ever there was a fellow capable of looking after himself, it's Monty. He probably took a walk to clear his head. I don't blame him. How about it, squire? My head could do with a little clearing.' The two men got up.

'We'll keep our eyes peeled for Monty.'

'Mother, aren't you going to do anything?' said Celestria irritably. 'I'm going down to the beach to see if he's there!'

'Oh, really, darling, you're being overly dramatic!'

'Well, someone has to look for him. If he took that boat out in the storm, he'll most certainly have been drowned. Now how does your coffee taste?' She stalked out of the room.

'Well, I always said she was made for the stage,' said Pamela once she had gone.

'What a morning!' said Julia with a sigh. 'Now there's nothing left of the party but rubbish to be cleared away. Still, it was worth it. Archie loved it, and that's what it was all about.'

'The girls loved it, too, rather too much judging by the look on Melissa's face,' said Pamela with a chuckle.

'They're young,' said Penelope. 'I remember my first kiss to this day.'

'Do you? Who was it?' Julia asked, flicking ash into the glass ashtray Soames had placed in front of her.

'A man called Willy,' Penelope replied, then gave a little snort.

'I hope kissing you was all Willy did,' said Pamela dryly. 'A woman can never trust a willy!'

★

Celestria hurried down the path to the sea. Harry, Wilfrid, and Sam followed her, although they didn't share her concern. Monty was the most reliable, solid man they knew. He was the hero who always saved everyone else. When there was a trap to be laid, Monty knew how to set it and where to place it. If there were camps to be built in the woods, Monty knew the best tree and how to stuff the cracks between the logs with hay. He knew how to light fires with flint and how to roast chestnuts. He could shoot rabbits from a distance, skin them, and fry them for dinner. Besides, he was a master sailor. Once he had made a pirate ship out of his small boat and taken them out into the middle of the sea in search of vessels from Spain, heavy with gold. They had worn eye patches and striped shirts and carried bottles of lemonade Monty called 'liquor.' No one understood the tides better than Monty. It was unthinkable that he had drowned at sea.

Celestria now knew why the sea had pulled at her that morning. It hadn't been because of Bouncy, but because it had just digested her father. The serenity of its surface was simply the sleep of a satisfied belly. The air was damp and salty, the sun warm upon her face, the sky a resplendent blue, washed clean by the rain. Celestria felt a sickness in her stomach in spite of the perfection of the morning.

While Celestria stood in the middle of the wide beach, a figure dwarfed by cliffs and rocks, gazing forlornly out to sea, a fisherman, drawing in his net, raised his eyes to where a small boat bobbed about on the horizon. 'Oi, Skipper, you see that out there?' he shouted to his friend. Merlin, nicknamed Skipper, stood a moment, shielding his eyes from the sun with a calloused hand.

'Looks like a boat,' he replied slowly.

'A fishing boat?' repeated Trevor.

'Motorboat,' said Merlin knowledgeably. 'See anyone in it?'

'No, 'less he's sleepin'.' Trevor grinned, revealing a large hole where his two front teeth had been knocked out in a brawl outside the Snout & Hound a few years before.

'We'd better go take a look,' said Merlin. 'Let's get this lot in first.' They finished their business, pouring the fish into large barrels, where they wriggled about, gasping for breath, slowly dying. Then they motored over to the boat. They drew their vessel up alongside, causing the small boat to rock about on the swell.

'Well, I'll be damned,' said Trevor, leaning over the side to take a better look. 'It's empty.' He rubbed his bristly chin thoughtfully.

'Not a soul,' said Merlin in wonder.

'Where's he gone to, then?'

'Dunno. Eaten by a big fish.' Merlin began to laugh at his own joke. Trevor joined him. He thought everything Merlin said was funny.

'What d'you make of it?' Merlin asked after a while, shaking his head.

'Silly bugger got drunk and drowned. Look, there's a bottle over there.' Sure enough, a champagne bottle lay discarded in one corner, rolling about under the seat.

'Any left?'

'Looks empty from where I'm standing.'

'What's that, then?'

'What?'

'That gold thing, by the bottle.'

'I'm gonna have to get in, aren't I? Bugger!' Trevor stepped over into the little boat. He leaned down and picked up a gold watch on a chain. 'Nice!' he said, turning it over. 'Pocket watch. Very posh!'

'Does it work?'

Trevor snapped it open as if it were an oyster. 'Tells the time like a lady.' He gave a whistle of approval.

'You know my joke about the lady?'

'Go on, then.'

Merlin began to laugh even before he told it. 'You ask a lady for a date. If she says no, she means maybe; if she says maybe, she means yes; if she says yes, she ain't no lady!' Trevor turned the watch over.

'R.W.E.M,' he read, squinting. 'Who's that, then?'

'Gold watch like that? Can only be one family round here.' Merlin's face grew serious.

'Who's that, then?'

'Robert Montague.'

Trevor whistled and raised his eyebrows. 'Blimey,' he said with a smirk. 'Let's go back and break the bad news.'

'You have no idea how bad it's goin' to be,' replied Merlin gravely. He wasn't laughing now.

Chapter 7

When *Princess* was dragged into Pendrift harbor, people began to gather on the quay, drawn by curiosity and the smell of tragedy that blew in off the sea. Merlin tied her to a bollard while Trevor clutched the gold watch. 'What's happened to Mr Montague, Skipper?' a man shouted. 'That's his boat, if I'm not mistaken.' Merlin did not know how to reply. Instinctively, he knew the family should be the first to know.

'Nothin',' he replied cagily. 'Broke down, that's all.'

The crowd began to mumble among themselves, and Merlin knew they didn't believe him. He hurried up the road towards the Snout & Hound. White with black beams and small dark windows laced with flowers, the Snout & Hound had welcomed weary fishermen and smugglers for well over three hundred years.

'I need to use the telephone,' said Merlin as he entered. The room fell silent, and, through the smoky air, they could see his anxious face and read in it that something terrible had happened. As much as he would have liked to have spoken to Mrs Julia in private, the telephone was at the bar, where a few of the locals were enjoying an early lunch. No one bothered to look like they weren't listening, and Merlin didn't have the will to tell them to mind their own business; they'd all know soon enough.

'I'd like to speak to the lady of the house,' said Merlin when Soames's condescending voice came on the line.

'I'm afraid Mrs Julia is indisposed,' he replied.

'Mr Archie?'

'As well.'

'It's urgent. It's about Mr Monty. It's Merlin here.'

Soames had recognized Merlin's rusty voice the moment he had heard it, but he didn't like to indulge in small talk with the locals. He wasn't about to bother Mr Archie, who was in the study with the door closed, and Mrs Julia was supervising the tidying-up operation in the tent, running about like Purdy in chase of pheasants. However, Merlin sounded very distressed, and Soames was aware that Mr Monty hadn't attended breakfast.

'Wait a moment, I'll go and find Mrs Julia,' he said, placing the receiver on the sideboard.

Merlin waited a good five minutes. He could hear Cook's doughy voice complaining about the amount of food left over from the party. 'It's indecent,' she was saying. 'This would feed an army. It wasn't so long ago that we were still being rationed.' Finally, Soames's voice came back on the line.

'She's taking your call in the sitting room,' he said. There was a click, then Julia's voice came on the line. Soames put down the receiver with some reluctance.

'Hello, Merlin?' She sounded anxious.

'Good morning, Mrs Julia.'

'What's happened?'

'It's Mr Monty's boat. We found it out at sea this morning.'

'Wasn't Mr Monty in it?'

'Only his pocket watch, Mrs Julia. Trevor's keeping it for you.'

'Good God!' she exclaimed. 'I'll send Archie down right away.' She hesitated a moment. Merlin saw that every eye in the pub was upon him. Mouths agape, eyes bulging with interest. Her voice was soft, as if she was afraid of her own words. 'You don't think he went overboard, do you?'

'There's a bottle of champagne rattling around in the belly of the boat, Mrs Julia. I think you should alert the coast guard.'

'Thank you, Merlin.'

Julia put down the receiver, barely daring to breathe. She moved across the room in a trance. Her legs felt as heavy as they did in nightmares when she tried to run from a nameless peril. She found Archie in his office. 'Something terrible has happened.' She stood in the doorway, as white as a ghost. 'Merlin found Monty's boat out at sea. Monty's nowhere to be seen, but his pocket watch was on board and a bottle of champagne.'

Archie jumped to his feet. 'Bloody hell! I'll call the coast guard immediately. You don't think . . .' His voice trailed off. The look in Julia's eyes was as good as a reply. He swivelled around and picked up the telephone. 'Go and tell Milton to meet me in the car,' he added, his voice urgent. 'We'll drive down to the harbour at once.' Julia did as she was told. All she could think about was those poor children. If something had happened to Monty . . .

Celestria wandered back up the snake path to the house, followed by the boys and Purdy. Harry didn't understand her anxiety. At twelve, he couldn't imagine anything rocking his secure little world. He chatted to his cousins as if nothing was amiss. Celestria felt nauseous. From the moment she had woken, the world had changed, as if it had shifted on its axis in the night, leaving everything looking the same but being totally different.

When she reached the house, there was pandemonium. Amid the chaos of the clearing-up operation, Julia was sitting on the terrace with Penelope, David, Melissa, and Lotty. She was smoking madly, her face pinched and grey. Celestria's heart stalled. She could guess what they were discussing because they spoke in hushed voices and stopped suddenly when they saw her. Pamela was nowhere to be seen. Neither were her uncles. When she reached the group, they said nothing, just looked from one to the other shiftily, their expressions as solemn as graves.

'Celestria,' said Julia finally, getting up slowly. There was no easy way to tell a child that her father was missing at sea, presumed dead. 'Your father's boat has been found.'

'And Papa?' the young woman asked, aware that her voice was little more than a squeak. Julia shook her head, then looked past Celestria to Harry.

'What's up?' he asked, shoving his hands into his pockets.

'It's Papa. I told you!' Celestria wailed. Julia rushed over to embrace them.

'They've found his boat, Harry. He wasn't in it, but his pocket watch was, which leads us to believe he was in it at some stage last night. He always wears it with white tie. Unless,' she added hopefully, 'he dropped it without noticing when he disembarked, before someone else stole the boat. That's a possibility, isn't it?'

Lotty put an arm around Celestria. 'The coast guard are out looking for him,' she said. 'I'm sure he's safe. We're all worrying for nothing.'

'There's probably a very simple explanation,' Julia agreed.

'Knowing my brother as I do, I would agree with Julia,' said Penelope. 'Monty's not the type to throw himself overboard. Life's much too good!'

'What was he doing out there in the first place? So early in the morning?' Celestria was baffled. 'Where's Mama?' No one spoke up. 'She doesn't know?' Celestria was shocked, though not surprised. They were all much too scared of her mother's reaction to be the one to break the bad news. 'Well, I'm going to find her,' she said, and stalked out.

Upstairs, Celestria found her mother in her bedroom, standing at the windowsill in her dressing gown, with Poochi in her arms. She was looking out over the sea as if she already knew it had swallowed her husband. 'Mama,' Celestria said. 'Papa's lost at sea. They've found his boat and his pocket watch.'

Pamela turned to face her daughter. 'What are you talking about?'

'Papa's missing. They've found his boat, but he wasn't in it.'

'Are you sure?'

'Certain. Uncle Archie and Uncle Milton have gone down to the harbour. The coast guard are already looking for him.'

Pamela dissolved into tears. 'They think he's dead?' She sank onto the window seat. 'I just don't believe it. Why would he take that darn boat out at such a god-awful hour of the morning?'

'Did you fight last night?'

Pamela was affronted. 'Of course not!'

'Were you drunk?'

'Not particularly.'

'Are you sure?' She recalled her mother's shaking hands and unsteady walk.

'Of course I'm sure. Okay, he might have been a little tipsy, but not enough to do something stupid. Monty isn't like that, as you know. Besides, he would have left a note.'

At that moment the doorknob rattled. Both women turned their eyes to the door in the hope that Monty might walk through it, but instead Harry's worried face peered around it. 'Is it true?' he asked in a small voice.

'Don't you worry, Harry, darling,' exclaimed his mother, floating over to embrace him in tuberose and pink silk. 'Your father's going to be fine. He's probably having a cup of coffee in town, reading the papers. You know what he's like. We must all stop worrying. What will he think when he finds us in such a state?' She gathered him into her arms, pressing her powdered cheek against his.

Down at the harbour Merlin was waiting for Mr Archie. A large crowd had gathered on the quay, mumbling among themselves, imagining all sorts of implausible reasons for Mr Monty's disappearance. The most likely, they all agreed, was that he had been kidnapped, possibly by pirates.

They fell silent when Archie drove up in his Rover, parking it in front of the Snout & Hound. The pub had now completely emptied of customers, barmaids, and the publican himself, who had joined the throng outside in the hope of seeing a body at the very least.

'Good God,' said Archie to his brother-in-law. 'What's going on here?'

They climbed out of the car and walked over. The crowd parted to let them through, the men taking off their hats to show their respect. Archie recognized most of the faces but didn't know them as well as his brother did. In spite of his class, Monty had enjoyed many a beer and a game of darts at the Snout & Hound and shared a great deal of laughter in his typically uninhibited way.

Merlin tipped his hat. 'Here she is, Mr Archie,' he said gravely, pointing to the boat. Trevor emerged from behind his friend and opened his hand to reveal the pocket watch. Archie took it.

'Well, this is certainly his watch,' he said softly, his eyes tracing the initials that their father had had engraved to mark Monty's twenty-first birthday. That now seemed like another life. He dropped it in his pocket.

'How did you find it, Merlin?'

Merlin scratched his beard. 'We were fishing. 'Bout nine

o'clock this morning. It was misty out here, which makes me think that if Mr Monty had been out early, he might have got lost.' Archie nodded thoughtfully. Merlin continued. 'Trevor saw it first. It was far out. Must 'ave drifted. When we got to it, *Princess* was empty but for the watch and the bottle.'

Archie raised his eyebrows. 'Bottle?' he repeated. He narrowed his eyes and glanced at Milton. Milton shrugged. Monty wasn't a boozer. Merlin nodded at Trevor, who climbed into the boat and dropped onto his knees to reach the champagne bottle that was hidden at the back, under the seat. He handed it to Merlin.

'Well, look at that!' he exclaimed, holding the bottle up for everyone to see. 'There's a note inside.'

'A letter in a bottle?' said Milton incredulously. 'It must be a joke.'

'If it's a joke, it's in poor taste,' Archie added, his eyes sliding over the curious throng. He took the bottle from Milton and tried to shake out the piece of paper, but the note remained firmly inside the bottle.

'You're going to have to break it, Mr Archie,' said Merlin. The crowd began to get impatient. The mumbling grew louder. Perhaps it was a note from the kidnapper. Or a prank of his own. They all knew Monty could be a bit of a prankster.

Suddenly the crowd was forced to part as a police officer fought his way through.

'Ah, Inspector Trevelyan,' said Archie, shaking the man's hand.

Inspector Trevelyan was unmistakable, with a white foamy moustache and wild grey eyebrows, a distended bottom lip that never smiled, and a shiny nose that looked like a lump of melted wax. In his tweed cap and beige raincoat he was as much of a landmark as the Snout & Hound, having been a part of Pendrift for longer than anyone could remember.

'No sign of him, I'm afraid,' he informed Archie grimly. 'We've got a team scouring the cliffs, and the coast guard are out at sea. So far, nothing.' Inspector Trevelyan turned his attention to the bottle. 'What's that in there?'

'That's what we're trying to find out,' Archie replied. 'The damn thing won't budge.'

'You'll have to break it, sir,' said Inspector Trevelyan.

Archie wasn't certain he wanted the entire town to witness what was in the note. If it was indeed a prank, he'd look very stupid. If it was worse, they had no business knowing. He waded through them like he often waded through his herd of cows, pushing them apart with his hands. Then he bent on one knee and knocked the thin end of the bottle against the rocks beneath the quay. The top came off in one piece and dropped into the sea with a plop. Careful not to cut himself on the broken glass, he withdrew the note.

It was a single piece of paper taken from the house. From Archie's study, to be precise. Top left-hand drawer, where he kept his writing paper and cards. On it were written two words. Two words that made no sense at all, but in Monty's handwriting.

Forgive me

Milton looked over his shoulder. 'What on earth does that mean?' he said, baffled.

'God only knows!'

'Surely not suicide? Of all the people least likely to take their own life it was Monty. Why on earth would he do such a thing?'

Archie didn't feel anything at all except confusion. He would have felt sad had he been convinced his brother had committed such an act. But he wasn't. First, Monty was the happiest man he knew. Second, he was a devout Catholic. Third, he loved his wife and children. Three very good reasons not to end it all. 'This is madness!' he exclaimed in fury. 'When he bloody well turns up, I'm going to kill him myself!'

He showed Inspector Trevelyan the note. 'That looks like suicide to me,' he said, handing it back.

'It would appear so,' agreed Archie, 'had it been written by anyone other than my brother. I simply don't believe it.'

'We'll continue the search,' said Inspector Trevelyan. His shoulders hunched, tense with the grim business of his job. 'If anything turns up, we'll come straight to the Hall.'

'Thank you,' said Archie, frowning.

Archie and Milton returned home in bewilderment. Merlin and Trevor sat in the pub, telling the story over and over again, while everyone else gave their opinions on what they believed had really happened. Nothing united the community better than a good mystery.

When the Rover drew up at Pendrift Hall, the rest of the family spilled out onto the gravel, desperate for news. Archie shook his head. 'Damn fool!' he spluttered. 'Left this silly note in a champagne bottle. Why the devil would he go and do something like that?'

Pamela took the note. 'It's his writing all right,' she said. 'You don't think he's . . . He wouldn't. Not Monty. This is a joke!' It was too late to protect Celestria and Harry. The note was already being passed around and dismissed as preposterous.

'Perhaps what started as a joke, when he was drunk and being silly at the end of the party, finished in disaster,' said Penelope.

'You're saying he's dead?' said Pamela angrily.

'I'm saying he might have fallen in and drowned unintentionally.'

'That's still saying he's dead. Why doesn't anyone admit it? My husband and the father of my children is dead!' She put her hand to her forehead and swooned. 'Oh Lord. I must go lie down. I feel like I'm about to throw up my heart!'

Julia and Penelope rushed to her aid, taking an arm each and leading her back into the house. Celestria and Harry watched them go. Neither felt the desire to follow. When Pamela took one of her turns, it was better to stay out of the way.

'I need a stiff drink. Soames!' Archie stalked after them. 'Soames!' Soames appeared in the hall, his expression impassive, as he hoped not to reveal that he had been listening to the entire conversation through the pantry window. 'Get me a whiskey right away. And one for Mr Milton, too.'

Celestria and Harry, supported by Melissa and Lotty, Wilfrid and Sam, followed David and the two men into Archie's study. It was a library of bookcases up to the ceiling, with a gaping fireplace surrounded by a burgundy leather club fender and two worn leather sofas. Archie's reading chair had been moulded into the shape of his body, and a hole was wearing through in the seat, revealing its foam insides like the guts of one of the boys' dead rabbits. The air was musty, as if the window hadn't been opened in a long time. Celestria recalled, with a stab of pain to her heart, the grim look on her father's face the night before, when she had watched him unseen from the door.

She flopped onto the sofa next to Harry, who had gone very quiet and pale. She put her arm around him and pulled him close. He was as flat as a deflated balloon, and his eyes shone with fresh tears. Melissa and Lotty squeezed in either side of them.

Celestria looked at Archie. 'Mama's right, isn't she? Papa's dead.'

Soames brought the drinks in on a tray. Archie took a swig and gulped it down miserably. It was all very baffling.

'I'm not writing him off until I have a body,' he said, his

moustache twitching defiantly. 'Or at least some evidence of one.'

'What about murder?' David suggested, sinking into his uncle's armchair. Archie was too agitated to sit down. Milton walked over to the window, his hands in his pockets, and stared out as if expecting Monty to wander across the lawn.

'What motive?' said Archie.

'Money,' David replied with a shrug.

Archie dismissed it with a firm shake of his head. 'Absolutely not. He might be rich, but he's not Croesus.'

'Maybe Penelope's right,' Milton conceded. 'What started as a prank ended in disaster.'

Celestria looked over at Wilfrid and Sam, who sat on the sofa opposite, in shocked silence. 'What did you all do when you went out in his boat?'

'We played pirates,' replied Sam.

'Did you ever put notes in bottles?' Wilfrid and Sam looked at each other pensively. She turned to her brother. 'Did Papa ever play silly pranks, like pretending to fall overboard?'

'We pretended to shoot at Spanish merchant vessels,' said Harry.

'We never put messages in bottles, but we did talk about it,' said Sam. 'Uncle Monty told us that if we were lost at sea it was the best way to get a message home. The tide would take it to the beach.'

'Charming,' said Archie sarcastically. 'I doubt that note was written in the boat. The paper was out of my desk, for a start. I think he wrote it here, found an empty bottle, and set off with the intention of doing something silly.'

'You know he liked to play treasure hunts on the sand. What if the note in the bottle was part of a game he was planning?' said David.

'Then why write "Forgive me"?' Archie drained his glass. 'That's a suicide note if ever I saw one.'

'If Papa was going to kill himself, which I very much doubt,' said Celestria impatiently, 'he would have written a longer note. Have you ever known him to say a few words when a dozen would do? He wouldn't have left us in doubt. He would have said, "I'm unhappy, this is the only way out." Or something along those lines. He wouldn't have been so cryptic. Papa has never been cryptic.'

They were all silent for a moment. Everything pointed to suicide, but none of them believed it possible. Then a small voice piped up.

'Papa wouldn't want to make us sad. He loves us.' Harry's pitiful face remained immobile, but for a single tear that trickled down it, leaving a thin, shiny trail.

They were jolted from their thoughts by the urgent ringing of the doorbell. No one moved. The room seemed to hold its breath as Soames's footsteps were heard tapping across the stone floor as he made his way to the front door, followed by the murmur of low voices as he exchanged a few words with the caller. A cold wind swept in and slid across the floor and into the study where the small party waited anxiously for news. Celestria shivered and folded her arms. She felt a gradual tightening around her throat and the shameful inability to cry. It was as if her anguish had blocked her power to express emotion. The draught was damp and smelled of the sea. Had it finally given up her father's body?

At last Soames knocked on the study door. 'What is it?' Archie asked, his voice tense.

'It's Inspector Trevelyan,' Soames replied. Archie's eyes fell a moment onto the younger children. He wondered where Nanny was and why Julia hadn't sent them all off somewhere out of the way so they wouldn't have to endure the agony of waiting.

'Show him into the drawing room,' he said. Celestria rose in protest. 'I'll see him on my own,' he replied, his tone resolute. They all watched him leave the room and close the door behind him.

'They've found the body,' said Celestria resignedly, rubbing her throat. 'I know they have.'

'Let's not jump to conclusions,' Milton suggested, unconvincingly.

'Quite,' agreed David.

'Don't be silly, Celestria,' said Lotty. 'I don't believe he's dead. It's all a terrible misunderstanding. Daddy's right, we're leaping to conclusions when we know nothing.'

'We have a note,' Celestria snapped. 'There is no alternative conclusion to leap to.'

It seemed a very long time before Archie returned to the study. His face was grey. 'They've found his shoes,' he said. 'Washed up on rocks.'

Celestria gasped.

Harry sobbed. 'Does that mean Papa is dead?' he asked. Celestria exchanged looks with her uncle. He shook his head sadly.

'I'm afraid it's almost certain,' he replied.

'But wouldn't one take off one's shoes to swim?' said Melissa.

'He wasn't planning on taking a swim, silly!' Celestria retorted.

Archie shook his head. 'I'm afraid that the note in the bottle, his pocket watch, and the shoes, all indicate that he took his own life. As incredible as it seems, Monty has committed suicide.'

Chapter 8

Father Dalgliesh cycled up to Pendrift Hall the moment he heard the news. It had been Miss Hoddel who broke it, though she hadn't realized at that stage the enormity of the gossip she had picked up. 'Mr Monty got drunk and fell overboard last night,' she had said, relishing the idea of a scandal. 'Everyone's talking about it.' A mole, sprouting three long black hairs, quivered on her right cheek as she attempted, in vain, to disguise her delight.

Father Dalgliesh had been too shocked to question her further and, besides, already he knew that her news was often gossip, distorted and exaggerated like a game of Chinese whispers. He waited for her to finish emptying the bin by his desk, a chore she dithered over, hoping to be questioned, then watched her leave the room with a loud, exasperated sigh. He had telephoned the police station at once and spoken to Inspector Trevelyan's office to discover that Miss Hoddel wasn't as misinformed as he had hoped. Monty hadn't been seen since the party the night before. Now the discovery of his shoes had left Trevelyan in no doubt that the poor man had indeed drowned, leaving two children fatherless and a wife without a husband to look after her. It was a terrible tragedy. An accident, no doubt. The family must be shocked to the core. Father Dalgliesh thought of Celestria, that beautiful, carefree girl who walked with a dance in her step, and he knew he had to go to her.

Once again he cycled across sunbeams, now amber in the fading light of the dying day. Long shadows fell across the road, and a light scattering of orange leaves reminded him that summer was drawing to a close. It was less than a week since he had cycled this same road, his spirits high as the warm August sun had shone down upon him. He could not have foreseen the tragedy that would send him riding up the same winding lane again, with a heart as heavy as stone. He turned his thoughts to Mass the following morning and silently asked God to guide him as to the best way to comfort the Montagues.

His journey was interrupted by a slow herd of soft brown cows ambling up the lane ahead of him. Flies buzzed about their scruffy heads as they mooed irritably, like a bunch of fat-bottomed ladies in the fishmonger's on a Saturday morning. A young lad with a stick encouraged them to move faster, but they stubbornly refused to do as they were told. Father Dalgliesh waited patiently for them to turn into the field, followed by an excited sheepdog clearly not doing his job very well.

With the help of prayer and meditation, he had managed to dispel all improper thoughts of Celestria, that captivating girl. He had been caught off balance; it was as simple as that. He knew that when he saw her again, he would no longer be dazzled by her beauty but would see inside the pretty casing to the human soul that was now in dire need of comfort. He was ashamed of his weakness, but aware that his life's journey would be peppered with temptation. He resolved to rise to each challenge with courage and conviction. His weakness would only make him stronger and remind him that he was a frail sinner like everyone else. It would teach him humility.

These were Father Dalgliesh's thoughts as he arrived at Pendrift Hall. The front of the house was cast in shade, as the sun hung low behind it. Purdy didn't leap out to greet him as he had done the first time. But it wasn't long before the door opened and Soames stood like an aged sentinel on the top step, shoulders back, chin high, eyes wary as he cast his gaze down the slope of his long, imperious nose. He breathed in through dilated nostrils and, without smiling, nodded to invite the priest inside. It was a grim welcome echoed by the house itself, which seemed already in mourning.

'Please wait in the hall,' said Soames. 'I will inform the family that you are here.'

'If they do not wish to see me, I quite understand,' said Father Dalgliesh tactfully.

The butler stepped slowly across the flagstone floor and knocked on the drawing room door. He entered, closing the door quietly behind him. Father Dalgliesh strained his ears but heard nothing other than the rhythmic ticking of the grandfather clock and finally its tinny chiming as it struck six. He pushed his glasses up his nose and wiped the sweat off his forehead. It had been hard work cycling uphill.

With an eerie creak, the drawing room door opened and Soames stood aside to let Father Dalgliesh enter. Julia sat on one sofa with Penelope, while Melissa and Lotty sat on the sofa opposite. Celestria was positioned at the piano as if about to play.

'Father,' said Julia, rising to greet him. 'I'm so grateful you have come.' If she was at all bothered by his sudden appearance, she didn't let it show.

'I wanted to offer my sympathy,' he said, his eyes wandering to the piano, where Celestria watched him impassively. 'I heard the terrible news.'

'Please sit down,' replied Julia, gesturing to an armchair. She sensed his awkwardness and attempted, in her usual bright way, to put him at his ease. She, however, felt as far from bright as a drizzly Cornish sky. 'It is all rather confusing.

Monty left a note asking us to forgive him and supposedly threw himself into the sea. The trouble is it's so out of character none of us wants to believe it.' She reached for her cigarettes.

'Play something cheerful, dear,' said Penelope to Celestria. She looked at the priest. 'It's been a trying day.'

Celestria began to play, her music dominating the room so that Julia had to raise her voice to be heard.

'I've sent the little boys out with their cousin David to shoot rabbits. Anything to distract Harry, poor darling. He worshipped his father.'

'How is his wife?'

Penelope spoke without thinking. 'She's in bed with a migraine. I doubt she'll ever get up again.'

'Will she come to Mass tomorrow?' Father Dalgliesh asked.

'Goodness no,' replied Julia hastily. 'She's not a religious woman.' She didn't want to repeat the things that Pamela had said about the Church. It wasn't fair to show her in a bad light to a stranger. However, if Father Dalgliesh hoped to give her comfort, it would have to be delivered by prayer alone.

'Archie's gone to tell our mother, and Milton is out searching for the body,' said Penelope in her loud, booming voice, regardless of her niece. 'If there were shoes, there are bound to be feet. If there are feet there must be legs. Monty is out there somewhere, unless he's in the belly of a fish.'

Suddenly Celestria stopped playing and stood up. Her face was deathly white, emphasizing the clear grey of her eyes. Her hair, drawn off her face and clipped up on top of her head, cascaded down her back in waves, making her look younger and fragile.

'I don't think he drowned at all,' she said. 'Why would lace-up shoes come off all by themselves? I'd believe it if the shoes had feet in them.'

'I agree with Celestria,' said Melissa.

Lotty nodded emphatically. 'I think he's been kidnapped.'

'Then why leave a note?' said Julia kindly.

'He was forced to write it,' Celestria replied. She walked past the priest and joined her cousins on the sofa.

'But the paper came from Archie's study,' protested Julia, dragging heavily on her cigarette. This was all giving her a headache.

'Then someone broke in and made him do it.' She looked at her aunts in a sudden fury. 'Papa didn't commit suicide.' She turned to the priest. 'He's a religious man. He believes in heaven and hell. Everyone knows that taking your life is no shortcut to heaven but to eternal damnation. Why would eternal damnation be any better than life?'

She glanced down to his feet and noticed he was wearing odd socks. Father Dalgliesh followed her eyes with a sinking feeling. He had done it again: one red sock and one yellow sock. They looked at each other, and Celestria gave a wan smile. In spite of the tragic tone of the day, the priest couldn't help but smile back.

'Then one has no alternative than to wait,' said Julia with a sigh.

'And pray,' Father Dalgliesh added gravely. 'Whatever happens is the will of God.'

'Or the will of Monty,' said Penelope dryly.

When Elizabeth Montague heard the news, she wouldn't at first believe it. 'It's not true. Robert would never be so self-ish!' she raged, her face flushing the color of a fresh bruise.

Archie tried to rationalize. 'I know. It's implausible. But it's the only explanation. Monty has disappeared. The note in the bottle, the shoes in the sea, the boat left to drift – they all point to one thing: that Monty has taken his own life.'

'Robert would never do such a thing. Even if he were unhappy. Which he wasn't, because I'd know about it. I'm his mother, for God's sake. This has got to be a prank. A sick joke. Or kidnap.'

Archie sighed. He'd already had this argument with David. He rubbed his forehead wearily. 'I'm afraid, Mother, at this stage we have nothing else to believe but the worst. How or why, we may never know, but Monty is most probably dead.'

Elizabeth sank into the sofa. 'If that is the case, then it won't be long before I join him,' she said, her voice tight with restrained grief.

Archie poured her a glass of gin, then walked over to the window and stared out into the diminishing light. The dower house was a short walk down the garden from the Hall and overlooked the sea. It was a pretty white house with large windows, built at the same time as the main house but not as loved and uncommonly damp. It bore the same chilly expression as its mistress and required fires to be lit throughout the summer. Outside, the ocean was calm beneath a flamingo-pink sky. Feathery clouds drifted on the horizon, turning a deep shade of grey as the sun dipped beneath it.

'Why the note? *"Forgive me."* Forgive you for what, Monty? For leaving your family bereft? For not communicating your unhappiness? For bottling it all up? For never asking for help?' Archie seemed to be talking to himself.

'He wasn't unhappy,' Elizabeth snapped then took a large gulp of gin. 'He was jolly. He's always been jolly. There's no side to Robert. *No surprises.* He's always been like that. Like his father. Straightforward. A more honest man one simply couldn't find. If he is dead, then it wasn't because he sought death. Death found him and snatched him away.' She straightened, her jaw stiff as if struggling to contain her emotions. 'But I won't believe it until there's proof. No funeral until the body is found. Until then, my Robert is still alive.'

Archie turned to face her. She was a broad woman, with

wide hips and a strong, formidable face and yet, in that cold room, she looked very small.

'Why don't you stay at the Hall for a while?' he suggested kindly, even though Julia wouldn't thank him for suggesting it. His mother looked at him sternly.

'I might be old, but I've survived on my own for fourteen years. There's no reason to be a burden to anyone now. I shall join you at Mass tomorrow as usual, and then I would like to see Father Dalgliesh alone. If Robert is dead, then only God will be able to comfort me.'

As Archie left the room he heard the sound of breaking glass. He hurried back to find his mother on her knees, picking up the pieces with trembling hands. He knelt down beside her. 'Leave me alone,' she growled. The ferocity of her reaction stunned him, but he did as he was told. He looked back a moment to see her sink to the floor and bury her face in her hands. His natural instinct was to comfort her, but she would not be comforted. He left with the sense of inadequacy that had dogged him all his life. How come Monty had admired *him?* What was there to admire?

Father Dalgliesh reached for his bicycle. The dusk was heavy, the air cooler, the first smoky smell of autumn carried on the wind with the scent of the sea. He paused a moment, wondering if his visit had done any good at all. Father Hancock would have known exactly what to say. But not him. He didn't have the vocabulary or the delivery.

Suddenly he felt a presence behind him. Still holding the handlebars, he turned around. There, sitting on the doorstep, sat Celestria. She struck a match and lit a cigarette, and her lovely face was suddenly illuminated in the dusk.

'Mama hates me smoking. She says it's unladylike.'

'I think she's probably right,' replied Father Dalgliesh.

'I think it's excusable today of all days, wouldn't you agree?'

'I'm very sorry, Celestria.'

'So am I. It's a crying shame. I'm being driven mad in there. Going round and round in circles: "It looks like suicide, but how unlike Papa. Why would he do it?" And on and on and on. I want to close my ears to it all. As for Mama, she's in bed with a migraine again, and there's no Papa to put her out of her misery. Aunt Penelope's right, she'll never recover.' She raised her eyes, blowing out a puff of smoke. 'What drives a man to take his own life?'

'An unbearable unhappiness,' he replied. 'A depression so heavy that the alternative, whatever he believes that to be, is better than living.'

'You see. That's what I don't understand. Papa was so happy. All the time. He always smiled. He had time for everyone. No one was too small or insignificant for him to take trouble with. You know, he cared about people. He cared about us. He loved life. Why would somebody like that write a note, put it in a bottle, motor out into the middle of the ocean, and then jump overboard?'

Father Dalgliesh leaned his bicycle back against the wall and went to sit down beside her. He felt she needed to talk and was pleased to have the opportunity to be of use.

'Do you cycle everywhere?' she asked, and he suddenly caught the scent of bluebells grown warm upon her skin. There was something alluring about the smell of spring that made his stomach flip over.

'While the weather is nice, I do,' he replied.

'What about when it rains?'

'I shall get wet or take the car.'

'So you *do* have one?'

'I do.' He smiled diffidently. 'But I don't like to drive.'

'Are you afraid?'

'A little nervous, shall we say.'

'When I learn to drive, I think everyone else is going to be a great deal more nervous than I.'

She held the cigarette to her lips and watched him through the smoke as she exhaled. 'Does one go to hell if one commits suicide?' she asked.

'The life God gave us is not ours to take away.'

'That's what we're taught. Do you believe it?'

'I do. Life is sacred. It is not ours to dispose of. We have to accept whatever God gives us with gratitude. Only God has the right to take it away.'

'So if Papa has killed himself, is he damned for eternity?'

'He is in hell until God decides to forgive him. We must pray for him.'

'Does God listen?'

'That's why we pray, because He listens.' He pushed his glasses up his nose. 'Look, if you did something wrong, would your father hold it against you forever?'

'Of course not.'

'Then you have answered your own question. God is a forgiving father. I don't, however, believe that one gets away with murder, any less the murder of oneself.'

'I've attended Mass all my life because of Papa. Mama couldn't care less. She's not religious and thinks the whole thing is manufactured to keep simple people on the straight and narrow. I can't say I've ever really thought about God.'

'But you're thinking about Him now.'

'That's because I'm forced to. If Papa is dead, he's in a place where I can't reach him. God rules that place, so I might as well try and speak to Him.'

Father Dalgliesh felt his heart swell. 'That's one way of looking at it,' he replied with a tentative smile. 'God can be a great comfort in times such as these.'

'I'm still hoping, though,' she said, turning away and flicking ash onto the gravel.

'That's only natural. Until there's proof, there will always be hope.'

'My grandfather used to tell me that dead people become stars.'

'It's a nice idea.'

'I wish he were here how.'

'Your grandfather?'

'Yes. He'd know what to do. He's the sort of man who knows everything.'

'Where is he?'

'In New York.' She took one final drag of the cigarette, the end lighting up like a firefly. 'Harry has always been Mama's favourite, after herself, of course. But I'm special to Grandpa.'

'And your father?'

'Papa? Everyone's special to Papa.'

Father Dalgliesh said goodbye to Celestria and watched her walk inside. He was left alone in the dark with nothing but the faint smell of bluebells. A shadowy figure stood watching him from an upstairs window. Pamela wrapped her shawl around her shoulders and shivered. She did not move until the priest had turned the corner and disappeared down the drive. Then she raised her eyes to the sky, wondering whether there was a heaven after all.

That night Celestria felt a strong urge to visit little Bouncy in his bed. It was late. Everyone had retired. She felt drained and weepy and strangely angry. She remembered the morning scouring the beach for Bouncy, unaware that the sea had taken her father instead. She crept down the corridor to Bouncy's room, decorated with cream wallpaper on which were depicted pale blue elephants. Bouncy adored elephants; he called them 'fanties.' She opened the door as quietly as she could. There, in the pale yellow light of the little candle that burned eucalyptus oil on the dresser, Bouncy lay in his bed, his arms up by his ears, his legs spread in their blue pyjamas, the blanket tossed off in his sleep. His eyes were closed, his skin translucent, his full lips sensual in the warm comfort of his dreams. She gently replaced the blanket, putting his legs beneath it one by one. He didn't even stir, but continued to breathe deeply and slowly, as only children do. Suddenly, she felt tears fill her eyes and spill over onto her cheeks. He looked so beautiful and innocent.

She heard a movement and turned. Julia stood in the doorway in her dressing gown. Celestria smiled through her tears. Julia tiptoed over and put an arm around her niece.

'This morning we thought it was Bouncy,' Celestria whispered.

'I'm ashamed to feel grateful, now that God has taken Monty,' replied Julia. 'My heart is full of gratitude and sorrow.'

'He's a treasure,' said Celestria. 'It's consoling to see him safely sleeping in his bed. He gives me hope. We found Bouncy; perhaps we'll find Papa.' They remained in silent thought for what seemed a long while. Finally, Julia spoke.

'You're not alone, Celestria, darling,' she said. Celestria was too moved to reply.

She allowed herself to be drawn against her aunt and rested her head against her shoulder. They both gazed upon the sleeping child and wept.

Chapter 9

Pendrift had talked of nothing else since Mr Monty's boat had been discovered the previous morning. No one believed Monty had committed suicide. On that they were all agreed. Everyone claimed to know him intimately, for he had been a man happy to pass the time of day with anyone who offered their company. No, the Monty they knew was a man content with his life and only too ready to share that contentment with the rest of the world.

Indeed, Monty was as much a part of the little Cornish town of Pendrift as pasties and clotted cream. He enjoyed reading the papers over a cup of coffee in Maggie Brewick's Tea House, buying cigarettes in the corner shop, and drinking beer in the Snout & Hound. Everyone greeted him warmly, and he knew them all by name – from the secretary in the doctor's surgery to old Talek, who sat on the bench gazing out to sea, day in day out, like a discarded coat, getting shabbier with each rainfall.

He took an interest in the most minute details of their lives: a wife whose husband had strayed, a sick dog, trouble with the plumbing, a child who'd won a prize at school, inflation, government, royalty, the way things were always better in the old days. Even Archie wasn't aware that Mrs Craddick's son had been hospitalized with polio. Mrs Craddick ran the post office and wouldn't have presumed to chat with Archie or Penelope, but Monty lingered if there wasn't a queue and although he now came down from London only in the summer, he remembered everything about her family and asked after them all more kindly than her own husband did. His compassion had once reduced her to tears. She had confided in her friends, and he had grown even more in the affections of the community – although perhaps not in those of Mr Craddick.

Pamela, on the other hand, had never visited the post office, and Celestria only went into town to buy things she didn't need, just for the small pleasure of shopping. It never occurred to her to speak to the locals. They'd stare at her with wonder in their eyes, for her beauty dazzled them. 'Good morning, Miss Montague,' they'd say, the men tipping their hats, the women nodding politely – she knew she was a swan among geese. 'Regards to your father,' they'd say, and she'd throw them a gracious smile that they'd devour hungrily, but forget them the minute her head was turned. The first family of Pendrift might be respected and admired from a distance, but Monty was one of them.

It was Sunday morning. While most of the town were Church of England, some, like the Montagues, were Catholic and attended Mass in the Church of the Blessed Virgin Mary, one of the few original Catholic churches left standing after Henry VIII had brought the majority crashing to the ground. However, this particular Sunday saw a vast increase in the number of attendants, while the Protestant Church of All Saints was virtually empty. The Reverend Woodley scratched his head in bewilderment and wondered where they had all gone.

Celestria, dressed in black, accompanied the rest of the family to Mass. Harry had barely spoken since their father's disappearance. His face was sad, but his eyes were empty.

Pamela had remained in bed, demanding that Soames telephone the vet because Poochi was off his food. 'He's
depressed,' she said. 'And I don't blame him. I'm depressed,
too.' David walked ahead with the young boys, but there was
no point in trying to cheer everyone up. Julia held Bouncy's
hand while Nanny walked alongside, noticing that the child's
shoelace was coming undone but not wanting to delay the
party by bending down to tie it. Elizabeth walked with
Archie, using him for support in the place of Monty. She,
too, had chosen to wear black. 'I'm still in mourning for
Ivan,' she explained when Archie arrived to collect her. 'I
don't want to be mourning Robert, too. He survived the
war, he can survive this.' Milton walked with his wife, who,
in the great English tradition of grieving, showed no emotion.

Lotty and Melissa walked on either side of Celestria, like a
pair of funereal bridesmaids, their discreet black hats lost
beside the flamboyant spray of Celestria's black feathers. Lotty
had been so consumed with sorrow over the disappearance of
her uncle that she had crept out of bed in the middle of the
night and written to Francis Browne. Having restrained
herself for weeks, she now allowed all the pain and longing to
pour out of her heart and onto the page in her small, neat
handwriting. Sitting alone in her uncle's study, using the same
paper that Monty had used to write his suicide note, she
wondered whether Celestria was right that it would be far
easier to run off together and elope than to reveal the truth to
her parents. In the face of death she felt brave and fearless.
Why spend a lifetime with a man she didn't love, just for the
sake of being comfortable? Francis might not have money,
but he was rich in all the qualities that truly mattered to her.
'I have realized,' she wrote, 'that life can be snatched away at
any moment. I don't want a life of compromise. I want it all,
and you are everything.' The letter now smouldered in her
handbag, waiting to be posted the following morning.

When the Montague family walked down the aisle, every eye turned to watch them, and people bowed their heads with respect as they passed. Julia squeezed Bouncy's hand, for large crowds of people made him nervous. The little boy reached out for Nanny, who took his other hand and rubbed the soft skin with her thumb. Julia caught eyes with Merlin. He took off his cap and pressed it to his chest, wishing that he could turn the clock back and find her brother-in-law asleep in the boat, instead of that dreadful note in the bottle.

The family took their places in the front two pews. Celestria sat beside her brother and held his hand. He continued to stare ahead as if he hadn't noticed her. It was hard for both of them, for, while there was no body, there remained a glimmer of hope. Yet that glimmer, like a ray of light, was impossible to hold on to.

Celestria's mind began to wander, as it always did in Mass. She understood no Latin and found its monotony soporific. She had come because she knew her father would have liked her to and, while that small hope of his survival remained, she believed God still hadn't made up His mind whether or not to recall him. Perhaps He needed a little persuading, in which case prayer might just do the trick. However, when Father Dalgliesh stood before her, his godly presence enhanced by the splendour of his green vestments, her mind stopped its aimless wandering. The priest looked quite different from the awkward man she had talked to on the doorstep the night before. He had authority and a presence that filled the church. She blushed, suddenly wishing she hadn't asked him such silly questions, as if his celibacy was something to be laughed at.

'Before I begin Mass, I would like to welcome you to church today. I know many of you are here to pay your respects to Robert Montague and his family at this sad and difficult time. I welcome you all and thank you for your support and comfort.' His eyes settled on Celestria, his expression full of compassion. 'We ask God that, through prayer, Robert Montague may be delivered safely back to his family and that, through love, we can all unite and give strength to those who need it.'

Celestria noticed Harry's bottom lip begin to tremble, and her own eyes stung with tears. Suddenly it all felt so real. He hadn't come back, and nothing had been heard of him. Although her heart told her it wasn't possible, her reason began to accept the fact that everything pointed to suicide. Everything but her father's nature, which perhaps she hadn't known as well as she thought.

At the end of Mass the congregants spilled out into brazen sunshine that seemed to mock the solemnity of the day. The people of Pendrift paid their respects to Elizabeth, Julia and Archie, Penelope and Milton, smiling sadly at the children, who stood around like animals in a zoo, trying to ignore the assault of curious spectators. Celestria stood apart from the crowd with Lotty and Melissa, who were determined to save their cousin from having to talk to the locals. 'As if you haven't been through enough,' said Melissa sharply, watching her mother shaking hands with people she had never seen before.

'That's the penance for being the most important family in town,' said Lotty with a sigh. 'Everyone feels they own a part of you.'

'No,' said Celestria, shaking her head so that the feathers of her hat floated up and down as if about to fly off. 'It's because Papa was so loved. Everyone here believes they were his intimate friend. They haven't just lost a distant member of the community, but a friend. I barely recognize them, but Papa knew them all by name. And the older ones, like Old Beardy over there,' she pointed to Merlin, who stood, hat in hand, talking to Archie, 'I bet he knew Papa when he was a boy.'

Suddenly a middle-aged woman broke away and

approached the three girls. She was buxom and attractive, with hair the colour of a field mouse drawn into a bun beneath a navy blue hat. Celestria knew she had seen her somewhere before, but she couldn't place her. The woman hesitated a moment and seemed to wilt under Celestria's imperious gaze. Hastily she squared her shoulders, spurred on by the respect she felt for the girl's father. 'I'm Mrs Craddick,' she said in a soft, girlish voice that curled around her vowels like wood smoke. Celestria extended her hand. 'I just wanted to tell you how sorry I am about your father. He was a good, kind man. The best.' She smiled and lowered her eyes as the apples of her cheeks flushed pink.

'Thank you,' Celestria replied, wishing the woman would go away. Instead, Mrs Craddick lifted her gaze, now glittering with tears, and continued.

'You see, my little boy's been very ill. Very ill indeed. We thought he might die. But your father, Mr Montague, found the best doctor and paid for him to be treated. He told me never to tell anyone. Well, he didn't want to embarrass my husband. You see, I don't want his kindness to go unnoticed. It's only right that you and the rest of the family should know what he did for others. He was a selfless man, Miss Montague.'

'How is your son now?' Lotty asked.

'Oh, he's on the mend, thank you, Miss Flint.' She looked at Celestria again. 'If it weren't for your father, my Rewan would . . .' She stopped suddenly, catching her breath. 'Well, I won't keep you.' She turned and fled, melting back into the sea of dark suits and hats.

'Did you know about that?' Melissa asked Celestria.

Her cousin shook her head. 'No.'

'What a dark horse Uncle Monty was,' said Lotty, impressed.

Celestria narrowed her eyes, recalling the conversation she

had overheard between Julia and Monty in the library. 'So dark he's invisible,' she added dryly. 'I'm beginning to think I don't know my father at all.'

When Celestria returned to the Hall, she went straight up to see her mother. Pamela was sitting in bed in a cashmere cardigan and nightdress, trying to feed Poochi a piece of bread and pâté. When she saw her daughter, she raised eyes that were red-rimmed and shiny. 'He won't eat.'

'He will when he's hungry,' Celestria replied, unbuttoning her coat.

'He's lost his appetite.'

'Haven't we all.'

'I never thought Poochi cared for your father. But he's obviously devastated.'

'Have you sent a telegram to Grandpa?' Celestria took off her hat and began to pick out the pins in her hair in front of the mirror on Pamela's dressing table.

'I don't want to bother him until we know for sure.'

Celestria's shoulders hunched, and she fiddled with one of the pins absentmindedly. 'Oh, I think we do know for sure.'

'Until there's a body I refuse to believe it.'

'There might never be a body, Mama. As Aunt Penelope so tactfully put it, he might be inside the belly of a fish.'

'They don't have fish that big off the coast of Cornwall,' Pamela objected. 'What does that silly woman know, anyway?' Suddenly she began to cry. 'Oh, for goodness' sake, you silly pooch, eat!'

Celestria perched on the edge of the bed and took her mother's hand.

'What are we going to do?' Pamela howled. 'I can't go on without Monty. He was everything to me. How could he put me through this? If he was unhappy, he could have told me.

We could have worked it out. But to go and kill himself is so unbelievably selfish.'

'We'll just have to make do,' said Celestria, having to be strong for her mother. 'Harry will go back to school. We'll return to London. Life will continue as it always has. Papa will no longer be there, that's all.' There was a long silence as Pamela digested her daughter's words. Then suddenly she grabbed Celestria's hand.

'Oh, Celestria. I've lied to you.'

'Lied to me? What about?'

'Your father and I. The night he disappeared. We did have a fight.'

'What about?'

'He's a terrible flirt.'

'Papa?'

'Oh, darling. You're too young to know about such things. You're innocent, naïve.' Celestria thought of Aidan Cooney but felt nothing but an unbearable emptiness inside. Pamela ran a hand down her daughter's cheek. 'He loves beautiful women. Of course, I'm used to his flirting and turn a blind eye most of the time. But it doesn't mean it doesn't hurt, to watch him turn those honey eyes on someone younger and prettier than me. No one can resist him when he looks at them in that way. It's like he's seeing right through you and into you and knows what you want and what your life is lacking. But the other night, it was the straw that broke the camel's back. We got upstairs, and I flew at him. I told him that he was too old to go around chatting up young girls, that it made him look a fool.' She drew her fingers across her eyes to wipe away the tears. Her nails were long and red and perfectly manicured. 'Then I told him I didn't want him to spend so much time travelling. That it wasn't fair to leave me alone so often.'

'What did he say?' Celestria asked in a small voice.

Pamela's face crumpled with distress. 'He got so angry, he didn't look like himself at all. It was like a stranger had suddenly got inside of him. He told me his flirting was harmless. That it was just a bit of fun. It made him feel alive, he said. He argued that he worked his backside off so that you and I could have nothing but the best, and that Harry could have the finest education England has to offer. He raged that Elizabeth pushes and pushes him to be perfect and that her standards are so high he can't possibly meet them all of the time. He said he was weary of being corroded by us, like a rock in a vast sea of demanding people, wearing him down little by little until he'd have nothing left to give. He told me I was spoiled and greedy.' Her shoulders began to shake. 'He said the sooner you married, the better, because you were only going to turn out like me, driving him insane with your demands.'

'He said that?'

'He said some terrible things, darling. It must have been the alcohol. I swear, I have never seen him like that before. Now it's going to haunt me for the rest of my life because that is the way I will remember him.'

Celestria sat in silence, a frown lining her brow. She felt as if her mother had just cut out the bottom of her world, sending her tumbling into a hole where there was nothing to grab hold of to stop her falling. She swallowed hard and tried to ignore the ache in her throat.

'Did he kill himself to punish us?' Celestria asked. Her voice came out thin and reedy. 'Because we made too many demands? Well, that's nothing compared to the hell he's putting everyone through, is it? Father Dalgliesh says that suicide is a mortal sin and that he's gone straight to hell.'

'He said that?' Pamela asked. 'Monty is in hell?'

'I don't know why you're looking so surprised, you don't believe in heaven and hell.'

'No, I don't. There is no hell, just other people.' She laughed cynically.

Celestria sighed and stood up. 'Well, Mama, don't forget to wire Grandpa. He needs to know. I'm going to write to him myself.'

That afternoon, Celestria sat at her uncle's desk and opened the top left-hand drawer. Inside, in neat piles, were letterheads and cards for correspondence. She tried to imagine her father's frame of mind as he had sat there in the middle of the night, deliberating what to write in his suicide note. Surely, she thought, if one is about to take one's life, one would want to explain to one's family, to leave them with some peace of mind. Instead, her father had written two meaningless words. Forgive him for what? Taking his own life? Putting his family through hell? Fighting with his wife? For saying such horrid things about his daughter, who was determined never to turn out like her mother, by the way?

She pictured him standing by the window, where she had found him the night of the party. He had looked so different. Solemn and troubled. There had been a ruthlessness to his face that had frightened her. When he had seen her there, his features had softened, restoring to her once again the ebullient father she loved. Slowly she began to put together the pieces gleaned from the conversations she had had with her mother and Aunt Julia and from the couple of times she had spied on him when he had not known that he was being watched. She was more certain than ever that while the rest of the family had blithely enjoyed their summer holiday, Robert Montague had been hiding a dark secret.

She pulled out a sheet of paper and took a pen from the tray on top of the desk. *Darling Grandpa,* she began. *Something terrible has happened, and I need your help . . .*

★

Elizabeth Montague stood in Father Dalgliesh's parlour, gazing out of the window into the garden. Her hand gripped her walking stick, and her face was rigid with indignation. He offered her a chair, but she would not take it. 'My son is not dead,' she declared, without looking at the priest. She sensed pity in his expression, and, if there was one thing she abhorred, it was pity. 'You don't know my son, do you, Father?'

'I haven't had that pleasure, Mrs Montague,' he replied.

'Well, let me tell you about him, then. He is an exceptional man – a wonderful son to me and a wonderful husband, father, brother, and friend. He wouldn't let us down like this. It isn't in his nature. He shines brighter than the brightest star. Everyone loves him. I'll wager there isn't a person in Pendrift who doesn't think the world of him. Now why would a man so beloved take his own life?' Her chin wobbled, but she restrained it with a determined stiffening of the jaw.

'I am at a loss,' he replied.

'He is a success. Everything he touches turns to gold. He has that Montague charm, like his father. Young Bouncy has it; Celestria, too, though what good is it in a girl as superficial as Celestria? It's wasted. You know, Robert made his first fortune when he was a very young man. He travelled the world determined to prove himself. Archie came into the world with a niche already carved out for him. His destiny was here at Pendrift. Robert had to carve his niche on his own. I never doubted he'd return in glory. Robert has more ability, intelligence, and wit than my other two children put together. He persuaded us to invest in a sugar venture in Brazil. We didn't hesitate, and we were right to trust him. Robert made us all rich.' She turned her rheumy eyes to the priest. 'I know a mother shouldn't love one child over and above her other children, but I do. I love Robert the best. He makes me very proud.'

Father Dalgliesh didn't know what to say. He stood

awkwardly knitting his fingers while this formidable woman stared at him defiantly. He wished God would inspire him with the right words to comfort her, but he heard nothing.

'It is in God's hands,' he said clumsily.

'Perhaps,' she snapped, turning to face the garden again. 'I expected to outlive my husband, but I never expected to outlive my son. My youngest child. My most beloved Robert. No, I will not accept it. If he was in trouble, he would have told me. I'm his mother. He would have come to me.'

'All we can do is pray for his deliverance.'

'Prayer,' she sniffed dismissively. 'I'm devout. I pray constantly. Where has it got me?' She shuffled past him. 'I was rather hoping you'd offer me a miracle, Father Dalgliesh.'

'I wish I were able to.'

'Well, if you can't turn water into wine, you had better pray. I shall pray, too, with the rest of my family. He's in God's hands now. There's nothing more we can do.'

Chapter 10

Three days passed and nothing was seen of Robert Montague. Pendrift descended into a state of mourning. There no longer remained any doubt of his suicide, not even in the Snout & Hound, that hotbed of gossip and intrigue. The family grieved for him, except for Elizabeth, who resolutely declared that no child of hers would ever do such a thing.

Father Dalgliesh spent most of his time counselling the townspeople. The air in his parlour was thick with the perfume of weeping women who had all loved Monty, not as a lover, but as a good and kind man who had always put others before himself. How, they asked, could a man who had everything to live for throw his life away? Father Dalgliesh answered as best he could, drawing on the training he had received at the seminary. During these visits he began to gain a better understanding of the man everyone knew as Mr Monty. He had touched each and every one of them in some way or other, from a simple chat in the Snout & Hound to paying young Rewan Craddick's hospital bills. Whatever form it took, there was no doubt that Mr Monty had improved people's lives. And yet, Father Dalgliesh was no wiser than they were. 'Why,' he asked himself, repeating the question he had been asked over and over again, 'would a man who had everything to live for throw his life away?'

Then, on Thursday morning, he received an unexpected visitor.

Father Dalgliesh was at his desk, seeing to his correspondence, for which he had had little time in the last few days, when there was a knock at the door. He heaved a sigh. Another troubled soul to attend to in the parlour, no doubt. He put down his pen. 'Come in,' he replied. The young curate, Howel Brock, poked his face around the door.

'I'm sorry to disturb you, Father, but there's a lady here to see you. She says it's important.'

'Did she say her name?'

'No. She says it's a private matter.' Father Brock raised his eyebrows. 'She's wearing a hat and dark glasses,' he added. 'Very mysterious.'

Father Dalgliesh's curiosity was aroused. He got up, straightened his waistcoat, then proceeded to the parlour. Miss Hoddel was cleaning the tiled floor in the corridor with a shabby mop. When she saw Father Dalgliesh, she stood up and leaned on the handle, wiping a grubby hand on her floral apron.

'You've got Greta Garbo in there,' she said with a chuckle. Father Dalgliesh ignored her and opened the door.

The strange woman perched awkwardly on the edge of the sofa, a small, fluffy dog lying sleepily on her knee. She was strikingly beautiful in a black tailored jacket and skirt and black lizard shoes that were pressed together at an angle to her body. Around her neck she wore a pearl and diamond choker. Her hat was small and pinned to the side of her head, from where a thin veil of netting fell down to her nose. When she saw him, she did not smile, but took off her dark glasses to reveal icy blue eyes that were cold but captivating. Father Dalgliesh's heart missed a beat. She was the image of her daughter.

'My name is Pamela Bancroft Montague,' she said in an American accent. 'My husband is Robert.' At the mention of his name, she lowered her eyes so that her long black lashes almost brushed her cheeks. She was very carefully made up, but powder and lipstick could not disguise her distress. She stroked her dog with a gloved hand.

'I'm very sorry for your loss, Mrs Bancroft Montague,' said the priest, sinking into the armchair opposite.

She inhaled with difficulty and shook her head. 'My husband was a devout Catholic, as I'm sure you are aware.'

'Indeed.'

'I, on the other hand, am nothing. I'm an atheist.'

'You don't believe in God?'

'I don't know,' she mumbled, not able to look him in the eye.

'Then you are agnostic.' He smiled at her reassuringly.

'That doesn't sound so bad, does it?'

'God is there, Mrs Bancroft Montague, whether you believe in Him or not. He waits patiently for you to open your heart and eyes. His love is unconditional.'

'I want to believe, Father. I do.' She heard Miss Hoddel knock her mop against the door. 'This will remain confidential, won't it?' she murmured.

'Of course.'

'I don't want my husband's family to know that I have come.'

'One moment,' he said, getting up. Father Dalgliesh walked over to the door. When he opened it, a blushing Miss Hoddel almost tumbled in. She straightened up and smoothed down her apron. 'Would you be very kind, Miss Hoddel, and make us a pot of tea. Perhaps you might tidy my study afterwards. I have noticed it's got quite dusty lately.'

'I'll have to clean around your books, Father,' she replied irritably.

'I'm afraid I still haven't had time to sort them all out.'

'As you wish,' she said, bending down to pick up the steel bucket of dirty water. 'Though it does my back no good at all.' As she moved away she cast a glance into the parlour, where the strange woman sat with her back to the door.

'I've got no one to turn to,' Pamela continued when Father Dalgliesh returned to his seat. 'I have to be strong for my children, you see.'

'Celestria and Harry,' he said, nodding.

'You've met them. I'm afraid the day you came for lunch I was suffering from a migraine. I get them occasionally. Well, Monty was my rock, Father. He was my whole world. Now he's gone, I feel I'm all alone.'

'What about your husband's family?'

'They're all terribly British, if you know what I mean. Penelope acts as if nothing has happened. Milton's gone very quiet and contained. Archie's tormented and not very strong. Julia, his wife, is as distraught as I am, but it's that stiff-upper-lip thing. It's all very dignified and what one would expect from a Montague, but my feelings are laid bare for everyone to see, and I feel I'm such a burden to them all.'

'What about your children?'

'Oh, Harry is easily distracted, thank heavens, but Celestria now thinks her father has been murdered. But she would, wouldn't she? Little girls always adore their fathers. Well, most of them do.' She lowered her eyes.

'Celestria mentioned a grandfather who lives in New York,' he said. 'I assume that is your father.'

'Yes, he's my father, all right.' Her face grew hard. 'I have a troubled relationship with him. Celestria adores him. I took her to America for the duration of the war. Harry wasn't born then, so it was just the two of us. My father has always been a rather distant figure in my life, the kind of man who never had the time, but thought gifts would make up for it. He was too busy making money. Besides, he wanted a son. A Richard Bancroft III to take on his empire after he retired. Well, he got a Pamela instead. That wasn't good enough. I think by the time Celestria came to stay, he had realized what he had missed out on, because, boy, did he shower her with love and affection.' She chuckled bitterly. 'I've never forgiven him for that. But Celestria thinks the sun shines out of—' She stopped suddenly, remembering where she was, and added, 'She thinks he's perfect.'

'I can't imagine you get to see him very often.'

'We used to spend a week with him at this ridiculously flamboyant castle he owns in Scotland, but I hated the cold. So did my mother, who prefers to stay in America. We haven't been for years. And we used to go spend the whole of July in Nantucket, which was where I spent my summers as a child, but we haven't been for the last two years. What with one thing and another . . .' Her voice trailed off.

'Celestria must miss him.'

'She was devastated when we returned to London at the end of the war. She didn't recognize her father and missed her grandfather dreadfully. Monty tried so hard, and, in the end, they got on like a house on fire. Well, he had that charm. It was impossible not to love him.' Her voice grew quiet as she spoke about him. 'London was a grey city in comparison to New York. Post-war rations and all that. It was hard to adjust. Then Harry was born. My darling Harry.' Her eyes lit up. 'He loved his father, too, but he's always been my little boy. Children have a way of just getting on with life, don't they? Harry's not moping about in a heap, like me. He's back in the woods with his cousins, trapping vermin and shooting rabbits with David. I wonder what goes through his head at night when there aren't any distractions.'

'Children might seem to handle bereavement better than adults, but it doesn't mean they aren't scarred by it. They just have a different way of coping, that's all.'

'My heart bleeds to think of the pain my husband has caused him. Didn't he think of that the night he took his life?

It's the most selfish act imaginable. My children are left father-less, and I'm a widow.' She began to cry. 'Black really isn't my colour, either.'

'Mrs Bancroft Montague,' Father Dalgliesh began, but Pamela cut him off with a melodramatic sob.

'What am I going to do? How am I going to go on? He should have taken me with him.'

'You have your children to think of. They need you now more than ever.'

'I'm of no use to anyone. That's the truth of it. I'm a hope-less mother.' She clicked open the black handbag on the sofa beside her and pulled out a white handkerchief. Dabbing her eyes, she continued, 'Monty was never around, you see. He travelled so much on business. When we first married, it wasn't like that. He'd invest in some scam, which would either make him a lot of money or it wouldn't, but he was around. Then after the war he established an office in Paris, spending half the week there and half the week in London. Those weeks then turned to fortnights. He became hard to pin down. I could never get hold of him. Then he'd return and try to be a good father and husband, and in many ways he was. He bought me beautiful gifts, told me how lovely I was, took Celestria to tea at Fortnums and Harry to Hamley's, where he treated him to a new train set or something. He was perfect, and yet so damn *imperfect*. I look back now and realize that he was only skating on the surface of our family life together, never pene-trating beneath because he never gave us his time and he never shared his thoughts. He was always so . . .' She struggled to find the right word. 'Detached, as if his heart and mind were somewhere else – yet always charming, always funny, the life and soul of every party. I was the envy of every wife in London, believe me. The reality was less glamorous.' She sighed and sniffed delicately. 'I just wanted him to be around. His business grew. More time in Paris. He seemed to have his fingers in every pie. Perhaps I shouldn't begrudge him; after all, he was working so hard – for us. You'll think I'm awfully spoiled, Father, but sometimes I felt he gave so much of himself to people he barely knew, he had little to give to us.'

'I don't think you're spoiled at all,' said Father Dalgliesh kindly. 'I think you're lost, that's all.'

'How will I ever find myself?' she asked, stifling a sob. 'I don't know where to look.'

'God will help you.'

'If I can't see Him, how do I know He's there?'

'Close your eyes and look inside your heart.'

'But they all say that. How can I look inside my heart? I don't have eyes on the inside of my head.'

Father Dalgliesh wanted to laugh. But Pamela was deadly serious.

'Next time there is a beautiful sunset, stop a while to look at it. Next time you see a beautiful view or a magical dawn, hear the birdsong at the end of the day, next time you are struck by the magnificence of nature, when your heart is flooded with that melancholy feeling of awe, turn your mind to He who made it all. Let His love flow into your heart. Stand up and say "I open my heart to You, God, so that You may fill it with Your love and make me whole."'

She sniffed and put the handkerchief back into her handbag, clipping it shut. 'I'll try,' she said softly. 'I trust God can find all the pieces.'

Miss Hoddel knocked on the door and staggered in behind a tray of cups and teapot, complete with a yellow tea cosy she had knitted herself. Father Dalgliesh leapt up to help her. 'I'll go and put my feet up now if you don't mind. I did your study yesterday and don't wish to repeat the exercise until I absolutely have to. Might help myself to a cup of tea. These are trying times.' She feasted her eyes on the elegant visitor, hoping to woo her into conversation. There was almost a scuffle as Father Dalgliesh had to push her through the door.

'You certainly deserve a cup of tea, Miss Hoddel. Thank you very much for ours.' Miss Hoddel returned to the kitchen scowling and sat eating cake while Father Dalgliesh remained in the parlour for another hour.

Finally, they emerged and Father Dalgliesh showed Mrs Bancroft Montague to the door. 'You are most welcome to come and see me any time you need to. Perhaps you will come to Mass on Sunday. I think you'll find church a great comfort.'

She turned to him and took his hand in hers. 'I want you to know, Father, I'm not a good person.'

'I don't judge people, Mrs Bancroft Montague. That is not my right nor my interest. I guide them in the way that I believe is right. We are all sinners.'

'The eye of the needle and all that,' she replied with a chuckle.

'So you do know your scriptures.'

'Some,' she said with a smile. 'One picks it up in a family like mine.'

As she walked down the road she was surprised to find that she felt a lot better.

No one wanted to begin the painful task of sorting out Monty's affairs, least of all Pamela, who'd rather have gone to ground like a bear. However, the matter was taken out of their hands by a telephone call from the family solicitor, Mr Scrunther, who requested a meeting most urgently. It had been over a week since Monty's disappearance. Nothing more had been recovered. The waters had swallowed all trace of him, along with the secrets of his last moments, forever sealed in the sea's impenetrable bed of rock and stone.

Mr Scrunther's office was in the nearby town of Newquay,

on the main street above an estate agent specializing in pretty seaside houses for rent. Archie accompanied Pamela and Celestria, as neither of them knew the first thing about Monty's business, though he was pretty vague himself. As an executor of his brother's will, it was right that he should be there, although Monty could not officially be pronounced dead due to the absence of his body. There would be an investigation, no doubt, and a petition to court in order to receive a death certificate. Monty had acted most irresponsibly. The very least he could have done was leave them with a body to bury.

Mr Scrunther greeted them unhappily, shaking their hands and muttering his regrets through his bushy white beard. 'This is a sad day indeed,' he said, ushering them into his office. It was dim and smelled of damp wool and stale cigar smoke. 'I knew Mr Montague when he was a young man setting off to Brazil in search of gold. He was a man of courage then. Who could have predicted this?'

'Shame he didn't have the courage to face his problems, whatever they were,' said Archie, taking a seat.

Mr Scrunther walked stiffly around to his own chair. Cornwall was no place for a man with arthritic bones. He sat down carefully and leaned back against the leather, the buttons on his waistcoat almost popping under the strain of his capacious belly. He took off his pebble glasses and proceeded to clean them with a white cloth before replacing them on his large potato nose.

'I'm afraid Mr Montague had a whole mountain of problems,' said Mr Scrunther, looking like a headmaster discussing a wayward child with his parents.

'Monty?' said Pamela. 'Problems?' Mr Scrunther leaned forward and opened a large black file. He lifted his chin and glanced down his nose, upon which a small sprouting of curly white hairs was visible.

'As I'm sure you know, Imperial Amalgamated Investments

folded two years ago.' He paused as he heard Pamela's sharp intake of breath.

'His business folded?' repeated Archie, horrified. He turned to Pamela. 'Did you know anything about this?'

'No.' She frowned, looking bewildered. 'He must have begun something new because he's been working incredibly hard for the last two years.'

Mr Scrunther shook his head and raised his eyes over the rims of his glasses. 'I'm afraid his other businesses folded in the last six months. The Buckingham Trust Company and St James's Holding Company. There is no easy way to tell you this, Mrs Montague. Your husband was in terrible debt.'

'There must be some mistake,' interrupted Archie. 'Why, only a couple of weeks ago he was away on business in Paris.'

'He said he had a million pounds under management!' Pamela argued. 'Surely he didn't lose all that?'

Mr Scrunther shook his head gravely. 'He lost most on the stock market. Every investor lost his money. The rest he withdrew himself.'

'What did he do with it?' Pamela asked.

'That, I'm afraid I cannot tell you, Mrs Montague, because I don't know. He came to see me Thursday before last. He wanted to settle his affairs in the event of his premature death. Of course, I suspected nothing of his intentions.'

'He came to see you the day before the party? What did he say?' Pamela glanced at Celestria, who was sitting quietly, listening to every word. Her mouth was fixed into a grim line that did not soften when she returned her mother's look.

'He was anxious. He said he had lost everything. Perhaps that is why he had gone to Paris, in order to see what he could salvage.'

'Why didn't he tell me?' said Pamela, shrinking into her chair. 'If all his businesses went bankrupt, what the devil have we been living on?'

'Savings, investments . . .' Mr Scrunther paused. 'Your husband used to have a lot of money, Mrs Montague.'

'Then where's it all gone?'

Mr Scrunther shrugged. 'I don't know. I only know what he told me. That he doesn't have anything left.'

'Well, that explains why he took his life. He couldn't bear to disappoint us,' said Celestria. 'All anyone ever talks about is the wonderful Monty, getting them all out of trouble, and where did it get him? Into trouble himself. He just couldn't say no to anyone. He even offered to pay for your birthday party, Uncle Archie.' Archie looked puzzled. Julia had kept her promise. 'Yes, I overheard Papa and Aunt Julia talking in the library about a week before the party. She was crying. Well, Papa said he'd help her out.'

'Monty once more to the rescue.' Archie breathed in through his nose. He didn't like to discuss his problems with outsiders, and it humiliated him to think of his own wife grovelling for money.

'He also paid for Mrs Craddick's son's hospital bills,' Celestria continued, glancing at her mother. 'It seems that Papa was looking after everyone but himself.'

'Helping everyone? What with? If he had no money of his own?' Suddenly the colour drained from Pamela's face. Her jaw dropped, leaving her mouth hanging open like a shark's. 'Oh, my God!' she exclaimed in horror. 'He's gone through mine as well. I just know it.'

Mr Scrunther cleared his throat. 'Two years ago Mr Montague put the house in Belgravia in your name, Mrs Montague, thereby avoiding any inheritance tax in the event of his death.'

'Did he do that at the time Imperial Amalgamated Investments collapsed?' Archie asked.

'He did.'

'At least he cast a thought to us,' said Pamela with a sniff. 'I'd hate to think of us being destitute.'

'Mr Montague's death may have come as a complete surprise to you all. However, I would imagine he had planned it very carefully. I'm sorry he kept you in the dark. Perhaps I should have said something.' He scratched his beard.

'You couldn't have abused his trust, Mr Scrunther,' said Archie diplomatically. 'We completely understand.'

'If it meant we could have avoided all of this, it would have been worth it,' answered Mr Scrunther.

On the way back in the car, Pamela sat staring out of the window in silence. Now, at least, they had a motive, however incomprehensible it was. Archie gripped the steering wheel. Pendrift Hall was suddenly in grave danger. He had hoped to ask Monty for help. Now there was no possibility of help from anywhere, only heaven. His wife hadn't told him that she had already divulged their money problems. She couldn't have known that he was on the verge of doing exactly the same thing himself. He had felt emasculated by the thought, but desperation had left him no alternative. Now he didn't know what to do, or whom to turn to. Celestria watched the raindrops wiggling down the window as the drizzle fell from low grey clouds. It was bleak outside, and it was bleak within. No one spoke, each in his or her own silent world, trying to come to terms with the knowledge they had gained about the man they had all thought they knew.

'Why didn't he tell me?' said Pamela after a while. 'It makes me so mad. If he wasn't dead, I'd kill him myself!'

'Would you have understood?' said Archie, not meaning to be unkind.

'He obviously didn't think so,' Pamela replied. 'I didn't question him about his affairs. We never talked business. He said that was men's talk, better left for discussion over a glass of port at the end of dinner. I suppose he had enough of it at White's. There was no need to bring it all home with him.'

'You don't know Papa's gone through your money,' said Celestria. 'Anyway, how could he touch it?'

'Because he set up the account, darling. Of course he had access to it. I never even looked at it. I just spent when I felt like it. Your grandfather gave it to me when I married. Back then it seemed such a large sum; I never believed I'd ever get through it. I certainly never expected my husband to!'

'What's happened to innocent until proven guilty? Isn't that the law in this country?' Celestria was angered that her mother was already accusing her father of robbing her.

'I'll call the bank as soon as we get home,' said Archie through gritted teeth. 'Don't worry, Pamela, we'll get to the bottom of it.'

'I can't bear it,' she said melodramatically, a tear trickling down her ashen face. 'I thought I knew the man I married. I've lost everything. If he's been through my money, what are we going to do? What will I do about school fees and our home? Without money, how will we maintain it, and God, all the staff, how will we pay them? We're going to be destitute. Homeless. Why didn't Monty think of that before he threw himself into the water?'

'That's precisely why he killed himself,' said Archie. 'Because he couldn't bear to let everyone down.'

'What will your mother say?' Pamela exclaimed. 'Rather a lot, I should imagine.'

'I'm not going to tell her,' said Archie firmly. 'Why give her unnecessary pain?'

Pamela raised her eyebrows in disapproval. 'Don't worry, I'll carry it all for her,' she said sarcastically.

Archie ground his teeth. The woman was pushing his patience to the limit. It was a wonder he hadn't lost his temper. She didn't know the meaning of the word *destitute*.

He and Julia were in real danger of losing Pendrift Hall, without a soul to turn to for help, while pampered Pamela was
screaming poverty. Had she forgotten her millionaire father?
Or was the lead in the current drama too tempting to resist?

That night Archie dressed for bed in his dressing room adjacent to his wife's bedroom. Classical music wafted out from
the gramophone, along with the floral scent of her bath oil.
Everyone had gone to bed, exhausted and emotionally wrung
out. The shock of nearly losing Bouncy had sent Julia into a
frenzy of devotion. She read him stories, cuddled him at every
opportunity, and visited his room five times a night to check
he was tucked up in bed. Monty's suicide had been a terrible
blow for everyone, but he knew his wife thanked God the sea
had taken him and spared her son. To her the two were inter-
linked. The man for the boy. As if there lurked below a
monster to whom a soul must be sacrificed, like some ancient
Greek myth.

He wandered into her room. She was brushing her hair at
her dressing table, her gaze lost somewhere in the space
between herself and the mirror. When she saw him enter, she
blinked and shifted her focus.

'Darling, are you all right?' she asked, as if she had only just
noticed how troubled he was.

He nodded bravely. He clearly wasn't. She stood up and
walked over to him. He didn't move away, but let her put
her arms around him.

'Is it Pendrift?' she whispered.

His breath was staggered as he tried to repress his misery. 'I
don't know what to do,' he replied. 'I'm letting you down.'

'You're not letting me down. I'd be happy in a hovel, as
long as we're all together.'

'You don't mean that, darling. Pendrift Hall is your greatest love after your children.'

She pulled away and frowned at him. 'After my children? After my children and you. You're my greatest love, Archie. I loved you before I loved them, remember?'

'That's very sweet of you.'

'I'm not being sweet. I'm being honest. I'd rather you sold everything and we lived in contentment than living like this, with worry, barely communicating, forgetting about each other.'

'If I sold Pendrift, neither of us would be happy. You know that as well as I. Pendrift is in our blood. It's a part of us, like another child. It would be like tearing off a limb, or scooping out a piece of our hearts. Can you imagine young Bouncy, or Wilfrid and Sam, being anywhere else? Pendrift is all they've ever known. I'd rather sell the paintings and the furniture than lose their home. No, there has to be another way.'

'I was thinking, Archie. Nanny's getting old now. It's time to let her go. It's got nothing to do with the other morning, or that we need to save money; I'd like to look after Bouncy myself. Perhaps we could settle her into one of the farm cottages, give her a small pension.'

He looked at her quizzically. 'Are you sure?'

'I nearly lost Bouncy. He's so precious. I don't want to miss a minute of his growing up.'

He kissed her forehead. 'If it's what you want, I support you. Bouncy would rather be with his mother.'

'I'm so pleased you agree.'

'If you're happy, darling, I'm happy.'

'We'll find a way to save Pendrift. I know we will.'

'I'll never forgive Monty for betraying us all. He's left one hell of a mess behind him.'

'A widow and two fatherless children, too,' said Julia.

'They'll survive. Richard will sweep them up to that castle of his. But what about us?'

'Let's not think about it, darling,' Julia urged, leading him to bed. 'Let's get some sleep. Everything always seems worse when one is tired. Let's lie together and take comfort from each other. I thank God it wasn't you, or one of the children. I'm so grateful that we're alive and together. Nothing else really matters but our family.'

They lay in the darkness, their arms entwined as they had so often lain in those early years of marriage before the children had come to squeeze in between them. Julia nuzzled her face into his neck, and he stroked her hair. 'What would I do without you?' he said softly. 'You're very strong and resilient, darling. I'm lucky to have found you.'

'Don't be silly. We're lucky to have found each other. It'll work out, you'll see. Every cloud has a silver lining. We just can't see it yet. Wait until the sun comes out, then it'll shine so brightly it'll put everything right.'

'When you're around, the sun's always shining, Julia,' he said, kissing her forehead. 'I don't tell you as often as I should. But I love you, old girl.'

'And I love you.' She chuckled sleepily. 'Silly old man.'

Chapter 11

God, it's so humiliating!' wailed Celestria, throwing her clothes into her suitcase without bothering to fold them first. Lotty and Melissa lay on the bed watching her, not knowing how to comfort her. 'Papa's gone through not only his own savings but Mama's, too. We haven't a penny left in the world. In fact, we're totally skint. That's my inheritance out the window. God, it makes me so mad!'

'But surely your grandfather will bail you out? Isn't he one of the richest men in America?' said Lotty.

'Of course he'll bail us out. He'll bail *Mama* out, but what about me? I had an inheritance, not to mention a happy sum just waiting for the ring and those marriage vows. Now it's all gone! Just like someone set fire to it. You know, Papa hasn't had a job for the last two years. His business collapsed. He's been living off savings.' She pulled her silk dresses off their hangers. 'Well, I shan't be needing these anymore if I'm to be a social pariah!' She cast them into a suitcase already over-flowing with stockings and shoes.

'You're overreacting, Celestria,' said Melissa calmly. 'You'll probably find there's money put away somewhere. Uncle Monty wouldn't leave you with nothing. After all, who does he expect to pay Harry's school fees?'

'Grandpa!' Celestria chuckled cynically. 'Papa married money, don't forget. Perhaps he knew he was unreliable all along. Anyway, Uncle Archie telephoned the bank. There's nothing – just a large overdraft. I can't believe Papa killed himself because of that! Can you imagine what people are going to say? The whole of London's bound to be talking about it. Who's going to want to marry the daughter of a suicide who doesn't have a penny to her name?'

'Tragedy will just make you more glamorous,' said Lotty kindly.

'On the contrary. I think they'll all give me a wide berth in case the disease is genetic or, even worse, catching. Take note, Lotty, being poor is very unpleasant.' Melissa looked inquiringly.

'Grandma's taken it very badly,' Lotty said quickly, blushing profusely. 'She refuses to believe it. Just sits at the window staring out to sea, hoping he'll walk back up the path as if nothing's amiss.'

'Don't feel sorry for her,' said Celestria, wandering over to the window. 'She'll be joining him soon enough.'

She gazed out across the ocean to where low clouds and fog mingled with choppy waves and sea spray. A pair of gulls wheeled on the wind like gliders. 'I don't think I'll ever enjoy the sea again,' she said quietly. 'I'll always remember it for having taken away my father and bringing us all such unhappiness. The sooner I get to London the better.'

'Why the rush? Harry doesn't go back to school until the ninth of September.'

'Because I can't be here any more.'

The two sisters remained silent. They'd be returning to London shortly, too: Melissa to the arduous task of finding a husband, and Lotty to her affair with Francis and the decisions she'd ultimately be forced to make. She didn't want to think about them.

'Poor Harry,' said Lotty with a sigh. 'How dreadful to lose one's father so young.'

'A boy needs a man in his life, to set an example,' agreed Melissa.

'A fine example our father set,' Celestria scoffed, spraying on perfume before putting it in her spongebag. The scent of bluebells filled the room, but an autumn wind blew in through the open window. 'It's all over,' she said, and her voice had a sharp and furious edge. 'The summer, our childhoods, Cornwall – everything's been turned on its head. I want to go through Papa's things; that's why I'm leaving. I want to find out what else he was keeping from us. Where he's been running off to for the last two years, supposedly on business. I don't feel I know him any more.' She placed her spongebag on top of the clothes that lay in a messy heap in the suitcase. 'Now, Lotty, you sit on top, and Melissa and I will zip it up. Damned suitcase, it's not big enough.'

It proved an impossible task. Celestria had brought far too many clothes, many of which she hadn't even worn. Finally, she decided to leave all her beachwear in the cupboard. 'Where I'm going these shan't be needed,' she said grumpily, watching as at last Melissa managed to fasten the suitcase.

As she stepped into the hall, Soames opened the door holding a silver tray of letters. 'Miss Celestria,' he said, eyes falling to the suitcase she had dragged down behind her. 'You should have let Warren carry that for you; it looks heavy.'

'It *is* heavy. Full of sorrow, Soames.'

'Indeed.' He cleared his throat. 'I have about a dozen letters for you.'

'Really? Probably all saying what a wonderful man my father was.'

'And they are right,' agreed Soames, who had always held Mr Montague in the highest regard.

She sniffed dismissively and took the letters. 'Can you find out train times to London, please. I'll leave this evening.'

'So soon?'

'Don't worry Soames, I'm leaving Mama with you.' Celestria laughed, but Soames didn't find it funny at all.

In the drawing room Julia sat smoking over old photograph albums while Penelope did a crossword and Wilfrid, Sam, and Harry worked quietly on a jigsaw puzzle Archie had set up for them on his velvet-topped card table. It was a cosy sight. Had it not been for the tragedy that cast a shadow over every moment of pleasure, Celestria would have relished such a scene of familial harmony. Archie, Milton, and David had gone to play squash with friends who lived on the other side of Pendrift, and little Bouncy was having tea in the nursery with Nanny. Pamela was in bed with Poochi, who, to her intense relief, had begun to nibble on a biscuit.

'I'm returning to London tonight on the sleeper,' Celestria announced on entering the room. 'I've received tons of letters,' she added. 'I suppose one's father committing suicide isn't a daily occurrence.'

Julia looked up from pictures of Monty as a boy. 'Today?'

'Yes.'

'Alone?'

'Yes.'

'Is that wise?' She looked at Penelope, whose attention was entirely focused on a clue. 'Penelope, do you think it's wise for Celestria to go up to London on her own?'

Penelope raised her eyes over her spectacles. 'We're going next week. Why don't you wait and we can all travel together?'

'I can't wait,' Celestria said, flopping into an armchair. She began to flick through the letters as if shuffling a pack of cards. 'Do you think I should open them now, or will they make me cry?'

'What does your mother say?' Julia persisted.

'About what?' Celestria chose the one with the prettiest

handwriting and tore open the envelope. It was from Mrs Wilmotte.

'About you going up to London?'

'I haven't told her. Besides, I don't think she cares. She's only thinking of herself. I don't imagine she'll be moving very far from her bed for a long time.'

'Doesn't she rather need you?' Penelope asked, beginning to take an interest.

'I don't think so. She's got her wretched dog, hasn't she? He's eating, by the way. Thought you'd all be pleased.'

Julia noticed an anger in Celestria that wasn't attractive. She wished Archie were there to back her up. What was she going to do in London all on her own, in any case? She hardly had the money to hit Bond Street.

'Look, I know what you're all thinking. I'm not in my right mind. Well, you're right. I'm not. I'm devastated and shocked. Papa's let us all down. We can't have a funeral because there's no body. We can't even confirm he's dead until some bloody court somewhere gives us a death certificate, not that there's anything left anyway. Why he didn't shoot himself or something, I can't imagine. At least then we'd have a body to bury. Yes, I'm angry and upset. Isn't it natural that I should want to be at home? Grandpa will look after us; he's got pots of money, and anyway, if push comes to shove, I'll go and live in New York with them. He was my father for the best part of my childhood, anyway.' She shrugged as Julia and Penelope both stared at her.

Julia was too shocked to speak, but Penelope put down her pen and lifted her chin, taking a slow, deliberate breath through her nose. She took off her spectacles and folded them into her lap.

'Well, my dear. You've made your feelings very clear, haven't you? I should go up to London if I were you and spend some time on your own, to reflect. Perhaps you might direct some of that energy into compassion rather than hate, and remember that it's Monty who's enabled you to have everything you want in life, and spent the last two decades raising you and giving you the best education money can buy.'

'I didn't mean it like that,' Celestria mumbled, looking at her feet.

'I'll get Archie to drive you to the station,' said Julia tartly, hurt by Celestria's callous disregard for anyone but herself. She glanced at Harry, appalled that his sister had allowed herself to say such dreadful things in front of him.

Sensing a suddenly lowered temperature in the room, Celestria decided to walk out on the cliffs alone. She donned a macintosh and Wellington boots, thrust her hands into her pockets, called for Purdy, and slammed the door behind her. No one understood. Not even Aunt Julia, who had always been so kind. Didn't they realize that the man who had drowned was someone totally different from Robert Montague? He was a man who had squandered his wife's fortune as well as his own, *and* his daughter's inheritance. He was a man who lied. A man who hadn't done a day's work in two years. A man who took regular business trips to Paris and Milan with no business to be done. He was thoughtless and selfish and a terrible coward. He had shattered their lives into hundreds of fragments that no one would ever be able to put back. That man was a stranger; he wasn't her father at all. So where was Monty, the man they all knew and loved? Whatever had happened to him? Had he ever existed? As she trudged along the wet path that wiggled its way around the cliff top like a snake, she knew she had to find out. What's more, her intelligence told her that there must be someone else involved. Someone, somewhere, had driven him to it.

The drizzle that sprayed her face tasted of salt. It wasn't cold, but the damp seemed to penetrate her clothes and cause her bones to ache. Purdy trotted along beside her, nose to the ground, bracing himself against the wind that flattened the fur on his back. Celestria put her head down and stared at the path, her mind pondering her miserable predicament.

Suddenly she heard a voice calling her name. She turned around to see Father Dalgliesh hurrying up the path towards her. Purdy recognized him immediately. He wagged his tail and trotted up to greet him, thrusting his wet nose into the man's coat.

'Father Dalgliesh,' she said, not having expected to see anyone up there on the cliff top.

'Miss Montague, I thought it was you walking ahead. I recognized Purdy before I recognized you in that coat and hat. I've just been with your grandmother.' His glasses were covered in little droplets, and his hat and coat were soaked.

'Don't tell me you didn't take the car?' She screwed up her nose in disbelief.

He shook his head. 'I thought a brisk walk in the drizzle would be just the thing to raise my spirits.'

'I thought men of God were always happy.'

'This is a sad time for us all,' he said seriously.

'I know, Papa's in hell. It's sad for him, too!' Father Dalgliesh heard the resentment in her voice and knew that God had brought him to her for a reason. They began to slowly amble together.

'I didn't say he's in hell, Miss Montague.'

'Please call me Celestria. Miss Montague sounds ridiculous!'

'It's God's prerogative to decide where he is, Celestria. There are many things to be considered. Whether it was in fact suicide, whether he was driven to it, whether he was himself when he did it.'

'Oh, I don't think he was himself, whatever "himself" means.'

'Why do you say that?' Father Dalgliesh asked. Celestria

told him about their visit to Newquay and how her father had been living a lie for the previous two years, perhaps more, for all she knew.

'I'm going up to London to get to the bottom of it,' she said. 'Someone, somewhere must know about his affairs. What he's been up to all this time. Aunt Julia thinks I should stay in Pendrift. Aunt Penelope just thinks I'm horrid. Uncle Archie's as useless as an umbrella on a sunny day, and Uncle Milton would rather forget it all with a game of tennis. They don't understand. They don't understand *me*.' Father Dalgliesh heard the desperate cry in her voice, and his heart buckled. In the rain, sodden to the bone, she appeared lost and alone. He stopped walking and looked at her with such compassion that she began to cry. 'Oh, dear,' she sobbed. 'I'm so sorry.'

'It's good to let it all out,' he said kindly, touching her wet arm.

'I don't think I've cried since Papa disappeared.' Now she had started she didn't know whether she'd be able to stop. It felt as if her heart had burst open, releasing tons of poison.

'Then it's about time you did.'

'You see, no one understands me but you.'

'I'm sure they do,' he said, thinking how mother and daughter were very much alike.

'You don't know them. Mama's more interested in her stupid dog. Grandpa's in New York. The minute I tell everyone how I feel they all go cold on me, like I've said something terrible. The fact remains, Papa's been bloody selfish.' She put her hand to her lips. 'I'm sorry for swearing.'

'That's all right. Nothing I haven't heard before.'

'I've got no one to turn to. I'm all alone in the world, and, what's more, I have to be strong for everyone else when all I want is for someone else to comfort me for a change.'

Father Dalgliesh hesitated a moment, rummaging around

for the right words. He was becoming increasingly used to weeping women, but none was as heartbreaking as Celestria. *'There, there, dear, you'll feel better soon,'* just wouldn't do for her.

'Why don't you come back to the presbytery?' he said instead. 'Miss Hoddel will make us both a cup of tea, and we can talk where it's warm.' He smiled, and his face radiated such kindness, Celestria was unable to refuse.

Purdy was happy to stretch out on the rug in front of the fire that Miss Hoddel had had the foresight to light while Father Dalgliesh had been out. 'I won't have that dog messing up the house,' she had complained when she saw Purdy's dirty, wet fur. 'He can lie on an old towel in front of the fire to dry off. Fires in summer, we'll be having a heat wave at Christmas next!' She had bustled off to fetch a towel while Celestria and Father Dalgliesh took off their coats and hats.

'What a day!' he exclaimed, shaking the water off his coat. 'It really feels like the end of summer.'

'The day my father died was the end of the summer and the end of my childhood,' she replied dramatically, giving her coat to Father Dalgliesh to hang up on the peg in the hall.

Miss Hoddel brought a tray of tea and a plate of biscuits into the parlour. 'Will there be anything else, Father?' she asked, hands on hips.

'Nothing else, thank you, Miss Hoddel.'

'Father Brock told me to tell you that he won't be back until six; he's nipped into Newquay.'

'Thank you, Miss Hoddel.'

'Right, I'll be in the kitchen if you should need me. I have to rest my legs, if you don't mind, and my back is killing me slowly. It's a marathon every day in this house, and I'm on my own.' Her eyes lingered a while longer than was polite on the young woman who looked even more beautiful with wet hair and no makeup. She didn't like her much, though; a bit snooty, she thought. Not like her father. Now, he was a real gentleman. He always had a smile to give and a kindly word. With a snort she left the room, closing the door behind her.

'I feel so wretched, Father, and so confused,' said Celestria, sipping her tea. 'It's like my whole life has been a sham.' Her grey eyes grew dark with tears.

'That's normal, and you shouldn't feel ashamed. It's not uncommon to feel anger and resentment and a sense of betrayal. Suicide is a very difficult thing to come to terms with. Those left behind feel guilty because they couldn't help. They feel rejection because their loved one would rather die than be with them. They feel unloved and worthless. The fact is that a suicide considers no one but himself. His despair is so great that he thinks only of a way out. Nothing else matters.'

'Which is why I have to find out what really happened. I was with him the night he died, and he was as far from a man in great pain as he could possibly get.'

'Which is why you feel angry.'

'Yes, I feel angry because of that, but also because I have loved someone who didn't exist. According to my family, I shouldn't be angry. I should be mourning him in a dignified way, like all of them.'

'Stiff upper lip?' He repeated her mother's very words.

'Yes. I want to shout and scream, and they're all going about their day grieving quietly with great dignity, as a Montague should. The worst is that it's just going to go on and on and on because, until there's a body, there's no funeral, therefore no end to it all. Perhaps Old Beardy will catch a big fish in his net with Papa in his belly and we can all be done with the whole sad episode.' Her shoulders began to shake, and she let out a loud sob. 'I can't stand it here any longer. I was bored by the summer as it was and longing to return to London. Now I'll return to gossip, and no one's going to marry me because I'm poor. I haven't been poor yet, but I know I'll hate it.' She bit her lip, aware that she was lying in the presence of God. He'd know for sure that her grandfather would never allow her to be poor. 'If not poor, then the daughter of a disgraced man!' she added hastily.

Celestria was such a sorry sight, with her hair all wet and tangled, her face smarting from the wind and tears, her shoulders hunched with dejection, that Father Dalgliesh followed his impulses and sat beside her on the sofa, where her mother had sat the previous Thursday, and took her in his arms. She rested her head against his chest and sobbed like a child.

The little seed that had been planted in a secret corner of Father Dalgliesh's heart now stirred in the warmth of physical contact and began to grow. He sensed that stirring, but didn't push her away. To his shame, their closeness felt pleasant. He inhaled the scent of damp bluebells and felt his head swim. He knew God had sent him a challenge. It was far bigger than he could have anticipated. But Christ resisted temptation and so would he.

However, he wasn't prepared for Celestria's abandonment to her own impulses. He felt her soft lips on his neck and her warm breath brush his skin. She was no longer sobbing, but breathing softly. For a second he remained frozen in the moment, his mind numb, his tongue mute; his senses were more alive than ever. He felt the sweat gather on his brow as his body grew hot. His senses were besieged by feelings he had never experienced, but overriding them all was a sinking feeling of shame. How had he let it happen? Had he weakened because of vanity? He was humbled. Vanity itself was a cardinal sin. Gathering the little strength he could find, he gently pushed her away.

'No, Celestria,' he whispered, trying to see past the beautiful face to the soul inside. 'You mustn't.'

Celestria stared at him. Suddenly she recoiled in horror, as if she had seen something ugly in those deep, compassionate eyes. She stood up, dizzy with confusion, and, ignoring his protests, ran to the door. Purdy stretched reluctantly and followed her out into the rain.

'Celestria!' Father Dalgliesh shouted after her. 'Celestria!' But it was too late. She had grabbed her coat and hat from the hall and slipped into her boots before he had been able to stop her. He watched her go, disappearing up the street and into the fog that had now descended over Pendrift.

Chapter 12

Celestria lay on her father's dressing-room bed and buried her face in the pillow. She had endured the journey back to London with difficulty. It had been uncomfortable on the train, not to mention lonely on her own for such a long time. She wished Lotty or Melissa had accompanied her, but Penelope would not have even considered it. 'What are you going to do up there all by yourself?' she had asked, and her tone had weighed heavy with disapproval. However, her mother had been surprisingly understanding, overruling them all so long as Celestria telephoned every day. In any case, it was only a week before they all joined her in London, and Mrs Waynebridge, the housekeeper, would be there during the day to look after her.

Every time Celestria thought of Father Dalgliesh, her toes curled with embarrassment. He had been so kind and sensitive, taking time to listen to her, to see her point of view and not condemn her, that she had mistaken a sense of profound gratitude for love. She recalled the look on his face. She'd never forget it as long as she lived, and she'd never get over the shame. He had suddenly grown bigger, like he had that Sunday morning at Mass, and his eyes had become distant and unfamiliar, setting him apart and out of reach. She had been a fool to try to bring him down to her level. She considered the food chain and decided that Father Dalgliesh wasn't an animal at all.

Even a lioness wasn't capable of catching a ray of light. 'Oh, what must he think of me?' she groaned.

She rolled over and stared at the ceiling her father must have stared at a hundred times, when Pamela had banished him to his dressing room because he had drunk too much or smoked too many cigars, the smell of which she couldn't abide. It was hard to believe that he was dead. His room was still full of his things, as if he had been there only the day before. His suits hanging clean and pressed in the cupboards; his shoes neatly placed in rows, polished until they shone; an ashtray on his dressing table full of coins, golf tees, and cuff links; a blue shirt draped over the back of a chair; his ivory and silver brushes all lined up in a row; his burgundy dressing gown hooked onto the back of the door; slippers beside the bed; book on the bedside table left unfinished. The air still smelled of him. Outside, the low hum of motor cars was a reminder that the world continued to turn as it always had. That everyone was busy with their own lives while Celestria was grappling to make sense of hers.

Mrs Waynebridge brought her breakfast on a tray, puffing like an old steam engine as she mounted the stairs. 'There you go, love,' she said kindly, placing it on the ottoman at the end of the bed. There was something wonderfully comforting about Mrs Waynebridge's soft Yorkshire accent; it was as familiar to Celestria as hot Marmite toast and warm milk and honey. 'I don't imagine you got much sleep last night in that train.' She straightened up and smoothed down her white apron. She was soft and round like a marshmallow, with dove-grey hair and a warm, fleshy face. Her brown eyes were red-rimmed and shiny from crying, though she didn't want Celestria to know how much she had wept.

'I don't know what to do with myself,' Celestria sighed, climbing off her father's bed. 'It's like he's still here, isn't it, Waynie?'

'When me father died I spent a whole day in his room just going through his things.' Mrs Waynebridge smiled sympathetically. 'Every item suddenly took on greater meaning, because it had belonged to him. The trick is to remember all the things you loved about him. To dwell on the good times, not on the empty years ahead.' She swallowed hard, trying in vain to follow her own advice. She had sensed something was afoot when a single magpie had alighted in the garden back in July. In vain she had searched for a second . . . one for sorrow, two for joy, but the damn thing was all on its own.

'I want to understand why he did it.'

'That's something you might never find out. Only he knows that.'

'There have got to be clues,' Celestria insisted. 'I'm going to go through every inch of this room and his study. There'll be a trace of it somewhere, I promise you.'

'I'd let sleeping dogs lie, if I were you. Nowt good will come of it.' Mrs Waynebridge watched Celestria bite into the piece of toast and honey she had made her. The honey came from Archie's hives in Pendrift. 'That's me girl,' she said, her eyes now filling with pleasure. 'Get some food down you. What you need is nourishment and some tender loving care.' She knew the girl wouldn't have had much of the latter from her mother. 'I'll cook you a nice omelette for lunch and leave you something in the fridge for your dinner.'

'Thank you, Waynie.'

The old woman's eyes began to glitter. 'I've known you since you were a baby,' she said, then closed her eyes a moment in an effort to contain her emotions. 'We all survived the war and the loss of those we loved. I survived the Blitz. Didn't leave this house for a moment, even though me sister tried to convince me to stay with her in Yorkshire. The point is, Celestria, bad things happen. We push through them because there's no other way. You may never know why your father took his own life, but it won't have had nowt to do with you or Harry, or Mrs Pamela, either. Men are laws unto themselves, governed by things we women don't understand. I loved me Alfie, but by Jove I didn't understand him and his silly ways. You've grown into a fine young woman. You'll find a good man to love you and look after you and have children of your own. Life takes on a different dimension when you have your own family to think of.' Celestria was already opening the drawers in her father's bedside tables.

'Lord knows what I'll find in here. I don't even know what I'm looking for.'

'You'll find everything in order, that's what you'll find. Mr Montague was a stickler for order and tidiness. He ran his home like a military operation. I always have to tidy up after your mother, but Mr Montague, he was something else.' Celestria was already in her own world, taking out books and glancing over old photos and letters bound with string. 'Well, I'll go back downstairs,' said Mrs Waynebridge, hesitating in the doorway. 'Leave you to it, then.'

Celestria glanced up. 'Thanks, Waynie. Don't know what I'd do without you.' Mrs Waynebridge's spirits soared at the compliment, and she happily padded back down the stairs.

Celestria spent all morning in her father's dressing room. She found a board game that looked as though it had never been played and a faded green photo album of his childhood, full of pictures of the family at Pendrift. Her father seemed always to be in fancy dress, his wide face beaming a monkey grin, showing off with a cane or an umbrella and hat. To Celestria's surprise, her grandmother smiled, too; her joy rendered her barely recognizable. There were boxes of badges and buttons, souvenirs and postcards, history books and old comics, but nothing that indicated unhappiness. Everything was placed carefully in drawers as if he needed to know where each item was in case he required it urgently. For a man so meticulous about detail, Celestria found the loose ends left by his suicide highly uncharacteristic. She finished her tea, stood with her hands on her hips, and looked around. The room was cosy in spite of the spirit that had left it, and contained only the paraphernalia of a contented life. *This just reinforces my theory*, she thought to herself. *Papa didn't wish to end his life. He had no choice. Somebody pushed him into it. And I'm going to find who if it's the last thing I do.*

She rifled through his study, a large room with tall sash windows that gave on to the garden. One wall was entirely made up of bookshelves, stuffed full of history books and classic novels, though she didn't recall ever seeing him read anything other than newspapers. The grate was empty, yet the nutty smell of smoke mingled with the scent of his cigars, embedded in the upholstery of the deep crimson curtains and sofa. His velvet armchair looked large and empty, the footstool placed in front of it expectantly, though he'd never put his feet there again. There was a portrait of his father, Ivan, on the wall above the mantelpiece, gazing down with deep and loving eyes, and on the mantelpiece a large walnut clock ticked away, chomping through the minutes with tireless regularity. Now her father was as dead as that portrait, and time continued to pass regardless.

She opened the desk drawers and rummaged through them. She didn't know what she expected to find, and finally, by lunchtime, she realized to her frustration that she'd probably never be able to prove her theory. Mrs Waynebridge cooked her omelette at the stove, her stout fingers deftly handling the frying pan and eggs with the efficiency of a woman whose life has been dedicated to serving others.

'I've looked everywhere, Waynie,' said Celestria, crestfallen. 'I can't find anything suspicious. I might as well forget the whole thing and mourn him like Aunt Penelope.' She articulated her aunt's name with emphasis.

'You sound just like her,' chuckled Mrs Waynebridge.

'I don't think she believes there's anything suspicious about Papa's suicide.'

'What were you hoping to come across?'

'Oh, I don't know. Something that might indicate he was unhappy?'

Mrs Waynebridge took the frying pan off the stove and turned to face Celestria, who was lying across the table, her head resting on her arm. She looked pale and tired, the dark circles around her eyes almost purple. 'There is a box of papers in the pantry,' Mrs Waynebridge said with a shrug, wanting to be helpful. 'I doubt it's what you're looking for. Mr Montague gave it to me to throw away a few weeks ago, before he set off for Cornwall. He was in a terrible hurry. But as it's heavy I haven't got around to doing it. I thought I'd wait until Jack Bryan comes to sharpen the knives. Your father had a good tidy-out of his study, you see. He was about to put all the rubbish in the grate, but I reminded him the last time he did that he nearly set the house on fire!'

Celestria sat up and looked at Mrs Waynebridge quizzically. 'He cleared out his study? Why would he do that if everything was so tidy already?'

'He had so much stuff. It was all in order, I'll grant you. But he just couldn't stand throwing anything away. He was like a magpie. I don't know why he didn't keep it all in his office.' *Because he didn't have an office,* Celestria said to herself. He knew he could trust Waynie not to read anything, for she was illiterate. Celestria bit the skin around her thumbnail, debating why her father would choose to throw away all his papers in the middle of the summer when his family were down in Cornwall? *Unless he was taking the opportunity to destroy things he didn't want anyone to find after his death.*

Celestria ate her omelette in a hurry. 'You eat like that and you'll get indigestion,' said Mrs Waynebridge, taking a small mouthful.

'Was Papa acting oddly?' Celestria asked, her mouth full of egg.

Mrs Waynebridge narrowed her eyes as she tried to remember. 'He were very busy,' she said. 'I wouldn't say that he were acting oddly, not odd. But distracted, perhaps. Hurrying around, trying to get everything done before leaving for Cornwall.'

'Getting what done, exactly?'

'He were on the telephone a lot. I left him cups of tea on a tray in his study. He barely touched them. Didn't want to be disturbed. He closed the door.'

'Why didn't you tell me all this this morning?'

'As I said, there were nothing odd about him. He were a busy man, your father.'

'Did you hear anything? Anything at all?' Celestria persisted.

Mrs Waynebridge looked affronted. 'You don't think I listen through keyholes, do you, Celestria?'

'Of course not. No. I'm just piecing together a picture of his last days, that's all.'

Mrs Waynebridge sighed heavily. 'He were talking to a woman,' she volunteered with some reluctance.

Celestria raised her eyebrows. 'A woman?'

'Yes. He said, "You're a darling, Gitta." Then he hung up. It struck me as strange because for one, I expected the woman to be Mrs Pamela, and for two, the name is foreign. That's why I remember it, you see.'

Celestria shook her head in amazement. 'Good Lord, Waynie, it's like getting blood out of a stone. Anything else you haven't told me?'

Mrs Waynebridge's white skin blushed pink. She lowered her eyes. 'I were afraid to tell you in case your father were . . . you know . . .'

'Seeing another woman?' said Celestria casually.

'By gum, Mr Montague wouldn't do that,' she replied in a fluster.

'Don't worry, Waynie. I won't tell Mama. It'll be our secret.'

Celestria opened the box in the pantry with anticipation. She felt she was beginning to uncover evidence of foul play. If her father was seeing another woman, perhaps the woman's husband bumped him off? With mounting excitement she began sifting through the papers inside. There were letters that meant nothing to her. Letters from the bank about investments, and from people with foreign names. Some of them were sent to a PO Box in South Kensington, others to the house in Belgravia.

One letter caught her attention because it contained a photograph of her father standing in what looked like a cloister, with the sun on his face, his panama hat sitting crooked on his head. He looked carefree, his mouth twisted into a half smile as if he had just told a joke. The letter was from someone called Freddie, who, according to the address on the letterhead, lived in a convent in Italy. *'My dear Monty,'* it said in neat, looped handwriting. *'It was a pleasure to see you again. You brought light and love into our home. I just wish you could have put a smile on Hamish's surly face. Sadly, at the moment, that is one miracle too far. I apologize for his appalling behaviour, but I know you understand. I only wish you could have stayed longer. I'm writing to tell you that due to our present circumstances, my husband and I have decided to open the Convento as a bed-and-breakfast. Hamish is against the idea, for obvious reasons, but it is the only way. If he would just sell some of his paintings, or even show them, we might climb out of this hole, but he won't hear of it. If anyone should mourn, it is I. What about the living? It is not healthy to live among the dead. I also want to thank you, dear Monty, for your generosity. You really needn't have put your hand in your pocket. I am ashamed and humble in my gratitude.*

My fondest love, Monty. May God bless you and keep you safe. Freddie.'

Celestria stared at the letter for a long time. Was this another woman besotted with her father? Had he given her money, too? Was she a lover, a mistress? What was he doing in Italy? She looked for a date on the letter, but there was none, and the postmark was illegible. There was clearly a good reason why her father hadn't wanted anyone to find it – she just didn't know what that reason was yet. She put the letter aside, slipped the photograph into her pocket, and continued her search.

It wasn't long before she seized upon bank statements, a few dozen of them, tied up with string. They were all in order, as if some efficient secretary had kept them all neatly filed. She scanned them, not quite knowing what she was looking for. Then her eyes fell upon long numbers that had left his account. To her amazement, they were all cash transfers to a name she didn't recognize: F.G.B. Salazar. *So this is where all the money's gone,* she thought, her heart thumping with excitement. The sums were large and regular. She gasped at the quantities. She didn't fail to notice, either, that in the last two months, they had been bigger and more frequent.

She was so engrossed in the bank statements she failed to hear the telephone ring. A moment later Mrs Waynebridge filled the doorway. 'It's for you, Celestria. Mr Aidan Cooney.' Celestria left the papers with reluctance and took the call in the kitchen.

'Aidan,' she said.

'Darling, I'm so sorry to hear about your father. What a tragedy!'

'I know. It's ghastly.'

'I telephoned Cornwall. A snooty butler told me you were here.'

'Soames.' She smiled. 'He is rather pompous, I'm afraid.'

'Are you on your own?'

'Yes. I couldn't stand being there a moment longer. You can't imagine how awful it is down there. Everyone mourning. No body. No funeral. Just a dreadful limbo. I had to get away.' The words tumbled out in a rush.

'Let me take you out for dinner,' he suggested. 'Just the two of us. I'll look after you.' His voice was rich and granular, like brown sugar. She felt the tears welling in her eyes and an urgent longing to be in his arms.

'I'd love that,' she replied, grateful that he didn't seem to think any less of her due to her father's suicide.

'I'll pick you up at seven.' He hesitated a moment. 'You know my number if you need me. I'll come over the moment you call.'

'Thank you. I'm fine, really. I'll see you later.' She hung up and smiled. Aidan Cooney was exactly what she needed. 'Waynie,' she shouted. 'I'm out for supper.' Mrs Waynebridge appeared from the other end of the house, panting.

'Anyone nice?' she asked, hands on hips.

'Yes, he *is* nice. Mama would certainly consider him marriage material, though I'm not sure I would.'

'What do you consider marriage material, then?'

'Oh, I don't know.' She sighed and shrugged. 'Someone altogether more unpredictable. Someone who doesn't look at me in that doe-eyed way.'

'I wouldn't look a gift horse in the mouth if I were you.'

'That's it. I'm not sure he isn't a rather wonderful horse.'

'Now you've lost me.'

'I'm looking for a lion.'

'Sounds like trouble.'

'Exactly,' Celestria said with a smile. 'That's what I'm after.'

Mrs Waynebridge shook her head. 'What do you want me to do with all them papers?' she asked, noticing them strewn all over the pantry floor. If Mr Montague were still alive, he'd be exceedingly unamused.

'Nothing. Just leave them there. Tell Jack Bryan to sharpen those knives. I might be needing them!'

Celestria took a cab to Coutts Bank in the West End, where she asked to see the manager. 'Mr Smithe is out for lunch,' the cashier informed her.

'It's a matter of some urgency,' said Celestria, tapping her fingers on the counter with impatience. 'My name is Celestria Montague.' To Celestria's irritation, the cashier did not seem to recognize her name.

'You'd better speak to Miss Bentham,' the woman said, aware that the haughty young lady was someone of importance. 'I'm new here.' She coughed apologetically and disappeared to look for her colleague.

Celestria looked about at the tall ceilings and rich wooden counters, stone floor, and big, heavy doors. The place had an air of formality and grandeur that reminded her of her father. She could see him in here, in his dark suit and coat, his briefcase in one hand, Brigg umbrella hooked over his arm. The bank was almost empty, except for an old man in a suit and bowler hat writing a cheque in the corner.

Finally, Miss Bentham appeared. She was middle-aged and wore a conventional suit and sensible shoes with sturdy heels and thick brown stockings. When she saw Celestria, she smiled. Her face, hard in repose, softened with animation. 'Miss Montague,' she said, extending her hand well before she had reached her. Celestria took it, and Miss Bentham shook it emphatically. 'Come into my office, where we can talk in private.' Celestria followed her, those sturdy heels tapping across the polished floor, the sound echoing about the near-empty room. The old man in the bowler hat turned, his attention caught by the beautiful young woman with the dancing walk. Celestria caught his eye, and her gaze was so imperious the old man was caught off guard and hastily looked away.

Miss Bentham's office was a handsome room with an ornate cornice running along the top of the walls and a large sash window that gave out onto a quiet back street. She invited Celestria to sit on the upholstered chair and offered her a cup of tea, which she politely declined.

'I'm here to talk about my father,' she said, placing her brown crocodile handbag on her knee.

'Mr Montague is a very good client of ours,' Miss Bentham replied, although a shadow of anxiety swept across her face.

'*Was* a good client,' Celestria corrected.

'I don't understand?'

'My father is dead,' she stated impassively.

Miss Bentham gasped.

'I'm afraid he died in a boating accident in Cornwall.'

Miss Bentham brought her hand up to her mouth. 'When?' Her voice was a mere husk, and Celestria knew instinctively that her father had meant more to Miss Bentham than money. 'Oh, God! Forgive me. This is such a shock.' She collapsed into her chair.

'Last week.'

'I'm so sorry. This is dreadful.'

'It is a terrible time for all the family, as you can imagine. I have come up to London to sort out his affairs.'

'Absolutely. If I can be of any help. Any help at all.' Miss Bentham withdrew a white cotton handkerchief from her sleeve and dabbed her eyes beneath her glasses. Celestria noticed that her hands were shaking. 'He was such a good man, Miss Montague. He always had time for a chat. Most don't, you see. It's understandable. Everyone's busy. But Mr Montague.' She smiled and blushed. 'He was a gentleman. I looked forward to his visits.'

'I'm interested to know why these large amounts of money were being transferred to F.G.B. Salazar.' She handed the statements to Miss Bentham, who pushed her glasses up her nose and composed herself. She took a while, her eyes running up and down the pages. Finally, she shook her head and gave the statements back to Celestria.

'I'm not able to enlighten you, I'm afraid.' She hesitated, as if weighing her feelings for Mr Montague against her loyalty to the bank and its principles. Celestria smelled weakness and pounced on it.

'My mother is in hospital due to the terrible shock, and my darling little brother, Harry, hasn't uttered a word since Papa died. He's only small, and he worshipped his father. I really need to know.' Celestria had no qualms about lying. She lowered her eyes to enhance the effect and heard Miss Bentham let out a long sigh.

'Well, I can tell you that he's in the south of Italy,' she said in a hushed voice. 'I don't know where. It was none of my business. You should ask Countess Valonya.'

'Who?'

'Mr Montague's secretary. I haven't seen Mr Montague for a few months, but Countess Valonya came in weekly to arrange the transfers and transactions.'

'Do you have an address?'

Miss Bentham took off her glasses and rubbed the bridge between her eyes, suddenly wilting. 'I'm afraid not. If it helps, I often sent things around to her at the Hungarian Club in Hampstead.'

'Thank you, Miss Bentham. You have been most kind. My father obviously trusted you a great deal.' Celestria slipped the statements into her handbag and stood up.

'He was a gentleman, Miss Montague. His passing is a loss to us all.'

Celestria left Miss Bentham wiping her eyes with her tidy little hanky, clearly in shock. It had been fortunate that Mr Smithe had gone out for lunch; he might not have been so forthcoming. She looked at her watch – time enough to make a quick visit to the Hungarian Club.

Chapter 13

The plot was thickening like cream. Celestria had never heard of Countess Valonya, but maybe she was the Gitta that her father had been talking to on the telephone.

Celestria hailed a cab and thirty minutes later alighted at the foot of the steps leading up to the Hungarian Club. The place was dimly lit, with high ceilings and a dark wooden floor of wide, polished boards. The old staircase swept extravagantly up to a landing where a vast gilt mirror hung. The air was heavy with the sour smell of rotten flowers. There was no one downstairs, but the low murmur of voices could be heard on the floor above. She climbed the stairs, clutching her handbag, not knowing what to expect.

Upstairs were two enormous rooms with a landing in between where a couple of old ladies in hats and gloves sat on a crimson velvet divan, talking in hushed voices, moving their hands vigorously to demonstrate outrage. When they saw Celestria, they stopped chattering and watched her warily through hooded eyes. Ignoring them, Celestria wandered into the first room, where small clusters of people were sitting around tables, drinking coffee and *plinkas* and smoking in the gloom. The atmopshere was grim, as if their sorrow had transformed itself into a grey mist that hung over them, refusing to lift.

Most were old and very elegantly dressed. Some of the ladies had feathers in their hats and wore fur stoles in spite of the warm weather. Their necks were adorned with pearls, and diamond brooches glittered in the weak light. A small gathering of gentlemen in hats and suits sat playing cards, chuckling bitterly where once there might have been laughter, and in the corner, by the bar, a string trio played gypsy music. An elderly couple danced slowly in the gloom. Some of the people spoke Hungarian, others English with heavy, doleful accents, but their conversations were all the same: *'Revolution ... they have betrayed their country ... brave men have lost their lives ... we are old, the least we should expect is to die on our own soil ...'* Celestria sensed she was being watched, especially by the women, whose animosity was as thick as their misery. It was understandable; she was an outsider, intruding. Having decided that it would be more prudent to approach the men, she strode over to the table where the four codgers sat playing cards, assuming a confidence she didn't feel.

'Excuse me,' she said in her sweetest voice. 'I'm looking for someone.' One of the men raised his bushy eyebrows, fluffy and red like foxtails, and nodded. Celestria continued. 'Countess Valonya,' she stated. At the mention of her name the four men immediately exchanged shifty glances. Foxy eyebrows shrugged and puffed on his pipe.

'The countess hasn't been here for a week,' he replied.

'Do you know where I might find her?' She forced a self-conscious smile.

'Who wants her?'

'My name is Celestria Montague.'

'Count Bādrassy,' replied the man, extending his hand. He didn't smile. 'Do you want to sit down and make an old man happy?'

'I'm not staying, thank you,' she replied, not wishing to offend him. 'It's a matter of some urgency.' Count Bādrassy said something in Hungarian to his companions, and they all laughed, clearly at her expense. Celestria felt her frustration mount. Then she had an idea.

'It's her family,' she said deliberately. 'I have some terrible news.'

They grew serious: those words were as familiar to them as death. Count Bādrassy spoke around the pipe that hung out of the side of his mouth and picked up his cards to indicate that their conversation was coming to an end.

'She lives in Weymouth Mews. I can't remember the number, but you will know it when you see it.' She understood that this was as much information as she was going to get.

Outside at last, she was relieved to breathe the warm London air again and leave the disillusioned old people behind to stagnate. Weymouth Mews was a taxi ride away, a small cobbled street with pretty window boxes and red-tiled exteriors bathed in the warm light of late afternoon. A white fluffy cat slept on a windowsill, tail twitching as it dreamed of milk and fat mice, and a young woman rattled a pram over the stones towards the main road. Count Bādrassy had said she would know the house when she saw it. She wished she had asked a few more questions because she didn't know what to look for. The young woman with the pram was now too far away to ask, and she found herself alone with the cat, who clearly wasn't going to be much help.

She decided to wander up the street and look into every window. Perhaps Countess Valonya had stuck a Hungarian flag on a pole outside her door, though Celestria wouldn't have recognized it. She walked for a while until, finally, the last house on the left grabbed her attention. It was the same size as the others. What set it apart was the winding wisteria bush that climbed up it, covering the entire façade in rich green leaves. There was barely enough room for the windows, which struggled to peer through the thicket of foliage and the flock of birds that lived in it, obviously encouraged to nest there by the little wooden houses fixed to the branches and scattered with grain. From the outside it looked pretty; from within Celestria imagined it must be quite claustrophobic.

She stood in the shade for a moment, deliberating what she was going to say to the countess. Before she could gather her thoughts, however, the door opened, and an extravagantly dressed blonde creature swept out in a fury. 'Are you trying to steal my birds?' she hissed, her voice deep like a man's and heavily accented. She screwed up her face so that the makeup she had caked onto it cracked like dry clay. Celestria's eyes dropped to her décolletage, which was white and brazen, exposing a vast bosom squeezed into a tight blue dress that gave her a tiny waist and a shortness of breath.

'No, of course not,' she replied, taking a step back in horror.

The woman snorted. 'I should hope not. There are some rare species in there. I nurture them, so they belong to me. You understand?'

'I apologize, Countess. My name is Celestria Montague.' She recalled her mother's advice always to respond in the opposite tone of one's aggressor, in order to wrong-foot them. It worked. Countess Valonya was, for a moment at least, speechless.

'You had better come in,' she replied at last, retreating into the dark little house. Celestria followed, catching in the air behind her the acrid stench of alcohol, along with the sickly sweet scent of musk.

The house was as cluttered as the façade and resembled a flamboyant boudoir. The sofa was draped in silk throws of pale greens and pink; purple velvet curtains were trimmed with lace and hung like the elaborate curtains of a theatre. The floor was adorned with Persian rugs, and on every surface were plants in pots on lace tablecloths. Celestria noticed the open bottle of gin on the round dining table, and the absence of a glass. The smell of alcohol was strong, as if the woman were sweating gin and trying to mask it with lashings of musk. Celestria, who had a sensitive nose and a delicate stomach, felt the bile rise in her throat. She was thankful when the countess lit a cigarette and the air was at once infused with the smell of tobacco.

'Take a seat,' she said, draping herself over the upholstered chair that was placed in front of the empty grate. 'Did your father send you?' Before Celestria could reply, the countess staggered to her feet and leaned on the mantelpiece cluttered with porcelain figurines. 'Or was it your mother?' She cackled meanly.

'He is dead,' Celestria replied, trying to fathom the relationship between this unlikely woman and her father. She was certain that they had not been lovers. Her father would never have sunk so low. The countess swung around, her pale eyes full of blame.

'Dead?' Her mouth hung open. She seemed not to have the strength to pull it shut. 'No, that is not true. You deceive me.'

'It is true,' Celestria replied, opening her bag to find her own cigarettes. The sooner she got outside, the better. She placed a cigarette between her lips and flicked her lighter. 'He died in a boating accident in Cornwall last week,' she added, blowing the smoke into the foul-smelling air.

The countess's eyes rolled about in their sockets as she tried to remember. 'I spoke to him last week,' she retorted. 'He was very much alive.'

'Clearly you spoke to him before he died.' She didn't look capable of recalling what she had done that morning, let alone the week before.

The countess's face opened into a triumphant smile. 'You cannot stop me from seeing him, you know. Love is made all the sweeter when it is forbidden.'

Celestria sighed with impatience. *God,* she thought wearily, *another woman besotted with Papa.* 'I'm not interested in how you feel about my father. In fact, I simply couldn't care less.

The fact is, Countess Valonya, I'm not the one preventing you from seeing him. He committed suicide, if you really want to know. He rejected us all.'

Countess Valonya was silent for a while. She stared into the half distance, isolated by her own tormented thoughts. Celestria took a moment to plan her next move. While the countess sat entranced, she smoked quietly on the sofa, watching her. In repose, her face melted and fell, as if the clay was still wet. Her full lips sagged, pulling her chin with them. Celestria noticed the dark roots of her hair beginning to grow through, making the blonde look even brassier. She seemed to wilt and grow smaller. Finally, she turned and stared at Celestria with shiny eyes. 'You come to tell me that?' she hissed. 'That he is dead? Is that why you have come?'

'Yes,' Celestria said. 'And to track down the money that you have been sending to Italy for him.' At the mention of money, the countess's shoulders stiffened.

'I don't know what you're talking about.' She now looked suspicious, as if this were a trap and Mr Montague was testing her loyalty.

'Why hide it? Weren't you my father's secretary?'

The countess was affronted. 'Secretary?' She forced a laugh. 'You think that I, Countess Valonya, was a mere secretary?' Now it was Celestria's turn to be confused.

'You had weekly meetings with the bank,' she said, trying to hold her ground.

'Yes, I worked *with* your father. I was never a secretary. I was vital for him. None of it would have come off had it not been for me. Looks can be deceptive; surely you know that? For a well-bred young woman, you are very rude.'

'What was your business?' *Papa hasn't had a job for two years,* she thought to herself, more bewildered than ever.

'If your father never discussed business with you, it is not my place to enlighten you. If he sent money abroad, it was for good reason. If you hope to get that money back, then . . .' She shrugged. 'God help you, it is not my duty to.'

The countess stood up. She swayed a little on her feet and steadied herself by holding the mantelpiece again. She threw her cigarette butt into the grate and weaved her way over to the dining table where, with trembling hands, she picked up the gin bottle and put it to her lips.

'I rarely drink,' she said aggressively, taking a gulp. 'I loved Monty. It is a love you could not possibly understand, being so young and spoiled. If you had lived through what I have lived through, with death always one step behind, then you would understand that love is the only thing you take with you when you die.' She took another swig and swallowed loudly.

Celestria recoiled. She hated that sound more than any other. It reminded her of Aunt Penelope, who couldn't eat or drink without slurping like a pig.

'I would do anything for your father.' Her head nodded like a puppet. She steadied herself by grabbing the back of a chair. 'Anything. But you wouldn't know. I wager that you didn't even know your father. As for your mother, ha! Monty was a stranger to her. I knew him better than all of you. Do you understand? All of you!' She had begun to slur her words. Celestria watched, transfixed, as she made her way to the stairs, holding her side and wincing in pain. 'If death takes me, too, we shall be united in heaven.' She put her foot on the first step, faltered, and fell with a thud.

Celestria remained frozen for a moment, not knowing what to do. The countess was slumped on the floor in a position that looked exceedingly uncomfortable, not to mention undignified. She knew she should telephone for help, but her head was surprisingly cool. She walked over and felt the woman's pulse. She was alive, but unconscious. Instead of doing the right thing for the countess, Celestria did the right thing for herself: she started searching the house, and this time she knew what she was looking for.

She began upstairs. She didn't know how long she had before the woman came round, so she worked swiftly. On opening the bathroom door she was appalled to find a dead squirrel in the lavatory. The window was wide open. Ignoring the squirrel, Celestria took a gulp of air. She couldn't understand how somebody could live like this, but even more baffling was how her father could have been associated with such a woman.

There was nothing in the bedroom, except a bottle of morphine hidden beneath a chamber pot in the bedside cabinet. That was obviously the motive for her sudden attempt at climbing the stairs. Celestria hurried downstairs and began to rifle through a pile of papers on top of an upright piano. She glanced at the countess, who twitched a couple of times. Her face was now deathly pale. Celestria sensed that she was slipping away. Torn between compassion and ambition, she hurriedly sifted through the papers, hoping the countess would hold on at least until she had found what she was looking for.

'I'll telephone for an ambulance in a moment, I promise,' she said, knowing the countess couldn't hear her.

Finally, she seized upon a pile of counterfoils addressed to none other than F.G.B. Salazar in Puglia, southern Italy. Puglia – that rang a clear bell. She recalled the strange letter from Freddie. She lived in Puglia. There were also medical bills from addresses in Harley Street. Most were for morphine, some for medications whose names meant nothing to Celestria, all paid for by Salazar. There were also money transfers from the same place. What on earth was the connection between her father, Salazar, the countess, and Freddie?

She folded the papers and slipped them into her handbag. The countess was completely still. Celestria picked up the telephone and dialed 999. After giving the necessary details, a guess at the address, and a false name for herself, she left without checking whether the woman was alive or dead.

At seven o'clock the doorbell rang. Celestria had just had time to bathe and change, but barely to reflect on the day's findings. The bills and other papers were still in her handbag, to be examined later when she had time to think about them and their consequences. She spared no thought for the tragic countess, whose murky role in her father's life was yet to be fully uncovered. As she pressed her cheek to Aidan's and inhaled the scent of shaving cream that lingered on his skin, she allowed herself to settle into the present moment with some relief. 'It's so good to see you, Aidan,' she said as he kissed her.

'I've missed you, darling,' he replied, and her stomach flipped as his voice in her ear reminded her of their delicious encounter in the conservatory. If anyone was capable of helping her to forget the hideousness of the last week, it was Aidan.

'I've booked a charming little place on Pimlico Green,' he said. 'It's cozy and quiet. I didn't think you'd welcome a noisy place bustling with people.'

'I couldn't possibly bump into anyone I know tonight,' she said, taking his arm and allowing him to lead her down the steps to his car. 'I'm not ready.'

'Of course you're not, darling. I'm so pleased you're here, where I can look after you. I hated to think of you being holed up in ruddy Cornwall, for God's sake.' As they reached Aidan's shiny green Austin Healey, he opened the door for her, allowing his eyes to run lazily up and down her body with admiration. 'I don't think I've told you how beautiful you look tonight.' His voice was deep and earnest. Celestria smiled at him gratefully. For the first time in her life she felt unsure, as if her father had taken her self-esteem to the bottom of the sea.

The restaurant was indeed cosy. Tables were set up in the little square, alongside a flower shop that was still open. The scent of lily and rose fused into the balmy London air, giving the city a foreign feel. 'This could be Paris,' said Aidan merrily as the waiter pulled out Celestria's chair.

'There's even a red rose on the table,' Celestria added, picking it out of its little glass vase and sniffing it. 'Shame, it's one of the non-smelling variety.' Aidan put his elbows on the table and rested his chin on his hands. His blue-green eyes twinkled as he gazed at her fondly.

'I'd like to take you to Paris,' he said.

She smiled and tilted her head to one side. 'Perhaps I'll let you,' she replied.

'After a couple of glasses of wine, "perhaps" might become "yes,"' he said, flicking his fingers in the air to call the waiter. 'A bottle of Sancerre,' he instructed, without having looked at the wine list. Once the waiter had disappeared into the restaurant, Aidan took Celestria's hand and held it across the table. 'We don't have to talk about your father if you'd rather not.'

'I've done nothing but talk about him for days. My head aches with it all.'

'I can imagine. It's the not knowing that's the worst. They still haven't found him, have they?'

'And they won't. Not now.'

'I liked your father enormously. He was the sort of fellow one simply couldn't dislike.'

'That's why this whole thing seems so surreal. Papa would never have taken his own life. I think he was murdered.'

Aidan's eyes grew large. 'Murdered?' he repeated. 'By whom?'

Celestria shook her head. 'I don't know. But I'm beginning to learn a lot about my father that I didn't know.' Celestria shook her head. 'I don't want to talk about it at this stage. I'm not sure what to make of it all yet.'

'Then let's drink and talk about other things,' he suggested. 'How about I enlighten you on the misfortunes of others?'

Celestria grinned and withdrew her hand. 'That sounds like an interesting distraction.'

'Oh, the secret lives of our fellow Londoners. One simply wouldn't believe it, were it not for my extremely reliable sources.' The waiter poured a small amount of Sancerre into Aidan's glass. He swirled it about, took a sniff and then a gulp. 'Perfect,' he said. 'This is just the ticket!'

Aidan told Celestria all the scandal he knew, then made up the rest. They threw their heads back and laughed, and Celestria forgot all about her father and the dreaded message in the bottle. She drank the wine, which was so light she barely noticed the quantity she consumed until her head became so dizzy and her spirits so buoyant that she no longer cared.

Aidan was handsome in a smooth, glossy way, with sandy hair and sleepy eyes the colour of Cornish rock pools. He was tall, with broad, manly shoulders and muscular legs that had powered up and down the rugby pitch in his Eton days. Adored by his mother, Mary-Rose, he had been indulged by women all his life. He knew how to endear himself to ladies of any age and was deemed the perfect son-in-law by his friends. Celestria found his confidence exciting. He had a way of looking at her that made her stomach lurch, as if he was making love to her with his eyes. She remembered his touch, the wickedness of it, and reached out for his hand and held it. 'Tonight is just what I needed, Aidan,' she said, and her voice sounded husky and far away.

'It's only just beginning,' he replied, squeezing her hand. 'Look, it's not even dark yet. You can't go home until the night is over.' His eyes grew heavy. They rested on her lips that parted with the thought of what was still to come. 'I won't let you,' he added in a low voice. Celestria found herself blushing at the inevitability of their encounter and lowered her eyes beneath the weight of his stare. 'I'm going to take you home with me. I don't think it's right that you should be alone at the moment.'

'Then you'll have to have me for a week,' she laughed, toying with his fingers across the table. 'Mama doesn't come back until next Tuesday.'

'Then I'll have you for a week. I'll have you for two, or for the rest of . . .' He hesitated, his expression suddenly serious. 'I'll have you for as long as you let me,' he said, smiling away the sentence he failed to finish.

He paid the bill and drove the short distance to his flat in Chelsea. The sun had sunk below the buildings, turning the sky a misty shade of pink. It was warm, the air sticky and humid, no breeze. The streets were quiet but for flurries of fat pigeons that dropped out of the sky to peck at pieces of food that had been tossed onto the pavements. People were still away on holiday, the schools still on their summer break. London was ghostly. No parties, no dinners, no grand lunches at the Ritz to distract her from having to think too hard about life. Celestria looked out of the window and wondered whether things would ever return to the way they were. Then a terrible thought entered her head: did she want them to? Suddenly a vision rose up in her mind: parties, engagement, marriage, children, more parties, a never-ending cycle of frivolity. She shook it away with an impending sense of disillusionment. *It must be the wine,* she mused, feeling the air rake warm fingers through her hair as Aidan drove into Cadogan Square. *I obviously didn't have enough!*

Aidan's flat was large, with tall ceilings and elegant French doors that led onto a balcony overlooking the square. Celestria stood in the diminishing light and stared out into the dusk. 'It's a beautiful night,' she said, as the pink hue paled to grey. Aidan stood behind her and put his arms around her.

'It's nothing compared to you,' he whispered, planting a kiss on her neck. She turned, her eyes suddenly filled with sadness.

'Kiss me, Aidan. Kiss me so that I don't have to think about anything else but you.'

Aidan took her face in his hands and lowered his lips. She closed her eyes and savoured the taste of him, all other thoughts expelled at last. His kiss was soft and tender, his breath warm on her skin. His arms wrapped around her and drew her close so that she no longer felt insecure. Aware that they were on the balcony in full view of anyone who happened to be walking down the road, Aidan led her inside. There, on the brown velvet sofa, they lay entwined, and she didn't protest at all when his hand travelled beneath her dress and caressed the skin above her stockings. She didn't even spare a thought for Rafferty because with Aidan it felt familiar. Besides, she needed him. She didn't want to think about her father or delve too deeply into her own feelings of loss and abandonment. She wanted to lose herself in Aidan and soak up the love he was only too willing to give her.

'I want to make love to you,' he murmured. 'Let's get married, Celestria, darling. Let me take care of you.' His voice was insistent. 'Say that you'll be mine forever.'

'Oh, yes, Aidan,' she replied, hoarse with desire, allowing fate to carry her along like a empty shell on the tide. She seemed to have forgotten about her father, the missing thousands, and Countess Valonya. Nothing mattered any more but Aidan and his wide and generous arms. *He'll look after me,* she thought drunkenly as he stood naked before her. *And I'll never be alone again.*

Chapter 14

Celestria awoke with a throbbing headache at about two in the morning. It took her a while to work out where she was. The room was unfamiliar, the sofa strange, her state of undress a little worrying. Then she recognized Aidan, sleeping contentedly in the half-light that shone in from the street. He was lying beside her, his face nestled into the curve of her neck. She stared at the ceiling, trying to piece together the events of the evening before. They had made love. That, she remembered without any trouble. For a start, she felt uncomfortable between her legs. She couldn't remember whether she had liked it or not, which was a shame given that it was her first time. She recalled having gotten carried away during the preliminaries. Aidan was rather gifted at those. She would have smiled at the recollection had her head not hurt so. No doubt it had been wonderful at the time. However, she now felt rather shoddy. As she struggled to get up without waking her lover, she remembered he had said something about marriage. She couldn't recall having responded.

She managed to find her clothes, carelessly strewn around the drawing room. Her knickers were under the sofa, one shoe in the corridor. She dressed hastily and tiptoed out of the room without a backwards glance. *That's two people I've left unconscious in the last twenty-four hours,* she thought to herself. *But this time it's I who feel used.*

She walked towards Pont Street. The road ahead was empty but for the odd taxi that sped past, its yellow light shining in the dark. She hailed one without any difficulty. Conscious of the dishevelled way she looked, she didn't attempt to make small talk with the cabbie. Instead, she stared out of the window feeling empty inside. Making love was meant to be something sacred and special. A union between two people who love and cherish each other. Not a drunken night on the sofa and a hazy recollection the morning after.

Celestria Montague, twenty-one years of age and no longer balancing precariously on the edge of womanhood, crawled between her own sheets, pulling the covers over her head in order to blot out the world about her, and sank into a deep, dreamless sleep.

She awoke six hours later to the insistent ringing of the telephone in her mother's bedroom next door. Where was Waynie? she thought grumpily, waiting for her to pick it up. The ringing continued. With a groan she rolled over and placed the pillow across her ear. It was too early to face Aidan. Besides, she didn't know how she felt about him. Better not to feel anything yet. *I'll think about it later,* she thought and drifted back to sleep. At 11.25 a.m. she was awoken again by the telephone. It rang and it rang. *Oh, Lord, he's keen,* she complained, unable to ignore it this time. Dragging her sleepy body out of bed, she staggered into her mother's bedroom and picked up the receiver. To her amazement, the great booming voice of Richard W. Bancroft II shouted down the wire. 'Fox? I've been telephoning you all morning.'

'Grandpa?' she replied, stunned. 'Fox' was the nickname he had called her since childhood.

'No, Santa Claus! Who else?'

'Where are you?'

'I'm at Claridge's.'

'You're here!' It was as though she'd been injected with a shot of adrenaline.

'Would my granddaughter do me the honour of having lunch with me today at the Ritz?'

'This is such a surprise.'

'A good one, I hope. From what I gather, you've had a rather nasty one recently.'

'To put it mildly.' She laughed huskily.

'You can tell me all about it over lunch. Twelve-thirty prompt.'

'Have you spoken to Mama?'

'That's how I knew where to find you, Fox. Hiding up here all by yourself. Thought you could do with a bit of company. Don't be late!'

She heard him chuckle and imagined him sitting in the splendour of his suite at Claridge's, puffing on a cigar, wrapped in his burgundy dressing gown with silk lapels. Around him would be photos of him playing golf with Eisenhower, opening a city library with Bernard Baruch, kissing Maria Callas after a show in Rome. Her grandfather was the last of the robber barons, an oil king. An American who loved Britain so much he had bought the most extravagant Scottish castle he could find and decorated it to the hilt. He travelled with his own crystal and silver cutlery, and his rooms at Claridge's were adorned with pale orchids and lilies in advance of his arrival. Richard W. Bancroft II was not a man to do things by halves. He liked to surround himself with beautiful things, and only the highest quality would do.

Celestria sank onto her mother's bed, trying to unscramble the muddle in her head. She felt as if she had a ball of wool instead of a brain. She looked at her watch: eleven-thirty. She had less than an hour to bathe and dress, and she knew that for her grandfather, Fox had to look her very best.

As she submerged herself in the bath and let the bluebell-scented water wash over her, cleansing her body of the previous evening's wickedness, she began to feel the enormous relief of her grandfather's presence. At last, he had arrived to look after her. She could tell him everything, and he would listen with those wise grey eyes. What was not right, he would put right, because Richard W. Bancroft II was a man of great power and wealth. He might not be able to bring her father back, but he would rescue them from impending poverty. She might even go and live with him in New York, find a nice rich American, and live in Manhattan and have a holiday home in Nantucket. That thought appealed to her enormously. By the time she had slipped into a pale summer skirt and yellow twin set, lustrous pearls around her neck and on her earlobes, she was feeling almost completely restored. Her hair was pinned up at the sides, falling in waves over her shoulders and down her back, mascara and lipstick carefully applied. On her way out she glanced at her reflection in the mirror in the hall and wondered whether she looked different now that she was a real woman, having laid bare the mysteries of sex. Or maybe her sudden metamorphosis was due to her mother's crimson lipstick and pearls.

Celestria arrived at the Ritz by taxi. As she alighted onto the pavement she felt a frisson of excitement at the sight of the shiny red Bentley that had drawn up at the door, purring like a very grand cat. An immaculately dressed chauffeur in black hat and gloves stepped out and opened the rear door with the help of two uniformed doormen from the Ritz, pink-cheeked with excitement, for Richard W. Bancroft II was not only a very important guest, but a famously generous tipper. Celestria stood and watched in amusement as Rita, her grandfather's assistant, stepped briskly out of the front passenger door as her boss climbed carefully out of the back, greeting the Ritz door-men with characteristic aplomb. As thickset as a bear, he stooped at the shoulders and walked with the slow stride of a man forced to concede to the ravages of age and time. However, he had thick silver hair, sharp intelligent eyes, and the vital wit of a man many years his junior. He raised his hand to thank the chauffeur and proceeded up the steps. Rita, who accompanied Mr Bancroft everywhere, stalked on ahead to alert the manager that Mr Bancroft had arrived. She needn't have bothered. Mr Windthorne was already standing in the entrance hall to receive their esteemed guest.

Celestria followed the party through the doors, wondering how long it would take them to notice her. She was a regular guest at the Ritz and knew most of the staff by name. While Mr Windthorne shook her grandfather's hand he happened to glance over his shoulder, his attention momentarily distracted by the beautiful blonde girl who hovered in his peripheral vision. 'Mr Bancroft,' he said with a flush of pleasure, 'Miss Montague has arrived.'

Richard Bancroft turned around slowly and grinned at his granddaughter. 'On time and as radiant as ever!' he exclaimed in a thick American accent, holding his arm out for her to slip in and kiss him. Celestria embraced him with affection, pressing her face to his with a delicious sense of sailing into harbour from a choppy, uncertain sea.

'You smell of bluebells, and it's not even spring,' he said with a chuckle, suddenly feeling a great deal younger. She slipped her hand through his arm, and he patted it fondly.

'Good morning, Miss Montague,' said Rita a little frostily. Having worked for Mr Bancroft for the last fifteen years, she never liked to see him close to other women, especially his granddaughter. When he was with Celestria, he almost forgot Rita existed. 'Mr Bancroft would like to go straight to his table,' Rita informed Mr Windthorne importantly, stalking ahead on precariously high heels.

'In the most beautiful dining room in London we won't have any reason to move until late afternoon,' Mr Bancroft added, proceeding down the corridor towards the restaurant. 'Glad to see nothing's changed in a year, Mr Windthorne.'

Celestria caught sight of herself in the large gilt mirrors as she passed and thought what a handsome pair they made. She envisaged walking down the aisle of the Catholic church in Farm Street on the arm of her grandfather. At least she still had someone to give her away.

'Now, Fox, what the hell is going on?' Richard Bancroft looked straight at his granddaughter, his expression grave. Rita and Mr Windthorne had retreated, leaving Mr Bancroft to enjoy his granddaughter and the excellent wine at the discreet round table in the far left corner of the dining room by the window.

'Papa has supposedly committed suicide,' she replied. 'A note was found in a bottle in his boat with the words *Forgive me* written on Uncle Archie's writing paper. They also found his pocket watch in the boat, and a pair of shoes washed up on the rocks, though how a pair of lace-up shoes could come off on their own is a mystery to me! If you ask me, he was murdered.'

Richard Bancroft chuckled and took a sip of Bordeaux. 'Full-bodied. I like it,' he commented appreciatively. The sommelier filled their glasses. 'Now let's not run before we can walk, Fox. A good detective studies all the facts before making a judgment like that.'

'Well, we went to see the solicitor, who told us that Papa hasn't had a job for two years and that his business went bankrupt. Meanwhile, he's been travelling "on business" all over Europe. What business can that be? I ask myself.'

'Indeed.'

'Not only had he gone through his own money, but Mama's as well.'

'I see.' Richard Bancroft narrowed his eyes and a shadow passed across his face in spite of the sun that shone with brilliance through the tall glass doors. 'Go on.'

'He's spent my inheritance, Grandpa. Mama, Harry, and I have nothing to live on. We're as poor as church mice.' Her grandfather laughed and shook his head.

'You talk a lot of nonsense!'

'Aren't you appalled?'

'Finish the story.'

A waiter hovered by the table, ready to take their order. Without consulting his granddaughter, Richard Bancroft ordered for both of them.

'You need something nourishing; you're as pale as death,' he said to Celestria. 'A little red meat is what this doctor orders. And have some wine; it'll put the colour back into your cheeks.' Celestria took a half-hearted sip in order to please him. She felt she had drunk enough wine the night before to last her a month. 'So far it's looking bad,' he said. 'Tell me more.'

Celestria continued, grateful to hand the mystery over to someone better qualified to deal with it. 'I couldn't stand being down at Pendrift another moment. Mama has taken to her bed, complaining that Poochi is having a nervous break-down with all the stress. I found the atmosphere claustro-phobic. Without a body there's no funeral. There might never be a body. Then what do we do? When will it all be over?'

'So there's no evidence, beside what the solicitor told you, of Monty's unhappiness?'

'None whatsoever. In fact, I'd say he was the happiest man alive!'

Richard Bancroft nodded thoughtfully. 'But there's more, isn't there?'

'I found a box of rubbish in the pantry at home. Waynie said that Papa had tidied out his study before coming down to Cornwall.'

'So, what did you find, Sherlock?'

'I found a love letter from a woman called Freddie, who lives in a convent in Puglia, as far as I can tell. It contained a photograph of Papa, looking incredibly pleased with himself. There was no date on the letter. Then I found bank statements that showed enormous amounts of money being sent out to Italy. Where did it all go to? I wanted to know. So I went to the bank, only to be told that it was all confidential information. But . . .'

'You used your charm, didn't you, Fox?' He grinned lopsidedly, clearly impressed.

'I found out the name of Papa's assistant, though she claimed to be his partner. Countess Valonya, who is the most frighteningly grotesque woman one could possibly meet. She's the one who deals with the bank and Lord knows what else. I tracked her down through the Hungarian Club in Hampstead. She lives in this odd mews house covered in bushes and birds. She'd make a fascinating fairground attraction. She refused to tell me anything. The most ridiculous part is that she tried to convince me that she had seen Papa alive recently. Of course I didn't believe her. She was clearly drunk. She thought it was a ploy of mine and Mama's to stop her seeing him, as if she were his secret mistress or something. I'd like to think Papa had better taste than that. Judging by the outpouring of grief from half the women in Pendrift, he certainly had a wealth of choice, had he been so inclined.'

'He was a ladies' man, that's for sure,' said her grand-father. 'There's no crime in that.' Celestria reached for her bag and delved inside for the bills. She placed then on the table in front of her grandfather.

'I found these in her sitting room. She's addicted to morphine, clearly. She was drinking, too, out of a bottle of gin, neat. Must have been disgusting. This Salazar person obviously pays her bills, perhaps a salary, too, and what's more, he lives in Puglia, the same place as Freddie. Coincidence? I don't think so. He's the one Papa was sending all that money to. I want to know why, and I want the money back. It's our money. Do you think he was blackmailing Papa? Perhaps Papa was paying to keep him quiet about something. The point is, I think this Salazar creature is the person responsible for Papa's death. Maybe he was having an affair with this Freddie and paying Salazar to keep quiet. One thing is very clear – Papa didn't want us to know any of it.'

Richard Bancroft studied the papers for a while, lost in thought. He sipped his wine, then leaned back in his chair to allow the waiters to place a plate of foie gras in front of him. Celestria looked down at her own dish of veal scallops and felt her stomach rumble with hunger. She hadn't eaten since the night before. Her spirits rose, thanks to the reassuring presence of her grandfather, and she merrily tucked in.

'Well, Fox-Holmes, I now know for sure that your best qualities you've inherited from me.'

'And my worst qualities?' she asked with a smile, for she already knew the answer.

'From your mother.' Celestria would have laughed heartily, had she not suddenly remembered her mother's fight with her father the night he disappeared: *'He said the sooner you married, the better, because you were only going to turn out like me, driving him insane with your demands.'* Her grandfather's joke was no longer funny.

'Do you agree that it all sounds rather suspicious?' she asked.

He shrugged, handing her back the bills. 'You're the detective. It might be nothing, but on the other hand, it might be a great deal.'

'I want to go to Italy and track down this Salazar creature.'

'I thought you might.'

'Am I wrong?'

He took her hand and his wise old eyes looked at her with understanding. 'Perhaps, but you're never wrong to follow your instincts. Where would I be today if I hadn't followed mine?'

'Did you start with a hunch, Grandpa?'

'I started with a hunch, just like you. You don't realize where I come from. You wouldn't believe what I have done to get to where I am today.' He considered his empire. From coal mines in Pennsylvania to oil in California, newspapers in Chicago, and the ski resort he was building in Colorado. 'I would have achieved nothing had I not followed my instincts. Gone with the hunch.' He paused and smiled the smile of a gambler. 'I'll fund your investigation, Fox.'

'You will?' she exclaimed brightly. 'What will I tell Mama?'

'As little as possible. You're taking a holiday. You need to get away from it all.'

'I knew you'd look after us, Grandpa,' she said happily.

'What? Going to Italy? Whatever for?' Pamela was indignant.

'Grandpa says I need a break.'

'Your whole life is a break,' said Pamela, feeling a stab of jealousy. Her father wasn't sending *her* to Italy.

'I need to recover from Papa's death.'

'Don't we all? It's hell down here. We're all in a dreadful limbo. I'm longing to come back to London next week and put darling Harry in school. He's out all day with David and the boys. Thank God for David. I don't know what I'd do with Harry if David weren't around to distract him. I'm suffering the most terrible headaches. The shock of it has done me in.'

'Grandpa will look after us. We're not going to be poor.'

'Money can't heal the sense of betrayal. I feel cut to the quick. The man I loved, with whom I shared the best years of my life, has lied to me and squandered my fortune. I thought

I knew him. You have no idea how that feels. Lord, he's shared my bed for over twenty years. So when are you planning on leaving and where are you going to stay?'

'I'm going next week.'

'You're not going before I've seen you. Anyway, why the rush?'

'Why not? London's dead at the moment. There's no one around. It's frightfully dull.' She thought of Aidan asleep on the sofa and wondered whether he'd been trying to call her while she was out having lunch with her grandfather.

'Where are you going to stay?'

'In Puglia.'

'Puglia? Where is Puglia?'

'Southern Italy. Down on the heel.'

'Why don't you go somewhere civilized, like Tuscany? I'm sure your grandfather has friends you can stay with.'

'He has friends in Puglia who live in the Convento di something or other, I can't remember. Apparently, it's very beautiful there and cut off, which is what I need. It's by the sea.' She bit her lip, hoping her mother wouldn't catch her out.

'So is Pendrift,' said Pamela dryly. She sighed heavily. 'Who's going with you?'

'No one. I can go alone.'

'You certainly cannot. I'm not having my twenty-one-year-old daughter travelling across the world on her own. You'll be abducted or something.'

Celestria's heart sank. 'Who could come with me?'

Pamela hesitated. For a terrible moment Celestria thought her mother might suggest herself. 'Waynie,' she said finally, clearly pleased with the idea. 'You can take Waynie. I don't think she's had a holiday in years.'

'But she's never been farther than Yorkshire!'

'She's the perfect chaperone. No greasy Italian will get past Waynie.'

'She can't read or write!' Celestria protested.

'What difference does that make? It'll all be in Italian.'

'Suppose she won't come?'

'I pay her salary.' Pamela hesitated, remembering she had no money. 'Your grandfather can pay for her to take a holiday, too. She can consider it a bonus!' Celestria visualized Waynie getting in the way of her investigation and felt her enthusiasm deflate.

'How long is Grandpa staying at Claridge's?' Pamela asked, changing the subject.

'He didn't say.'

'I'll probably see him before he goes up to Scotland, then.' She didn't sound too excited by the idea. 'Maybe now I've lost my husband, I'll get my father back.'

'How's Aunt Julia?' asked Celestria, ignoring her mother's barbed comments.

'Smoking like a chimney. Even she is finding it hard to smile at the moment, so imagine what it's like for the rest of us, without her natural buoyancy. Archie spends a lot of time with Elizabeth. She refuses to believe Monty's dead. She had a meeting with Father Dalgliesh and told him in no uncertain terms that he wasn't to presume her son's death. Until there is a body she won't hear of it. She says she's wearing black to mourn his disappearance, not his death. Lord knows what she thinks has happened to him. Running around the country with amnesia, I suspect – shoeless! Really, these have been the worst few weeks of my life. I don't think I'll ever recover.'

'You could try going to Mass.' Celestria didn't know why she bothered to suggest religion to a woman who believed in nothing, even though it was clear that, with Monty gone, the only person capable of lifting her mother out of her depression was God Himself.

'Maybe,' she replied. Celestria was surprised. Pamela's response was uncharacteristically benign. 'I really must go. Telephone me tomorrow, darling.'

Pamela put down the receiver with a sigh. She couldn't possibly tell her daughter that she had already had a meeting with Father Dalgliesh. She couldn't admit the degree of her desolation. Standing at the window, she watched the sunset. It was a beautiful evening. The sky was watery blue, the sun a rich amber gold, melting into the horizon like liquid honey. She remembered Father Dalgliesh's advice: *'Next time there is a beautiful sunset, stop a while to look at it.'*

'Where are you going in such a hurry?' asked Penelope as Pamela rushed past her in her dressing gown. Pamela hadn't emerged from her bedroom for the last three days.

'I'm going to watch the sunset,' she replied, making for the cliffs.

Good God, Penelope thought to herself. *The woman's finally gone mad.*

Chapter 15

Celestria discovered that the events she had put into motion the previous night were now gaining a momentum of their own. Aidan turned up at her house weighed down by the most enormous bouquet of roses. She smelled their sweet perfume long before she saw him, which brought on a vague memory of a proposal. Celestria wasn't a person easily forced into doing something against her will. In fact, she was quite ready to make her excuses, blame the wine, her confused heart, whatever it took to erase the agreement she might have made. However, Aidan's expression was so full of anxiety that she buckled.

'You're not regretting last night, are you?' he asked, the words he'd carefully rehearsed tumbling out in a hurry. 'You weren't there when I woke up. I telephoned you constantly. No one answered. I've been sick with worry. I hope you don't think I took advantage of you. I would never—'

'Silly old thing! Waynie doesn't work on weekends, and I was asleep,' Celestria chided affectionately. 'It wasn't proper for a young lady to wake up in a man's bed. I'm not that sort of girl.'

'Of course you're not,' he said, his shoulders dropping with relief. 'You'll still marry me?'

She hesitated a moment before shaking her head of any misgivings. 'Yes. I do and all that. You see, you needn't have worried.' She took the flowers and walked back into the hall. 'These are lovely. I adore roses.'

Perhaps last night hadn't been such a mistake, she conceded. Aidan would make a fine husband, after all. He was rich, handsome, charming, funny, and well respected. What did it matter that she didn't love him? She could always take a lover further down the line if she felt so inclined. Practically speaking, he would look after her, and that was the most important . . . She would want for nothing, and he was awfully good at the preliminaries, which was the second most important requirement of a husband. Her mother would be relieved to be shot of her, and, besides, they all needed something happy to distract them from the recent horror of Monty's suicide. She placed the roses on the table and turned to face her fiancé. She allowed him to take her in his arms.

'Are you happy, my love?' Aidan gazed down at her and stroked her face with his eyes.

'Very,' she replied. It was true. She no longer felt shoddy about the night before; Aidan was to be her husband, after all, and her grandfather had arrived just in time, like a lifeguard with a rubber ring to stop her from sinking. She was as happy as she could be in the circumstances. She returned his gaze in rather the same way she had looked at those adoring adults in her childhood, her eyes full of affection, her heart as empty as a pretty bubble. Aidan smiled with pride. *She really loves me,* he thought with gratitude.

'I can't wait to spoil you, darling. We'll buy a glorious house together and fill it with children. You'll be Mrs Cooney. How does that sound?' *Honestly? Not very glamorous,* she thought, but the Mrs part appealed to her. 'I need your mother's permission,' he added seriously. 'When does she come back from Cornwall?'

'Ah,' said Celestria, pulling away. 'I need to talk to you.'

'What's the matter?' He followed her into the sitting room.

'Mama gets back on Tuesday, but I'm going to Italy.'

'Italy?' He was shocked. 'When?'

'Next week.'

'You never told me.'

'I only thought of it today. My grandfather's in town, and he suggested I take a holiday.'

'You're not going on your own, surely?'

'Mrs Waynebridge, our housekeeper, is coming with me, though she doesn't know it yet. Grandpa will organize everything. I'll be taken care of. Don't you think I need time to get over my father's death?' She sank into the sofa, spreading herself across it like a sleek white cat.

'Of course you do. I'm being selfish. How long will you be away?'

'Not long. A fortnight, a month. I don't know. No longer than a month.'

Aidan relaxed. 'I suppose I'll manage without you.'

'Of course you will, darling.' Celestria pulled him onto the sofa and covered his face in small kisses.

'You won't fall in love with an Italian while you're out there, will you?'

'I don't like Italians,' she said, unsure whether or not she had ever met one.

'I'll just have to wait until you get back, then. It'll be the worst month of my life. Knowing I'm engaged to the most beautiful girl in the world and unable to tell anyone.'

'You can't possibly tell anyone,' Celestria gasped in horror, unconsciously carving a little hole in their arrangement in case she might need to escape through it.

'My parents will love you,' he continued. 'I can't wait for them to meet you.'

His enthusiasm was a little disconcerting, the idea of meeting his parents rather alarming. If one considered the food chain, he was certainly near the top as far as wealth and class were concerned, but she wasn't sure he was a lion. It didn't matter. Lion or stallion, at least he wasn't a wildebeest. Anyway, she didn't have to think about it now. For the time being she could ignore her doubts. She was leaving for Italy in a week.

'Where shall I take you for dinner?' he asked.

'Later,' Celestria murmured. Aidan pressed his lips to hers and began to kiss her deeply. *Later,* she thought to herself, *I'll think about it later.*

Pamela stood on the cliff top, staring out over the sea that had swallowed her husband only a week ago. It was still incomprehensible. She felt as if she were walking in a nightmare, waiting to wake up, but that blessed moment never came. She was incarcerated in it forever. The water below her was calm, lapping innocently onto the sand as if it were incapable of drowning anyone. She raised her eyes to the sky, which exhibited the magnificent colours of sunset. The sun itself was a rich gold, enflaming the horizon with blood reds and fuchsia pinks, setting alight the wispy clouds that wafted across it like puffs of smoke. She waited to feel something, but her heart was heavy with the hatred she felt for all around her: for the duplicitous sea and her careless husband. She expected God to appear in the sky in an angel-drawn chariot or a flash of light like Paul saw on the road to Damascus. She expected to feel the weight lifted off her shoulders at the very least. But she felt nothing, just the same wearing sense of desolation.

Julia watched the sunset, too, from the terrace where she was alone with Purdy. She smoked a cigarette in the still evening air and reflected on the terrible repercussions of her brother-in-law's suicide. She and Archie had little money. The aid that Monty had promised had all been castles in the sky. He had had nothing to give them, just empty promises.

Is that why he killed himself? Because he had pledged so much to so many and couldn't live with the shame of not being able to deliver?

There was no one they could turn to. Elizabeth did not have much, either. There were cottages on the farm, but they brought in a meagre rent. Pendrift Hall was a terrible burden. Part of the roof needed mending, for a start. The upkeep of such a house was a struggle, not to mention the children's school fees. And yet they all loved it so much. It was the only home the children had ever known, and little Bouncy just adored the seaside. He was growing in confidence, beginning to explore the house and its many corridors and rooms on his own. She smiled at the recollection of finding treasures posted in strange places: pieces of jigsaw puzzle slipped into drawers in the spare room; a fluffy toy under a bed; Nanny's reading glasses dropped carelessly into a flower pot; a trail of mischief she was able to follow all over the house. Julia began to cry. She didn't bother to restrain the tears that now welled in her eyes and spilled over her cheeks.

What were they going to do? The prospect of having to sell Pendrift Hall had already seeped into her subconscious a long time ago, but now it surfaced as a shocking reality. If only they could find the money to pay off Archie's debt. But that sort of money wasn't easily come by. She considered working herself: she had a good eye for decoration and design, but where to start at her age? Besides, it would take a while to build up the business; they needed the money now. She thought of Wilfrid and Sam and her darling Bouncy. What future did they have if Pendrift Hall was sold off? It was all very well for Pamela, crying poverty for no reason. Her father would undoubtedly step in and give her bank account a hefty cash injection. Julia had no father to bail her out. The only person who could help them now was God.

★

Father Dalgliesh watched the gradual fraying at the heart of Monty's family with sadness. He prayed for them and did his best to comfort them when they sought him out in the presbytery. Elizabeth Montague expected him to know whether her son was alive or dead, and had looked appalled when he had told her that his communications with God were only one-way. 'I feel God in my heart,' he explained. 'He doesn't give me news bulletins.'

Elizabeth didn't understand. 'He was my favourite, you know,' she had said, her steely grey eyes glittering with emotion. 'He was so like his father. I will have little to live for if God has taken Robert, too.'

Pamela Bancroft Montague wanted someone to lean on. Her husband was gone, she was estranged from her father; there was no one left but the Church, for which she had previously felt contempt. She hadn't attended Mass following their meeting, probably out of fear or pride, having ridiculed it in front of her husband's family for so many years. Father Dalgliesh prayed she'd open her heart and let God in during the silence of her own contemplation. Maybe then would she feel ready to join her family in the front pew without embarrassment.

Julia Montague, of whom Father Dalgliesh had grown fond, was a godly and kindhearted woman. She visited him frequently to unburden her thoughts. 'I worry about Harry; he's so young. As for Celestria, she's like her mother, far more worried about herself.'

Father Dalgliesh recalled his last meeting with Celestria. He could still see her running off into the fog, her face enflamed. He had heard nothing since, but something told him she was no longer in Pendrift. He couldn't *feel* her there.

'She's not a bad person,' he said carefully. 'She's just lost.' He felt the colour burn his cheeks as he spoke of her.

'Oh, I don't think she's bad, Father, she's just too pretty for her own good. The trouble is she's been terribly spoiled by her mother. She's never had to think of anyone but herself.'

'Life has a funny way of moulding us. She's young, and the death of her father must have hit her very hard. If she hasn't grieved for him yet, she will later.'

'Her grandfather has arrived in London. That's a huge relief. He's an extraordinary man. A wonderful man. He's taking care of her. Pamela tells me he's sending her off to Italy for a holiday.'

'Italy?'

'Yes. Poor darling Harry will languish at boarding school while his sister basks in the sunshine in Italy.' She shook her head. 'I don't think that's fair, do you?'

'School is probably the best place for Harry at the moment. He'll be surrounded by his friends, and the routine of classes will be a distraction.'

'Celestria's like her mother, Father Dalgliesh. Every time Pamela has a problem she goes to bed with a headache. Celestria's just avoiding facing up to Monty's death by hiding out in Italy.'

'We all react in different ways. However far we run, we can never run away from ourselves.'

'But she's so selfish.'

'She has a big heart, Julia.'

Julia gave him a wry look. 'That's because you're a priest. You see the good in everybody.'

If you had seen the desolation in her eyes as I had, you would understand that she is in a dark place, he thought to himself, but instead he said, 'To every black cloud there is a silver lining.'

Father Dalgliesh wished he knew the truth about Monty's death, but he had to remind himself that he wasn't a detective; his job was to pick up the pieces for those the man had left behind. The job would be a whole lot easier, however, if

there was a body to bury. It was all very distressing for the
whole community. The only person deriving pleasure from
the scandal was Miss Hoddel, who had her own explanation.
'If you ask me,' she said, ignoring the fact that nobody had,
'he's killed himself to be rid of Mrs Pamela.'

'Now why would he want to do that?' asked Father
Dalgliesh patiently.

'Well, if you were married to Mrs Pamela, wouldn't you
want to kill yourself?'

Father Dalgliesh had to leave the room. He'd never heard
anything so preposterous in his life.

Mrs Waynebridge was astonished and a little nervous when
Pamela telephoned her to request that she accompany Celestria
to Italy the following week. She flushed pink, then turned
grey before her colour settled into a pasty white, like mashed
potato. She put down the receiver and waited at the kitchen
table until Celestria returned home at teatime. She placed her
crocodile handbag on the sideboard. Mrs Waynebridge got up
slowly. 'You don't look well, Waynie. What is it?'

'Your mother has asked me to travel with you to Italy.'

Celestria's face lit up. 'Oh, good! You will come, won't
you?'

'Doesn't look like I have much choice.'

Celestria rushed over and took Mrs Waynebridge's hands
in hers. 'It'll be fun, Waynie. We've never been to Italy.'

'I've never been farther than London. I'm Yorkshire born
and bred. Strong in th'arm, thick in th'ead!' Mrs Waynebridge
looked as though she was about to cry. 'What'll I do in Italy?'

'Lie in the sun and be treated like a queen.'

'Oh, I don't think I'd like that. Where will we stay?'

'At this divine little bed-and-breakfast in Puglia. It's on
Italy's heel.'

'That doesn't sound very appealing.'

'It's by the sea. Think of all that Italian food and wine. We'll have a ball, you and I.'

'You know what they say about Italian men?'

'They're charming. Forget the war; it's been over for years. Besides, you might fall in love.'

Mrs Waynebridge flushed again. 'Really, Celestria. At my age!'

'We'll look after each other. Besides, don't you think it's about time you saw a bit of the world?'

'I'll make that tea,' she said, withdrawing her hands and shuffling over to fill the kettle. 'You'd better watch out for those wops, Celestria. Your mother will have a heart attack if you fall in love with one of them.'

'So will Aidan,' Celestria added under her breath, delighted that Mrs Waynebridge had decided to come. She sat down, kicking off her shoes. 'No, I'm not going all the way to Italy to stay there. God forbid! I can't imagine anywhere more isolated than the heel of Italy! No, I'm going to find out who drove my father to take his life and then I'm going to dish out the most horrible helping of revenge. You, Angela Dorothy Waynebridge, are going to help me.'

'Sometimes you talk a lot of nonsense, love.' Mrs Waynebridge placed the kettle on the stove.

Celestria laughed. 'That's what my grandfather says!'

Elizabeth Montague stood on the cliff top and let the salty wind bellow about her. She steadied herself by leaning on her walking stick and bracing her shoulders. Her black cape fluttered in the air like bat's wings, but she stood unmoving, staring out over the murky Atlantic. It was evening. The sky was a milky grey, descending into muted shades of pink and orange where the sun had sunk below the line of the sea, melting to liquid gold. She stuck out her jaw defiantly, but her grief burst through the tender flesh of her heart and filled her body with despair. She blinked away the tears, ashamed to be giving in, and felt her lips begin to tremble. She hadn't cried when Ivan died. She had stuffed her pain to the very bottom of her soul and shut it with a cork, allowing nothing out but also allowing nothing in. Now the cork was released and it all came frothing and bubbling forth, the old sadness mixed with the new in one great unstoppable flow. Her hand clenched her stick so the knuckles turned white and the veins stuck out like blue worms under her skin. She didn't take her gaze off the sea. The treacherous sea. She had lived by it all her life. As a young woman she had sailed, swum, and paddled in it; as an old woman she had taken comfort from its rhythms and tides, the little treasures it washed up on the sand and the wild birds that lived off it, diving into the waves like falling angels. This is how it repaid her love: with death.

She remained there until she was cold right to the marrow in her bones. She felt weary and yet strangely at peace. She wiped her face with the back of her hand then hobbled towards the Hall thinking of little Bouncy, the only one of her grandchildren who wasn't afraid of her. With a growing sense of urgency she reached the house and stumbled through the French doors into the drawing room. She didn't bother announcing her arrival. As she crossed the hall she heard low voices in Archie's study. Julia and Archie were in deep discussion. She paused a moment, long enough to hear the words *sell the house*. Her heart stumbled. It wasn't possible. Were they talking of her house? The Hall? The tears welled in her eyes again as she started up the stairs towards Bouncy's room, hoping she had misheard. Nothing good ever came of eavesdropping.

Nanny was sitting on Bouncy's bed reading the child *The Little Engine That Could* when the imposing black figure of Elizabeth Montague appeared in the doorway. Nanny looked up and stopped mid-sentence. She couldn't remember the last time Elizabeth Montague had ventured upstairs. The old woman looked bloodless, her grey hair wild, her eyes glittering with tears. Nanny stood up.

'Are you all right, Mrs Elizabeth?' she asked, remembering the handsome woman she had worked for in her early days.

'I've come to see my grandson,' she announced, hobbling forward. Nanny moved aside so that Elizabeth could sit on the edge of the bed. Then she hurried as fast as her old legs could take her to find Mrs Julia.

Elizabeth leaned her stick against the wall by the headboard and settled on the bed. The warmth of the bedroom seeped through her clothes and onto her cold skin. Bouncy looked at his grandmother and smiled. 'Don't be thad, Grandma,' he said, and his innocence brought a lump to her throat. She took his hand, so small and plump, in her withered one, and stroked the soft skin with her thumb.

'I'm not sad any more,' she replied, and a tear trickled down her cheek, getting caught in the deep lines that extended down from her mouth.

'Then why are you crying?'

'Because I'm happy to see you,' she said, and smiled. The little boy looked confused. 'Sometimes grown-ups cry when they're happy,' she explained.

She heard the sound of footsteps along the corridor. A moment later Archie and Julia appeared in the room. 'Are you all right, Mother?' Archie asked. He looked at his wife, who returned his stare with a shrug.

'I came to say good night to my grandson,' she said. She picked up the book. 'Ah, *The Little Engine That Could*. My favourite book. Shall I read it to you?'

Bouncy nodded, raising his big brown eyes to his parents, enjoying the attention. Elizabeth began to read, her voice full of animation. She read without pause, except for a moment's hesitation when Bouncy put his hand on hers and ran his fingers over the surface where it was still smooth but covered in brown liver spots. 'I'm making it better,' he whispered.

Elizabeth's voice wavered, but she stiffened her jaw and continued. 'Thank you, darling. It's already much better,' she replied.

Julia took Archie's hand and led him away, drawing Nanny with him. She sensed her mother-in-law needed to be alone with Bouncy. If anyone could mend her heart, it was her three-year-old son. Perhaps it was something to do with the dishevelled hair and watery eyes, but she was certain she could already feel it thawing.

Chapter 16

Pamela arrived back in town to find the house filled with red roses. 'Goodness me, people are so kind,' she said, dropping her suitcase on the hall floor.

Celestria didn't have the heart to tell her that they were all from Aidan and all for her. She didn't tell her that she was engaged, either. She'd wait until she had come back from Italy. Right now, she was unable to think of anything but solving the mystery of her father's death.

Godfrey, the butler, had returned from his summer break to the dreadful news of his master's suicide. A wiry man with silver hair and a nose like a beak, he had worked for Mr Montague almost as long as Mrs Waynebridge had. With the formality that came with years of loyal servitude, he offered his condolences to Mrs Pamela in a few short sentences, his expression as grave as an undertaker's, placed a silver tray laden with letters on the hall table, and proceeded to carry her suitcase upstairs. When he reached her bedroom, he remained a while in the doorway that led into Mr Monty's dressing room. The air still contained his scent embedded in the upholstery, where it would now begin to fade. Like a lost dog he lingered there for a long time, not knowing what to do.

'It feels so empty without your father,' said Pamela to her daughter, sensing a coldness in the rooms that hadn't been there before. Harry strode past her and dragged his suitcase up the stairs. Cornwall had been the scene of unhappiness, but also a much needed distraction. Now he was home, the house echoed with the dreadful loss. The rooms seemed larger, the ceilings taller, the air unfamiliar, and his father's memory a ghostly presence everywhere he looked. He sat on his bed and let the sense of desolation wash over him like a gigantic wave. He was now the man of the house, but inside he felt like a little boy, barely able to keep afloat.

Pamela had scarcely had time to catch her breath when the doorbell rang. It rang persistently, as if the caller was in a terrible hurry. 'Where's Godfrey?' she snapped, raising her eyes from the pile of letters she was shuffling through.

'He's upstairs,' Celestria replied.

Pamela huffed. 'Can't he hear the bell?'

'I'll get it.' Celestria rolled her eyes; the door was only a few paces away.

'Tell Waynie to take Poochi into the kitchen. He could do with a little something.' Pamela wandered off, distracted by the handwriting on one of the envelopes.

Celestria opened the door to find Lotty on the doorstep in a cloud of Chanel No 5. 'Good Lord!' Celestria exclaimed, pulling her cousin inside. 'What are you dolled up for?' She took in the red lipstick and coiffed hair.

'I need to talk to you,' Lotty hissed, her eyes darting across the hall like those of a hunted animal.

'What's happened?'

'Where's Aunt Pamela?'

Celestria turned around. 'She was here a minute ago.'

'Tell her I'm here, just so she knows.'

'Oh, *I get it*. You're off somewhere else. Mama, it's only Lotty!'

She heard her mother shout back from the sitting room. 'Don't forget Poochi, and your grandfather is coming at six.'

'Let's go upstairs,' Celestria suggested.

'No, I can't stay. I'm meeting Francis.'

'So, you want me to cover for you?' said Celestria with a smile. 'You've made your decision, then? Are you going to elope?'

Lotty looked flustered. 'I'm not sure. I mean, I don't know. I need to talk to him.'

'I don't think talking will get you anywhere. That kind of talking just gives me a headache. Besides, you've had the whole summer to think about it. If my father's death has taught me anything, it's that a girl needs to be looked after, if not by her father, then by her husband. I wouldn't recommend being poor to anyone. It was ghastly. Fortunately, I have a rich grandfather.'

Lotty found her cousin's melodrama grating. She had no experience of poverty, on any level.

Celestria lowered her voice and grew serious. 'I never want to go there again, Lotty, and I wouldn't want you to.'

Lotty changed the subject. 'Melissa and Rafferty are getting serious, by the way. They're very in love. I thought you'd like to know.' Her voice sounded flat.

Celestria looked mildly concerned for a moment. 'Oh,' she replied tartly. 'Just as well, considering how she compromised herself at the dance.'

'What do you mean?'

'He ravaged her like an animal.'

'Did he?'

'Of course. You could see it in her eyes. One simply can't behave like that with a man and not marry him. One can so easily get a bad reputation. London is a small town.' Lotty looked confused. 'Anyway, he's undoubtedly rich and handsome; he'll make the perfect husband. It's not all about love, you know.'

'I think it is,' Lotty replied in a small voice. 'I think love is more important than money. Life is short . . .' Her voice trailed off. If Monty's death had taught *her* anything, it was that nothing but love had any worth at all.

'You're a hopeless romantic. No, one should have a cool head when deciding one's future. There's time later on for the hothead to take precedence. Marry Eddie, Lotty, but love Francis. It's very easy. That way you get the best of both worlds.'

Lotty looked offended. She straightened up, nostrils flaring. 'And you, Celestria. What are you going to do about your future?'

Celestria turned away. 'Marry for comfort, like I told you. I might even grow to love him. If not, I'll love someone else, discreetly. Nothing wrong with that. Papa used to say the eleventh commandment is "Never get caught." Well, he's right about that, and I don't intend to.'

'Well, you and I are very different, Celestria. Please cover for me. You will, won't you?'

'Of course I will.' She opened the door. The street outside was bathed in sunshine, the little communal garden a froth of green on the point of turning. She remembered her forthcoming trip to Italy and felt her heart swell with excitement. In that state of happiness it was easy to be generous. 'Whatever you decide, Lotty. I'll always stand by you.'

'Thank you, Cousin. I hope your trip to Italy is a success.'

'Don't worry, I'm already on the scent.'

'You will write to me, won't you?'

'If you write back and tell me what you decide. You can always join me in Puglia if it all gets too much. I can't imagine Aunt Penelope taking to Francis.'

They embraced warmly, and Celestria watched her cousin hurry off down the street towards Belgrave Square. *We are very different, you and I,* she thought smugly as Lotty turned the corner. *I will never give up my comfortable life for love.*

★

Pamela began to unpack. All her clothes had been washed and ironed, so she had only the simple task of putting things away. She dared not venture into Monty's dressing room. The sight of the empty room would give her another migraine. Usually she'd be unpacking for him, too, which she'd always found a bore. Now she longed for his socks and shirts to put away. It was while she unpacked that she discovered that the star brooch she had worn for Archie's birthday party, the one that Monty had given her, was missing. At first she thought nothing of it, figuring it had probably dropped to the bottom of the case. But when she pulled out the last few items, it wasn't there.

'Celestria!' she shouted out to the landing. 'Have you seen my brooch?' Celestria wandered into the room.

'No.'

'I can't have left it in Pendrift.'

'Did you have it after the dance?'

'I remember very little about what happened after the dance. It's the shock.'

'It's only a brooch,' Celestria consoled her.

'No,' retorted Pamela sharply. 'It was much more than that.'

That evening Richard W. Bancroft II arrived at number 13 Upper Belgrave Street. His chauffeur remained outside in the red Bentley, waiting for an opportunity to smoke a quick cigarette beside the gates of St Peter's Church, next door to the house. Godfrey opened the door and showed Mr Bancroft into the sitting room, where his daughter and grandchildren were waiting for him. Celestria was the first to embrace him, and he patted her affectionately on the back, planting a kiss on her forehead. Harry didn't know his grandfather as well as his sister did and felt awkward, unsure whether to kiss him or shake his hand now that he was the man of the house. But

Richard Bancroft was not a man of indecision. He scooped the boy into his arms and kissed him, too. Harry blushed, but it was the first physical contact he had had with another man since his father died and he liked it.

'You've grown into a fine young man,' said Richard. He rested his gaze on his grandson for a long moment, admiring his intelligent face and pitying the dreadful loss that was reflected in his clear grey eyes. 'I bet your father was very proud of you. He had a right to be.'

Harry was unable to reply. He felt the tears sting his eyes but was able to restrain his emotions by stiffening his jaw and shedding none.

Pamela, Poochi under her arm like a handbag, took her father's hand in hers and kissed his ruddy cheek. 'Hello, Pa,' she said. In spite of their difference she was grateful he had come.

'I'm sorry, sweetheart. I'm sorry for you all.' He sat down. Godfrey poured Pamela a glass of sherry from the drinks table that stood behind the sofa, where golden liquids glittered in crystal decanters beneath a large potted jasmine. 'Pour me a whiskey, Godfrey. Straight, no ice.' The butler did as he asked and brought the glass over on a silver tray.

'Would Sir like anything else?'

'Not for the moment, Godfrey. Why don't you take a break?' He took a swig and watched the butler leave the room, closing the door softly behind him. When he was sure that they were completely alone, he lowered his voice and spoke solemnly.

'This is a dreadful business, but I want you all to know that even though I am unable to bring Monty back, I can at least support you financially so that life can continue as it always has. When do you go back to school, Harry?'

'On the ninth,' Harry replied, feeling a great sense of relief that his grandfather was assuming control of things.

'I'll telephone your housemaster this evening. You're the head of the family now, son. It's a heavy duty on the shoulders of one so young, but it could just be the making of you. Death comes to us all eventually, and your father gave you the best years of his life. You know the Jesuit saying? "Give me the boy until he turns seven and I'll give you the man." Those seven years are the most important. They're the foundation blocks from which you will build your future, and yours, my boy, are very strong. You're thirteen now, a young man. This can only make you stronger. You understand?' Harry looked doubtful. His grandfather chuckled. 'You will.'

He pulled a fat white envelope out of the inside pocket of his jacket and handed it to Celestria. 'This is the itinerary for you and Mrs Waynebridge. You leave on Thursday. Rita will come over tomorrow morning to go through it all with you. Fred will drive you to the airport. The arrangements have been made to the last detail. I didn't think your mother would like me to leave anything to chance.'

Celestria felt a frisson of excitement. 'Thank you, Grandpa!' she exclaimed, thrilled that only she and her grandfather knew the real reason for her trip.

It had not escaped Richard's notice that Pamela had so far said little. She was sitting on the club fender, her white fingers stroking her dog, listening to everything he said, her face taut with discomfort. 'Now, why don't you both leave your mother and me to discuss the boring stuff,' he said, draining his glass. Celestria and Harry left the room.

'Thank God we're not going to be poor,' said Celestria to her brother as they climbed the stairs. Harry clicked his tongue. His confidence had returned with the wave that had swept in his grandfather.

'You and Mama are ridiculous sometimes,' he replied. 'We were never going to be poor.'

Richard Bancroft studied his daughter. He knew her so

well, even though in the last twenty years he had slowly lost her. 'What's eating you, girl?' he said. 'I can only read so much from your silence. Have I done something to offend you?'

Pamela's cheeks stung pink, and she swallowed. 'I feel so wretched,' she said in a soft voice, lowering her eyes. 'I haven't asked you for a dime in twenty years!'

'You might be married, Pam, but I'm still your father.'

'Monty stole everything from me.'

'He knew I'd look after you.'

'He didn't think of the shame he'd bring on us.'

'There's no shame, Pam. Those who love you sympathize.'

'There are plenty who don't, believe me.' She laughed bitterly.

'If he was in a mess, I doubt he thought of anything but escape. He must have been at rock bottom to kill himself.'

'It was so unlike him.'

'We're not all black and white.'

She raised her eyes and looked at him steadily. Suddenly the question that had been lurking in a far recess of her mind for over twenty years rolled to the front. She had never dared ask it, fearing his answer. Now that her husband was dead, it no longer mattered. It would, however, shed light on a great many things. 'Did you see beneath the surface?'

Richard nodded slowly. He had always been good at looking into the hearts of people where lay their intentions, ambitions, and desires. Monty was no exception. 'I never liked him,' he replied, shaking his head.

'I thought as much,' Pamela said, feeling the wall between them dissolve in the light of honesty. 'Why?'

'I never trusted him.'

'When everyone else did? Why were you different?'

'Because you meant more to me than you did to everyone

else. You're my only daughter, Pam. He wasn't good enough for you.'

'Did Mama like him?'

'She couldn't see beyond his charm and good looks. When you and your mother get something into your heads, there's nothing that can stop you. I let you go. It was the only thing I could do. I hoped I'd be there to pick up the pieces.'

'You couldn't have foreseen that it would end this way.'

'Of course not. Right now, I can't even put my finger on why I never trusted him. Maybe because he was too good to be true. There were no cracks. Everyone has cracks, even me, and I'm pretty perfect.' They both laughed. The tears spilled over Pamela's cheeks and dropped off her chin onto her pale yellow cashmere sweater.

'You are pretty perfect, Pa. I'm sad that we've drifted apart over the years. It must have been hard for you to have seen me with Monty, when you sensed faults in his character.'

'You're pigheaded, Pam, like me. I couldn't blame you for marrying the man you had set your heart on. I'd have done the same, no matter what my father might have thought. No one can tell me what to do. I admire that quality in you.'

'I feel so betrayed, because I loved him.'

'But you're not alone. Come and sit next to your pa.'

Pamela snuggled up against her father and breathed in the scent of her childhood. It was the smell of home, no matter where she was. 'What am I going to do?' she asked. 'Harry's at boarding school. Celestria's off to Italy. I'm all alone.'

'Celestria and Harry need you.'

'What about *my* needs?'

He kissed the top of her head and chuckled at her selfishness. 'You don't change, do you, Pam? You're young and beautiful. When you're ready, you might fall in love again.'

'I don't think my heart could take it.'

'Oh, I think your heart is full of secret compartments you've never even looked into.'

Pamela sat up suddenly and stared at him. 'Do you believe in God, Pa?'

He shrugged. 'Of course I do. There's got to be some greater power than me.'

'I mean, really. Do you *really* believe?'

'Yes, I do.'

'Why don't I?'

'Perhaps you haven't found Him yet.'

'You sound like Father Dalgliesh.'

'Father Dalgliesh is obviously a very wise man!'

'I don't want to believe that after all this struggling, there's nothing. I want to believe we all go somewhere. That Monty is somewhere.'

'If you're good, you'll go to heaven no matter what you believe.' He sounded as if he were talking to a child.

'But that's the problem, Pa. I'm not at all good.'

He looked at her with affection. 'It's never too late to start.'

'But it's so awfully difficult.'

'Not if you try. I started this morning, and it's not as difficult as I imagined it to be.'

She laughed, both irritated and amused. 'You're teasing me!'

'I don't know the answers, Pam. Even your Father Dalgliesh doesn't know. You have to find out for yourself and have your own belief that comes from here.' He placed his hand on his heart. 'Not from what other people tell you.'

'You are good, Pa! You've rescued us.' He hadn't seen his daughter look at him with such fondness in twenty years. He felt his old heart give a little flutter, like a phoenix rising from the ashes.

'It's a start,' he said with a chuckle. 'I've got *sixty* years of not being good to make up for. How else do you think I built my empire? You can't make an omelette without breaking eggs.'

Mrs Waynebridge packed her bag. She didn't have many clothes, being a woman of simple tastes and means. The thought of flying terrified the life out of her, even though Celestria had assured her they'd be flying first class. They still had to be in the air, whichever class they travelled in, and those machines didn't look right in the sky. 'It's against nature. If God had wanted us to fly, He would have given us wings,' she had complained. However, she had to admit that a large part of her was excited by the idea of adventure. If she could overcome her nervousness, she might actually enjoy herself. She had watched two magpies alight on her small terrace that morning . . . one for sorrow, two for joy . . . That had been very encouraging.

She was a widow and life was lonely, set into a comfortable but not very exhilarating routine. She wasn't sure about the Italians, but Italy was famously beautiful. She folded her cardigan and placed it over her Sunday dress. It was the end of summer, Celestria had said, but the evenings could be cold. She wasn't expected to take her apron. She stood up and stared down at her small suitcase. The sight of it made her tremble. It meant leaving home. Leaving England. Setting off for somewhere unfamiliar. She carried the case downstairs and put it in the little entrance hall, where it would remain until Mr Bancroft's chauffeur came to pick her up on Thursday morning. She went into the sitting room and perched on a chair with her hands neatly folded on her lap, feeling a mixture of excitement and sickness. She was relieved she couldn't see the case. It was getting dark outside. She looked at her watch. It was eight-thirty. She was too nervous to eat or even to heat up some soup. Sliding her eyes over the furniture in the small

Fulham house, she suddenly felt quite lost, as if everything that belonged to her was drifting off on an unseen tide. Would it all be here when she got back?

Celestria didn't pack. She knew Waynie would help her the following day. Instead, she lay in a hot bubble bath, feeling a sense of serenity wash over her with the bluebell-scented water. She had told Aidan that she was tired. The truth was that she was tired of hanging around waiting to go to Italy. Aidan had suggested a flick, but she didn't feel like necking in the back row. She'd retire to bed early and get her beauty sleep. She needed all her energy if she was going to find the person responsible for turning her world upside down.

The sun set and the sky grew dark above London. The same sky grew dark above Puglia, but the stars were much brighter there, and the moon, full and round like a ball of mozzarella, was not obscured by the clouds that gathered over England, but shone phosphorescent over the Aegean Sea, turning it a milky green.

There, on Italy's heel beneath that all-knowing moon, a small flame was kept alight in the fragrant city of the dead that stood over the track from the Convento di Santa Maria del Mare. It was quiet, but for a light breeze that rustled through the pine trees, casting dancing shadows across the grassy square and paving stones that led through the rows of silent crypts. The scent of lilies filled the air, and the little candles cast flickering gold shadows across the stone walls where the spirits of the dead rested in peace. Except for one spirit, who was not allowed to rest. The man knelt before her tomb and wept. By the sheer force of his grief he kept her little flame alive. However much she tried to move on, she could not.

PART TWO

Chapter 17

The journey to Puglia took two days. Mrs Waynebridge had barely drawn breath since they had left London in the early hours of Thursday morning. It had been raining. Large, steamy drops landing on parched pavements and running down drains choked with early autumn leaves. Mrs Waynebridge had been ready and waiting an hour before Celestria was due to pick her up in her grandfather's chauffeur-driven car, clutching her handbag on her knee, raincoat buttoned up to her chin, hat containing her soft grey curls, her face pinched with anxiety. In her hand she held the passport Rita had managed to obtain for her with Mr Bancroft's far-reaching connections. She had watched the clock above the fireplace with mixed emotions: part of her felt like a turkey on Christmas morning, awaiting the chop; the other part like a turkey endowed with magic wings, waiting to fly for the first time. Whichever turkey she turned out to be, she was still a turkey for having allowed herself to be coerced into embarking on this ridiculous adventure in the first place.

She had glanced around the house she had shared with her husband of forty-six years and then remained in as a widow, and knew that she was leaving behind everything that was familiar, but most frighteningly, her routine. How would she exist without structure? She'd lived a structured life from the moment she had entered into domestic service as a mere sixteen-year-old. She'd be like a body without a skeleton. What on earth was she going to do with herself with no daily map to follow? But Celestria had arrived half an hour late, smiling confidently, and her worries had been swallowed into the girl's enthusiasm.

They had left the grey skies and low-hanging clouds behind and arrived in Rome, where the air was thick, hot, and caramel-scented. Above them the sky was bluer than either had ever seen before, the clamour of birds in the umbrella pines rising above the roar of traffic in a merry cacophony, and, suddenly, after having chattered all the way on the airplane out of nerves, Mrs Waynebridge had been rendered speechless. For once she had no comment. It was all too beautiful.

They had taken the train from Rome to Spongano, changing at Caserta, Brindisi, and again at Lecce. Celestria had read Maupassant's *Bel Ami,* a present from her grandfather. Mrs Waynebridge knitted a cardigan for Celestria, who thought the shade of green she had chosen the ugliest ever seen. Mrs Waynebridge called it 'parrot green,' explaining that the parrot was a very lucky bird. Celestria concentrated on her novel, repressing her desire to point out that practically any other colour would have been preferable to parrot green, regardless of superstition. Mrs Waynebridge gazed out of the window and let her eyes wander over the cypress trees and olive groves and small clusters of sandy-coloured houses that shimmered in the midday heat. She was careful not to interrupt the girl's reading; Celestria hadn't the patience for interruption. But when they went to eat in the restaurant car, she chattered away with the enthusiasm of a dog let off her lead.

'I should like to have seen the world,' she said, toying with the wedding ring she still wore. 'But a goose wandered into church on our wedding day, so I knew I were destined for the home and hearth and not for a life of adventure.'

'A goose?'

'A goose. It just waddled in out of nowhere. It were a sign, you see. I knew it, of course, because of me understanding of the secret nature of birds. It was no coincidence. Alfie thought me more than a little soft in the head, but he never did take me nowhere. Perhaps he took advantage of me superstitious mind. Had I not noticed the goose, we might have had a more interesting life.' She sighed wistfully.

'I think you're a silly old goose, Waynie, for believing such rubbish.'

'When you're older, you'll know what I mean. The world is full of messages, if you know where to look for them.'

'I won't allow superstition to direct my life.'

'No, love, you have a mind of your own.'

'I'm not sure travelling is going to appeal to me, Waynie. I've sat on this train long enough to never want to sit on another.'

Waynie disagreed. 'First class, love. I could sit in first class for a week and not grow bored.'

Celestria felt she had seen as much of the world as a city girl on the brink of marriage could desire to see. Nothing compared to New York and London. Her mother had taken her to Paris a few times and been as bored by the Louvre as she was. Once she returned home, she doubted she'd be tempted farther than Cornwall. This was to be an adventure in search of truth. Having exacted unspeakable revenge on the person responsible for her father's death, she would go back to her cosseted life in London, where Aidan would look after her in suitably grand style until her dying day. She considered Aidan with a growing sense of unease. There was something unsatisfactory about the whole situation. She reminded herself that love wasn't the objective; she could find love later if she desired. The important thing was that he loved her. The more she thought about it, the less she believed her own reasoning. She picked up her fork and toyed with her pasta as if it were a helping of garden worms.

As the sun waned, the train screeched to a halt. Waynie and Celestria disembarked wearily, alighting on a small platform where only a few miles of dirt track separated them from their journey's end. They inhaled the pine-scented air and felt themselves a little restored. The silence was soothing after the rumble of the train, the sea breeze a blessing after the heat of their carriage. Celestria stretched, savouring the sight of a pretty blue bird that watched them with interest from the top of a carob tree. Now, *that* colour would have made a lovely cardigan.

Their attention was caught by a short, stocky man in a beret and waistcoat who was striding purposefully towards them. He greeted them in Italian with a smile so charming that Mrs Waynebridge once again lost her voice. His shiny blue eyes belied his advanced age. They twinkled like tourmalines in rock, reflecting the light with a mixture of sincerity and mischief.

'*Vengo da parte dalla signora Gancia, dal Convento di Santa Maria del Mare,*' he said, and his voice was as soft and light as flour.

'*No parlo Italiano,*' said Celestria, drawing on her French education and slapping an 'o' on the end. The man chuckled and nodded energetically.

'*Io, Nuzzo,*' he said, pressing his hand to his chest and articulating his name slowly and clearly as if speaking to the hard of hearing.

'Hello, Nuzzo,' Celestria replied. 'My name is Miss Montague, and this is Mrs Waynebridge.'

Nuzzo frowned, drawing together two feathery eyebrows. He glanced at the muted Mrs Waynebridge, and his face softened with sympathy. She looked grey and tired. He said something incomprehensible, then bent down to pick up their bags. Mrs Waynebridge had her one small case, but Celestria had three navy blue Globetrotters littered with stickers. Nuzzo made several journeys, and his jovial smile never faltered.

Celestria was astonished to find they were to travel in a horse-drawn cart. The sturdy beast stood patiently in the evening sun while fat flies buzzed about his head, which he shook every now and then in an attempt to shoo them away. Nuzzo piled the cases on top of one another on one seat, then gestured for the ladies to mount. Mrs Waynebridge thought nothing of it, having grown up with similar transport, and took Nuzzo's hand for support. For a moment she hesitated, unsure whether her tired legs would function as they ought. Nuzzo encouraged her with words she did not understand, but his tone was gentle and persuasive and his grin so endearing, she felt herself blush and heaved herself into the cart. Celestria was appalled. It was a terrible come-down from her grandfather's swish red Bentley. As if in response to her snobbishness, the carthorse lifted his tail and released a foul-smelling expulsion of wind.

'Good Lord!' she exclaimed in distaste. 'I didn't come all the way to Italy for this! We have come to the end of the world, Waynie,' she said, waving her hand in front of her nose.

'I think it's lovely,' replied Mrs Waynebridge. 'If this isn't paradise, I don't know what is.' Nuzzo took the reins, and the horse slowly set off up the dusty track. 'I don't think I've seen anything as beautiful in all me life!' She watched Nuzzo's broad back as he hunched over the reins, his white sleeves rolled up to reveal strong brown forearms, grey and white tufts of hair sticking out of his beret, and found his presence surprisingly exhilarating.

As they proceeded down the coast they stared in silence at the rough, arid terrain of Puglia. It was not the lush, green hills they had seen in photographs of Tuscany, but relatively flat, scattered with white rock and herds of sheep grazing on grass and wild capers. The crumbling stone walls that divided the land reminded Celestria of Cornwall, and yet the scents of thyme and rosemary were altogether more exotic. Below, sheer chalk cliffs descended into the glittering turquoise sea that stretched all the way to Albania. Positioned on top of these cliffs stood ancient lookout towers, once used to keep watch for foreign invaders, but now nothing more than useless and deserted decorations. They passed through little villages of sandstone houses with flat roofs and iron balconies, where stray dogs roamed cobbled streets lined with shady pines and cherry trees: old women stood in doorways, dressed in black; and elderly men in berets lingered on benches in village squares, watching the shadows lengthen, puffing on pipes and old regrets. Grey olive groves grew out of the dry, rugged earth where goats roamed freely and children played, ignoring their mothers, who called them to bed.

They were both weary and overwhelmed by the distance they had travelled. At the sight of the unfamiliar terrain Celestria began to wonder why she had come. Surely, it would have been better to have accepted her father's death as suicide and moved on, she thought bleakly, her spirits sinking as her energy flagged. It had all seemed a very good idea back in England. Nuzzo spoke no English, and her Italian was limited to a few phrases. She was ashamed that she had presumed all foreigners spoke English. What if this Salazar character spoke as little as Nuzzo? Would she ever manage to get anything out of him? She reassured herself that there would surely be someone at the Convento who would be able to translate. Mrs Waynebridge sensed Celestria's unease and began to feel nervous herself. She rested her eyes on the dependable shoulders that were guiding the horse home and felt herself immediately comforted.

At last they arrived in the small town of Marelatte. They were met by a pack of mongrel dogs, sniffing the ground in search of scraps and wagging their thin tails. *'Dei cani della signora Federica Gancia,'* said Nuzzo, nodding. *Ah,* thought Celestria, recalling the letter she had found in the pile her father had intended to burn, *the famous Freddie, no doubt.* The cart turned off the track and stopped beside a plain, unremarkable sandstone building attached to a pretty church with tall oak doors below an arched stained-glass window. Sitting proudly on the pink-tiled roof above was a square bell tower ready to summon the people to worship. Nuzzo climbed down a little stiffly and motioned to the wide door of the Convento, inside which was another, smaller door. *'Il Convento di Santa Maria del Mare,'* he exclaimed, catching his breath.

Mrs Waynebridge stood unsteadily in the cart, unsure how to get down. Nuzzo hurried to assist and held out his hand. As she took it they momentarily caught eyes, and the sparkle in his, so bright and infectious, caused her heart to stumble and a small smile to spread across her delicately flushing face. *'Va bene, signora,'* he said kindly as she placed her aching feet on the dry, dusty ground, grateful for its solid lack of motion.

'Thank you,' she replied, regaining her composure.

'Fa niente, signora,' he said, his gentle gaze lingering on her a little longer than necessary.

Celestria climbed down without help, too busy with her own thoughts to notice the flirtatious communication between Nuzzo and Mrs Waynebridge. She strode over to the door, pressed the bell, and waited. For a while nothing happened. Then she heard the scuffle of feet, the unbolting of locks, and finally the little door opened to reveal the wide, handsome face of Federica Gancia. To her relief, Celestria knew at once that this woman had not been her father's mistress; she was far too old!

Federica Gancia settled her warm, whiskey-coloured eyes on Celestria's pale face and smiled, revealing delightfully crooked teeth. 'Welcome, Miss Montague. Do come in; you must be tired.' Her English was perfect, with only the slightest hint of a foreign accent. She looked behind Celestria to where Mrs Waynebridge hovered in her shadow, clutching her handbag to her chest. 'Did you have a pleasant journey? We are a long way from England.' Mrs Waynebridge was startled that the woman was addressing her, and hastily nodded. Federica thanked Nuzzo, and Mrs Waynebridge risked one last look back as he shook the reins and proceeded up the track into town. 'I hope he made himself clear,' said Federica, still waving. 'Nuzzo's a wonderful character, but he speaks no English. I would have sent my husband, Gaitano, but he is in Brindisi this evening.'

Celestria and Mrs Waynebridge stepped into a cobbled courtyard surrounded on all four sides by a cloister. It was lit with a dozen large church candles that blazed in the twilight, illuminating the deep red colour of the walls. Under the arches there were piles of fat, brightly coloured cushions embroidered with gold thread that caught the light and glittered. A couple of cats watched them, their eyes bright and unblinking, like silver coins. Above them the pale sky revealed the first twinkling star and, in a small window cut into the wall, a soft grey dove cooed sleepily. Mrs Waynebridge gasped when she saw the bird, for the dove symbolizes love. She glanced at Celestria. She was certain that love wasn't destined for her, at her age, and was about to say so, but she was suddenly too weary to speak, and, besides, her young companion was gazing around her, silenced by the strange magic of the place that vibrated in the hypnotic glow of the flames and lingered on the air that was heavy with the scent of lilies.

In spite of her exhaustion, Celestria's heart suddenly warmed and expanded, filled with something unfamiliar but delicious. She knew instantly why her father had loved it there; it felt like home.

'Welcome to the Convento. I'm so pleased you have come to stay. Your father is a dear friend of ours.' Celestria stared at Federica, suddenly aware that she had not heard about his death. For a moment she hesitated, unsure how to break the news. She glanced at Mrs Waynebridge. Her face was sunken with fatigue, and Celestria knew that she would receive no help from her. Federica's expression grew solemn. 'What is the matter?' she asked, her hand clasping the Madonna pendant that hung over her large bosom.

'My father is dead,' said Celestria.

Federica stared at her. 'I don't know what to say,' she murmured. She took a deep breath, a frown lining her brow and pinching the skin between her eyes. She stared at Celestria for a long moment as if fighting to make sense of what she had just heard. Finally she placed a hand on Celestria's arm, and her voice, when she spoke at last, was thin and hoarse. 'I am sorry for your loss and for my own. You must both come inside for a drink and something to eat. You must be tired.'

Federica took them across the courtyard to a little door that led to a narrow passageway and out into the kitchen garden, where large terracotta pots of basil and sage stood in clusters, a cosy home for a young family of sleek black cats. Celestria looked up and caught her breath at the sight of the enormous moon, suspended seemingly only yards from where she stood, a phosphorescent sphere in the darkening sky. Never before had she seen a moon so pregnant and so vast as the one she saw that night over Marelatte. Without comment Federica opened the kitchen door. Inside, the air was fragrant with the aroma of freshly ground coffee. One wall was decorated with a collage of rough wooden breadboards, another with black ladles hanging in a row. The long shelf that ran above the sink and sideboard was weighed down by cheerful-looking pots and jugs of varying size and colour, like one might find in a Moroccan souk. Celestria would soon find out as she explored the place that Federica Gancia was an avid collector. If she fell in love with an object, to buy one wouldn't do; she had to buy the lot. From coffeepots and breadboards to African art and Mexican dolls, she bought in large numbers and arranged them together in clusters. Each room was themed and more beautiful than the last. She had a unique sense of colour and texture, creating warmth and vitality in the rooms that had once been simple monks' cells. At the other end of the kitchen was a door that led out into the garden and the orange grove beyond.

'Can I offer you some wine, or perhaps coffee?' she asked, her golden eyes tired and troubled. 'Luigi has left hot soup and prosciutto for supper. We bake our own bread, and it's delicious.' Mrs Waynebridge waited for Celestria to lead the way, hoping she'd ask for tea.

'A glass of wine for both of us, Signora Gancia,' Celestria replied, and Mrs Waynebridge's heart sank. Alfie had drunk like a sailor, but she had always been careful to limit her own alcohol to a glass of sherry in the evening, at the end of a busy day. It made her garrulous, which wasn't appropriate in Upper Belgrave Street, where discretion was paramount, nor at home, where Alfie had liked to be quiet. Since being widowed she had never dared drink on her own, lest she start to chatter and not know how to stop. Now she was too tired to care.

'Please call me Freddie; everyone does. Signora makes me feel old.'

Celestria didn't know why the woman minded feeling old: she *was* old – she must have been well into her sixties. She poured the wine and led them through the dining room, decorated with vast bowls of fresh pomegranates and pears, into a room with low vaulted ceilings where scruffy, threadbare sofas and armchairs were arranged around a fireplace that, at this time of year, remained unlit. Two places had been laid for supper at a round table that probably seated eight. Celestria's mouth watered at the sight of prosciutto and freshly baked bread. They sat down and tasted the wine. Mrs Waynebridge felt her spirits rise. Wine had never tasted so good, she thought, taking another large gulp. Federica sat down and poured herself a glass. She took a sip and a moment to compose herself, then turned gravely to Celestria.

'I am so terribly sorry to hear that your father has died. In reality, it is a shock. I was so deeply fond of him. He was almost like one of my family. You have no idea. How can I possibly explain?' She sighed heavily, and her eyes glittered in the mellow candlelight. 'May I ask how he died?'

'He drowned at sea. It was an accident.' Celestria was too ashamed to look at Mrs Waynebridge. She took a large swig of wine and consoled herself that her lie was only a small one.

'How terrible. You must be distraught!' The older woman touched Celestria's hand. 'Why did you choose to come here?'

'Because my father loved it so much. I want to feel close to him. I also need to get away from England and have some time on my own. It's been the hardest summer of my life.'

Federica's eyes softened, and she smiled sadly. 'I'm so pleased you chose Puglia. Your father fell in love with this place. He came whenever he could.'

'Did he have business here?'

Federica laughed. 'There is no business here, my dear. He came like you. To escape the world.'

Mrs Waynebridge was so delighted by the feeling of a full belly and light head that she didn't care how much Celestria lied. Besides, she understood. Suicide wasn't something one necessarily wanted shouted from the rooftops. 'He were a busy man,' said Mrs Waynebridge, and at the sound of her voice, it was Celestria's turn to look startled. Mrs Waynebridge hadn't uttered a word since they arrived.

'I'm sorry, we haven't been properly introduced,' said Federica to Mrs Waynebridge, extending her hand. 'The sad news has made me forget my manners.'

'This is Mrs Waynebridge,' said Celestria, her mouth full of bread and prosciutto. 'She has worked for my family for Lord knows how long. How long, Waynie?'

'Over forty years. I lost count about ten years ago. You see, I worked for Celestria's grandmother when I was only a girl. I looked after Mr Montague like me own son. I never had children; it wasn't me destiny. There were once a dead robin in the birdbath, which said it all, really. Dead robin: a barren womb. Alfie thought me mad, but I weren't wrong. It's logic, isn't it? Nowt good will come of a dead bird. Or a dead anything, for that matter, but I never learned the meaning of dead animals, only birds.' Celestria gazed at Mrs Waynebridge in horror. After having barely uttered a word since Spongano, she was now unwilling to stop.

'Mama wouldn't let me come on my own, so poor old Waynie has had to join me. She's never travelled farther than London!' she said, hoping to curb her companion's loquaciousness.

'It's a pleasure to meet you, Mrs Waynebridge,' said Federica, and Mrs Waynebridge smiled happily, if a little unsteadily. She was glad she had come.

While they ate, the pack of dogs that had been out on the hunt when they arrived now trotted into the sitting room. Federica welcomed them affectionately. 'These are my four-legged friends: Pompea, Fiametta, Primo, Cyrus, and Maialino. I found Pompea first, and little by little the others followed. I have a growing family.'

'Do you and your husband live here alone?' Celestria asked, watching her lean down to pat them. They were all mongrels, but Federica seemed to love them nonetheless.

'We had a daughter who lived with us, but she died three years ago. She is buried across the road in the mausoleum we built especially for her. Her husband, Hamish, continues to live with us.' A shadow passed over her face. 'You see, I, too, am familiar with the bitter taste of death.' She reached out and held Celestria's hand. 'I understand your loss because I live with my own.' Her voice was a husk. She swallowed, withdrew her hand, and gazed for a moment into her wine-glass while she collected herself. Pompea nuzzled beneath her arm, and she lifted it to let him in. He rested his head on her lap with a heavy sigh.

'The loss of a child is far worse than the loss of a father. At least Papa had enjoyed a little of life,' said Celestria, putting down her soup spoon.

'One cannot stop living, although at times, God knows, it would have been easier,' said Federica, rubbing the silver Madonna pendant between her thumb and forefinger.

'Do you have other children?'

'I have a son who works in Milan and another daughter, who lives with her husband and children in Venice. Natalia was my youngest. Then, of course, I have my guests, some of whom, like your father, become family, too.' She lowered her eyes again and stared at the embroidered flowers on the tablecloth.

Celestria watched Federica. She was a handsome woman with fine bones and soft, fair skin with remarkably few lines. Her long grey hair was drawn up and clipped to the back of her head in a thick, untidy ball. She wore no makeup, just shiny yellow beads, the silver Madonna pendant, and large gold earrings on fleshy lobes. She wore olive-green slacks with flat shoes and a long green cardigan that reached her knees. Celestria had assumed Italian women were dark-skinned and raven-haired like Sophia Loren. Federica didn't fit the stereotype at all.

After supper, Federica showed them to their rooms. They crossed the courtyard again and climbed the wide stone staircase that led up to the bedrooms. An irregular corridor followed the line of the cloister, around three walls of the building. The floor was covered with rich Persian rugs piled high with unsteady towers of books, and a small grand piano was placed at one end in a niche in front of a window.

'Hamish plays,' she said. 'Or should I say, used to play. He hasn't played in a long time, but if you are fortunate enough to hear him, it will take your breath away.' As she passed the books she muttered under her breath. 'These are beginning to get in the way. Thank goodness Gaitano is turning the little folly in the garden into a library. They are gathering in precarious towers all over the Convento. Books are his passion. He is never happier than when he is surrounded by books. To him they are like pets, to be stroked and caressed and cared for.' She opened a small wooden door that led into an exquisite bedroom. 'This is your room, Celestria. Your father always stayed here.'

Celestria followed her inside and was at once enchanted by the scent of lilies that filled the room. There was a four-poster brass bed covered in brightly woven textile throws of pinks and greens and yellows. The stone floor was covered with a rug, and at the other end of the room there was a large iron bath and a window that looked down to the courtyard.

'I've never been so happy to see a bed!' she exclaimed happily. 'It's beautiful!'

'Your father liked it, too,' Federica replied quietly. A shadow passed rapidly across her face. She gave Celestria a long hard look before inhaling through her nose, as if dismissing the thought that had just popped into her head. 'Just to let you know, I have one other guest here at the moment, Mrs Halifax. She's English, too. A painter. A charming woman. I

think you'll like her. She's very eccentric. She wears a different pair of shoes every day, and they're very . . . colourful.'
She smiled in complicity and raised her eyebrows. 'I don't
know what to make of her, but I like her enormously.'

'How many guests can you accommodate?' Celestria asked,
noticing that someone had already brought her bag upstairs
and placed it in the room.

'Eleven, but at the moment, being the end of the season,
it's rather quiet. In the summertime we're always full. I have
another lady arriving next week. Poor Gaitano and Hamish;
they're going to be quite outnumbered by women. Not that
it matters. I don't see much of them as it is. Hamish, well . . .
what can I do?' She shrugged and forced a smile, but it was
clear that there was something that bothered her greatly about
her son-in-law. Her face tensed whenever she mentioned his
name, which, for some reason, she felt compelled to do
frequently. 'Let me show you to your room, Mrs
Waynebridge,' she suggested.

Mrs Waynebridge was dazzled by the rich colours and
smells of the place. The wine had softened her exhaustion,
but had also robbed her of her balance. She took Celestria's
arm, suddenly feeling very old, and hobbled down the corridor behind Federica.

Mrs Waynebridge's room was smaller, but, like Celestria's,
it was decorated with vibrant textiles and a large double bed.
The walls were bare but for a few wall hangings and three
small windows with shutters that gave out onto the courtyard
below. 'Your bathroom is down the corridor, first door on
your right. The door after that is Mrs Halifax's room. I hope
you won't mind sharing the bathroom with her.'

'Don't mind at all, Mrs Gancia,' Mrs Waynebridge replied,
suddenly longing to climb between the sheets. 'If you don't
mind, I think I'll retire to bed. For an old bird what's only been
as far as London, Maray – whatever, is a long way to come.'

Federica smiled sympathetically. 'Good night, Mrs Waynebridge. Sleep well. Breakfast will be in the dining room from eight o'clock, but feel free to come down whenever you are ready. Luigi will see that you are looked after.'

'I might never wake up,' she replied, trying in vain to smile. Her cheeks sagged like the water balloons Celestria and Harry used to make as young children. 'You sleep well, too, Celestria. I'm just next door if you need me.'

As Celestria and Federica hovered in the corridor, Celestria asked the question she had been burning to ask all evening.

'Does the name Salazar mean anything to you?'

Federica nodded. 'Of course. Francesco Salazar is a rather pompous lawyer here in Marelatte.'

'I've been trying to tidy up my father's affairs. I have correspondence from him and various things that I need to clear up. I thought perhaps I could do that while I am here.'

Federica frowned, and, for a moment, a shadow of suspicion darkened her face. 'Of course,' she replied with a shrug. 'I will get Nuzzo to accompany you.'

'Monday would be good,' Celestria replied, wishing they hadn't arrived on a Friday. What on earth were they going to do all weekend? As charming as it was here, she didn't want to stay any longer than was necessary. 'You didn't by any chance meet a Hungarian called Countess Valonya, did you?'

Federica shook her head. 'I'm afraid not. I would remember a name like that.' She narrowed her eyes. 'Are you looking for anyone else?'

Celestria shrugged. 'One never can tell.' She gave a little sniff and stepped into her bedroom, flopping onto the bed with a yawn.

'Of course. If you need my help I will be happy to do all I can. You only have to ask. *Va bene,* I hope you sleep well.' Federica remained in the doorway, her mouth open as if about to say something else. Celestria turned and looked inquiringly, but the older woman closed her eyes and shook her head with an apologetic smile. *'Niente,'* she said, turning away. 'See you in the morning.'

'Good night,' Celestria replied, getting up to close the door. She knew that the wine, the soup, and the fresh sea air had prepared her for a long night's sleep.

Chapter 18

Celestria awoke to the bright Italian sun streaming in through the two small square windows behind her bed and the sonorous sound of bells from the church next door calling the people to worship. The song of birds filled the air, and a dog barked outside in the road. She inhaled, smelling the scents of pine and rosemary that were carried on the breeze, and the lingering bouquet of lilies. She stretched contentedly and gazed around her. In the light of day the room looked even prettier. The bold colours of the textile throws mixed with the muted reds and browns of the rugs gave the room warmth. Federica had clearly chosen the items out of love and not to match some rigid colour scheme. She knew her father would have liked it as much as she did. She rolled onto her side and considered him. Alone in the room that only she shared with him, she allowed herself to miss him. Not in the way she had missed him in England, avoiding the pain and considering only the practicalities and inconveniences of his death, but the sadness of his absence. The fact that she would never see him again.

She closed her eyes and pictured him. He must have lain here in his pyjamas, breathing the same scents, listening to the same sounds, escaping the world as she was. Had he come here when his business had collapsed to hide from the reality of not having a job to go to? Had he perhaps dreamed of escaping forever? If he loved it so much, why seek death? Why such finality when there was so much to live for? These thoughts strengthened her resolve, and she climbed out of bed and dressed in a pair of white slacks and a pale blue shirt, a silk Hermès scarf around her neck. She brushed her long blonde hair off her face so that it fell in waves over her shoulders.

Downstairs Federica's dogs rushed at her excitedly. A couple of maids smiled as they wandered past with clean towels and sheets. They were small, with brown faces and glossy black hair cascading down their backs. Clearly impressed, they broke into chatter the moment they passed her. Waynie was already eating breakfast in the dining room, at the long refectory table that was laid out with bread, prosciutto, and fruit.

'Good morning, Celestria,' she said brightly. 'I don't think I've ever slept so well in all me life. That bed beats the old one Alfie bought when we moved into Anselm Road. He got it off Pete Duff what owned a warehouse in Harrogate, full of God knows what junk, in exchange for a bit of plumbing. Alfie never paid for nowt if he could help it. Even me ring.' She looked down at it and smiled. 'Makes no difference to me. It's the thought what counts.' Celestria wandered past the sideboard, gazing hungrily at all the pomegranates and figs piled high in wooden bowls.

'I do like it here, Waynie,' she said emphatically, helping herself to a pomegranate.

Waynie smiled. 'You know, I never expected to. I was very nervous, to tell the truth. But there's something magic here.' She lowered her voice, glancing about the room suspiciously, and leaned forward. 'Can you smell the lilies? I haven't seen a single lily since I arrived. That's magic.' She straightened up and spoke normally again. 'I can't put me finger on it, but I feel years younger already. Don't the bells sound lovely? Not at all like bells in England. I should have slept like the dead, but I woke with excitement in me belly. Something extraordinary is going to happen, I can feel it.'

'Is there a bird to corroborate this feeling?' Celestria teased, sitting down.

'Now you're pulling me leg, and that's not wise. It's old and might come off!'

They both turned as a tall, silver-haired man strode in, accompanied by a younger man who grinned toothily. 'Welcome,' said the older one. 'My name is Gaitano; I'm Freddie's husband.' Like his wife, he spoke good English, but his accent was more pronounced.

Celestria extended her hand, which he took in his as he bowed again, almost bringing her hand to his lips, his small brown eyes settling on her warmly from behind a pair of fine silver glasses. Her heart lurched with longing; the only other man to have ever greeted her like that was her father. In a sudden cascade of memories she recalled that day on the beach when he had gone out in his boat with Harry and their small cousins; he had kissed her hand then. She could still remember the affectionate twinkle in his eyes as he had offered her a place in his boat. She pushed the painful image from her mind and concentrated on Gaitano. His face was noble, with a straight Roman nose, chiselled jaw, and high cheekbones, still a devastatingly handsome man.

'And this is Luigi, the most talented cook in Puglia. Luigi speaks no English,' he added, patting the young man's back affectionately. 'But food is a language common to us all, wouldn't you agree?'

'Naturally!' Celestria nodded, liking Gaitano already. 'This is Mrs Waynebridge,' she added. 'Neither of us speaks Italian, but we both like our food!'

Gaitano bowed, but Mrs Waynebridge was too nervous to extend her hand. She felt it wasn't her place. She thrust it into her lap, where it remained until the danger had passed.

'Ah, Mrs Halifax,' said Gaitano as a plump elderly woman walked into the dining room, aided by a walking stick that rang with the tinkling of tiny bells. She had a jolly, round face, seamed with laughter lines and lines of sadness as her full and active life had impressed itself in all its diversity onto her peachy pink skin. Celestria remembered Federica's comments about her guest's shoes and slid her eyes down the crushed velvet housecoat to her feet. They did not disappoint, neatly clad in green velvet slippers decorated at the toes with furry gold balls.

'Good morning, young man,' she said to Gaitano in a voice that was thick and smoky. 'Goodness, we have company. How very nice. Are you American?' Celestria wondered how the old woman had deduced that just by looking at her. Mrs Halifax explained. 'I heard you talking outside my room last night.'

'Oh,' Celestria replied. 'Well, my mother's American but my father's ... He was English.' Mrs Halifax noticed the hasty change of tense and discreetly moved on.

'Well, it's lovely to have the company of fellow countrymen.'

'This is Mrs Waynebridge,' Celestria added.

'Pleased to meet you,' said Mrs Waynebridge, putting down her teacup and allowing her right hand to slide up from her knee to shake Mrs Halifax's.

'Oh, you must be from Yorkshire,' said Mrs Halifax, resting her stick against the table and taking the chair that Gaitano pulled out for her. 'I have spent some wonderful times up north, near Skipton. Do you know Skipton? It has a glorious old castle. The Fattorini family are dear friends of mine, you know.' Mrs Waynebridge nodded. She knew the castle, it was famous, but she had never been there, and, as for the Fattorini family, she would never have presumed to make their acquaintance. 'Salt of the earth,' Mrs Halifax continued.

'They speak their minds with a good dollop of warmth and humour.' She shook her head, sending the little cluster of purple feathers she had pinned in her hair into a floating dance. 'I'd love a cup of coffee, Luigi,' she said. 'And an egg. Could I trouble you for an egg? Four and a half minutes and a piece of toast, lightly browned, not burned. I do hate it when they burn the toast, don't you?'

Luigi, who understood her request only because it was what she had ordered every morning for the last month, went into the kitchen, leaving Gaitano alone with the women.

'If there is anything you want, Luigi will be happy to oblige, and Nuzzo will take you anywhere you wish.' He directed his speech to Celestria, but it was Mrs Waynebridge who blushed at the mention of Nuzzo's name. 'He can be your personal guide.'

'That would be very kind. We'd like to take a look around, wouldn't we, Waynie?' Mrs Waynebridge nodded enthusiastically.

'He will be back at midday. I have had to send him into Castellino on an errand. Might I suggest a ride up the coast and a picnic lunch on the beach?'

'Sounds just like Cornwall,' she replied. 'We'll be waiting in the courtyard at twelve.'

'Good. Luigi will prepare something to eat. Now I shall leave you to get to know one another,' he said, bowing again. His face twitched with an ironic smile. The three women must have seemed to him a rather incongruous group.

Luigi brought Mrs Halifax her egg and a small cup of black coffee, the smell of which was too much for Celestria to resist. 'I don't usually like coffee, but that smells delicious!' she said, leaning across the table to breathe it in.

'They grind it fresh, you see. They don't make it so well anywhere else in the world, I assure you. Why don't you try it with hot milk?' Mrs Halifax suggested. 'It's like hot chocolate.'

'That's a good idea, I shall. Luigi?' When Luigi returned, Celestria pointed at Mrs Halifax's coffee, then at the jug of milk. 'Lots of milk, *mucho mucho*,' she said, tossing him an enchanting smile. As she turned her charm on him, his ears turned red and his stomach flipped over.

'*Si signora, molto latte*,' he replied enthusiastically. He returned to the kitchen with the intention of making her the best *caffé latte* ever made.

'Have you been here before, Mrs Halifax?'

'Yes, every summer for the last four years. I met Freddie and Gaitano when I was staying near Pisa about six years ago. They used to live in Tuscany, you see. Then they discovered this wonderful place and bought it. It's been a labour of love putting it back together again. It was a ruin. Recently things have gotten difficult, and they've had to open it to paying guests.' She lowered her voice. 'With all due respect to nice people like you, I don't think it's been easy for them. They won't ever leave it, though. Too many memories. That's another story, and it's not my place to tell it.' She sighed heavily and straightened up. 'I like to paint, you see. I find a place I like and return every year, like a swallow, I suppose. I used to travel with a couple of friends, but then Debo passed away, and it was too miserable just being the two of us. Besides, Gertie and I fought all the time. It worked when we were three – Debo was a good buffer – but then just being two, I don't know, it wasn't the same. I've tried many different places, but after Maurilliac in France, nothing was as lovely or as special until I found the Convento. Freddie and Gaitano are like family to me now.'

'Did you live in France?' Celestria asked.

'No. We painted there after the war, at a gorgeous château that had been converted into a hotel. England was so grey and miserable. France was beautiful. We returned the following year, but it had changed.' She looked sad, as if her jolly face had suddenly melted, and took a sip of coffee. 'I'm a silly old woman with too much attachment to the past. It's a long story, and one evening I might tell you if I feel up to it.'

'I'd like that,' said Celestria softly.

'So this is your first time here?' Mrs Halifax rallied.

'Yes.'

'There's so much to see. The church next door is lovely, and over the road is a rather magical city of the dead.'

'City of the dead?' said Mrs Waynebridge a little uneasily.

Mrs Halifax's eyes lit up. 'The cemetery. It's simply magical. Can't you smell the lilies? You must go and visit. It calms the soul. I have painted it a few times. It looks different depending on the light. I find it feeds something inside me and fills me up. I don't know, perhaps as I am old, it gives me a rather reassuring feeling about death.'

'Who's buried there?' Celestria asked, crinkling up her nose at the distasteful idea of death.

'Everyone from around here. It's a walled city of beautifully built white stone and marble crypts: big ones, small ones, communal ones, plain ones, ornate ones, all alive with candles and flowers. The extraordinary thing is that you won't find a single dead flower there. Not one. They take care of their deceased with love and devotion. That's the way it should be. Not like in England, where graves are left to rot.'

Celestria was immediately curious, though Mrs Waynebridge was more than a little spooked by the idea of a city of dead bodies. Graveyards were lonely, bleak places where she didn't like to linger if she could help it. A whole city of graves was another matter altogether. 'I think I'll let you go on your own,' she said to Celestria.

'Don't be silly, Waynie. You're coming with me whether

you like it or not. It's important for you to soak up the whole experience.'

'Don't imagine it's anything like English graveyards, Mrs Waynebridge,' interjected Mrs Halifax. 'It's nothing of the sort. You'll see. It's magical.' She smacked her lips. 'Simply magical!'

After breakfast, Mrs Halifax hobbled off to paint, leaving Celestria and her companion to the wonders of the city of the dead. They stepped out of the building into the dazzling sunshine. Celestria, already hot, untied her scarf and threaded it through the belt loops of her slacks, tying it at the side. She slipped on a pair of sunglasses and breathed in the scent of the sea, which she could now see sparkling in the distance behind the cluster of little houses that had been built outside the walls of the city of the dead. Mrs Waynebridge put on a white hat and withdrew a handkerchief from her sleeve to dab the sweat that had already begun to seep through her face powder and gather in little drops on her nose. All was quiet; the people of Marelatte were attending Mass in the little church attached to the Convento.

The road was empty, leading out of the town into the wild, rocky countryside of little brick walls and sheep. They passed a pack of stray dogs, tails high, noses to the ground, ribs showing through their thin coats. The city of the dead rose up before them, its walls warmed to a pale yellow in the morning sunshine. The gates were large and imposing, open to people and dogs alike, but there seemed to be no one there. Celestria and Mrs Waynebridge wandered inside in silence. They both stopped to gaze at the long paved walk-ways that ran between the rows of little mausoleums built out of stone that contained the remains of the once living. 'Come on,' Celestria hissed, afraid of breaking the tranquillity. The smell of lilies, warm wax, and pine was intoxicating. Mrs Waynebridge followed nervously, fearful of intruding.

Celestria walked on, her light walk almost a skip. In the centre was a grassy square of tall pine trees, their branches full of twittering birds, their deep green needles bristling in the breeze. The sun filtered through them, throwing a kaleidoscope of dazzling sunspots onto the neatly cut grass below. 'You see,' said Celestria with a laugh. 'It's not frightening at all. In fact, it's beautiful. When I die, I'd be happy to rest in a place like this.' She sighed. 'It's so serene and heavenly, don't you think?'

'It's still eerie to think that all them houses are full of dead people,' said Mrs Waynebridge with a shiver.

'Oh, I think there's something rather romantic about it. Let's take a look inside one of them.'

'I don't think we should,' Mrs Waynebridge protested. 'They don't belong to us.'

'I don't imagine anyone would mind. Besides, the dead aren't in any position to complain.'

Celestria disappeared up some steps into a communal crypt. Row upon row of little plaques marked the graves, and each grave was decorated with a vase full of fresh flowers. They covered both walls right up to the ceiling. Entire families were buried alongside one another. When Mrs Waynebridge entered, she found Celestria running her hand over the words thoughtfully. 'Look, here's a whole cluster of a family called Salvatore.' Beside each name there was a small photograph. 'These were all old people. Rather nice to live a long life and then end up here. I don't think I'd like to see a young person. Much too close to home.' At the end of the crypt stood a small altar covered in candles, their flames flickering gently amid the heavy aroma of flowers. She thought of her father, dead like these old people. Unlike them, he had had a good many more years ahead of him. 'I wonder if we shall ever have a body to bury. Somewhere we can come and remember him. I can't imagine him lying in a coffin, lifeless.' She turned to Mrs Waynebridge, her voice a whisper. 'I can't imagine him dead, you see.'

Mrs Waynebridge wrung her hands anxiously. 'Let's get out. There's too much death here. Gives me the willies,' she said in a wavering voice.

Celestria followed her into the sunshine. As they wandered back Celestria noticed a crypt that stood out from the rest. It was up a few steps, a little apart, and looked as if it had been built recently – the stone was whiter and newer than the others. It wasn't that it was bigger, just that it some-how overshadowed the place where it stood. It was plain but for the initials N.MCC. engraved into the marble above the door. Without saying a word Celestria felt herself drawn inside.

Within, two candles burned on a small altar, beside which a photograph stood in a silver frame dominated by an enor-mous vase of white lilies, their scent more pronounced than ever. Celestria moved to take a closer look. The photograph was of a young woman. Her face was radiant and smiling and breathtakingly beautiful, set against the deep blue sky, as if she was already in heaven, smiling down with love. Her hair was rich brown, blowing in the wind, the expression in her eyes light and carefree. Celestria turned to the stone tomb that contained her coffin. It was made out of marble and carved with a relief of a vine heavy with grapes. She wondered who the girl was and how she had died, suddenly saddened by the loss of such a young and vibrant life.

Without warning, a shadow fell across the doorway. She turned with a start to see the tall, arresting figure of a man. His face was grey with fury. He leaned on a stick, but he wasn't old. His hair was fair and unruly and much longer than was fashionable. He shouted at her in Italian, his voice deep and granular like the growl of a bear. He stepped aside so that she could leave. 'I'm sorry, I was just curious,' she apologized hastily, her hand immediately shooting up to her chest in mortification. 'I didn't mean to intrude.'

'Bloody American!' He switched to English. 'You're all the same. Why can't you mind your own business?' Celestria had never been spoken to in such a rude manner. She didn't know how to respond. She wasn't equipped to deal with this sort of person. He stared at her, his pale green eyes ablaze with indignation. She felt her face throb with embarrassment, and, to her shame, her eyes began to water. Suddenly, the man seemed to check himself. His fury abated, and he said quietly, gesturing to the door, 'Just leave.'

Celestria pushed past him. He was very tall, well over six feet, and broad shouldered so that as she swept past he dwarfed her. Mrs Waynebridge waited for her outside, pale with shock. The city of the dead spooked her enough as it was, without some scruffy, unshaven demon rising up out of nowhere to shout at them. Celestria took her arm and hurried away. She felt him watching her, his eyes burning holes into her pale blue blouse. She waited until they were far away before she risked a glance back. To her horror, he was still standing there, his face grim, his gaze fixed upon her. Celestria turned away and hurried on.

'Good God, the rudeness of that man!' Mrs Waynebridge exclaimed when they were outside the gates. She took off her hat and fanned her hot face with it. 'I'm all shaken up like a jug of cream.'

'He was horrible,' Celestria agreed. 'I hope we don't bump into him again.' Her legs were trembling. She wiped her eyes with her hand. 'How dare he speak to me like that? He's certainly no gentleman. I thought Italian men were meant to be charming.'

'He's no more Italian than I am,' said Mrs Waynebridge with a snort.

'Where's he from, then?'

'Scotland.'

'He's Scottish?'

'I'd recognize that accent anywhere, I would.'

'I was too shocked to notice.'

'What's a Scotsman doing down here, I ask myself?'

'Probably looking after those sheep we saw yesterday.'

'I didn't even see him coming.'

'I was only admiring the crypt.' Celestria's voice grew quiet. 'She was beautiful.'

'A young woman, was she?'

'Yes, his daughter, perhaps. I was intruding. You were right, Waynie, I shouldn't have gone in there. It was none of my business. Oh, Lord, I've made a fool of myself.'

'You're trembling.'

'I'm shaken up like a jug of cream, too,' she replied, relieved to reach the safety of the Convento.

'You haven't made a fool of yourself, love,' said Mrs Waynebridge reassuringly, pulling a sympathetic face. 'You won't be seeing him again. And if you do, just walk on t'other side of road. That's what I do to them I don't wish to speak to.'

Celestria fell through the door with great relief. The dogs rushed up to greet her, and she crouched down to press her face into their fur to hide her tears. Getting up, she glanced at her watch. It was half past eleven. 'Nuzzo will be here shortly. I'm going to go upstairs to freshen up.' She fled before Mrs Waynebridge could see her crying.

Celestria closed her bedroom door behind her and leaned back against it for a moment. She shut her eyes and took a deep breath. 'Oh, Lord!' she groaned, her limbs still quivering from her encounter. 'What am I going to do?' She rubbed her face with her hand, then began to chew on the skin around her thumbnail in agitation. She walked over to the window and looked out, deep in thought. From there she could see into the courtyard below and on to the bell tower of the little church next door. She couldn't see the city of the dead, although it rested just beyond, but she could smell the lilies from that crypt as if they meant only to mock her.

She had never, in all her life, been spoken to in such a rude manner. She felt humiliated, angry, and, to her horror, a little afraid. She hoped to God she never laid eyes on that man again. *Let's get the job done and go home,* she thought to herself. *I don't want to be here a moment longer than I have to.*

Chapter 19

Half an hour later she stepped into the courtyard, feeling a great deal better, and found Mrs Waynebridge talking to Nuzzo. He was dressed in a smart black suit with a waistcoat and pressed white shirt, and held his beret in his hands, leaving his thin grey hair to stick up in curly tufts. He gave a roguish smile, exposing large gaps between rather small teeth, raised his round, tourmaline eyes to Celestria, and bowed politely. *'Buon giorno, signorina,'* he said in a voice as soft as demerara sugar. Mrs Waynebridge was clearly taken with him, for the apples of her cheeks blushed with the hue of a young girl discovering love for the first time.

'Good morning, Nuzzo,' Celestria replied, wondering how Mrs Waynebridge had managed to communicate with him despite his lack of English. He seemed to read her thoughts.

'Io parlo leetle English,' he replied, illustrating with his forefinger and thumb, which he held up to his eye like a pair of tweezers.

'A little is better than nothing,' Celestria said briskly. 'Are you ready, Waynie?'

The older woman nodded, clutching her handbag. 'As ready as I'll ever be,' she said breathlessly, following Nuzzo outside into the sunshine.

Celestria closed the heavy wooden door behind them with a loud clank. Once outside, she cast a quick glance across the dirt road to where the city of the dead stood in stillness and serenity, half hoping, half fearing, that the rude Scotsman would suddenly stride out. Nuzzo waited beneath the avenue of pine trees that lined the road leading into town.

Nuzzo helped them into the cart with great gallantry, as if he were an old-fashioned knight. Mrs Waynebridge gave her hand willingly, and a little feebly, Celestria thought, in order to prolong the moment. Celestria stepped up swiftly. Nuzzo, however, gave her minimal attention; he had eyes only for Mrs Waynebridge. Once they were settled, he withdrew a paper bag from inside his jacket. '*Mele,*' he said, revealing two shiny red apples.

'How thoughtful,' sighed Mrs Waynebridge, taking one and handing the other to Celestria.

'I thought you mistrusted Italian men,' Celestria hissed.

'I do,' she replied, turning the apple around in her fingers. 'But I'm enjoying the fuss. I haven't received the attentions of a man for, God knows, fifty years. Alfie gave up once he'd won me. That's what men are like. It's all in the chase.'

Cypress trees rose up to a clear blue sky, where a few large-winged birds floated on the air above the cliffs. The sea undulated gently, waves glittering like sequins in the sunshine. After a while little bells rang out across the fields where sheep grazed, dropping their white heads to chew on the rough grasses and herbs that thrived there. Mrs Waynebridge's heart grew light with pleasure as the new sights filled her spirit with the taste of adventure. She liked the heat, she liked the smells of thyme and rosemary that flourished among the rocks, and she liked the sight of Nuzzo as he turned and smiled at her with tenderness.

Celestria thought of her father and what he'd think of her travelling so far to seek vengeance for his death. She hoped he would be proud. Even if she found nothing, at least she had tried.

Out in the fresh air that swept in off the sea, Celestria shook her head and allowed the breeze to blow through her hair, leaving a faint trace of pine. The sun shone warmly on her skin, and the horizon stretched as far as she could see, stirring within her something sweet and melancholy. A group of grubby children mucked about among the rocks, waving to Nuzzo as they passed, and a skinny mongrel chased the cart, snapping at the wheels playfully. A few other horses and carts trotted by, and Nuzzo stopped for a chat, laughing heartily with an elderly man whose horse pulled a large load of timber destined for Gaitano's new library.

Finally, Nuzzo drew up alongside a path that led down to a secluded cove. The path was well worn by the footprints of children who liked to play there after school. Today it was quiet. Nestled against the cliffs, it lay in tranquillity like a secret bay. As they stepped onto the stones a trio of white birds flapped their wings and scattered into the sky, leaving to the waves the remains of the seaweed they had been pecking at. 'Isn't this charming,' said Mrs Waynebridge, taking off her hat and patting her hair to check it was still in place.

'I should have brought my bathing suit,' Celestria replied. 'I can't strip off here in front of our friend, can I?' Nuzzo didn't understand. He found a spot in the shade and put down the picnic basket Luigi had prepared for them. Unfolding a rug, he gestured to Mrs Waynebridge.

'Thank you,' she said, smiling.

'*Grazie,*' said Nuzzo, nodding at her with encouragement. She shifted her eyes to Celestria, but she was busy taking off her shoes to walk in the waves.

'*Grazie,*' Mrs Waynebridge repeated.

'*Brava!*' enthused Nuzzo, nodding excitedly. '*Grazie.*'

'Thank you,' said Waynie with a chuckle.

'Sank oo,' said Nuzzo.

'No, no. Thank you,' Mrs Waynebridge repeated, emphasizing the 'th.' 'Th . . . th . . . thank you.' Nuzzo copied her, placing his tongue against his top teeth.

'Thank you,' he said, pleased with himself.

'Very good,' she exclaimed, clapping her hands. Nuzzo opened the basket and pulled out a bottle of wine and two glasses.

'Oh, how very nice,' said Mrs Waynebridge in surprise.

'*Vino,*' he said, holding out the bottle. '*Vino.*'

'*Vino,*' Mrs Waynebridge replied. '*Grazie.*'

'*Bravissima!*' he said with such exuberance that Mrs Waynebridge found herself roaring with laughter. He poured two glasses and gave one to Mrs Waynebridge.

'*La signorina?*' he asked, looking over to Celestria, who was now in the water, holding up her trousers so they didn't get wet.

'Leave her,' Mrs Waynebridge suggested, touching his arm. He looked down at her fingers on his arm and grinned. Mrs Waynebridge pulled her hand away, appalled at her own forwardness. She took a hasty sip of wine.

'It's very good. Go on, have some. *Vino,* you.'

'*Io?*'

'Yes, you. It's very good.' She took another sip. Nuzzo sat down beside her and brought the wine to his lips.

'Good,' he said.

'Good,' she repeated.

'*Buono,*' he added.

'*Buono,*' she repeated.

'*Lei è brava e buona,*' he said, his shiny eyes twinkling at her, knowing she wouldn't understand. '*E bella,*' he added under his breath. '*Buona e bella.*'

'The water's cold!' Celestria called out, smiling broadly. 'But it's lovely.'

'Come and have something to eat,' Mrs Waynebridge shouted back.

'I'm not hungry,' she replied. 'Besides, I'm too excited to eat.'

'Excited about what?'

Celestria sighed. 'I don't know. I feel excited, and I don't know why.' Her toes tingled, her hair danced on the breeze, and, to her surprise, she felt her heart inflate with happiness. 'This place is just adorable. I want it to belong to me. My own special bay.'

'I think, love, this is one thing your grandfather can't buy you.'

Celestria turned around and faced out to sea. How different the water was from the navy water of Cornwall. She closed her eyes and let the sun warm her cheeks. How far she was from England, her mother, Uncle Archie and Aunt Julia, Uncle Milton and Aunt Penelope, her grandmother and the boys, David, Lotty, and Melissa – she was hundreds of miles from home. Down on that secluded bay, so removed from the grim events that had brought her here, she was overcome by a completely new and exhilarating feeling. She felt free. She sensed her father right here with her. He had belonged in Marelatte. Whatever it was that had drawn him here was now drawing her, too.

'I think we should eat,' said Mrs Waynebridge to Nuzzo, feeling her stomach twisting with hunger. 'It's just you and me.' She rested her eyes on his irregular features and smiled with pleasure. 'And I couldn't be happier with the company.'

They arrived back at the Convento at teatime. Mrs Waynebridge went upstairs to tidy herself, the sea wind having messed up her hair. Celestria, who hadn't eaten lunch, was now ravenous. She made her way across the courtyard, past sleeping dogs, through the kitchen garden, where the young family of black cats snoozed among pots of sage and basil, into the kitchen. Luigi was washing up. She could smell the risotto. 'Is there any left?' she inquired, lifting the lid off the saucepan. 'Lord, it smells good!'

'*Lei vuole mangiare?*' he asked, holding out a bowl.

'Lovely,' she exclaimed.

'*La Signora Halifax mangia a tavola,*' he continued, gesticulating through to the dining room. Celestria understood the word Halifax and skipped through.

'Ah, Mrs Halifax. You're eating late, too!'

'I was out painting and completely forgot the time,' she said. 'I think I've burned my nose. It feels awfully sore.' She rubbed it self-consciously.

'It is a little red. I burned my cheeks; they're smarting. I don't care, though,' she said, sitting down. 'Mama would scold me for ruining my skin. She thinks brown skin is very common and ugly.'

'She's wrong. It suits you,' Mrs Halifax replied. 'You'd suit anything, dear. You're blessed with a lovely face, whatever the colour of your skin.'

Luigi brought her a bowl of risotto and some bread. When he offered her wine, she took it without hesitation.

'Have you had a pleasant morning?' Mrs Halifax asked, watching Celestria take a forkful of risotto, closing her eyes in pleasure.

'Actually, I've had the most enchanting day, in spite of a shocking start.'

'A shocking start? My dear, that doesn't sound good.'

'You know you said that I should visit the city of the dead?'

'Isn't it marvellous!'

'It's beautiful. In fact, Waynie and I were so moved we even went into one or two of the crypts.'

'I bet you didn't find a single withered flower in the entire place.'

'No, but I did find the rudest man in Italy.'

Mrs Halifax raised her eyebrows in surprise. 'Goodness, he must have been very rude indeed; the Italians are an outspoken lot. Who was he?'

'I don't know. He was so unpleasant, I didn't introduce myself.' It felt exciting to talk about him. Perhaps Mrs Halifax would shed some light on his identity. 'I was simply admiring the beautiful photograph on the little altar when he shouted at me, bellowing from the doorway like a monster.' Mrs Halifax put down her fork and tried to interrupt, but Celestria ignored her. 'I imagine the girl was his daughter. He was Scottish. What a Scotsman is doing down here, I can't imagine. Perhaps it's the sheep. There are sheep in Scotland, aren't there? I have to say, I have never been so insulted in all my life. He hadn't even bothered to brush his hair. He was a sight.'

Before Mrs Halifax could utter a single word in reply, they both became aware of the man who now filled the archway that led through to the little sitting room with his dark, unruly presence.

Celestria dropped her fork into her risotto and gasped. 'Oh, Lord!' she exclaimed. 'It's you!'

He strode over and extended his hand. The sleeves of his white shirt were rolled up, revealing brown, muscular arms covered in light brown hair.

'My name is Hamish McCloud,' he said, unsmiling. 'I can't say it's a pleasure to make your acquaintance.'

Chapter 20

Celestria was at a loss for words. As if by remote control she introduced herself and allowed him to take her hand. The sensation of his skin against hers caused her stomach to flip. She returned his stare with defiance, but her entrails turned to jelly.

Finally he spoke, his Scottish accent soft and smoky. 'I should apologize for shouting at you, but in my defence, you were trespassing. The woman in the photograph was my wife. As for sheep, I have little to do with them unless they are on my plate, medium rare, with a little mint sauce and red currant jelly. I don't brush my hair very often; I don't see the point. I'm an artist, not an office clerk. If you don't like it, don't look at it. I'm sure we can avoid each other if we try. I hope I have answered all your questions. If I see you again, I will endeavour not to shout.'

Celestria didn't know whether or not he was joking. His expression was deadly serious. How could she have known that he was next door, listening to her every word? When she didn't reply, he turned on his heel and left through the kitchen, disappearing out into the gardens. Celestria felt as if she had been hit by a tornado.

Mrs Halifax picked up her fork and continued to eat the risotto. 'Well, my dear,' she said casually, 'I tried to warn you, but you did plough on.'

Celestria's appetite had disappeared. 'What's he doing here?'

'He's Freddie and Gaitano's son-in-law.'

'Ah,' said Celestria. It all made sense. 'He was married to their daughter.'

'Natalia. She died three years ago. It was a terrible tragedy. She fell from the cliff. Killed instantly.'

'My intrusion was unforgivable.'

'Not at all,' said Mrs Halifax kindly. 'The city of the dead is open to everyone. You are free to wander wherever you desire as long as you treat the place with respect. I can't imagine they'd welcome a band of noisy children kicking footballs, but you and Mrs Waynebridge weren't causing any trouble. No, I'm afraid Hamish has been deeply troubled ever since his wife fell from that cliff. He used to be the funniest man you could ever meet. He had a wonderfully infectious sense of humour and a lightness of spirit that was a joy to be around. He's a gifted pianist and painter, but I don't think he's painted much since Natalia died. Dark scenes, I fear. A pity, when he's surrounded by such beauty.' She watched Celestria for a moment. 'Don't worry, his bark is worse than his bite. He's just uncomfortable with himself, that's all. Death is a hard thing to get over. He must feel abandoned and alone. He loved her so very much.' She lowered her eyes and finished the last of the risotto. 'My little boy died of polio. I've never got over it. Somehow the years pass, we look and sound older, but inside we're still the same, with the same hearts. I miss him as much now as I did that first, terrible year. I understand poor Hamish. But he will move on, eventually. Of course, he doesn't know that, does he? We all have to move on in the end. Life is for living, and the moment we all meet up in the next world will come soon enough.'

'I'm sorry about your son.'

'He was a dear little boy.'

'What happened to Hamish's leg?'

'He fell off his horse, hunting. It was years ago, when he was in his twenties. It's given him trouble ever since. Some days are better than others. He doesn't always need that stick.' She gave Celestria a conspiratorial look. 'He's attractive, though, isn't he?'

'He's rude,' Celestria corrected petulantly.

'Yes, he is, but he can be so very charming.'

'I don't think I want to know.'

Mrs Halifax smiled into her wineglass.

Federica was in the small stone folly that was to become Gaitano's library when Hamish's shadow fell across the floor. 'You gave me a fright,' she said, forcing a smile. She knew why he was so cross and felt guilty for not having warned him.

'What is she doing here?'

'You mean Celestria?'

'Celestria Montague. What the devil is she doing in Puglia?' Gaitano took a tape measure to the wall.

'Hold the other end,' he instructed his wife, ignoring Hamish's indignant tone. If there was one thing Gaitano hated, it was confrontation. His son-in-law had been like a bear with a thorn in his foot even before Natalia had died. Gaitano had grown used to rising above it.

'I don't know.' Federica shrugged, taking the tape measure and holding it against the right-hand wall. 'Why, have you just met her?'

'She waltzed into Natalia's tomb like the ghastly American tourist that she is. Without consideration.'

'It's a beautiful tomb. You should be proud of it.'

'That's not the point. She wasn't there to admire it.'

'I suppose you were rude.' She handed the tape to her husband while he jotted the measurements down on a notepad.

'She's Robert Montague's daughter,' he growled. 'I hated the man.'

Federica looked nervously at her husband. 'You had no reason to hate him,' she said, walking out into the sunshine.

Hamish followed her. 'No, the women in my family threw themselves into his web with joyous abandon. Why should I hate him? I should have loved him, too?'

'You never knew him!' Federica hissed, glancing shiftily into the folly.

'I missed nothing.'

'You know why? Because your heart is closed, Hamish. Do you think that is what Natalia would want? You guarding her tomb like a dog, biting anyone who dares go near? Life is passing you by. She's gone. Either you live or simply exist, but the fact will remain: Natalia is dead, and you can't bring her back. None of us can. You think I live with my heart full of joy? No, my child is dead. I'll never hold her again. I'll never smell the orange blossom in her hair. I'll never touch her skin and feel that unique sense of being a part of another human being. I carried her in my belly, and I nurtured her into womanhood. I saw the happiness you brought to each other, and I saw your future together cut short. Do you think I don't regret her death every day? But I don't blame you. I resent your self-pity and your hatred. If Natalia is watching you, she will lament the loss of the man she fell in love with and married. Sometimes I don't recognize you, Hamish, and that hurts, because you are the part of my daughter she left behind. No, I don't live with my heart full of joy, but I try to be happy as a woman who has lost a limb tries to be happy. I suggest you do the same because your fury changes nothing.'

'You don't understand,' he said quietly, shaking his shaggy head.

'I'm tired of trying.'

'This isn't about Natalia. It's about Robert Montague.'

'Why don't you just talk to Celestria? You might find you like her.'

'You know nothing, Freddie. You see her through the same pair of rose-tinted glasses as you see her father.'

She stared at him suddenly, biting her bottom lip. 'I think you'll find she's a very sweet girl,' she said quickly.

'I know the type, and I don't like it at all.'

Federica sighed. 'Oh, what is the point? Your heart is so full of hatred. I just don't understand you any more.'

Hamish hesitated a moment, during which time they glared at each other. Finally he spoke, and his voice was raw and sad. 'I'm unable to enlighten you,' he replied. Leaning heavily on his stick, he began to walk away.

'I won't have you being rude to her, Hamish,' Federica called after him. 'And don't forget, Gaitano needs you to help with the library.'

'What was all that about?' Gaitano emerged into the light, squinting behind his glasses.

Federica shook her head. 'That boy!'

'He's a man,' corrected Gaitano.

'But he behaves like a boy.'

Gaitano put his hand on his wife's shoulder. 'He's young. He'll fall in love again and look back on Natalia's death with more perspective.'

'Who'll want him, for God's sake?'

Gaitano chuckled and raised his eyebrows. 'There's someone out there, trust me.'

She swung around to face him. 'If you're thinking Celestria Montague, think again.'

'She's a beautiful girl, and a challenge for the strongest man, I should imagine.'

'She's the daughter of the man he hated.'

'Hated? Why anyone would hate a man like Robert Montague is beyond me.'

'Me, too,' Federica agreed quietly, walking back into the folly. Gaitano remained, watching his son-in-law's hunched figure disappear through the little gate, into the road where the city of the dead lay peacefully overlooking the sea, and scratched his head. It was all very baffling.

Celestria found Waynie in her bedroom. She had taken off her shoes and was stretched out on the bed, smiling contentedly.

'Waynie, you'll never guess who I've just met!'

Mrs Waynebridge sat up with a start. 'Good God, you made me jump out of me skin!'

'I'm sorry, Waynie, but I have to talk to you.'

Mrs Waynebridge patted the bed. 'You'd better sit down, then.'

Celestria sank down beside her. 'You'll never believe it. That horrid man who shouted at me in the cemetery is none other than Federica and Gaitano's son-in-law, Hamish.'

Mrs Waynebridge gasped. 'Well, I never!'

'I was sitting at the dining table with Mrs Halifax, telling her all about our unpleasant encounter this morning, when who should emerge from the sitting room but the very man I'm telling her about. He had heard every word.'

'Oh, dear. He didn't shout at you again? Not with Mrs Halifax sat beside you, surely?'

'No, but he wasn't very pleased. I hadn't spared a single detail of his rudeness. He extended his hand and introduced himself coldly. He told me that Natalia was his wife and that if he sees me again he'll endeavour not to shout. I don't think he was joking.'

'He should have apologized at the very least,' said Mrs Waynebridge indignantly. 'Where are his manners?'

'I don't think he's got any at all. He didn't say a word to Mrs Halifax.'

'How uncouth. You're both guests in his home.'

'Oh, I don't care, Waynie. I'll ignore him. I have no time at all for people like him. He's got no class, clearly. Mourning is no excuse for forgetting one's manners.'

'Quite right, my dear. It'll be his loss.'

Hamish knelt before his wife's tomb. He felt alone and lost. No one understood, not even Natalia. He considered Robert Montague. He remembered the handsome man in the panama hat and linen suit. His easy smile and laughing eyes. The attractive crow's-feet that dug deeply into tanned skin and that air of nonchalance that seemed to draw people to him like the smell of nectar drew butterflies. He remembered the way Federica giggled in his company, as if she were a young girl again, blushing and throwing him coy looks, playing with a stray wisp of grey hair between her fingers. He remembered Natalia watching him quietly, like a mouse mesmerized by a scheming cat. Curled up on the armchair in the garden, biting her thumbnail anxiously, gazing across from under thick eyelashes, her expression grave, barely blinking in case she missed something. How he had resented the man then – for stirring something dark and dangerous in his wife, something that would not have surfaced had the two never met. What did it matter now? Natalia was dead.

He closed his eyes and leaned against the hard stone surface of the tomb. He could still see Natalia's broken body at the bottom of the cliff, her mouth agape, blood trickling down her white cheek, her eyes wide open in surprise. Surprise at her sudden fall, or surprise at what she had become?

'Oh, Natalia,' he groaned, beating his brow on the stone. 'What did you do?'

That evening Federica sloped off, dressed in a simple black dress, carrying her bead rosary in her pocket. Gaitano was with Hamish, who was helping him build the library. It was still warm, the sun a fiery ball of amber, sliding down the sky, turning it a watery shade of blue. The dogs tried to follow her, but she left them inside, closing the door on them so they wouldn't bark in the road and chase the cats in the cemetery. The air was thick and pine-scented, the dew already settling into the grass and foliage to make it sparkle. She crept around to the church door and slipped inside.

She was greeted by a miasma of smoke from the candles and incense, through which Padre Pietro turned to see who had entered his church. He glanced at his watch. Confession wasn't until eight o'clock. When he saw it was Federica, he replaced the Bible on its stand and smiled at her. The smile she returned was uneasy. She stepped lightly up the nave and crossed herself in front of the altar, kneeling devoutly as she did so.

'What troubles you?' he asked.

'I need to confess,' she replied gravely.

'But you are early. Confession isn't until eight o'clock.' He was a man who liked the comfort of routine.

'I know, Father, but I am unable to come then. I have guests to entertain.'

'I see.'

'Please, Father. I need to unburden my sins.' She looked at him, and the desperation in her eyes moved him.

'If it is a matter of urgency, then you must confess.'

She breathed deeply with relief. 'Thank you. Thank you very much.'

On Sunday morning Celestria awoke once again to the sound of the church bell summoning the people of Marelatte to Mass. She lay in bed and stretched, not feeling in the least bit inclined to fulfil her Sunday obligation. She recalled Father Dalgliesh, a distant figure in her thoughts, so far away. Having removed herself physically, she had detached herself mentally, too. It felt good to be alone where no one knew her, except Waynie, of course. The sense of freedom was intoxicating. It filled her body with bubbles, so she felt light and buoyant and happy as never before. She closed her eyes and listened to the light chatter of birds, the sound resonating from the little stone bell tower and the sudden sporadic burst of barking from Federica's pack of dogs. The light morning breeze brushed her skin with the floral scent of lilies, and she lay unmoving, prolonging this moment of peace.

Federica and Gaitano had gone to Mass. Mrs Halifax was drinking coffee in the garden, reading *An Enchanted April,* while Mrs Waynebridge wandered down the avenue of orange trees, lost in pleasurable thoughts. The dogs trotted in, panting from their morning excursion, tails wagging at the satisfaction of once again marking their territory and frightening off would-be intruders. Celestria bent down to pat Maialino, who snuffled her feet like the little pig he was named after. Mrs Halifax raised her eyes briefly, then lowered them again, not wanting to be interrupted from reading her delightful book.

Celestria grabbed an apple from the bowl in the dining room. She wasn't hungry. She walked down the gravel path, past pots of herbs and borders of pink roses enjoying the last of their bloom. Maialino followed, leaving the other dogs to lie in the shade, drink water from the fountain, and gaze hopelessly at the large orange fish that swam there. She opened the gate into the road and stood a moment, gazing across at the pale walls of the city of the dead. The scent of lilies was stronger than ever. She turned and closed the gate behind her. She felt her heartbeat accelerate, certain that, even though she couldn't see him, Hamish was there, haunting his wife's crypt more jealously than the dead.

She began to walk beneath the paved avenue of pines that led into town. She hadn't been into Marelatte itself since she arrived. There was nothing else to do on a Sunday but explore.

At that moment a movement over the wall caught her attention, and she turned. Hamish was standing outside the little stone folly that was to be Gaitano's library. He was wearing only a pair of khaki trousers hanging low on his hips and a crumpled straw hat that cast a shadow across his face. His body was muscular and tanned the colour of leather. She couldn't help but catch her breath at the sight of him. She stopped and put her hands on her hips, silently challenging him. They stared at each other for what felt like a very long while. She tried to make out his expression. Even though his features were shaded she could see a pensive twist on his lips. He raised his hand and rubbed the bristles that grew on his cheeks. For a second she was sure he was about to walk over to her, and she braced herself expectantly, ready for confrontation. He made a slight movement. She felt a stab of adrenaline. Then he changed his mind, expelled the thought with a subtle shake of the head, and walked inside.

Celestria was deflated and furious. Why was he avoiding her? Had her intrusion been so dreadful? Maialino snuffled her feet again. She clicked her tongue, resisting the temptation to follow him, and turned around and made for the little gate. She no longer had the desire to explore Marelatte. Her morning had been spoiled.

Hamish stood in the cool shade of the folly, the saw in his hand hanging limply against his trouser leg as if he had forgotten all about it. He heaved a sigh, took off his hat, and rubbed his forehead, which was hot and itchy. The mere sight of Robert Montague's daughter inflamed his heart with fury. What was she doing here? Why had she come? How did she dare? He wasn't taken in by her beauty or her obvious charm, like Federica. She was like her father. She had the same superficial beauty, the same shallow light in her eyes, the same petulant mouth of someone used to flattery and adoration. He despised her as he despised her father, and he resented Federica now more than ever. Once again, she had made a grave misjudgment of character.

With a decisiveness typical of the old Hamish, the Hamish he was before Natalia's death had knocked the confidence out of him, he hastened to Gaitano's dusty Lancia Flaminia, which sat outside the Convento in dire need of a wash. He drove to Castellino, his jaw set in a determined grimace, his thoughts so full of Celestria there was room for little else. He hadn't visited Costanza in over a month; he hadn't had the will. Now he was wound up like a ball of string, he needed her soothing touch to untangle him.

Costanza had returned from Mass. A voluptuous woman of easy virtue, there was an awful lot for her to repent of. She was a widow, her husband having died of gangrene ten years before, leaving her alone and childless. However, she had grown to relish her independence and had no desire to marry again, even though she could boast countless offers. There was a jealousy in Italian men that she found unsatisfactory. They wanted to possess their women. Costanza was now her own keeper, but she was happy to loan herself out periodically, when the right man came along. She had various lovers, but none as handsome and vigorous as her Scotsman, nor as tormented.

She was delighted to see him when he appeared in her garden. She tossed off her black hat and veil and any remaining residue of repentance and allowed him to take her in his arms. He wore only a pair of trousers. The skin on his shoulders was hot and tacky with sweat. She kissed him, laughing at the surprise his visit had given her and tasting the salt on her lips. They didn't speak. She took his hand and led him through the house to her bedroom, which was as familiar to him as his own. He walked with the support of his stick, feeling the stiffness in his knee joint more keenly than ever.

They lay naked together and made love. She kissed him tenderly and stroked his hair, opened her velvet body to him, and let him release his frustration with energetic thrusts and rasping groans that came from the very depths of his being. He took her with a fury that Costanza mistook for passion, and several times. Then they parted with the same wordless understanding: a kiss, an affectionate look, a smile of gratitude, a wave of the hand. She watched him drive off with regret. He never stayed very long. He never talked to her. She longed to penetrate his thoughts and understand him. She knew she could make him happy if only he'd invite her in. But he had lost his beloved wife. Perhaps he had lost the will to love again. She waved until the car had turned the corner, then returned inside with a smile; in all the times they had made love, he had never been so ardent.

Chapter 21

Celestria spent a fitful night, her belly aching in anticipation of her meeting with Salazar the following morning, her spirit disturbed because Hamish hadn't dined with them yet again. She knew she shouldn't focus on him but on seeking vengeance for her father's killer, but she was unable to evict him from her thoughts. He filled them and dominated them and made her blood simmer with fury.

'Right, are you ready to take me to meet Salazar?' said Celestria to Nuzzo, standing in the courtyard the following morning.

'Salazar, *si signorina*.' He nodded eagerly, then turned to Mrs Waynebridge. *'Ciao, signora,'* he said, a wide smile spreading across his face.

'Good morning, Nuzzo,' she replied, watching him make for the door, his gait bow-legged, as if he had spent most of his life on a horse. Celestria raised her eyebrows at her friend.

'I think he rather likes you,' she said.

'He's quite a charmer,' Mrs Waynebridge conceded.

'Don't fall for it. I've heard that Italian men can't be trusted.' Mrs Waynebridge looked crestfallen for a moment, before noticing the ironic look on Celestria's face.

'Did I say that?' she gasped, the colour restored to her cheeks.

'You did.'

'Oh dear, I'm ashamed of myself. I like the Italians.'

'You certainly like one of them.'

Mrs Waynebridge cast her eyes up to the little window in the convent wall, to where the dove had cooed the night they arrived. Could the bird have sat there for her?

'Good luck, love,' she said, patting Celestria's arm. 'I hope you find what you're looking for.'

'So do I,' Celestria replied. 'Then we can go home.'

Mrs Waynebridge's face fell. Celestria wished she hadn't said it, because she didn't want to go home, either.

Celestria slipped on her sunglasses and followed Nuzzo through the little wooden door into the burning hot sun. Nuzzo pointed out small attractions he thought the *signorina* might enjoy. She threw a glance at Gaitano's little folly, half expecting to see Hamish there with his saw in his hand and his brown torso glistening in the sun.

Marelatte was dominated by the Piazza della Vittoria. Tall palm trees stood among olive and orange trees, paved walkways lined by iron benches, stone water fountains, and borders glittering with brightly coloured flowers. The trees were alive with birds, chirping loudly from the branches. A young couple walked hand in hand across the shadows, and a pair of toothless old men sat on a bench in the shade, watching them enviously. Celestria and Nuzzo walked on past the piazza, up a wide street where the baroque town hall stood proudly in the centre, larger and more ornate than the more humble buildings that surrounded it. A narrow street branched off to the left, where a plain-fronted house stood, its iron balconies hanging with terracotta pots of red geraniums, and, beyond, a pale pink church rested in the shade, the curvature of the pediments on the roof giving the skyline a pleasing harmony.

Nuzzo greeted people as they walked. Celestria noticed the appreciative glances in her direction. A group of small, brown-faced boys stopped kicking their ball, their playful squeals fading as they stood in a huddle, watching the angelic blonde lady with wide, curious eyes. She smiled at them, and they proceeded to nudge one another, fighting to lay claim to her affection. '*I ragazzi* like you,' said Nuzzo, grinning. Celestria laughed, not understanding the words they now began to shout after her.

Finally, Nuzzo turned off down a cobbled street where the sun didn't reach. It was cooler there in the shade. A cat scratched her grey back against the wall, hopping lightly off on her three good legs when she saw them approach. Nuzzo stopped outside a wooden door on a plain-fronted, flat-roofed building. The window to the right was misted by a net curtain, but Celestria could make out the vague lines of an office. '*Ci siamo,*' he said. On the wall beside the door was a bell and a brass plaque: F.G.B. Salazar. Celestria hesitated a moment, gathering herself. She hadn't worked out what she was going to say. Now she had no time. She pressed the bell and, with a racing heart, waited for a reply. After what seemed like a long time, the door opened and an anxious-looking woman peered out.

'*Buon giorno, signora, è arrivata la signorina Montague per il signor Salazar,*' said Nuzzo, taking off his hat respectfully.

'*Non c'è,*' the woman replied, shaking her head. Nuzzo made some inquiries. The woman replied briskly, shrugged, and closed the door.

'What did she say?' Celestria asked.

Nuzzo looked at her sympathetically. '*Il signor Salazar,* no.'

'He's not here? Well, when will he be back?' She stared at Nuzzo irritably. The poor man pulled a face. He didn't understand her question, and, even if he did, he was unable to reply in English. 'This is ridiculous!' she snapped. 'I've come all the way out to Italy to see him. How long is he going to be away? How long do I have to hang around waiting for him?' She was filled with disappointment. Nuzzo looked terrified. Celestria felt sorry for him; it wasn't his fault. 'Let's go back to the Convento and ask Federica,' she added more gently.

'*Convento? La signora Gancia?*' Nuzzo's eyes lit up. He replaced his hat and strode into the sunshine. '*Andiamo!*' he said, beckoning her to follow. She remained a moment staring at the window, willing Salazar to appear. With an impatient sigh, she set off after Nuzzo.

Celestria arrived at the convent hot and irritated. She found Gaitano in the courtyard talking to the old man with the cart full of timber that Nuzzo had chatted with on the road the day before. Gaitano smiled at her, and the old man took off his hat respectfully. They wound up their conversation and parted, the old man delighted to find Nuzzo hovering in the entrance hall with nothing to do. Gaitano raised his eyebrows kindly.

'You don't look very happy,' he said as Celestria approached.

'I was hoping to have a meeting with Mr Salazar today,' she replied. 'He's wasn't in. No one speaks English around here. Can you ask Nuzzo what the lady said?' Gaitano shouted across the courtyard. Nuzzo broke off his conversation with his friend and hurried out of the shadows. They exchanged a few words. Gaitano nodded gravely. He turned to Celestria and shrugged apologetically.

'This is Italy for you. He's away on business, and she doesn't know when he's going to be back.'

'What am I to do? I have to talk to him. It's important.'

'I'm sure he'll be back in a few days,' said Gaitano, trying to sound positive. The girl's face remained taut with frustration. Gaitano nodded at Nuzzo, who disappeared back into the shadows.

'In a few days? What am I going to do while I wait?'

'Do you like books?' Gaitano asked.

'Yes,' she replied sulkily.

'So do I. I'm in the process of constructing a library in the garden. Come, I'll show you my English collection.' He led her across the stones to a small door that opened into a large, vaulted room full of books. They were piled against the walls, on the tables, and balanced in unsteady towers in the middle of the room.

'These are all English?' she gasped in astonishment.

'I like to read in the original language where possible.' Gaitano gazed upon them lovingly, as if they were his children.

'I can see why you need to build a library,' she said, feeling better in the cool, out of the sun. She wandered among them, bending down to read the spines, forgetting all about Salazar.

'I see you like books, too.'

'I lose myself in literature,' she replied, picking up a book of poems by Wordsworth. 'My grandfather buys me books. He has the best taste. He has never given me a book I haven't loved. I've always loved Wordsworth.' She ran her fingers over the dusty cover in a caress. *'I wandered lonely as a cloud/ That floats on high o'r vales and hills,/When all at once I saw a crowd,/A host, of golden daffodils . . .'*

'Beside the lake, beneath the trees,/Fluttering and dancing in the breeze,' Gaitano finished the verse for her. His eyes lit up with admiration. 'Which is your favourite book?' he asked.

'The Count of Monte Cristo,' she replied without hesitation.

'Alexandre Dumas,' said Gaitano, raising his eyebrows. 'That's Hamish's favourite book, too.'

'Oh,' she muttered dismissively, finding it hard to believe that such a crude man could appreciate good literature.

'Did he read it in the original language?' she asked, replacing Wordsworth on his pile.

Gaitano laughed. 'I very much doubt it. When he arrived in Italy, he spoke nothing but English. However, he discovered a talent for languages, which wasn't a great surprise to me because he is musical. Musical people are often gifted linguists.'

'My grandfather made me read it in French, but I have to confess I read it again in English later. It was only then that I fell in love with it.'

'That, of course, is the test of a good book. You can read it over and over and find new things each time. A good book never loses its appeal.'

'That is so true.' She threw him an enchanting smile. 'Which is your favourite?'

'Proust, *A la Recherche du Temps Perdu*.' His French was flawless. 'I love many, but I love Proust the best.'

'I wish I could read them all in their original languages,' she sighed, picking up *Anna Karenina*.

'Russian defeats me,' he said, watching her with new eyes. 'Latin languages are very easy for us to learn. They are all very similar. Russian, on the other hand, is a world away. I have to read Tolstoy in English.'

'I think the job of the translator is a much underappreciated skill. They are unsung heroes. It is thanks to them that I have enjoyed so many foreign books. I'm ashamed to say I wouldn't know any of the translators by name.'

'Let me lend you a book to keep you entertained while you wait for Salazar to return,' he suggested enthusiastically, wandering around the books in search of one that would please her.

'I would love that. Thank you,' she replied, feeling the familiar sense of excitement at the thought of a new book.

'I find the experience of diving into a new world the most exhilarating of sensations,' he said.

'I agree. Each book is like a little world. You can carry it in your hand, and, yet, the space it creates in your mind is infinite.'

He stopped, crouched down, and traced his fingers up the spines of another stack. 'This is my American section,' he said. 'Have you read *The Age of Innocence?*'

'Edith Wharton. "Americans want to get away from amusement even more quickly than they want to get to it."' She laughed huskily. 'I've read it.'

'So I see.'

'My grandfather is American.'

'Then perhaps that is not the section I should be looking through.' He walked to the other side of the room, pushed his glasses up his nose, and bent over. 'This is my English, twentieth-century section,' he announced, then proceeded to mutter to himself as he glanced up and down thoughtfully. Finally he seized upon the perfect novel. *'The Forsyte Saga.'*

'I haven't read that,' she said, watching him ease it out then rearrange the books so the towers remained standing.

'John Galsworthy. A fine writer. You will enjoy him.' He passed it to her.

'This will keep me entertained for days!' she exclaimed. 'It's the size of *War and Peace.*'

'But infinitely more readable!'

'If I disappear for a week, I will blame you.' She laughed.

He looked at her fondly. 'If you disappear for a week, Celestria, I will blame myself!'

He watched her cross the courtyard. *What a surprise,* he thought, dazed from the pleasure of their encounter. *I would never have taken her for a reader.* He was still grinning when Hamish found him.

'I've been looking for you,' he said to his father-in-law.

'Oh?' Gaitano replied, taking off his glasses and slipping them in his breast pocket.

'I need to know how deep you want those shelves.'

'I've just been talking to Celestria,' he said casually. 'We've been sharing our love of books.' Hamish didn't reply, so Gaitano continued. 'Guess what her favourite novel is?'

'I don't know.' He shrugged dismissively.

'The same as yours.'

He looked taken aback. *'The Count of Monte Cristo?'* Hamish frowned. He couldn't imagine a girl as superficial as her getting through a novel like that.

'She read it first in French. She quoted Wordsworth and Wharton.'

'I don't suppose she has anything better to do than lie about, reading.'

Gaitano looked at him quizzically. 'Is there anything better to do?'

Hamish ignored him. 'Will you come and take a look at those shelves? I don't want to make them too shallow.'

Gaitano followed him into the courtyard. 'I want to be able to fit two rows of books on each shelf, otherwise I just won't get them all in.'

'We'll have to find you another folly.' Hamish chuckled.

'Freddie says I should give some away.'

'Doesn't she realize you have one of the best collections in Italy?'

Gaitano sighed melodramatically. 'She's not a lover of literature like you and me, Hamish. Silly woman doesn't understand. It would be like giving away parts of myself.'

Hamish patted him on the back vigorously. 'Don't worry, we'll fit them all in, and if we don't, we'll build you shelves in the Convento. She'll just have to free up space by getting rid of some of her own collections.'

'If it comes to that, Hamish, it won't be me who tells her but you. You're the only person with a growl that makes her bark sound like a baaaa!' They both roared with laughter.

★

Celestria heard the rumpus in the courtyard below and peered out from behind the curtain. She saw Hamish and Gaitano wandering across the stones to the front door. Hamish had his arm around his father-in-law, who looked frail and bald beside Hamish's brawny physique and thick shaggy hair. There was something very touching in the way that Hamish patted his father-in-law on the back, as if they were two friends equal in age and strength. But how could Gaitano love him? So far she had witnessed nothing of Hamish's charm, of which Mrs Halifax had spoken in such glowing terms, nor found in him any evidence of the man who loved Dumas's great novel. He had been ill-mannered and gruff when he should have been courteous. She watched them disappear with a mounting sense of outrage. If he was charming to Mrs Halifax and affectionate to Gaitano, why couldn't he be kind to her?

She lunched with Waynie, Federica, and Mrs Halifax, complaining bitterly about her thwarted plan to meet Salazar. 'He might not return for days!' she exclaimed.

'Then your ill fortune is our good fortune,' said Mrs Halifax. 'Because we will enjoy your company for a little longer.'

'At least Gaitano has lent me a novel.'

'Ah, Gaitano has discovered another book mate,' said Federica with a wry smile. 'He will be pleased. I don't have the patience to read. Natalia was like me; she had no desire to plough through a novel. She preferred pretty things she could wear. Hamish, however, loves books, too. He and Gaitano can spend a whole evening discussing a single novel.'

'My grandfather calls it "pecking the flesh" of a good novel,' said Celestria, ignoring Federica's reference to the rude Hamish. 'We like to peck the flesh well into the small hours. There's something magical about that time when the dawn is breaking and everyone is asleep, just the two of us, entering another world together.'

'I know exactly what you mean,' exclaimed Mrs Halifax, taking another slice of prosciutto. 'I prefer the early hours of the morning, or dusk, when the light is most subtle, when one is utterly aware of the transience of it all. That one's life is but a blink on the eye of time. I like to be alone to experience it without distraction. That way I can reflect on my life and appreciate it.'

'Do you read, Mrs Waynebridge?' Federica asked. Mrs Waynebridge blushed and shook her head. She wasn't about to confide that she was illiterate.

'She knits the most beautiful sweaters,' interjected Celestria, sensing her discomfort.

'I'm knitting Celestria a jersey,' Mrs Waynebridge added. 'Parrot green.'

'Parrot green?' repeated Mrs Halifax. Her eyes shone with delight. 'Parrot green is my favourite color. I have the most delightful pair of shoes in parrot green, decorated with purple sequins. Aren't you lucky, Celestria? I can't wait to see it on.' Celestria managed a thin smile at the thought of having to wear parrot green.

'Oh, it won't be ready for ages,' she said hopefully.

Mrs Waynebridge shook her head. 'On the contrary, if this Mr Salazar keeps you waiting, Celestria, I'll have it done in a jiffy!'

That evening, Celestria bathed and dressed in a fever of agitation. She was certain that Hamish would be at dinner. She was uncertain, however, of the best way to treat him. Should she ignore him? Should she return his rudeness? The thought of having to talk to him was worse than any she had ever had. No one had disliked her before. The novelty was an exceedingly unpleasant one.

She pulled on a pair of pale blue slacks and a light cashmere sweater, for the nights could be chilly, and tied her hair into a ponytail. She didn't wear makeup; she didn't want him to presume she was dressing up for his benefit.

As she walked down the stairs she resolved to treat him coolly and with indifference. Maialino and Fiametta were lying under the cloister on the pile of crimson cushions. They no longer jumped up when they saw her, for they were accustomed now to her presence at the Convento. The candles were already lit, although it was not yet dark, and the smell of beeswax combined with the salty smell of the sea. The light was dusky and pink, falling through the little window in the wall and onto the stones in the courtyard that hadn't yet been swallowed into shadow. She wandered through the kitchen and out into the garden, where the rest of the group was enjoying a glass of wine.

Hamish stood head and shoulders over everyone, even Gaitano, who was tall. When Celestria stepped out, he raised his eyes and watched her. She made a conscious effort not to look at him, although she felt the discomfort of his stare. Federica brought her a glass and led her to where Mrs Halifax was chatting to Mrs Waynebridge, commenting on the beauty of the sky, noting the pink clouds that drifted on the breeze like puffs of candyfloss.

'You can see why I love to come here and paint. The sky is never the same one day to the next. Nature is continually miraculous.' She turned to Celestria. 'Ah, my dear girl. You look lovely tonight.'

'Thank you,' she replied, then caught sight of the eccentric pair of shoes beneath Mrs Halifax's long purple dress. 'Parrot green!' she exclaimed with a chuckle.

'My favourite shoes. I've worn them especially for Mrs Waynebridge,' she said.

'Perhaps you should knit the sweater for Mrs Halifax, Waynie!' Celestria suggested.

'If we stay long enough, I'll knit one for both of you,' Mrs Waynebridge replied.

'Oh, would you!' Mrs Halifax exclaimed. 'I would adore a jersey in parrot green, and perhaps a little purple to match my shoes.'

'It would be my pleasure,' gushed Mrs Waynebridge, feeling the dizzy effects of the wine.

Celestria's attention was drawn to Gaitano, who was talking to Hamish. She raised her eyes, stumbling at once into Hamish's gaze. She recoiled, as if burned, and shot him her most haughty look before turning her full attention on Mrs Halifax.

Federica walked over to her husband and son-in-law. 'Are we to have the pleasure of your company for dinner?' she asked Hamish.

He shook his head. 'I'm not staying,' he replied.

'Don't you think you're being a little childish?'

'I'm under no obligation to fraternize with the guests,' he retorted.

'This is a family business, and you are family. I would like to see you at the dinner table once in a while.'

'Then once in a while it shall be. But not tonight. I've made other arrangements.' He drained his glass. 'I'll see you tomorrow.'

'Are you going to leave without even greeting her?' Federica was furious.

'I don't think she has the slightest desire to be greeted, Freddie. And neither do I.' With that he stalked past her into the kitchen.

Celestria stepped back, as if she had been tossed aside by a sudden wind, and looked to Federica and Gaitano for an explanation.

'Leave him alone,' Gaitano said to his wife.

'He's so rude,' she replied crossly.

'It'll pass.'

'You've been saying that for months.'

'I never said it would be quick.'

'He should pull himself together.' She felt Celestria deserved an explanation. 'Let's go and eat,' she announced, linking her arm through Celestria's. 'I'm afraid my son-in-law is a little volatile,' she ventured as they walked through the kitchen to the dining room.

'Please don't feel you have to apologize for his rudeness.'

'Some might take offence.'

'Rest assured, I'm not one of those. Gaitano,' she called out. 'I want to sit next to you so we can talk about books some more. I feel we have so much to discuss.'

'So do I,' he agreed, pulling out her chair. 'We have merely scratched the surface.'

Celestria was glad of Gaitano's company. Pecking at the flesh of a novel was the only distraction powerful enough to take her mind off the man, who, for the slight misdemeanour of trespassing on his wife's grave, was determined to make her his enemy.

Chapter 22

Hamish sat in Saverio's bar playing Scopa with old Leopoldo, his son Manfredo, and his good friend Vitalino. The sun had set; the dusky road outside was quiet but for the odd stray dog crossing the shadows in search of scraps. Saverio leaned over a cup of black coffee, moaning to a couple of sympathetic friends about his wife's sour humour and refusal to make love to him any more. He cast a glance at Hamish, whose tormented face was partly hidden by the hand of cards he was pretending to study, and felt a stab of guilt; at least he had a wife to complain about.

Hamish was looking at the cards, but he wasn't seeing them. He felt disgruntled, as if someone had pulled him out of his body and carelessly stuffed him back in again so that nothing fitted properly. He shuffled on his chair in an effort to settle back into his skin, but to no avail. He still felt troubled and uncomfortable. Vitalino watched him carefully. He was the first friend Hamish had made on arriving in Italy five years before, and he understood him better than anyone. He wanted to catch his eye and give him an empathetic smile, but Hamish was lost in thought.

Hamish had been a very different man before Natalia's death, Vitalino mused. He had painted with flamboyance, played the piano with flair and passion, and held everyone in his thrall with his talent for making the most mundane task of the day into the most hilarious story. No one could laugh like Hamish. A real belly laugh, throwing his head back and roaring like a bear. He rarely laughed like that these days, and Vitalino hadn't seen a painting in months. Yet recently Hamish had slowly begun to re-emerge. As if he had made a mental decision to begin the long climb back up the cliff from where Natalia had fallen to her death. He had started to paint again, and the task of building Gaitano's library had filled him with enthusiasm, for, like his father-in-law, books were one of his great loves. Until the last few days, when, for no apparent reason, his climb had suddenly been frustrated. The pallor had returned beneath his tan; the haunted expression once more seeped into the lines around his eyes. He had that furtive, hunted look again, like in the days following Natalia's death, when malicious whispers condemning him of foul play had lingered in the pauses between declarations of condolence.

Old Lorenzo caught his son's eye and shrugged. It was unlike him to resist a quip to shake Hamish out of his mooning. Leopoldo looked to Vitalino for guidance. It was no use. None of them knew what to do. If Hamish was reluctant to share his troubles, there was nothing that could persuade him.

'Let's buy another round,' Vitalino suggested, patting Hamish's back playfully.

'I'll have coffee,' Hamish replied, placing his cards on the table. He noticed the look of concern on the faces of his companions. Shifting his eyes from one to the other, he gave them a wry smile and sat back in his chair. 'What's going on?' he asked.

'You're not yourself,' said Leopoldo, his crusty voice surprisingly gentle. 'Are you all right?'

Hamish sighed. 'My mind's not on the game tonight. I'm sorry.'

Manfredo folded his cards. 'Let's abandon the game, then. It's no good for your morale to lose all the time!' He pulled a smile, which Hamish returned halfheartedly. Vitalino called out to Saverio, who tore himself away from his bitter soliloquy to make them coffee.

'It's that blonde woman, isn't it?' said Vitalino. Hamish looked startled. 'We've all seen her. She sticks out like a swan among swine.'

'She's a beauty,' Leopoldo agreed, shaking his grey head. 'You have to move on. It's been three years. Natalia is with God.'

Hamish's face grew red with anger. 'You don't know what you're saying, Leopoldo,' he growled. 'Besides, she's not my type.'

'Then I will have her,' quipped Manfredo.

'You're most welcome,' Hamish replied, standing up. He threw some lire on the table. 'For the coffee. It's my turn.' He made for the door, gasping for air.

Outside he stood in the moonlight, leaning heavily on his stick, breathing deeply. The door opened behind him, and Vitalino appeared, his face full of concern. 'She's rattled your cage, hasn't she?' he said.

'Yes,' Hamish groaned. He set off up the road. Vitalino accompanied him.

'You have to learn to love again, my friend. You're young . . .'

'Save it!' Hamish snapped. 'Leopoldo doesn't know what he's talking about. He doesn't know her.'

'Who is she?'

Hamish stopped and turned to face Vitalino. He gathered himself a moment, as if it cost him to mention that hated name. 'Robert Montague's daughter.'

Vitalino recoiled. 'My God, what's she doing here?'

'I don't know.' He continued to walk again. 'But I wish she'd leave.'

Vitalino thought for a moment. He had noticed her strolling through the town with Nuzzo the day before. He had been struck by her loveliness – as pale and graceful as an angel. The whole town was talking about her. 'Look,' he ventured. 'She's not Robert Montague. I don't think it's fair to condemn her just because she shares his blood.'

'I can't bear to look at her.'

'That's easy,' said Vitalino.

'This isn't a joke.'

'Aren't you making a mountain out of a molehill?'

'I thought you of all people would understand.'

'I do. But she's not her father. She's an individual. You should treat her as one. Have you spoken to her?'

'Not really.' Hamish shrugged off their first encounter in Natalia's crypt; he was too ashamed to speak of it.

'So you don't know her at all?'

'No,' he conceded.

'You've prejudged her.'

'Yes.'

'For an intelligent man, you're a fool!'

Hamish shook his head. How could he expect his friend to understand when he didn't know the whole truth? Only he and Natalia knew what was too dreadful to share.

The following two days Celestria walked through the small town of Marelatte in the hope of meeting the elusive Salazar, only to find the same woman with the same flustered expression on her increasingly gaunt face. As Celestria waited for the man to return, she whiled away the time by sitting in the garden reading *The Forsyte Saga,* which distracted her from her sorry situation, as Gaitano knew it would. Another family's trials helped her temporarily to forget her own. Her head ached with thinking about her father. The book was a relief, like ice to lower a fever. She felt Hamish's brooding presence in the Convento even though she rarely glimpsed him. She knew he was working on Gaitano's library but dared not venture near, even though her fury at being ignored made him hard to disregard. His arrogance was unbelievable and aroused in her a nagging curiosity.

She had been at the Convento for five nights, during which time she had barely mentioned her father. He existed only in her thoughts, shoved aside by the Forsyte family and any other means of distraction that enabled her to avoid feeling any pain. On the fifth night, however, the frustration of not finding Salazar, combined with Gaitano's grandfatherly attention, Hamish's rudeness, and too much wine, filled her with an overwhelming sadness. She went to bed heavy-hearted, wanting nothing more than to cry into her pillow, but the tears would not come. She pulled out the photograph of her father in his panama hat that she had found with Federica's letter, and held it to her bosom.

Unable to sleep and longing to express her pain, she shrugged on her dressing gown and padded down the corridor to the piano. She sat on the stool in front of the window, through which a silvery beam of light entered to illuminate the keys. The piano had called to her from the first moment she had seen it. Yet she had not dared play in case someone overheard her. She didn't desire to play the tunes she had laboriously learned since childhood, but her own made-up songs that she heard in her head and yearned to sing.

She knew she wasn't a good singer. Her voice was not clear but husky and unsteady. Sometimes she didn't even make the notes. But it was the most satisfactory way of expressing her feelings. When she sang, she felt a loosening in her chest, a pouring of something warm and healing into her heart, and a lightness of being. It was her secret pleasure. She had never needed it more than now.

Leaning the photograph on the music stand, she placed her hands over the keys. Slowly she began to play. She was careful to play quietly. She didn't want to wake anyone up. As her fingers pressed the chords she felt a melody emerge and began to hum. The hum grew into words and the words into phrases as she sang of her love and her sorrow, climaxing in a chorus that she repeated over and over until the tears seeped through her eyelashes and poured down her cheeks.

Unknown to her, Hamish had been restless, too. He had avoided seeing her by working on Gaitano's library and dining with Vitalino and his large, demonstrative family. Yet his friend's advice stuck in his mind. He was unable to shake it off because Vitalino was right. It was unjust to judge a woman by the actions of her father. Hamish had trouble sleeping, tossing in the heat of his room, plagued by night terrors and an unquenchable frustration. He had escaped to the coolness of his studio, up a small flight of stairs not far from the piano. At first he thought he was dreaming when he heard the soft notes wafting down the corridor. He had suspended his brush and raised his eyes to the door, listening intently.

No one played but him. He couldn't hear the voice, but he knew instantly who was touching the keys. Drawn by curiosity, he tiptoed down the corridor and peered around the corner, making sure he remained in shadow so she wouldn't see him. What he saw moved him deeply and unexpectedly. Celestria sat in the pale moonlight, her face shining with tears, singing softly to herself. Her hair fell about her shoulders in waves, tumbling over her white dressing gown, loosely tied so that it revealed her smooth chest and the lace top of her negligée. She played a sad tune, stumbling on the keys, hitting the odd wrong note, but seemingly unaware. Her voice was deep and smoky, and it didn't matter that she sang a little out of tune. She looked beautiful but, most notably, vulnerable. He forgot his prejudice and wanted simply to hold her against him. He remained for a long time staring in awe at the sight of the woman he had believed to be hard and arrogant. The overriding feeling, however, was one of shame. Vitalino was right; he was a fool.

He watched her for an hour, oblivious of the time. Finally, she heaved herself up, drained from weeping. She wiped her face on the sleeve of her dressing gown, gently closed the lid of the piano, and returned to her room. Hamish retreated into the shadows so that she didn't see him as she passed. He inhaled the faint smell of bluebells and watched her open her door and disappear inside. Overcome with longing, he crept over to where she had been sitting, as if the warmth of the seat would bring him closer to her. Suddenly he saw the photograph on the music stand. He recognized the man at once. Taken there at the Convento, he was unmistakable in his pale suit and panama hat. He picked it up and asked himself: Why is she crying for her father?

Celestria was in bed when the photograph was slipped under her door. She heard the rustle as it was pushed through the crack. She sat up and stared at it, too frightened to move, for she sensed who was behind it. What flustered her the most, however, was that not only must he have heard her singing, but he must also have seen her cry.

Chapter 23

The following morning Celestria awoke to see the photograph on the floor by the door. Daylight flooded the room with sunshine and banished the demons from the shadows. She no longer felt afraid or ashamed. Perhaps it had been Gaitano or Federica, neither whom would think any less of her for shedding tears. She picked the photo up and put it on the dresser, leaning it up against the mirror so she would see it every time she brushed her hair.

She breakfasted early and, infected by the enthusiasm of the dawn, made off for Salazar's office. Surely today would be different?

She rang the bell and waited for the woman to open the door. To her surprise, she barely recognized her, as she was now fully made up with red lipstick, coiffed hair, and a little too much rouge. The woman smiled and beckoned her inside. Celestria's heart soared. The elusive Mr Salazar had returned. The woman said something incomprehensible in Italian and gently pushed her into the waiting room. There were a sofa and a couple of armchairs, a single painting of the sea, and a vase of yellow flowers on the coffee table. She offered Celestria a drink. *'Caffè?'* Celestria shook her head. She was much too nervous to waste time drinking coffee. 'Please wait,' said the secretary, obviously struggling with her poor English. Celestria sat down, attempting to look confident, and picked up a magazine. The secretary disappeared. She could hear the murmur of low voices down the corridor. Finally, the door opened and a handsome middle-aged man strode in, wearing a pressed ivory suit and shiny, two-toned brogues. He was short, with sleek black hair, a low, unwrinkled forehead, thick eyebrows that resembled furry caterpillars, and the large, oleaginous smile of a man used to slipping through people's defences with his charm.

'Signorina Montague,' he gushed, opening his arms as if about to embrace her. 'It is a pleasure to finally meet you.' His English was good, though flamboyantly accented. His bitter chocolate eyes appraised her with admiration. 'You are more beautiful than your father,' he said with a laugh. 'Please, come into my office.'

She walked past him, through a cloud of sweet cologne, into a room that was wood panelled, with a bookcase filling one wall, a pair of mahogany filing cabinets between two windows that gave on to a small cobbled courtyard, and a wide English desk more suited to a city chairman than a provincial clerk. He offered her a seat before sinking into his own leather chair. 'I, too, have daughters,' he said, pointing to the family photographs that rested in silver frames on the desk amid piles of papers and a smart leather briefcase. 'Italian women are beautiful, but you, *signorina*, put them in the shade.'

Celestria was not in the mood for his empty flattery. There was even something insulting about his assumption that she would be grateful for it. 'I am here about my father,' she said briskly.

'Of course you are. Signor Montague was a good client of mine.' Celestria was surprised. She hadn't expected him to know he was dead.

'Who told you he had died?' she asked. It was Salazar's turn to look shocked.

'Dead?' He shook his head and straightened. 'I never said he was dead.'

'You used the past tense.'

'So?' he shrugged. 'We no longer do business together.' He rubbed his chin thoughtfully. 'So, he is dead?' The smile had slipped off his face, leaving his mouth loose and shapeless.

'He died at sea.'

'How?'

'In a boating accident. He drowned.'

'Drowned?' Salazar's eyes widened in horror. He had suddenly gone very pale. 'I am sorry for your loss.'

'So am I.'

'How can I help you?' He loosened his tie as he was beginning to sweat, and forced a smile that hung unsteadily on his face.

'I am sorting out his affairs. I know nothing of his businesses. I do know that he sent money out to you on a regular basis. I'd like to know where that money has gone.'

Salazar hesitated a moment. He reached for a silver box, opened it, and took out a small cigar. 'You don't mind if I smoke?' Celestria shook her head. He fumbled in his jacket pocket for a lighter. She knew he was playing for time. 'Life is all fog and smoke and mirrors,' he said with a shrug.

'What do you mean?' Celestria was irritated.

'His business collapsed. He took what little there was left and disappeared. What can I tell you?'

'Where did all those thousands of pounds go?'

'Sunk, my good lady. I suppose, one could say, drowned, like your father.' His small eyes shone maliciously.

'I don't understand. What business was it?'

Salazar heaved a sigh and took a long puff before placing his cigar on the edge of a glass ashtray already filled with ash. He leaned forward. His face was now red and sweating. '*Signorina*, it is a man's world. If I were you, I would leave business to the boys. Besides, you have already admitted that you don't understand. I have not the time nor the patience to enlighten you.'

Celestria was affronted. He stood up and opened a drawer in one of the filing cabinets behind him. Celestria looked out into the courtyard. An iron gate stood at the top of a small incline of steps, opening into what looked like a pretty orchard of apple trees. The steps made her think of the mausoleum in the city of the dead, and her thoughts once again wandered to Hamish. Salazar turned, bringing a file with him, and sat down. He placed it on the desk and opened it. Celestria peered over. He was flicking through what looked like correspondence and lists of numbers and names. 'This, my good lady, is all I have left of your father.' He slapped a page with the back of his hand.

'What are they?'

'Lists of creditors.' He looked at Celestria and raised a bushy eyebrow. 'Your father left nothing behind but angry people demanding money.'

At that moment there was a knock on the door. The secretary appeared, looking flustered. *'C'è una signora alla porta che dice di volerti vedere, dice che è urgente. E' arrivata direttamente da Parigi.'* He smiled at Celestria, but loosened his tie again.

'Tell her I am busy,' he replied frostily. 'Tell her to come back tomorrow.'

The secretary nodded and closed the door behind her. Celestria frowned.

'It seems I am besieged by women today. I am a lucky man.' He picked up his cigar and puffed on it again. 'Now, where were we?'

'My father's business. Was it his alone?'

'No, he had a partner, and the countess, of course.'

'The countess?' Celestria screwed up her nose. 'Countess Valonya?'

There was another knock on the door. The secretary didn't
wait for Salazar to respond but opened it in a fluster. *'Dice che
la vedrá. E furiosa.'* He chuckled nervously. The secretary was
very pale, wringing her hands. She spoke at great speed, her
voice a note or two higher than before. After she had left, he
shrugged again.

'The woman is in love with me,' he sighed pompously.
'What can I do? Frenchwomen are very pushy. They don't
like to take no for an answer. She has telephoned me daily
from Paris, demanding to see me. Can you imagine?' He
took a puff, pausing for a moment. 'I deal with all sorts of
people, *signorina*. From the ex-king of Italy to the present
king of olive oil. I treat them all the same. With respect.
My job requires discretion. My clients are important men
of means and position, and they don't take very kindly to
being played with.' He narrowed his eyes and gazed at her
through the diaphanous screen of smoke. 'Your father was
a gambler. Some he won, some he lost, but he played a
little too hard. Do you understand what I'm saying?'
Celestria nodded slowly, though she wished he would
make himself clear.

'What part did the countess play in my father's affairs?'

'I never liked her. Let's just say she was a lugubrious character. He sent her out when he could not come himself. A
shadow that blended in with the night.'

Suddenly a loud crash resounded through the building.
The secretary hurried in. There was a terrible commotion.
Salazar stood up and dialled for the *carabinieri*. Celestria peered
around the corner, to where the front window was broken.
Shattered glass lay all over the floor. Within minutes a couple
of policemen in khaki uniforms had arrived. Salazar strode
past her. He let off a round of staccato Italian phrases at the
woman who was now being marched away by the police. She
hurled back abuse, straining to free herself.

Celestria caught sight of her. She was beautiful, middle-aged, her shiny brown hair parted on the side and carefully tied into a tight chignon at the back of her head. She wore an ivory suit, the jacket nipped in at the waist, the pencil skirt reaching just below her knees. Her heels were high, and of pale leather to match her handbag. She didn't look the type to throw a brick through a window; more likely to have a champagne glass in one hand and a cigarette holder in the other.

Salazar shook Celestria's hand. She knew he was withholding information. But he was as slippery as the grease he used to slick back his hair. For the moment there was nothing more she could do.

She left with reluctance, aware that she had learned nothing at all. So the countess had done her father's dirty work, but what exactly had that involved? Salazar had given nothing away. She had no means of knowing whether the money had indeed been withdrawn, and, as far as she could tell, there was no way of finding out. Lord, she wished her grandfather had come with her. She wasn't equipped to work all this out on her own.

She wandered into the piazza and sat on a bench in the sunshine. A horse plodded past, pulling a cart of pine furniture. She watched him and envied the man who led him, for he appeared to have not a care in the world. Her stomach rumbled, and she realized that it was two in the afternoon and she hadn't eaten since breakfast. She thought of the vast sum of money her father had supposedly withdrawn the week preceding his death. To whom had the countess given it? Was he being blackmailed? If so, what could it be that he hadn't wanted anyone to know about? He hadn't had a job for two years. He had squandered his family's money. Where had it all gone to? What was he running from?

She stood up to make her way back to the Convento and she noticed the police station at the other end of the piazza.

Curiosity overrode her hunger, and she walked around to see what had become of the Frenchwoman. There seemed to be no one about. She looked up and down the road, then stood at the foot of the steps leading up to the door and listened. She heard a burst of laughter, then a woman's voice, smooth and silky like condensed milk. She recognized it at once. Perhaps, if Celestria could solicit her help, she might shed some light on the mysterious Salazar. Celestria felt she had nothing to lose by trying.

She entered the police station to find the Frenchwoman sitting on a chair surrounded by a group of eight enraptured policemen. One was lighting the cigarette she held to her crimson lips, another handing her a little cup of coffee. They were all laughing at whatever she was saying. Her Italian seemed flawless. When she saw Celestria, her eyes narrowed and the smile turned into a scowl. *'Chi è lei?'* she said, nodding towards Celestria.

'I was having a meeting with Salazar when—'

'I threw a brick through his window.' Her English was good but heavily accented. 'What is it to you?' She took a drag and blew out the smoke, watching the younger woman with disdain. The policemen were clearly bemused.

'I think we are in the same boat.'

'You can think what you like, *chérie*.' She showed no willingness to collude.

'Can we talk in private?'

The Frenchwoman laughed meanly. 'I am under arrest, or perhaps it has escaped your notice.' She ran her eyes over her audience and straightened the cap of one of them, before patting it playfully. 'Why don't you go away?'

Celestria was stung. The woman began to speak to the men in Italian. They all turned to Celestria and laughed. She spun around and hurried out, her cheeks burning with humiliation.

Folding her arms against her chest, she strode back beneath the pine trees to the Convento. 'This has been a huge mistake coming out here,' she muttered to herself crossly. 'Why is everyone so horrid?' She cast her eyes over to the city of the dead.

As she stepped through the door into the Convento, she bumped straight into Hamish. Without deliberating her words, she stiffened and, to his astonishment, said exactly what was on her mind. 'Oh, Lord, it's you again! The one person I do not wish to see today.'

'I—' he began, but she cut him off with a loud sigh.

'Save it. I don't know what it is about this place, but it is filled with very rude people. Where I come from people are good-natured and polite. And you know what? It's not the Italians who are rude. No, Nuzzo is a darling, and Freddie and Gaitano are charm personified. It's the Scottish and the French, who should really know better.'

'I should apologize,' he said, frowning heavily, visibly disturbed by her outburst.

'It's too late for that. You've had ample opportunity. Anyway, I really don't care. I have business to see to. I'm not here on holiday, you know. It is really of no consequence whether or not I get on with people like you. My mission is altogether more important. Why don't you go and shout at someone else? I'm in a hurry.' She folded her arms and stared at him defiantly. 'In fact, you should meet the Frenchwoman with whom I've just had the misfortune of colliding. You'd get on like a house on fire!'

Hamish stepped aside with reluctance. He was bewildered. He hadn't anticipated such rudeness from her, and it had wrong-footed him. He watched her march across the courtyard and disappear up the stairs without a backwards glance. She hadn't even accepted his apology.

Chapter 24

After lunch Celestria composed a telegram to her grandfather. She wrote that Salazar had been extremely unhelpful, most probably hiding the truth. She had no way of finding out. She didn't speak Italian and had no 'connections' to rely on. She also mentioned the Frenchwoman and the brick she threw at his window. 'Where do I go from here?' she wrote, then ventured into town to find the post office.

Mrs Waynebridge and Nuzzo walked along the top of the cliffs, where the stony ground gave way to tufts of rough grass and sprigs of herbs. Fluffy sheep grazed on the vertiginous hillside, apparently unafraid of falling into the sea. The air was sweet with the medicinal scent of the eucalyptus trees, and the sound of the waves lapping the rocks below lent a musical accompaniment to their promenade. Nuzzo had taken off his jacket and rolled up his sleeves, revealing his muscular brown arms. His beret protected his head from the sun, but the skin on his face was thick and weathered due to having lived most of his life out of doors at the mercy of the elements.

Mrs Waynebridge was hot beneath her hat and welcomed the breeze that swept in off the ocean. The sun was high in the sky, and she could already see her white skin turning pink on her freckled forearms. Nuzzo playfully endeavoured to teach her Italian by pointing things out and stating their names with the same clarity with which he had introduced himself on their first night.

'*Pecora,*' he said, pointing to the sheep.

'*Pecora,*' she replied.

His face lit up excitedly. '*Pecora, brava!*' He looked about for something else. '*Mare,*' he said, pointing to the sea. '*Mare.*'

'*Mare,*' she replied.

'*Brava, signora. Mare.*' Mrs Waynebridge felt her heart swell. Nuzzo's enthusiasm made her feel young again.

'*Cielo,*' he said, waving his hand up at the sky. '*Cielo.*'

'*Cielo,*' she repeated.

He shook his head, impressed. '*Bravissima!*' he exclaimed. Then he bent down and plucked a small yellow flower that nestled between two white stones. '*Fiore,*' he said, handing it to her.

'*Fiore,*' she repeated softly. He gazed at her, his eyes full of affection. '*Bella,*' he said bashfully.

Mrs Waynebridge swallowed. Even she knew what *bella* meant. She looked down at the flower. '*Bella,*' she said.

'*No, signora.*' He shook his head, gesticulating at her. '*Lei è bella.*'

Mrs Waynebridge blinked at him. 'Me?'

'*Sì, signora. Lei è bellissima.*'

Celestria returned from the post office and wandered through the kitchen to sit on a bench in the garden, surrounded by terracotta pots of lavender. Amid the aromatic tranquillity of the herb garden she pondered her next move. Her meeting with Salazar had come to nothing. She had no option but to await her grandfather's instructions. As much as she tried, she was unable to ignore Hamish's insistent face, which leapt into her mind at every available opportunity, demanding to be noticed. She dismissed him with a snort as Mrs Waynebridge finally returned from her excursion, flushed and bright eyed, a lively bounce to her walk. In her hand she twirled a small yellow flower.

'I found out nothing,' Celestria told her flatly. 'I'm at a loss where to look now.'

Mrs Waynebridge sat beside her, grateful for the shade of a large canvas parasol. 'Maybe you're looking for something what isn't there.'

'There's something there, all right. The bugger won't tell me, though. He played with me like a cat with a mouse. I don't speak the language. I have no way of knowing whether he was telling the truth.'

'Why don't you just lie back and enjoy a holiday?' Mrs Waynebridge smiled secretively, taking off her hat to fan herself. 'It's a beautiful place. *Bella, pecora, cielo, mare, fiore, bella . . .*' Her voice trailed off.

'Because I won't rest until I find out why my father killed himself. I suspect it was blackmail.'

'Blackmail?'

'I'm sorry, Waynie. I can't expect you to understand when I haven't kept you in the picture. My meeting, though, bore no fruit, but I met a frightful Frenchwoman who threw a brick through Salazar's office window and was dragged away by the police. He's obviously not very popular. This town is full of the rudest people.'

'And some very nice people, too.' Mrs Waynebridge stared out over the orange grove that extended from the garden to a small cluster of houses fighting for shade beneath towering pine trees.

'More flirting, I presume. Really, Waynie, I'm shocked. You've not even been here a week!'

Mrs Waynebridge played with the little flower. 'No harm in a little flirting. I don't think I've looked at another man since me Alfie passed away. That Nuzzo is a right so-and-so.'

'How do you communicate? He doesn't speak English.'

'We get by.'

Unable to sit still, Celestria suggested they go for a walk. Mrs Waynebridge, tired from her morning excursion, declined. She was happy to sit in the sun, alone with her thoughts. She hadn't had such nice thoughts in a very long time. So Celestria headed off alone. To her annoyance, she caught herself looking for Hamish everywhere she turned her eyes, but instead she found Mrs Halifax on the cliff top, painting a small, disued fortress.

'You know,' she said, gazing out over the sea. 'Puglia has been dominated by the Greeks, the Romans, the Byzantines, the Normans, the French, the Spanish, and the Neapolitans. These lookout points were built to keep watch for approaching Turks. They would send signals down the coast by lighting fires, alerting one another of attack. Terribly romantic, don't you think?' Celestria sat down on the dry, spiky grass and looked out over the sea. 'You'll find some beautiful Moorish buildings here, too. It's a great melting pot of different cultures. I do love it.'

'I expected it to look like Tuscany.'

Mrs Halifax laughed. 'Most certainly not. That's the charm of it.'

'You paint very well,' said Celestria, glancing at the canvas.

'I've had years of practice.'

'Don't you get bored?'

'Certainly not. Why would I get bored? Every scene I paint is different.'

'But you're on your own all the time.'

'I'm surrounded by the wondrous beauty of nature. It fills my soul. Besides, I like to be alone with my thoughts. I remember the past. That makes me happy.'

'Why didn't you return to France?'

'Ah, I aroused your curiosity.'

'You said you'd tell me.'

She stopped painting. 'I fell in love.'

Celestria looked surprised. 'You fell in love?'

'I know what you're thinking. Old ladies don't fall in love. Well, it's not what you think. I fell in love with a little boy who lived at the château.'

'Ah.' Celestria nodded.

'His mother worked there. He was mute. A dear little thing he was. So enchanting, with white-blond hair and these big, curious, intelligent blue eyes. He reminded me of my son.' She sighed and started painting again. 'Then one day, at Mass, a miracle happened. God gave him back his voice.'

'A real miracle?'

'Yes. They do happen, you know, very occasionally. If you let them.'

'What happened to him?'

'He went to live in America. His mother fell in love with an American who came to stay. I don't blame her. He was a dish if ever I saw one. After that the château held little charm for me. Without Mischa the place seemed cold and empty and joyless. I never went back. But I remember him always. There's a place in my heart where he resides along with my son and husband.'

'It must be a painful place,' said Celestria.

'Painful? No, my dear, it's the happiest place there is, full of memories of the people I have loved. You'll learn that love comes in many different disguises. It strikes when you least expect it and often when you really don't want it. Sometimes it's so quick to take you over, you don't believe it. In the end there is nothing as important as love. It's the only thing you take with you when you die.' Mrs Halifax gazed out over the sea, a wistful smile warming her face with the sun.

'It's very quiet here, isn't it?' said Celestria after a while.

'It'll take some time to get that dreadful city out of your system.'

'Oh, I love London,' she said brightly.

'I like it, too, in very small doses! Do you want to paint something?'

'Oh, I don't think I'd be very good.'

'Why not have a try? Look in my bag; there's a small sketch-pad. Why don't you grab a piece of charcoal and have a go. You don't have to show it to anyone, if you'd rather not.'

As there was nothing else to do until her grandfather arrived, Celestria sketched Mrs Halifax. The old woman sat beneath a straw sunhat, in the shade of a withered evergreen tree whose branches were low with prickly, unfriendly leaves, holding her brush in front of her nose every now and again to measure distances. While Celestria drew, she entertained Mrs Halifax with stories of her family in Cornwall. Mrs Halifax laughed out loud.

'Oh, dear, you are a funny girl,' she said, wiping her eyes. 'Your Aunt Penelope sounds quite a card.'

'She's very fruity,' said Celestria, watching Mrs Halifax laugh again. 'Like a bowl of rich red plums!'

Celestria's drawing was terrible, but it didn't matter. She discovered she enjoyed the tranquillity of the afternoon, the gentle sound of the sea lapping against the rocks below, and the distant barking of a dog. She enjoyed Mrs Halifax, too. 'You're a pretty girl, Celestria. You must have a suitor or two back in England?'

Celestria thought of Aidan. 'Not really,' she replied, then decided there was no point in lying to someone who had nothing to do with her life back home, so she added, 'Well, I have agreed to marry someone.'

'Oh, dear, you're going to have to break it off then, aren't you?'

Celestria looked surprised. 'Why would I want to do that?'

'Because you're not in love. That's obvious.'

'But he's very nice.'

'If *nice* is the best adjective you can come up with, I should definitely avoid the trip to the altar. Weren't you forbidden to use that word at school? I was. My dear, if the earth doesn't move, it isn't right.'

'But, Mrs Halifax, the earth has *never* moved.'

'Good God, dear, you're still a child! You've plenty of time for earth-shattering moments. Believe me, the earth will move. It will tremble and shake and shift on its axis, leaving you in no doubt that you are head over heels in love. By the way, please do call me Daphne.'

That evening, back at the Convento, Celestria bathed and dressed for dinner. She wondered what her grandfather had made of her telegram and hoped he had decided to join her. She spent a long time in her room, rubbing oil into her body and painting her toenails pale pink. Then, a now-familiar voice rose up to her window from the courtyard below. She wrapped a towel around her and hurried over to peer down between the shutters. There, talking to his father-in-law, was Hamish. Her stomach lurched. He was pointing to various places beneath the cloister, and Gaitano was rubbing his chin thoughtfully. They were speaking Italian.

Celestria dressed, her body quivering with the sudden rush of adrenaline. Confronting him had been the right thing to do. She didn't feel furious and defensive; rather, her assertiveness had empowered her. She slipped into a pretty white sundress that reached midcalf and showed off her slim shape, and a pale blue cashmere cardigan. She rubbed her bluebell scent into her wrists and under her ears. She was certain that since their confrontation earlier, he would attend dinner tonight, if only to have the last word.

She skipped down the stone staircase and out into the courtyard. She cast her eyes to the little door through which Hamish and Gaitano had disappeared only minutes before and hoped they'd step out again. She bent down to pat Primo, who was lying sleepily on one of the crimson cushions that were piled up under the cloister beside a low table of elaborate hand-embroidered dolls from Afghanistan. She played for time, but they did not emerge. Finally, as the courtyard grew darker, she knew she should make her way to the dining room.

Mrs Halifax was already deep in discussion with Mrs Waynebridge and Federica. There was no sign of the men anywhere.

'I'm sorry I'm late,' Celestria apologized, taking the seat beside Federica, opposite the two other women.

'There is no "late" at the Convento,' said Federica. 'You are our guests, and you can come and go as you please. Besides, you are not the last.'

'You look lovely, Celestria,' said Mrs Waynebridge. 'Don't you think so, Mrs Halifax?'

'Oh, to be young again, able to wear such pretty, feminine things,' the older woman replied, smiling at Celestria. 'I compensate by wearing silly shoes.' Celestria noticed there were two more places laid and presumed they were for Gaitano and Hamish. She felt her heartbeat accelerate at the prospect of colliding once more with the darkly alluring Scotsman.

'A telegram came for you this evening,' said Federica. 'I should give it to you before I forget.' She delved into her pocket and pulled out a white envelope. Celestria opened it with excitement.

'It'll be from my grandfather,' she said happily. Then her face fell. 'He's not coming,' she muttered, disappointed.

'What does he say?' Mrs Waynebridge asked, hoping they wouldn't have to leave now she was beginning to enjoy herself. She had already pressed the little yellow flower between the pages of her book.

'*My dearest Sherlock, if anyone can get to the bottom of it, you can. Use your guile and your imagination. Isn't it about time England made friends with France?*'

'Whatever does he mean?' Mrs Waynebridge asked.

'I know what he means. I was just rather hoping he'd come out and help me. You see,' she said to Federica, shoulders drooping, 'I haven't simply come out for a holiday. I've come to find out why my father killed himself.'

Federica blanched. 'He killed himself?'

'I'm afraid I didn't tell you the whole truth.'

'Don't apologize,' said Federica gently, touching her hand. 'There's nothing to apologize for.' But the older woman's face sagged with sorrow. 'Wouldn't it be better to leave him in peace?'

'Absolutely not. I am determined.'

Before she could say another word, the Frenchwoman Celestria had last seen in the police station now entered through the kitchen. 'What a day,' she said huffily, 'they don't get much worse.'

'That makes two of you,' said Mrs Halifax.

Celestria stared at the Frenchwoman in horror. She had changed out of her cream suit and was wearing a pair of navy blue slacks and a blue-and-white-striped top. Around her neck she had tied a silk scarf. Her hair was pulled off her face and fell in a ponytail down her back. Just above her lip was a thin white scar that almost reached her nose.

'I don't think you've met Celestria,' said Federica. The Frenchwoman's eyes fell upon the younger woman. She recognized her instantly.

'We have met. I'm afraid I was rather rude. I apologize. My name is Armel.' She held out her hand. 'I was just having a bad day.'

'Didn't look so bad to me,' said Celestria dryly.

'Yes, well, appearances can be deceptive. You don't know the half of it.' She sat down. Luigi poured her a glass of wine. She sniffed it first, then took a sip. 'Very nice,' she said, 'for Italian wine.' Federica ignored her comment, which Celestria considered immensely rude. 'What were you doing with that cheating rat?' she asked Celestria. Celestria felt herself stiffen. It was none of her business. However, she remembered her grandfather's advice and decided that nothing would come out of nothing. She decided to throw some bread onto the water.

'I believe he has stolen my father's money,' she said, looking at Armel steadily.

Federica shook her head. 'I'm afraid I wouldn't trust Salazar as far as I could throw him.'

'He's a pompous ass!' Celestria added.

'You and I do have something in common,' said Armel darkly, knitting her long brown fingers. 'I believe he has stolen my husband's money.'

'Do you think he has women throwing bricks through his window every week?' said Celestria with a small smile.

'This is most extraordinary!' Federica exclaimed. 'You both turning up at the same time.'

'This Salazar character can't know what's hit him,' said Mrs Halifax, chuckling huskily.

'I tried to get information out of the police,' said Armel seriously, settling her hooded brown eyes on Celestria.

'I thought you were just holding court,' said Celestria. Armel didn't smile.

'With a little persuasion, I hoped to find he had a record of this sort of thing.' Celestria must have looked incredulous, for Armel clicked her tongue and added sulkily. 'I can't do it on my own. I have no connections in Italy. It is only by coincidence that I discovered my husband had been sending money to Salazar. I want to know where it has all gone. Salazar said that he withdrew it. It is not true.'

Celestria stopped smiling. She felt light-headed as the blood drained from her cheeks.

'Your husband is sending money to Salazar?' she repeated slowly.

'*Was* sending money to Salazar. My husband is dead.'

Federica looked from one to the other. 'Now I am afraid,' she said, clutching the beads that hung against her chest. 'This is madness.' Celestria felt the room spinning around her. She stared at Armel.

'We have more in common than you would imagine,' she said. 'My father is also dead.' Armel's cool façade now crumbled. Her eyes glistened, and her lips began to quiver.

'Forgive me,' she whispered. She took a moment to compose herself, during which time Celestria and Mrs Waynebridge looked at each other in bewilderment. Mrs Halifax didn't know quite what to make of the sudden turn of events, and Federica's fear mounted. Something very sinister was going on in Marelatte. 'We need to talk, you and I,' Armel said at last. 'Perhaps we are not alone.'

'You think there may be others?'

'For sure. Why not?' She shrugged. 'Salazar is a crook. I believe my husband was murdered. I believe Salazar was behind it.'

'What are we going to do?' Celestria asked, gnawing the skin around her thumbnail. Armel's beautiful face now looked older and less hard.

'I don't know. But we have each other.' She managed a thin smile, but her eyes revealed nothing but hopelessness.

'Don't leave us out,' said Federica, the colour returning to her cheeks. 'You have us, too. Don't forget, I'm Italian, and I have connections.' She turned to Celestria, the suspicion that had cast a shadow across her face now dispelled. 'I want to help,' she said. 'I *really* want to help.'

At that moment Gaitano entered the room, followed by Primo and the other dogs. 'Forgive me,' he said brightly, taking the last seat. Celestria felt a wave of disappointment as she realized that Hamish was obviously not joining them for dinner. 'I had a few things to discuss with my son-in-law. This building is an ongoing project. A labour of love.'

'We are still converting rooms,' Federica added, trying to shake off the sinister feeling that that these two foreign women had whipped up in the room. Her cheerfulness couldn't fool her husband, however.

'What is going on?' he asked solemnly, shifting his eyes across the faces of the four women. Federica sighed and told him the whole story.

'It is very strange,' she said finally. 'One Englishman and one Frenchman both die, having transferred enormous amounts of money to Salazar.'

'My husband wasn't French,' interjected Armel. 'He was English.'

'My father did a lot of business in Paris,' said Celestria.

'My husband did a lot of business in London.'

'You don't suppose . . .' Celestria's voice trailed off. It was too much of a coincidence, surely.

'That they knew each other?' said Armel. She took a gulp of wine. 'Now you come to mention it, why not?'

Chapter 25

After dinner, Armel put out her third cigarette and drained her wineglass. 'I can tell you that I will not leave until I have uncovered my husband's murderer,' she said, standing up shakily. She was far removed now from the brittle, arrogant woman Celestria had seen in the police station. She looked fragile and desperate, the shadows under her eyes emphasized by the amber glow of the candlelight. Gaitano pushed out his chair.

'Allow me to escort you to your room,' he said, and she didn't decline. Mrs Waynebridge suggested Celestria have an early night.

'You've had a long day,' she said kindly. 'What you need is a good sleep.' Celestria didn't argue. Her eyes suddenly felt heavy with exhaustion. Federica and Mrs Halifax bade her good night and she left the room with Mrs Waynebridge shuffling out behind her.

As she walked down the corridor she noticed a little staircase leading up to a room she hadn't seen before. The door had been left ajar. Inside, the light was on. But there seemed to be no one there. She could just make out a table of paint pots. Her heart stumbled. It must be Hamish's studio, she thought, discovering a hidden source of energy as her disappointment evaporated. Mrs Waynebridge left her in her room. She stood in front of the mirror in her pretty white dress and looked at her reflection. *All dressed up and no place to go,* she thought. There were no parties in Marelatte. Only Hamish with his dark, enigmatic presence. He was clearly still avoiding her.

Without another thought, she left her room and tiptoed down the corridor to where the little staircase promised proximity to the man who had inflamed her imagination. She looked about her to make sure there was no one around and then climbed the steps. With a thumping heart she pushed the door a little, and it opened with a gentle whine. Inside was a square room with a small window looking out over the sea. The moon was full, lighting up the water below it with bold silver strokes. On the left was a table, covered in dried paint, and coloured pots and tubes of watercolours and oils. There were muddy jars of brushes and thin brown boxes piled one on top of another. On the right were large canvases stacked against the wall. She wandered over to take a look. To her horror, many were grim and dark pictures of ghoulish faces. Some were so abstract she couldn't make out what they were. Daphne Halifax's paintings were heavenly compared with the hell of Hamish's compositions. She pondered the state of mind necessary to produce such tortured pictures. She rested them back against the wall and turned to the canvas that was placed on an easel. The paint was still shiny and wet. He must have painted it that day. Like the others, it was dark. A man sat hunched at the bottom of the painting, shrouded in a black cloak, facing away so that she couldn't see his face. In front of him, in the right-hand corner of the picture, there was a door left ajar. Around the door was a golden light coming from the other side. It seemed so bright compared with the dimness of the world inhabited by the crouching man. She extended her hand and touched the canvas. The paint was still sticky. She withdrew her fingers, rubbing them together to erase the paint stuck to her skin. With a shiver that rippled across her flesh, she felt his desolation and the desire to open the door and enter the light. The picture stirred in her something strange and unfamiliar, a deep sense of compassion.

Suddenly, she heard footsteps coming down the corridor. She froze. There was nowhere to hide. She turned around, her mind cranking up a suitable excuse for once again intruding. Before, she had felt so bold. Now she felt foolish. As the shadow of a man fell across the door, she grew hot with fear, her heart beating loud and fast. To her immense relief, it wasn't Hamish but Gaitano. He looked at her quizzically.

'I'm afraid my curiosity got the better of me,' she admitted, looking sheepish.

He smiled and shook his head. 'You're daring in your curiosity.'

'Perhaps too daring. He despises me for intruding into his wife's crypt. He'd probably strangle me if he discovered me here, looking at his paintings.'

'Natalia's tomb is a sacred place for him.'

'I know that now. I was in the wrong. It wasn't right to go there. I was walking on her grave.'

'I don't believe in holding on to the dead. One has to let them go.'

'Judging by these pictures, I don't think he's ready to let her go.'

Gaitano sighed. 'That is because he does not want to. He is wracked with guilt because he was with her when she fell off the cliff. He believes it was his fault. Freddie and I don't throw blame. It was an accident.'

'I'm so sorry.' Celestria stared at the painting, now understanding why he couldn't reach the light behind the door. He felt he didn't deserve to.

'Natalia died three years ago. She would not have wanted us to remain in a state of mourning. She was a bright, carefree spirit who believed in the world beyond death. She didn't fear it, so neither should we.'

'My father's death has devastated my family' she said, wanting him to know that she understood bereavement. That she wasn't an outsider, preying on someone else's misfortune. 'My mother's inconsolable. My father was the world to her. She's lost without him.'

He turned to her, rubbing his chin thoughtfully. 'If I can do anything to help you and Armel, I will. Let's sleep on it. Everyone has chinks in his armour, even Salazar.'

'Thank you,' she replied.

'Don't let Hamish intimidate you. He's very soft beneath his hard shell.'

'Oh, he doesn't intimidate me at all. We can easily avoid each other.'

Gaitano smiled knowingly. 'Of course you can.'

As they left the little room, Gaitano switched off the light and closed the door. Celestria longed to ask where Hamish was, why he hadn't joined them for dinner. But she felt it was none of her business. Gaitano escorted her to her room and said good night. She undressed and brushed her teeth. As she was getting into bed she heard the banging of the front door and footsteps in the courtyard below. Something compelled her to move to the window. As she peered through the crack in the shutters, she saw, to her astonishment, Hamish staring up at her bedroom window. He ran a hand through his hair, hesitating a moment as if deliberating what to do next. For a second their eyes met. She jumped away as if scalded, her cheeks hot with embarrassment at having been caught watching him. She remained petrified, wishing she had had the sense to peer through the shutter, waiting for the footsteps to continue and disappear.

Finally, she climbed into bed and switched off the light. That moment of silent communication embossed itself on her mind like a still from a film: his face, set in a grimace, suddenly handsome in the light of the moon. She sensed they were somehow linked, as if he were pulling her towards him like a furious magnet. She lay alert to every sound. It wasn't long before she heard his footsteps along the corridor outside. She froze in her bed, barely daring to breathe. There was no reason why he should knock on her door, or even pause outside her room. Yet, as the footsteps neared her room, she was sure they slowed down. Her pulse thumped in her ears. The footsteps were now right outside her door. She could feel his eyes upon it, burning through it, as if he could see into the dark room to where she lay trembling in her bed. Then they continued, and she was left wondering whether she had simply imagined it.

The following morning she found Armel in the garden, hiding behind a large pair of sunglasses, a sunhat upon her head, a small cup of coffee in her hands. She wore the same pair of navy blue slacks she had worn the night before. When she saw Celestria, she raised her hand and waved.

'*Bonjour,*' she said, her voice friendly. 'Why don't you join me?' Celestria sat on the wicker chair beside her.

'Have you seen Waynie?'

'I believe she went into town,' she replied.

'Alone?'

'No, some retainer was with her.'

'Nuzzo,' said Celestria, with a grin. 'I think Waynie has found love.'

'Lucky her,' said Armel dryly. 'I have lost mine.' She took a sip of coffee. 'I drank too much last night. My head aches.'

'There was a lot to take in,' Celestria conceded. 'What are we going to do, Armel?'

The older woman shook her head. 'I don't know.'

'Surely we can do something. We're stronger as a team.'

'I exhausted myself last night, trying to work out a way of sneaking into Salazar's office, but if there was anything incriminating in his office, you can be sure that he has got rid of it.'

'He looks like a Mafia boss with those funny two-toned shoes.'

'I suspect he did some sort of business, or investment, with my husband and your father, probably others, and ran off with the money. No one would connect two deaths in two different countries.'

'What was your husband called?'

'Benedict Devere. We met in Paris at the races before the war. He was so handsome I could barely take my eyes off him.'

'Do you have children?'

'No. I wanted children, but it wasn't to be. Now I am too old. I wish I had something left of him. A child that was a part of him. At least you are a comfort to your mother.' She twisted the rings on the third finger of her left hand. One was a large diamond solitaire.

'I have a little brother, too.'

'You have each other.'

'One only realizes how much one relies on someone after he is gone.'

'Salazar has not only stolen my husband, but he has left me without a penny to my name. Only the house in Paris and the jewellery Benedict gave me over the years, which I am pawning little by little. Soon I will have nothing left. You see, it is vital that I get that money back.'

'What was Benedict's business?' Celestria asked.

'He was an entrepreneur. He bought and sold art, the odd racehorse, property.'

'Sounds like my grandfather,' Celestria said.

'It was only after he died that I had to look into his affairs. It seems that he gave every last penny to Salazar.' She frowned and drained her cup. 'He must have discovered some major invest-ment opportunity out here. That is the only answer. But what?'

'Do you suppose Benedict and Papa were in it together? I don't know exactly what Papa did. But I did discover that his business went bust a couple of years ago. All the while he was supposedly in Paris on business, he was here. Did Benedict ever mention Papa? His name was Robert Montague, Monty for short.'

Armel removed her sunglasses, and her dim eyes lit up with recognition. 'Yes, I know that name very well. Monty was your father?'

'Yes. Did you meet him?'

'No. But Benedict spoke about him. I had no idea they did business together, but he was definitely a friend he had in London. Your mother is Pamela?'

'Yes.'

'Of course. She's American, like you. Benedict told me about her.' Now she smiled at the memory. 'He said she was very beautiful, but very demanding.'

'I'm afraid she needs a lot of attention. She hated it when Papa travelled. That's why it was so upsetting to discover that he hadn't had a job for the last two years.'

'Perhaps not the job he had originally, but if he was in business with Benedict, he was working, believe me. It might not have been the desk job he had had before, but it would still have required him to have travelled.'

'That's a relief to know,' said Celestria, her heart surging with gratitude. 'That's been bothering me so much. To think that my father might have been travelling to avoid being with us.'

'Listen, Benedict was secretive about what he did and where he went. It was all part of the job. Some he lost, some he won. I didn't get too involved. He was an independent spirit. He didn't want some nagging wife making demands on him all the time.'

'I think Mama made Papa crazy with her demands.' She remembered with a bitter aftertaste the last conversation her mother had had with her father: *He told me I was spoiled and greedy. He said the sooner you married, the better, because you were only going to turn out like me, driving him insane with your demands.'*

'Do you smoke?' Celestria took a cigarette from Armel.

'Mama doesn't know what to do with herself now that Papa has died. You see, not only did he give Salazar his own money, but Mama's as well, not to mention what by right belonged to me and Harry.'

'Mon dieu!' Armel shook her head and blew the smoke out of the side of her mouth. 'It must have been an incredible opportunity to risk so much.'

'So you don't think he stole it?' Celestria was ashamed they had all jumped to that conclusion.

'Not necessarily. Perhaps he thought he was going to make you all a fortune.'

'We already had a fortune,' said Celestria.

'Maybe he thought he'd double it. If he was anything like Benedict, I doubt he ever thought he'd lose it. Benedict invested my money for me. Most of the time it was worth it.'

'Did he give your money to Salazar, too?'

'I had so little, Celestria. In the end I didn't consider it mine. He looked after me. Now he is gone, I'm alone. There is no one to look after me. I'm forty-five years old, and I have nothing. I will have to sell the house and buy a small apartment. You can imagine. I have been used to a certain standard of living. Now I have to begin all over again.' Celestria inhaled deeply. To be bereft was bad enough; to be bereft and poor was unthinkable. At least Celestria had her grandfather.

Armel and Celestria had no option but to bide their time.

Armel was sure that, with Freddie and Gaitano's help, a chink in Salazar's armour could be found. Celestria was content to wait. The longer she waited, the more likely she was to bump into Hamish, who now dominated her thoughts almost more than her father did.

She spent the afternoon with Mrs Waynebridge and Daphne Halifax, accompanied by the playful Nuzzo. He and Mrs Waynebridge seemed to have a joke that only they shared, for they ribbed each other teasingly, stating words in their own language for the other to repeat. They walked into town. The locals all greeted them warmly. The children with the same curiosity, giggling behind brown hands, followed them in small, mischievous groups, like elves.

They entered a little shop that sold food and postcards. A young woman stood behind a counter; her aged mother, dressed in black from head to toe, embroidered a shawl in the corner on a stool, while two small children played in the doorway. They shared banter with Nuzzo, who took off his beret when he entered. They laughed, even the sad-looking old lady, who cackled at Nuzzo's impish charm. Celestria bought postcards to send to Lotty, Melissa, and her mother. She chose one for Aidan, out of guilt, because Daphne was right; she wasn't missing him.

Mrs Waynebridge bought some postcards, too, while Daphne exchanged a few words with the shopkeeper in broken Italian. After that they ambled along the coast, taking pleasure from the rocky coves along the way. Nuzzo picked flowers to give to the women, but Celestria knew they were all plucked for Waynie. She wanted to ask where Hamish's wife had died. The cliffs were high and sheer the whole way along. It could have happened anywhere. Nuzzo would know. However, she felt she shouldn't ask.

★

Hamish did not appear that evening, either. Celestria was frustrated. She saw so much of Freddie and Gaitano; how was it possible for him to avoid her? She wished they had never met in that dreadful place. Then he wouldn't have overheard her talking about him with Daphne in the dining room. They might even have become friends.

During dinner, the conversation turned unexpectedly to Hamish. Federica mentioned Saverio's bar in town, where he went every night, staying until the early hours of the morning, playing Scopa with the locals. Celestria was struck with a crazy idea. After dinner, she said good night to Mrs Waynebridge, but, instead of going to bed herself, she crept out of the Convento and made her way into town.

She walked briskly under the pines. The moonlight was bright, casting shadows across the paving stones as if it were a silver sun. The air was thick with the scent of wood and herbs from the Convento's garden, and the smell of lilies was carried over the wall of the city of the dead on a cold breeze blowing in off the sea. Celestria shivered, wondering whether she should go back. What would he think of her turning up like this? She knew no one. What if he wasn't there? If he was, what on earth was she going to say to him?

She arrived at the bar. Small groups of men were sitting outside, playing cards, smoking, and drinking. She noticed at once that there were no women. One by one they lifted their eyes. Some glared at her with hostility, others with ill-disguised delight. She tried to look confident, but inside she felt lost. She knew she was not welcome. Suddenly a familiar voice called her name. She turned to see Salazar standing behind her in a coat that was extravagantly lined and had a wide fur collar, wearing those old-fashioned two-toned shoes. He looked ridiculous.

'Miss Montague,' he said, amused to see her in such an unlikely place. 'It is a pleasure to see you again.' His smile was broad and somehow indecent. He held out his arms again, as if about to embrace her. 'Let me buy you a *limoncello*. It is only right to welcome you to my town. I must apologize for our hasty meeting. That woman has been a plague.' He shook his head, lifting his hand to escort her into the bar. Celestria feigned confidence, knowing it was the only way to get her through what was clearly a terrible mistake.

'She was very rude,' she replied, hoping to draw him into a false sense of friendship.

'Frenchwomen have no manners. I much prefer doing business with the British.' As she walked in, she felt more pairs of eyes upon her, indignant, as if she had walked into a private party uninvited. Salazar ordered a *limoncello* for her and a coffee for himself. 'So,' he said, appraising her with unguarded appreciation, 'you are very brave to come here on your own. Saverio's wife only serves behind the bar during daylight hours, and she's as ill-humoured and tough as a donkey.'

'Oh?' she replied coolly, noticing his predatory eyes slipping over her body, as if deciding which part he'd devour first. 'Do Italian men turn into vampires the moment the sun sets?'

He chuckled. 'Didn't your mother warn you? Night-time is not safe for little girls.'

'Should I be worried?'

He shrugged. 'Not now you are with me. Salazar will take care of you.' He raised his eyes to a group of people in the corner laughing raucously. Celestria turned around to see Hamish at a table, playing cards with a group of men in caps. He was throwing his head back, roaring with laughter like a lion, his hair falling about him in a shaggy mane. Her heart surged with relief. However, he couldn't see her because he was facing the other way. She turned back to Salazar, who was beginning to make her extremely uncomfortable. 'Did you come here alone?' he asked.

'Of course,' she replied defiantly. 'This is a small town; I'm hardly likely to get lost.'

'As long as you don't walk in the shadows.' He laughed and puffed on his cigar, blowing smoke into her face. *'Poverina!'* His eyes lingered on her lips longer than was polite. 'This is no place for a girl; why don't I walk you home? Where are you staying? At the Convento?' Before she was able to reply, Hamish's voice spoke from behind her.

'That's okay, Salazar. I'll walk her home. She's staying with us.' Celestria was too relieved to feel foolish. She spun around to face him. 'Shall we go?' he asked, raising his eyebrows in amusement, his mouth displaying the beginnings of a smile.

'I'm ready,' she replied.

'Che peccato,' said Salazar, putting the cigar between his lips. 'We were just getting to know each other.'

'Tell your wife,' said Hamish, placing his hand in the small of her back and leading her out into the street.

'Thank you,' she said, folding her arms and shivering, more from fright than nerves.

'What? For not shouting at you?' He smiled cynically.

'No, for saving me from Salazar.'

'You're a foolish American,' he replied, leaning on his stick with one hand, putting the other in his trouser pocket. 'Where do you think you are? In Manhattan?'

Chapter 26

They set out down the road towards the Convento. Hamish leaned on his stick, his limp preventing him from walking very quickly. Celestria was aware of every fibre in her body, her nerves alert like an animal braced to react, uncertain whether he was friend or foe. However, one thing was certain: he was unable to avoid her now.

'What on earth possessed you to come to the bar?' he asked gruffly.

'I was bored at the Convento. I wasn't ready to go to bed.'

'Do you make a habit of wandering the streets at night on your own?'

'Certainly not! What are you implying?'

'I'm joking. This might be a small town, but I wouldn't consider it safe for a girl like you.'

'A girl like me?'

He glanced at her. 'You're more suited to the Ritz than to a small-town bar frequented by rough countrymen.'

'You misjudge me.'

'I never misjudge anyone.'

'You're going on appearances. You don't know me at all.'

He stopped and looked her up and down as one might appraise a mare for sale. 'Expensively cut, well-conditioned hair. Blonde, which is rare in these parts. Manicured nails, polished skin, clean clothes, a fresh dress every day, smart leather shoes, painted toenails, elegance, refinement, and an air of snootiness, too, which comes from being spoiled by your parents. Don't pretend you felt you blended into Saverio's, because you stuck out like a swan among swine.' Flattered that he had noticed her in such detail, Celestria hid her pleasure behind a veneer of defiance.

'If one was to judge simply on appearances, you wouldn't come off too well yourself.' She looked him up and down with the same arrogance. 'Hair that could do with a good wash and a brush; a shave wouldn't go amiss, either. Stooping shoulders, which denotes a man ill at ease with himself or his height, which should be an advantage. Scruffy clothes more suited to a shepherd than an artist, who should really have more taste. The shoes could do with a polish, too. But I don't judge on the outside alone.'

'You don't know what you're talking about.'

'You're wrong. But you are right about one thing, I didn't like the bar at all.'

He continued to walk. 'That's because you got hooked by the crookedest man in Marelatte.'

'And unhooked by the angriest man in Marelatte.'

He glanced down at her irritably, but her smile was surprisingly infectious; he couldn't help but smile, too. Celestria felt a wave of triumph.

'I have good reason to be angry.' His face crumpled into a frown. 'But I don't owe anyone an explanation, least of all you.'

'I think you're old enough to do as you please.'

'How old do you think I am?'

She laughed, though every muscle in her face and neck was taut. 'I don't know. Older than me.'

'Most of Marelatte is older than you. You're just setting off, like a beautiful sailing boat. I imagine this is the first time you've left the safety of your cove. I should stay with the oldies. It's safer within the walls of the Convento.'

'With you in residence, I don't think that particular cove is very safe at all.'

'You can't be afraid of a man with a limp? Even though he's a little rough around the edges.'

'I gather it was a hunting accident,' she said.

He looked at her quizzically, and she realized that she had unwittingly revealed that she had been asking about him. She was sure his lips twitched with amusement.

'I haven't ridden since,' he replied, looking straight ahead.

'Do you miss it?'

'Damn right, I miss it.' He shook his head. 'I don't think I've experienced such freedom as I felt on a horse. Flying like the wind. Jumping whatever stands in my way. I was good at it, too.'

'I've never even sat on a horse.'

'No?'

'Now taxis, I've been in a lot of taxis. Yellow ones in New York and black ones in London. That's something I'm really good at, along with painting my nails and sitting in the hair salon.' He chuckled, the lines around his eyes and mouth deepening into his weathered skin. She felt a sudden yearning to run her fingers over them.

'But you love books,' he said softly, and she realized to her joy that he, in turn, had been asking about her.

'Gaitano says we share a favourite book,' she ventured.

'*The Count of Monte Cristo.*'

'And the terrible Château d'If,' she added with a grin.

'What else do you love?'

She sighed ponderously. 'I love dancing, playing the piano . . .'

'Yes, I know.'

She felt herself blush and hastily moved on. 'Freddie told me you're the only one who plays.'

'Not any more.'

'Why not?'

'Because it makes me sad.'

'I find the melancholy tunes uplift me the most.'

He turned and looked at her curiously. 'Do they?'

She knew then that he had witnessed her tears. She turned away. 'Yes. By expressing my feelings, I release them.'

They walked under the pine trees, across the dark shadows and silver slashes of moonlight that lit up the paving stones beneath their feet. The Convento loomed out of the night, seemingly impenetrable. The door was closed; the little window carved into the stone, where the dove had cooed the evening they had arrived, now blind and empty. The bell tower on the roof of the church caught the light and turned to silver. They both tasted the floral scent from the city of the dead across the road. Celestria didn't want the night to end.

'Do you want to come and look at the sea from the old fortress? It'll be beautiful in this moonlight,' he asked, stopping to glance across the road. His features grew suddenly serious, his brow lined and heavy, as if an invisible weight had at once smothered any joy.

'I'd love to,' Celestria replied, finding her eyes drawn there, too, knowing that he was thinking of Natalia. She felt jealous of the ghost who still laid claim to his heart. And yet they barely knew each other. She had no right to it. Again he put his hand in the small of her back as he accompanied her across the track, though there was little danger at this time of night from Nuzzo in his horse and cart. The warmth of his hand burned through her dress.

They walked past the gates in silence, the crypts dark in the tranquillity of the night. Hamish threw a troubled glimpse inside, to where the park was bathed in shadows cast by the towering pine trees and beyond, to where the eye could not see, to where the spirit of his wife remained, locked in that small, candle-lit mausoleum with the secrets that only they knew.

'Darkness is simply the absence of light,' he mumbled.

'Are you in a dark place, Hamish?' she asked gently, moved by the heaviness that now enveloped them.

'What do you know of darkness?' he retorted gruffly.

'I can feel it,' she replied, following him down the little stony path that led to the cliffs where the old fortress stood, silhouetted against the sky. 'I feel it when I'm with you.' He stopped and looked at her a moment, his eyes boring into hers as if searching for something.

'What did you just say?' he asked, leaning towards her. His voice was full of pain.

'I feel the darkness that surrounds you.' He didn't respond, but turned and continued to walk down the path.

Finally, he sat down on the dry grass where she had sat the day before while Daphne painted. The fortress was filled with shadows, desolate and empty like Hamish himself, plagued with demons and a deep, unfathomable sadness. They sat together, gazing in silence over the rippling sea and vast starlit sky. In that moment, sitting beside the man she now knew she loved, Celestria felt the gentle movement of the earth's plates beneath her.

'What are you doing in Puglia?' he said at last. She took in his profile, the strong line of his jaw, the long crooked nose, and the bright, almond-shaped eyes blessed with thick, feathery lashes.

'I have come to find my father's killer,' she replied steadily.

'Your father was killed?' He stared at her incredulously.

'My father apparently committed suicide in Cornwall a few weeks ago. He drowned at sea. They found his boat and a suicide note. But if you knew my father, you'd be as certain as I am that he would never have taken his own life. I have discovered that he sent large sums of money to Salazar, which is why I went to see him. Salazar claims my father withdrew it again, but I don't believe him. I think he stole the money and, somehow, got rid of my father.'

Hamish's head spun. 'I didn't know,' he murmured, toying pensively with the crook of his walking stick. 'You must be shattered.' Now he knew why she had been crying, and his heart filled with compassion. Like him, she was well acquainted with grief.

'Do you know what I'm most afraid of?' She felt emotion tighten her throat and the prickling sensation of tears behind her eyes. It was only because of the beauty of the night and because Hamish, too, suffered the pain of bereavement that she let down her guard. For the first time since her father died, she felt her heart buckle with sorrow, as if she had at last allowed it in. 'I'm afraid that I'm wrong. That he stole our money, then killed himself because he couldn't bear to live with the shame. If that's true, then I'm afraid that I never knew him.' She wiped away a fat tear that trickled slowly down her cheek. Hamish put his arm around her and drew her against him. She rested her head on his chest and closed her eyes. Perhaps it was the darkness, or the fact that he hurt, too, that enabled her to grieve without embarrassment.

'The people you think you know are often full of surprises. Those you hold in the highest esteem only disappoint you,' he said, his tone full of bitterness. 'Even those closest to you, the ones you think you know the best. You don't know them at all. All you have is your trust.'

Hamish withdrew his arm and began to toy once again with his stick. 'I hope you have some nice young man back in England to make you happy.'

Celestria was stung by his comment. She didn't want a nice young man as superficial as she was. In Hamish's eyes she saw great depths like oceans, stirred by sorrow, agitated by joy, but most of all unpredictable. She knew she'd never settle now for shallow pools and puddles where the stones below

were clearly visible. Her heart strained to reach him, longing
for him to hold her. His words made her recoil. If he really
believed that, then what was he doing sitting alone with her
in the middle of the night?

'There are plenty,' she replied, wanting to hurt him back. 'As
soon as my questions have been answered, I'll return home.'

'Girls like you are sure to marry well,' he said ironically.
'Not only are you taught to sing and dance, you're taught to
think in terms of wealth and estates. I spent most of my life in
England, and I know your sort. Well-educated girls like you
live in a rarefied, though I might add, disadvantaged, world.
You lick the fruit of life, but you don't bite into it and taste
the bitterness and sweetness of the flesh.'

'That's where you're wrong. When I fall in love, the earth
will shake, tremble, and shift on its axis, whether the man I
lose my heart to has money or not.' She stood up and made
her way down the slope to the fortress, surprised by her words,
which echoed with an honesty and sincerity she had never felt
before.

It was dark inside the fortress. The earth was damp, the stone
walls cold and hard. She could hear the sea below, lapping
against the cliffs with wet tongues. Her heart was thumping,
throbbing in her ears. She hoped Hamish would follow. She
hurried along the stones to the other side, where the wall was
crumbling but a tall window remained, giving on to the glittering ocean and navy blue sky, where a corpulent moon
hung low and heavy. She stood staring out, the wind raking
cold fingers through her hair, sure she could sense him
approaching her slowly from behind.

Then it was his fingers on the back of her neck, and not
the wind. Caressing the skin there, cupping her shoulder, and
turning her around to face him. He looked down at her, this
big, strong man with eyes as vulnerable as a child's.

'I'm sorry. I've been foolish. Playing a clumsy game,' he said, gently tracing her cheek and neck.

'Why play a game at all?'

'Because I don't want to love you.' He studied her face as if hypnotized by what he saw. 'I'm drawn to you. Don't think I haven't tried to resist you.'

'Why resist me? Don't you deserve to be happy?' He was very close now. She could feel the warmth of his body against hers, his breath on her forehead, his lips only inches away, and the delicious tingling in the pit of her belly.

'I don't think I can any longer,' he groaned, closing his eyes and kissing her. Aware only of him, she remained in the present moment, savouring the tenderness of his touch, the feel of his rough skin against hers, his smooth, warm lips, and the sense of being pulled into the eye of the storm, from where there would be no turning back.

They spoke no more. There was too much on his mind even to begin. He didn't know how to explain. He wasn't sure she'd understand. Right now, he, too, existed in the present moment, relishing the taste of this woman who had held him in her thrall since their first inauspicious meeting in the cemetery. He had secretly watched her, tried to ignore his fascination with her, fought to resist the power of her attraction, knowing all along that there was light behind the door, if only he could reach it. If only she were someone else. Anyone other than Robert Montague's daughter.

He knew he shouldn't kiss her. But what man could resist the warm translucence of her skin, the sensuality of her lips, the startling brazenness of her sexuality set against the cool stiffness of her class, like cream on stone? He had fought against his reasoning and lost to his instincts, like an animal with nothing but his five senses. How blissful it would be to lose himself in her, to forget his past and the tragedy there that would inevitably poison any cup of joy he attempted to drink from.

Finally, he pulled away. 'Come, I'll take you back to the Convento.' His voice was full of regret, betraying the confusion that tore him in two.

He took her hand and the stick that he had leaned against the wall, and they walked back up the path. They passed the walls of the city of the dead, and, even though no words were spoken, the fact that he made a conscious effort not to look there told Celestria that she had lost him. When they reached the Convento, the little window in the wall was no longer empty. Not one but two fat doves slept in the moonlight.

He turned the key in the lock and opened the door for her. She realized that had she not met him in the bar, she would not have been able to get back inside. Once within the sanctuary of those walls, they crept across the courtyard and upstairs without exchanging a word. Celestria wished he would say something. They had crossed an invisible line. It wasn't possible now to step back. Quietly, he escorted her down the corridor to her bedroom. With her fingers on the handle, she hesitated, longing for reassurance.

'Where do we go from here?' she said at last, turning to face him.

He shook his head and frowned, his face cast in shadow. 'I don't know.'

'You can't allow yourself to wither away, loving a ghost, Hamish.'

His eyes grew hostile. 'You don't know what you're saying,' he whispered.

She reached out and touched his arm. Her hand looked out of place there. 'Do you want to pretend this never happened?'

'It happened because we both wanted it to happen. But you don't want me,' he said, without self-pity. 'Trust me, your suitors in London are a much safer bet.'

'Don't play that old card with me. So you're in your late thirties, you have a limp, you need to brush your hair and learn some manners and a little patience; I can live with all of that. But I can't compete with a woman who's not around to play fair.'

At the mention of his wife, the air stilled around them. He glared at her, suddenly distant, the intimacy they had shared in the fort all but completely evaporated.

'You don't understand,' he began, closing his eyes as if to control his fury. 'You're young. You know nothing about love.'

'If I don't understand, it's because you haven't explained it to me. You're right, I am young, but I know about love.'

'You do?'

'Yes, I do now. Because I realize the love I thought I felt before has been all about me. I want to run my fingers over your wounds and heal them. I want to kiss away the past and bring light and happiness to your future.'

He was disarmed by her candour. 'You don't know me,' he said incredulously, a little afraid.

'But I love you regardless.' She gazed at him steadily, absolutely sure of herself. 'I don't care about your past; it has nothing to do with me.'

'Oh, God,' he groaned. 'It has everything to do with you.'

They stared at each other for a long moment. Finally, he touched her cheek with his rough and calloused hand, shaking his head in bemusement. 'I don't know what to make of you,' he said.

She turned and kissed the palm of his hand. 'I'm the light behind the door.' He looked at her in surprise. 'You're in a dark place entirely of your own making.'

'I wish that were so. Good night, Celestria,' he said, leaning down and planting a lingering kiss on her forehead. Then he turned and walked away.

Chapter 27

Cornwall

Back at Pendrift Hall, Archie and Julia waited anxiously for the car. It was a beautiful sunny day, so the house would be shown off to its best advantage. Wilfrid and Sam were at school, and little Bouncy had been sent to his grandmother's for the morning so that the prospective purchasers could look around in peace. The estate agent had valued it far higher than Archie had predicted, but neither of them wanted to sell. Archie had lost his temper, Julia had sulked, but they had both come to the conclusion that they were left no option. The debts had to be repaid. They were struggling to keep afloat. Neither had had the courage to tell Elizabeth.

Archie tried not to become sentimental. It was bricks and mortar, after all. Julia, however, couldn't help but cling to the memories of her boys' young lives that lingered in every corner, beneath every chair and table where they had played, in the gardens and down on the beach. The air still vibrated with their laughter and the laughter of their father and his siblings. She couldn't bear to tear her children away from the only home they had ever known. She knew she'd shatter their security. In an uncertain world, she wanted to give them that one certainty from which they would set off to make their own way. Whatever life threw at them, nothing would ever take away that magical foundation. Now, her hopes were dashed.

At last a silver Mercedes convertible drew up outside the Hall. Soames waited for them on the steps that led up to the front door. He stood stiffly in his black tailcoat and shiny shoes, rocking gently back and forth, holding his chin up so that he could peer down his nose in a supercilious fashion. Three people climbed out: Mr Townley, the slick estate agent, in a pinstriped three-piece suit and tie, and Mr and Mrs Weavel, the prospective buyers, who Soames thought looked frightfully common.

Reluctantly he showed them into the hall, reeling at the sweet cologne that Mr Weavel had clearly bathed in that morning, and apparently swallowed, too, for it seeped from every pore. Archie and Julia knew they had arrived, but remained seated in the drawing room, pretending to read the papers. Both were too nervous to read. Julia smoked her third cigarette of the morning while Archie rubbed his fingers over his moustache. They caught eyes as the sound of Soames's footsteps crossed the hall. Julia stubbed out her cigarette and Archie's fingers froze on the thatch of hair that had now been smoothed so much it shone.

'Come in,' called Archie in response to Soames's knock. The butler entered, looking as unhappy as they did.

'Mr and Mrs Weavel and Mr Townley.' Archie folded his paper and stood up. Julia followed suit, throwing her newspaper onto the coffee table in the centre of the room.

'It's a pleasure to meet you,' said Archie, extending his hand.

'You have a beautiful house,' simpered Mrs Weavel, laying her hand limply in his like a dead pigeon. 'It's everything I hoped it would be.'

'We have been very happy here,' replied Archie, aware that Julia was almost too distraught to speak. It was so out of character for her not even to manage a smile.

Mr Townley shook hands firmly and with enthusiasm. This
would be a big sale for him. The Weavels were very rich.

'Do you have children?' Julia asked, watching with indignation as Mrs Weavel wandered about the drawing room in her
tight little grey flannel suit and stilettos, peering into everything. Didn't she know they weren't selling the furniture?

'No, we don't,' she replied. 'Paul and I don't really like
children very much.' She laughed falsely, giving a little sniff
and a shrug by way of an apology.

'This really is a family home,' Julia added with emphasis.

'Oh, goodness me, we're not going to live here ourselves,'
Mrs Weavel said. She looked at her husband, who chuckled
at the absurdity of the idea. 'No, didn't Mr Townley tell you?
We're going to turn it into a hotel.'

Julia glared at Archie. Archie looked away. What did it
matter what they did to it?

'Why don't I show you around?' he suggested, striding
into the hall. 'It's a large house, and I'm sure you're busy
people.'

Mr and Mrs Weavel followed him. Mr Townley was put
out. He'd rather have done the showing around himself. It
was always easier to sell a property if the owners made themselves scarce.

Julia heard them talking in the hall. She remained standing with her hands clenched, wondering where she could
go and hide. Those damned people were going to go into
every room in the house. How dare they rifle through all
her things, trample on her memories? She couldn't bear it.
They didn't even like children. Mrs Weavel was so arid Julia
doubted her womb would be capable of conceiving, and Mr
Weavel was beyond belief with that disgusting scent. It
made her eyes water, and, worse, it was already lingering in
the soft furnishings. She'd have to open the windows the
moment they had gone.

She sank onto the sofa and stared into the half distance. So this was to be a hotel? This beautiful drawing room would be a tacky lounge full of cigar-smoking strangers paying large amounts of money to taste a bit of history. She could imagine the crimson-and-gold-patterned carpets and tables of magazines. The thought of what they would do to the children's bedrooms was more than she could stand. She put her head in her hands and wept. *If only Monty were alive, none of this would be happening. He would have thought of something.*

After an hour Archie stepped into the hall, followed by a delighted Mr Townley, rubbing his hands together with glee. The Weavels loved it. They adored the views. They'd have to cut down a few trees, of course, in order to accommodate the gazebo, and that pond would have to go, as would the little square lawn at the front of the house, because they'd need a car park for guests. There was plenty of space where the terrace stood for a conservatory. Mrs Weavel was very fond of conservatories. 'That way the guests can enjoy the garden even when it's raining,' she had said. Mr Townley had commended her flair.

They stood in the hall, all smiling, except for Archie, whose expression was so pained it was more of a grimace than a smile.

'It's perfect,' gushed Mrs Weavel, taking her husband's hand.

'I would like to make you an offer you can't refuse,' said Mr Weavel. He was clearly the sort of man who liked to talk big. He expected Archie to look pleased. Archie looked miserable.

'You won't be sorry,' said Mr Townley, breaking into a sweat. 'It's a rare piece of England. A jewel, and it comes with the charming little town of Pendrift.'

'We appreciate that,' replied Mr Weavel, puffing out his chest. 'And our guests will appreciate that, too. It's a shame when these old houses are allowed to go to ruin because the grand families who live in them don't have the cash to maintain them. That's where we step in. We'd like to throw you a lifeline and rescue your house.' He glanced up at the pretty mouldings on the ceiling and shook his head. 'To think that this beautiful place has been hidden from view for three hundred years. Damn shame, if you ask me. Now it will be enjoyed by everyone.'

Archie's face grew redder and redder as he tried to contain his anger and humiliation. He had never been so insulted in his life. He focused on the debt and the offer they were about to make him and tried to ignore their oafishness.

Suddenly the sound of Bouncy's piping voice rang through the house, making Archie's heart leap. However, the feeling was short-lived, for holding the boy's hand was Elizabeth, her bottom lip protruding with fury.

The three visitors turned as Elizabeth Montague's large frame filled the door that led into the hall from the kitchen wing.

'Mother!' Archie exclaimed, looking aghast. 'What are—'

'How dare you not inform me that you are intending to sell Pendrift! I have to find it out from my grandson.' She banged her stick on the floor, as if her furious face was not enough to convey her outrage. Bouncy stared up at his grandmother in wonder, for her ears had turned bright red.

'Please excuse me,' Archie said to the Weavels, hoping to usher Elizabeth into the drawing room. Like one of his stubborn heifers, she would not budge. 'We were going to tell you once it was all settled,' he explained gently, through gritted teeth. Julia, who had heard the familiar boom of her mother-in-law's voice, hurried out into the hall. Suddenly, the appalled expression on Mrs Weavel's perfectly made-up face made her want to scream with laughter. Soames, who was hiding in the pantry, heard everything and he, too, smiled to himself. With any luck, Elizabeth Montague would put off any buyer unfortunate enough to meet her.

Elizabeth turned on the visitors. 'Do you know how long I have lived in Pendrift? Almost sixty years. Sixty years! Do you know how long my late husband, Ivan Montague, lived here? His whole life. This house has been in my husband's family for three hundred years. If you think I'm going to stand back and let a pair of upstarts snatch it from under my nose, you've got another think coming.'

Mr Townley looked on the point of fainting. It was all too horrendous. The Weavels would never buy the place now.

'And you!' she glared at Mr Townley, who visibly shrank with fright. 'I don't want to see your face in this house again. Do you understand me? I may be old, but I'm a formidable opponent with my stick.' She banged it on the floor again to prove her point. Bouncy stuck his tongue out at Mrs Weavel, who recoiled.

'Darling, we're leaving,' she said to her husband. Mr Weavel remained rooted to the spot. 'Right now!' she shrieked, making for the door.

Soames appeared out of nowhere to open it for them. He was unable to hide the pleasure that put a glow in his sallow cheeks. Mr Townley said nothing. He followed Mr Weavel, scurrying into the back of the car like a scalded rat. The wheels spun on the gravel for a moment as Mr Weavel hit the accelerator with too much force. Then they were gone.

Julia began to cry with happiness. Without premeditating her actions, she ran over to Elizabeth and threw her arms around her. 'I love you!' she cried. Elizabeth looked startled for a moment, but then her mouth twitched a little before breaking into a broad smile. Julia could feel her shaking beneath the hulk of her body.

'As if I would ever let anyone buy Pendrift. Over my dead body.' She would have hugged Julia back had it not been for Bouncy, who still held one hand, and the stick, which remained in the other. It felt good to smile, to feel her heart inflate with joy. She remembered that feeling now. How she had missed it.

'I'm ashamed, Mother,' said Archie, looking down at his feet.

'Are you in so much trouble?' she asked gently, hobbling over to him.

'I'm afraid we are,' he said, running his fingers over his moustache again.

'Then why didn't you come and talk to me?'

'We didn't want to upset you.'

'Codswallop. I'm more upset now than I've ever been.' She shook her head. 'I love this house and everyone in it. This is where Wilfrid, Sam, and little Bouncy belong. They're Montagues, don't forget.' Bouncy looked pleased to be mentioned and ran off to jump on the sofas in the drawing room. Since Nanny had retired to a small cottage on the estate, he spent an awful lot of time springing about in the grown-up parts of the house. His mother was too kindhearted to tell him to stop, or perhaps it gave her pleasure to see him so happy. 'I'm hurt that you felt you couldn't talk to me. Am I such a monster?'

'What are we going to do?' said Julia, looking anxious again.

'I don't know, my dear,' said Elizabeth, straightening up, ready for battle again. 'But whatever it takes, we will not sell Pendrift. Something will turn up. We'll stand firm, and we'll never surrender. Your father would turn in his grave if he thought of this place passing into the hands of those clods, and it would just about finish me off. Actually,' she said, grinning sheepishly, 'I think the excitement has given me another lease on life. Soames, a gin and tonic, please, and make it snappy. Let's go and sit in the drawing room. Where's Father Dalgliesh? It's about time he made a direct call to the Lord. We need a little divine intervention!'

Julia raised her eyebrows at her husband, who frowned back in bewilderment. He had never seen his mother in such good form.

Penelope, on the other hand, was not in good form. Lotty had run off with Francis Browne. She couldn't understand what had taken hold of her daughter that she would give up her future for the love of a man of no means. Talent was worth nothing if it didn't put food on the table. 'One has to be realistic and keep one's feet on the ground,' she explained to Melissa, who was as shocked by the news as her mother.

She wasn't sure which upset her more: the fact that her sister had run off with a man, or that she hadn't let her in on the secret. The whole thing was compounded by Monty's death. Two disasters in one family were more than anyone should have to take.

'In this day and age it is far more important to be comfortable than to be in love. One can grow to love one's husband. I did. Milton and I are a picture of happiness.' (This wasn't entirely true, but she was terrified Melissa would copy her sister and run off with the dreaded Rafferty, who was almost as unsuitable as Francis Browne.) 'Besides, all-consuming love really doesn't last. It's like a fire. It consumes everything in the first rush and then diminishes to embers. Friendship is more lasting and true. Poor Edward; he'll be devastated when he hears the news. Of course, if the whole thing blows up in her face, he won't have her back. No one will have her. I don't suppose she thought of that when she decided to run off with Mr Nothing.'

'It isn't too late,' said Melissa. 'She might change her mind.'

'I hope she doesn't,' retorted her mother fruitily. 'The damage is already done.'

'You can't let her be penniless!'

'She has made her choice; let her suffer the consequences. We will have to suffer the shame.'

'Everyone will talk about it,' said Melissa miserably.

'They're already talking of nothing but Monty's death. Really, we have never been so fascinating.' She heaved a sigh, her bosom rising to meet her third chin. 'Don't you dare entertain ideas of doing the same thing, Melissa. I can only suffer this once.'

Melissa thought of Rafferty O'Grady and simply nodded obediently.

That evening, Father Dalgliesh dined with Archie, Julia, and Elizabeth Montague in the dining room at the Hall. He arrived on his bicycle and leaned it up against the wall. As was his custom, Soames appeared in the doorway, but it was a very different Soames from the sour butler who never greeted him without a scowl. There was something different about his face. His nose seemed to have grown smaller. Father Dalgliesh looked at him more closely as he climbed the steps. It was then that it struck him. The butler was no longer looking down his nose.

'Good evening, Father,' he said, and even his voice was different. It had a slight bounce to it, as if his words were made of rubber.

'Good evening, Soames,' Father Dalgliesh replied. 'This is a pleasant surprise,' he added, referring to the late invitation to dinner.

'It is indeed, Father. Mrs Elizabeth insisted you come.'

Father Dalgliesh felt his stomach churn. He was rather intimidated by that overbearing woman. But Soames led him into the hall, and there was no time to dwell on their dreaded meetings in the parlour. To Father Dalgliesh's surprise, the drawing-room door was open, and laughter spilled out. He heard the voice of a child, and his spirits rose; he couldn't help but love that little boy who ran tirelessly up and down the nave every Sunday morning.

'Ah, Father,' said Archie, getting up. His face was ruddy and his eyes red-rimmed, but he was smiling enthusiastically. 'Do come in.'

Julia and Elizabeth were sitting on the large sofa, watching Bouncy jump off the upholstered coffee table onto the smaller sofa. He wore blue-and-white-striped pyjamas, and his hair had been brushed with a side parting. His chubby face was rosy, and his brown eyes sparkled. It was a joyous sight. What surprised Father Dalgliesh the most was that Elizabeth was smiling. He had never seen her smile. It was unexpectedly captivating.

'Do come and watch Bouncy,' she said, waving him over. 'We put him to bed, but the little monkey escaped and made a break for it.'

'I'm pleased to see him,' said Father Dalgliesh.

'Oh, we are, too. It's always a joy to see that darling child!'

'Hello, Father,' said Julia. 'He'll go back to bed shortly. He's very tired.'

'That's because he's played with me all day,' exclaimed Elizabeth proudly. 'He's my little friend, aren't you, Bouncy?' The child grinned at her before launching himself off the table and landing on the sofa with a squeal of glee. When he smiled like that he looked so like her younger brother.

'How are you all?' Father Dalgliesh asked, sitting down in an armchair, his view of the two women obscured every few minutes by the flying child.

'Actually, not good,' said Archie, rubbing his moustache. 'Not good at all.'

'Oh, dear,' he replied.

'We're in a bit of bother,' Archie began, then stalled.

'We are struggling to maintain the house,' Julia continued. 'We don't want to sell it, of course, but we're going to have to do something if we want to keep it.'

'Oh, dear,' said Father Dalgliesh again. 'Can I help?'

'Of course you can!' exclaimed Elizabeth heartily. 'You say yourself that the power of prayer is very strong. Well, you can put in a good word for us. Prayer couldn't bring Monty back; I was a fool to think it could. One has to accept what has happened and move on. However, my son and husband would turn in their graves if they got wind of us struggling to hold on to their family home. No, it simply won't do. You're our last resort.'

'God usually is,' said Father Dalgliesh dryly, pushing his glasses up his nose. 'I will do my best. I find that miracles do happen, but in the most unlikely ways. If God grants you your wish, expect to be surprised.'

He was uneasy that they were pinning all their hopes on him. He averted his gaze, resting it quite by chance on a photograph of Celestria that stood in a frame on the table beside him. She was radiant and smiling, her blonde hair blowing in the breeze, dressed in her polka-dot halter-neck top, sitting on the sand with the sea glittering beside her. His heart stumbled a moment as he remembered that awkward moment in the parlour. It had shaken him to the core, not because of any wrongdoing on his behalf but because, deep down, in the pit of his belly, it had excited him.

'Isn't that a lovely picture of Celestria?' said Julia, pulling Bouncy onto her lap. 'That was taken before her father died. She was still happy.'

'How is she now?' he asked, hoping that the tremor in his voice did not betray him.

'She's still in Italy. I haven't heard a squeak. But no news is good news.'

'The distance will be good for her,' he added, pulling his eyes away. *The distance is good for me, too,* he thought with a sense of relief. *And when she comes back I will be strong again.*

Chapter 28

Marelatte

In the morning Celestria found Armel and Federica talking in the garden over cups of coffee, their voices low. When they saw her, they stopped talking and smiled broadly. 'Come,' said Federica excitedly, waving her over. 'I have something to tell you.' Celestria took a seat beside them. *'Luigi, un caffè latte per la signorina, per favore,'* she called to Luigi, who immediately spooned ground coffee into the *caffetiere* and placed it on the stove. 'We have some developments,' she said, toying with the large silver Madonna that lay on her bosom.

'It is all thanks to your son-in-law,' Armel added. 'The mysterious Hamish.'

Celestria felt herself blush. However, the two women were so absorbed by their discovery that they failed to notice.

'This morning, while I was preparing the table for breakfast, Hamish came in looking quite a different man,' said Federica. 'He asked me about Salazar. He said he saw you with him yesterday and was worried. Salazar is a very dubious character. Not to be trusted. I hope you don't mind, but I told him the whole story, as I understand it, and he said that if we want to learn the truth from Salazar we have to elicit the help of his mistress, Rosanna.'

'Salazar is a family man,' continued Armel, her fingers running absentmindedly up and down her scar. 'He has five children and a good and loyal wife whose family are well respected in this region. He would not want them to know about Rosanna.'

'How do we persuade her to help us?' Celestria asked.

'Because she is Nuzzo's sister,' said Federica.

'Nuzzo knows?'

Federica nodded. 'Not only does Nuzzo know, but he is in love with Mrs Waynebridge. He will do anything for her. He has told Luigi, and Luigi's wife has told me.'

'The Marelatte grapevine,' said Celestria. At least the grapevine had not yet communicated her night-time adventure to the bar.

At that moment, Luigi emerged from the kitchen with a silver tray carrying Celestria's milky coffee. They paused while he put it down on the table, asked if there was anything else they required, then returned inside.

'What do we do?' Celestria said impatiently.

'Nuzzo will talk to his sister today.'

'What if she doesn't agree?'

'We are going to appeal to her, together. Women to woman,' said Armel.

'We Italians take death very seriously, Celestria,' said Federica gravely. 'If Salazar has indeed induced the suicides of two men, Rosanna will not want to shelter him.'

Celestria stared at Armel in confusion. 'Benedict committed suicide, too?' Armel nodded. 'You didn't say.'

'I didn't think it relevant.' She shrugged.

'The parallels are too striking to ignore.' Celestria shook her head. 'There's a pattern, but I can't make it out. Am I alone here? Can you see something I can't?'

Armel shook her head. 'Only that both men were not the type to take their own lives. I say they were murdered.'

'So do I,' Celestria agreed emphatically.

'Let's get to the bottom of it,' said Federica, rubbing her hands together energetically. 'Besides, I've never liked that man. He's much too pleased with himself.'

Armel lit a cigarette and blew smoke into the warm air. She narrowed her eyes. 'If Salazar killed my husband,' she said solemnly, 'I will kill him.'

'There are ways to take revenge without resorting to violence,' said Federica seriously. 'It is far harder to live with guilt than escape it through death.'

Celestria thought of Hamish and knew that was true. Did he often wish to escape? Is that why he spent so much time in the mausoleum, praying for death to unite them and rid him of his guilt? Was death the light behind the door?

That evening, as Celestria was changing for dinner, she heard the melancholy notes of the piano. She knew at once that it was Hamish. She hadn't seen him all day, in spite of having looked for him in every shadow. With growing disappointment she had sensed his pulling away. This was not the reaction to their kiss that she was expecting. With Hamish, there was no internal map to follow; she had only her instincts and the faith that they were destined to be together. She slipped into a pale blue dress and hurried down the corridor, her heart suspended until she knew whether or not he wanted her.

The sound grew louder as she turned the corner. There, amid the piles of books and the figurines his mother-in-law collected, he sat at the piano on a stool that was far too small for his long legs. She smiled tentatively and he smiled back, as if there had been nothing odd about his absence.

'Where have you been?' she asked, leaning on the piano lid. He continued to play.

'In my head, thinking of you,' he replied, and her stomach leapt with joy. He lowered his eyes, his fingers finding the chords with ease, and grew suddenly serious as his whole body moved with the music, now more dramatic.

'You're playing a sad tune,' she said.

'But I feel happy. You're right, music is a release. It penetrates the soul and relieves it of pain. It fills me up inside and makes me believe that anything is possible.' He closed his eyes and continued to play for a few minutes.

Suddenly he stopped, midphrase. 'Come,' he said, rising from the piano and taking her hand. He led her down the corridor to the little stairs that took them up to his studio. The paint smelled fresh. She realized that this is where he had spent the day. She longed to see what he had done, but the easel was facing away from her.

He closed the door behind her, swung her around, and kissed her hungrily. She wound her arms around his neck, melting against his body, no longer feeling out of place. In the studio, with the window wide open to the soft evening sunlight and calm sea, there was no darkness for him to hide in, no night to blame for his rashness, no moon to fabricate a magical limbo in which reality is suspended. He kissed her honestly and openly and without regret.

Celestria no longer compared him with other men she had kissed; there was no comparison. He was a different beast, as removed from the London food chain as it was possible for him to be. And there, in the succulent, pine-scented air of Italy, she, too, felt removed from all that she had left behind.

'You're an angel, Celestria, come to drag me out of myself. I misjudged you. I see that now.' He nuzzled his face in her hair. 'I need you.'

'And I need you, too,' she conceded.

'Let's not dwell on the past. It's time to let it go.'

'If that is what you want.'

'It is what I want. I want you and I to start afresh. I want you to forget that I ever shouted at you. And I want to forget, too.'

Celestria longed to ask him about Natalia. She wanted to know how she died, why he felt such guilt. But she knew not to push him. If he wanted to tell her, he would, in his own time. For now, she was content just to be with him, even though she sensed that those two candles burned brighter than ever in the mausoleum across the road, unwilling to be ignored.

That night, after dinner, they sneaked out to light a fire on the beach in the little bay that had captured her heart that first day. It was sheltered against the cliffs like a haven from the rest of the world, big enough only for two people and the dance they made together. The light of the moon bounced off the ripples on the sea, and the fire crackled and burned, sending sparks into the damp and salty air.

'I'm sure living by the sea does my leg no good at all,' he said, holding her close as they moved slowly across the stones. 'I should have remained in the highlands.'

'Why do you stay here?'

He shrugged. 'Because my past is here.'

'But your past is sad. Why don't you move away? Start again. Leave it all behind.'

He looked down at her, his eyes tender and full of affection. 'Because I love it. I love the sounds, the smells, the peace. It has a deep magic embedded in the soil that holds me to it.' He turned his gaze out to sea and frowned. 'I could never leave it.'

'You said I was your angel to take you out of yourself. Perhaps I'm your angel to take you away from all this.'

He grinned at her and stroked her cheek with his fingers. 'Perhaps, but I'd always come back.'

'You don't miss Scotland?'

'Not at all.'

'You don't feel the desire to go back, ever?'

'There is nothing in the world that would make me go back there. All the happiness I have ever known is here. I lost it for a while, but you've brought happiness back into my life. You brought it here, and here it will stay.' His smile faded, and he grew suddenly serious, his eyes wandering over her features. 'You know, I could love you,' he said in a very quiet voice. 'I could love you very much.' Before she could dwell on the significance of his words, he kissed her again, and she forgot all about them, lost in the milky light of the Marelatte moon.

The following morning Celestria met Rosanna in the little church that stood next to the Convento, with Federica, Armel, Mrs Waynebridge, and Nuzzo. The daily Mass had been celebrated. The priest had retired. Only the candles remained lit on the altar, representing whispered prayers and solemn wishes, flickering among the spirits who hovered about to gather them. Celestria followed them down the aisle of simple wooden chairs, her espadrilles padding softly across the mosaic floor that depicted, surprisingly, the signs of the zodiac. She crossed herself before the altar and lit a candle. She thought of her father and mumbled a prayer: that his spirit rest in peace, wherever it was. Glancing to her right, she noticed Armel do the same, but her eyes filled with tears that squeezed out between her lashes when she closed them.

They sat in a small chapel that was separated from the rest of the church by a black railing and gate. The altar was covered in a white cloth, on top of which were placed two fat ivory candles and a large silver platter beneath a marble statue of Christ on the cross. She wondered what Father Dalgliesh would make of their plotting in God's house and felt a stab of guilt as she recalled the moment she had compromised him as well as herself. However, she hadn't time to dwell on Pendrift, for Rosanna appeared at the gate, dressed in black, with a black lace shawl draped over her head, hiding her face. She appeared nervous, hunching her shoulders, darting her head from side to side like a bird to check that she was not being watched. Nuzzo sprang to his feet and took her hand, introducing her to Armel and Celestria. Rosanna's hand was small but soft, with neatly manicured nails. She did not lift her veil, but sat down beside her brother, interlocking her fingers in her lap.

Federica did most of the talking. Armel's Italian seemed flawless, and she interrupted Federica every now and then in a loud hiss, gesticulating wildly, unable to hide her fury or her grief. Celestria noticed Mrs Waynebridge's attention was permanently focused on Nuzzo. His face was mischievous, in spite of the solemnity of the occasion and place, as if it cost him to be serious.

Mrs Waynebridge had changed, Celestria observed. Nuzzo had given her back her youth, her independence, and her spirit of adventure. Celestria had rarely seen her since they arrived. She spent the days out exploring the countryside with Nuzzo in his horse-drawn cart, returning with an enlarged vocabulary of Italian words and more flowers to press in her book. She looked so much lighter now she was no longer weighed down by apprehension, and the twinkle from Nuzzo's eyes was now reflected in hers.

Federica began explaining Benedict's and Monty's deaths and how they connected to Salazar. Rosanna listened, saying nothing, her large eyes blinking behind her veil. Then Nuzzo said his bit, his voice persuasive and beseeching. He raised his palms to the sky, shrugged, pulled faces that were intended to look sad, but still his mouth turned up at the corners. Finally, there was silence. They all looked at one another. Celestria was afraid that she wouldn't help. She seemed far too timid.

Slowly she raised her hands to her veil and lifted it. Beneath the disguise her face was the colour of *caffè latte,* with thick eyebrows and long, glossy lashes around big brown eyes. Her lips were sensual and bow shaped, enhanced by the red lipstick she had carefully applied to match her fingernails. Her face was full and soft, and it was clear from her compassionate expression that she was moved by their story and fearful of her lover. Celestria could deduce from the urgency of her voice that she was giving them vital information. Rosanna then replaced the veil and stood before the altar, crossing herself. In a blink she was gone, like a bird flying off into the shadows.

The small group left ten minutes later and congregated in the Convento, where Federica debriefed Celestria and Mrs Waynebridge. 'She took a little persuading. She is afraid; Salazar is a dangerous man. However, she has agreed to help us. She meets him in a little house in Castellino. You and Armel must be there at five o'clock this evening. I will send Hamish with you. He is a big man. Salazar would not want to get into a fight with him.'

'Will Salazar know that Rosanna has betrayed him?' Celestria asked, worried about the woman's safety.

'No. She will pretend that she is as surprised to see you as he is. You must not give her away. That is most important.' Then she added carefully, 'Salazar is a pompous man, but he is not necessarily a murderer. I cannot imagine what happened to your father and Armel's husband, and you are right that there are parallels too striking to be ignored, but remember, Salazar might be innocent in all of this.'

'Maybe,' said Celestria. 'But I choose to believe he's as guilty as the devil.'

Nuzzo returned to his work and Federica to the daily tasks that kept her busy in the Convento. Armel sat with Celestria and Mrs Waynebridge in the sunshine, debating Salazar's innocence.

'I want Salazar to know that I think about my husband every moment of the day. It is like a dagger to my heart that is twisted and twisted over and over,' said Armel bitterly. 'He has stripped me of my life. My reason to go on. You know I told you that my husband was an entrepreneur?'

'Yes.'

'Well, he was that, of course. He also worked for the government. He was a very important man. However, he was a shady man. Complex. A man with many layers, like an onion. At his core, I'm afraid, he was a criminal.' She raised her eyes wearily. 'It was only when I looked into his affairs after his death that I discovered he was an arms dealer, too. He bought and sold arms to Israel. To both sides. I am ashamed, but it doesn't stop me loving him.'

'How did you make the connection to Salazar?'

She chewed her cheek for a moment, then sighed heavily and lit a cigarette, drawing the nicotine into her lungs, visibly relaxing. 'I found various accounts in his name, paid for by Salazar. Then there was this revolting Hungarian woman. At first, I thought it was an affair. My husband had an eye for the ladies, and I'm sure I was not the only woman in his life. I am French. We Frenchwomen understand that a man has his needs. But when I saw her—'

'Countess Valonya?'

'You know Countess Valonya?' Armel looked surprised.

'I had the misfortune of meeting her, yes. She worked for my father.'

'She worked for my husband, too.'

The two women stared at each other, barely able to voice the fear that now seeped into their hearts like acid.

Mrs Waynebridge suddenly snapped out of her trance. 'Sounds to me like your husband and Mr Montague are one and the same person.' She laughed at the absurdity of her thought, but Celestria and Armel didn't laugh.

'Do you have a photograph of your father?' Armel asked quietly, her face as pale as a funeral lily.

'You don't think . . . It's not possible!' Celestria could barely utter the words; they stuck in her throat, which now felt as if it were full of cotton wool.

Light-headed with terror, she ran upstairs to her room. 'Oh, please, Lord!' she murmured as she gazed upon the face of the man she was losing, little by little. Soon she wouldn't know him at all. When she returned, Armel had lit another cigarette and was smoking feverishly. Without a word, Celestria handed her the photograph. Armel let out a long rasping sound, like a death rattle, and bent double, laying her head on her hand.

'*Mon dieu!*' she gasped.

Celestria sat down, feeling suddenly very small and frail. 'Is that Benedict?' she asked in a whisper, although she already knew the answer. 'We should have guessed.'

The birds twittered in the trees, the dogs barked in the road outside the Convento, and the sudden neighing of a horse agitated the still, midday heat. Marelatte continued as it always had, and yet, for Armel and Celestria, the world had shifted.

Federica emerged from the kitchen. 'What has happened?' she asked, for Armel was still hiding her face in her hand, the ash on the end of her cigarette drooping like a long grey caterpillar, about to burn her fingers. Celestria could barely speak. She had lost her voice. She tried, but nothing came out, just a weak hiss.

'I suggested that Armel's husband and Celestria's father were one and the same man. I didn't think I were right for a moment. By gum, I didn't.' Mrs Waynebridge clutched at her chest and shook her head. 'This is such a shock.' Her eyes sparkled with tears, and the youthful glow Nuzzo had settled on her cheeks turned to dust.

Federica sank into a chair, her own face devoid of colour. She stared at the ground without blinking. 'Well, that explains a lot, doesn't it?' she said bitterly, as if she were talking to herself.

'I suppose it does,' Mrs Waynebridge agreed, gazing anxiously at her.

'I'm so sorry,' Federica said, reaching out to touch Celestria's arm. The girl remained still.

'Did you bury him?' she croaked.

Armel lifted her head, and the ash broke off onto the paving stone below. 'No. Did you?'

'No.'

'So, there was no body?'

'No. He drowned at sea.'

Armel nodded. 'Benedict drowned at sea. He must have planned it very carefully.' She blinked at Celestria, as she was suddenly struck with an extraordinary idea. 'Are you thinking what I'm thinking?' Her eyes suddenly hardened and grew as cold as slate.

Celestria nodded, her jaw loose as she floundered to make sense of it all. 'Could it be true?'

'You've lost me,' said Mrs Waynebridge, turning helplessly to Federica. 'Have they lost you, too?'

'I daren't say,' replied Federica, pulling on her pendant in agitation.

'I'm thinking the impossible.' Armel shrugged. 'That Benedict Devere, Robert Montague, is not dead at all. That he planned his own death, transferring money to Salazar, which Countess Valonya withdrew on his behalf so that he could start a new life somewhere else. If he is capable of leading a double life, why not a triple life?'

'If that is true, he underestimated us,' said Celestria, her voice steady.

'He certainly did,' agreed Armel. 'If he is alive, we will find him.'

Federica got up and walked hurriedly into the kitchen. She stood a moment with her back against the door, clutching her chest, her breathing staggered and shallow. A few moments later, she had composed herself. She reached for a bottle of wine, crossed herself, and silently asked for forgiveness.

Celestria ran down the little path to the fortress. Her throat was tight, her breathing laboured, her head bursting with the need to cry. Finally, in the seclusion of the old stone ruin, she stood at the window, rested her eyes on the soothing rise and fall of the sea below, and let out a loud sob, like the cry of a wild animal. Once she had started, she couldn't stop. It was as if all the hurt that had built up over the weeks following her father's disappearance had now found a crack in her resistance and burst forth. She felt utterly broken by his deceit. As if he had taken an eraser and rubbed out her past and the very ground she stood on. *The most terrible discovery of all was that he hadn't included her. He had shut her out. The father she loved had never truly existed.* The tears burned her cheeks and dropped off her chin onto her pretty white dress. She clutched the windowsill for balance. That is where Hamish found her.

Without a word he enfolded her in his arms and let her cry against him. With tenderness he stroked her hair and wiped away her tears, kissing her in a vain attempt to put her back together again. After a while her breathing grew regular, and she stopped crying.

'Federica told me,' he said. 'I'm sorry.'

'He lied to me all my life. He married Armel just after the war, when Mama and I came back from America. All the while he was off on business he was building another family.' She pulled away and gazed up at him. 'I trusted him blindly. I loved him unconditionally. But he didn't love us at all. If he loved us, how could he bear to leave? What is Mama going to think? Harry, too? My God, what will my family do when I tell them? It will destroy us all.'

'Think very hard before you tell them,' Hamish suggested gravely.

'But he's alive,' she said, frowning. 'He's alive. He's not dead at all. I've been mourning him for nothing.' She grew angry. 'I've shed tears over him. I've damned the sea for snatching him. I worried about the pain he might have suffered. I prayed for him to be rescued from hell. Yet he planned his death with care. He planned to make us all suffer. He cheated us out of our money so that he could enjoy a future somewhere else. What about *our* future?'

'Your future is here with me,' he said suddenly, holding her very tightly. 'Your future is in Marelatte. This is where you belong.'

'I don't know who to trust any more,' she replied in a small voice.

'You can trust me.'

She looked into his deep, unfathomable eyes and noticed how different he was from her father, Aidan, Rafferty, and Dan. There were no smooth edges to Hamish: no gloss, no wide, enchanting smile, no pretence. Hamish's honesty was raw and natural. Of that she was grateful.

Chapter 29

Hamish drove Gaitano's Lancia Flaminia down the dusty road to Castellino, a small, Moorish-looking town south of Marelatte. Armel sat in the front beside him, Celestria in the back. The vibrations in the car were strained, almost giving off a sound, like the high-pitched squeaking of violins. They arrived in town, their faces grim with determination. The buildings were constructed in the same pale stone as those in Marelatte, with flat roofs and tall, brown doors behind which secret courtyards were concealed from passers-by. However, in Castellino, the Moorish influence was plain to see: arched façades, twisted candy pillars, and intricate trellis balconies that would not have looked out of place in Morocco. Eucalyptus trees rustled in the sea breeze. A few old men sat on benches watching the setting sun, not knowing how many more sunsets they would live to see, and a group of stray dogs trotted casually by in search of dustbins, in hope of scraps.

The house Rosanna had directed them to was small, pale yellow, and set apart from the rest, built on a slope that descended to the bleached white cliffs. It was not an impressive house. In fact, it looked half built, as if the owners had run out of money and had to stop building mid-project. Hamish looked at his watch. They were slightly early. He swivelled around to where Celestria sat quietly in the rear seat and took her hand.

'Are you okay?' he asked, concerned.

'I'm feeling sick. How about you, Armel?'

'Me, too. A cigarette will calm my nerves. Do you want one?' She rummaged about in her leather bag.

'Definitely,' Celestria replied, gaining strength from the warmth of Hamish's touch. Her hand, settled into his large rough one, made her feel safe.

'At least you will learn the truth,' he said, then turned his eyes away with a frown.

'Perhaps I should have stayed in England and mourned him with the rest of my family. Ignorance is bliss.'

'What if we find him?' Celestria continued, leaning towards the flame that Armel held out for her. The end of her cigarette lit up like a firefly before dying away.

'I don't know,' Armel replied softly, shaking her head.

'It would be better if he were dead. At least there would be some certainty,' said Celestria, her voice hard.

'And no humiliation. He can't have loved us very much if he was prepared to fake his own death in order to be rid of us.' She chuckled cynically, her gaze lost in the half distance.

'You don't know the truth,' said Hamish. 'You may never find out. It might be better that way.'

They climbed out of the car and stood in the orange sunlight. They stamped their cigarettes into the sandy earth and proceeded to walk slowly towards the house. Hamish took Celestria's hand. If Armel noticed, she said nothing, but stared grimly ahead. They were on a mission, and nothing would distract them from it.

As Rosanna had promised, she had left the door ajar. Hamish took the lead and stepped inside. The hinges made no sound as he pushed the door open. Inside the air was cool and smelled of freshly ground coffee. The floor was made of flagstones, the walls plain white. Only a simple wooden crucifix hung above the fireplace. There was no staircase to climb, as the house was built on one floor. Hamish turned to the women and nodded. They were ready. Celestria felt her stomach ache with fear. She was grateful that Hamish had come. She would not have had the courage to come alone with Armel.

Voices could be heard in the room at the end of the corridor, then the ripple of Rosanna's laughter. The smell of cheap perfume seeped under the door. Hamish crept quietly over the tiles and stopped outside the room. He paused a moment, as if to gather himself. Then he flung open the door. Inside, Rosanna lay on the bed in a cream satin dressing gown, her brown hair cascading over her shoulders in lustrous curls. Salazar stood in his underpants at the foot of the bed. To add to his humiliation, he was wearing socks, fixed at the knees by elastic black garters, and his polished two-toned shoes.

At first he looked furious, his smooth face mottled with anger. Then he looked surprised, and finally afraid, as he realized why they had come. Never would he have imagined that Celestria would align herself with Armel. He shouted at them in Italian. Hamish replied calmly, throwing him the green dressing gown that lay over the chair. Rosanna curled up at the end of the bed, feigning terror. She was a good actress. Salazar begged for them to respect her honour and let her go. Hamish agreed, and Rosanna ran to the bathroom, where she dressed quickly and left without a word. It was clear that he didn't want his mistress to hear what he had to say.

'So,' said Armel briskly, sitting on the end of the bed and crossing her legs, 'you have a mistress.'

'It is none of your business,' Salazar snapped, visibly rattled.

Hamish strode over to the window and folded his arms. 'Don't worry. It won't be anyone else's business. If you do something for us.'

'I've told you all I know!' he protested.

'You said Robert Montague had a partner,' Celestria asked. 'Who was he?'

'Benedict Devere,' Salazar replied. Armel caught Celestria's eye and nodded. Salazar looked uncomfortable. His hair was no longer sleeked back with grease but falling over his forehead in thick tentacles. He ran his hand through it, ashamed and humiliated to be seen like that. '*Senti,* I never met him. I dealt with Robert Montague and the countess. I received my instructions by letter, telephone, and telegram. Countess Valonya acted on behalf of them, and she was paid from my office. It is she who carried out their dirty work. I just brokered the deals to keep them on the right side of the law.'

'What deals did you broker for them?' Hamish asked.

'Planes. They sold used American and British fighter planes to the Egyptians.'

'*Mon dieu!*'

'Since when?' Celestria asked.

'Eighteen months ago. Devere was already in the business of selling arms. I met Robert Montague while he was staying at the Convento. We agreed to do business together. There was this hangar. Devere had acquired planes. He met the Egyptians at the casino in Monaco. They wanted to buy them. I have connections in Italy. They needed me. If they are dead, I did not kill them. The Egyptians did or the Mafia.'

'Why?' Hamish asked.

'You want to know why? Then let me take you to the hangar, and you'll see for yourselves. I, too, have been misled.' It was clear that Salazar had no idea that the two men were one and the same. Celestria sensed that he was telling the truth. He had acted as go-between. He probably didn't suspect, like they did, that her father had faked his own death.

They drove farther south until they reached a large white hangar that stood isolated in the middle of an expanse of dry, rocky ground. There were no houses as far as the eye could see. Salazar led them to the large sliding door. He opened the padlock with a key, then pulled the door open. It rattled in protest. 'Take a look!' he exclaimed triumphantly, striding inside. 'It is not surprising that the two men have been killed. No one wants rusty, useless planes that can't fly!'

'How the devil did they pull it off?' Hamish asked, gazing around him in amazement at the motley array of shabby planes disintegrating in the gloom like bones in an elephants' graveyard.

'It is very simple. Child's play! Montague and Devere raised the money to buy the planes. The Egyptians paid a deposit. Devere and Montague took the money and disappeared. Now I'm left with creditors who do not take kindly to being played with. Do you understand what I'm saying?' He stared at them in desperation. 'Salazar does not have blood on his hands.'

'He's not dead!' snarled Armel, treading lightly across the floor to take a better look. 'He's in hiding. If you value your life, you don't mess about with people like that and hang around.'

'He?' Now Salazar was confused.

'For God's sake, wake up, you silly little man!' Armel had lost her patience. 'My husband and her father are the same man!' Salazar scratched his head. He suddenly looked tired. 'That Hungarian bitch did their dirty work for them so no one would ever know "they" were "one."' He's brilliant. I half admire him now that I know he pulled off such a daring scam. He fooled me. He fooled all of us. And you, Salazar,' she laughed meanly. 'In all your deals he took two cuts. How do you feel about that?'

Salazar scratched his head again. 'I don't believe you.'

'Then you're a fool!' she exclaimed, her voice shrill. 'But he has not got away with it yet.'

'Hell hath no fury . . .' said Hamish, catching Celestria's eye and pulling a sympathetic smile.

'We can assume he is alive, then. He is not running from us, but from the Egyptians,' said Celestria quietly. 'That is at least something.'

'Oh, he had two wives! What is to stop him having more? He has started a new life somewhere with our money.'

'With the Egyptians' money,' said Salazar. 'I hope, for his sake, that he is never found.'

'I hope, for your sake, that you don't become a scapegoat,' said Hamish to Salazar. 'I'd hate to think what the Egyptians would do to you.'

For a moment Salazar looked suitably hunted. Then he shrugged, regaining his composure. 'Life is all fog and smoke and mirrors. You win some, you lose some, but there is always business for a businessman like me. Now, if you don't mind, I have wasted the afternoon. I do not wish to waste the evening, too.'

Hamish drove back to Castellino and dropped Salazar off at his love nest.

'I still think he's as guilty as sin,' said Celestria, watching him walk back into the house and close the door behind him.

'He's guilty of stealing money, I'm sure. He's got *crook* written all over his face,' said Armel. 'But he's not guilty of murder.'

'So where's Papa?'

'That, my friend, is the million-dollar question.'

That evening Hamish and Celestria sat beside the old fort, watching the pinky glow of sunset that reflected off the water. Hamish leaned against the gnarled evergreen tree, his arms around Celestria, who lay against him.

'He could be anywhere,' she said. 'I've been gazing at the sea, imagining him drowning in it. He's put us all through hell, and he's probably living it up on a golden beach somewhere.'

'If he's running for his life, he'll have no life.' Hamish's voice had a bitter edge.

'He's not very clever, is he? I've sent a telegram to my grandfather. He'll be amazed.' She chuckled cynically. 'He didn't cover his tracks very well.'

'He probably never expected you to doubt him.'

'I knew he couldn't have committed suicide. The rest of the family accepted it. But I knew in my gut. It just wasn't like him. Think what he's done to my poor mother and to Harry. They believe he's dead. He's ruined their lives. What would Mama think if I told her he had another wife? It would destroy her. I wish now that he *had* killed himself. Death is better than betrayal.' Hamish said nothing. But Celestria felt him stiffen. 'I'm ashamed of him. I thought he'd be smarter than that!'

'Well, he underestimated you.'

'Now what? I can't scour the globe for him. Besides, he doesn't want to be found. He's probably as far away from here as a man can possibly get.'

'You have to let him go.' Hamish kissed her temple.

'You can bet your life that Armel won't.'

'She's got nothing else. You've got family and your life ahead of you.'

She looked at him steadily. 'Do you love me?'

Hamish paused, then chose his words very carefully. 'I know that I *could* love you.'

'I love you. I probably fell in love with you the first time I saw you.'

'Even though I shouted at you?'

'Maybe *because* you shouted at me. You were honest; I realize now that I haven't had much honesty in my life.'

He laughed. 'You have a funny way of loving.'

'I saw your pain, and all I wanted to do was make it go away.' She leaned forward and planted a kiss on his lips. 'You see, I've never considered anyone else but myself. That's how I know I love you. Because I care about you more than I care about me.'

'There are no fancy parties in Puglia.'

'I've had enough fancy parties to last me the rest of my life.'

'I have no money.'

'You're rich in talent.'

'That doesn't put food on the table.'

'It does if you sell it.'

'I carry a burden of grief.'

'It'll be lighter if I carry it with you.'

He paused, holding her with the intensity of his eyes. 'Do you know what you're taking on?'

'Let's not speak any more. Love me, Hamish. That's all I ask.'

She pressed her lips to his again. Unable to resist her, he wrapped his arms around her, kissing her ardently, blotting out the tragedy that dwelt in the darkness of his own shadow. Hoping that by making love to her, he could fill his soul with all that was good and joyous.

The sun sank below the earth, turning the sea inky black. Hamish peeled off her dress, revealing the ripeness of her flesh, pale in the phosphorescent light of the moon. He traced his fingers over her skin, around her breasts that were heavy with youth and the promise of motherhood, and knew that in her lay a future that was fertile and full of light, if only he could allow himself to take it. Celestria sensed his disquiet, but this was the one thing Natalia could no longer give him. She unbuttoned his shirt and slipped it over his shoulders. He was hairy, muscular, and brown. The contrast with her own body gave her a frisson of excitement. Daphne was right: with the right man the earth shook. It trembled, and it shifted on its axis. In those tender moments Celestria believed that nothing could come between them. That Hamish would choose life over death, light over darkness, and a future instead of the past. But those candles continued to burn in the city of the dead, and only he could put them out.

Chapter 30

Celestria lay in bed, her eyes closed, her ears taking in the light twittering of birds and the sporadic barking of dogs. She smiled at the memory of the night before and stretched. They had made love. It had been wonderful. She was filled with uncontrollable joy. She wanted to shout out of the window, let everyone know how happy she was. For a moment she felt guilty. Her father had betrayed her and her whole family; it was indecent to be so happy while they were all at home suffering. And yet her love for Hamish overrode all other feelings.

She slipped into a pale blue polka-dot sundress. Her eye caught the photograph of her father that she had left on the table, among Federica's collection of hand-painted clay figures. There he was, smiling out at her, his panama hat sitting crooked on his head, his smile wide and raffish, with the arches of the cloister behind him. Her hand hesitated above it for a moment. She was flooded with sadness. The man grinning out at her might just as well have been a stranger, someone she had met a long time ago but knew little about. No, that wasn't her father. Not the man who had taken the boys off in his little boat to play pirates, drawn trails on the sand for them to follow to find treasure, and made her mother's migraines disappear. No, her father, the man she loved, had died that day in Cornwall. Of that she was now certain. It was right that they should mourn him, because he was never coming back. She placed the photograph in the pocket of her dress and left her room.

As she stepped into the corridor, Daphne Halifax was leaving her room. She wore a long purple and turquoise dress and the oddest-looking shoes, fashioned in violet with gold feathers on the toes.

'Good morning, my dear,' she said, smiling warmly. 'You look lovely today. You're glowing.'

'Thank you! I'm happy.'

'Any particular reason?'

'Oh, Daphne, can I come into your room a moment?' she asked, longing to tell someone.

'Of course. Though I think I can guess.'

Celestria followed her inside and flopped onto the bed. 'I'm in love!' she enthused. 'The earth moved, it really did. As you said it would!'

Daphne sat on the end of the bed, clearly delighted. 'I knew you and Hamish were made for each other. I can tell you in confidence that Freddie did, too. The moment you arrived she said, "That's the girl for Hamish."'

'She did?'

'Of course. Sometimes we old people see things that the young are unable to. Remember, I've lived a long time.'

'He's moody and unpredictable, but I care about him in a way that I've never cared about anyone. His pain hurts me; it's as if I feel it, too. But when he smiles, the whole world lights up. He has the most enchanting smile. And his charisma, it fills the room like a light. Oh, Daphne, I'm unable to think of anything else. My mother would have a heart seizure, if she knew. In fact, my whole family would disapprove.'

'Why on earth would they?'

'Because he's about fifteen years older than me. He's been married before. He's penniless. He doesn't brush his hair.

Mama would most certainly tell him to cut it. Aunt Penelope would ask him where his estate was and be appalled to discover that he doesn't have one. Only Grandpa would approve, because he started out with nothing, too.'

'Hamish's family have a beautiful estate in Scotland.'

'They do?'

'He fell out with his family and left for good. I don't think he's been back in years. You see, he's a free spirit. He found convention there too stifling. He despises the British obsession with class and money. I don't blame him. It's terribly shallow.'

'I don't think he'd like my family very much.'

Daphne paused a moment, her expression suddenly concerned. 'He'll never go back, Celestria. He was very unhappy in Scotland. You do know that, don't you?'

'Yes, I do.'

'If you take him on, you'll have to compromise in a very big way.'

'I'll do anything for him.'

Daphne touched her hand. 'Loving isn't all about sacrifice. I hope he makes you happy, too.'

'Oh, he will. We're both moving on now.'

'Oh, yes, your poor father. What did you discover?'

'That he was an arms dealer. He was selling rotten American airplanes to some Egyptians he met at a casino in Monaco. He must have made a lot of money and run off with it.'

'Are you suggesting he isn't dead?'

'I'm not sure. But I'm convinced he fabricated his own death in order to disappear.'

'Good God! Freddie hasn't told me any of this.'

'Didn't she tell you that he was also married to Armel?'

Daphne looked horrified. 'To Armel?'

'Yes, can you imagine how terrible? He was leading a double life.'

'But, my dear, how did you discover that?'

Celestria pulled out the photograph and handed it to her. 'I showed her this. As well as being Robert Montague, he was also Benedict Devere.'

'What a ridiculous name!' Daphne scoffed. 'Anyone would have known *that* was invented. Really, the man should have had more imagination! Let me put on my glasses. Ah, now I can see him clearly.' Suddenly her jaw dropped. 'Well, I never!' she exclaimed, raising her eyes to Celestria. 'Good gracious!'

'What is it? You weren't married to him, too, were you?' Celestria teased.

Daphne didn't laugh.

'What?'

'Well, I don't think I should say.'

'Say what?'

Daphne thought about it for a moment, pursing her lips tightly, working out where her loyalties lay. Finally, she handed the photograph back. 'My dear child, this whole business is nothing to do with me. However, I believe in telling the truth no matter what. You have a right to know.'

Celestria felt her stomach plummet. 'Go on.'

'I saw this man two days before you arrived.'

'Are you sure?'

'Absolutely. It's the way he wears the hat, you see. Slightly crooked. And the smile. One simply couldn't mistake that smile.'

'Did he stay here?'

'No. I don't think he meant me to see him.'

'What was he doing, then?'

Daphne sighed heavily. 'He was with Freddie.'

'With Freddie?' Celestria repeated in astonishment. 'Two days before I arrived?'

'That's right. I was painting near the old fort. He was here when I arrived. He seemed a little agitated, now I come to think about it. He couldn't stand still. He lit a cigar and toyed with it between his fingers like this.' She moved her fingers to demonstrate.

'That's definitely my father,' said Celestria, discovering that he was capable of snatching her joy after all.

'Then Freddie appeared, and he smiled. That's when I noticed the smile. Unforgettable.'

'Please don't tell me they're lovers!'

Daphne shook her head. 'I don't know. They embraced and talked for about an hour. The more they talked, the more agitated he became, until he cried in her arms. I was terribly moved. A man like that reduced to tears. Freddie looked destroyed. Then he gave her a small package and left. I don't know if he had a car waiting somewhere, or whether he walked. He just disappeared, leaving Freddie sobbing on that grassy slope where you sat the other day with me.'

'What was in the package?'

'I don't know. She didn't open it there.'

Celestria folded her arms and clicked her tongue angrily. 'So she has known all along that Papa didn't kill himself.'

'I suppose she has.'

'Do you think she knew that he was married to Armel as well?'

'I don't know.' Daphne shrugged. 'I don't know how much she knew. Perhaps he kept her in the dark in the same way that he kept you and Armel in the dark. There does seem to be a pattern to this.'

'But she was the only one who knew he wasn't dead. He faked his death in France as well as England. Why was Freddie different?'

'Perhaps it wasn't an affair. She's much older than him, and she's married to Gaitano.'

'I'm going to find out.' She noticed the frightened look on Daphne's face. 'Don't worry, Daphne, I will keep your name out of it.'

'Thank you,' she replied, relaxing her shoulders. 'Dear me, this is a horrid mess, isn't it?'

Celestria left Daphne's room, her stomach knotted with anxiety. The one question she hadn't been able to ask now tormented her. Did Hamish know about this, too? Had he known all along and not told her? Is that why he held back? Not because of the woman buried in the city of the dead, but because of his own guilty secret?

She went downstairs to find Armel in the courtyard, her bag at her feet, surrounded by the dogs. She was talking to Federica. Celestria stiffened. She wanted to confront her now, but she knew that caution would serve her better. If Federica was capable of putting on such a brilliant act, then she would do better. Feigning a smile she didn't feel, she walked up to the two women.

'Are you leaving?' she asked Armel.

'I'm afraid I am. There is nothing left for me to do.' She sighed sadly. 'I will return to Paris and endeavour to get on with the rest of my life.'

'I'll miss you,' said Celestria truthfully. 'We are a good team.'

'And I'll miss you. Look me up if you come to Paris, won't you? Our meeting is one of the good things that have come out of the disaster.'

'I promise.'

'What are you going to do?'

'Mourn him, like everyone else. As far as I am concerned, he is dead.' Celestria glanced at Federica, but the older woman didn't flinch. 'I prefer to remember him the way he was before he disappeared. I will not allow the things I have learned to tarnish my memory of him.'

'You are right,' said Federica. 'One has to look forward.'

Armel left. The dogs followed the cart up the road for as long as they could. The cloud of dust grew smaller and smaller until it disappeared out of sight, the horse's harness catching the light and twinkling in one last goodbye.

'The place will be incomplete without Armel,' said Federica, running her hand down the string of shiny pink crystals that hung down to her waist. 'I've grown fond of her.'

'Do you grow fond of all the people who stay here?' Celestria asked.

Federica didn't blink. 'Yes, I think I do. You see, it's not a hotel. It's a home, and you are our guests.' She walked back inside. 'I'm going into Castellino for the morning. Would you like to come?'

Celestria followed her into the courtyard. 'Thanks, but I think I'll go find Waynie. You haven't seen her, have you?'

'She had breakfast with Armel, then went out.'

'I've lost her, haven't I?'

Federica laughed. 'I'm afraid you have. Italy has a funny way of stealing people's hearts. I hope it has stolen yours as well.'

Celestria didn't reply. In spite of the woman's treachery, she couldn't help liking her.

She waited for Federica to leave, then went to search her room. Her father's little package had to be somewhere. She hesitated outside for a moment, looking about her and listening for the sound of footsteps. In the last couple of weeks she had turned into quite a detective. She felt very different from the frivolous girl she had been in Cornwall. Her father's 'disappearance' had propelled her into adulthood, and it had brought her Hamish. The death of one relationship, the birth of another.

The walls of Federica's room were decorated with paintings that caught her attention. The brushstrokes were bold, the colours vibrant, the scenes evocative. She realized where she had seen that style before: in Hamish's studio. She stepped closer and ran her fingers over the paint. It was rough and lumpy. Below he had written his initials: *HMcC.* How different these scenes were from the dark and lonely canvases that lay against the wall in his studio.

At the end of the room was a large iron bed, draped in a multicoloured quilt, covered in crimson and fuchsia cushions. The bedside tables were piled high with books. The windows were open, linen curtains blowing in the wind; a dressing table below, heavy with little bowls of rings and necklaces; a large mirror over which she had draped more beads. In the centre of the room there was a table laden with large wooden bowls of crystals of every colour and size, on strings and loose. It was like a magical shop. Against the walls were wooden wardrobes where her clothes hung in no apparent order, and on the floor there were rugs, placed one on top of another, almost covering the flagstones. If Federica had hidden the little package her father had given her, there was no way Celestria was going to find it among all this clutter. She didn't know where to begin. She didn't know what she was looking for, either. He could have given her anything.

With a sigh of desperation, she began to look through the drawers of the dressing table. Each drawer was filled to the brim with more beads and necklaces and rings and other knick-knacks she had collected from her travels. Celestria's heart sank.

She couldn't confront Federica without the box because she had promised not to bring Daphne's name into it. She searched the wardrobes and the cupboards in the bathroom adjoining. Then she sat on the bed, her shoulders hunched, certain that she was going to have to leave without it.

Suddenly, she heard Federica's voice in the courtyard below, talking to Luigi. She peeped out of the window to see her laughing, bending down to pat the dogs, the basket she carried over her shoulder full of shopping. She must have changed her plans. Celestria felt her frustration mount. As she turned to leave, her eye caught a familiar red box partly hidden in one of the bowls full of crystals on the centre table. She shoved her hand in and pulled it out victoriously, pressing it to her nose with delight. She was sure she could smell the scent of tuberose. There, glittering in the light, two diamond stars twinkled at her. Her mother's missing stars. The stars her father had given her, then stolen so ruthlessly.

She closed the box and returned to the bed, where she sat down and waited for Federica to appear. Her heart was hopping about in her chest like a cricket, but Celestria had never shirked confrontation. Perhaps now she would learn the whole truth, and even discover where her father was. She watched the door without blinking until her eyes stung. Finally, the sound of footsteps and the rapid panting of dogs invaded the silence. Federica opened the door and stepped inside, giving a start when she saw Celestria sitting calmly on her bed, holding in her hands the little red box.

The dogs followed her inside, dispersing to different parts of the room. Federica closed the door, put down her bag, and turned to face Celestria. She didn't seem angry at finding the girl in her room, nor was she defensive: she just looked sad.

'Papa gave this to my mother,' said Celestria angrily. 'He said he had to find stars big enough to outshine the stars in her eyes. This is how I saw my parents, like two glittering stars. But to him, their marriage meant nothing.'

'I'm sorry,' Federica said, taking the place beside her on the bed. 'I didn't know.' As much as Celestria wanted to hate her, she couldn't.

'So, tell me, how much *did* you know?'

'Almost as little as you. Only that he wasn't dead. Forgive me.'

'Why didn't you tell me?'

'Because he told me not to tell anyone that I had seen him. My loyalty will always be to him, because I love him.' She took Celestria's hand. Celestria let her take it, but it lay limply in the older woman's palm. 'When you arrived and told me he was dead, I was so torn. I didn't know how to handle it, so I did the best I could. It was the hardest act I've ever put on. Then when you announced that you were here to discover the truth, I was given a window of opportunity. I took it. I encouraged you because I was unable to tell you myself. I thought perhaps the truth would bring him back.'

'Nothing can bring him back – least of all the truth.'

'I hoped,' she said hoarsely.

'Anyway, I don't want him back.'

'Celestria. In spite of all that he has done, he is still your father. His life is in danger. He had to run away. He got himself into trouble.'

'Before or after he married Armel?' Federica flinched. He was indefensible. 'So you told no one?' Celestria continued.

'No one.'

'Not even Gaitano?'

'Not even him.'

Celestria swallowed hard. 'And Hamish. Did he know?'

'No.'

The knot in Celestria's stomach released. 'That is at least something. So where is he now?'

'I don't know. I haven't heard from him since, and I don't expect to.'

'Was he your lover? Did he jilt you?'

Federica laughed at the absurdity of the question. 'Of course not! I'm almost old enough to be his mother. No, I love him like a son, Celestria. I'm not saying that if I wasn't younger I wouldn't fall in love with him. But I'm old and married, and I know my limitations. We have an understanding that transcends words.'

'That's what they all say. You know you're only one of a large number of women who believe he loves them.'

'Perhaps.' She shrugged. 'It doesn't matter. He brought happiness into the Convento. After our daughter died I was lost. With your father's help I found myself again. I learned to love her memory and let her go.' *Shame Hamish can't do the same,* Celestria thought, feeling miserable again.

'He's like Dr Jekyll and Mr Hyde. Two people. One who spreads happiness wherever he goes, the other who lies and deceives and spreads pain.'

'Your father is a charming, charismatic man. But he is also deeply flawed. He cannot help but try to please everyone. He wants to be Mr Wonderful to everyone he meets. Of course, it is impossible to be everything to everyone. Not even Monty can do that. In trying, he has created all these different worlds in which he is always at the centre.' She looked at Celestria with tenderness. 'For a while he was in the centre of my world, too. I can only guess at the others. There may be many. Too many to control. Your father is not a good man, Celestria. But I love him in spite of all his faults.'

'Why is he so flawed? Uncle Archie and Aunt Penelope are normal! Where did their parents go wrong?'

'Sometimes people are born flawed. I don't think your grandparents are to blame. However, from what he has told me, I know that his mother put a great deal of pressure on him to excel. He was her golden boy, but her love came at a price. It was conditional. He was the magnificent Monty, yet inside he felt inadequate and undeserving and guilty.'

'Guilty? What of?'

'Of resenting his family.'

'He resented us?'

'He resented the expectation everyone placed upon him. It was too much to bear.'

'So he started another family because he was sick of the old one?'

'I don't know.'

'You seem to know an awful lot about him,' said Celestria grudgingly.

'I was like a mother to him. Someone he could talk to. Someone who thought the world of him, without strings.'

'I despise him,' she replied.

'Don't hate him. Pity him.'

'I pity myself. The more I try to remember him as he was before he disappeared, the less I trust my memories. Everything I have learned about him undermines the father he was to me. He was my papa for twenty-one years, and yet who was he? He loved Mama, and yet he gave you the stars he bought for her, the gift from him that she cherished. His heart is empty.'

'Or perhaps it is too full. Take the stars back to your mother,' said Federica sadly, handing her the box. 'Tell her you found them under the bed. Don't tell her the truth. As you have realized yourself, the truth is far worse than the lie.'

Celestria closed the box and stood up. 'We have all been betrayed,' she said.

'But we have found one another.'

'Yes, we have,' she replied, thinking of Hamish. 'And I found Marelatte.'

Back in the solitude of her bedroom, she wrote to her grandfather, telling him everything she had discovered. He had trusted her instincts. He had supported her need to get away, to learn the truth. Now she needed his advice. Was she a fool to love Hamish?

Chapter 31

That afternoon, Celestria found Mrs Waynebridge in the garden. She was sitting in the sunshine, talking to Daphne. They were both laughing beneath their sunhats. When they saw her, Mrs Waynebridge waved and Daphne got up stiffly. 'I'll leave you two together,' she said, picking up her crocheted bag where she kept her book and reading glasses. 'I must go and do some painting before the light goes.' Celestria sat down in Daphne's chair.

'I've hardly seen you, Waynie,' she said, regretfully. She was on the point of telling her about the diamonds when she realized that Mrs Waynebridge was no longer interested. The housekeeper had a faraway look in her eyes.

'Nuzzo has asked me to marry him,' she said finally.

'How did he do that? Playing charades?' Celestria hadn't meant to sound unkind. 'Or has he taught you some Italian?' she added more gently, hoping she hadn't taken offense.

'We understand each other perfectly,' replied Mrs Waynebridge, lifting her chin proudly.

'Did you say yes?'

'I did.'

'Waynie, I'm so thrilled for you!' She leaned across and hugged her.

'Are you really?' Mrs Waynebridge had been worried

about telling her. She didn't like to think of Celestria travelling back to England on her own.

Celestria tried to look happy. 'I really am,' she said, but then the tears spilled over and she could no longer hide her feelings. 'I'm sorry. I'm so selfish. You've found happiness with Nuzzo in this beautiful place, and all I can think about is myself.'

'Don't be sorry. I understand. Remember, I've known you since you were a baby.'

'It's been an awful week. I came out to find Papa, but I found love instead.'

'You've found love?' Mrs Waynebridge had been so distracted by her own inflating heart that she hadn't noticed Celestria's. 'Who with?'

Celestria looked sheepish. 'Hamish.'

'I thought you didn't like him?'

'I changed my mind. I like him very much.'

'What made you change your mind?'

'I got to know him.' Her face flushed, setting her eyes alight. 'It was all a misunderstanding, Waynie. But we're past that now. Mrs Halifax was right: he's charming and intelligent and funny, too. When we finally talked, we clicked together like an engine and carriage that were made for each other. When I'm with him, it feels right. I feel safe with him.' She sighed. 'I really love him, Waynie. I don't yearn to return home to London. I want the simple life here with him. I want to walk up the beach holding hands, dance in the moonlight, watch him paint. I want to play the piano and sing, work my way through Gaitano's library, and give Hamish children who'll love the simple things, like we do. I want to make him happy.'

'Then why are you crying?'

Celestria wiped away a tear. 'Because I don't know what to do. Do I stay here? Do I go home? I haven't had a marriage proposal.'

'Give him time; you've only just met.'

'What if he's still in love with his dead wife?'

'That won't get him anywhere.'

'Gaitano says he feels guilty because he was there when she fell off the cliff. He thinks it was his fault. He won't stop blaming himself.'

'Time will heal, love.'

'He's had three years! How much longer will it take?'

'He's only just met you.'

'But I'm here. I'm a living, breathing person, loving him. Natalia can't love him from where she is.'

'What are you going to do?'

'I don't know. There's nothing to keep me here now. Do I stay, or do I go?'

'You stay, Celestria, and you fight for what you want,' the older woman replied fiercely.

'Perhaps I don't belong here. I should return to London and marry Aidan and forget that I ever met Hamish.'

'Then you'll live half a life.'

'No, I'd live half a life here with Hamish. Natalia would have the other half.'

The decision, however, was taken out of her hands by a telegram that arrived as hers was sent to Scotland. It was from her mother. Celestria read it. Then she read it again. She tried to read it a third time, but her eyes had blurred with tears: 'YOUR GRANDFATHER PASSED AWAY THIS MORNING STOP COME HOME STOP.'

She sank onto the cushions beneath the cloister, pulling Primo and Maialino onto her lap for comfort. Hamish sat beside her and took the telegram from her trembling fingers. 'God,' he murmured, kissing the top of her head. 'You loved him like a father, didn't you?' She nodded but couldn't speak. They sat there, in the shade, for a long while. Primo and

Maialino sensed unhappiness. Finally, she drew away and folded up the telegram.

'I have to go home,' she said, wiping her eyes with the back of her hand.

'I know.'

'What are we going to do?'

'I'm going to be here when you come back.'

'Do you want me to?' She looked at him with a frown, longing to be certain of his affection. Wanting to have it all for herself.

'Yes.' He took her face in his hands and kissed her lips, taking his time. 'I want you to come back very, very much.'

Mrs Waynebridge was brokenhearted for Celestria. 'She has lost not only her father, but her grandfather, too, who she loved more than anyone else in the world, even her mother. Which isn't really surprising, if you know her mother,' she told Federica and Daphne.

'But what about Hamish?' said Daphne, recalling their morning conversation.

'I'm hoping she'll come back,' replied Federica. 'He needs her, and they could be so happy together.'

'She'll come back,' said Waynie, with a knowing smile. 'A woman is never the same after experiencing Italy.'

That night Hamish made love to Celestria beside the old fortress. There were no stars, and the moon was hidden behind thick clouds and mist that hung low over the sea. The air was strangely warm and humid. A storm was brewing. They lay on a rug and loved each other, their hearts heavy with melancholy, unsure of what the future held for them.

In the morning Celestria packed her suitcases and waited in the courtyard for Gaitano, who was going to take her to

Spongano. It was raining. Large drops fell onto the paving stones and dripped off the arches of the cloister, where the dogs lay. Mrs Waynebridge and Daphne had said goodbye to her in the dining room, both too emotional to watch her drive away. Hamish was nowhere to be seen.

Suddenly Federica appeared in a flurry, wringing her hands. 'Hamish told me to tell you he's in the cemetery. He wants you to go and see him before you leave.' She looked anxious. 'He says it's important.'

Celestria ran across the road, the rain drenching her dress and shoes and flattening her hair against her face. A couple of black cats had taken shelter in the entrance of the cemetery, huddled together to keep dry. She hurried through the gates, into the city of the dead, where the rain had fallen on the warm earth in the little park and filled the air with the sweet scent of damp pine. Birdsong resounded up and down the little avenues as the birds fluttered about to find shelter, and the heady smell of lilies emanated from the little mausoleums mingled with the smell of candle wax. She reached Natalia's crypt and climbed the steps. Inside, Hamish stood with his hands on her tomb, staring at the floor. When she entered, he looked up. His face was ashen, his eyes redrimmed. For a moment she thought he was going to shout at her.

'I'm letting her go,' he said. 'I want to make a commitment to you. But first I want you to know everything. I should have shown you earlier.'

Without saying another word, he led her outside. The rain had become a light drizzle. He took her down the little path towards the old fortress. He walked with his stick, but his limp was less noticeable. Instead of turning right to the fort, he turned left and led her along the cliff top. Her sodden dress clung to her legs like seaweed, and her canvas shoes squelched with each step. After a few hundred yards, he stopped.

'This is where she died,' he said, dropping his stick and taking her by the shoulders.

Celestria looked down. It was a long way. Natalia hadn't stood a chance; she would have been broken on the rocks before she had known what had hit her. He looked at her intensely, his eyes full of pain.

'She was having an affair, Celestria. She was in love with another man.' His tone was brittle, like the scrunching of fragmented glass. 'I found out and confronted her. She accused me of being moody and self-obsessed and claimed I had driven her to it. We had a fight. She was as volatile as me. We were like two sparks in a fire, maddened with anger and hurt. I told her she had to choose between me and him. But she couldn't choose. She loved him, even though she knew he would break her heart. Perhaps he had broken it already.' He inhaled as if he needed to find the courage to continue. Then he gripped her shoulders and said: 'The other man, Celestria, was your father.'

Celestria was horrified. She recoiled, catching her breath as if she had been winded. 'My father?'

'I should have told you.'

'My father? Having an affair with your wife?' She took a step back. 'It's not possible.'

'I'm afraid it is.'

She took a moment to digest the awful truth. 'That's why you hated me. Because I was his daughter. It makes perfect sense.'

'But I fell in love with you.' He gazed at her in desperation.

'But you lied.'

'No. I never lied. I just didn't tell you the whole truth.'

'So why are you telling me now? When I'm on the point of leaving?'

'Because when you come back, I want to start with a clean slate. I want to put it all behind us: Natalia, your father. I want us to begin our life together untarnished by the past. You're the only person who will know the truth. But there's more.'

'More?' Celestria's features were contorted with pain.

'Natalia claimed she was unable to choose between me and Robert because she was carrying a child. She didn't know whose child it was.' His eyes filled with tears. Celestria felt her own tears gathering, ready to unite with the rain that trickled down her face. 'She was carrying a life inside her, Celestria. It could have been mine. How could she not know? I lost my mind. I shouted at her, and she just looked at me, full of defiance, as if relishing the power she had over me. She showed not a grain of remorse. How closely related are love and hate. In that moment I loved her so much I hated her. The next thing I knew was that she slipped and fell. I didn't push her. I swear to God, I didn't push her. But I don't remember clearly. It's all a blur. Could I have pushed her when she was carrying a child?'

'So you haven't only been mourning Natalia, but the child who might have been yours.'

Hamish nodded. Celestria's heart buckled.

'Oh, Hamish, I'm so sorry.' She wound her arms around him and held him close. 'I don't doubt you,' she whispered.

Celestria sat on the train in the dry clothes she had changed into before she left. Now she watched the Italian countryside flash past her window. In her bag she carried the diamond stars she would return to her mother. She wouldn't tell. She would keep it all to herself, a more generous act than her father deserved. Pamela would never know the truth. She would believe he had only ever loved her. Harry would grow up with happy memories of his father building him traps in the woods above Pendrift, constructing sand castles on the beach, and taking him out in his little boat to play pirates. By not telling them the truth she would safeguard their past and protect their future. It was the right thing to do.

She rested her head against the seat and closed her eyes. She saw her grandfather's large face and twinkling eyes. She could almost run her fingers over the deep lines in his skin and over his knobbly nose. How she loved him. He had been such a strong presence in her life. Just knowing he was there gave her an immense sense of security. Now he was gone, she felt alone.

She realized now that he had been the only man in her life to love her honestly. While her father had breezed in and out, armed with presents and compliments, her grandfather had taken a deeper interest. She had never penetrated her father, but he, in turn, had never penetrated her. It was her grandfather who had made it his business to know and understand her. He had encouraged her as a little girl, and it was in the small things that he had shown he cared. While her boyfriends had celebrated her beauty, her grandfather had been proud of her spirit, her intelligence, and her wit. After her father's disappearance, his had been the only arms she had wanted to hold her. How she wished she could have shared with him her experience of Italy. He would have admired her courage in discovering the truth about her father's fake suicide, and comforted her when her past had unravelled like a ball of pretty ribbon to reveal the ugly truth within. Now he would never know, and she'd never again feel his reassurance.

Chapter 32

Pamela went to church. It didn't matter that St Peter's wasn't a Catholic church; as far as she was concerned, God was damn lucky that she was going at all. She sat on one of the chairs at the front and contemplated the most extraordinary happening of her life. It had all begun the night before last. She had gone to bed, having drunk a cup of hot cocoa, feeling miserable. Harry was at school, Celestria doing God knows what in Italy, and she was all alone with just Poochi for company, feeling extremely sorry for herself. Her father was in residence in Scotland. In his vast, over-decorated, gothic castle, surrounded by servants and friends he had acquired over the years. She had spoken to him that day by telephone. He had been stalking with the Earl of Rosebury. He was feeling fit and well and very pleased with himself. Now, after years of estrangement, Pamela felt close to him again.

In the middle of the night she woke. It was dark but for the golden glow of the streetlamp outside the house. She blinked into the darkness as a figure appeared before her eyes. To her astonishment, it was her father. His form was ghostly, not entirely solid, but in colour. He looked younger, too. He didn't speak, but she sensed him communicating and understood him. He was saying goodbye and wrapping her in love.

She felt her eyes well with tears, willing him to stay. He smiled his characteristic broad smile that extended across his whole face. 'I'm ready,' he said silently. 'I'm done here. But I'll always be around.' She sat up, determined to hold on to him. But then he was gone. At eight o'clock the telephone rang. Her father had suffered a heart attack in the night and was dead.

Now she sat in church, knowing that her vision had been nothing less than the soul of her father saying goodbye as he made his final journey to heaven. She no longer had any doubt. There *was* life after death, and there *was* a God. He had heard her and given her this gift. She couldn't wait to tell Father Dalgliesh. She would telephone the presbytery as soon as the service was over.

It was strange. She had lost her husband and her father in less than two months, and yet she no longer felt alone. She knew they were with her in spirit, and that certainty gave her great comfort. After years of not believing, she now understood why people went to church. There was so much more to life than the glamour of the material world. There was a spirit world, an existence beyond death, and that gave her life a whole new meaning. Besides, if she was going to be judged, she'd better start making up for her bad behaviour.

Celestria returned to London. The excitement of being back home was spoiled by the sadness of her grandfather's death. She stared out of the taxi window, feeling nothing but a terrible emptiness. She felt sorry for herself, having lost two men in the short space of a few weeks. However, once she was home, lying on her mother's bed, hearing about Lotty's flight with the piano teacher and how Penelope was so incensed she could barely speak about it, she felt better.

'Dear Lotty has made a terrible mistake,' said Pamela. 'What sort of life will she have with a simple piano teacher? Where will they live? I can't imagine her being very happy living in Maida Vale.' Celestria admired her cousin's courage. It was no easy feat to defy Aunt Penelope.

'Why do you all think one has to be rich to be happy?'

'Because money buys freedom.'

'Not freedom from her mother!' said Celestria with a chuckle.

'I'm trying to be good, so I'll pretend I didn't hear that.'

'Why are you trying to be good? Isn't it a terrible effort?'

Pamela sniffed and placed her dog on her lap. 'I've found God,' she said. Celestria snorted in disbelief. 'Don't mock me, darling. I saw a vision the night your grandfather died. He came to me.'

Celestria grew serious. 'He did?'

'Absolutely. He was grinning his great big grin, and he told me that he'd still be around. It was very clear. Undeniable. Then I was woken by the telephone saying he'd died in his sleep. So God is up there somewhere, and your grandfather is there, too. I am as surprised as you are. But I've made a pledge to be a better person, because when I die I want to join him. No good being in hell with your father when I can be in heaven with Pa.'

'Mama, Papa's not in hell!'

'Of course he is. Not for long, of course, because we'll pray for his soul.'

Celestria so wanted to tell her the truth, but she knew her mother couldn't take it. 'When is the funeral?'

'On Saturday. Ma is coming over from New York. She's miserable that she wasn't there when he died. Anyway, you have a few days to recover from your trip before we go to Scotland. We'll stay in the castle. I'll have to sell it, of course. Ma won't want it.'

'Are you sure you don't want to live there?'

Pamela shot her a look of mock contempt. 'It's a ghastly pile. I don't know why he bought it in the first place. He spent so little time there.'

'I had so much to tell him,' said Celestria sadly. Then, with a pang of horror, she remembered the letter she had sent him. He hadn't lived to read it. What if her mother found it? She swallowed, resolving to find it and destroy it the moment she arrived in Scotland.

'I'm sure you do. He's around, if you feel like sharing it with him.'

Celestria stared at her in amazement. 'You sound like someone else!'

'I am someone else,' she said seriously. 'I've shed a skin, metamorphosed. How was your trip, darling? Did Waynie survive those Italians she was so frightened of?'

'Mama,' said Celestria carefully, 'she's still there.'

'You came home on your own?'

'I'm not a child, Mama!'

'What's she doing there, for goodness' sake?'

'She's marrying one of those Italians.'

Pamela stopped stroking Poochi and placed her hand across her mouth. 'You can't be serious! Waynie?'

'I'm afraid it's true. Waynie isn't coming back.'

'What's gone wrong with the world? I'm losing everyone.' Celestria knew she couldn't begin to tell her mother about Hamish.

'She's very happy. You've found God; she's found love. They're very sweet together, actually. It's taken years off her.'

'You're different, too,' said her mother, narrowing her eyes suspiciously. 'I hope you didn't fall in love.' Celestria lowered her gaze and ran her fingers over the bobbles on her mother's crocheted bedspread.

'I had a good rest.'

'Harry's back at Eton. The best place for him. His house-master called me to say that he's fine, surrounded by his friends and all the distractions of school. By the way, Aidan

Cooney has been telephoning, wanting to know when you were coming back. Why don't you give him a call? He's definitely at the top of the food chain. I must go, darling, I'm having my hair done. Don't want to be late.'

Celestria knew that she'd have to face Aidan sooner or later. Even if she took Hamish out of the equation, she couldn't marry Aidan. Daphne was right; why commit to a lifetime with a man who didn't make the earth move?

Celestria telephoned him, and he suggested they have lunch in Knightsbridge.

'Darling, I'm dreadfully sorry about your grandfather; the old boy had a good innings, though!'

'Thank you, Aidan.'

'You're an heiress now. I don't need to save you from poverty.'

Celestria felt uncomfortable. Not because of Aidan's brashness, but because she realized how much Italy had changed her. A couple of weeks ago she would have laughed at his comments. 'I miss him so much.'

'I'm going to take care of you now, my darling.'

Celestria put down the telephone and realized that she didn't want anyone to take care of her. She was quite capable of looking after herself. She ran a bath and soaked in it. When she closed her eyes, it was Hamish who rose out of the mist, his wide face solemn, his green eyes deep and troubled, his hair wild and unkempt. It wasn't the rose oil that filled her senses but the memory of pine and the sound of birds in the almond trees, dogs barking in the road, and the peaceful stillness of the city of the dead. Puglia had refashioned her so that now her shape no longer fitted the old mould. She felt at odds with her London life. Yet there niggled at the back of her mind the fear that Hamish's love was not enough. Perhaps the gamble was too great, even for her. Would life not be simpler if she tried to pick up the pieces of her old life?

She waited for Aidan in the hall. The house no longer felt like home. Without her father it felt empty, as if he were the vital note without whom the chord clashed. When the doorbell rang, she picked up her handbag, expecting it to be Aidan, but to her surprise, it was a deliveryman with the largest bunch of lilies she had ever seen. She pressed her nose to them and inhaled the scent; it reminded her of Italy.

'Typical Aidan,' she said, handing them to Godfrey. 'Will you put them in water? I'd like them in my room, please. They're beautiful.'

'Of course, Miss Celestria,' Godfrey replied, longing to ask about Mrs Waynebridge. Was it true that she was never coming back? He hesitated a moment. Celestria sensed the reason.

'Mrs Waynebridge is getting married to an Italian she met in Puglia,' she said. The old man's eyes widened. 'Italy has changed her, Godfrey.' She sighed wistfully, her gaze resting on the lilies. 'It has changed me, too.'

Godfrey disappeared with the lilies. Celestria continued to wait. Finally Aidan arrived, jumping up the steps to the front door two at a time. His face expanded into the widest smile. Celestria had forgotten how handsome he was.

'Darling!' he exclaimed, wrapping his arms around her. 'You look beautiful. God, it's good to have you back, old girl!' He kissed her lips, and Celestria was so taken aback she forgot to thank him for the lilies. 'I'm taking you to the Ritz,' he said. 'Only the best will do for my fiancée!' There was something very reassuring about being in his arms again. It was as familiar as an old pair of slippers.

'I thought we were going to have lunch in Knightsbridge?'

'I changed my mind.' Celestria would rather not have gone to the Ritz. It would only remind her of her grandfather. 'I've got a surprise for you.' He smirked, pleased with himself.

'You needn't have gone to the trouble,' she said, wondering when would be the best time to tell him that she couldn't marry him. He opened the car door and helped her in. There was a time when she had relished his shiny green Austin Healey; now her heart longed for Nuzzo and his horse and cart.

They arrived at the Ritz to be welcomed by the doorman, who took her hand in both of his. 'I had great respect for Mr Bancroft, miss,' he said, his eyes brimming with sympathy and regret. 'We shall all miss him here.'

'Thank you so much,' she replied, wishing they had chosen anywhere else in London but here, her grandfather's favourite dining room. Mr Windthorne swept across the carpeted floor to greet her.

'We are all so dreadfully sorry, Miss Montague. London shines less brightly without Mr Bancroft.'

Aidan took her arm, and they were escorted along the corridor, past the tea room where she had often eaten scones and jam with her grandfather, and into the dining room.

'I have chosen a table around the corner so you can be private,' said Mr Windthorne, with a wink at Aidan. Celestria suddenly had the most dreadful feeling. They were conspiring together. She remembered Aidan's mention of a surprise for her. Surely he wouldn't have announced their engagement without telling her first?

As they turned the corner she was welcomed by a long table of family and friends. Celestria's heart sank. This was not the time to meet his parents. Everyone stood up and clapped, their faces aglow with delight.

'Darling, why didn't you tell me?' Pamela cried, rushing over to embrace her. 'I'm so pleased! A spring wedding; I've already booked the church.' Celestria felt faint. It had all gone too far. Her mother's arms wrapped around her like tentacles, and she was enveloped in a cloud of tuberose. 'You shall have the most spectacular wedding, darling. It's what Pa would have wanted.' Celestria knew that her grandfather would have only wanted what *she* wanted. Slowly, she moved around the table, greeting everyone with a smile and a kiss, while inside she wanted to die.

'It's a pleasure to meet you,' said Aidan's mother sweetly, kissing her. 'This couldn't be a happier day.' Celestria was about to make it the most miserable day. Aidan's father kissed her, too, and Celestria felt sorry. Had things been different, she would have loved Aidan's family. 'Really, Aidan,' she said finally, sitting down. 'The flowers were enough.'

He looked at her quizzically. 'Flowers? What flowers?'

'The lilies that arrived this morning.'

Aidan looked put out. 'I didn't send you any flowers.' He appealed to Pamela. 'Do you know who sent my fiancée flowers?'

'Oh,' Celestria replied with a shrug. 'Perhaps they weren't for me. I didn't read the note.'

'They'll be for me. I've received so many letters of condolence. People are so kind,' said Pamela, too excited to dwell on something so trivial. But Celestria was staring into her champagne glass. She knew they weren't for her mother. She recalled the scent of lilies that rose out of the city of the dead, and a smile crept across her face.

'I think a London wedding, don't you, darling?' her mother continued blithely.

'London?'

'Well, word has it that Archie's selling Pendrift,' she hissed under her breath.

Celestria was jolted out of her daydream. 'Selling Pendrift?'

'I shouldn't say,' Pamela added quickly, wishing she hadn't said anything. Her daughter had suddenly blanched on what should be the happiest of days. 'I think the blossom in London is simply stunning in springtime . . .'

Celestria stood up. 'Please excuse me,' she said, clearly flustered. Aidan frowned, Pamela looked sheepish, and the rest of the table looked on puzzled as they watched her leave the dining room.

'I'll go,' said Pamela, getting up. 'It's overwhelmed her. Don't worry,' she reassured Aidan. 'We'll be back in a minute.' Pamela found Celestria in the hall, waiting for her coat. 'You can't go!'

'I'm not marrying Aidan!' Celestria replied. 'It's all a dreadful misunderstanding. I'm in love with Hamish.'

'Hamish?'

'Hamish McCloud.'

'Who in the devil's name is he?'

'He's Scottish.'

'I don't even know him!' Pamela clutched her neck as if finding it difficult to breathe.

Celestria tried in vain to suppress a smile. 'Well, he's in his late thirties, a widower, walks with a limp, doesn't brush his hair, is a talented artist without a penny to his name, and makes the earth tremble and shake and shift on its axis. He has a vile temper but a raw and passionate heart, and, in spite of my efforts not to, I lost my heart in an instant.'

While Pamela struggled to reply, Aidan strode up to join them. 'What's going on?' he asked, watching Celestria shrug on her coat. 'Where are you going?'

'You shouldn't have told anyone!' she retorted crossly.

'It was a surprise. I thought you'd be pleased.'

'I can't marry you,' she said, finally managing to look suitably solemn.

'Why not?' Aidan looked distraught.

'Because I don't love you, Aidan. I like you, but like is not enough.'

'I can make you happy,' he said in desperation, taking her in his arms. Mr Windthorne watched the unfolding drama from behind the reception desk.

'I know you can,' she said, pulling away. 'But I want more than that, and so should you.'

'But I love you.'

'I'm sorry.'

'Darling, you need to think about this,' interjected Pamela, finding her voice at last. 'It's not too late to change your mind. You've lost your father and your grandfather. It's not surprising that you're not yourself. Let's go home and talk it through calmly, where we're not being watched by all the staff.' Mr Windthorne looked away with a cough, pretending not to notice them.

'There's nothing to talk about. I've made my decision, and, believe me, I've never been of sounder mind. If death teaches you one thing, it's that nothing matters in this world but love. You can't take your wealth with you when you die.' It was then that she was struck with an idea. 'Mama, you never told me Uncle Archie was in trouble.'

'It's not our problem.'

'If Papa were alive, he'd never let them sell Pendrift.'

Aidan clenched his hands, furious that they had digressed.

'But he's not alive. Anyway, he had no money; you know that as well as I do,' Pamela snapped.

'But *we* do.'

Her mother narrowed her eyes. 'You are now a very wealthy woman. I bet your Harry McCloud will be happy about that!' She grabbed Aidan's wrist. 'This young man has the means to look after you, Celestria, irrespective of your grandfather's inheritance. I think your Harry McCloud will find it very humiliating being supported by a woman!'

'Well, that's easy to take care of, isn't it?'

'What do you mean?'

'If I don't have money, we'll be equal. By the way, Mama, he's called *Hamish* McCloud.' She turned to Aidan. 'I'm sorry. I really am. But I have to go now.' She hurried off without a backwards glance. Aidan and Pamela watched her go in silence.

Celestria arrived at Upper Belgrave Street in a flurry of excitement. Her joy inflated her like a hot-air balloon so that she was barely able to keep her feet on the ground. She called for Godfrey. The old man staggered out, having enjoyed rather too much wine with his lunch. 'Godfrey, the note that came with the flowers, where is it?'

'I threw it away, Miss Celestria.'

'Well, get it out. I need to see it.'

Godfrey disappeared, and Celestria paced the hall, unable to remain still. After a few minutes he returned.

Celestria opened the little white envelope. Written on a simple card were the words, *'You are the light behind the door.'* She pressed the card to her lips. 'Daphne!' she said with a smile, knowing that the old woman would have arranged this for Hamish. Godfrey stared at her in bewilderment.

'Is there anything else, Miss Celestria?'

'Yes, Godfrey. After the funeral on Saturday I'm going back to Italy. But today, I'm going to Pendrift.'

'Pendrift, Miss Celestria?' Now he was really confused.

'Please tell Mama that I have taken the train and that I will be back in time to travel with her to Scotland.'

'You will be very tired, Miss Celestria,' he said, overwhelmed by her travel plans.

'One doesn't get tired when one is happy, Godfrey. And I am very happy.'

Chapter 33

When Celestria appeared at Pendrift Hall, Julia and Archie were in the drawing room having coffee with Elizabeth, who had joined them for dinner. She stood in the doorway with her small suitcase, looking as radiant as if she had just enjoyed a full night's sleep.

'Hello, everyone!' she said, beaming, relishing their surprise.

'Good God, Celestria!' exclaimed Archie, standing up. 'Where did you come from?'

'The station,' she said. 'I got a cab.'

'It's so late. You should have telephoned,' said Julia, rising to greet her. 'This is a lovely surprise. You do look well.'

'Hello, Grandma,' she said, bending down to kiss her. The old woman smiled, and Celestria noticed the change in her immediately.

'When did you get back from Italy?' Julia asked.

'This morning.'

'You must be exhausted,' she said, noticing her niece's eyes shining with unusual brightness.

'Not at all. I slept on the train.'

'To what do we owe this pleasure?' said Archie. It wasn't like Celestria to make an impromptu visit.

'I'd like a drink first. A glass of red wine would be nice,' she said, looking around the room she had lived in every summer but never really noticed. Archie walked over to the drinks table and poured her a glass. 'Pendrift Hall is a magical house,' she said.

'It's special, isn't it? There's none other like it,' Archie replied, his eyes full of sadness.

'It's special because of the people who inhabit it,' said Elizabeth firmly, looking on her son and daughter-in-law with pride. 'We all imprint ourselves onto it over the years. It's certainly been loved.'

Archie handed Celestria the glass. She took a swig and felt it trickle down into her empty stomach.

'Mama tells me that you are thinking of selling.'

'How does she know?' Archie asked, affronted.

'She probably knows the ghastly Weavels,' said Julia, lighting a cigarette. 'Nothing about Pamela would surprise me.'

'It's true,' said Elizabeth stoically. 'Pendrift Hall is in trouble; that's all there is to it.' Now she looked more like her old, disgruntled self.

'Well, I'd like to honour my father's promise,' said Celestria. The three of them stared at her.

'What promise?' interjected Elizabeth, glancing at Archie.

'I heard you talking in the little sitting room,' she admitted to Julia, unabashed. 'Papa said he would help you out.'

'Ah,' said Julia, looking embarrassed. 'Monty was always there.' She raised her eyes to her husband. 'Now he's not, and everything falls apart.'

'I am now very rich. I've inherited my grandfather's fortune, along with Mama and Harry. I can't keep my share all to myself; it's more than even *I* could spend in a lifetime, and I certainly won't need it where I'm going!' The wine made her feel deliciously light-headed. 'Papa would never have let you sell Pendrift.'

'He most certainly would not,' agreed Elizabeth, clicking her tongue.

'So neither will I.'

Julia blinked, her eyes now shining with tears. 'You really want to save our home?' she asked, dazed. 'I didn't think you liked it here.'

'It's not just your home, it's *our* home. All my happiest memories are here. I just never knew it.'

'My dear girl,' said Elizabeth. God had indeed performed a miracle. Father Dalgliesh had been right; help had come from the most unexpected place. 'I thought you the most selfish of all my grandchildren.'

'Papa thought so, too,' Celestria replied. 'And perhaps I still *am* selfish, because this is giving *me* pleasure. You see, I'm in love. He's highly unsuitable, and Mama is furious. But Grandpa would have celebrated it and encouraged me to follow my heart. I haven't changed that much, after all. If I were unselfish, I'd marry Aidan Cooney to make Mama happy. But as it is, I'm going to return to Italy after Grandpa's funeral and make Mama very unhappy indeed.' She shrugged unapologetically.

'Good God, girl!' Archie exclaimed suddenly, turning pink. 'Your father would be very proud of you, Celestria.'

'Thank you,' said Elizabeth humbly. 'And thank you, God, for giving Celestria a big heart. Now, tell us about your young man? What does he do?'

Perhaps it was the wine, or the fact that Celestria no longer needed approval from anyone, but she told it to them straight, without reserve, and although Archie dropped his coffee cup and stained the carpet, no one was in any position to criticize.

The following morning, Celestria awoke late to the sound of Bouncy in the garden below, kicking a ball across the lawn with Purdy. She stood a while at the window, gazing out. Bouncy made her smile, running over the grass on his short legs, laughing with abandon. It gave her pleasure to know that, thanks to her, he would grow up here. Maybe he'd never know how close he'd come to leaving it. She raised her eyes to the sea that glittered innocently in the pale light of morning. Of the family, only she knew that her father hadn't drowned there. Only she knew the extent of his deception. But by saving Pendrift, she was somehow erasing some of his malice, preserving his memory as she would have liked to remember him. No one would be any the wiser. They'd all thank her, assuming that she was simply taking up where he left off, doing what he would have done himself, had his life not been so cruelly cut short.

But *she* knew. Not a day would go by when she wouldn't wonder where he was and what he was doing, and whether his duplicity had brought him happiness. She doubted it was possible to build happiness on foundations that were warped with pain. He had selfishly sought pleasure without considering the hearts he had broken along the way. Well, she wouldn't allow him to hurt her family any more. The knowledge that she was preserving their memory of him gave her the deepest sense of satisfaction.

As she walked across the lawn to the snake path that led down to the sea, she was suddenly hit on the shin by the football. Little Bouncy squealed with laughter. 'Thorry,' he said, his lisp as sweet as ever. Purdy came bounding over the grass to catch it.

'You kick very well. I think you're going to be a skillful footballer.' The little boy jogged over to her. 'I see you now have Mummy all to yourself,' she said, recalling the time Nanny nearly lost him to the sea.

'Mummy'th my betht friend,' he replied as Purdy ran past, almost knocking him to the ground. Bouncy ran after the dog, trying to catch his Labrador tail.

'And Grandma?' added Celestria, a little mischievously.

'Grandma playth with me, and Daddy throwth me in the air.'

'I bet Grandma doesn't play football.'

'Grandma is very old,' he said innocently. 'Wilfrid and Sam play with me, and Purdy,' he added, springing up to run to the ball. He gave it a good kick. It flew over the grass. Purdy ran after it, and Bouncy ran after Purdy.

Celestria raised her eyes to one of the drawing room windows, where Julia stood watching them. For her, Celestria's gift was even more precious. Pendrift wasn't just her home; it was her children's home.

Down on the beach Celestria sat on the sand, enjoying the solitude and the gentle rhythm of the waves. She allowed her memories to take her back to the summers of her childhood, knowing that she would never spend another summer here again. One chapter had closed; another was about to begin. She didn't know where it would take her, but she was confident that, with courage and patience, she would find happiness with Hamish.

Suddenly she heard a familiar voice behind her. She swivelled around to see Father Dalgliesh striding across the sand. 'I was told I could find you here,' he called out above the sound of the sea. 'Do you mind if I join you?'

'Please do,' she replied, watching him sit down.

'This is a surprise,' he said, catching his breath. 'Julia tells me you've saved Pendrift. Your gift is generous.'

'Not really,' she replied. 'My grandfather has made me very rich. I'm just pleased I'm in a position to do it. It's what Papa would have wanted.'

'Of course,' he said. 'I'm sure he'd be very proud.' There was a long silence. He took off his glasses and pulled out a handkerchief with which to clean them. 'How was Italy?'

'It was beautiful,' she replied.

'I don't know Puglia. What's it like?'

'Dry, stony, flat, cliffy. There are parts that remind one of Cornwall, except the sun shines, and the sky is that incredible blue.' While she told him about the cemetery, the little church attached to the Convento, and the old fortress, she grew more certain than ever that Puglia was where she belonged, in spite of all the unhappiness Hamish had suffered there. If it hadn't been for Natalia, he wouldn't be the man he was today. Because of Natalia, she loved him. If it hadn't been for Freddie, Gaitano, and Daphne, she might never have changed. What was the point in running away from all that?

'You look very refreshed,' he said, putting his glasses back on. It was true. She was more beautiful than he remembered her. She was no longer troubled, as if in Italy her spirit had at last found peace. 'I've wanted to talk to you ever since you ran off,' he began, but Celestria stopped him by touching his hand.

'Father, please. I'm so ashamed. I was misguided, not to mention foolish.'

'You were confused; it was understandable. I wanted to tell you because I didn't want you to feel embarrassed. But you were gone—'

'I remembered your eyes for days afterwards.'

'My eyes?'

'Yes, you looked at me with such compassion, and yet in your eyes I saw a reflection of my own ugliness.'

He shook his head. 'You're beautiful.'

'Perhaps on the outside, but I was ugly on the inside. Even my own father thought me spoiled and demanding. Mama thinks she's changed because she saw a vision of my grandfather the night he died.'

'She did?'

'She might have found God, but she's still the same person. Some people are too old to change, or perhaps too set in their ways. I'm not, and Italy has changed me. As much as I love Pendrift, I feel disconnected here, as if I no longer belong.'

'That's because so much that was familiar to you has changed.'

'I know. My father was such a big presence; without him it just feels empty.'

'Give it time.'

She shook her head and her hair fell over her shoulders in yellow curls. 'No. I'm going back to Puglia.'

He raised his eyebrows. 'You're going back?'

'Yes. I met a man, Father.'

'Ah.' He fought his disappointment.

'He needs me.'

'And you? Do you need him?'

'More than I realized.'

'Then you must go. But you'll be missed.'

She smiled at him knowingly. 'You'll miss me, won't you?'

He smiled bashfully. 'Yes. But I'll be happy to know that you are happy. Perhaps it's too much to expect you to remain in a place that has brought you so much unhappiness.'

'No, that's not true. This place has made me grow up. I love it more now than I ever did. But I love Puglia, too. I thought I'd want to leave it and start afresh somewhere new, but I don't want to run away from the place that has offered me another chance.' She chuckled, knowing that Father Dalgliesh couldn't possibly understand. 'If it hadn't been for Puglia, I would have turned out just like Mama, and imagine what a fright I would have been! Mama was bad before, but now she's found God, she's even worse. You wait, she'll be down here soon enough arranging the church flowers and collection bags.'

'When are you leaving?'

'Tomorrow morning.'

'Then we have time for a walk?' he suggested.

'I'd like that,' she replied, standing up.

'So would I. At least this time it's not raining,' he said, setting off along the beach towards the path that led up to the cliff top.

'I see you're wearing a matching pair of socks.' She laughed, slipping her hand through his arm.

'You noticed?'

'I always noticed, Father.'

Hamish sat in Saverio's bar playing Scopa with Leopoldo, Manfredo, and Vitalino. It was raining. The air in the bar was thick with smoke and condensation. The men of Marelatte gathered around the small tables to drink coffee and complain about their women. Hamish remembered the time he had suddenly seen Celestria talking to Salazar. He recalled the sense of outrage that Robert Montague's daughter had invaded his inner sanctum that had combined with the overwhelming urge to protect her from the situation in which she was so clearly out of her depth. He stared blankly at his hand of cards and recalled how deftly Celestria had crept under his skin from the first moment he saw her running her fingers over the vines on Natalia's tomb. Her allure had shone out as brightly as those two candles. It had disarmed him. He had been ashamed of his outburst and, for the first time in three years, painfully aware of what he had become. When he had discovered she was the daughter of the man who had seduced his wife, there was no other option but to avoid her. He knew himself well enough to know that she would be hard to resist. He wanted to hate her, but he couldn't help falling in love with her. She had opened his heart and poured honey on the wounds with her humour and compassion, and suddenly he had felt hopeful again. He had rediscovered a sense of romance. Beauty had sprung out of tragedy like a flower sprouting from a rock. He had

believed her carefree smile and clear grey eyes incapable of
such selflessness. He had misjudged her, and he had misjudged
himself. He now felt a different man; but would she come
back to him?

'What's on your mind, Hamish?' Leopoldo asked gruffly,
rubbing his bristly chin. 'Your eye hasn't been on the game
tonight.'

'It's love,' said Vitalino with a smirk. 'Another drink to
drown your sorrow, friend?'

'I have no sorrow,' Hamish replied, smiling devilishly. 'I'll
outwit you all, you'll see!'

'You think your luck's in?' Manfredo teased. 'You've lost
every game so far!' He caught his father's eye and shrugged.

'Can't you see he's shaved his face? Only a woman could
do that to a man. It's a tragedy, it really is.' Vitalino laughed,
shaking his head. 'His eye's not on the game because his mind
is on a beautiful angel of a woman.'

'If she can make you shave, how much lower can she drag
you?' Leopoldo growled.

Hamish laughed, throwing his head back like a shaggy
lion, but inside he was riddled with doubt. 'She has the power
to do anything she chooses,' he said, giving in.

'Even take you away from us?' Vitalino ventured. His
smile sat uneasily on his face. 'She wouldn't do that, surely?'

'Would you miss me?' Hamish joked, slapping him on the
back.

They all laughed, but Hamish remembered his promise to
Celestria with foreboding. He belonged in Marelatte.

He left the bar with Vitalino. The rain had stopped, leaving the wet earth sugar-scented and glittering. The clouds had
drifted out to sea, exposing a great black hole in the sky studded with stars, and there, shining in the midst of such splendour, was the moon. Hamish knew that that moon would
always make him think of Celestria.

'I'm going crazy,' he confided to his friend. 'Marelatte seems incomplete without her.'

Vitalino chuckled. '*You* seem incomplete without her.'

'I'm afraid.'

'Afraid?'

'That I didn't give her a good enough reason to come back.'

'Aren't *you* a good enough reason?'

'I should have told her how I feel.'

'Didn't you? Women need to know.' Vitalino considered himself an expert.

'Not enough.'

'Women need a bit of poetry. You've lived here . . . how long? And you still haven't picked up the Italian way of wooing women? It's all in the words and the way they're spoken. That's why the Italians are the best lovers in the world. We're famous for it. You're too economical with your words, that's the problem. Perhaps it's because you are Scottish. But trust me, women like it laid on with a trowel.'

'You talk a lot of shit, Vitalino.'

'It's shit that works.' He puffed out his chest, but Hamish still dwarfed him. 'So you think she'll return to her world and forget about you?'

'Yes.' Hamish's voice cracked. 'It's only when they leave you that you realize how much they mean to you.'

'Don't be so hard on yourself. If she loves you, she'll come back.'

'She's very young. The young are fickle.'

'They also love with passion.'

Hamish smiled, recalling the times they had made love on the slope above the old fortress. 'That is true.' He turned to his friend and shook his head apologetically. 'I'm doubting myself. I've found someone special. I'm terrified of losing her.'

'I understand. I envy you. No sooner have I settled my heart on one woman than another steals it away. I spend my life chasing it around town!' They both laughed. Vitalino noticed that Hamish walked without his stick. 'Where's the old man's wand?' he asked.

'Don't need it,' Hamish replied.

'I'd get it back if I were you. Women are suckers for a vulnerable man.'

'I can't. Saverio's wife has flown off on it!'

Vitalino chuckled affectionately. 'You might have lost your heart, but at least you haven't lost your sense of humour!'

Chapter 34

The day of Richard W. Bancroft II's funeral it rained. The sky was heavy with thick grey clouds and drizzle that fell without pause. The countryside looked bleak. The trees were shedding their leaves, and the sodden ground was covered with rotting foliage. But on her lapel, Pamela's diamond stars shone as if they contained rainbows.

The funeral took place in a cold stone church in the nearby village. Pamela had organized flowers, but still the church looked austere. Everyone from the estate attended, and many people from the town, even though they had never met the eccentric American who owned the big castle but rarely visited. Neighbouring gentry, with whom he had shot grouse and stalked deer over the years, stepped out of shiny cars in black hats and suits to say farewell to a man whose large but rare presence had nonetheless left a big indentation in their world. Harry comforted his grandmother, who had flown over from America. Pamela assured her father in her prayers that she would give him a big memorial service in New York, where he would be remembered in a way that was more fitting than this miserable place. But her father was now in spirit and no longer cared about such earthly trifles.

To Celestria's delight and surprise, Lotty and Francis attended. Pamela greeted them warmly, determined to be a good person, especially in God's own house. The cousins embraced, realizing that they now had more in common than they ever had. Lotty showed off the small engagement ring she wore alongside her gold wedding ring.

'We married two days ago in Kent,' she said. 'It was small but utterly beautiful. Mummy and Daddy didn't come, which was their choice, but David and Melissa did. Oh, Celestria, I'm so happy!'

'How is Melissa?'

'If you're wondering whether she and Rafferty are going to follow in my footsteps, I'm afraid Melissa has backed out.'

'The romance is over?'

'She's buckled under the pressure.'

'Aunt Penelope?'

Lotty nodded. 'She was always going to do the right thing.'

'Not necessarily,' Celestria said with a smirk. 'There's still plenty of time for her to do the wrong thing.'

'I've missed your barbed sense of humour, Celestria. I feel we've been apart for a very long time,' said Lotty. They sat together in the pew, and Lotty held her hand.

Back at the castle they drank cups of tea and shared stories. Lotty was delighted that Celestria had also broken away from convention. 'It makes me feel better that I'm not the only rebel in the family,' she said.

'They didn't expect it of you,' said Celestria. 'You were Miss Goody Two-shoes. I was always going to do something rash.'

'Like marrying a prince or a duke. No one expected you to fall in love with a penniless artist, like I did.'

'Mama still hasn't got over it. She's appalled. What is it about our family?'

'It's not *our* family; it's *your* father. If he hadn't died, I would never have been bold enough to run off with Francis. Uncle Monty's death taught me that life is short and precious and that one should seize the day. I'm so happy that I followed my heart and not your advice. Eddie Richmond could never have made me happy.'

'Aidan Cooney could never have made me happy, either,' Celestria agreed. 'I created a few ripples there, I can tell you. I hope he forgives me one day.'

Lotty leaned forward. 'Tell me, Celestria. What is Hamish like?'

'He's like no one else,' she replied. 'Grandpa would have approved!'

Pamela sat in her father's library, in the worn leather chair he must have sat in after dinner to smoke a cigar beside the fire, and contemplated her life. Celestria's decision to return to Italy to marry a man who had been married before had come as a great disappointment. She should have followed her mother's advice and married Aidan, but she'd find that out later. Pamela always knew best. At least Harry hadn't flown the nest. He was a sensible boy, right at the very top of the food chain, like his father.

While she was ruminating, she noticed a small pile of letters on the desk. She stood up and walked over with the intention of throwing it all into the fire. However, an envelope, addressed to her father in Celestria's handwriting, caught her attention. She picked it up and looked at it for a long moment. Her daughter hadn't bothered to write to *her* from Italy. She felt mildly offended and turned it over, sticking her nail into the fold to open it. As she did so, she was suddenly aware of her error. She was, after all, trying to be a good person. The letter was not addressed to her; it was none of her business. She heaved a sigh, her curiosity mounting with her frustration. *I bet she told him all about this Harry McCloud character,* she thought crossly. She tapped the letter on the palm of hand, deliberating what to do, struggling between the bad person she was and the good person she longed to be.

She raised her eyes to the fire that flickered in the grate. 'God,' she said in frustration. 'It's so bloody difficult being good.' She strode over to the fireplace, longing just to take a peek at the first few lines. Celestria would never know, and she was her mother, after all. But God would know. She sighed again and shook her head. 'This better get me to heaven,' she said, looking up to the ceiling. Closing her eyes, she threw the letter into the fire and watched the flames consume it. Feeling virtuous, she returned to the reception. *Now I have to celebrate my daughter's decision to marry McCloud,* she thought to herself. Then, as an afterthought, she muttered, 'With this one, God, you just might be pushing your luck!'

Pamela wandered back into the hall to find a large bear of a man standing dripping wet on the rug. His hair was long, his skin brown, his clothes shabby. On his feet were light summer shoes, impractical for Scotland and splattered with paint. She looked horrified and stopped a good distance away, in case he was a tramp who had found his way in uninvited.

'Who are you?' she demanded, looking him up and down with distaste.

'Never mind,' he growled, turning his attention to the drawing room, from where the drone of voices drifted out on the smoke-filled air.

'You can't go in there!' she exclaimed. 'Good Lord!' At that, he turned and stared at her, narrowing his eyes. A glint of recognition lit up his face and he smiled in amusement. Pamela was startled by the sudden transformation, and felt the colour rise in her cheeks. His smile had the devil's charm. She crossed herself. 'Don't be alarmed,' he said. 'I've come for Celestria.'

'My daughter?' she gasped. 'You've come . . . for Celestria?' Pamela felt faint. The devil himself had come to carry off her child.

'The name's Hamish McCloud.'

Celestria was still sitting on the sofa with Lotty when Hamish's unruly presence filled the doorway. She stopped mid-sentence, sensing a change in the air. Lotty looked past her to the door, and her jaw dropped. She gasped. 'Who is he?' Celestria felt her heart stumble even before she turned to look. Scarcely daring to hope, she turned around. She saw him before he saw her. He was searching the room, a deep frown lining his brow. Her heart flooded with joy and compassion; he looked so out of place, standing there in his odd clothes, among funeral guests dressed in their very best. She stood up. He saw her at last, and his expression softened and a wide, infectious smile flowered upon his face. With outstretched arms he strode through the throng of people, who parted in bewilderment to let him through.

'You've come for me,' she gasped, allowing him to wrap his arms around her, sweeping her off the ground so her black heels hung suspended in the air. She raised the veil pinned to her hat and pressed her lips to his. The smell of him brought back all that was good about Marelatte. She closed her eyes and felt the tide moving slowly within him, pulling her back to the old fortress, the little bay, and that special place beneath the gnarled evergreen tree.

'You've come to take me back,' she murmured happily.

'No, I've come to be with you.'

She drew away and stared at him in disbelief. 'You'll stay here for me?'

'I love you, Celestria. I just want to be with you. I no longer care where that takes me. I just want to make you happy. You see, your happiness is intertwined with mine.'

She saw in his eyes something fresh and new, like the sparkling blue sky the morning after a storm. 'I thought you said you'd never leave Marelatte?'

'Only you could make me leave.'

Pamela stood in the doorway, staring at them with the

same bewilderment as the rest of the guests. A hush had fallen over the room, and a brightness had filled it, as if the sun had finally come out and tumbled through the windows. Yet outside, it was still raining. So this was the man who had stolen her daughter's heart. She sighed, gazing at the strange, golden light. He wouldn't have been her personal choice, but, she conceded, sensing the loving presence of a spirit, her father would have approved.

'Let's go home,' Celestria said, her feet touching the ground again.

'And where would that be?' Hamish asked, taking her hand.

'Marelatte,' she replied nonchalantly, watching for his reaction.

He looked astonished. 'Marelatte?'

'Yes. We belong there with all the memories, good and bad.'

'You mean that?' The happiness on his face filled her with joy.

'I'm not making a sacrifice, Hamish. I want to belong there. I want to raise our children on that pebble beach. I want to show them that vast mozzarella of a moon. You said our happiness is intertwined. Then Marelatte is where we both belong.'

'Then you'll marry me in the church beside the Convento?'

'Waynie can be my bridesmaid,' she replied with a mischievous laugh. They stopped in front of Pamela, who still looked like she had just met the devil. 'The name's Hamish McCloud,' he repeated, extending his hand. 'We haven't been properly introduced.'

Pamela liked Puglia. The journey had been long, and Gaitano's Lancia Flaminia could have done with a good cleaning. But the weather was warm, the Convento enchanting, though rustic, and the wedding one that neither she nor Harry would have missed in a million years. Celestria looked as beautiful as Pamela had on her own wedding day, even though her dress had a rather homemade charm about it, having been made locally. She found Hamish a little alarming, but he made her laugh, which she hadn't done in a while, and he made Celestria happy, which was the most important thing. Her daughter might have saved Pendrift, but she hadn't given away all her inheritance. It was terribly romantic to be married to a painter, but his forthcoming exhibition in Venice might not lead to anything, and the two of them needed to live. Though, judging by the simplicity of their life in Marelatte, they wouldn't need much.

She visited the city of the dead on the suggestion of that eccentric lady, Mrs Halifax. The place smelled of pine and melting wax and was very peaceful. She was pleased to feel God in the narrow avenues of stone crypts and surprised by the warm allure of the place. She came across a crypt that was set apart from the others and climbed the stairs to take a look inside. There was a small altar and two candles, whose flames had not been lit in a while. Although pretty, the place felt empty and smelled of damp. She turned to the stone tomb that depicted a vine heavy with grapes. It made her think of fertility and immortality.

Celestria and Hamish sat alone on the bank above the old fortress, gazing over the sea that stretched out before them, as they would do in the many years to come. She rested her head on his shoulder, and he held her hand in his, toying with the simple gold ring that she now wore on her finger to symbolize a bond that would never break. They said nothing. Words were superfluous when their hearts were so full.

A bright crescent moon rose into the darkening sky. It didn't matter that it wasn't full; there would be many more full moons above Marelatte. Celestria closed her eyes and let him wrap his arms around her, knowing that at last she had come home. Home was where he was.

Father Dalgliesh pondered the rapid passing of time. It had been five years since Celestria had gone to live in Italy. Little had changed in Pendrift. Merlin still told bad jokes in the Snout & Hound, and Trevor still laughed at them. Julia had begun to redecorate Pendrift Hall, and Archie had made some good investments for a change, with which he bought more land without the need for a loan. Wilfrid and Sam were at university, and in the summer, when Harry came to stay, they still set traps and still failed to catch anything, though they boasted great heaps of corpses to the pretty girls they met on the beaches of Rock. Elizabeth and Bouncy had grown very close. Now that she was going blind, he would sit with her on the lawn outside the dower house and tell her what he had learned at school. Often he would read to her from his school books, and she never grew bored.

Father Dalgliesh often thought of Celestria. They always toasted her at dinner up at the Hall. She had saved it, and for that they would be forever grateful. Monty's death was never discussed, not because of shame but because they all liked to remember him in their own way, quietly. Occasionally, Father Dalgliesh would catch one of the family staring wistfully out to sea and know instinctively what was on his or her mind. But he never asked. He rarely thought about Monty himself, except for that one time in Mexico.

Father Dalgliesh had travelled to the remote village of Zihuatanejo on a charity mission, to spread the word of God. On the second day of his visit he had taken a walk along the beach.

He was alone, savouring the solitude after the rigorous demands of the day. He was standing with his hands in his pockets, looking out to sea, when a man sitting on the sand caught his attention. He was waving to two dusky-skinned children who were playing down by the sea with their young mother in a red cotton dress. They waved back before continuing their project.

Father Dalgliesh walked closer. There was something strangely familiar about the man. He wore a panama hat set at an angle on his head, and in his hand he held a smoking cigar, toying with it between his fingers. He looked up at the priest. His eyes lingered on him for what felt like a very long time. Suddenly he raised his hat. Father Dalgliesh caught his breath, for he had surely been recognized. He had seen Robert Montague only once, at Archie's fiftieth birthday party, but this man, with his insouciant air, had to be him. It can't be, he thought to himself, stunned, trying to decide what to do. But the man had gotten up from the sand and was striding over to his children. Father Dalgliesh shook his head. It couldn't be. It was impossible.

The evening sun was still very hot. The priest began to sweat. Should he go and talk to him? Or should he pretend that he hadn't recognized him? Was the similarity between the two men perhaps a horrendous coincidence?

While he deliberated, the man stood a moment, gazing out to sea, lost in thought. Then he crouched down and dragged his finger through the damp sand. He hesitated a moment, then turned to the priest, his eyes squinting in the sun. Father Dalgliesh watched in amazement as he got up. Taking the smaller child's hand, he left the beach and wandered up the track, followed by the woman and the other child. He didn't look back.

Father Dalgliesh watched them go with regret. Then his eyes turned back to the place where the man had written something in the sand. Something he clearly wanted Father Dalgliesh to see. He wandered over, his stomach churning with the sense that he had missed an opportunity that would never come around again.

It was then that he noticed two words written in the damp sand: *Forgive me*. Just as soon as he had finished reading it, a rogue wave surged up the beach and washed the words away.

Acknowledgements

When I was deliberating where to set this book, I had the good fortune of being invited to stay in Puglia, southern Italy, with one of my oldest friends, Athena McAlpine, who, together with her husband, Alistair, has made the most enchanting home and bed-and-breakfast out of an ancient sanctuary once inhabited by monks. I was immediately captivated by the magic they have made of their small corner of Italy and set about basing much of the book there. I extend to them my deepest gratitude, for without *Il Convento di Santa Maria di Costantinopoli* this book would never have been written.

I would like to thank my sister-in-law, Sarah Palmer-Tomkinson, and her mother, Christina Millard Barnes, for answering my questions on Catholicism, but I'd like to make it quite clear that they are in no way responsible for what I have written! I also thank Victor Sebestyen, author of *Twelve Days – Revolution 1956*, for helping me on the small Hungarian section; my friend the psychologist, John Stewart, for helping delve into the minds of my characters; and Jayne Roe, Karen and Malcolm Weaving, and Dorothy Cosgrove for inspiring in me a love of Yorkshire and Lancashire. I thank my mother, Patty Palmer-Tomkinson, for taking the trouble to read the early drafts; her comments were invaluable.

Thank you to Suzanne Baboneau and her brilliant team at

Simon & Schuster for republishing this book with a beautiful new cover, and to my agent, Sheila Crowley, for her wise counsel.

As always, superlative thanks to Sebag. I wouldn't be writing without him.

THE SWALLOW AND THE HUMMINGBIRD

Santa Montefiore

Rita Fairweather has been waiting for George Bolton, her childhood sweetheart, to return to Devon at the end of the war. She wants their future to be a continuing reassurance of their past. But George comes back as a man changed by the horrors he has experienced.

Unable to settle back into a small town life, George decides to travel to Argentina. And Rita promises to wait. But George faces irresistible temptation and an agonising choice. As the years pass, Rita keeps her word, but how long should she wait for the love of the life?

'The novel displays all Montefiore's hallmarks: glamorous scene-setting, memorable characters, and as always deliciously large helpings of yearning love and surging passion' Wendy Holden

Paperback ISBN: 978-1-47113-206-3
eBook ISBN: 978-1-47113-207-0

MEET ME UNDER THE OMBU TREE

Santa Montefiore

Sofia Solanas grows up on a beautiful ranch in the middle of the Argentine pampa. In a world of old-fashioned values, she carves out a place as a rebellious polo-playing young woman. But eventually, as her mother fears, Sofia's stubborn nature leads her to trouble . . .

Anna discovers that Sofia has embarked on a forbidden love affair. To save the family from shame, she sends Sofia to Europe – away from her friends and family and the man Sofia loves for twenty years. But then, a family tragedy calls Sofia home, and she must discover if her passion still lives on . . .

'All the ingredients of a classic romantic read – thwarted love, exotic locations and lifestyles of the rich and famous'
Daily Mail

Paperback ISBN: 978-1-47113-212-4
eBook ISBN: 978-1-47113-213-1

THE FORGET-ME-NOT SONATA

Santa Montefiore

In an Anglo-Argentine community in Buenos Aires,
two sisters – Isla and Audrey – spend their days playing
tennis, riding horses and enjoying picnics in the summer
heat. Isla is spirited; Audrey dreams of love.

When two handsome brothers arrive, Audrey loses her
heart to the wrong one. Louis Forrester, a troubled man
and gifted pianist, composes a brilliant piece of music
for her: the forget-me-not-sonata. Amidst their secret
love affair, tragedy strikes and Audrey is faced with a
heart-breaking dilemma. Will Audrey allow herself to
marry a man supposedly so wrong for her?

'The kind of book you can't wait to get back to' *Tatler*

Paperback ISBN: 978-1-47113-208-7
eBook ISBN: 978-1-47113-209-4

THE BUTTERFLY BOX

Santa Montefiore

Federica Campione adores her father.
No matter that Ramon, a distinguished traveller and
writer, spends months away from their home on the exotic
Chilean coast; as soon as he's back, his daughter has eyes
for no one but him. When he gives her a magical box from
Peru she believes he will always be there for her.

As she grows to womanhood, Federica attempts
to recapture that long-forgotten sense of security in the
arms of the debonair Torquil Jensen. From the sanctuary
of a seemingly perfect marriage, she embarks on a painful
journey of self-discovery. But can Federica ever truly escape
her gilded cage and learn the true lesson of the butterfly box?

Paperback ISBN: 978-1-4711-3210-0
eBook ISBN: 978-1-4711-3211-7

THE FRENCH GARDENER
Santa Montefiore

Nestled deep in the countryside, surrounded by beautiful
gardens, Hartington House is the perfect escape from
city life for Miranda and David Claybourne.

But Miranda misses the glamour and excitement of the work
and friends she has left behind, and David, often away in
London, treats their home as a weekend retreat.

Then an enigmatic Frenchmen arrives on their doorstep.
Jean-Paul, mysterious and charming, restores the garden
at Hartington to its former glory. He also transforms the
lives of Miranda and her children. Soon Miranda discovers
a journal, and an untold story unfolds of secrets planted
long ago with love . . . secrets that are ready to grow again.

'Intricate and well-written – perfect for a rainy bank holiday'
Company

Paperback ISBN: 978-1-47113-198-1
eBook ISBN: 978-1-47113-199-8

THE HOUSE BY THE SEA

Santa Montefiore

Ten-year-old Floriana is captivated by the beauty of the magnificent Tuscan villa just outside her small village, and dreams of living there someday. Then one hot afternoon, Dante, the son of the villa's owner, invites her inside and from that moment on Floriana knows that her destiny is there, with him. But as they grow up they cross an unseen line, jeopardizing the very thing they hold most dear . . .

Decades later and hundreds of miles away, a beautiful old country house hotel on England's Devon coast has fallen on hard times. Its owner, Marina, hires an artist-in-residence to stay the summer and teach the guests how to paint. The man she finds is charismatic and wise and begins to pacify the discord in her family and transform the fortunes of the hotel. However, it soon becomes clear that he is not who he seems . . .

'A gripping romance . . . it is as believable as the writing is beautiful' *Daily Telegraph*

Paperback ISBN: 978-1-84983-106-2
eBook ISBN: 978-1-84737-932-0

THE SUMMER HOUSE

Santa Montefiore

'I couldn't put this book down' Julian Fellowes

Antoinette's world has fallen apart: her husband, the
man she has loved for as long as she can remember, has
died tragically in an accident. He was her rock, the man
she turned to for love and support, the man she knew
better than she knew herself. Or at least so she thought . . .

For as she arrives at the familiar old stone
church for George's funeral, she sees a woman
she has never met before.

Phaedra loved George too, and she could not bear to
stay away from his funeral. But as she sits before his
wife, she knows that what she is about to reveal
will change all their lives forever.

'Sweeping' *Glamour*

'Gripping' *Daily Telegraph*

Paperback ISBN: 978-1-84983-105-5
eBook ISBN: 978-1-84737-929-0

SECRETS OF THE LIGHTHOUSE

Santa Montefiore

She longed for a fresh start. But her past
would not let her go.

Ellen Trawton has run away from London to the
sweeping landscape of Connemara, hoping to find a
place she can cut off all contact with the past. But
beneath the wild beauty of the Irish landscape lie
secrets which have been hidden for years . . .

Conor Macausland cuts a dark, lonely figure. His
young wife, Caitlin, died tragically at the old lighthouse,
and her loss has devastated him. But when he and
Ellen meet, a connection sparks between them.

Ellen soon realizes that Conor's past is not all it seems,
and there's more to her family history than she knew too.
As the secrets are finally revealed, the truth must be told . . .

'One of our favourite authors, sweeping stories of love and
families spanning continents and decades' *The Times*

Paperback ISBN: 978-1-4711-0097-0
eBook ISBN: 978-1-4711-0098-7

THE BEEKEEPER'S DAUGHTER

Santa Montefiore

Dorset, 1932: Grace Hamblin is growing up on a beautiful rural estate. The only child of the beekeeper, she knows her place and her future – until her father dies unexpectedly and leaves her bereft and alone. Alone, that is, except for the man she loves, whom she knows she can never have.

Massachusetts, 1973: Grace's beautiful, impetuous daughter Trixie Valentine is in love. Jasper is wild and romantic, a singer in a band on the brink of stardom. Then tragedy strikes and he must return to his home in England, promising to come back to Trixie one day, if only she will wait for him . . .

Weighed down by memories, unaware of the secrets that bind them, both mother and daughter are searching for lost love. To find what they are longing for they must confront the past, and unravel the lies told long ago . . .

'A superb storyteller of love and death in romantic places in fascinating times' *Vogue*

Hardback ISBN: 978-1-4711-0099-4
eBook ISBN: 978-1-47110-102-1

FIND OUT MORE ABOUT SANTA MONTEFIORE

Santa Montefiore is the author of eleven
sweeping novels. To find out more about
her and her writing, visit her website at

www.santamontefiore.co.uk

Sign up for Santa's newsletter and keep
up to date with all her news.

Or connect with her on Facebook at

http://www/facebook.com/santa.montefiore